SAMUAL

Greg Curtis

Samual

SAMUAL

Paperback Edition.

Samual

Dedication

This book is dedicated to my mother Ruth and my sister Lucille, my biggest supporters, harshest critics and all round cheer team, and without whom this book would not have been written. It's also dedicated to my father gone too soon but not forgotten.

Cover Art

The wonderful cover art was created by Stefanie Fontecha of Beetiful Book Covers.
https://www.facebook.com/beetifulbookcovers

Samual

Prologue

The attack that night was one that would live in the legends of the elves of Shavarra for thousands of years to come. And in the nightmares of countless children for the rest of their lives. Those that survived to speak of it would speak of its suddenness, ferocity and the strange and terrible steel creatures that caused such death and suffering. But above all else they would speak of the creatures' eyes. Their glowing red eyes that told of certain death in the night.

It was the sentries who saw them first, though there were precious few of them to begin with, and far fewer of those survived the sight to sound the alarm. As in all elven lands, there had never been a real need for guards or sentries in the towns and cities. These were peaceful lands; peaceful people. No one had ever attacked them before, and perhaps because of that they weren't as alert as they should have been.

Shavarra was the eastern most of the elven provinces. The youngest of them too, the land having been tamed from wilderness less than a thousand years before. The capital city was also called Shavarra and it was the only true city contained within the mighty Shavarran Forests for which it was named. It was a land famed for its beauty as much as the fine horses, great craftsmen and bounteous food it produced. And like all elven lands, it was known for its peaceful ways and good people. In all its recorded history there was not one record of its people ever having gone to war or done anything else so ugly. But then it had no need to. Its neighbours were also peaceful.

To the north lived the dwarves of the Iron Bridge clan, and though they were a boisterous and often bad tempered people, they were still the traditional friends and trading partners of the Shavarran elves. For many centuries the two regions had traded weapons, steel and precious metals for food, horses and high quality hand crafted goods. It was a relationship that was important to both peoples. Without it, neither province could have flourished or protected itself. Besides, neither people had any desire for the other's land. Dwarves liked mountainous regions and elves their great forests. The most trouble they ever had between them was the occasional fight among competing traders, and of course the tavern brawls the dwarves were famed for.

South of Shavarra – thankfully very far south – was the poisonous swamp land known as Racavor, the home of ogres, goblins, saurana and other unpleasant creatures. It was also the home of one of the great sylph cities; Istantia. But the sylph did not travel let alone go to war and fortunately the creatures of the swamps that surrounded their mountain city found the fresh air and open forests of Shavarra as unappealing and hostile as the elves and all other peoples found their swamps. Similarly, the denizens of that region did not generally have the ability to organise into armies of conquest. Instead they tended to band together in small hunting groups, little more advanced than wolf packs. For the most part they did not stray far from Racavor and their next meal, while the elves did not enter their swamps. A fortunate happenstance that had been in place since before recorded elven history.

Further to the east lay the great oceans, inhabited some said by the merfolk. The elves however, were neither keen sailors nor fishermen, and never having settled near the sea had little knowledge of them. All they had was the word of mouth of the various travellers who passed through the region, and there were precious few of them.

Finally to the west lay the nearby human kingdom of Fair Fields, another ancient trading partner of the elves, although one that they had occasionally had some differences with. The humans sought to cut down trees and forests so they could use the wood to build their houses and the land to raise mighty farms, something that the elves found abhorrent. The forests were more than just trees and homes to wild creatures to the elves; they were their homes. Fortunately the humans had respect for the law as well as a love of farming and building, and over the centuries many laws had been written and agreements signed to stop the humans ever coveting the elves' forests. After all it was what kept the various fiefdoms and baronies from constantly warring with one another.

Besides which, while the elves might not have an army of conquest, their border patrols and guards were more than able to take care of troublemakers, and the people of Fair Fields knew it. A single elf well concealed in the forest with a long bow could take down a dozen men in armour safely. Further, any attacking army would have to stick to the main trails, leaving itself utterly exposed to them. And that was without reckoning on the elves' most powerful weapon; their magic. Save for the sylph the most powerful wizards in the world were elven. The cost of an invasion would be high, even if it was successful, and there was little hope of that.

Thus Shavarra had never needed a true army to defend its borders. Only guards to keep the odd unruly travellers in check, and border patrols to intercept the occasional bandits or outlaws moving into their territory. Similarly the city itself had never needed many sentries. Why would it? It was a peaceful city contained deep within the forest heart of a peaceful land.

But this new enemy cared for none of that. He was none of that. Where their neighbours and threats were flesh and blood, his soldiers were steel claws and cold murderous teeth, and there was no reasoning with them. Nor did he have a clear attack plan as would an opposing army. There were no lines of cavalry or soldiers, no horse drawn cannon such as the humans might use, or even generals. Instead there were hundreds or perhaps thousands of wolf sized steel rats that snuck into the city undetected. Stealthy as thieves in the night. But then it seemed he wasn't trying to take the city or overwhelm its guards. His plan simply seemed to be to kill the elves. *All of them*. His was an army of assassins.

The sentries didn't stand a chance. They had never anticipated an attack of this nature, and for the most part they never even saw their attackers as they wove their way through the forests. Often they were attacked from behind as the steel fiends managed to encircle them. Their only warning was the sudden scrabbling of steel claws on the ground as they charged.

A few had time to turn, perhaps even to scream, before the creature was on them. And then they died. None had the time to draw their weapons, though precious little good a light steel sabre or bow would have been against a solid steel rat the size of a wolf. An axe might have been of more use, but none carried such things other than for chopping firewood. No more use was their traditional white leather and chain mail armour, as the sharpened claws and teeth of the beasts tore straight through their protection and then through to their hearts. Full steel plate might not have fared much better.

Unlike flesh and blood creatures these made no sound as they tore their victims to pieces. There was no growling as would come from a wolf pack, nor the squeaks that would come from rats. They did not roar in savage triumph, nor cry out when injured. No more did they stop to feed as would wolves. They attacked for one reason only. To kill.

It took the rats only a very short time to take out the sentries before moving on into the city itself. Using their unnatural stealth they quickly found the trees that were the heart of the city, and began climbing them. Unlike the elven inhabitants, they had no need to use the spiralling staircases or the hanging walkways to reach the higher homes. They climbed the trees directly, their claws digging deep gouges into the ancient bark, and then crept out along the overhanging branches, slowly getting themselves into position.

With the ability to climb and to remain perfectly silent as they homed in on their prey, they were the perfect weapon to attack an elven city and murder its people. Any other attacking force would have been heard leagues away in the dense forest. They also would have probably had to have used the main stairways and walkways suspended among the great redwood trees to access the city, and thus would have raised the alarm. This enemy however, suffered no such problem.

In too short a time hundreds – perhaps thousands – of the steel vermin were poised above all of the major buildings and many of the residences in the government sector, waiting for the command to attack. The city was home to over thirty thousand elves, most of them sleeping, and none of them had any idea of the doom that was literally hanging over their very heads.

That would soon change.

The command was given, a silent order that was heard by every one of the rats, and immediately the creatures attacked. Dropping down from the highest branches, they landed directly on and then burst through the thatched roofs of all buildings, the roofs proving unable to support their weight. In a heartbeat the rats were inside the homes of the inner city elves, most of whom were asleep. The unfortunate occupants had no chance to defend themselves. Few even managed to make it out of their beds before the rats were upon them. But in their fear and suffering their screams proved to be the alert that saved much of the rest of the city. For there were far more homes than rats.

By the time the steel rats had finished with their first victims – most of them elders, advisers and masters of magic

– many of the elves from the surrounding homes were awake. And though at first they had no idea what was happening they quickly gathered their weapons and put on armour as they rushed outside to find out what was happening with their neighbours. Meanwhile those in homes or buildings with more sturdy wooden or slate roofs had a little more time to defend themselves or flee as the rats had to work to break through them, and they became the first among the elves to see their attackers and survive.

These elves were to become the back bone of the fight back against the steel vermin. Even before the guards had been fully roused and the soldiers dressed, they were fighting, learning the strengths and weaknesses of the enemy, and taking the fight back to them. Many years later in the retellings of the battle, the elves from the government sector of Shavarra would be remembered as those who spearheaded the defence. If not for their courage, warning and quick wit, the casualties from the battle would have been many thousands more.

Of course, they paid a dreadful price for that reputation, with more than half the ruling council slaughtered in their beds, along with the master artisans, spell casters and scholars. The enemy had selected their initial targets with care, hoping to destroy the elves' ability to fight or even flee in the opening skirmishes of battle. But he hadn't counted on the basic resilience of the elves, or their innate fighting spirit.

As the long night passed a thousand pitched battles ensued between the steel rats and the elves. One that the elves very slowly lost, although in their defeat they managed to make the rats pay a huge toll.

The rats were dangerous and immune to most weapons, for only the heaviest axes could break their steel shells. But they were also outnumbered by at least twenty to one. And while one sword might break on them, or one arrow bounce off their metal hides, twenty were a different matter, and slowly the elves managed to inflict some casualties of their own upon them.

Moreover the few spell casters that chose to live in the city, and who had survived the initial assault, soon showed their ability to turn the battle. Nature mages reformed the trees around the rats, trapping them in their wooden clutches. Weather mages brought down lightning and wind to smash the rats into small pieces, while the very few fire mages still living, all sadly students, blew them to pieces where they stood. Wizard fire was highly effective against them as the rats simply exploded as the balls of fire touched them.

Elves with quarterstaffs soon learned a valuable lesson in fighting the steel monsters as well. The rats could be flipped over, and their undersides were much less sturdy than the rest of them. Better still, once on their backs they seemed to have difficulty righting themselves, giving the defenders a good chance to kill them.

Had there been more spell casters in the city to begin with the battle might have been won. But sadly there were few magic users living in the city itself, as most chose to live out in the more rural settlements where their skills were of more use. And few of those wizards in the city were masters of fire to begin with. The demand for that skill was greatest among the border patrols and the smelting, forging industries of the southern settlements.

For his part the commander of the rats proved cunning; his army silent and vicious. The rats continued with their tactics of stealth, climbing above the heads of the defenders and dropping on them from above, catching more than a few spell casters by surprise. Or finding places to hide and then leaping out upon unsuspecting, injured and unarmed elves fleeing from the battle. Worse still, they obeyed none of the rules of warfare. Where a soldier would spare mothers and children while looking for armed assailants, the rats saw them as easy targets and went for them wherever possible. Their orders were to kill everyone.

And so the battle raged through the night, with the elves slowly losing both ground and people, but saving as many as they could.

As the sky finally began to lighten the sky, those elves still fighting felt a sense of hope. They had survived through a night of blood and death and with the rising sun they thought the worst might be over. Because the rats' ability to hide and skulk in the shadows, would be gone. Without it and with their numbers already dwindling, the elves hoped that the tide of battle would turn back to them, and they would drive the rats from the city.

For a while it seemed that the elves' hopes were coming true. Especially when the battles were dying down. When the sun's rays showed the remains of many thousands of fallen steel rats all over the main concourses. Many more could be seen on the forest floor. They had already paid a terrible price with thousands of elven bodies scattered like leaves from the trees throughout the city, and countless more lying dead in their homes, their bodies still waiting to be discovered. But at least they had been able to dream they had been winning. For a while a few brave souls had even found the courage to smile and give cries of victory.

But then came the calls from the elves on the higher walkways, and they knew the city's doom was upon them. For far out to the east they could see a line of silver and steel heading towards the city. A line many leagues long. Reinforcements were coming.

One by one the surviving elders and war masters climbed to the lookouts and tried to guess just how many of the steel rats were coming before eventually giving up. It had to be in the thousands they knew, but how many beyond that was impossible to know. Ten thousand, twenty – it was all just a guess. But it didn't matter. What did was that it was too many to fight. Hopes fell and hearts plummeted as the defenders realised that there was no chance of winning back their city in the face of such overwhelming numbers. Not when they had already lost so many people, soldiers, wizards and civilians, and all to a force far less than half the size of the army approaching.

They had to run.

But at least they had time. Perhaps half a day in which they could either prepare to die or flee. And some did want to stand and fight. Leaving meant abandoning their cherished homes, their city, and their hopes and dreams to a steel evil, but they would at least survive as would their kin.

It was not an easy decision to make by any means, and some refused to leave even when the guards and surviving elders had made it for them. It might seem crazed to many, but to an elf to abandon their homes and their lives and everything they loved was almost worse than dying. Nor did leaving promise them safety. The elves had no guarantee that the golems, as the wizards named them, would stop attacking once they had taken the city. After all, they had no idea why they'd attacked in the first place. What would giant steel rats want with a city anyway? And yet clearly all they wanted was an empty dead city. Unless – though few dared to give voice to the thought – all they had really wanted was dead elves? Nor did they know if they would even be fast enough to escape the rats if they did give chase.

Fleeing was simply the only chance they had.

Before the sun had risen even a quarter of the way into the sky, more than fifteen thousand surviving elves had packed up as many of their belongings as they could and were preparing to depart their home, by horse, wagon or foot. The survivors quickly grew into a mass of horses, elves and wagons, which in turn and with a lot of shouting became a caravan.

Then, before the sun had risen much higher, the order was given and the city's residents began their long journey to safety. A very long journey since even then they knew or feared that their nearest or only refuge would be in Golden River Flats, at least four months travel across hostile terrain.

It was a caravan of suffering as over a thousand of those fleeing were badly wounded. Many of them would not survive the journey. Adding to the distress there were only a few dozen healers with the caravan, as many of them had been killed. So many went without healing as they travelled. Too many would not survive the day let alone the journey.

It was a caravan of despair as elf after elf looked back at the glorious city of Shavarra slowly disappearing into the forest behind, and knew that they might never see it again. For most the city had been the only home they had ever known, or ever wanted.

It was a caravan of fear as the survivors, burdened down with the sick and the dying, wondered if the rats would leave them alone, or if they would give chase. Few if any were still up to the contest of battle, and the horses were overloaded. They couldn't run and they couldn't fight.

It was a caravan of mourning as there were few elves who had not lost someone in the attack.

But most of all it was a caravan of questions. Who had attacked them? Why? And what would they do once they got to Golden River Flats? Sadly there were few if any answers. But as that first terrible day grew into a longer and more painful night many promised themselves that they would eventually get those answers. And then, though it was unelven, they would exact a terrible revenge on the master of the rats.

Chapter One.

It was the sound of horses that woke him. The steady clip clop of their well-shod hooves on the hard packed clay road. They were still a distance away but were coming steadily closer. The sound wouldn't normally have bothered him, except for the number and the hour. There had to be dozens of them, and it was at least four hours past sun down. Lots of horses travelling late at night, and coming from the East. Possibly from the city. That had to mean trouble. But of what sort?

As always Sam woke easily, and quickly had the dagger he always kept under the pillow in his hand. He had reason. Over the years Sam had discovered that the sound of horses late at night usually meant trouble, and more often than he would like, assassins. More than a few had been sent in search of his prized scalp over the years and some of them had found him. Thus far they'd all failed badly at killing him, mostly at the cost of their own freedom, limbs and sometimes lives as they attacked with all the fury of a rabid dog. Fortunately he was a knight of Hanor as well as a wizard and the king's son, and he could fight. They kept forgetting that. And at least some good had come from their losses, as their defeat had provided him with some more weapons, armour, horses and anything else of value they had on them, which he could then sell for good coin.

He'd also sold those assassins that survived into slavery, figuring it was a more than suitable punishment for those who chose to kill others for coin; especially his half-brother's coin. A life for a life was his thought. There were still a few slavers who plied the trade path that ran along the Shavarran border down to the seaport of Schist Harbour. It was probably a dangerous thing for him to do, but despite the risk that his would be killers might talk, leading to yet more bounty hunters and assassins on his tail, he thought it also the right thing to do. He wasn't a murderer which was the only alternative he had. He also enjoyed the irony of making a profit at his half-brother's expense. It was somehow fitting, and it kept him fed and sheltered.

Assassins though usually only came in ones and twos, and mostly they had the good sense to at least muffle their horses' hooves with sacking, if they were foolish enough to bring them into ear shot at all. These he realised, as he heard more and more of them, were not assassins.

Nor were they visitors from the nearby town of Torin Vale or Torin Endess mi Idril – the Vale of Torin's Tears – as it was more properly called in High Elvish. They would call out to him as they arrived. He had lived among them for five years. Long enough to know many of them.

Puzzled rather than alarmed, Sam threw off his covers, pulled himself out of bed and walked over to the window in the main room, a genuine glass window he'd bought especially for his little cottage. All it had cost him was a brace of poisoned stilettos – another of his half-brother's generous gifts to one of the many assassins he'd hired. Heri had no doubt expected the man to stick the dagger in his chest. Sam had had other ideas. It pleased Sam to know that even his half-brother's hatred and evil could be used to build him a home and keep him warm and comfortable.

His might not be a particularly proud cottage, barely large enough for him to have a separate bedroom upstairs from the living area and kitchen, but it was home and whenever he had a few coins to rub together, he liked to spend some of them on it.

In the five years since he'd found the abandoned building and made it his home, he'd increased the size of the main room and put in a sleeping loft. Then he'd re-roofed the entire cottage, replacing the old rotting thatch with new oiled planks. He'd also bricked out a new internal fire place so that he could cook inside, an absolute must when it rained so often, and replaced the rotting rope stairway leading up to it with a sturdier, permanent staircase spiralling around the oak tree's massive trunk. Finally he'd purchased glass for his windows; all four of them.

Then there were the extensive gardens and orchards which he'd planted, both for food and income, and the stables around the tree's base. It was still a modest cottage, certainly not large enough for his wife and the hoped for children he would by now have had, had it not been for Heri. But it was comfortable, it kept him fed, warm and dry, and above all else it was home.

So who was outside it?

Sam stared out the window and from the light of the nearly full moon, not to mention the torches the group were carrying, he could just make out the horses and their riders. And the moment he set eyes on them he knew there was trouble. Riding at night by torch light usually meant trouble in itself. There was too great a chance of a horse putting a foot down a pot hole to risk it unless the need was very great. But it was the number of torches he could see that truly worried him.

"Alder's hairy tits!" He swore quietly as he took in the sight. He didn't know what he was seeing but he was sure it had to be the doing of the god of mischief. It certainly wouldn't be the doing of the elves' precious Goddess. She might not be the All Father who he followed, but she was still a good goddess. And nothing of this looked good.

In the darkness he could see a trail of torches almost a league long, winding back like a glowing serpent into the blackness. A league of torches! Sam tried to estimate the number of horses and elves that had to equate to and failed. At the very least it had to be in the thousands, maybe in the tens of thousands.

That sent a shiver running down his spine. Thousands of elves, wandering along a darkened trail at night, a mere twenty leagues or so from the capital of the province. That had to be bad. Worse, the direction they were travelling suggested they were coming from the city itself. Then again, where else would you find thousands or even tens of thousands of elves in one place to form a caravan to begin with? Shavarra was a realm of small towns and villages and there was only one city.

Grabbing his cloak from the wall and dropping the knife back on the bed, he hurried down the stairs and out onto the balcony to greet the first of the riders and find out what was going on. The "balcony" was actually a widened platform at the top of the stairs which he'd extended around all sides of the cottage. He'd added it to his home a couple of years before, mainly so that he could drink a hot mug of tea in the evenings while listening to the bird song all around. This elven land was truly a marvel to a boy raised in the human cities of Fair Fields, and he loved to simply spend time enjoying it.

He might no longer have wealth and titles, the comfort and warmth of a soft bed at night, the luxury of plush woven floor coverings underfoot, servants to do his bidding, or even the company of his good wife and the promise of family to come, but the beauty of the land could give him back a lot. It was exactly as Ryshal had promised him so long ago when they had first planned on coming here. He only wished that she were here with him instead of in a dungeon. He prayed each night, even as he despaired, that one day he might somehow rescue her, and bring her out here to her enjoy this beautiful land with him. Having her here would be his definition of paradise.

On the nights when he mourned the most for all that he'd lost, the beauty of the land still brought him a measure of peace. A peace that it seemed was now under threat.

Sam rushed back inside, grabbed a lantern from the shelf and lit its paraffin soaked wick with a spark from his fingers, so that he could both see and be seen by those approaching. He then hurried back onto the balcony, prepared to meet them. Years of looking over his shoulder made him grab his trusty greatsword as well – just in case. These were safe lands normally – the elves were a very law abiding people and they didn't tolerate any sort of crime – but this caravan from the city was anything but normal.

As the first of the riders approached – city guards by the look of their uniforms – he wondered if his worst fears hadn't been terrible enough. Because the grim determination, pain and sorrow that showed in the faces of the guards, together with the ripped and torn uniforms, and the bandages covering so many of their arms and legs told a terrible story. By the light of their torches he could see perhaps twenty guards clearly, and all of them wore at least one bandage. Too many wore more blood soaked bandages than clothes. Seeing them like that Sam put his greatsword down. These people needed his help, not his suspicion.

There was of course only one explanation for such a caravan to a soldier born and raised; they'd been in a fight. A major battle. And considering that they were city guards, it had to be Shavarra itself where the battle had been waged.

Shavarra; the only major city in the region, and the shining star in the elves' list of most beautiful places in the world. A battle there was unthinkable. But worse than that, these didn't look like people who had won a great battle. If they had won they wouldn't be here. They'd be at home, celebrating and tending to their wounded. These looked like refugees.

Thousands of refugees. Which left Sam with the obvious questions. Had the city itself fallen? If so how? When? And above all to whom? Who would attack Shavarra?

"Hail." Sam called out to the closest of the riders, and for his trouble received only a lack lustre wave as they carried on past down the curving trail. Apparently they were set on their course, which had to be the nearby settlement of Torin Vale. A lone peasant wasn't going to be allowed to distract them. Besides, a caravan a league long couldn't stop easily. But towards the rear of the leading bunch a single rider peeled off from the caravan and headed towards his cottage. Apparently he was at least going to receive one visitor, and hopefully some answers.

Quickly the rider reached the base of his staircase, and dismounted gingerly. Saddle sore, or carrying some injuries, he couldn't be sure of which and he didn't like to ask. Either way it wasn't enough to stop his visitor, and he quickly walked up the stairs winding around the tree until he was on the balcony facing Sam. Unlike the others holding the torches, this soldier was a member of the border patrols. The emblem on his chest – a pair of fighting griffins – told Sam that. Unfortunately the soldier's manner confirmed everything he'd feared; the battle had been lost. It was in his posture, his sloping, tired shoulders, his head bent with shame and the complete lack of a spring in his walk. He was both defeated and exhausted.

Moreover the soldier seemed no more friendly than his emblem. His helmet stayed firmly on, the side pieces covered his neck. He even kept the face guard down as if he could not stand to be seen. In the dark, even by the light of his lantern, Sam could see little more than two dark eyes glowing out of his visor.

"Hail." Sam used the traditional greeting once more, this time with the raised sword hand to show he wasn't holding a weapon. Normally he wouldn't have bothered except on formal occasions, but the last thing he wanted this night was a tragic misunderstanding.

"Well met cousin."

Sam started as a woman's voice came out from under the helmet. That was one thing he would never get used to in Shavarra; women serving among the soldiers. Such a thing would never be accepted anywhere else. Or at least not in Fair Fields. There the men fought and the women ran the house as was proper. But this was not his land, even though it was now his home, and it certainly wasn't his place to say anything about it. Besides, Ry would have told him off at great length had he ever dared say such a thing in public. Or at all. At least the woman used a relatively friendly greeting, addressing him as cousin, as all elves considered themselves. But then it was dark and she was obviously tired. She hadn't had a chance to notice his human sized bulk or listen to his thick accent.

"Good soldier –", he knew it was always best to be polite, "– what is this? Has something happened to the city? And where are you all going in the middle of the night?"

"Elf friend –", apparently she'd realised from his thick accent that he wasn't elven, or at least fully elven, "Shavarra has fallen to the enemy. Much of it is destroyed and many, many of our people are dead. Those that survive with us are now refugees, fleeing the city and the enemy, heading first for Torin Vale. But our scouts tell us the enemy is still pursuing us, his evil golems only a few leagues behind our stragglers. You must gather your family and join us lest you be butchered in the night like so many others."

"Fallen? How?"

But he only whispered it. In a single word she had confirmed all he had feared, and yet even looking at her and the column of refugees passing his front door, he still didn't understand how it could be. Shavarra was a well defended city, having a standing defence force of over a thousand soldiers. It was known far and wide as a place of peace and beauty. Surely no one would ever want to attack it? Certainly not its neighbours.

Could it be some sort of jest? He found himself wondering that because the words were simply too impossible to accept. The elves were extraordinarily fond of their word games. Their sophistry as his father would have called it. Strange in a people so enamoured of the truth. But he couldn't find anything amusing in what the soldier had told him. And he could see for himself the proof of what she had said.

Eventually his soldier's training finally returned to him, and made him ask the questions he needed answers to. And she had spoken one word that he didn't understand.

"Golems?"

They were all but mythical creatures created by dark wizards to do their heavy work. But if they were the enemy, he had to think it was significant. At the least it suggested that they had been attacked by a wizard. He'd heard tales of such creatures and their incredible strength, but only ever seen one. And while it had been a powerful creature – a lump of steel shaped roughly like a man – it hadn't been that tough to kill. His brother had sent it after him in the first few days of his exile from Fair Fields, and even though Sam's magic then had been weak, he had destroyed it easily enough. It had been slow and it had melted. Whatever wizard Heri had used to create it and send it after him had been paid too much gold for his services. Still, Sam had never heard of golems being used as soldiers or hunters. They were simply too stupid and too slow for that.

"Giant steel rats. Thousands of them. They hunt in packs

like wolves and kill like assassins, dropping from above, creeping around the sides or crawling under things to pounce. They tried to kill everyone. Men, women and even children. Especially the children. They didn't attempt to take prisoners, they didn't obey any rules of war. Instead they just attacked and killed, attacked and killed. And they didn't stop until they were destroyed. Most weapons won't do more than scratch them and unless you punch a dozen arrows in them. Light swords are not much better. They're true steel. Shavarra was attacked by an army of steel rats with glowing red eyes. And they're still chasing us."

"Gather your family. You must leave before the sun rises. That is all the time you have before they will be upon us here."

Without another word the soldier pivoted on her heels and took the stairs back down to her horse. Apparently she had said all she wanted and wasn't prepared to waste any more time.

Limping still, probably from an injury he decided, she made good time back to her horse, mounted up and quickly hurried back to her group. The warning given, her duty was done and she appeared anxious to return to her post.

"I thank you for the warning good soldier," Sam called out after her. "And please tell any who want it that they can harvest all the fruit and vegetables they need from the gardens."

The elf gave no sign that she had heard. Perhaps she hadn't. More likely though given the events of the previous couple of days she had no interest in the thanks or aid of a common citizen. Especially the thanks of a half elf.

That was the trouble with living in an elven homeland. While he was officially welcome here as were all people of good heart and civil manner, as a half elf he was considered as something less than either human or elf. All other races and those of mixed race for some reason seemed more at home, more accepted in the towns than him. So there were gnomish and pixi traders everywhere, even a few dwarves, and many of them had taken elven partners, something too that seemed to be accepted. But for a human to do so seemed to be something else entirely, and their offspring, more so. He didn't know why. He hadn't worked up the courage to ask anyone lest he make things worse. But he knew it was so.

Coming to these lands five years ago hadn't been an easy decision. He'd known before he even set foot in them that he would be looked down upon. Those few traders he knew who plied this land had told him that at length the moment they'd seen his ears sticking out of a human looking face. But he also wanted to see the land of his mother, maybe even meet some of her kin, and he knew from his father before he'd passed away that his mother had been well connected in elven circles. At least before she'd run off with a human, and then died in childbirth not too many years after his own birth, without ever being officially wed.

It had surely been a disgrace for her, and a lifelong regret for his father, especially after her death, but as the king he could never have married an elf. His loyalty to his people would have been placed in question, and that could never have been allowed. It would have placed his rule in jeopardy and his people's well being at risk. It would have set the kingdom up for a coup and given his enemies the very cause they dreamed of to overthrow him.

Thus far he'd had little luck in finding his mother's family, mainly because the few times he'd made it into Shavarra itself he'd felt as though he was carrying some sort of disfiguring disease, and had limited himself to the trading he had come to do, before fleeing back to his cottage. How could he even approach his mother's family if that was how the normal elf treated him?

Still, there hadn't been a lot of choice at the time. He'd had to leave Fall Keep in a hurry. It was that or be responsible for the death of his wife at his own half-brother's hands. And none of the other lands had seemed particularly appealing either. Nor safe. He still hoped that one day he might meet his mother's family, and that they might even welcome him. But that wasn't why he stayed here. What kept him here was that while he remained in Shavarra he was at least certain that fewer assassins would find him here than anywhere else he might live. The border patrols would pick up such people very quickly, and their fate would not be a pleasant one. Only the smarter, more cunning ones were getting through, and those few he could deal with.

Now though it appeared he had to leave regardless, something he was loath to do. He might not be the most welcome person in the realm, but over the years it had become his home. If he wasn't close with any of them, he was at least accepted by the local elves. They didn't bother him much, they traded fairly with him, and sometimes, just sometimes, he could share a conversation or a drink with them; pass a joke and forget his troubles as they forgot his parentage. He had learned not just Elvish but High Elvish, even if his accent was coarse. And he had learned many of the stories and much of the history of the land. It had taken five long, hard years to reach that stage. But now that life was in jeopardy.

But where should he go? If he went home to the human province of Fair Fields to the west his face would still be known by too many, including all of the royal guards. He could never live there unknown or unnoticed, and the cost to Ryshal of his being seen would be beyond his ability to stand. Heri would have her executed. He dreamed of going home, but that was something forever denied to him.

Further west again – much further, and across several other realms – lay the elven forest province of Golden River Flats. It was the largest elven province on the continent, with three major cities and dozens of large towns. It was also the nearest elven province to Shavarra and no doubt the destination of the elves.

The Golden River Flats were very similar to Shavarra in their people and lands, except for their size. The Flats had three major cities, each of fifty or a hundred thousand elves, and scores of large towns. It was also far more welcoming of travellers, and while there he had met with not just humans, elves and dwarves from afar, but also dryads, gnomes, pixies and even halflings. Their market places were simply teeming with strangers. Yet, though it might have been partly his youth at the time, he had never felt welcome there either. Elves everywhere had looked at him twice every time he'd taken his helmet off to reveal his pointed ears sticking out the sides of a human face, and after that they'd tended to give him a wide berth.

He could live there much as he had lived in Shavarra; as an outsider. But at least he could live there in relative peace. It would however, mean starting over. Here at least, the people had become used to him. They might not be overly friendly, but no more were they openly intolerant. Actually he was probably being too harsh; some of them were his friends, and the children liked him as well.

South and east of Fair Fields, and across a treacherous mountain pass lay the dwarven land of Ore Bender's Mountains. It was a bustling, vibrant land filled with traders and travellers. He had been there once in his youth, and found it fascinating. Especially the ports. Fair Fields being a land locked region, he had never previously seen a port. Ore Bender's Mountains though had three, and he had spent many long hours watching the ships coming and going, the wind filling their great white sails as they sailed sedately out across the endless blue ocean.

But on the other hand, to live among dwarves for any length of time was to ask for trouble. They were such a naturally garrulous people who took offence over the slightest of things. The chances were that if he lived there and that even if he tried to avoid trouble, that combat would become a way of life. Besides, the city was wide open, the people unfailingly good at giving directions, and any assassins would find him in a heartbeat. It was why he hadn't gone there when he'd first had to flee Fair Fields.

North and west of Fair Fields lay the gnomish lands of Fedowir Kingdom, a vast expanse of hard scrabble farms, stunted forests and deserts and swamps, where only the toughest survived. Conditions were harsh, and although the people were friendly, they would have little use for a wandering soldier. Raising food was more important than waging war, and if he couldn't plough a field or find another useful trade, he would quickly find himself redundant.

South and west of Fair Fields lay the Dead Belly Wastes, so named because the few explorers who'd crossed them and survived kept remarking on how many dead creatures they'd found, all with their bellies facing up to the sun. The Wastes were home to many ruined cities and lost temples, but no one had ever bothered to explore more than a few of the closest. The land was simply too tough. There was no water, a vast variety of deadly lizards, snakes and insects, and being so featureless and full of sand dunes, it was far too easy to get lost and die.

Between the two lay only a narrow strip of no man's land; the Dead Creek Pass. It was a rough trail that led to Golden River Flats. According to legend the pass had once been a vast river which had flowed through the wastes themselves, allowing great cities to flourish. But over many thousands of years it had become little more than a dried up strip of land, with a few wells dotting it while the Wastes had turned into sand.

Once in his youth he'd travelled through them as part of a troop of trainee knights, learning their craft and riding to Golden River Flats. It had been a most distressing time as they had constantly had to ration their water, always giving more to the horses than themselves, and living with the aura of death all around them. But after three long hard weeks of riding they'd reached the elven homeland, and perhaps enjoyed it even more for its gloriously abundant life after having passed through such death.

Further afield still lay the lands he'd only heard of, but of which there were many. In fact there were more human kingdoms, elven provinces, gnomish, dwarven and pixie lands than could be visited by any one man in a lifetime. As a student he'd been taught the names of all twenty seven provinces and realms on the Great Continent of the Dragon's Spine. He knew the dozens of island nations that surrounded it by heart. He even knew their rulers and the main details of their peoples, lands and trade. But he'd never been to them and had met very few representatives from them, other than those closest to Fair Fields. In all truth he had never planned on visiting them.

Nor did he intend to now. Human, elven, or other; kingdom, province, collection of villages, rich or poor, they simply weren't home. Fair Fields had once been his home. Shavarra was slowly becoming a home. They weren't.

Which brought him back to only Golden River Flats as being a safe and moderately acceptable alternative place for him to live. His best bet he thought, was to stay with the elves as they made their way slowly there. He had no doubt though that the road ahead would be hard, with unknown threats ahead, and an all too deadly one nipping at their heels.

It would be a lengthy journey to get to the Flats. One fraught with difficulties for the elves. For a start they were four hundred leagues from their destination at a minimum, and they had to first cross the hundred leagues or so of Shavarra just to reach the border with Fair Fields. For the moment it was safe territory, but the roads and trails through the forests had never been designed for speedy travel, and with thousands of wagons on them, the elves would have their work cut out just trying not to tear them apart even if they weren't being chased by these golems.

After that it would be a hundred and fifty more leagues to cross Fair Fields. They were good roads to travel, cobbled in parts as the local farmers pooled their efforts together to make their trips to the markets as quick and easy as possible. But the nobles of the various baronies and fiefdoms would no doubt demand a fee for crossing their lands, and the prices for food and goods would undoubtedly be high as the merchants saw an opportunity they could exploit. Worse still, they would have to deal with one noble after another. Fair Fields wasn't a true kingdom, his half-brother the reigning king notwithstanding. It was more properly a collection of misfit lords who came together mainly for defence and trade. But each noble, each house had its own agenda, most of which came down to increasing their wealth and power at the expense of their neighbours.

After that they would travel a further hundred and fifty leagues along the arduous Dead Creek Pass as they cut their way between the Dead Belly Wastes and the Fedowir Kingdom. A winding and sometimes steep dirt track in place of a road, the Pass had few resources along it other than the odd trading post or well. It was also reputedly littered with bandits. Though he couldn't imagine them attacking a party of this size, any stragglers might not be so fortunate. And the caravan would be slow as it had to carry not just food but also water with them. On horseback a rider could make it through in three weeks. But a caravan with overloaded wagons would be lucky to do it in a month and a half.

After that they would finally arrive at Golden River Flats, and hopefully find a place to live. Maybe the Shavarran elves would find an area to settle; perhaps they'd be broken up into smaller groups to be spread among the other elves? But even there the elves might not be safe. With an army of golems nipping at their heels – something that until that night he would never have thought possible – and the caravan crawling, their enemy could perhaps chase them all the way to the Flats and beyond. Though it made no sense that they would, neither did anything else the soldier had told him.

If the golems had already taken the city, why were they chasing the elves? Because he had no doubt from her words that they were. Did that mean that their goal was not the city at all, just the elves themselves as she'd said? Was their goal purely murder? And if so why? What sort of enemy lived only to fight and kill but not to take? But then what sort of army was made of steel rats?

The soldier in him said that if they were truly golems then they served another. A master wizard who was directing them from somewhere else. But then why would a wizard want a city? Or, if the wizard didn't want the city, why had he even attacked it? And if all he really wanted was the elves' dead as it appeared, then what could drive him to take such action? Was it some sort of vendetta perhaps? Revenge for past deeds?

Sam couldn't believe such a thing. While there were undoubtedly some nasty wizards around, surely none could hold a grudge against the elves. They were a law abiding people; peaceful almost to a fault. They never turned away those in need and they never attacked without cause. And they hadn't been to war in all the centuries the province had been inhabited. And yet try as he might Sam could think of no other possible reason for what he'd been told.

It was a riddle and a half to solve, and one that he knew was probably beyond him for the moment. He needed more information. Still, in the morning he decided he would find out more as he followed the caravan of elves west.

Until then, it was time to pack.

Chapter Two.

In the morning, before first light Sam did much as he'd been instructed. He'd already packed up his house the previous night and made it weather tight, making sure it would be there if and when he was able to return to these lands. Assuming the golems didn't destroy it. That only left himself and his horses to worry about.

Donning his full armour, (which still bore the crest of the House of Hanor on the banded blue chest plate despite his efforts to erase it) Sam gathered his weapons and mounted his war horse Tyla. He tied the reins of his other horse Aegis to the saddle, stuffed Elsbeth the milking goat into one of the oversized saddle bags, something she wasn't particularly happy about, and then left his home for what could be the last time.

The only thing he did different from what he'd been told to do was that he set off east instead of following the elves west to the village of Torin Vale as he'd originally intended. Straight into the heart of the enemy's advance as they chased the elves.

It wasn't a casual decision, nor he hoped a mistake. He was after all a warrior and a fire wizard both, and was more than capable of dealing with most threats. Although truthfully, he wouldn't have categorised giant steel rats or golems as most threats. And from what he'd heard from the soldier the previous night he knew he would have to be cautious. Yet even if the danger was greater than he could handle, he had to go. It was his duty.

Whether or not he was truly welcome among these elves, they were good people and they were innocent. And since he chose to live among them they were also his people. It was his duty as a knight of Hanor to protect them with his dying breath. They were also his mother's family, and his wife's as well. Running from battle was not the way to protect kith and kin. At the very least he had to scout out the enemy. He needed to look for his lairs; his strengths and his weaknesses. That information would be invaluable to the elves. And if he could bloody their noses a little, so much the better.

There was anger inside him. It had been bubbling close to the surface for five long years but so far he had kept it under control. During that time he had concentrated on his studies and used it as he worked on drawing ever more magical strength. But he had always kept it under tight control. Now though for some reason, it had started breaking loose. It had come boiling up through the night as he packed, and it was all he could do not to scream with rage. He wanted to strike out and destroy the enemy. Such was neither the way of a trained soldier nor an honourable knight, and yet a very primitive part of him still wanted nothing more than a good fight. A chance to hit back at something. To finally strike out at anything instead of just taking the loss and suffering as he had had to do these past five years. And like it or not, these golems would make perfect targets for his rage.

All through the night as he'd made ready for the morning, he'd felt that rage growing within him, so much so that it frightened him a little. And right behind it was his fire magic, whispering its sweet song of destruction. Even if the golems ran away he might well roast them, right or wrong. After all, they had committed a terrible crime and they had no souls. They were fair game.

Yet there was still more than just honour, rage and a need to find out what had harmed his kin that set his path that morning. There was also a strange feeling in the pit of his stomach that as bad as this attack was, there was more to it than just a battle or a war.

It was the reference to golems that had triggered something deep within him, and he simply had to see them with his own eyes. It was a memory, or a fragment of one that had been dancing in the back of his mind for hours as he'd watched the last of the elves pass by his home. He still couldn't quite place it even now, though he knew it had something to do with his training in the arcane arts. And with all the readings of the various prophecies. A line from one of them kept echoing in his thoughts:

"– and when the golems hunt,
the cities shall fall,
and the people shall know fear."

He only wished he could remember the rest of it, or even which book of prophecy it was from. There were so many in the library of Fall Keep – thousands in fact – and it had been many years since he'd read them.

Maybe it was just the despair and hopelessness he'd been living with for so long which was driving him mad. Or maybe not. Either way he had an uncomfortable feeling in the pit of his stomach that that prophecy was a foreseeing of what was happening now. But if it was, then this was only just beginning, and dark times lay ahead. He hoped that by seeing at least one of the golems for himself that it would trigger the rest of those memories, bringing them to the surface and telling him what was to come. Or that at the least he would learn how to kill them. First though he had to see one.

Sam let the horses take their time as they wandered slowly back down the road, while he spied ahead for the first sign of trouble. He had no need to hurry, he knew. The rats would come to him even if he sat and waited outside his home. It would just take a little longer for them to reach him.

Samual

It wasn't a hard road to travel. The trail had been regularly graded and the ruts from the wagon wheels had been filled in. In the wetter, muddier areas, stones and cobbles had been laid out, and wide stone bridges crossed the few streams that ran through the land. As with everything else in Shavarra, the elves took great care to make sure the roads were well looked after. But emotionally it was a tougher ride as he had to balance his anger against his nerves. Sam needed to keep his wits about him. That was the difference between a soldier and a berserker. A soldier had to be always clear thinking and have a plan. And more often than not, a soldier would win. Reason and strategy would overcome passion.

Sam needed to win. To put an end to these steel demons. Too much of him though just wanted to pound them with his axe. Still, he remembered his training, somehow managed to keep his cool, and slowly made his way towards the front without incident.

Using his eyes, his ears and his nose as his instructors had taught him, he searched for anything out of the ordinary. Anything that might tell him that he was entering an enemy's domain. But the trouble with the steel golems, if he truly understood what the soldier had told him last night, was that he didn't know what those signs might be. All he knew was that they would not approach as an army. They would not march in formation. They would scurry and sneak like assassins in the dark. No more would they give off any odours as might a man or an animal. Nor would they make unnecessary sounds as they conversed among themselves.

As well as using his physical senses, Sam cast his mind's eye ahead. It was one of the senses that sharpened with advanced training in the arcane arts and he used it to look for signs of magic. He knew that if there was one thing that golems would give off, it was surely the smell of magic. Great and terrible magic.

Such creatures hadn't truly been seen in the lands for centuries, and even then they hadn't been common as they could only be created by the greatest of alchemists. Mostly they had been kept by the alchemists as glorified pets and servants. Symbols of their power. And now there was suddenly a whole army of them? Golems who were able to act independently of their master? Such things had to mean magic of the highest order. Magic that any spell caster should sense from many leagues away.

But while Sam couldn't detect the magic of the golems, what he did note was the quiet of the forest. Normally these lands were filled with creatures. And while his nature magic was limited, it was enough to detect the more magical of them. The unicorns, griffins and pegasi. He seldom saw them, but such was their presence that he felt them. Always. Not this morning though. Wherever they were, they weren't nearby. That worried him.

It was a long slow trip, and for the longest time he could neither see nor sense anything of the enemy. He did however see the occasional peasant or soldier coming up the trail at speed, no doubt trying to catch up with the caravan. Many were frightened, some were wounded; all were in a hurry. Too much to have any time to stop and talk, though he asked all of them if they had seen the enemy behind them. None had – though all thought they were being chased – and none wanted to stay with him for any length of time to tell him of what they had seen. Not when he was clearly travelling the wrong way. The elves were like any other people in that regard. No one wanted to talk to mad men.

In truth they all probably thought him mishin li or moon crazed, but right then was not the time to argue with a human in full armour, riding a giant black steed, and with a second the same size beside him, loaded down with weapons and a goat. They hurried on. No doubt they would tell any others that they met of the mad warrior they had passed.

The sun had well and truly risen by the time Sam first felt the tingle of magic ahead, and he knew his enemy was approaching. It was only then that he fully accepted that this enemy was real. Because up until then despite everything he'd seen, his mind had kept telling him that it couldn't be. Armies of golems? That was madness. But then feeling the mass of distant magical energy, he knew it was real. They were still many leagues away, but the magic still raised the hairs on his neck, much like the charge in the air after a lightning bolt had just struck close by. Sam kept the fire in his centre hot and ready for use though he knew he had time. He didn't have to fan the flames of his magic just yet.

Three hundred yards further on he stopped the horses in a clearing, distracted by an unexpected emotion. He could still feel the enemy a good distance off, though closing in remorselessly, but he was sensing something else as well:

Fear.

Sadly it was not the golems' fear – metal magical constructs didn't have any. But even if they had, Sam could sense that the source was much closer than them. Nor was it that of the animals of the woods as the golems passed them by. They hid, and though they knew something strange was among them, they had no concept that it was a predator. Then again for them it wasn't. The golems were hunting people. And what he was sensing was the fear of those being hunted.

It had been some time since he'd encountered anyone by then, and even when he had it had only been a straggler here and there. But this was more than that. This was a full party. Opening his senses wide Sam could feel men, women and children close by. There were a lot of them. Apparently not everyone had made it out of the city with the main caravan. Nor had they all made it out alive. These elves were grieving as they fled, and they were terrified.

Sam was torn. Part of him – the part that was soft and emotional – wanted to go to them and help. He knew he could. He had a couple of horses, some weapons and most important of all he had magic. But the soldier in him knew better. Where he stood was the perfect place to meet the enemy. The clearing he was in was perhaps only a hundred yards across, but it was enough to stop the golems from creeping up on him unawares. And that according to what he had been told, was how they liked to strike. It was also enough space to use some of his more powerful weapons and spells safely, if he needed to. And he knew he would. The magical stench of the enemy was already growing. He could not yield this spot.

In the end the soldier won through as he usually did. The years of training were too hard to ignore, while the fear of the elves coming towards him wasn't yet overpowering. Nor were they in as much danger as they feared. They were still well ahead of their enemy and they would remain so for a while. Long enough to reach him and safety. He would let them come to him.

Soon enough he heard the first sounds of the elves arriving. Hooves beating erratically as tired horses galloped. The shouts as the frightened elves called to one another, urging each other on as they tried to stay ahead of the rats. The nickering of frightened horses as they picked up on their masters' fear. The sounds of twigs breaking as they broke through bush and scrub.

"Hanor!" Sam let loose his family's ancient war cry as loudly as his lungs would let him. He wanted to let them know that there was someone ahead of them. Someone who would provide them with help, even if they didn't know what sort. And in truth it was good to finally be able to shout his name out loud, admitting all that he had kept hidden for so long, while remembering happier times. It was a good name, a proud name; not something to be hidden. Immediately he felt their spirits raise as they heard him. They didn't yet know anything about him but they knew they weren't alone any longer.

Thirty or forty heartbeats later they broke through the last of the bushes before hitting the clearing. It seemed they had left the trail, perhaps hoping to evade the golems or make better time through a short cut. Arriving in the clearing they saw him standing there in the centre of the trail ahead. It must have come as a shock to them. A tall human dressed in full armour and astride a massive black horse, with a second beside him. And if any of them knew their heraldry they would have noticed the crest of Hanor on his armour and the blue of his honour. A knight of Hanor was surely the last thing a party of fleeing elves would have thought to come across in their own lands. But they weren't foolish enough to stop and wonder.

Sam in turn studied them as they galloped towards him, saddened somewhat by the sight. Even more than the others, the stragglers confirmed all that the soldier had told him the previous night and more. The same sorry tale of battle, loss and death. They were a rag tag group. A party of soldiers – possibly a border patrol by the looks of their armour – with a group of civilians in their midst. Traders were also in the group, complete with two trade wagons. But instead of wares in the backs of their wagons, they had women and children. At least a dozen.

Too many of the soldiers were wounded for his liking, and few had had time to dress their injuries, while those bandages that had been tied were blood soaked. Meanwhile many of the civilians were wounded as well, and the fear and sorrow on their faces was enough to tell him that even those who were uninjured were carrying a heavy burden of pain and grief. They had lost people, friends and family. Their feelings added to his anger.

"To me!" Even as he called to them, Sam was drawing his spare greatsword and battle axe from Aegis' pack. They were all he really needed, while the rest of the supplies she carried – mainly food, clothing, some spare armour, medicine and of course his goat – they could use. Well, perhaps not the armour, though they could probably sell it for coin. Three full sets of blackened snake scale armour would be of little use against steel golems. Its value was in the way it allowed its wearer to creep up on his prey silently. Besides, it wouldn't fit.

When the first of them reached him, he told them to take Aegis and anything else they needed and keep going up the trail as far and as fast as they could. He would catch them up. They didn't try to talk him out of staying once they saw him with weapons drawn and fire already dancing off his blades. They could see he was both a wizard and a warrior and they understood he was planning on fighting. They would not interfere.

Two of the women from the wagons jumped on Aegis, lessening the load on the other horses a little, and in a few more heartbeats they were behind him, galloping away as fast as they could. No doubt a few looked back as they fled, staring at his armoured back and wondering who he was. But they weren't foolish enough to waste time in conversation.

A few moments later the clearing was once more silent and Sam was alone. But the enemy was closer. He could feel them, like tiny charges of lightning dancing over his skin. He could almost see them in his mind. Happily he knew they were still at least half an hour away, but to feel them this strongly from such a range meant that they were even more powerfully enchanted than he'd guessed. It was time for him to prepare his magical defences. And by then he knew he had to. This would not be a simple battle, it would be war.

His initial thought had been that there would only be a few of them. The advancing scouts chasing down the stragglers and clearing the region of enemies. That at least was a logical military action. But sensing them as they approached he realised that that was not the case. He could feel perhaps several hundred of them, maybe even more. They were hunting as a pack and were chasing the elves hard. These weren't the scouts he'd expected. They were the first wave of an army, harrying their defeated foes, and preparing the way for a larger force to follow. Hand weapons and the odd fire ball as he'd planned to use against such numbers would be useless. Instead he began preparing his most powerful magics, concentrating as he never had before.

Knowing he would need every ounce of strength he could muster to fight so many at once, and yet relishing the fight like one too long soaked in blood, he began by channelling all the fire he could find. He drew heat from the sun above, and the warmth from the ground below. He also pulled some of the life spark out of the forest. With only half an hour to prepare himself and plenty of need, Sam used every scrap of his strength that he could to draw in the fire, and quickly found himself channelling more fire than he had ever held in his entire life.

Normally he channelled no more than enough to launch a few good fireballs, plenty to take on most enemies, or to practice with. This time he was gathering enough to knock down a castle, and just hoped that it would be enough. Yet strangely it was no more difficult. The stakes were perhaps slightly higher in that if he made a mistake, there was the likelihood that he would explode like a blocked cannon, levelling the entire clearing in the process instead of just burning himself to a cinder, but the effort involved was no greater. That surprised him.

After nearly five years of daily practice with the arcane texts, struggling to master the complex exercises, and learning to hold ever more sophisticated shapes in his thoughts, he'd reached some form of plateau. A level beyond which he could not progress. In fact for the last few years he'd almost thought himself sliding backwards in some areas as his hopes had faded and his mood darkened. Particularly in terms of increasing his strength. Sure, his control might have been improving, but it had seemed he was paying a price for that control in terms of raw strength.

That had scared him for a while, because he knew that only when he had his magic at full power would he ever have a hope of rescuing Ryshal. And that was his goal. In fact it had been his only purpose in training, even though he knew in his heart that he had no real hope of doing that. Because to get to her he'd have to get to his brother first, and to get to him he would have to go through an entire keep of soldiers and wizards. And even if he did finally manage to get to him, one of Heri's guards would only hold a sword to Ryshal's throat until he let him go. Despair had set in after a while and he guessed that that was part of what had held him back. But even knowing what it was, he had not been able to fight it. Until now. Now for some reason, the power he needed was coming to him in leaps and bounds.

Perhaps he had been getting stronger as his studies progressed, something his instructors back in Fair Fields had always promised him would happen if he worked at it. Perhaps it was just the need and the imminent danger that was giving him the extra strength. Possibly it was the ever growing anger as he thought about what these things were doing to Ryshal's kin while he was still exiled here, unable to rescue her. It could even be the relief as he finally had an enemy to strike at instead of simply turning his anger inwards. Or maybe it was just that the drawing of the fire had never been the hard part. Whatever it was he didn't care. He couldn't. Not when the magic was singing so sweetly in his veins.

Sam felt a darkness in his soul, and it revelled in the power. It sang at the thought of what it was going to do with that power. It screamed of vengeance and might. Sam was scared – of it as much as the enemy – but not as much as he should have been. Because that same darkness would not allow it. The power that he'd struggled to attain for so long had finally arrived. In fact there was suddenly far more than he'd ever dreamt of. And he was going to use it to destroy his enemies. *All of them*. Instead of worrying about the danger, or even the rightness of his actions, Sam simply let the magic build and concentrated only on hanging on to it until it was time to be used.

All around him the temperature fell drastically, and soon the clearing had a frost forming all over it, as well as the nearer trees. In fact the only place not turning white was the patch of green on which he and Tyla stood. Winter was suddenly coming to the forests on a beautiful summer morning. It was something he'd seen many times before, though never on such a scale. All fire magicians had seen this from time to time. It was simply fire and ice – two sides of the same magical coin. After all, they had to draw their fire from somewhere.

In time Sam knew he had drawn enough fire to handle anything that came. He had enough fire magic to level a mountain. If what he held within him couldn't destroy them, then nothing could. It was time to start focussing it.

Draw, shape and release. Those were the three steps in using any elemental magic, and he had practised them all until he had fallen asleep on his feet on too many nights. This was no different except for its impossible scale. Now that the drawing was done it was time to shape it. To make it into the weapon he needed.

First he began by preparing his weapons to serve as spell founts. These would be able to store and release the magic in controlled bursts. Normally for a wizard, the shaping was held within the wizard himself, but as Sam also had a good grounding in Earth magic as well, he'd discovered over the years that he could impart small amounts of the magic into solid objects and use them to shape and hold it. It was what the common folk and hedge wizards called enchantment.

Few other wizards were also enchanters, something for which he could be grateful since for a wizard at war, enchantment was one of the most useful weapons he could use. With enough time he could enchant a legion of weapons and traps; enough to devastate an army before he even had to ready his own defences.

Enchantment was some of the most delicate and complicated wizardry he had ever studied, and yet he'd found over the years as he'd practised it, that it wasn't difficult for him. A sign perhaps of his increasing control of the magic. But never before had he tried imparting such huge amounts of magic into any weapon.

First he imbued his favourite greatsword with the fire scythe enchantment and enough power to slice through a mountain. He gave it all that the sword could take without exploding, which was a lot. The sword was well made and had not a single imperfection along its gleaming length. It had to be to handle the power he was channelling into it. Despite his concerns the sword held the power perfectly, and he re-sheathed the blade with extreme care. With so much magic within it, even a small dent from a fall could result in the weapon exploding.

Next came the battle-axe. He gave it the thunder fire storm enchantment. The axe itself was almost too large to use as a weapon even for him, its double-sided head weighing twice as much as even a greatsword. But that same mass made it perfect for holding a tremendous amount of fire magic, while its shape added focus to the enchantment. And this particular sorcery was his preferred magical attack as much for the spectacular fire storm it created as for its effectiveness.

Both of those were enchantments he had practised and cast many times before, and other than the unusual amount of power he was instilling in them, he knew the weapons could handle the magic. The bulk of the magic though could not be released into a weapon or other inanimate object. Instead it had to be shaped and released. Only a wizard could hold and use such power. As a spell caster he had to hold it, shape it and release it into himself. And this time it would not just be a few small fireballs that he held. This time he would hold on to an inferno.

With some trepidation Sam focussed the rest of the fire magic into his hands. Holding it apart in two equal and opposite measures he knew that the world around him would be safe – until they touched. Then, when the time came and provided he was strong enough and brave enough – and maybe desperate enough – he would release the fire ring conjuration. It was something he'd never tried before. It wasn't just the power that was dangerous about the spell, but the release of that particular shape directly from his own flesh. The spell was one of the most dangerous possible for a wizard, and with the power he was holding anything could happen. But if it did he guessed, he would never know anything about it.

That done he waited, desperately trying not to fidget as his patience was strained. Nor could he stop himself from shaking, as the magic strained to be released. And with all that power literally coursing through his flesh and his steel, who could blame him if he couldn't sit still? For once he forgave himself his poor self-control, though he made sure he didn't let his hands touch.

To keep himself from thinking about it, Sam spent the next little while simply counting the passage of time. Using it as something to concentrate on instead of the magic inside him, demanding to be released. He'd nearly reached a thousand before the first of the steel rats reached the clearing. But then when they finally did, he smiled and let out a sigh of relief. Soon he would be able to release all the fire coursing within him, and it would be glorious. But not yet.

"Alder's balls!" He swore to himself when he saw the first of the rats appear – but not out of shock. The soldier had told him what to expect. Instead for once he meant it as a promise. He was going to rain down all the fury of the twisted god of mischief upon their steel heads, and when he was done none would remain. It seemed fitting somehow to use the god's name. He was said to be twisted; part man, part beast, part male, part female, both hairy and scaled. A jumble of bits and pieces all held together by his divine presence. Soon these steel creatures would be the same. A jumble of parts.

They came from the direction of Shavarra as he'd expected, but only a few dozen at first. Behind them however, he could feel many, many more, spread out in a long column. All would soon be dead. Assuming they were ever truly alive.

For some reason the rats stopped briefly in their advance when they approached the clearing and spotted him. After a moment's thought he even knew why. He could feel it coming from them. Confusion. They had never before seen their prey standing still before them and waiting. Normally they either jumped on their prey while it was unaware of them or they chased it. This was different. They didn't know what to do. So they asked.

Sam couldn't have explained how they asked. Couldn't even have described the manner in which they spoke, or who they spoke to. But he heard them sending their question back to their master so far away, and he heard the response just as clearly. Kill! As if there should ever have been any doubt.

Samual

No sooner had they been given their orders then the first dozen or so of the steel rats charged at him like rampaging lions, attempting to cover a distance of a full hundred and fifty or more yards of open land as quickly as possible. It was a mistake.

Sam lowered the sword until it pointed directly at them, and with a simple command a blast of magic streamed from it, like a scythe made out of fire. It hit the first of the rats dead on, slicing them in flaming halves. The golems exploded as though they were filled with gunpowder and the steel fragments fell everywhere. The sight filled him with relief as well as satisfaction. It was a good sign. It meant that as strong as the rats were, they were also vulnerable, something he hadn't truly been sure of until just then. It could only be because they too were imbued with too much magic. Once their form or their function was altered even a little, it became unstable, and they exploded. That was a weakness which could be exploited.

The rats either didn't seem to understand that, or if they did then they didn't care. A second pack of the rats charged directly over the bodies of their former pack mates, only to meet a similar fate. A heartbeat later they were followed by a third. The golems it seemed weren't bright – but they were obedient.

All up at least a hundred steel rats surrendered their insides to the fire scythe spell before somewhere a halt was called. Their master, having sensed something of their sudden unexpected losses, stopped them before they could lose the rest. Obviously he could see something through their glowing red eyes. Enough at least to see the problem and form a plan.

Realising that his army was facing a wizard, and probably guessing he was using some form of scything spell, the golem master reasoned that Sam wouldn't be able to get all of them if they came in small groups of three or four each, from all directions at once. He was right too. The scythe spell couldn't handle such an attack very well. But then Sam had expected that the rats would learn from their mistakes. It was just a pity he hadn't got more of them before they'd changed tactics. The sword still had at least half of the fire magic spell raging within it.

As he felt the rats circling the clearing, gathering into their groups and preparing for the order to attack Sam sheathed the greatsword and raised his battle-axe high above his head. Did the rat master guess his intentions? Sam didn't know. But what he did know was that it was already too late as he saw the first of the rats entering the clearing and knew it was time. Even before the rats had been given the order to attack, he released all of the fire magic that he'd stored in the axe in a single glorious strike, and watched with satisfaction as a fire storm appeared somewhere over his head.

A spinning, screaming ball of fire, it spat out bolts of liquid fire in every direction, like a thousand insane archers with flaming arrows. Yet each of those bolts found its way unerringly to its target and at least fifty more rats went up in flames in the forest in a single stroke. Even Sam was impressed by the potency of the enchantment. Never before had he seen the spell work so effectively. His enemy no doubt wasn't so pleased.

A hundred and fifty odd golems destroyed in only a matter of moments by a single human. All that work and magic that had gone into making them; lost. Sam could almost hear the scream of rage that came from the rats' master so far away, and he tried not to smile too much. At least not yet. The battle was far from over.

Then his enemy showed his inexperience in battle. Angered beyond reason the master brought out all his remaining rats, at least another three or four hundred and tried a mass attack. He was trying to overload the power of the fireball spell with sheer numbers. He needn't have worried about it. Sam had used every last ounce of fire magic in the axe in that one blast. He'd had to to kill so many steel rats at once from such a distance. But he wasn't worried. Not by the golems anyway. Not when he'd already seen the results of his opening attacks and felt his new found power.

Even as he watched the rats streaming towards him like a sprawling river of steel teeth, red eyes and claws, Sam sheathed his battle-axe beside his sword, and raised his arms above his head instead. It was time to see if the fire ring could do as much damage as his studies had told him it could. Once five thousand or more years ago before the Dragon Wars, fire rings had been considered among the most powerful of all a wizard's attacks. But the devastating losses of people from it and other such magics had been terrible. According to some it was these very magic shapes that had helped bring the Dragon to power and ultimately nearly destroyed the world.

The Dragon Wars had brought the ancient world to an end. Empires and realms had been shattered. Lands had been destroyed. According to some even the ancients themselves had been broken. Because once they had been one people. After the wars they had evolved into many different races. All that was left of those ancient times were scraps of knowledge, legends and ancient artefacts. The fire ring was one of those scraps of ancient knowledge that had survived. One he had studied carefully.

Properly used it was supposed to be able to destroy an army. Improperly used of course, it would destroy him. Concentrating furiously on holding all that raging energy coursing through his hands together while trying to shape the final form, Sam brought his hands ever so slowly and smoothly together. His timing was perfect.

When the closest of the rats was less than fifty yards from him, his palms touched, and a screaming fire breathing monster broke free within him. Suddenly he had to hang on for dear life as something more powerful and wild than he had ever imagined possible ripped loose from his body and coalesced just over his head and all around him.

The forces involved – the heat and the light – were almost unbearable as the fire ring screamed its way free of him. It started to spin violently and briefly Sam had to shut his eyes to keep from going blind. He panicked a little. But only for an instant. It was far too important to keep his concentration so that the flow of magic into the spell was smooth and even. To give in to fear was to die. He could not give up his own life fire in the process. And to allow himself to give in to the spectacle or the pain was to do just that. That was the true danger in wizardry. That in giving of his essence to bind the magic to him, the wizard would release his life force with the spell. More than a few spell casters had died trying to use a spell far too powerful for them.

But not this wizard. And not this day. Sam held on for dear life and felt the magic leave him cleanly.

A heart beat or a thousand hours later his battle with the spell was over and Sam watched with immense relief and awe as a living circle of fire spread out from him in all directions, as fast as an arrow could fly. It was like a ripple in a pond spreading out after a stone had been cast. But this ripple came from the very depths of the underworld itself; an inferno of rage as it ripped away from him like a demon released.

The rats didn't stand a chance, but neither did they care. Even through the rapidly departing fire wall he could see their steel faces and red eyes as they continued to charge at him, stupidly running directly into the oncoming fire. But only until the two touched. Then the rats exploded. Hundreds of glorious explosions that looked like cannon fire.

In mere heartbeats the battle was over, the rat army had

been completely vanquished without a single survivor, and Sam knew a moment of complete triumph. But only a moment as that feeling quickly turned to one of shock and horror. The fire ring was even more powerful than he'd guessed, and more than it needed to be; far more. Sam watched with horror and awe as it reached the end of the clearing and then just kept advancing on through the forest. A raging juggernaut of savage and yet strangely beautiful destruction.

The effect as it hit the nearby still frozen trees was staggering, as they too exploded with enough force to make the ground shake, before raining smouldering sap and bark everywhere. But at least they didn't catch fire. Further on out most of the trees did, exploding into fifty or a hundred foot high fire balls that turned the sky orange, and unleashed thunderclaps that shook the ground in all directions. And all the while the wall of fire that was the ring's edge just kept travelling further and further away from him.

Finally, perhaps only a dozen beats of a frightened heart after it had begun its insane rampage, Sam watched the fire ring disintegrate, turning into brief flashes of glorious light and thunder before disappearing up into the sky like ascending angels streaking for heaven itself. But they were no angels. Nor were they demons either. They were the remnants of something far more powerful. In that short span of time the fire ring had done more damage than any dozen hurricanes.

Left behind in the clearing where he stood and for half a league of forest in every direction lay a scene of utter destruction. In the distance trees, pines, oaks and even great redwoods stood broken. Many had been smashed into kindling. Many more were sending up clouds of black smoke, as the wet sap tried to catch fire, while others had become raging bonfires. Nearer to the clearing many of the once proud trees were little more than stumps in the ground, while their blackened branches had formed into piles of debris scattered like fallen leaves around them.

For the longest time Sam simply stared at the carnage around him, stunned at how much damage he'd wrought, and wondering how he could have created something so terrible. What he had just released had to be a dozen, perhaps a hundred times more powerful than anything he'd ever done in his life. It was much more than he'd intended. More than he'd even known was possible. In fact there was only one word for what he had wrought; devastation. It would be years if not decades before the forest recovered from his magic. He also wondered if the elves would ever forgive him for destroying one of their forests.

Where had the power come from? As he sat there on Tyla's back staring, that question echoed through his mind. Because what he had done, wasn't just more than anything he'd ever been able to do before. He suspected it was more than any mere wizard could do. More surely than even a master could achieve.

Yet at the same time as he sat there staring in awe, there was also a feeling of savage pride and triumph running through him. After all, there were no rats remaining. Not a single one had survived the fire ring. Five hundred, six hundred – perhaps even more – golems had been turned to scrap metal in a single blast and the first wave of the enemy's attack had been destroyed in a single battle. The next wave, if it had yet been formed, wasn't even on the horizon. He had just won a major victory for the elves. Maybe the elves would take that into consideration if they ever thought about judging his actions.

Though it was wrong, there was also a certain feeling of satisfaction running through him as he surveyed the carnage all around him, and discovered his true strength. No longer could he regard himself as a student. Power on this scale, though its effects might have been terrible, could only be found in a master. Despite the endless pain and suffering he'd felt as he'd struggled to learn the spells and to carry every more fire within him, this here was proof that he had reached a new level. Mastery.

The satisfaction of having destroyed an enemy, and of having finally found such incredible power after so many years of trying was a wonder to him. But it was more than that. It was hope. Looking around and seeing all he had wrought he knew he had finally found all the power he needed to rescue Ry. He could level her prison, the keep and everything around it should he choose and his brother and his armies could do nothing to stop him. It was now only a question of tactics.

Once he had thought his strength in reclaiming her would be as that of a soldier, with the might of steel to be his anchor, and magic as an aid in the fight. Now he realised, his magic had become far more powerful than any steel could ever be, and it was a good feeling. He knew finally that not only could he do it, but that none could stand against him. The time to reclaim his wife from her prison and punish his half-brother for his evil was upon him. Very soon his life would be whole once more and he could barely contain the excitement at the thought. Soon Ryshal would be back in his arms.

But not this day.

The price for his spell casting was already demanding to be paid. He knew it even as he sat there staring in speechless awe at what he had achieved. While his life essence was still strong, his magic wasn't. He had spent an incredible amount of magic in forming that ring, and his own fire was subdued, almost asleep. He had no more spells left in him for the moment, and soon he would fall asleep where he sat as his body and soul tried to regenerate the magic. He had just done the equivalent of running twenty leagues in the time it took to walk a dozen paces, and his flesh and soul needed time to recover. He couldn't afford to be here when that happened, or the next wave of golems might catch him sleeping. He had to leave, and soon.

Dismounting quickly, Sam gathered together as many parts of the dead golems as he could, hoping to have something to study later. Something to bring to the more learned masters of the arcane arts. But what remained was almost unrecognisable. The rat bodies were twisted. Many had torn and melted from the heat of the fire and the force of the explosions. In the end he gathered half a dozen of the best heads, tossed them in the already over full saddle bags and made off after the last elven party.

Finding his way after them wasn't an easy job either he discovered, as his horse had to pick her way gingerly through more than half a league of blackened, wind strewn branches which were so thick that they actually obscured the length of the trail. Despite her sure footedness, Sam found he had to lead his mare through the worst of it on foot, clearing the path ahead with what little remained of his magic, and his boots as they went. Later, when he was through the worst of it, he found that smaller pieces of the trees were dotted along the trail all the way back to his home.

It was a difficult trip back, but it was still a good journey, knowing that at least one enemy had been vanquished, and that the power he had searched for, for so many years was finally with him. It was a vital journey too when exhaustion was galloping up on him. He had given too much into that final spell, and he was drained. It was still only late in the morning, and the sun was high, yet already he was dreaming of a nice soft bed. It was difficult to stay alert. He needed to get to the safety of the elves.

As he rode, he tried to stay awake by concentrating on what he'd learned of the enemy. Not only from facing them in combat, but also from finally seeing the golems with his own eyes. And he realised that he had learned something.

Something important. More than just their strengths and weaknesses, or even their strange method of communication with their master. He'd looked into their glowing red eyes at some point and seen what surely anyone should have known, but apparently no one else was prepared to admit. These things weren't actually golems. They were machina.

True golems had nothing of life or machinery in them. They were inanimate lumps of whatever material they were created out of, until they had a spark of magic and a dose of alchemy breathed into them. But these were machina. Machines created with moving parts and a shadow of life. Even without having magic imbued in them they still were nothing like golems. They remained inanimate but were able to be moved into positions as a child could move the limbs of a doll. And once someone had breathed their magical shadow life into them, they became much more than any mere golem.

They had far greater mobility for a start, as the elves had already found to their cost. Where a golem would usually plod along as though every movement was a major exertion, these things could run, jump and climb as well as any living animal. More troubling then that though was that they had far greater autonomy. A golem practically had to be ordered to carry out every little movement. They were too stupid to be able to follow complicated commands. But these things could be given an order and then be left to carry it out. They could even ask questions. Unlike golems they had a simple intelligence. They were machina.

The only problem he had with the understanding of their nature was that there were no machina left. The last of them had been created and destroyed in the terrible Dragon Wars, more than five thousand years ago. A time when the forces of a warlord known only as the Dragon, had created an army of machina, tens or even hundreds of thousands strong, to lay waste to the entire world. But he had eventually been defeated, his armies destroyed, and the secrets behind their creation lost to time. Not a single one had ever been seen since. Until now.

Which left him with only a few frightening possibilities. The first and potentially the least dangerous, was that someone had found the remains of part of his army, and somehow reanimated it. Bad enough, but still manageable as it meant the enemy's strength was limited. More limited now that Sam had destroyed so many of them. The only problem with that theory was that according to all the legends, the Dragon's entire army had been destroyed, and whatever might have survived should have rusted away long ago.

Of course artefacts from the ancient ages before the Dragon wars were still around, and occasionally turned up in various ruins or were dug up in fields. And many of them still had magic. Powerful magic. So much so that many wizards would spend fortunes trying to acquire the ancient treasures.

The second possibility was that someone had discovered the secrets behind the making of the machina, in which case they could surely create many more of these monsters, and many other types as well. The history books and sagas had spoken of some machina that flew and others that burrowed under walls. That was more worrying, as it meant that the enemy could make more of these horrors as he needed them. And Sam had no doubt that he would.

Yet even that compared poorly with the third option. The possibility that the warlord himself, the Dragon, had returned after five thousand years to re-conquer the world. And while it was surely impossible, a little voice in the back of his head kept reminding him that the warlord had never been killed. After more than ten years of battle, with the numbers of dead people reaching in the millions if not the tens of millions, his armies had finally been destroyed, and the warlord had been defeated. But according to the legends he had cheated death and had chosen to flee even while sickening from a poison spell, rather than be executed.

That was one of the great mysteries of the Dragon. He had come out of nowhere with a mighty magical army of steel, and returned to it afterwards, with no one having ever even seen his face. There were so many mysteries about him. For a start if no one knew what he looked like, then no one knew if he was human, elf or dwarf, or any other sort of mortal. Scholars had debated that very point for thousands of years. And they certainly didn't know where he had come from. After all, he had magic stronger and stranger than any ever known. Magic that wasn't even being studied anywhere else, let alone mastered. And his goal didn't seem to be conquest so much as death. The total obliteration of all people. Perhaps he had truly been a demon instead of a man as some claimed. And if he had been, could he return? Sam wasn't even sure if demons actually died.

The truly horrible thing though was that these machina had acted in exactly the same way as the Dragon's machina of old. They had continued to kill even after attacking and taking the cities. For it seemed they'd never wanted the cities; only the death of the people who called those cities home. Could he truly have returned after five thousand years? There was of course no answer. Not yet. But what there was he knew, was a pattern. Or the beginning of one at least.

Though Sam didn't want to admit it – and the elves might not want to hear it – this new enemy, be he the Dragon returned or a replacement, was following the same pattern so far. Attack by stealth, kill everyone he could, and then leave the cities deserted and dead without any apparent reason. And if the pattern held he would then strike again, somewhere else. Somewhere far away. Next time Sam knew, it would probably not be the elves who were hit. It might be a human land or a dwarven province. It might be the gnomes or the pixies. Sam had no way of knowing who would be attacked or when.

Samual

All he did know as he kicked his mare in the sides to hurry her up, was that there would be a next time. Conquering Shavarra had never been their enemy's entire dream. Every fibre in his being knew that. He was merely getting started.

And Sam knew that wherever the enemy next struck, he had to be there.

Chapter Three.

Ryshal lay on her tiny mattress in her dark cell, crying.

It wasn't for the pain, though that was cruel. This new guard who'd turned up – she didn't know his name, and hadn't even seen his face as he always wore a black studded leather mask – was a monster, and the beatings were becoming worse by the day. He hit her as no one should hit another, and not just with his fists. That had only been for the first month or so. Now he used whips and sticks, and some days the blood poured down her back. But she was an elf and a dancer both – she could withstand pain.

The terrible conditions she was held in weren't the reason for her tears either. For five long years she'd been locked away in her dark underground cell, the only light coming from a tiny barred window high above that showed her the sun for only a few precious moments every day. Yet she could bear that too. A few moments of sunlight were enough to drive away the cold from her bones for a while. And though the damp and fungus ate at her lungs, just as the fleas and lice bit at her skin, she had the strength to withstand that too. Even the starvation was tolerable. A few scraps of mouldy bread and water were enough to keep her going. For a while.

What hurt her so was none of those things. It wasn't even the fear of what was coming. It was the horror of why it could finally be allowed. She had listened to the raucous laughter of this new gaoler day after day while she lay bleeding on the rack, heard his plans to continue to beat her until there was nothing left, and she knew that time was running out for her.

It hadn't been. Until recently she'd known that this nightmare would one day end. She'd known that Samual would come for her, and her life would return to how it had been previously. She would recover in the arms of her husband and family. She would learn to dance again. She would teach again. She would raise her own children. That was her gift – faith. She prayed constantly and the Goddess spoke to her some days. She whispered in her ears that everything would be all right. That this, her suffering was all a part of her divine plan. And that she would be rewarded tenfold for her torment. It was her faith that kept her strong in this hellish place and she clung to it with a determination stronger than steel.

But suddenly things were different. This new guard had arrived and had started beating her, and she knew that meant that something had changed up above in the keep. Heri had not dared to beat her so badly before. In fact he had for the most part left her completely alone. For all his evil he'd known better than to harm her. He knew how terrible Samual's vengeance would be when he found out, and he knew enough to fear it.

So she had been given if not good food, then at least enough simple gruel to keep her going. She had been allowed to bathe, and to wash away the insect pests that assailed her. She had been given some thin blankets to keep her warm at night. If she became ill the healers or the priests of Phil the White were sent to her. And she had not been beaten. In truth the gaolers had been almost respectful, knowing why she was there, and knowing that they never wanted to face the wrath of her husband if she died at their hands. She was Ryshal Hanor after all. They did not want to face her husband. Ever.

But something had changed, and all she could think was that either Heri was no longer in control of the realm, or for some reason he no longer feared his half-brother. And there was only one reason he would not fear Samual.

If Samual was dead.

That was why she cried. Her husband, her beloved, and the father to her children yet to be conceived; dead. It could not be. It could not be tolerated. But as the days went by and the beatings continued and even grew worse, the fear returned to haunt her like a ghost in the night.

She prayed of course. Prayed constantly to the Goddess. But she heard nothing back save that she was her child, always. And to keep with her faith. It was all part of the plan. And that her husband would come for her. This, the Goddess promised, was the hardest part. It was always hardest just before the end. And the end was close.

Ryshal told herself that it was impossible that Sam was dead. She knew her husband, she knew him for the warrior he was. No matter how many cut-throats his brother sent against him he would always survive. He would always win. He did not know how to lose. With a sword in his hand and fire in his eyes, he was unstoppable. A warrior such as the world saw only once in a generation.

The guards had told after she'd first been brought down into this nightmare, that more than a hundred of the king's royal guard had fallen to his blade and his fire when he'd first been told of her capture. That he'd gone mad with rage as they kept him from returning to the keep to rescue her, and that only their sheer numbers and the threat to her life had held him back. That would not be enough forever.

And every day he was apart from her, she knew he would be training. He would be practising his magic and his craft, planning her rescue, making himself ready, so that when that glorious day came, there would be no mistake.

Samual would come for her. He could not die. He could not be dead.

But still she cried.

Chapter Four.

The Court was full that morning. There were a dozen petitioners asking to be heard, many of them linked with either the noble houses or the merchant guilds, several emissaries from the nearby realms seeking an audience, and five or six disputes needing to be resolved. It was a long list of duties to get through in a morning. And all Heri really wanted to do was check his soldiers, count his treasury's gold, and listen to the reports of his spies. Those were the things that really mattered. Those were the things that kept him in power.

The rest of this – the polished wooden floors and walls, the grandeur of the huge vaulted ceiling in the throne room, the massive stained glass windows with their depictions of his family's heroic acts, the assembly of overdressed courtiers attending him – they were nothing. Theatre. They were what made him look like a king. But in the end it was always about power. About being able to force his will upon others. And that was done through force of arms, economic might, knowledge and cunning. Looking the part merely helped him keep the throne.

But Heri was surrounded by enemies. Smiling, polite, elegant enemies dressed in all their finery, all of whom would happily stick a knife in his back if they thought they could get away with it. Especially if it would gain them the throne.

Prince Venti was currently standing to one side chatting with some of the ladies. He called himself a prince but really, he was no prince at all. He just claimed the title since his father had been the king before Heri's father had taken it. The man was stupid, but he had a powerful army.

Seeing him standing there posing like a king, Heri had to

fight the impulse to have him killed on the spot. Or even to do something cunning like invite him into his private sanctum and introduce him to his little horse head statue. The man would do well as a horse he thought. And it was about time he made some use of that ancient artefact instead of just letting it sit on his shelves. But he supposed someone would notice the prince's absence and know he had last been seen with the king. It would also be difficult getting a horse out of his sanctum through the underground tunnel.

Lord Cameral stood in the background, holding a drink and giving the impression he was there simply to socialise. And yet Heri noticed he didn't take a single sip of his drink. He pretended to be just a guest enjoying himself, but really he was there to see what he could learn. Watching and listening carefully to everything around him and looking for any piece of information he could exploit. The man was a plotter and a schemer. Luckily his lands were weak. He could cause Heri trouble but ultimately could not take the throne and he knew it.

And then there were the Fallbrights. The entire accursed family was here, all of them stuffed into fine clothes that they looked distinctly uncomfortable in. They were a bunch of brigands – though they called themselves soldiers – who had seized an estate a generation or two back, and held it ever since by force of arms. Naturally they had no respect for him since he wasn't the warrior they wanted, and they weren't afraid to point that out. They weren't going to enjoy today's session of the Court Heri promised himself. That would be his only joy today.

To make matters worse, it was also a celebration – the archaic festival of the midsummer sun or some such thing – and so there were a number of white robed priests of the All Father currently littering the marble tiled floor with their presence and intoning prayers. He hated the priests, and if the gods truly existed he didn't like them much either. But he needed their support so he publicly followed the All Father and pretended faith. He spent good gold keeping the All Father's poxy great temple in good order, and insisted that the people follow the observances of the king of gods. He even kept an adviser from the temple on hand, though he never listened to him.

But at least it was the king of gods that he supported publicly. A worthy god for a king to worship. Not some miserable little god like Vineus or worse the god of one of the other races like the elves' pathetic Goddess. He allowed the worship of the other gods – a king had to indulge the weak minds of his subjects – as long as they didn't go against his rulings. So the priests of the Red God of War and Vineus could be seen walking the streets freely. Phil the White had his own temple in the city. Healing was always a valued gift. The priests of Draco however had been banned from the realm. He had nothing against dragons as long as they stayed far away from him, but their priests liked to play with fire literally and that threatened the safety of everyone. Naturally none of Draco's priests were in attendance.

But as if to make up for their absence there were minstrels. He hated minstrels. Their singing tore at his ears, the sounds of their harps and lutes were pure torture. Adding insult to injury he recognised them as nothing more than a bunch of thieves and beggars who told endless lies about him across a thousand inns. He would have had them all put to the sword had it been allowed. He regularly prayed to the All Father to have them struck down by some plague. But of course that never happened. The gods – if they truly existed – did not do as he asked. And to kill them himself would simply have been seen as a king gone mad, and would have stirred up the people against him. So he had to tolerate them. As the king he had to be seen by the people as at least fair. They were never going to love him as they had loved his father, but if he was considered fair, then at least they wouldn't turn on him.

Heri's mother had taught him that, before she'd turned against him and he'd imprisoned her in the towers with the rest of his enemies. Stupid woman, she'd actually thought that she could control the throne through him. Now she had plenty of time to reflect on her mistakes. He was the king and she should have known better. But still, he visited her and listened to her advice from time to time, one piece of which was to hold regular public courts. His subjects needed to know that their king still lived and that he still held the reins of power tightly. That their lives were his.

They also needed to know that he was beyond them in all the ways that mattered. And so the castle was kept in perfect order, the throne room and all the antechambers were polished daily and the most extravagant of artworks hung from the walls. Naturally most of them were portraits of him, looking down regally over his subjects.

The cannon throne that he'd had carefully crafted in precious metals was another symbol of his power. He had had his golden high backed chair draped in the most expensive furs he could buy and then placed securely on two bronzed cannon. Those cannon in turn stood on a raised dais of marble overlooking the chamber. He thought it emphasized both his wealth and his military might.

Then too he held a dozen balls a year, more than he needed to and far more than he wanted, but he had to demonstrate his wealth at every opportunity.

The guards in their expensive finery and bearing their more than serviceable weapons were also sign of his power, as was the army he kept and the regular patrols he sent throughout the realm. The people had to know he was more than just a man; that he would not be easily overthrown, and that when the time came if they tried, he would crush them. There was a reason he kept the heads of those who had dared to stand against him on a garden of pikes outside the front gates. There was also a reason that there were so many of them.

More important than the people of course, the nobles had to know that he was king. Fair Fields was less a kingdom than a collection of baronies, fiefdoms, principalities and estates that had come together for trade and mutual defence from one another. The throne was a prize that all of them wanted. And they all wanted to see Heri fail so that they could lay claim to it.

He would not fail though. And today every noble house would see once again that he had a way of dealing with those who challenged him. It would keep them in order for a while. And the people would think nothing of it save that the king was supporting them. Today would be a good day for him. If he could just get through it.

Heri sat on his throne, idly clutching his gold and jewel encrusted sceptre, surrounded by his court and tried to look attentive as his mother had schooled him. A king had to be seen to be concerned with affairs of state, even when he wasn't. Like today for example.

Usually he was. Usually he liked being king. He liked having the nobles of the realm bow to him. He liked setting down the law, and watching them grit their teeth in pain as they had to obey. He liked raising taxes for the same reason. Not because of the poor people who also had to pay them. They were nobodies. But the nobles, the pretentious, treacherous lords and ladies of the court – most of whom were always looking for a chance to slip a dagger in to his back – they mattered, and he loved seeing them suffer. He loved seeing the impotent fury in their eyes as they surrounded him, bowed to him, while all the time masking their rage with fake smiles.

This day however, wasn't a good one. First there had been news from his spies that the elves of Shavarra were on the move. No one could tell him why, save that it didn't seem to be a military posture. But the one thing they could tell him was that the elves were heading this way. West towards Fair Fields. Every pigeon they had sent had said the same thing. He didn't like that. He especially didn't like that there could be a war coming. So he had had his patrols start riding the border and now waited impatiently for more news from his spies.

To add to his worries Augrim had been making noises about some huge magical event in the world. He too could tell him little about it, save that it was immense and it heralded major changes in the world. The man might be his magical advisor and highly respected as a wizard, but some days Heri wondered if he was really worth what he paid him. True the wizard had found him a lot of ancient magical treasures for his sanctum, but often his divination skills didn't seem to be the most reliable. And the cost of all those scrolls of magical knowledge the wizard wanted in exchange for his services was excessive. Besides, he hated the wizard's stupid looking beard.

Then a messenger had come from the dungeons with some disturbing news. His prisoner was poorly. That was a worry. He didn't really care in truth whether Ryshal lived or not. She was inconsequential, especially since she'd spurned his advances years before. There were plenty of other wenches happy to share his bedchamber and a whoring elf didn't matter to him. But if she died his hold on Samual died with her, and that could be dangerous.

Samual had magic, which was bad enough. He'd used it against him once, and Heri had counted himself lucky to have been ready for him. Even so it had been close. A lot of men had fallen that day and Heri had nearly fallen with them. But if Samual had been thinking he would have known that his magic wasn't his greatest weapon. Nor was his blade. He was a knight, one of the dearly loved knights of Hanor, and he had a following within his order. People who would blindly follow him. Others would follow them in turn. And they would do so not only because they loved Samual but also in memory of their father – the only king of Fair Fields to have been elected by the people of the land and not the nobles. That made Samual much more dangerous than a few sparks flowing from his fingertips.

It also didn't help that his half-blood brother was fair of face. He stood tall and he smiled and people flocked to him. They listened as he spouted his noble words. They believed in him. The bastard had been favoured by the All Father.

Heri hated him for that. He always had. Samual had been his father's favourite. He had always had everything given to him. Worse still, things came easily to him. Whether it was swords, or warcraft, learning or magic, he had been given everything. For as long as he could remember Heri had always wanted Samual dead. It had just never seemed to happen.

Heri for his part wasn't loved by the people, and there was nothing he could do to change that. The people wanted a hero. Or a worthy king. At the very least they wanted someone they could understand. Feel a little kinship with. But using the shortened version of his name had not been enough to do that. Samual called himself Sam and the people flocked to him because of it. He shortened his name and they lost what little respect they had for him to begin with. And now instead of Heriott he was eternally Heri. As for the Court they hated him. An older brother, even if he was a bastard son without a legitimate claim to the throne could still pose a serious threat to his rule if he was loved. Heri couldn't afford threats.

Lose the throne and lose his life. That was one of the facts of life his mother had taught him, and Heri had learned the lesson well. He had no interest in dying.

That was why Heri had locked Samual's elven whore up in the first place. Samual had made a pretence of leaving Fair Fields with his new wife and her parents. He had loaded up wagons and made all the right noises. But it had been a lie. Heri had seen through to the cold, calculating heart of his pox ridden half-brother. Samual had been making a play for the throne. He had only pretended to be leaving. In truth he had been fomenting revolution. His plan had been to make the people protest and beg him to stay. He had even amassed a following. It wouldn't have been long Heri knew, before Samual had graciously acceded to the people's demands and taken the throne from him. That could not have been allowed.

So he had abducted Samual's wife and locked her away. Then he had sent his royal guards to kill Samual. They had failed. Badly. But his hostage had saved him. Even at the end Samual had not been able to kill him. The whore was his weakness. And Heri knew he had to keep her. Always. He could not afford her getting ill.

The girl had to live, at least until his brother had died. But Samual kept refusing to die, so his miserable elven whore had to live. For the moment. Because if she died it would be war. And Heri had no idea how strong or cunning Samual had become. How many allies he'd gained. All he knew was that until his assassins who he paid a hefty amount of coin for had finally done the one and only job he paid them to do, she had to live. Then she could hang.

If only he could find him! Heri was almost certain now that Samual was somewhere in one of the nearby elven realms. He was half elf so where else could he go? But finding one man who was presumably using a false name in either of the two nearest elven realms was proving extremely difficult. Samual could be anywhere, gathering his power and preparing his plans to take his throne. The whore had to live.

He'd sent a messenger back down to the dungeons with those very instructions, and a healer as well, but they hadn't yet reported back. For all he knew the elven wench could already be dead. Then there would be an underworld of trouble. Especially if the nobles realised.

He had gone to great lengths to make sure that they never found out about his prisoner. Because the instant they did, his brother would have an ally. And if she died, then the nobles would have an angry fire mage, knight and a prince at their side. It would become a revolution.

"Highness?"

Heri looked up as his major-domo finally caught his attention, reminding him that he had a decision to render. The man was an irritation some days with his simpering words, and Heri hated the way he watched him all the time with those calculating eyes. But he could be useful, especially when he reminded him that he was supposed to be hearing a dispute instead of fretting. A dispute between a merchants' guild and the Fallbrights. Which reminded him in turn that he had already made up his mind – in fact he had done so well before the hearing – and he couldn't be bothered listening to anything more from the two of them. The morning was marching on and Heri had had enough. It was time to give his decision.

"Fallbright, attend me." He commanded the ageing Baron with an imperious wave of his hand, and watched with not particularly well-concealed glee as the noble limped his way to the foot of his throne. He was an old man, his hair very grey if not completely white yet, and he'd suffered an injury a year before falling off his horse. An injury that would not heal. But then it wouldn't when the Baron's own healers were in the pay of Heri, and had been commanded to keep him suffering. With luck he'd never walk properly again. But that was the price for disloyalty. After all, the man had openly questioned his will. Now it would be good that the rest of the court should witness his dominion over the noble, and learn some respect.

"Highness." Baron Fallbright bowed low to him as was required, despite the obvious pain it caused him. But then he probably knew that bad news was coming, and he didn't want to make it any worse.

"Your roads have been closed too long, the taxes you demand of the merchants passing through, too high. This will change. From the morn you will halve your taxes on the merchants, and your lands will be open to all."

"Yes your Highness." The Baron bowed again, probably hating him with every breath of his weakened body, while the rest of the court clapped politely. No doubt at least the merchant cartels would welcome his decision even if the nobles hated him for it. But Heri hadn't made his decision for them. Nor for trade. It was always about strategy. Fallbright had defied him, openly questioned his decisions in front of the court. He had to pay and he had to be seen to pay.

With the income from the merchants halved, the Barony of Fallbright would find itself in a difficult position. They could not afford to continue spending as they did, which meant their small army would become smaller again. Their spies and assassins would be reduced in number as well, and most importantly, their influence in the court would suffer.

Of course they'd fight back. They'd find some other devious method for gaining coin, and start once again to rise to the top of the pile of noble houses through a careful programme of assassinations and espionage. They'd probably also make a few more attempts on his life, never realising that their assassins were also in Heri's pay, or that their spies told them exactly what Heri wanted them to hear. The Barony was a big house and a rich one, but not that clever. Still, perhaps this would be a good evening to sit in his sanctum and spy on them through the Window of Parsus.

Heri dismissed the Baron with a casual wave and watched him limp back to his place in the queue of attendees to stand with his advisers, happy with his work. It would perhaps have been more satisfying to kill the old man, whether officially or through his own assassins, but that would bring its own problems in the form of his sons. The Baron had three of them and all of them were nasty in their own right. Each had trained as soldiers, although the two elder sons were none too bright. When their father died there would be a grab for his seat, and when one of them claimed it, trouble would begin. Bainbury – their main town – would be in turmoil – and there would likely be battles in the street as soldiers loyal to each of the three sons fought. And no matter which one of them finally succeeded and took the reins of the barony all three were just about ambitious and stupid enough to actually try to form an alliance against him and march on the citadel. The eldest two anyway.

They would lose of course. Fall Keep was ready for them – and even if it wasn't he had one or two toys in his secret sanctum that would destroy them completely – but they wouldn't be clever enough to realise that in advance, and there would be trouble until then. It would lead to his people panicking. Nobles and merchants would all be busy trying to take advantage of the discord, and of course, there would be more threats against him as people took their chances. The old man was a nuisance, but at least he wasn't stupid.

The youngest son though, Harmion, the weasel, now he was clever. Cunning like a rat. Or like one of Alder's followers as Heri sometimes suspected he was. Who else could the weasel follow but the God of mischief? If Harmion somehow took the seat when his father died, things would be worse. He wouldn't make the same mistakes as his older brothers. He would use subtlety and guile, and that was far harder to defend against.

Maybe, Heri thought, it was time that the weasel had an unfortunate accident. A crossbow bolt in his back. And while he was at it, Samual too could finally die. His assassins had failed repeatedly against him, causing him no end of annoyance, but there were always more to hire, and some of them surely were better skilled.

Sooner or later one of them would have to get through. Sooner or later Samual would die and he would finally be rid of him.

Heri tried to concentrate on that joyful thought as he listened to the next petitioner – a trading consortium upset about the market fees in one of Lord Cameral's towns. But really he couldn't. Not when Samual was so well hidden from his agents and all he wanted to do was kill him.

Now there was a prayer he would offer to the All Father.

Chapter Five.

Life was pain for Sam. It had been for a day and a half.

His woes had begun from the very moment he'd finally caught up with the elves after the battle and he was beginning to wonder if that had been a mistake. Despite the exhaustion of their mounts they had made good time and were very nearly at Torin Vale by the time he and Tyla had reached them. Sam by that stage had been almost asleep in the saddle. Only his horse's smooth gait and his feet bound firmly in the stirrups had stopped him from falling to the ground. The fire within him had seemed to have been drained by the battle – more so than ever before. He knew he couldn't have launched another attack for at least a week. Fortunately he figured the enemy had been badly hurt and his remaining machina a long way behind. He would need time to recover. The elves would have time to flee.

It was lucky he had a well-trained steed. He could set her off on course, and Tyla would carry on even though he had given her the lead. True to her nature, Tyla once on the path had quickly located her daughter Aegis' scent ahead, and had tracked her down and even given chase. By the time he truly awoke he was already in the midst of the fleeing elves. Elves who understandably had questions.

Despite the distance, they had seen and heard much of the battle, if only from the shaking of the ground under their feet, the thunder that echoed for leagues and the great balls of flame that seared the very sky. But from at least several leagues away, that was an incredible testament to just how massive that last spell must have been. Though Sam had been at the very heart of the blast, he had been sheltered from the worst of it by the channelling itself. So even what he had witnessed had been limited. The true force of the magic only the machina and the forest had known, and they weren't talking.

Half asleep on Tyla, Sam had answered a few of the Elders' questions as best he could while they rode the last few leagues into Torin Vale together, before he had collapsed completely in the saddle. By then he knew he had gotten as far as he could under his own power, and others would care for him until he was awake again. Half elf or not, the elves did not abandon anyone. Besides, if they hadn't, they wouldn't have been able to interrogate him. And he was beginning to realise the elves were curious.

He had awoken to find himself in the town itself and was soon being interrogated by a veritable menagerie of wizards and war masters, all of whom were desperately trying to work out what had happened. Even from the town they had seen and heard some of the battle, while the wizards – especially those with any sensitivity to fire – had felt it. The elves he was with were of course only too happy to tell them what they knew, which naturally only wetted their leaders' appetite for answers. The only part of which he could tell them before he had collapsed again was that the nearer machina were gone, and the rest were a long way off. He had bought them some time.

That was when he'd finally done the intelligent thing and fainted. Unfortunately he'd foolishly woken up.

He had awoken in the middle of the morning to find himself lying on a wagon and being carted out of town as the people of Torin Vale itself were packing up and joining the caravan. But he hadn't been lucky enough to be in one of the wagons peopled with villagers. Instead he had been left to sleep in the midst of a bunch of wizards, war masters and elders, all of whom were more than a little curious about him and what he'd done, and actually seemed to be happy to threaten torture to find out. To make matters worse he'd awoken with a headache vicious enough to make the idea of torture look good.

Of course while he was still asleep they had started doing a little sleuthing of their own. It was a polite way of saying they'd searched him thoroughly. They'd started by removing his helmet and discovered his half human half elven nature, something that naturally enough hadn't gone down well. Then they'd moved on to his armour, quickly identifying the crest of the House of Hanor, as well as the fact that he'd tried to remove it. They'd put two and two together and soon decided that he was some sort of rogue knight. It was actually close enough to the truth, even if he still remained true to his vows and was in good standing with the Order of Hanor.

After that they'd gone through his saddle bags and kit, examining first his weapons, and then finding his books of wizardry. Things that should not exist outside a guild. Such books should they fall into the wrong hands could be dangerous, and for that reason alone they were closely guarded. The wizards were understandably upset by the discovery, the more so when they saw that some of the books were of the higher levels of fire and ice magic as well as earth magic and nature magic, and that all were written for warring wizards. Thus with a single discovery he'd gone from being a rogue knight to a rogue wizard and possibly a criminal from another land. But at least the books weren't from any of the elven guilds. That would have been proof of a crime in their lands. But the books weren't written in Elvish and he had been cleared of that accusation at least.

Their pet theory had become a near certainty when they'd gone through all that Aegis was carrying in her packs. He'd loaded the poor horse high with valuables before he'd left, just in case he needed to find some coin on the way. Perhaps that hadn't been such a clever idea after all.

The three sets of blackened snake scale armour they took

as evidence of his antisocial nocturnal activities. Only thieves and rogues had such armour they reasoned, and only the most successful ones at that. The others couldn't afford it. The brace of stilettos and vial of dragon bane poison bore testament to another grisly trade. Then they'd found the shadow cloak, and all their theories had somehow become proof. After all, none but the most exclusive and expensive assassins would have such a cloak. Their cost was beyond anyone else's means. By the time Sam awoke fully he'd practically been convicted.

The only reason he wasn't being punished – other than for the fact that they no longer had a gaol, a labour camp, a court, or for that matter evidence of any crime – was that their own scouts had managed to confirm the few details of the battle that he had given them the previous day. That steel rats by the hundreds had been destroyed, along with their precious forest, and that no more machina were nearby. According to their far-seers the nearest rats were still rebuilding their numbers slowly in Shavarra itself. Thus he had saved them, and as far as they knew he had committed no crime in elven lands.

Meanwhile the wizards had determined he was suffering from the effects of having over exerted himself in combat due to his inexperience, and had prescribed rest and some of the worst herbal tea he'd ever tasted. That tea he rather imagined was the source of his headache. His own brain hated the taste so very much it was simply trying to claw its way out of his skull rather than remain anywhere near his tongue.

Of course a rock pounding headache wasn't about to save him from their interrogation once he'd awoken again, and for the rest of the day he had been subjected to their endless questioning. Who was he? Who had trained him? Where had he learned those spells? Where had he got those books? And above all else, what had he done?

It had been a very long day.

He had been given a brief respite for afternoon tea, when the entire train pulled to a stop. The horses needed rest and water, the people food and a chance to stretch their legs, and the wizards confirmed that there were no rats nearby. Something Sam, even in his weakened state could agree with.

Like the rest Sam too had been given a chance to get up and do the basics, naturally while being closely watched by the çity guards. But by the time he'd stretched and had some warm food inside him, he'd been beginning to feel a little like his old self. He'd been exhausted as he had never been before. The usual roaring bonfire of fire magic in his centre remained little more than embers, and he could find no way to fan it back into life. The elders had told him that it would return with time, for which he was relieved. The magic had been with him all his life and he didn't want to lose it. Especially not now when it had finally grown powerful enough to do all that he needed it to.

Actually he could already feel a little of his fire returning, but only a very little. There was a lot more to come. Much more than ever before. He knew that by the size of the hole it had left in him. A gaping hole larger than he had known could exist within him.

Unlike the other sick and injured though, Sam had chosen to dress himself for battle once more, and had pulled on his full armour and gathered his weapons to him. Exhausted or not he would not lie like a corpse in the back of a wagon when there might still be battles ahead. The wizards had disapproved of course. They'd told him he should rest. They didn't truly understand him. But the soldiers did and they'd made no move to stop him. He was a soldier, and no soldier ever born should have to face the enemy half naked. Besides, most of the elves by then had known something about what he had done from the gossip that had been flying around, and seeing him up and about was a morale booster for those in the nearer wagons.

Pulling his greatsword to him once more had also provided a surcease from his suffering. The sword still had some of the fire magic he'd imbued in it, and having it close helped to fire up his own energies a little. It wasn't much, but it was enough to brighten his mood a little.

Tea done, some warm stew and bread which had gone down happily if far too quickly, he'd spent the rest of the break grooming his two horses, both of which were tied alongside the wagon he was in. Both had been ridden hard, and both had been through a lot for little reward. They were due it, and he'd fed them from a bag of the best oats he could find and groomed them thoroughly. Elsbeth the goat had gone out to the bushes on the side of the road to chew away happily at some gorse, and he'd decided that she could ride on the wagon instead of in a saddle bag for the next part of the journey. She would like it better and at least his saddle bag would remain free of her deposits. While she'd eaten, a young boy had spent some time milking her, something she was quite used to, and her tail had wagged furiously with pleasure at the thought of the carrots to come. At least someone had been enjoying the journey.

Neither of his horses were presently being ridden as the elves seemed to have more than enough for their people. Also Sam suspected, the horses being both so large and black intimidated them. He wondered if any of them had realised that they were also fully trained war horses. Tyla had been trained by the stable masters for the Fair Fields dragoons, and Aegis by him. He hadn't told them. It would have just created more problems.

Grooming the horses had also given him the chance to study some of the other elves in the nearer wagons. A necessary yet upsetting chore. The soldier in him had needed to gauge their fighting strength, to know if they could defend themselves should the need arise; the knight had needed to confirm the truth of their plight. But the man simply wanted to weep as he saw their suffering. And their numbers.

Torin Vale was a large town with nearly ten thousand residents, while the city of Shavarra itself had held over thirty thousand more, but the caravan had swelled by at least twenty thousand more than that, as elves from the nearer towns and the outlying regions of the city had joined them. He gathered many more were coming. Unfortunately it had been easy to tell who had come from the city.

Sam knew many of the elves from Torin Vale, and by and large he recognised many of them among his neighbours. They were the ones with the better carts, the fresher horses, and the more generous supplies. The city elves were the ones wearing the bandages, crutches, slings and casts. They had the horses that had been ridden too hard for too long, and many pulled carts that would normally have been broken down for fire wood in due course. They were also the ones with the physicians hovering about, and whose faces were lined with terrible pain as they grieved for those they had lost.

Even worse than seeing them had been listening to their tales of woe, for they had suffered losses that no man should ever have to bear. Their kith and kin, their homes, their livelihoods, their pride and even their hope. He had known that first night that they were refugees, but it still hadn't prepared him for what that meant. Nothing could. It wasn't even as if he'd asked them of their troubles. He'd simply listened as they'd spoken among themselves, and he'd known that they spoke the truth. They weren't deceiving him for some typically incomprehensible elven reason. To them he wasn't important enough to even notice, and he hadn't broken into their grief with his sympathies. His words could not have helped. Instead he'd just listened quietly.

After the break, when the wagons had started rolling

again, Sam's woes had been redoubled as his interrogation had started in truth. Choosing to ride alongside the wagon instead of in it hadn't helped him. His questioners having decided that he'd had enough rest and that they had the time to spare, had been both relentless and merciless. Moreover, they had already known enough about him by then, to make it damnably near impossible to hide anything.

By the first hour he'd practically retold them every single detail of the battle a hundred times over. By the second they'd known almost the entirety of his life. The only thing he managed to hold back was his family name, though they'd known he was keeping it back and had been far from happy about it. But it was a matter of honour, not to mention safety, and Sam had stayed firm.

While in Shavarra he had used his mother's maiden name and had been known as Samawain Ellosian. It was even more vital that if they entered into Fair Fields lands, as he assumed they would, that they use only that name. The creator would have to have mercy on them all if any of the people of Fair Fields ever realised he was Samual Hanor.

But slowly they'd at least started to accept his assertions that he wasn't a criminal. That those suits of blackened snake scale armour were from those who had hunted him. After all why else would he have had three, only one of which might even have come close to fitting him? Or so many poisoned stilettos? Persuading them that the tomes of fire, earth and nature magic were his by right had been more difficult, as he still couldn't give them his true name. But weak as he had been when he had fled Fair Fields, he had still been the ranking wizard in Fall Keep. As such he was the rightful custodian of the tomes and none could take that from him.

Though they might have listened to his words Sam was sure that they hadn't accepted his assertion that the tomes belonged to him. Least ways he hadn't noticed any of the wizards looking to give him his tomes back. Not without proof, and somehow he suspected, not even with it. Ranking human wizard or not, he was a half elven wizard of enormous power, and well intentioned or otherwise they clearly considered him dangerous. In their eyes he was a wild creature suddenly residing free among them. They didn't know the half of it. But then that was something his brother would learn instead and he'd let that knowledge sustain him.

When darkness had finally fallen on Sam's the day, the interrogation had finally ceased, but far from being able to breathe a sigh of relief, his woes had only begun to grow again.

The battle masters had left early on, having decided they could learn no more from him and had duties to attend to. And happily for him the priests had left too. They had duties to attend to. Though unhappily they had promised to return. But the elder wizards and members of the Ruling Council had remained. They too had learned enough of him to make their own judgements – often unfair ones in his opinion – and so instead of continuing with the questioning, they'd moved on to the chastisement phase of the ritual. And it was a ritual, though it had taken him a while to realise that. He recognised it in the way each new elder was given his own turn to berate him. It was like a pecking order among chickens, except that he was the only one being pecked.

The Council elders and particularly the wizards had taken it in turns to explain to him how badly he'd failed in everything he'd done. In coming to Shavarra, in having such books of power, in not having immediately spoken to the local guild about his talent and the books, in having lived apart from the elves and in having thought of the elves as hostile to him. In practically everything he'd done.

The list of his mistakes seemed to keep on growing, and not once had any of them mentioned the fact that he'd destroyed their pursuers and in doing so allowed them to travel more slowly and yet safely away from the enemy. Thanks to him the once panicked retreat had become a properly organised exodus. They had managed to spend some time however, decrying the devastation he'd caused to their beloved forest.

And so his long day had continued, as he'd had to listen to endless lectures about his many failings.

His sole comfort as the hour grew late was in the knowledge that he had finally found all the strength he needed and more to do what he should have done five years before. In a few days, perhaps a week he would be fully recovered, and regardless of what the elves wanted, he was going to reclaim his wife. Nothing could stop him any longer, not with the power he'd finally found within himself. Not his half-brother. Not his half-brother's guards. Not even the whole castle. He carefully kept that plan a secret though. The elves would not have approved, and they would surely have tried to stop him.

"Don't you know why those of half elven and half human blood are hard to accept?" Elder Bela, Master of nature magic and a member of the Ruling Council itself, began his turn chastising Sam.

"No Elder." Sam tried to sound as though he was listening, but really he wasn't. It was late and Master Bela was simply the latest in a long line of accusers. Unfortunately he might not have been convincing judging by the scowl that appeared on the Elder's already long face. But then he was growing tired and Master Bela's complaints were much the same as everyone else's. It was getting hard to keep his eyes open. And to remember not to speak.

"Because those of your blood are so powerful!" The Elder raised his voice a little, perhaps in frustration.

"Powerful?" That caught Sam's attention. It even woke him up a little.

"Those bolts you threw were so strong that every magic user in a dozen leagues felt them. And the fire ring, that's something that even an experienced master of fire would have trouble conjuring let alone surviving. Your power is immense. And you've been hiding out in our lands for five years, pretending to be a simple soldier – while all the time practising your magic without permission, and without even an instructor!"

"But –!"

"Creator have mercy on us all! You could have destroyed the whole town by accident!"

"But –"

Sam wanted to say, yet again, that he hadn't ever thought to unleash such power, hadn't even known that he could, and that had he known he would never have done it in or near the town or intentionally harmed any elves. But the Elder shut him up before he could say any of that, and he realised it wouldn't have mattered anyway. This wasn't about him defending himself. It was about him being told off. This wasn't a conversation.

"Don't interrupt me boy. I'm not finished with you yet!"

Sam was cowed once more before the Elder, who looked to be working himself up into a full blown tantrum. It wouldn't be the first of the day and probably not the last either. It was better just to take it in silence and glean the few pearls of wisdom he gathered from each master in turn as they berated him. Because despite everything else, these sessions were the first real chance he'd had to learn anything about why the elves disliked half elves so much.

"As I said, all human elven offspring often have potential strengths greater and stranger than either of their parent races for reasons we don't fully understand. They often have wild unpredictability with it. Sometimes it's physical strength or impossible health, and some of your most powerful knights and our finest soldiers carry mixed elven human blood in them. Sometimes it's magic. All the most powerful wizards in any land carry both people's blood. And just occasionally it's something else entirely, like speed or charisma as they move faster than the eye can see or persuade others to their cause, however insane."

"We call people with your heritage 'vero eskaline', which means storm blood, and refers to the fact that children of such blood are touched by the wild side of nature. Something I think even you can accept at least now."

Actually Sam had heard the phrase, whispered behind his back from time to time, and had wondered what it meant. It was a High Elvish term that had become part of regular Elvish. Unfortunately with his relatively poor mastery of the tongue he'd translated it as strong blood wind, and always thought it some sort of slight upon his character, though he'd never been game to ask. He liked the Elder's translation better.

"Our people don't detest you for your nature. Never did. They're simply frightened of you!" That at least woke Sam up from his fugue state. Frightened? Of him? That was something which had never occurred to him. He'd never posed any threat to the elves; never wanted to. All he'd ever wanted was to live in peace and rescue his wife.

"But –" His objection died on his lips as he saw the look in the Elder's eyes. He still wasn't finished with him.

"If you had been born in Shavarra, you would have been raised carefully. Watched over by elders and priests looking for any sign of the talents granted you by your blood. But you would never have been unwelcome. Far from it. As vero eskaline you would have been considered a blessing. A great boon to our people, and in time when your gifts became known, you would have been trained in them properly. Some of our greatest leaders, elders, soldiers and wizards carry the same blood as you, and they are honoured for it."

"Had you come openly as an adult and told our people of your talents – had you accepted the guidance of the elders – the same would have still been true. You would have been brought to our wisest and taught carefully. But you did no such thing."

"Instead you arrived as an outsider, and you remained as one. A dangerous stranger living within our midst. One whose gifts were unknown, whose friendship even was uncertain but who was known as vero eskaline. A warrior who didn't trust the people enough to tell them his true name. How would you expect our people to react?"

"If – and I say this with the utmost emphasis – if you were to live among the elves of Torin Vale – truly live among them and let them know you as you let yourself know them – you would be welcomed by them. They're not unfriendly people. They're just nervous around you. After all, they know you're half elven, half human. Therefore they know you're unpredictable and powerful. But they know nothing else about you. There's nothing about you that says you've adapted to our ways, or that you even want to."

"And that has to change." If he had been telling him off before, suddenly the Elder became even more forceful as he instructed him as he surely would any naughty student.

"You live apart from us in our midst. You dress like a human soldier at war when our lands have always been at peace. You even cut your hair like one, with that crude shaven skull."

It wasn't crude! But Sam stopped himself from protesting out loud. It wouldn't help. And if the Elder didn't understand that close cropped hair was valuable when you wore a helm, that was his failing he decided.

"You speak our language yet seem to understand little if anything of our soul. You keep your past a secret, thinking either that we would not realise how little you reveal of yourself, or that we should not know. No more do you carry any elven markings. You display nothing of your family or kin to show you belong among us; nothing of any elven academies attended or stations achieved, nor of any normal elven trade practised."

Sam would have objected to that too if he thought he could have got a word in, but the Elder had a point. He did perhaps stand outside the fold, by his choice as well as by theirs. It would have helped perhaps if he'd spent some time at the shrine in town. Perhaps offered a small tribute to the Goddess now and then. But he was from Fair Fields, raised all his life to follow the teachings of the All Father. Although he had nothing against the Goddess, it would have felt like a betrayal.

"You don't even tell us the truth of your name!"

Sam groaned briefly. Just when he'd thought things were coming to an end, they were back to that again. If there was one thing the elders hated even more than what he had done to their forests, it was not being trusted by him. And yet it was not a choice.

"Elder, that is for your protection as well as mine. If I did, if my birth name were made known, the consequences would be dire. For me, for my loved ones, and also for anyone foolish enough to be too near. You've already seen the wares of those who last came to kill me. There were many more before them. I have been attacked by assassins almost without number over the years, and they are only those who made it through the border patrols – the few who somehow managed to track me."

"Imagine how many more would come should my name become common knowledge and people know where I live. At the risk of being rude Elder, I repeat; I am not a criminal. I have committed no crime in any land. I have the books by right, and I mean no harm to anyone. I simply hide from those who would do me harm. And there are many of them." It had to be the hundredth time he'd said the same thing, and they still kept coming back to it, like a dog with a bone.

"In that at least Elder, I think he speaks the truth." A woman's voice came from behind him, and Sam turned to see that a rider on a roan mare had joined them. When she'd arrived, he didn't know. Between his tiredness and the endless tirades, she could have been there for hours without him noticing.

"I thank you for your support good soldier."

He thought he'd better acknowledge her defence of him as best he could. It was the only support he'd had all day. But secretly he was also curious. It sounded almost as though she knew something about him, and that could not be good.

"Save your thanks warrior wizard. You may not be so happy shortly." The terrible thing was that she wasn't making some sort of threat. From the look in her eyes she did know something about him. Something that would cause him pain, and she sorrowed for it. He was even more certain of it when she turned her eyes from him back to the Elder so quickly.

"There are some ahead who would wish to speak with the wizard Samawain Ellosian. They say they may know him, and if he is who they think, they will explain all." That puzzled Sam a little, until he realised it must be some of the elves from Torin Vale. Over the years some had become familiar. Some even knew a little of his life story. No more than he had told the elders, and none knew his true name. But they knew some of it, and that had to be a good thing if it supported his story.

"With your permission Elder?" She nodded to the Elder who was looking a little nonplussed, and he nodded back. The transfer of responsibility for the guest, prisoner, or wayward child had apparently been made, and in short order Sam found himself trotting beside his rescuer, as they headed closer to the front of the caravan.

Nothing was said as they made their way forward, partly because of the horses' fast paced trot which would have made it difficult not to have bitten their tongues as they spoke, but partly because of his guide's sombre mood. As they travelled, Sam paid his new – guard?, warder? – close attention, as she in turn scrutinised him. He had the feeling it was important. Also, he had the strangest feeling that he'd met her before. There was simply something familiar about her.

She was one of the border patrol from her armour, which consisted of a painted white leather breast plate over chain mail and over it all a padded jacket which fell down over leggings. It was the standard light armour for cavalry. From the twin laurels decorating her shoulders he realised she was an officer of the griffin troop. But he didn't know her from his conversations with any of the patrols.

She was tall for an elven maiden, standing probably very close to his own six foot in height at a guess, and she was more powerfully built too. Even with her long blond hair that hung in loose braids down her back, and the dark tanned skin of her people she would have stood out among them. Her face though, that was what would really have caused her to be noticed among the crowd. Not that she was blemished or in any way plain. She was every bit as beautiful as any other elven maiden he'd ever met. But she had what would politely be called a stern countenance. The severity in her eyes, the hardness of her mouth and the rigid set of her jaw line; all were far from normal, and the firelight from the torches did nothing to soften her look.

This was a woman he suspected, with a bitter past. Things had gone hard for her somewhere along the line. Perhaps she had lost family, despite her youth. Maybe she had suffered a loss of reputation or betrayal at the hands of good friends. Then again she might just have seen too much death these last few days. Whatever it might be, he knew that it was a part of her. It no doubt made her a capable soldier and he was certain she could handle her weapons with skill born of endless practice. Perhaps whatever had happened in her life was the reason why she had become a soldier in the first place.

Despite the fact that she looked so familiar, he knew he had never seen her before, even in a crowd, nor spoken with her one to one. If he had he would definitely have remembered those piercing brown eyes. They drew the watcher in like the talons of a bird of prey did a mouse. Yet still there was something familiar.

After a long, painfully silent trip they drew alongside a group of wagons loaded down with elven traders. Sam figured they were probably merchants caught out at Torin Vale. Certainly they did not appear to be wounded and the horses looked fresh. They couldn't have been in the city itself to be so fresh. But more than the wagons caught his eyes, as he soon spotted a pair of familiar faces among them.

"Alendro! Pietrel!" Without a moment's thought he kicked Tyla in the flanks and galloped towards them like a mad man, waving stupidly. In a matter of heartbeats he was with them, already clambering up the side of the wagon as he looped

Tyla's reigns over the side post, his escort forgotten.

"You're here! Free!" He picked up each of them in turn in a giant bear hug, so unbelievable happy to see them. It might have been extremely unelven, though they would never have objected. But he couldn't help himself. He was simply so overjoyed. Because if they were here, it meant Ryshal was free. Her parents would never leave Fair Fields without her. After five long years she was finally free!

Perhaps his brother had finally felt secure enough in his reign that he didn't need a hostage any longer? Maybe she had somehow escaped or been rescued? Either way he didn't care. It didn't matter how. All that mattered was that she was free.

And then he saw the haunted looks in their eyes, the grief written in their faces, and saw the priestess of the Goddess standing alongside the wagon. With a sense of dread he realised he had made a terrible mistake. There was always one other reason they would leave her. If she had already left them. And this day it seemed that the priests and priestesses of the Goddess were everywhere. Bringing comfort to those whose loved ones had left them.

"No!"

But his denial was in vain, and he knew it as the darkness clutched at his heart. As they told him what they knew of Ryshal's death, he refused to believe it. To have struggled and sweated for so long with only one goal in mind. To finally have that goal within his grasp and then be told it was too late! He couldn't accept it. He could never believe that his half-brother would be so stupid as to kill her. She was his leverage against him. She kept him safe and quiet. Surely he wouldn't have done such a thing?

Except it seemed that he had.

As they spoke, Ry's parents cried. They were clearly heartbroken and that more than anything else convinced him of the truth of their words. They wouldn't leave her for any other reason. Not unless they knew she was dead.

As he finally had to let their words in, he felt a yawning cavern of grief and bitterness opening up in his soul. One large enough to swallow him whole. And the largest part of him wanted nothing more than to jump in after. But another part, the angry part, refused to let him. As large as the cavern was, the anger was larger, and growing with every beat of his heart as he thought of what had happened to Ry. To the woman he loved. The one he was supposed to live with for the rest of his days. The one for whom he should lay down his life to protect. And that anger not only kept him from grieving, it began to take hold of his very soul.

Others could grieve; he could not. Not then, and not until he who was responsible for this evil was dealt with. Permanently.

"There will be blood!" Ry's parents looked up at him, surprised as the anger burst free from his mouth. They had obviously known of their daughter's fate for some time, and were well into their time of grieving. Besides, they were elves. Good and true elves. They hadn't expected his reaction. They probably didn't even understand it.

"But –"

Sam cut them off with a single look, and he watched them almost step back in shock as they saw it. The fury growing in his clenched jaw. The rage boiling in his eyes. The way his muscles were already rippling under his armour. They couldn't truly understand, he knew that. They never would. But one day, after he had done what had to be done, he hoped they could be friends again.

"Blood will be paid for the blood of the innocent that was spilt. My brother will burn in the Halls of the underworld for all eternity for this crime. That is my oath as Samual Hanor, son of Eric Hanor, Knight of Hanor. And none may nay say it."

Alendro and Pietrel looked shocked at his words. The soldiers that seemed to be coming out of the very woods at him from every direction on the other hand looked determined. Apparently they had known the news before him, and had prepared for it. They were going to stop him. His sworn vengeance was unelven. He could almost see the objections on their mouths. Killing Heri would not bring Ry back. He knew that. He also knew that it would cause trouble in the land they would soon be entering. That it was wrong. But he couldn't listen to them. No more could he allow them to stop him.

With a single deft leap he was once more mounted on Tyla, a move that surely caused them some surprise, as he showed himself to be more agile than even most elves. He hadn't practised with his sword and armour every day for most of his adult life for no reason. A second command with his knees had her taking off even as they began shouting at him. Shouting at those ahead to stop him.

He couldn't let them. And despite being close to exhaustion, he still had magic to burn. Magic he hadn't told the elders about, though they should have guessed when they saw the books. A silent command sent to every horse within three hundred yards caused them all to suddenly stop. Their riders, pressing their knees into their flanks, suddenly found their mounts unwilling to obey. A ripple of Earth magic behind him opened up a ten foot wide trench parallel to the caravan. A trench that their unwilling mounts would have to jump in the dark if their riders wished to give chase.

Somehow he thought they might not, as he heard their

surprised shouts behind him. Most didn't even know who he was, and those who did had thought him too weak to fight if it came to a struggle. But their surprise and even the tone of fear in their cries told him they had discovered their mistake. He had no doubt they would soon be running to the elders with the news. And all the while he would be putting the leagues between them.

It was fortunate that the caravan had stopped for the night in a region of open fields, with nearly all the horses untethered, as it allowed him to disappear quickly into the dark as he steered a path away from the elves. Somewhere up ahead he knew he would have to re-join the road, but hopefully that would be well past the front of the caravan. And with a little more magic he would be well beyond where the elves could expect him to be.

Touching his ungauntleted hand to Tyla's neck, he granted her a little of the stamina and strength of his nature magic and felt her respond, galloping even faster than before, and yet feeling nothing of strain with it. Actually she was revelling in the feeling of power that he had granted her, and he knew she wouldn't have stopped without a lot of urging on his part. And with the night vision of the owl which he was lending them both, she had no need to worry about potholes or trees. She could see as clearly at night as she could by day.

She snorted with excitement as she found the extra strength coursing through her veins, and true to her nature and his urgings, galloped even faster. Though she didn't know it, the mare had many leagues to travel and Sam was determined to cross them in as short a time as possible.

His brother could not be allowed to live one single heartbeat longer than absolutely necessary. He had already lived too long.

Chapter Six.

The keep was dark when Sam arrived, fairly much as he'd expected. His brother had a hatred for wasting anything, even paraffin, and so by the light of the stars Fall Keep was little more than a brooding mountain squatting on the land. A darkness stealing what little light there was. But here and there he could see the odd glow from a lamp as a sentry made his rounds on the battlements, and a couple of the higher windows had light coming from them.

It was a deception of course. Fall Keep was a city as well as a keep. The city was merely hidden behind the keep's massive walls along with the keep itself. It was the massive walls that someone approaching saw. Walls that in the darkness looked like a piece of the mountain that someone had simply carved into shape. That gave no hint that there was anything behind them. Or that there was any way through.

The original keep had been built maybe a thousand years before. It was a massive, hulking structure that sat between two hills. From the front it looked like nothing more than a giant wall of stone blocks. The keep itself lay behind the walls, concealed though it was really a true castle in its own right. It had been added to over the centuries, the keep growing ever larger and more intimidating as time had passed. Meanwhile behind it, sitting on top of the plateau between the hills was the city. It was home to anywhere from fifty to seventy thousand souls – no one had actually ever counted them. But none of that was visible from the front.

It was well built in truth, with its walls ten foot thick and made of solid blocks of stone which were held together by steel pins as well as mortar. It had been designed to take the fury of enemy war machines with impunity. And it was more than just a wall; it was also a battlement.

From the battlements atop the walls archers could rain down arrows all day and all night on anyone foolish enough to attack it. Cannon based in the buttresses that dotted the wall could do the same, and level an attacking army. Fall Keep was a true citadel and considered nearly impregnable by any army. But then it had never been attacked by a wizard. Least of all a master of fire. The rarest and most dangerous of all masters.

And why would it have to defend against such a wizard? After all, there were no such people among the humans. And those found among the magical races didn't much care for either war or the human realms.

Soon, Sam promised himself, the vaunted strength of the keep and its assumed invulnerability was about to be shown lacking. Walls would crumble and light would shine in the darkest parts of the keep itself, before it burned to the ground. Those who survived would speak of this night forever. They would curse Heri's name for eternity. Heri himself though would not survive. He would burn. He would scream for what he had done, and then he would burn until nothing of his evil remained.

Sam felt the fire raging in him as never before and knew it was simply echoing the anger burning in his soul. Anger that had only grown hotter with every hour and every day as he'd raced to Fall Keep. The darkness within his soul that had scared him in Shavarra no longer frightened him. He welcomed it, and it in turn powered him as never before.

His tiredness after that first battle had gone away as if it had never been the moment he had been given the black news, and his magic had returned with every hour as he rode, until he felt stronger now than he ever had before. Much stronger. Yet even his strength caused him pain, as he cursed himself for having only become strong enough to rescue her once Ryshal was finally beyond his reach. The self-hatred and anger fed each other until all that was left was a terrible, aching need for vengeance.

It was time to use a little of that strength. It might have been smarter to try and creep in. To use his skills and his magic to enter unobserved and make his way to his brother's bed chamber as he'd secretly hoped to do before. But that was when he had had to worry about the risk of Ryshal being harmed if he was seen. But she was beyond either harm or further pain now, and he wasn't feeling very smart right then. He was simply too angry, and had nothing left to lose. He was more angry and hurt than he'd ever been in his life, and nothing was going to come between him and his vengeance. Nothing!

Without a second thought he raised his left hand and sent a fireball flying toward the main gate. A blast of fiery fury that screamed with rage as it flew. When it hit it was as though the underworld had ripped its way through to the citadel.

It wasn't even a powerful blast compared to what he could have cast, and yet it did everything he'd dreamed of and much more, as it ripped the gate house apart and tore the draw bridge and portcullis behind it into shattered fragments of wood and steel. The force of the blast blew the foundations under the gate walls into stone powder and smashed a hole in the ten foot thick front stone wall wide enough to march an army through, all while shaking the entire castle and town behind it. Anyone who had been asleep before this had been suddenly and satisfactorily wakened. It was a good satisfying blast, and he'd barely even begun.

Heartbeats later Tyla hurdled the twenty foot wide moat as if it was just a puddle. She was naturally a powerful horse, and he was enhancing her strength and stamina with his own magic. He had been for the six long days and nights that they'd raced here. But far from minding the running, she enjoyed it. If he had never felt so strong, neither had she, and the chance to hurdle a small river was not so much a challenge for her as a joy.

They touched down well inside the gate and then galloped madly across the courtyard, heading directly for the stairs leading to the main halls of the castle.

All around Sam could see the soldiers from the barracks running for their armour and weapons, shouting at each other in confusion even as they tried to work out what had happened. A few were already dressed. They were the sentries on night duty. Some of them even managed to point at him and start running for him weapons in hand. But they were far too slow, and a simple ripple of earth magic turned the ground under their feet into six foot high waves which knocked them back on their butts. A second made the stone fully liquid and they sank into it up to their knees, before it reset around them. They would be no threat until the masons had chipped them out of the floor.

He launched two more fireballs at the side walls of the keep as a distraction, each more than three hundred yards away from him. But distance was no problem for him any longer. They could have been leagues away and he would not have been troubled. Each blast opened up a gap in the ten foot thick stone walls nearly fifty feet across. It would stop the archers reaching the courtyard battlements. It would also leave the keep relatively defenceless for months to come, and the simple power of the explosions as they rippled through the ground was enough to throw people from their feet again even as they tried to dress, gather their weapons, and work out what was going on.

By the time he'd crossed the courtyard, he was surrounded by confusion and chaos. Ironically it rendered him almost completely safe in its midst, as no one knew what was happening and they never connected it with him.

The stairs leading up to the first floor terrace were a little more difficult, but only because Tyla wasn't used to them and he had to take them slowly. But almost no one noticed him – a dark figure on a black horse riding up the huge stone stairs as they ran around in utter confusion. It was not long before he reached the terrace.

He could have taken the main entrance on the ground, knocking the front doors down and racing through, but he knew that there would have been a more substantial army waiting for him if he had gone that way. But Heri's quarters were close to the terrace where he liked to stand and wave to his long suffering people. Of course when he did so he had his archers posted on the battlements so they could take down anyone who looked dangerous as they entered the huge courtyard below.

The terrace proved no more difficult to cross than the courtyard, as the only two archers who'd actually managed to reach their stations on it had to throw their bows to the ground as they caught fire in their hands. Their screams as they desperately put out the flames that started licking at their sleeves followed Sam as he galloped past them. But he paid them no mind. Another small blast tore out the armoured doors leading from the terrace to the inside of the castle, and he quickly forgot about them.

Sam raced around the upstairs balcony that completely surrounded the main hall, dining hall, ball room and throne room, Tyla knocking over tables and chairs in her rush. But it was light weight furniture, items put there simply to look elegant and make Heri feel grand. In reality the only people who ever stood on the balconies were Heri's own guards, and like the others they simply stood there with their longbows at the ready while the court was in session, there to kill anyone who looked like threatening him.

At the far end of the balcony he reached the side stairs

leading to the royal wing and bed chambers and he knew his prey was close.

Tyla's steel shod hooves made an ominous racket on the stone floors, as she thundered along. A racket that could surely be heard in the royal bed chamber itself. But then his prey would have heard the destruction of the main gate and walls before this, and had probably guessed what was coming. Who was coming. He was probably trying to run even now. But he would be too slow Sam promised himself. Far too slow. The toad would not get away from him.

Up the two flights of stairs he galloped, and then into the hallway where a dozen alert and panicked looking sentries in full armour were posted outside his brother's bed chamber. It was a mistake as their presence told him exactly which of the chambers Heri was using. Obviously Heri had expected his company as the only possible response to his murder. But he hadn't expected it enough. He had assumed Sam would come as a knight and a minor wizard, sneaking in. He had never expected to face a true master of fire. Another small fire ball took out the door and walls to the bed chamber, and blew all of the guards to the floor at the far end of the corridor where they lay in a tangled heap of steel armour and fallen debris.

Were they dead? Sam wouldn't have thought so as he'd limited the fireball's size to only what he needed; just enough to spare them serious injury though he didn't truly want to. It was simply a matter of honour, though in truth he was too angry to really care. They were his brother's henchmen, no more no less.

A heartbeat later his brother was in his view. He was standing beside his bed with a pike in his hands, while a couple of concubines in linen night dresses cowered behind the bed.

"Why?!"

Sam bellowed the question at his half-brother's cowering form, even though he knew he'd never get a reasonable answer. Not for why he'd killed her. Not for why he'd even jailed her in the first place. As an illegitimate son Sam had never been in line for the throne. He'd never wanted to be. And he had said that since the day he was old enough to speak. His brother had never had reason to fear him.

Until now! Now he would know fear.

"You!" Heri grabbed for a lump of white stone on the bedside table, sounding shocked to see him. He was too slow. Sam had no thought as to what the stone was, save that he could feel magic streaming from it. Still, it didn't last long when he hit it with a blast of fire. The stone melted and the table caught fire.

"Be damned!" Heri cursed and leapt away from the burning table before suddenly raising his pike and pointing it at him, as if preparing to charge. His white stone was gone and the weapon was all he had left.

It was an incredibly stupid thing to do. Without even thinking about it, Sam stretched out a finger and his sword of flame cut through the pike and half his half-brother's leading hand. Heri dropped like a stone, screaming as he saw his fingers hitting the floor ahead of him, and for a long time nothing more than his screams could be heard in that room. In fact he could probably be heard throughout the entire castle. He screamed like a little girl.

Sam didn't mind though. He enjoyed it. It might have been wrong of him and no doubt the priests would have plenty to say about it at his next confession, but for five long years he had hated his brother with a passion, even as he had had to suffer the ceaseless agony of knowing his wife was locked up in a dungeon and being unable to go to her. Never truly knowing her fate. Not knowing her touch. Not even knowing if she was well. All he had known was that she would remain alive as long as he stayed out of the realm and away from local politics. As long as he stayed away from the other nobles who Heri truly feared.

Heri's screaming brought more of the guards to his bed chamber, and they sprinted in belatedly. Many were still half dressed, and even those fully who were dressed and armed posed Sam no danger. Not while he had fire like this raging through him. He simply put up a wall of flame around himself and his brother, cutting everyone else off and ignored them. They could not pass through it and nor could their weapons. Not even arrows. He watched more than a few of them hit the fire wall and turn to ash. Poorly trained troops. They should have known better than to waste their arrows.

A couple of fire wizards had also shown up, and he saw them preparing their own fire to attack him. But they were too slow and little more than novices. Where were the masters? Sam couldn't feel them anywhere. Not that they would have posed any risk to him. But right then he didn't care. His target was in his sight, and these mages posed him no threat. He had been carrying his fire for days, building it up by the hour until he was near to exploding; they had had but a few moments. It was ridiculously easy to rip their ice swords out of their hands with a noose of flame, and in the process cause them to collapse as their own life force was splintered by the shock. They would not wake up soon and then it would be weeks before they recovered what strength they had.

In time Heri looked up from the stone floor where he knelt screaming, and managed a few choked words of hatred, calling him a bastard and a half-breed. But then he had called him these things all his life and Sam paid him little mind. He only wanted to know one thing. Why had his little brother killed his wife? Once he knew that he would release Heri from his life.

"Why?" Once more he extended a finger and the fire sword streamed out until it stopped mere inches from Heri's throat, stopping the rant in a heartbeat. Meanwhile Heri became aware that his back was only a few inches away from the fire wall itself. Abruptly Heri stopped speaking altogether as he felt both his back and his neck cooking. No doubt he now realised he was about to die, and was preparing his prayers for the afterlife. But Heri would not die before Sam had charged him with his crimes. This might be vengeance – it was vengeance – but it was also justice. Ry's death had been murder, no more and no less, and her murderer had to be called to account. He had to know why he was going to die.

"I never wanted the throne toad! I said that to any and all who would listen from the very start. I still don't want it. And you knew that from the day you turned five. You knew it and you didn't care!"

He shouted it at Heri in faltering common – he hadn't spoken the tongue in years – and watched his brother's face turn deathly white behind his burning cheeks as he expected to burn.

"Instead you had to set me up, again and again and again. Sending in your agents, your spies. Looking for the first sign that I might betray you. And even when I didn't you still stole my newly wedded wife from me. You locked her up, exiled me on pain of her death, and even then sent assassin after assassin after me despite your promises. None of them will ever return, but you will meet them again shortly – in the underworld."

"And now, when you've finally got everything you wanted, when you're supposedly secure in your rule, what do you do? You kill her! You foetid, murdering pile of cow dung! You kidnapped and murdered my wife! And you thought to live through this?!"

By the looks of things his half-brother wasn't thinking of anything very much at all right then. He was simply shaking in fear, and there was some suspicious moisture running down his leggings.

"Why? How? Did you think I would not find out? Did you somehow imagine I would not act? Did you imagine you had any way to stop me? That perhaps somehow one of your hundreds of assassins had finally succeeded in killing me? Did one of them perhaps report success a little early? And so you thought you had gotten rid of one problem, you should also get rid of the embarrassment of having illegally held an innocent elf maiden of good station in your dungeons for five years as well?!"

He knew that had to be it. It was the only thought that had crossed his mind in nearly a week of hard riding. His brother was neither brave enough nor stupid enough to kill Ryshal otherwise. He had all the cunning of a rat in a dung heap. It was why he'd looked so surprised to see him.

"No!" Finally his brother spoke, if only to deny it all. But how could he truly deny anything? He was guilty of it all and far more. Sam watched the sweat on his forehead start dripping to the floor, and knew Heri was terrified. Good! Soon he would be dead.

"No little brother? No? I suppose you're going to tell me it was all some sort of accident? That she accidentally stabbed herself in the back with a sword." He turned up the heat a few more notches and watched his little half-brother start shaking even more violently in his fear. Soon he would be begging. But he would find no mercy in Sam.

"No! No! I'm begging you no! She's not dead. Never! I wouldn't hurt her. Never!"

For what seemed like ages Sam sat there on his horse, taking in the words he'd never expected to hear, and it left him stunned. Shaken so badly he even let some of the fire out of his shield. It was a mistake, as the archers sensing his distraction, a full score of them, fired everything they had at him. Most, badly charred by the weakened fire, bounced harmlessly off his armour but one found the gap between his breast plate and over lapping shoulder piece, skewering him neatly in the arm pit.

The sudden pain pulled Sam out of his shock, and quickly he raised his fire walls again. But for a heartbeat or two it could have gone either way. He could have dropped them completely as he reeled in the sudden pain. It was no doubt exactly as his brother had planned.

A heartbeat later he had his brother once more pinned between the sword and the fire wall, and was preparing to end it.

"So you lie again! Even at your end you show yourself to be a deceiver. Not a warrior, not a king, not even a man. Just a black hearted thief of words. You have always lied. From your very birth you learned deception with every sip of your foul mother's milk, and now even at the end you can't find the truth. How can such a miserable creature as you ever be my brother? Our father's son? Dishonour is your way, and I am grateful that our father is not here to see you like this. You expected me to believe you. Just enough so that you could get me to lower my defences, and then kill me. But guess what brother. It didn't work."

"You should have known better. Your plan has failed, and your death is near. It will not be an easy one." And just to emphasise his point Sam pulled the arrow free, threw its bloody wreckage at his feet, and then set it aflame, all the while keeping his wall hot. It hurt. But mere physical pain could not distract him.

"You have cost me five years of my life for nothing. Your evil has caused me more torment than you could even understand as you have held my wife apart from me. You have tormented her as well, and locked her away in a dungeon. It is unthinkable! And now foul demon, you have murdered her! The least you can do is scream for me. Scream as you have never screamed before!"

Immediately he began tightening up the fire wall behind his brother, burning the hairs off his back, and getting the desired reward as Heri screamed with all his worth. And yet he was still trying to speak, to lie his way out of trouble.

"No! She lives! I promise you! On my honour. On my life!"

"What honour? Sewer rats like you have none! Were our father still alive he would spit on you. He would cast you off the battlements and feed your remains to the pigs! But you are finally right about one thing. Your life is the coin that you will pay for your crimes with." Except that even as he was speaking he was looking into his brother's terrified eyes, wanting to see some sign of regret, and seeing instead the one thing he had never expected to see. The truth. Or at least a lack of lies.

Heri finally had nothing of planning or deceit left to him. He was just a frightened, screaming coward. Which gave Sam just enough room to hope. To dream for the first time in many long years. To plan. And to ask a question that had never occurred to him. Could it be? Could she be alive?

How? Her parents had received the death notice. They had visited the grave. And they did not lie. But could it all be some sort of mistake? It seemed impossible – or nearly so. But still, he had to wonder.

And he also had to understand that if his brother was finally telling the truth, then he was in the strongest position he ever would be. His unstoppable anger had somehow brought him all the way through to the king unharmed, and then let him capture him. This chance would not happen again. He had to find out if there was truly any hope.

"Tell you what toad. Bring her to me now, before I count to maybe a hundred, unharmed and I'll even let you live. Fail, and I shall start slicing you up, piece by piece."

And just to emphasise his point Sam guided the flame sword down his front, cutting through his night clothes. Sam started at the collar and worked his way straight down while Heri screamed with fear and pain as his skin started blistering. He had never had much in the way of courage, depending on others to do his fighting for him, and in the face of a fiery death, he had none at all.

"Quickly now. Before I begin to doubt you." And to emphasise his words he started counting – loudly.

It was as the flame sword tip reached his belly button that Heri finally had the presence of mind to stop screaming and start ordering his guards to do as he said. And once he started he couldn't stop. There was a mass exodus of feet as surely a dozen guards went running off for the dungeons as fast as they could, but Sam paid them no mind.

Instead he was simply trying to remain calm as his instructors had taught him to. But it wasn't easy. On the one hand he was praying – even daring to hope – that his brother was telling the truth, and the promise of a whole new wondrous life had suddenly been laid out ahead of him. On the other he knew his brother was most likely lying. He was desperate and would no doubt say anything, just to save his own skin for a few more moments. In between those two raging emotions, he had to keep concentrating. To fail was to let go of the fire, to release it along with his soul. To fail was to die, and maybe take out the entire castle with him.

Closing his eyes – it was something a soldier would never do in battle but in this case he simply had to – he concentrated on moving beyond fear and hope as his teachers had taught him. He looked to find the calm place in his thoughts, and to expand it until it enveloped him. Because it was only there that the wizard could rule. And he needed to be the wizard. Eventually some sense of peace returned to him. Not much, but enough.

Finally he opened his eyes to see his brother staring back at him, and saw both hope and fear written all over Heri's face. The sweat that had begun pouring off his brow was dripping everywhere, until his remaining night clothes were plastered to him, while a puddle was forming around his feet. Sam would have wagered good coin that it wasn't all sweat.

He understood Heri's fear, but why was he hopeful? That was the important question. If Ryshal was dead he had no reason to hope. He would die shortly regardless. And Sam wasn't about to let his walls drop again.

He mulled it over silently, desperately trying to remain calm, while they waited. Heri just stood there and sweated.

Finally, after the longest wait he had ever known, Sam heard the sound of heavy steel shod boots clanging on the stone floors as their owners returned at a run, and he turned to face them, filled with hope and dread. The pounding of his heart in his chest was unbelievable, and the sound almost deafened him.

Finally they came into view, and he saw the one face he had never expected to see again. Ryshal. His mouth dropped as he drank her beauty in. And haggard though she was, she was still beautiful.

Her normal dark tanned skin was pale, and there were blotches on her face. The result of too little sun and a poor diet. Heri had never fed his prisoners very well. Not even apparently, his hostages, despite his promises. Her normal graceful and lithe form had become painfully thin, and he could see her cheek bones sticking out. She also could barely stand. It would be a long time before she would dance for him again. Her beautiful long tresses of hair had been cut short, and what was left was unkempt and matted. She looked to have aged fifty years in just five. Yet still he saw the incredible love and joy that shone from her very soul. Some of the laughter might be gone, but not he hoped, forever.

"Merciful creator." He barely even knew he'd spoken until he heard the words come out of his own mouth, and then he wondered who said them.

"Ryshal. Beloved." Actually he called her aylin mi elle, Elvish for light of my heart. But in common it translated as beloved, and seeing her he was once more in Shavarra in his home with her.

"Samual."

Her voice still sounded of sunny days in forests filled with happy creatures and dancing waterfalls, and it took him all the way back to when they had first met. Of the way she had entranced him with her beauty and love until all else had seemed as nothing. The pain of his flesh as long days training in weapons had left him close to exhaustion. The ache in his very essence as he spent long nights being tutored in magic and science. Even the suffering in his soul as he mourned for his father, and learned to despise his brother. The only thing Heri saw in their father's death was his chance to rule early. But not till he turned eighteen, for which pain he had blamed everyone, but most of all Sam. And he had taken it amiss that Sam should take a wife while he suffered. But when Ryshal had arrived in his life, all of that had become as nothing to Sam. Only she had existed. And that still held true.

They had not been married long before Heri had struck and before that they had only courted for a year. But she had become his world in that time.

"Come." Sam lowered a section of the fire wall and held out his hand for her, but for some reason she didn't move. It was then that he finally noticed the dagger to her throat, and the way her arm was being cruelly forced behind her back by the guard. It took a few heart beats to restrain himself enough not to strike the man dead where he stood for such insolence. But he reminded himself; the man was only being loyal to his king. A virtue not an evil, even when the king was Heri.

"Soldier. I have already said I will release Heri unharmed. Unlike my verminous half-brother, I have always been a man of my word. My honour as a knight of Hanor. As the true son of King Eric Hanor. Let her go, and you may have this miserable worm back."

"But I don't want him back."

Finally enough of the guard's face emerged from behind Ryshal that he could see him. He was no guard. His shield bore a pair of snakes entwined with a sword, the insignia of the Fallbright house, and his armour, not just the breastplate, was inlaid with silver and gold etchings. He had to be one of the lords of that house.

"I want him dead."

Sam, caught by surprise, was spared having to say anything by Heri, who suddenly screamed at his guards to arrest the traitor. He had seen his hope of survival arrive in the form of Ryshal, and suddenly he was terrified that it was leaving him again in the form of a coup.

About half the guards suddenly grabbed their weapons and started moving toward the traitor, while a dozen new soldiers from the Barony of Fallbright suddenly entered the room, weapons already drawn. They brought with them a half dozen more of the keep's own guards, all fully dressed for battle. The rest of the guards just stood there, plainly wondering what to do, while the archers held their ground, bows at the ready, and wondered who to kill. It was a coup.

Everything stopped for the longest while, as everyone in the room stared at everybody else, wondering who was friend and who was foe. No one was willing to start anything, lest they get caught on the wrong side or be stabbed in the back by their former comrades. Lest they have to fight their friends, or die at their hands. The silence was complete as no one dared make a sound. And the murderous tableau held for what felt like a lifetime as the silence stretched.

Meanwhile the wheels were turning in Sam's head as he started putting the miracle of Ry's survival together with the report of her death and the Fallbright coup, and saw the entire picture. It came as a revelation to see just how badly the wheels of power and politics had turned in Heri's kingdom. But Sam couldn't allow that to distract him. He couldn't hesitate any longer. He had to take the initiative or risk losing it all. He was too close now to having everything he wanted in his grasp, to let it be lost in a pitched battle.

"Well, well, well little brother. It looks like all is not well in Fair Fields, and while you have been spending all your time and effort hunting and fearing me, those of your enemies a little closer to home have seen their chance to stick the knife in."

He mocked Heri with his words, and yet for once he heard nothing of complaint or disagreement from him. He was too frightened. All eyes were suddenly back on Sam as if he was a great leader. He was no such thing, but he knew he held the floor. With so many undecided men in the room, and a wizard capable of destroying them all in a heartbeat in their midst, they would listen, hoping he had a way out for them.

"And you young Lord of Fallbright. I take it you were the one who sent the messenger to Ryshal's parents saying that she was dead. You arranged the grave for them to visit. You hoped that they would find me and that I would kill Heri in my rage. A cunning plan, if a little dishonourable."

Not to mention rather flawed given that it hadn't come off, but he didn't say it aloud. The young Lord of Fallbright – assuming that was who he was – nodded in agreement. He even had the gall to smile; Sam could clearly see his white teeth showing through the slits in his visor. He still thought his plan was working. Foolish man.

"Then again you just might yet get your wish anyway." He heard Heri gulp behind him. "Because if you do murder Ryshal I will kill him – and you with him. But you will have the privilege of hearing Heri scream like a girl at least a hundred times, as he in turn will have the same of you, before you both make it all the way to the pits of the fiery underworld and the great beast sups on your bones. That is the only mercy I will grant either of you."

The smile vanished as if it had never been as the would be king finally understood he had outplayed his hand.

"But I -"

"Are equally responsible foul brother. You captured her, locked her up and chained her. You starved and abused her, and then allowed her to be used as a pawn by your enemies. I will not forgive you this evil; ever. Nor will I forgive your would be usurper. My mind is made up. You will both die together in flaming agony, and there's nothing either of you can do about it. Nothing all your soldiers can do, since they will all be dead in the first heartbeat. Nothing your wealth can buy since I will loot anything I want from your rotting corpses. And nothing your families can even beg for, since they will all be dead too shortly after."

As he told them that, Sam was staring directly at the newcomer, and for the first time he got a look at the eyes of the young lord. He watched them widen in fear, and knew he was making his point to him as well. The young Fallbright was attempting to take the throne. He wanted power, but he wasn't willing to die for it. Least of all in screaming agony. Just like Heri. He wanted power at all costs – as long as he didn't have to pay them.

"Or, I can spare you." Suddenly all eyes were riveted to him. "I can change things for you both. I can be merciful, or I can be the evil one himself."

"Kill my beloved and I can assure you, you will die in screaming torment. Both of you. And after that I will go on to destroy your families and friends as you've destroyed mine. I will make sure that they know why they are suffering such horrible deaths. I can't make any promises of course, but I will certainly try to ensure that they will die cursing your names. Praying neither of you had ever been born."

And that for any Fair Fielder was the ultimate curse. Most believed that people so cursed had their souls shrivel up inside them even before they died, and that when they did finally leave the world, the demons would sup on their flesh for eternity. True or not, they would not risk suffering that fate.

"Or you can let her go and take your chances with your swords against each other. I will even give you that option. The chance for each of you disreputable worms to salvage at least a fraction of honour in front of these good soldiers. A duel. A fight to the death. Man to man. I would spare your soldiers a flaming death. Likewise your families and loved ones. I will give both of you a chance of victory. A chance to be king by your own hand, or at least to die quickly. Against me you have no chance of any of those things. No more do your guards or your families."

It was a telling point. He was by far the most powerful man in the room, and both of them had suddenly realised they were outmatched. Later, if either survived, they might come to regret their decision to take him on. For the moment they just wanted to live.

"And at least it's honest. Both of you will be given the chance to take or keep the throne on your own merits, instead of trying to twist myself and others to your ends. And really Fallbright, with all these people present did you really think that using me to kill Heri would somehow leave your hands clean? Now everybody knows. It's too late for that plan. You have been exposed as a foul schemer just like Heri. Are you a coward like him as well? And if you can't face a wounded coward on your own, what true man would ever follow you anyway?"

Sam watched the faces of the soldiers, all of them in fact on both sides, staring at one another and silently asking the same question.

That was one of the major obstacles Heri had faced in becoming and remaining king. Unlike their father he was a coward and a betrayer and known for both. His men did not respect him. He overcame it by sheer cunning and absolute ruthlessness, ensuring their loyalty by other means. And by the looks of things, this newcomer would have to face those same obstacles and use the same techniques himself.

"Your word?" The newcomer had made his decision quickly, not that he truly had a choice. He had foolishly overplayed his hand in his childish ambition, hoping only that

Sam's uncontrollable fury would do what he couldn't. But when it hadn't and he had seen Sam's strength first hand, he had discovered his mistake, and seen death approaching on swift wings. Someone he most desperately didn't want to meet. Besides, he had seen his soldier's doubts about him as well, and he had to restore their confidence. He figured it would be easy. He was a skilled swordsman, Heri a wounded coward, and he just wanted to make a show of his valour. Therefore he accepted the right of combat as his chance to seize the throne rightfully.

"My word." Sam nodded, while somewhere behind him Heri spluttered with fear as he saw himself being skewered by his rival shortly. Out of the frying pan and into the fire.

On cue, the newcomer removed his dagger from Ryshal's throat and stepped back into his soldier's waiting clutches, pretending honour. It was all Sam had ever wanted as he fully opened the doorway in his wall and Ryshal stepped through. For once, no one tried to shoot him, and he closed the door a heartbeat after she was inside. She was safe and he would never let her go again.

"I knew you would come for me. The Goddess promised me." Ryshal smiled at him. But she looked frighteningly weak as she crossed the last few feet between them.

"I have prepared for this day with every hour that has passed. I'm sorry it took me so long." Sam reached down for her and she raised her arms to him. Finally, they touched. Fingers intertwined. For the longest time he did nothing but hold her in his arms after he lifted her so terribly slight frame into his saddle and kissed her. It had been so long, and he wasn't at all surprised to find tears in his eyes. For an age he did nothing but hold her tight, overwhelmed with emotion. Love, pain, relief, anger, hatred and joy. All of them were coursing through him at once. It was all he could do to keep the flame shield alight and not simply burst into tears. Yet his training came back to him, held him secure even in the midst of such overpowering emotion and kept them both safe for as long as they needed.

Eventually he heard coughing and returned to the world. He turned to see Heri standing there, still pinned between the flaming sword and the fire wall behind him. Without a second thought Sam opened a window in the wall behind him, and watched Heri scuttle back into his own guards' waiting clutches. A moment later, the wall was intact again, and Sam began guiding Tyla out of the chamber, while all around guards scattered as the fire shield approached.

"You can't leave me here like this! Kill him!"

Incredibly Sam heard his brother barking orders at him as if he was one of his servants. His half-brother actually thought Sam would help him! Not for the first time he wondered at his sanity. Sam did turn back though, briefly, if only to make sure he had actually said it.

Heri must have seen the look in his eyes, as he suddenly turned white again. At least he had the sense to finally be quiet.

"For the creator's sake, somebody get the toad a sword and some armour and then let these two finally do their own dirty work instead of using others for their twisted ends." At least a dozen heads nodded on cue, and he watched them jump on a young guard and then start stripping him down. At least someone was willing to listen to him. But then he realised, they knew he was still the power in the room, and they didn't want to risk offending him. Ever. In that at least they had more sense than their masters.

"Oh, and before I forget –" he turned back to the Fallbright Lord who had finally removed his helm as he prepared for a duel. It was Harmion Fallbright as he'd expected, the youngest of the three sons. The one they called the weasel. But not to his face. He had a reputation for vengeance, cruelty and cunning, not to mention attacking from behind.

"A little thank you from me. You dared to place a dagger against my wife's throat and use her as a bargaining chip against me. You caused her parents the most terrible pain by telling them she was dead." Even as Harmion opened his mouth to object or argue, he saw the anger in Sam's eyes, and then cried out as Sam sent a sliver of fire to him and cut off the fingers of his leading hand.

Like Heri before him he too fell to the ground, screaming like a little girl. It was strange how similar the two were Sam thought. It was stranger still how much he enjoyed the sound of his screaming as well. No doubt the priests would be busy counselling him after this should he ever admit what had happened.

"Good! Now you're evenly matched. Weasel against toad. Have a good fight, and whoever wins, don't ever darken my door again. In these last few years I have achieved true mastery of fire. Elven mastery. And as such I am far beyond your power. Far beyond anything you can imagine."

"What I've done this evening – the damage I've caused your keep – is minor. Scarcely a few heartbeats work for me. But it will take a few months hard work and tens of thousands of gold coins for you to make it look like new. Remember that. Because you really, really don't want to see me return."

If either of the two would be kings was listening, they gave no great show of it, each wrapped up in their own little world of pain and fear as they were. But their soldiers listened intently, hanging on every word.

But it wasn't enough. Sam needed these two to learn. He

needed them to know fear. Enough to last them a lifetime.

"Kneel before me now; both of you." Heri and Fallbright stared at him as he commanded them, and he knew neither of them understood. But in the end he knew they would both understand one thing. Fear.

"You can kneel before me now of your own free will, or you can kneel because I have cut your legs off at the knees. Your choice."

It didn't take any more than that for them to understand how bad things were, and they both quickly found their knees. Neither of them had any true courage. And their men would remember that.

"Good. Now hear my words worms. Know this until the day you die. I do not forgive you your crimes. Neither of you. No more will I forget them. All that I have done this day is to postpone your punishment. But only while you stay cooped up in your little keeps like frightened mice. Should you ever come into my lands however; should you ever come close to me or mine, or send any more assassins after me, you will not have a keep at all. Or a life. Or a family. Or a kingdom. Nothing will be left of you to bury. And you will die screaming. Wishing that you had never been born."

"Do you understand me?" He raised his voice a little and let them tremble with fear as they guessed what would happen if they didn't.

"Yes."

"Good." Without another look at either of them, Sam guided Tyla out of the room, down the corridor, and then down the stairs to the throne room.

It was time to leave for a new life, somewhere far away

from this evil place. Somewhere with people he could trust. Even if they didn't like him.

Leaving should have been a triumph for him. A time of supreme joy. Instead it quickly became another time of worry. In his arms Ryshal had collapsed, her brief spurt of strength having faded, and he realised with alarm that she was weaker than he'd guessed. In fact she was gravely ill. It would be a long time before he could take her health for granted. Even now she was moving in and out of consciousness as he carried her. It was just another sign of how poorly she'd been treated.

Obviously she had been starved, mistreated and abused. She had been too weak for too long, and there had been a lot of shocks this day for her to cope with. His first priority when they got out of this pit of depravity would be to nurse her back to health. His next might be to inflict some more suffering on his brother for his ill treatment of her regardless of his word. If he survived. Heri was not a swordsman, and Sam would have wagered good coin Harmion was an expert. Then again, neither of them had a right hand.

Sam didn't yet hear the sounds of swordplay behind him, but then he didn't expect to. Heri was still dressing and yelling orders at his guards, and Harmion was still screaming like a baby. He would likely be long gone before either of the two had worked up the courage to fight. Assuming they actually did. Sam was certain however, that each would try to persuade their own troops to fight for them. Sam only hoped the soldiers had the back bone to resist. Meanwhile he just wanted to leave – something that was proving more difficult than he'd expected.

It had been a long time since he had been in the castle and somewhere in his travels he must have got turned around. He knew that when he took an extra flight of stairs down and found himself on the ground floor, heading towards the throne room from one of the side passages.

And when he emerged from the passage it was to meet the rest of the palace guards who were standing in front of the throne itself. There must have been three dozen of them. Where had they been during the fight he wondered? Not that there had been much that they could have done. Sam paid them little attention, as they all scurried out of the way of the fire shield. But he did see something that caught his interest; the throne. It made him angry.

All the suffering, all the pain Heri had put him and Ryshal through, and just so he could sit on a chair Sam had never wanted. It seemed so insignificant. In the end it was just a chair. With an impulsive sweep of his hand he sent a spray of fire arrows directly into it.

The effect was immediate as the inlaid gold and velvet throne caught fire and exploded, followed by the ornate velvet curtains behind it and the tables for the receiving of tribute and taxes. Again it was but the most minor of blasts, and yet the ferocity of the outcome was far greater than he could have hoped for as the pair of bronzed cannon on which it sat began to melt. It was yet another sign of just how strong he had become this past week.

Meanwhile the stone underneath the throne room began to crumble and melt just before the cannon exploded. Apparently they weren't just real cannon they were loaded and Sam was grateful he hadn't been standing in front of them. The palace guards ran for cover as red-hot fragments of the stone dais and bits of metal shot out in all directions. Unlike the arrows some of them made it through Sam's flame shield but luckily none hit them. He did however, catch the sceptre which conveniently came flying his way in one of the subsequent explosions. It was twenty two pounds of solid gold and was encrusted with diamonds and other precious stones. And while it was somewhat twisted and a little melted Sam figured it would buy an awful lot of food, horses and wagons for the elves of Shavarra. And no matter which of the two survived their duel, they didn't deserve such wealth. Sam shoved it roughly into a saddle bag, determined that they would never see it again.

In short order, the throne, the dais, and everything else had turned into a ball of fire, and was slowly descending through the castle as the stone floor underneath it melted. In time Sam knew, there would only be a great black abyss where once Heri's butt had sat so proudly. It would be a long time before a new throne was built for whoever would sit on it. Perhaps that would serve as a reminder to whoever the new king was that he had no interest in power. They didn't need to fear his taking their throne – just their lives.

Sam turned his back on the spectacle and made to leave, but then stopped when he saw the corridor to one side leading to the royal library, and his sense of duty returned to him. Only a single very long week ago, he had discovered much that needed explaining. A new enemy, or perhaps a very old one, that threatened his future, his wife's future, and Shavarra. He had made a promise to himself to protect his mother's and his wife's families. And in any case he was a knight of Hanor and that was his duty. To meet that duty he needed to learn more about his enemy. This was his chance.

With a flick of the reigns Tyla made her way down the corridor, somehow ignoring the tapestry covered walls which had caught fire, and then turned into the reading room, which backed on to the library. It was here as a child he'd spent countless hours learning not only of magic and science, but of statesmanship and history, of tactics and warfare, and of heroes. It was one of the few parts of the keep which still held some good memories for him, and he chose not to allow it to burn down as his flame shield touched the books. Rather he let the shield go and instead used his earth magic to reshape the corridor behind him so that they sealed at the end. Similarly the windows he quickly turned into stone walls. He could use his fire for light instead, and the main door out to the courtyard he sealed shut.

"Love, rest here for a bit. I'll only be a short while." He doubted Ryshal heard him, she was so deathly tired and pale, but he made sure she was told anyway even as she collapsed forward over Tyla's neck. Though unconscious she was at least alive. Once her safety was assured, he dismounted Tyla, and made his way into the library proper.

The chamber was surrounded by any number of shelves filled with weighty tomes and scrolls which extended from the floor to the fifteen foot high ceiling on all four sides. In the middle sat a dozen heavy desks at which scholars might sit and read, and of course many more comfortable easy chairs. Lamps in their wrought iron frames were dotted everywhere around the chamber, while more hung from the walls. But perhaps because of the lateness of the hour, none were lit. And as always there was dust everywhere. It seemed to be a perpetual problem in the library for some reason.

Seeing it again brought him back to his childhood. He had been taught here by various tutors. He had spent many long hours with his head bowed over the tomes and scrolls, being questioned about everything he was reading. He had even been coached in his lessons of statecraft here by his father – before he had wed that highly stationed troll and Heri had arrived in the world. This was a good place filled with good memories. And yet all was not right. Tomes were out on the tables, left open and unread when they should have been shelved. The shelves themselves were messy and nothing looked to be in order. Some of the furniture was in need of repair, while the curtains were threadbare.

Seeing it, and the lack of care that the library had received, Sam found himself appalled. This was a place that needed to be cared for. Not left to rot. Not for the first time he wondered how it could all have gone so wrong. The people of Fair

Fields were good people. So was his father. Hard working, honest and open people. And yet somehow they kept finding bad seeds to become their kings. His father had been the single exception in a hundred years.

A seasoned soldier and knight of Hanor, Eric Hanor had been made king for acts of heroism, after he'd saved the realm from the invading army of an unscrupulous tyrant. As king he'd tried to bring taxes down and the law within the reach of the normal peasant. For that reason he had been known to the people as King Hanor the True, and to the nobility as a nuisance and a threat to their power. For which crime he'd eventually been poisoned by an assassin's dart.

Then had come Heri, his father's legal heir, but cast in his trollish mother's mould – manipulative, cunning and a liar. Heri in the end had proved to be exactly like all the other kings who had come before their father. Self serving, intolerant, arrogant and petty. He had quickly raised taxes and put the common law back in the hands of the nobles, to win support from them. If he died this night Sam would not shed a tear for him and nor would his people, though it was always possible that Harmion would make an even worse king. Thus far he had certainly seemed no better.

But that could not be Sam's concern. He was no longer a citizen of Fair Fields. He had never had any position of authority. And after tonight he would probably be considered an enemy. His concern had to be his wife and her people. And an army of steel rats.

Sam hurried round the shelves until he came to the section on prophecy and promptly grabbed a full two dozen of the major works. He scarcely took time to even read their titles, and instead just shoved them into a canvas sack as fast as he could, before moving on to the magical sections. The fact that he could even do so was a testament to Heri's self-serving machinations and paranoid stupidity.

The wizard guild had once had its own separate library, as was expected for wizards across the lands. It was believed that the knowledge contained within their arcane works was too dangerous and too precious to be allowed to go free to those not properly trained – a view his father had shared. But then Sam's mother had been a fire wizard before him. His father saw the value in having a strong wizard's guild to defend and support the people.

In one of his first acts as king, Heri had taken those tomes from the wizard's library and placed them in the general library. His actions were an attempt at both undermining the value of wizardry and symbolically removing the status of its practitioners. Heri saw the wizard's guild as a powerful body and a threat to his rule. It hadn't helped that his older brother was developing into a powerful spell caster even then. Heri had even destroyed many of the tomes over the years, claiming such knowledge shouldn't be permitted. Tomes and scrolls that had cost thousands of gold pieces and the sweat of hundreds of scribes each, had been destroyed in a fit of royal pique.

Thus the library had been pillaged and many of its most important magical works destroyed. All save those that Sam had managed to secretly gather to himself all those years ago. Of course that same act had ensured that Heri had had only minor magic users to defend him today. A good spell caster was worth his weight in gold, and could easily find employment elsewhere. And why would one work for a king who despised him? Then again, Harmion might well have had something to do with his lack of master mages as well. The weasel would realise that they might have been able to protect the king from him, and in so doing ruin all his plans.

Sam quickly found all the remaining tombs on wizardry – there were only a couple of dozen or so left – and scooped them into the sack as well, and then stuffed the rest into the saddle bags. They were mainly from the schools of air and water. Sam having none of those magics within him had chosen not to save them when he'd lived in the keep. It was quickly becoming a heavy load, but then there were things he could do about that, and he'd already decided that this was going to be a major robbery as much as a rescue. If he could bankrupt whichever of the pair survived, so much the better.

Next he moved on to the scrolls, the section where the truly dangerous spells and most potent prophecies were contained. But without a librarian to catalogue them, no one other than a spell caster would have realised that. Heri had had the man thrown in the dungeon long ago for objecting to his changes, and he doubted that the man still lived.

Sam managed to roll up around seventy or so scrolls into a single bundle and placed them in the bedroll on Tyla's rump. He then squeezed as many more as he could manage within the sack of books. He winced as he heard the aged parchment of some of them crumpling, but he had no choice. It was either that or leave them behind where they could be of no help to anyone.

Then, suddenly remembering what else he had learned of the elves' enemy, he moved on to the history sections and grabbed a few volumes about the ancient Dragon wars, which he stuffed into a bag he found sitting by one of the desks and then draped around Tyla's neck. It was only a shame he couldn't gather the rest, because somewhere in one of them he knew that that damned verse was written. And with every day that passed he knew with greater certainty that it was the key.

In short order he was once more mounted on Tyla, Ryshal in his arms and the reigns in his hands, and he knew it was long past time to leave. Ry needed a safe place to sleep tonight, some hot food and drink, and she couldn't travel for too long to reach it. He opened the sealed stone doors leading to the ground floor terrace and the wide steps from there leading down to the courtyard itself, and raised his fire shield as they trotted out into the night.

Soon they reached the courtyard where more soldiers lay in wait. This time there were hundreds of them, and they lined the battlements which they'd had to climb up to with ropes. These ones though were not so impressed by his magic, and proceeded to rain arrows down on them. Not that they had any effect as the arrows instantly become dust the moment they touched the shield. Sam felt no great animosity towards them, but then they posed no real threat to either Ry or him. He figured these soldiers knew little of what had transpired in the royal chambers. Nor would they know who he was or why a wizard was destroying the castle. All they knew was that the castle had been attacked by a wizard who was even now in the courtyard beneath them, and they were simply trying to defend their home. Sam paid the soldiers scant attention.

Instead his thoughts turned to transport. With the extra three hundred weight or more of books and scrolls he'd loaded down on poor Tyla, plus Ryshal, and himself in full armour, his mare would not be running very far for long, especially considering how far she'd already run without pause. What he needed was another horse to share the load.

But then why stop at one? Again, he felt no obligation to be sparing in his theft, and the elves desperately needed as many horses as they could get.

A single pulse of earth magic collapsed the outer wall to the royal stables, and a quick spell of calling meant that easily sixty more black war horses began following them along the courtyard. Many were still saddled, the sign of a lazy groom. But that too worked to his advantage. Let the soldiers try to chase them with all of their best steeds taken and many of their saddles as well. And it wasn't theft he told himself. It was self-protection, and the barest beginnings of compensation for what had been done to him and his wife.

Besides, when they reached the elves he would give them all the horses. They surely had the greater need.

Some of the soldiers when they saw the horses following Sam tried to give chase. They didn't want to lose their steeds. But they stopped hurriedly and retreated when Sam tossed a few tiny fire balls their way. Better to lose their horses than their lives. In the end it wasn't a difficult problem to deal with.

A bigger problem was the missing drawbridge and the moat. Sam didn't want to jump the moat again with Ryshal so weak in his arms. Nor did he want to have to exert himself by giving even more strength to all of the horses following. While the magic was still burning fiercely within him, he was strong. But he still couldn't risk running out of magic before he was well clear of the castle.

A fraction of earth magic on the moat bed solved the problem and soon he had a stone walkway wide enough to carry two horses and carts side by side across it. Of course it completely negated the protective value of the moat, and it would take the stone masons weeks if not months to dig it out again – after they'd repaired the gate and walls that was. But that was a small price to pay for Ryshal's comfort.

Once outside Sam set Tyla off at a steady trot back to the elves, a herd of Fair Field's finest war horses following. Whichever one of the would be kings prevailed, they would spend a fortune replacing their steeds and a second repairing the keep, before they could even begin to look at the cost of replacing the gold and gem encrusted throne and sceptre. It was something that brought a quick smile to Sam's face. The first in a long time. A faint groan from Ryshal however, soon wiped his face of it.

She was rousing again. She needed care, and she most definitely needed food. The gruel his brother served his prisoners was surely not enough to keep body and soul together, and it would be a long time before Ryshal was back to full strength. A goal that he knew he had to begin work on immediately.

Quickly he fished out a small bag of trail mix from his saddle bag. A tiny spark of magic from his hand warmed the bag up, and melted the cooked oats and the honey into a semblance of a thick porridge and brought the smell of vanilla, apricots and cinnamon to Ryshal's nose, rousing her more fully. Pulling some eating utensils out of his pocket Sam fed her a few spoonfuls with infinite care, washing each one down with a little fresh water. It was good wholesome food and he knew it would do her good. He hoped it would bring her some strength for the long days of travelling ahead.

"Samual?" Her voice was so weak, and yet so wonderful to hear after all those long years of silence. But her obvious confusion worried him. Had she already forgotten that he'd rescued her? What did that say about her health?

"Yes love. It's me. And you're free. You're safe too."

"Free?"

"Free! I'm bringing you home to your family, and your people. You'll be safe with them, and I'll be with you too. Forever. Rest easy in my arms. I will not let you go again. Ever." He whispered it to her, before her brief spurt of energy faded and she lapsed once more into sleep in his arms. But by the moon light he could see that she had a smile on her face. She was so weak and thin that it terrified him to think of how easily she could sicken and even die. But she was also alive and in his arms and he was overwhelmed with joy to feel her nestled there. It was time to make sure she stayed that way.

Knowing that the main danger they faced was being followed by soldiers or worse, assassins, Sam knew that he had to stop any thought of that from entering anyone's mind, be it the surviving king, his usurper, or his soldiers. Remembering the fire prison spell from one of his earliest books of magic, Sam shaped and released a gigantic wall of fire that surrounded the entire citadel. Usually such spells were only designed to hold a person, block a passage way, or simply keep two people apart and as such they were small simple magics. But this – this was something far beyond any of those childhood spells.

Despite the fact that he had never cast such a massive fire wall, it was surprisingly easy, and although the wall was neither as hot nor as dangerous as it appeared, it looked very impressive. It would also work well. Not many soldiers would dare try to run through a wall of flame fifty yards high, orders or no orders. In fact they would baulk if anyone dared to order them to go through it. It would be a foolish king who gave that command.

But the best part of the spell was that it would last for at least a day or two; maybe even longer. Once it was formed it drew no more strength from the caster, and its shape was held within the spell woven air itself, almost like an enchantment. No one would be following them.

And for every hour that it endured, either Heri or Harmion would only be able to stare at it and wonder that they'd ever dared to anger a fire mage. No matter which of them won their duel, they would not risk having their soldiers follow him.

Of course it still left him wondering. How did he have so much strength? Because he was burning so much magic, and yet always seemed to have more available. Where was it coming from? Was this simply the level of mastery? Or was it something more? He didn't know. But he did know that wherever it was coming from he was going to use it.

"The Goddess be praised." Ry opened her eyes once more

to take in the sight of a city surrounded by fire. "She sang to me of your growing strength. But I never knew."

Sam would have answered her. Told her that it wasn't as impressive as it seemed. But she collapsed into him again, the effort of even remaining awake too much for her.

The spell cast and Ry asleep in his arms, it was time to go. Sam held his wife close, still wondering that he even could, and thanked the All Father for the miracle of her survival, Then he kicked Tyla in her flanks and began the long journey back to the loving arms of her family.

Chapter Seven.

"Bring me Augrim!" Heri bellowed at his guards, angrier than he had ever been in his life. And he had the body to prove it.

The weasel lay at his feet, nice and dead. He had died badly, and that was the only good thing to have come out of the night. Harmion's soldiers had quickly made themselves scarce after he had struck the fatal blow. But it wouldn't save them. No matter that they had only been following their lord's orders; they had gone against their King. He would have all of them hunted down and hung for that. And though they didn't know it yet, his own soldiers would follow them to the gallows. They had failed him. They had even forced him to fight his own duel. And perhaps most terrible, they had seen him kneel to his brother. He would not forget that.

As for the weasel he was lucky to be dead. Had he not been, Heri would have made sure his death would have been far more terrible. As it was it had been a hard one. The dart he had thrown had only nicked the weasel's hand and the fool had stupidly laughed at his failure, thinking that he had the battle all but won. He'd laughed at the injury, and displayed the wound to his men as if it was a trophy. And then he'd started coughing. A few moments later his body had started burning from the inside out.

Basilisk venom! It was always a favourite of Heri's. Who said the Dead Belly Wastes had no value? They grew basilisks! That was value indeed.

Still, as his own armour had started burning away, the steel melting into a puddle on the floor beside him, he had to admit that the weasel had been more dangerous than he'd expected. Not only better with a blade, but smarter than he'd expected. And whatever he'd coated his sword with, it could have won him the battle. Unfortunately for him Heri was smarter again and his poison had been quick acting.

The weasel had died and his family would follow him to the underworld in due course. After a lengthy period of suffering of course. In the meantime he had another man he needed to kill. His brother. It seemed that his assassins had failed once again. Which was why he was now bellowing for his magical advisor. A man who he noted had been suspiciously absent during the battle.

Out of fear or treachery? That was the only question he cared about. But it didn't matter. If Augrim had been on the Fallbright side, he would return to him. The coup had failed and in the end the man only cared about one thing. Getting enough gold that he could continue his arcane studies. If he had been in the Fallbrights' pay he would no longer be receiving any gold from that source. In fact soon the Fallbrights would be unable to pay even their own guards.

But he suspected it was more likely fear that had kept Augrim away. When his brother had struck and the castle had been shaken to its very foundations, he'd surely guessed that a truly powerful wizard had arrived and had fled. His magic was in the subtle and poisonous. In the summoning of undead and monstrous creatures. In the consorting with demons and the learning of secrets. Even divination. He could not stand directly against a wizard of such power.

Which also explained why his assassins had failed. He'd never guessed that Samual had gained such power. As he'd dressed for battle the guards had told him of what Samual had done to the castle. Of the massive holes he'd smashed in the walls. And of the throne. His beloved throne! Gone!

Samual would die for what he'd done – but it would have to be done carefully. He couldn't use an assassin. Or even an army of them. Heri couldn't afford to use any agent that could be traced back to him. He would kill his brother by being clever and using magic and knowledge. Which was why he bellowed for his advisor once more and then sent soldiers after him when the miserable worm still didn't show.

It was an age before Augrim finally arrived. Far too long, and by the time he appeared Heri was thinking about having him killed too. His hand hurt, and the physicians were busy bandaging it though they could do nothing for the pain. Their salves were useless. The wound wasn't bleeding. It had been burnt closed. He wanted something to kill the pain, not simply cover the wound.

"You sent for me Sire?"

Augrim managed a small bow as he entered the chamber. Enough to seem respectful though Heri knew the truth. He could see it in his eyes as he surveyed the room, particularly as he studied the remains of the weasel. The man cared nothing for him; only his own research. He might not have taken the Fallbright's coin this time, but he would have happily continued working for them as advisor if Heri had been the one to die.

"Ages ago! Where have you been?"

"Looking at the view Sire."

Heri stared at him, almost speechless with disbelief. For a moment he wondered if he had heard the wizard correctly. Staring at the view? Was the man jesting? Why would anyone, least of all a wizard, want to stare at a ruined castle? Especially when he had just been summoned by his king? But the man looked serious. Of course he always looked serious. With that stupid little pointed beard of his that he constantly stroked and his black eyes, there was rarely any sign of levity in him.

"The castle has been attacked! Your King has been injured! And you are staring at the broken walls wizard? Do you deliberately seek to anger me?"

"No Sire. I seek to understand your enemy. Your brother from what I've been told. And you can learn a lot about a man by his actions."

The wizard continued to stroke his beard as he stared back at Heri thoughtfully. He had what the peasants called bacca pipes – long tightly curled ringlets made of greying whiskers that he was inordinately proud of. As a result he stroked them a lot. One day Heri promised himself he was going to shave his beard off – and his head!

Yet perhaps he had a point? Who knew when it came to wizards? And the man had his uses. He had found him a lot of arcane items over the years. Things which would destroy his enemies if he had the need. And the most precious of them was the sun burst. An ancient magical weapon built to end wars – permanently. It would level a small mountain; an enemy castle by comparison would be no problem. Where the man had found it or how he'd laid his hands on it Heri didn't know. But it was valuable and so perhaps was the wizard's knowledge. For the moment.

"And did you learn anything wizard?"

"Yes Sire." Augrim fixed him with a stare, his face sombre. "Your brother is far more powerful than any wizard I've ever heard of. The damage he's done shows strength such as I've never seen. And the fire wall shows that he can weave as well. This is not the untrained minor fire wizard that left the land five years ago. At the very least he's a master."

"I think everyone here knows that!" Heri snapped at him, annoyed to be told something he already knew. Especially when it was so obvious. Maybe it was time to shave the wizard. His whiskers and his throat!

"But not everyone understands what that means." Augrim stroked his beard some more. "A master, called so early to his strength speaks to his motivation. Of need and perhaps pain. And if what your guards have told me is correct, it speaks of his anger toward you. Make no mistake Sire, if you anger him again he will come for you. And none will be able to protect you from his rage."

That last caught Heri by surprise. It also angered him. Was it a warning? A not so subtle hint that he couldn't stand against Samual? That Augrim would not stand with him? Heri thought that it might be. That underneath his calm demeanour the wizard was frightened.

"But more importantly, the fact that he has learnt to weave such powerful magic speaks of training. Advanced training. He has spent these past years studying with someone, and he is not alone. To go against him it would seem is to go against others. It could be war."

"War?" That Heri heard even through his pain and rage. And he knew he wasn't ready to fight a war against wizards. Not when he had other enemies closer to home to defeat first.

"Against whoever has trained him. Other masters probably. Powerful wizards who are unlikely to be human. No human wizard is so strong. And your brother is half elf. I would think he was trained by them. Then again the sylph and the fairy are even stronger and it may be that he has sought them out. He would have sought only the most powerful."

"And then there are always rumours of the nameless."

"The nameless? The unseen?" Heri knew of them of course. But he doubted they had ever existed save as the tales of the bards. Wizards exiled. Turned away from their colleges and callings. Hidden, living alone, or perhaps in little communities. They were said to be the most powerful of all. And the most secretive. Who they were and what they could actually do, he didn't know. No one knew. As far as he knew they were just a legend. A story for the bards to sing about and parents to tell their children. Sleep tight or the nameless would get you. It was just nonsense. But every so often something strange occurred and the songs started up once again.

"Only a thought Sire." Augrim shrugged. "And it may be worse yet."

"Worse?" How could things possibly be any worse?

"Though I cannot detect the presence of the divine, the power suggests Draco, Lord of the Skies. Father of Dragons."

Heri immediately understood why he'd mentioned the poxy god's name. And the unseen before that. It was about fear. Augrim did not want to go into a battle with other wizards. As powerful and knowledgeable as he was, he doubted his chances against them. And he certainly doubted his ability to go against a god. If Heri suggested it he knew his advisor would run rather than fight. That was the point. It was a not so subtle statement that his loyalty went only so far. And probably that of his soldiers as well. He decided to change the subject. For the moment.

"Fire wall?" His guards had said nothing of such a thing.

"Perhaps it would be best if you saw it for yourself Sire." With no more than that the wizard turned on his heels and marched out of the bed chamber, leaving Heri with the unfortunate option of having to follow him. Chasing his advisor in his own castle! It was unseemly. And yet still he had to.

So he followed the wizard out of the chamber and into the hallway, the annoying physicians in tow as they continued to try to bandage his hand. The guards brought up the rear, weapons at the ready. Not that they would be of any use. They'd already proven that once this evening.

Out in the hall way he followed Augrim to the upstairs audience chamber where he greeted his private visitors and occasionally discussed strategy with his commanders. It was a good room, blessed with huge glass windows that overlooked the courtyard and the walls beyond. It was also a place where he could stand and watch unnoticed as his visitors came calling.

But this night he wasn't looking down upon the courtyard for visitors. Instead he looked over the broken outer wall to the fire wall beyond. Flames leaping into the air at least seventy or eighty feet high. Maybe more. In fact if the walls were forty feet tall and these were at least twice as high, almost certainly more. And when he turned his head from side to side he could see that they were dancing outside the walls of his keep to both sides and then on around the city for as far as he could see. According to Augrim they completely surrounded the city.

It was then that he understood why his advisor was frightened. And he knew that his soldiers and his people would likely be as well. Not a one of them would dare go against Samual. And not a one of them would stand by him if he gave the order. They would run. Or they would run him through. Anything to avoid facing down certain death.

"Alder's balls!" Heri cursed his brother, realising in that moment that there was nothing he could do. Not yet anyway. Not against that sort of power.

For the moment he would have to spend his time and

effort calming the people. That meant coin for street entertainers. More gold for the temples to hold services. And not just for the All Father's temple. He was a dour god. The priests of Vineus would need to be out in the streets. The people loved the god of wine. A festival in his honour might well be in order.

Heri was going to be busy he realised. Keeping the people calm while they stared at the wall of fire surrounding them.

Samual would die, horribly. Once he had a plan that was. And some people he could actually trust to do the job. For the moment he would have to content himself with taking his vengeance out on the Fallbrights. And with making sure that none of the other nobles harboured similar ideas of rebellion.

In fact that was going to have to be a priority. He was going to have to guarantee their loyalty – and he knew of only one way to do that. Taking hostages. It was not going to be popular. In fact the noble houses were going to protest. Maybe some might even think of refusing a royal decree. But given that this night he had been shown to be weak, it would have to be done. He could not allow them to think he was vulnerable. That his throne was there for anyone with the strength to take it.

It was his throne, curse them all! He would never yield it.

Samual would wait. But not forever.

Chapter Eight.

Ten days passed before Sam made it back to the elves. Or nearly back to them. Ten long, heavenly and yet harrowing days as he watched Ryshal like a hawk, seeing her health slowly improving. It was a slow and terrifying ordeal, and she was far from fit even at the end, but at least by then there was a trace of colour showing in her cheeks, the blotches on her skin were fading, and the very first hint of some desperately needed weight was appearing in her arms and legs.

It had been a glacially slow trip. Even with the extra horses carrying some of the weight, all of which were in remarkably fine condition, he had scarcely got Tyla up past a trot for any of it. Ryshal simply wasn't well enough for that. And they had to take lengthy rests throughout the day every day for her to eat and nap. But it was worth it to have her back in his arms, and despite his fears he hadn't seen a single sign of pursuit. The soldiers could have followed easily once the fire wall had died away. They hadn't which surely meant that the king, whoever he was, had decided not to risk it. Perhaps he'd taken a look at his castle gate or the wall of fire surrounding his entire keep, and thought better of it? Perhaps he'd just seen the ruin of his hand and wondered how much more he could lose.

Either way it was just as well. That first night, and the morning after had been one of tremendous difficulty for Sam. He'd been torn between the absolute wonder of having Ryshal back with him after so long, the horror of discovering again and again how close to death she was, and the boiling rage at discovering her mistreatment. Any of Heri's soldiers who had been stupid enough to approach would have been reduced to ashes in a heartbeat, regardless of their intent.

That first night had been difficult enough, feeling how thin she was. Seeing the illness that consumed her. Feeding her, and helping her to rest, terrified that each time she fell back to sleep she might not awaken. Still, the darkness and clothing had concealed much more than he'd guessed. The morning that followed had been worse as it revealed all that he had not seen.

It had begun with the bathing. He had camped by a stream that night, making sure the horses had plenty of fresh grass and clean water to drink, and in the morning he'd decided to wash the worst of the dirt off her before they made tracks for the day. She had been living in squalor for so long that it was everywhere. Caking her skin and her clothes. For Ry who had always been a finicky clean woman – one who would go over every part of their chambers after he had finished cleaning them, and clean them again – living like this would have been an anathema to her.

Creating a small dam in the river by fusing the river stones together to become stone walls, he'd built a bath just big enough for him to hold her in it and wash her and her clothes while she lay in his lap in the heated water. It had seemed the sensible thing to do. But he had never considered the horror of what he might find.

Hunting out the small cake of soap he always kept in his bulging saddle bags, he'd begun by washing the dirt out of her hair in the warm water, and watched with dismay as most of her hair washed away with the dirt. But what it revealed was worse as he realised she was close to bald, and her scalp was covered with festering sores. It was then that he'd realised that she had nits and was covered with lice, something he'd never known of her or any elf. They were always so careful with their grooming and they expected it of others.

Knowing there was no choice, he'd shaved the rest of her hair off with his belt knife, weeping as he did so. It was a terrible thing to do. For an elf, especially an elven maiden, her long, beautiful hair was considered a crowning glory and a sign of being truly elven. It was her rowell aylin or golden light. But with no hair the nits would die quickly in the sun, the sores would dry out and heal, and she would recover faster. He could only pray that her hair would grow back as it should.

Then when he'd tried to remove her clothes, they'd disintegrated in his hands. They'd been little more than rags, again something no elf would wear. He'd thrown their remains away, disgusted by what she had been forced to wear. But he was horrified by what he found underneath them.

The sores that covered her whole body from the endless flea bites. The bruises that seemed to cover every inch of her arms and legs. The evidence of a whip which had been used on her back and legs. And the terrible thinness that allowed him to see her every rib; her every bone. He wept as he saw the piteous wreckage that had been made of her body. She who had once been so beautiful. Her skin always so soft and perfect, was a mass of wounds and scars. Her breasts once ample and delightful, had become withered lumps of leather. Her graceful womanly hips and elegant long legs had turned into lengths of bones with painfully thin skin stretched taught over them.

He was a strong man, a soldier who had faced death many times, yet he could not bear to see her looking so ill, and for ages as he'd held her and wept for what had been done to her, he had had to look away. It was only when his sense of duty returned that he'd found the strength to carry on. To bathe her, dress her wounds with the salve he always carried, feed her, and make sure she knew how much he loved her.

Ever since then, every morning and every evening without fail, he had bathed her, caring for her wounds and desperately watching for the slightest sign of a little more weight being put on. And with the blessings of the All Father, it was happening. Too slowly but still, every day was a little better than the last.

He had tried to make her eat at least six times a day. Small meals; porridge, soups, bread and dairy, fruit and meats, whatever he could hunt or buy from the local farmers. He knew that eating was the only way back to health for her, and yet she was so piteously starved that she simply couldn't eat a full meal. Her stomach no longer had room for it, and sometimes – too often in fact – even the little he could make her eat came back up as her body could not digest it.

Sleep was another thing she desperately needed, and even though she spent most of her time passed out in his arms, he made sure that she got at least two decent sleeps during the day, as they stopped for morning and afternoon tea. Yet each time she slept, he still worried that she might not wake up, and he'd spend the entire time watching her, his heart in his mouth, making sure she was still breathing. Watching her chest rising and falling, listening to the air passing in and out, even feeling her heart beating. And somehow, despite his fears, she continued to live, and even to slowly recover.

Of course the real healing would only begin when she was back in the arms of her family, in a proper bed and under the care of proper elven physicians. He would have run the horses into the ground to reach them if he thought she could have withstood the journey.

He would have healed her too, if he'd had even a trace of the healer's magic. But that was one of the bitter ironies of his life. He was one of the most powerful fire mages there was as impossible as that seemed. And yet he was still completely powerless when it came to what truly mattered. He could not heal so much as a cut finger.

Yet while he was terrified for her and desperately wanted to get her into the care of elven physicians who were some of the finest healers around, the very slowness of the trip was its own reward as it gave him more time to spend with his wife. Renewing their love, renewing their memories. And with each day that had passed she would rouse for a little bit longer, and they could talk a little more.

If she had been healthier and he less angry, it would almost have been like a second honeymoon. If only he could be less regretful or more forgiving of what had been done to her. But he couldn't. Maybe it was the half human side of his nature, but Sam still ached for revenge. The only thing holding him back was that he wanted his wife more. So their conversations tended to be almost stilted, something that they had never been before. Yet at least they were finally able to talk.

As Sam had told her of his life for the previous five years, he had also shared with her his love and pain. The same love and pain that Ryshal had endured in her tiny prison cell. But even as she told him of her relief at finally being free, Sam just kept hearing more reasons to get angry. Many more.

It wasn't enough that his brother had imprisoned her, that he had nearly starved her to death. He had locked her up in a basement dungeon, one with barely a scrap of light from a high window, and left her to rot. That was surely the very definition of suffering for anyone, but for an elf who lived for the forest and the fields it was worse. Add to that her confinement in a tiny cell barely large enough to lie down in. For a woman born to dance under sunlit skies, it must have been torture.

Worse still, she had been allowed little in the way of visits from her family. The most they could do when they did get permission was to speak to her from the high window, and to pass her a few scraps of food through the bars. The good stuff went to the guards, another group he dearly wanted to punish. She had committed no crime and they must have known that.

Samual

There could be no excuse.

They had beaten her too, though that had only begun about three months before when a new gaoler had arrived, and Sam guessed that that was Harmion's doing. If she had actually died he would have won everything, so long as Heri didn't suspect and kill him first. But he couldn't kill her directly. Not without getting caught. So he had no doubt bribed or coerced the guards to allow his man in to do it for him. She was a hostage not a criminal, but that had apparently not stopped the blackguard in his criminal duty. And her bruises were recent. In as terrible state as she had been, he had still had her flogged until she just lay on the ground and no longer moved. It was a miracle she had survived as long as she had. Only her faith had allowed her to survive. To wait for him to save her. Sam envied her that faith. In her place he had no certainty he could have clung to life for so long.

In time maybe, Sam would find that blackguard and teach him a lesson in beatings. He so desperately wanted to. But not until after Ry was well again. Nothing could come before that.

The only indignity she had not suffered was rape. His brother would not dare to cross that line, though once, when he and Ryshal had first been married, he too had desired her. He had made an improper advance. That was the only time Sam had ever crossed him – until just a few days before of course. It had also been the first time he had ever used his magic against his own family, and he recalled vividly the shame he'd felt at doing such a thing. And in hindsight it had been a mistake.

But the flaming sword he had levelled against his brother's neck all those years ago seemed to have done the trick. Heri had at least learned fear. Nothing of decency or even family though. Enough so that he would not dare cross Sam again. Or so he had thought. Unfortunately he had been wrong. That had perhaps been the most stupid mistake of his life, and one he would not repeat again. If Heri crossed him again he would kill him. There would be no negotiation.

Recently Heri had learned a lot more of fear – assuming he still lived. His injury would remind him of the truth of that for the rest of his life, and his castle's repair might also remind him of what real power was. But even if he hadn't learned, Sam would never allow him near Ry again. He would kill Heri before he came within a thousand leagues of her. He swore it on his life.

Part of Sam knew that his anger was a mistake. He even understood what it was costing him. His future. His hope. His joy. She was his aylin mi elle. The light of his heart. And his rage obscured that light. Already he could see the harm in it. Once they had been able to talk forever of anything and everything as they danced their dance of love, oblivious to the world around them. Now, they spoke of their wounded love and the pain of their time apart until either Ryshal fell asleep again or he grew too angry for words. But he could not let his anger go. The best he could do was force it down into the darkness of his soul. That he promised himself, was something he would work on over the years, as long as he had Ry with him.

Revenge was only worthwhile for those who had nothing else, as his father had told him long ago. To spend his life on it would be to waste his life. And for the first time in far too many years, he had the promise of a life again. Perhaps when they reached the elves it would be time to speak with the elders about his anger. It had granted him great power for sure – he could think of nothing else that had allowed him to grow so powerful as a wizard. But power was not the equal of love.

He understood that best in the quiet times. At night while Ryshal slept and he held her close while studying the books and scrolls he'd recovered from the library. Every so often as he tried to read by the light of a fire brand, he would glance at her face as she lay curled up into him like a small child. She was so thin and so frail that he knew there could be nothing more important in the entire world than protecting her. He promised himself over and over again that he would keep her safe and happy while he made her feel the most loved woman in the world. All else compared to that was nothing.

Unfortunately protecting her and her people looked like being a major undertaking. Her people were refugees, and their enemy was likely still pursuing them, placing Ry and her family, in jeopardy. And even if they hadn't been his people as well, he would have been honour bound to have protected them.

But it looked like being a task more difficult than any other he had known, and his progress was limited. After more than a week of studying he still had still not discovered the source of the passage that stayed in the back of his mind, though its words would always return to haunt him in the quiet moments. But he had read and reread the histories of the Dragon Wars, and they had scared him. If the warlord was truly among them once more, what had been seen at Shavarra was but the merest fraction of his power. A test perhaps as he stretched his fingers out against a relatively weak and unready target. Exactly as the first Dragon had done five thousand years before. Soon this enemy would reach out his hand against one or other of the more powerful realms, and then another and another until the entire region was in conflict. Then the suffering would be far worse than any could know. Exactly as had happened five thousand years before.

Once a few of the more powerful kingdoms had fallen to him – if he followed the same course – he would begin his true assault, hunting down the people. Using the armies of machina he had created together with an army of mercenaries, he would plunder the resources of every land he conquered to feed his war machine. All the while seemingly bent on only one thing; murder.

How could he protect her people against power and evil on that scale? How could anyone? Any mage no matter how powerful? Despite his dreams of winning a legendary victory against their enemy, Sam knew it couldn't be so. No single warrior, no single spell caster could do that. All he could do was fight by their side.

The first time the Dragon had failed, he had lost for only one reason. He had moved too quickly from destroying just a few lands to trying to conquer the rest. He had let his armies and machina be spread too thin. He had compensated by using mercenaries. But they could be bought by the other side just as easily. It was a mistake that the Dragon – if he truly had risen again – or his successor would surely not make a second time. This time Sam guessed his armies of machina would be larger and stronger than before, his reliance on mercenaries less, and his planning more thorough. He would be harder to defeat.

So as the journey continued, Sam had spent his down time reading and rereading the ancient histories as he formulated his own plans.

Ryshal it turned out though, had plans of her own.

"Make love to me."

Ry made the request on their tenth night on the road, and of course Sam wanted to. He loved her so much, and he had missed her company for far too long. He had ached for her touch for five long, miserable, lonely years. But he was also scared. Even after ten days of being fed and cared for she was far from strong. It was true that the bruising was fading, the worst of her sores had healed over, there was a little more flesh on her bones, and some peach fluff was beginning to grow on her head. Best of all, she was finding her smile again. Even her laugh. She was definitely on the road to recovery.

But she was still too weak and he told her so.

In the morning he told her they would reach the caravan, which he could sense in the distance. He guessed that they were little more than a league or two away. Then she would be provided with better care as she would be attended to by their physicians. A week or two after that, he told her, she would hopefully be strong enough. Then they could begin their lives together anew. They had time.

But time was not what Ryshal wanted. She had never been patient about such things, and before his brother had interceded had demanded his attention often. Her passion was one of the many things he had loved about her.

"Hmmph!" It was one of her favourite noises she made when she was irked and for a few blissful moments it brought him back to better times. He couldn't help but smile and kiss her as he'd told her to sleep. Which was when she took him.

Surprised by her strength – though he shouldn't have been, she had always been stronger than she looked – Sam quickly found himself rolled over on to his back, while his wife lay on top of him, hurriedly working on the straps to his armour. And he knew she would not be denied. No more did he want to deny her. By the light of the fire he could almost pretend that she was returned to her old self. Certainly the passion was there.

Unable to resist, he quickly helped her to find and release the leather straps that held his breast and back plates together, and then slid the entire section off over his head, his vest following close behind. A few moments later she was working on the draw strings that held his chain leggings and leg plates secure around his waist, and shortly after that he was completely naked and pinned underneath her. And hungry. Exactly as she wanted.

"By the Goddess you've grown strong!" Ry told him, her eyes wide.

She was right too he realised, though he'd never really thought about it until then. Over the last few years he'd concentrated on little more than weapons and magic, and that coupled with a proper diet as Ryshal's mother Pietrel had always insisted he eat, meant that his muscles had grown large while his puppy fat had all but disappeared. These days he rippled when he walked.

"Strong enough for both of us my love. Until you're well again, I will carry you everywhere you need to go. It will be my pleasure."

"You will not have to carry me for long my husband, I promise you that. But for the rest of our lives I will gladly go anywhere with you."

"And I with you." He kissed her hand, renewing at least one of the wedding vows they had sworn together so many years ago.

"Now my husband, it's long past time to relive our wedding night."

Sam would still have objected, but he wasn't given the chance as Ry took him exactly as she had always intended, and the time for words was long past. Instead he responded as he always had, returning her passion with his own, thrusting into her softness again and again, causing her to cry out with joy, even as she collapsed onto his chest demanding more.

At the end Ry called out in rapture just as he gave her his seed, laughing, singing and crying all at the same time, under a gloriously full moon.

Afterwards, as always Ryshal seemed filled with joy, and

he knew she would have been dancing and singing if she was able. Soon he promised himself, she would be. But for the moment, instead of that she settled for giggling into his chest and kissing every inch of his skin she could find, even as she fell asleep still on top of him.

It was a position Sam knew he could happily spend the rest of his life in, and Ry wasn't the only one with tears of joy in her eyes. Instead of rolling over as he would normally, letting her sleep curled into him while he studied, Sam simply pulled the bed roll over the top of them until they were snugly wrapped up together, and let his eyes close as he thanked the All Father for his infinite blessings. He thanked the Goddess too, for her wonderful daughter and for keeping her alive long enough for him to save her.

But still the anger was there in his heart.

Chapter Nine

It was on the eleventh morning as they awoke in each other's arms – the first time in weeks that Sam had actually slept rather than cat napped – that the scouts for the Shavarran caravan came across them. Two of them arrived, riding dappled elven mares. They were fitted out in light armour as befitted soldiers who needed to be highly mobile, but most important to Sam was that neither was wearing bandages. Maybe they were simply the fittest of the surviving soldiers. Or maybe as he hoped, things were getting better. They both had the decency to cough discretely as they remained a respectful distance away.

It didn't particularly bother Sam to be caught in such a position. Once it would have been, but after the previous night he felt nothing but peace and happiness. For the first time he knew a measure of faith that Ryshal would recover fully. Already she was far stronger than she looked, and though she had fallen asleep almost immediately after making love, she had felt like her old self as she had demanded and received everything he could give her. Being caught naked was inconsequential compared with that wonder. The anger would return, but not for a time.

Out of modesty and respect for his wife, Sam made the scouts turn their backs as Ryshal dressed. Something they were only too happy to do when they saw the flames dancing from his hand as he snapped his fingers, though probably they would have anyway. It might have been improper to intimidate them like that, even though he had no intention of harming anyone, but he didn't care. His wife's modesty was at stake. Besides, it probably told them who he was, assuming they didn't already know. And he had the strong feeling that they did, even if thcy didn't address him by name.

The only thing strange about it was how easily the magic appeared. Without the anger, without the fear, without even the concentration it was just there. A part of him. Perhaps he had truly reached a new level in his mastery of fire. Something more than just strength and control.

Once Ryshal was covered once more in his rude night shirt – something else he was determined to change at the first opportunity – Sam made her eat one of the apples he'd foraged the previous day while he dressed.

She wanted to go directly to her people and her family he knew, and he couldn't fault her for that. But she would have skipped breakfast to do it, and that was something he couldn't allow. Her health was improving steadily, but he could not allow her to slide back. He even raided Tyla's saddle for some cheese and a little milk he'd bought from a farmer the previous day to make it a complete breakfast, and forced their visitors to wait until she was done.

The two scouts though showed great patience, for which he also rewarded them with apples. Perhaps they respected his power, or perhaps they were simply grateful for what he had done in Shavarra. Maybe they simply understood that Ryshal was not well and therefore understood why he insisted on her eating breakfast. Whatever the reason they didn't complain as they calmly munched on their apples.

While she finished off the last of her breakfast, Sam prepared Tyla for another day's ride. He covered her now pommelless saddle with a thick rug to allow Ryshal to ride more comfortably in front of him and gave her some good oats from his rapidly dwindling supply. He also promised himself he would give her a proper rub down and grooming when they made the caravan. She was a good horse, valiant and true, and it was the very least he owed her for the last few weeks of loyal service she had given.

Very shortly after that they were under way; back to the elves, and back to Ry's family.

It wasn't a long journey. He'd sensed the caravan ahead the previous day and known they were only a league or so away. But it was a difficult one. Ry was impatient. She wanted to see her family desperately. Meanwhile Sam was more concerned about the reception he might get. After all, he hadn't left under the best of circumstances, and the chances were that there would be some unhappy elders waiting for him. It was almost certain he thought that there would be more lectures. Perhaps long swathes of stories from the elven histories that would explain to him in detail why he had been wrong to do as he had done. He hated that – almost as much as the elves seemed to love reciting the ancient tales.

Worse though, he might have to face the priests. The elves never did anything official without the priests of the Goddess in attendance to bless everything. And they would be very thorough. There would be prayers, singing, personal testimonies and of course more chastisement for his many failings. Failings that began with his being a follower of the All Father.

Still, at least the journey was over. Ry could see her parents and get the medical attention she needed. And he could return to his duties as a knight of Hanor and help protect the people. From now on that had to be his focus. First though he would have to apologise to the elders. Endlessly. He might be a half human and a follower of the All Father, but some days he thought his life was one of the God of Mischief's jests.

Ry had also told him a little of what he could expect. And a little of what he had to say. He'd told her of what had happened to her people, and something of what he'd done and why he was in trouble. For the most part she'd just laughed, but she'd also made certain he understood what would be expected of him, and what wouldn't be acceptable. Naturally defending himself against their charges and complaints wouldn't be acceptable.

She told him that once more as they rode back to her people. The scouts heard everything of course, but carefully said nothing, choosing instead to study the surroundings as she spoke. He wasn't sure why but it worried him.

But he was sure that they'd ridden out specifically to find them and bring them back. He knew that the moment the scouts led them to the front of the caravan, where he found a group of elves waiting for them. A group comprised primarily of elders. Moreover the caravan wasn't moving, despite the fact that they should have been under-way several hours before. He was expected.

"Honey?"

Ry saw them too he guessed.

"It's all right. They're waiting for me."

He hoped that brought her a little cheer, knowing that no elf ever wanted to have to face the elders. It wasn't that they were scared of them. It was simply that they hated the thought of having done something that would have deserved being brought before them, whether for good or ill. Elves prided themselves on living modest, decorous lives. They were never too loud.

Unfortunately his actions had caught their attention. Or at least they had caught the attention of one elder in particular Sam guessed as he spotted Elder Bela standing at the head of the group.

"Elder Bela," Sam greeted him politely. Why wasn't he surprised to see the Elder at the front of the congregation awaiting him? In truth he didn't know, yet somehow it just seemed appropriate that his final examiner should be the first to greet him on his return. Even if he did look anything but pleased to see his former charge again. In fact he looked as if he'd just eaten a particularly sour lemon, his already long face drawn and twisted into a grimace. Yet for some reason Sam was actually glad to see him. He even managed a respectful nod. After all it was the very least expected of either an elf or a knight of Hanor – and he was wearing his blue and his crest.

"Prince Samual Hanor."

Hearing his correct name used Sam knew they'd been doing some digging. But then he'd expected that. Pietrel and Alendro would have told the elders everything. It wasn't in their nature or that of any of the elves to keep secrets from their elders. Sadly he was sure that that would mean the elders had yet more questions for him, and perhaps more telling off. He decided instead to take the initiative. He had more important things to do than to gossip. Somewhere in the caravan strung out behind them were Ryshal's parents, and he most definitely wanted them to be a family once more. They too had suffered at their daughter's wrongful imprisonment, and then more so at being told of her death. Besides, Ry needed to see them too.

"Samual Hanor at your service Elder. Exiled son of King Eric Hanor the First, though I've never claimed the title of prince before, and now I guess it would be strongly disputed if I did. And may I present my wife, Ryshal Hanor. Daughter of Alendro and Pietrel Moonmissel. But I would not use our real names as we pass through Fair Fields."

Why he wondered, couldn't he stop grinning? It took him a moment to remember. His journey had ended for the moment, Ry would soon be back in the arms of her parents and the healers, and all the words he had given the elders before were being shown to be true. This was a victory for him.

"But –"

It was rude to cut the Elder off, but right then Sam was in a hurry, and manners weren't very important to him just then. Besides, he knew what the Elder was going to say. That Ry was supposed to be dead. Later he guessed, he would pay for his rudeness.

"I thought so too, but I'd reckoned without the devious nature of politics in the realm. I never thought I'd be grateful for that evil."

Which was an understatement. The evil machinations of the nobles had been the very thing that had freed Ry from their clutches and the irony wasn't lost on him. But the elders didn't understand the true depravity and trickery of the nobles as they fought each other for power, and he wasn't sure they would even when he told them. He doubted anyone not of Fair Fields itself would have understood. Still, he tried to explain.

"One of the Lords of the noble houses tried to use me as a pawn in a coup by lying about Ry's death to her parents. He thought to make me my brother's assassin. That I would kill Heri in my wrath. His plan didn't work out quite as he expected. But I did not kill either him or Heri. They can fight their own battles and I assume that they have. The keep is still standing, though with some rather large holes in it, and there are a lot of soldiers who will likely still be being dug out of its stone courtyard. I am sure I will be the only topic of conversation in any of the inns for a hundred leagues, mainly as they fear that I may return. But for at least a little while, I don't believe anyone will be giving chase to us."

"However, I'm afraid I can't stay too long right at the moment. My wife is ill from her years of ill-treatment and she needs to be with her family and the healers soonest. In the meantime I've brought you some gifts, compliments of the King, whoever he is and even if he doesn't know it."

He couldn't help but let the smile gracing his face grow broader as he uttered the last, for which Ryshal scolded him gently. Such a thing was too close to revenge for an elf to accept. Or maybe it was just that they shouldn't say such things in front of an elder. The priests might be called!

"First, for the foot weary, sixty of Fair Field's finest war horses. All well trained in the ways of combat, some still saddled, and all in the peak of condition. They will carry your soldiers proudly into battle, or pull the heaviest of wagons." On cue the wizard looked up to see the black mass of horses behind him, all following Sam and the scouts happily. His face gave nothing away though – save maybe disappointment in a morally challenged half human's behaviour. Beside him though, War Master Seille looked at them appreciatively.

The horses were not what an elf would normally choose to ride, as they had been bred for strength and stamina rather than speed and grace, but for all that they were magnificent creatures and were both loyal and brave. At the very least they would be useful in that they could pull a heavy wagon. Perhaps with some dye, to change their appearance a little as they passed through Fair Fields.

"Also, for the journey ahead, some gold and precious stones to buy provisions." He tossed the sceptre at War Master Wyldred, a relatively young and fit elder who had carried out much of his initial interrogation at Torin Vale. Sam watched with satisfaction as the elf staggered back a step or two in surprise at the weight. It was a gentle reminder to the elves that Sam was a true soldier as well as a wizard, and not someone to be trifled with.

All around the War Master the other soldiers stared wide eyed at the golden sceptre, trying to calculate just how much wealth he had casually thrown at them, and what they could buy with it. Even Sam didn't know. He estimated the gold alone at being the equivalent of five hundred to a thousand pieces, and even a truly magnificent horse would cost less than one. As for the stones, only the buyers could tell them that.

"I should mention that the sceptre was lost in the same fire that levelled the throne room of Fall Keep, and a couple of floors underneath. It doesn't exist any longer as far as people know. I'd suggest that it would be best if it remained that way." Sam watched Elder Bela's eyes close briefly as he clearly tried to suppress a groan at his morally challenged ways, and chose to ignore him. The Elder hadn't been there, he hadn't suffered as had Sam and Ry, and he had no right to judge.

"Finally, for yourself and the other learned elders, the best part of the library of Fall Keep relating to either magic, prophecy or the Dragon Wars. In fact it is all I could gather at such short notice. It was a rather ... hurried visit!"

He wondered how long it would take for word of exactly what had happened in Fall Keep to reach the elves as they entered Fair Fields, and then no doubt for them to give him another dressing down. Probably not long. For all that they were strangers in a human realm, they were good listeners. And after that he was sure the priests would be annoying him day and night. It had been so much easier when he had lived some distance from town. But that was something for tomorrow to worry about. For the moment Ryshal's family came first.

He grabbed the reigns and gave them a flick as he guided Tyla on, but then pulled her up short as Ry nudged him in the ribs reminding him of the rest of what he had to tell them. Ry had told him what the elves would do if he didn't, and somehow had even managed to convince him of it. Despite the madness of it, they would return Sam's gifts to the king if they thought they were ill gotten. It didn't matter that the people needed them or what they could purchase with them. That they would end up suffering even more misfortune as the king sent an army of assassins and maybe even soldiers to them, having inevitably decided to blame them for his attack. The elves would do anything to be sure of the righteousness of their actions. And to accept wrongfully obtained wares was to accept the wrong that had been done to obtain them. They had endless stories from their history to support that view. And the priests had endless sermons!

"Lest you imagine otherwise Elder, none of these gifts are stolen. All are mine by right, mine to do with as I see fit."

"The books like the others you now hold are mine by right both as the son of King Hanor and the ranking fire wizard in Fair Fields. I did not steal them, and I am no rogue. They are mine to hold or to give away and no one may say otherwise."

"Likewise the horses and the sceptre were my half-brother's. He claimed ownership of them in his own name." Of course the reason he could do that was that Heri claimed ownership of nearly everything. He claimed ownership of all of the kingdom's taxes as his as well. It was theft of course. Pure and simple. But the theft was "legal" since the king also wrote the law.

"They were his, and now they are mine. They became mine by way of penalty that I as the elder brother have exacted upon him for his crimes against our family. Since our father is dead, I as the older brother am the head of the house of Hanor if not ruler of the kingdom. I claim the position of laurena of the family, and as such I have the right to decide his punishment."

It was perhaps unwise claiming the position. The laurena or trunk of the family was the one that supported the rest of the family. As such he was the one that held the final say on family decisions. And Ry was right that in order to claim the property of his little brother as his he had to claim the position. But claiming it also meant he was in some respects responsible for what Heri did. And Heri had committed a great many crimes, and not just against his family.

"These are merely partial restitution for all the wrongs he has committed against my wife and I, and against her parents. A slap on the wrist. Whether he would admit it or not, Heri is a wayward child who has wronged his own family. He valued these things because of the stature that he thought they brought him. So as laurena I claimed them as a lesson that no man is above the needs of his family. Their loss will bring him humility. I hope it will instil in him a valuable lesson." Of course the only lesson that Heri was likely to learn would be one of fear and hatred, but that was good enough for Sam.

"And though it may trouble you to hear this, these are but the beginnings of the reparations I will demand of him should Heri cross my path again."

The Elder didn't look too happy when he said that, but then he didn't have what could be called a naturally happy face. His features were too long and serious for that. If anything he looked thoughtful at best – though his thoughts could have been travelling to some unhappy places. But he didn't say anything as Sam continued.

"The loss of a few trinkets and a little face is but a very small beginning to his lesson, and had I not made a bargain with the little toad to free Ry, he would be suffering much more now. Assuming he still lives he could not nay say that in front of me or anyone else, and thus they are mine to give freely. Mine and my wife's. But again I wouldn't mention that to anyone in the Realm."

"My brother has always hated the truth and the thought

that anyone might have dominion over him, least of all me, would send him screaming further into the grip of insanity." His grin only became wider, and Ry nudged him in the ribs again as she saw it. It was not acceptable to take pleasure in another's suffering. But at least he was allowed to say it, because it was the truth. The priests might still be visiting though.

Yet there was still one more thing he had to say. A thing which had weighed heavily on his thoughts as they rode back, and which he would have much preferred never to be uttered aloud, least of all in the company of Ry.

"Lastly, as we travelled back here I did some reading of the books and scrolls from the keep. I had time to study many of them in detail. Everything in those histories tells me those golems we met were not golems. As I suspected, they are true machina. They match the descriptions perfectly. They even move in the same way. Plus those damnable glowing red eyes are mentioned in practically every telling. Worse still, their style of attack – raiding the smaller realms first, using the cover of dark, attacking without warning, and killing everyone they can for no reason is the same as that described of the Dragon himself thousands of years ago."

As was one thing more, though he didn't have to remind them of it. That the machina and the Dragon Wars had ended the entire world of the ancients. In fact they had destroyed it. The Elder knew that as did every child who had ever had a history lesson. Even though the ancients had survived and their descendants had rebuilt the world over the last five thousand years, the terrible destruction the machina had wrought could not be forgotten. And they had not struck in just one land, nor only once. There had been years of war and every land had been attacked.

"I know you don't want to hear this, least of all while trying to keep the people together after such a terrible attack that has slain so many innocents and devastated the spirits of those who survive, but I fear you must. This fight is not over. Far from it. This is a war. I fear that the attack on Shavarra was only the start of what is to come."

"This is more than a hunch. Every fibre of my being – and I have trained all my life in the tactics and strategy of warfare as well as magic and combat – tells me that this is only the beginning. I don't know who's behind this, what's happening out there in the rest of the lands, or even what's coming, but this battle is far from just one against a rogue alchemist. This enemy's far too powerful for that, and his goals are far from modest."

Sam took a deep breath before saying the next part. Speaking the words he did not want to speak and that surely no one wanted to hear.

"Perhaps this is the beginning of a new Dragon War, or perhaps it's something else. But whatever his intent, our enemy has greater plans in mind than we have yet seen." He took another deep breath to quiet his emotions and let his thoughts flow more easily.

"Also, I don't know why this stanza is important, but I believe it is:"

"- and when the golems hunt,
the cities shall fall,
and the people shall know fear."

"If somebody – anybody – could just remember which book of prophecy that verse is taken from I would be very grateful. It's been running around in the back of my head for weeks. Ever since the night I first heard about the golems, and even more so when I first saw them. I think it may be important."

"For now though honoured Elders, I must go. I apologise for my rudeness, but I must bring my wife safely back to the arms of her family and then on to the healers." He even managed another small bow to them, something Ry had schooled into him, just for this meeting.

The elders in turn nodded to him, unhappy he was leaving so abruptly he suspected, but acknowledging his need to go.

Everything he needed to say having been said, Sam flicked Tyla's reigns once more and they left the elders and made their way down the wagon caravan. A caravan that seemed to have grown since he'd last been there.

It was still perhaps only three or four leagues long, but the wagons were stacked three and four wide on the flat roads leading to Fair Fields. Which could only mean they'd evacuated some of the other towns in Shavarra. Whitel Lee, Espellen Vale, Braellar's Falls, and so forth. All up he guessed, if they evacuated the whole province they could have as many as two or three hundred thousand people, and what he was seeing in front of him could well have been that many. He just hoped that the rest of the towns hadn't come under attack before they'd chosen to leave.

"So many!"

If Sam had been taken aback by seeing so many more elves now in the caravan, he suddenly realised the shock must have been a hundred times worse for Ryshal who hadn't seen any of them at all before. He had told her of what had passed a week after they left the castle – once he thought she was strong enough to take the terrible news. But telling someone something and actually seeing it were completely different things.

Especially when so many of those they passed still showed the scars of the battle, even weeks later. Unless there had been another battle since? There were too many still wearing bandages as though they were clothes, many more missing arms or legs, and above all else, so many sad, tired and defeated faces. That last more than anything else was what told the sorry tale. Elves weren't known as a sad people. To the contrary they were a happy, merry people. There was always music being played somewhere, the children were constantly running around and dancing, while even their more correct parents hummed quietly now and then. But that wasn't happening on this journey.

Without exception as they passed by the countless wagons, they could see a story of suffering, loss and hopelessness in the faces of those they passed. It was something Sam hadn't quite taken in before. But then he'd only been with them on the trail for a day or so, most of that asleep and the rest being interrogated. Besides, at that time the predominant feeling had been one of fear as the elves had been worried about when the golems might catch up. At some point while on the trail though, that had clearly changed, and the elves no longer feared that. They knew they were safe. Now they were counting the cost of that safety.

Sam had seen that look on people's faces only once before. It had been in the village of Deep Vale to the south of Fall Keep after a party of bandits had gone through it, killing half the men, wounding the rest and kidnapping the young women. Those who managed to survive were left with nothing as the bandits burnt their homes and farms, and stole everything of value. The elves looked just like them. Defeated, still trying to cope with their loss, and at the same time wondering what to do with the rest of their lives. But those villagers had had one advantage there that these elves did not. They still had a home they could rebuild. Until the enemy was hunted down and killed the elves of Shavarra knew they could never return home.

"But they're all alive Beloved. That's what's important. They may be homeless and fleeing for their lives, but they are alive. And one day, when this evil is defeated, they can all go home. *We* can all go home."

He gave her the best comfort he could, but even he wasn't certain the evil would be so easily defeated. First they had to find out exactly what it was, and then who was behind it. Nor was he entirely certain that the elves had the strength to return if and when the enemy was defeated. But he was absolutely certain they didn't have the will to fight anymore.

"And I promise you now before the All Father, that I will lend all of my strength to their cause. My sword and my magic are theirs, and I will not rest until they are safe and home once again. Your people will be as safe as I can keep them. I swear that as both your husband and as a knight of Hanor."

"I know that my love. I've always known that. You don't need to swear something so obvious to me." Ry sighed with what sounded like exasperation, her moment of despair having passed, but she also kissed his cheek.

"You would do it anyway. It's not a matter of honour or even duty. You are your father's son, and just like him, a good and decent man. That's simply who and what you are. It's why I love you so much. It's why I married you. And it's why I pray that we can one day have a family together. Our children would be so blessed to have you as a father."

"And you as their mother. They will need someone to teach them of grace and beauty, of love and compassion; laughter, music and dance." It was only the truth.

"I will teach you to dance yet my beautiful man. That oath I will keep."

He laughed, it was so good to hear the laughter in her voice as she promised to teach him what she had tried to many years before. Unfortunately he was about as graceful as a drunken ox, and Ry had made it one of her missions in life from even before their marriage to teach him. She hadn't forgotten.

"Ahh my love, you might have better luck starting with Tyla. She has the natural grace of her kind, and at least the good sense not to trip over her own feet."

"Ryshal?" The woman's voice came from the wagons ahead, and they both looked up to see her parents staring at them, a look of wonder and hope slowly dawning on their faces.

"Mother! Father!" Even as she was calling out to them, Ry was trying to dismount. Sam though held her securely around the waist and wouldn't let her go. Instead Sam nudged Tyla and they cantered the last fifty or so yards between them.

Mere heartbeats later, Ry and her parents were reunited in an explosion of cries and happy tears, and as Sam lowered her carefully into their waiting arms, the tears and cries became even louder. But that was as it should be for such a joyous event. There were even tears in his own eyes as he finally knew he was home, and though he was a soldier born and raised he didn't begrudge them one little bit.

In that moment he knew his journey had ended. Or one journey anyway. He had got Ryshal back. Now he had a new journey before him. He had to keep her and her people safe, help defeat their enemy, and finally bring them home.

It was a much more difficult task than what he had already faced, a far longer and more treacherous road. But he vowed to the All Father and the Goddess both that he would travel it to the end.

Chapter Ten.

"It's not a prophecy."

Master Rease caught Sam by surprise as he was tending to the horses, and he looked up, startled.

"Pardon Master Rease?"

"Your line of verse. It's not from any prophecy at all."

Sam looked at the Elder quizzically, surprised to see him away from the rest of the elders. He was a greying elf, a sign that he had to be at least a hundred and fifty years old, maybe much more. Yet in all those years he had apparently never learned how to be polite. He just turned up out of the blue and made his proclamations as though everyone should already be waiting there just for him to arrive and speak.

Sam didn't mind the old elf's manners though. Not if he knew where that damned line of verse came from. And obviously if he knew it wasn't a prophecy and he'd come all this way to tell him, he also knew what it was. Sam raised an eyebrow in question and waited patiently for the Elder to tell him. He knew he would. The man was dying to show off his knowledge.

"It's a poem. A piece of free verse written nigh on a thousand years ago by an explorer by the name of Haggard. A human I believe. He was –"

"Of course! Thank you!" The Elder didn't need to say anymore because Sam finally remembered where he'd read the verse. It was like the opening of a door into his childhood. Some of his oldest and fondest memories.

"He was exploring the caves of Andrea, the fabled birth place of the warlord himself. I remember reading that he was looking for anything to confirm or disprove that the Dragon Wars were as terrible as legend said, or even that they'd actually happened. He spent his life doing it, hunting through cavern after cavern, opening buried chamber after buried chamber, and still never found the proof he was seeking. But he wrote three journals about his journey." Three journals that Sam had read as a child on his father's knee. Three wonderful, inspiring journals.

While Haggard had never found all of what he was looking for, the journals themselves were considered by many to be seminal works. Mainly because they showed the true meaning of dedication and perseverance. In nigh on thirty years of trying, faced with set back after set back – fires, rebellions, wars, bandits, disease and just plain depression – Sir Haggard the Staunch as he had later been known, had never once given up. His had become the standard against which all other knightly quests were measured and few could ever compare.

"Do you have the rest of it?"

For an answer the Elder began reading from the piece of parchment in his hand:

"When the sky is blue and the days are sweet,
When the moon is full and the night air at peace,
When the people are once more replete,
Their bellies full and their cares few;

Then shall the peace be shattered,
and the ground shall turn red with the blood of the innocent,
Then shall the golems taste their fill of soft, sweet flesh,

170

Samual

And I shall taste victory.

Then shall my steel find the tender heart
and my teeth the softness of flesh.
Then shall mothers mourn their children,
And kings their people.

And when the golems hunt,
the cities shall fall,
and the people shall know fear.

They shall know Me."

"Of course! How could I have forgotten?" Even as he heard it Sam remembered the verse as if it was yesterday when he himself had read it aloud to his father. He had been only seven or eight at the time and had been proudly demonstrating his reading abilities to his father. He also remembered the pride he had felt in having such a wonderful father. Even now the memory brought a tear to his eye.

"It's not a very good poem."

"It's not a poem at all," Sam replied. "Or if it is, it's at least not one by Sir Haggard. It's a translation. The original script was carved into the walls of the master chamber as he called it, thousands of years before he entered it. Written in old heraldic scripture, the only written language we can decipher from the time of the Dragon Wars. It took months to translate and even then there were several different translations made." Of course the scholar probably knew all of that, but it didn't stop Sam from continuing as he remembered the rest of it.

"Sir Haggard always believed, though he could never prove it, that the lines had been written by the warlord himself

171

before he unleashed his armies upon an unsuspecting world. He wrote it as a prophecy of his own triumph. Before he brought the entire ancient world to its end." But even as he spoke, the wheels were turning in Sam's mind as he thought of another possibility. One that he was somehow certain was the truth.

"But what if it was actually written after that? After the Dragon had lost and his armies had been defeated? The warlord was never killed according to the histories. His armies were defeated, the machina destroyed, the magic behind them broken, his mercenaries killed and he was struck down by a poison spell, dying. But they never found a body, nor any other proof of his death."

"Sick, perhaps even dying, his magic shattered and his protectors gone, he might well have returned to his ancient home as many believe the Andrea caves were. Certainly it was too strongly warded for any others to attack then. Even thousands of years later when the wards and the stone itself were crumbling with age, it was a long, hard fought battle to enter the chambers. It would have been a refuge for him when everything else was lost. A place for him to renew himself. What if he was prophesying his own return? And his eventual conquest of the known world?"

"You jest! ... Surely?" The scholar paled. Yet if he truly believed that why did the scholar sound frightened? Why did he try so hard to deny Sam's words?

"I fear that the enemy we now face is the same one that the ancients fought all those years ago. I have done ever since I fought those things. These golems are true machina, and they have a master such as him. Either the Dragon himself has returned, or he has a true successor. A descendant perhaps. When I fought them, I heard or perhaps felt the commands that came from their master, and I knew that whatever else he was, he was no mere alchemist. He has the Dragon's power, and his knowledge, and the will to use it. He sees himself as an emperor, a king among kings – perhaps even a god – and he wants his kingdom and his sacrifices. We are only at the beginning of a new Dragon War."

And by the All Father did he hope it wouldn't end the same way. The first Dragon Wars had brought the ancient world to its end. Cities without number had been destroyed. Millions of people had been slaughtered. And most of what was known in those ancient days had been lost. The world – or the Continent of the Dragon's Spine at least – had been recovering from the effects of those wars for five thousand years since. And Sam doubted that they had even yet achieved the same level of knowledge that the ancients had possessed. They couldn't face another war like that.

"The warlord is returned my love? The Dragon himself?"

Sam turned to see Ryshal standing behind him and briefly wished he could bite off his own tongue. The last thing she needed to hear right now were his wild fancies. As before he instantly held back the rest of what he suspected, if only because it was such a miracle to actually be able to see her at all. And to know that she was getting better was even more so.

And she was recovering. He knew it with every joyous fibre in his body. She had woken up once more from her slumber, and though it had only been three days since they arrived, already he could see the colour returning to her face. The healers had done wonders for her, filling her up with their strange potions, making her eat and helping her sleep. They had even given her gentle exercises to do. And all of it was working. The last of her sores were healed, she was continuing to put on weight, napping instead of fainting, and spending a lot more time on her feet each day. He could not thank the healers enough for their wondrous work. And whether the healers followed the Lord of Healing, Phil the

White or the Goddess of the elves, they deserved praise.

"Or someone with his gifts has found the remnants of his armies or the knowledge of his magic." He went to her immediately, taking her hand and kissing it, before wrapping her up in his arms. She was still terribly light, but at least a dozen pounds heavier than she had been when he'd first rescued her. Presently wearing one of her mother's dresses, she could almost take him back to the days when they had first met.

"You look much better Ry. I can now see some colour returning to your cheeks. But there is still much more resting and healing for you to do. Now is not the time to pay attention to my wild flights of fancy."

"My love, from the very first moment when I met you, when I fell in love with you and when I married you, I always knew one thing about you. You don't have wild fancies. That's my role in our marriage. You are the level headed one. The one who keeps us on the path. The rock upon which we stand. You are the ever serious soldier and I the dreamer. And this does not sound like a wild fancy to me. It sounds like a living nightmare, much like my people's waking lives these days."

It had been a shock he knew for her to arrive and find out just how bad things were among her own people. It had been a shock for him simply to return and find out how much larger the caravan had grown and how many more wounded there were. He might have stopped the main force of the rats, but others had been striking at the smaller towns and villages, which was why the entire province was being emptied.

But it had to be harder for Ry. And that shock had been made all the worse because for five long years as she had sat in her dungeon all she had dreamed of was returning home to him, to her family and to Shavarra. For Ry, it was as though she had been given the greatest gift imaginable, and then someone had stolen it away from her before she'd even opened it.

"Nevertheless it's still not something for you to concern yourself with now. For the moment you need your rest and healing. Leave the soldierly things to the soldiers, and the rest to the elders." Sam spoke as gently as he could, while still trying to be firm. Fortunately she seemed to accept it though he knew that would not last. Sooner or later she would return to the topic, at which point she would not let him off so easily. He turned back to the Elder.

Master Rease, I bid you take that tome and the other two volumes if you have copies, back to the elders, scholars, master spell casters and war masters, and go through them in detail. Whether this is the warlord himself or someone else following in his footsteps, there may be hints in Sir Haggard's writings as to the battle plan of our enemy. Strategies, strengths and weaknesses. Even some of the secrets behind the making of the machina. All of this will be vital information as to how to fight him.

"I will do as you ask young Samual, but first I must also ask you to do something in turn. Master Bela and the other spell casters have requested your attendance in the vanguard."

It was Sam's turn to groan as Master Rease turned and slowly made his way back to his own wagon, his bad news given. Being summoned by the elder spell casters was likely to mean another interrogation. They had held off for three long days as he had tended to his wife, and in truth he hadn't even seen them except from a distance, for which kindness he was grateful. But the physician's reports were good and they had no doubt run out of patience with him. Especially Master Bela after his rudeness.

"Samual, you know you have to go to them, lest they come here and annoy my family and me as well!" She laughed happily. Despite the suffering she had endured and the shocks of the previous week, Ry's sense of humour was returning by the day for which he was eternally grateful, and he laughed with her.

"I can't move – my feet have turned to rock!" Sam thought he should at least try to think of an excuse, no matter how poor it was.

"Hmmf – we both know it is your head that is full of rocks! Especially if you thought that would get you out of a meeting with the elders!" She laughed some more, but then kissed him merrily on the cheek.

"But you have nothing to fear from them. They mean well even if they sometimes have a gruff way of showing it. Be honest and stand up for yourself. You are my husband, the man I love and one day I hope, the father of our children. You are also a brave and powerful soldier in the defence of our kin, and a mighty spell caster. You have earned a true place among us and you should walk with your head held proud. The people fear you no longer. They welcome you."

If she was right Sam hadn't truly noticed it. But then he hadn't been paying attention to anyone other than Ryshal ever since they'd returned.

"I have you again. More than that I do not know and I do not care." Sam picked her up and carried her to the wagon tray where he laid her down so that she could get some more sleep. Though truthfully she didn't look as though she wanted another nap right then. Instead of lying down, Ry sat up stubbornly and looked him directly in the eyes.

"And I you, for which wonder I will spend the rest of my days thanking the Goddess. But I am telling you the truth when I say that you are welcome among our people. More than welcome. When they speak of the Fire Angel, it is you they speak of. It is a great honour. You are already seen as one of us. They think of you as our guardian. You would know that if only you raised your head once in a while to look at the people all around you. Perhaps you could even try smiling now and then." Ry could be stern when she wanted to be, and this was apparently one of those times.

Sam knew better than to argue with her and nodded instead.

"Now go. Lest you keep the elders waiting and they grow impatient and come looking for you here!"

On cue Ry's mother appeared from the nearby river where she'd been doing the washing, and quickly went to her daughter. Sam knew she'd be well cared for while he was away, even if it was as many hours as he feared. There was something about the caravan having stopped so early in the afternoon that was suddenly bothering him. It was almost as if some very important people had decided they wanted the time free for a very special purpose. He feared that purpose had something to do with him.

Nodding his thanks to Alendro he mounted Tyla and cantered off toward the elders' wagons. They were up near the front of the caravan, a place they had to keep by virtue of their skills and importance, and as that was about a quarter of a league ahead of them he knew it would be best to hurry. They weren't a patient group.

On the way there though, he did as Ry suggested and studied some of the other elves around him. He was surprised to see that she was right. For far from the reactions he had once got in Torin Vale when he'd first arrived, the people did seem more open to him. A few even smiled as he passed and he nodded politely back. It was a surprise. Obviously something had changed. And maybe, though he didn't like to admit it, the Elder had been right when he'd said that a part of

Sam's difficulties had been of his own making.

Eventually he reached the elders' wagons. They had pulled them up in a circle and he could see the elders sitting on the wagon sides discussing the business of the day. Apparently they were having an important discussion and sitting on the grass simply wasn't appropriate for such matters. Their families on the other hand weren't so fortunate, and sat on the grass enjoying a late breakfast, while they waited for their partners to finish. Then again, the children didn't seem to mind as they laughed and ran around gaily in the sun, and no more did their parents as they watched over them.

Normally when Sam approached an elder he would have dismounted and gone to them on foot. But given that they were already raised high off the ground on the wagons, he decided that staying in the saddle was the better option. As Ry had said, he was a powerful wizard; he should hold his head high. It wasn't however, a sentiment that all of the elders seemed to agree with, and he watched a few give him disapproving stares as he remained on his horse.

There seemed to be more elders than he had seen before, and all of them were spell casters. Sam would have guessed that over thirty men and women sat on the wagon sides, waiting patiently. Clearly more had joined them from the other towns as they had travelled. And all of them were staring at him as if he were an interesting new spell to master. For the first time in weeks he felt nervous. But at least there were no priests with them.

"You sent for me Elders?" He thought it best to be polite as he bowed his head to them. It seemed he wasn't their most favourite person right then.

"Indeed we did Samual Hanor. Young Ryshal is doing well?"

"Yes Elder, she is recovering from my brother's malice even more quickly than I dared hope. The healers are doing wonderful work with her and I am deeply grateful for their care and skill."

"As are we for yours. In these past few weeks you have saved many of our people, and given us the chance to turn a panicked stampede into a more orderly march. You have brought us wisdom and wealth as well to help us on our way. And all for no recompense."

Elder Bela caught him somewhat off guard with his words. He hadn't known the Elder could even think that way about such things. The elves weren't exactly concerned with matters of wealth or payment. They had coin but for the most part did not use it. Property was not owned by any one person or family. People were just recognised as living in certain places. Homes were built according to need and by the town. And the basics of life such as food were free. It was only the little luxuries that coin was for. The unusual and sumptuous foods like the fruit from his trees. The more elegant clothes. The more ornate furniture. Heri would have died here!

Of course that was a difficult thing for a Fair Fielder to deal with. He never knew what to give away and what to sell, nor how much to charge. Now that Ry was back with him he planned on letting her deal with that part of life.

"None is required Elders. I am a knight of Hanor and it is my duty as well as my honour."

"Nevertheless, we are grateful and we would show that gratitude to you in the way we best can. We offer you a gift of magic, if you would do us the honour of accepting it."

A gift of magic? Sam had absolutely no idea what that might mean, but he knew enough to know it was obviously very important to the elves. So many elder spell casters didn't come together just to see one half elf for any small matter. Besides, he already knew he didn't want to annoy any more elders for at least a little while. They tended to be cranky.

"I would be honoured." He bowed again.

"As would we. But first we must learn what it is we can give you."

If anything the weight of all their eyes on him suddenly seemed to grow, and Sam felt himself being pressed down like a mouse under their gaze. Not for the first time he wondered just what exactly he had gotten himself into.

"And now my young soldier, we shall see what we shall see." The Elder's words were nothing if not cryptic, unless perhaps they were threatening. But before Sam could even think to ask what he meant, his world went dark. Very dark.

Caught by surprise Sam spun around in his saddle, trying to see what had happened to the light. He soon realised however, that it wasn't just the light that was gone. So was everything else. He wasn't in his world. Nor was he even on his horse. Tyla was nowhere in sight.

It was impossible. Only a moment earlier he had been on a meandering path running through a green rolling section of the glorious country side that comprised the start of Fair Fields. Now – if the fields full of torches were any indication – he was standing in the middle of a dry and dusty flat plain. One made of loose dirt and by the looks of things, bits of ancient white bone. Here and there he could see larger pieces of bone, and skulls in the dirt. As for the sky, it was black. The sun had gone away and no moon or stars had arrived to take its place. The sight made him nervous and he felt a shiver run down his spine. What was happening?

It was night time. But darker than any true night. With no

moon and no stars it was almost as though he was in some sort of giant cave. One where the only light he could see came from torches. All around as far as the eye could see were torches. Burning brands on wooden shafts standing maybe six feet high and extending for many leagues in every direction. How could that be? How could there be so many torches? If nothing else, who lit them and changed them when they burnt out?

But none of that mattered he realised suddenly when it came to him that this was a trap. He didn't understand that. The elders had said they were going to give him a gift of magic. And they hadn't seemed particularly upset with him. This time. And yet as more shivers travelled down his spine, he knew it was so.

Instinctively Sam reached for all the magic he could find nearby, and surprisingly found plenty. He could feel it in the black sky above but also in the ground under his feet. He could feel the fire flowing freely, and the living magic of the world and the creatures that lived upon it.

His feet? Sam looked down to see that he wasn't standing as he'd thought. Instead he was sitting on the saddle of a small rock, his feet touching the ground. How had he missed that? In fact he realised suddenly as he peered through the darkness, he was sitting on the only rock in the whole damn dead desert as far as he could see.

Standing up carefully, worried that he might sink into the dust, Sam began to explore his new world. First he walked over to the nearest torch some thirty yards in front of him. The ground crunched under his feet as the hard sand crust of the desert gave way, but it held and he sank no more than an inch. Clouds of fine dust puffed up with each step he took. That didn't bother him as much as the little particles of bone he could see in the dirt and which he knew his feet were sinking into.

Shortly he reached the torch and confirmed his worst fears as it let him see everything about the ground around it. The bones were human as he'd suspected, and by the looks of things, they were from at least half a dozen different people. But worse than that he realised they weren't all ancient, dried out bones. Some of them still had the remains of flesh on them. Dried out tendons and gristle that the scavengers had left behind.

This was a killing ground! That was the immediate thought that crossed his mind. Followed by the understanding that it was still in use. But why would the elders send him here? Was Ry wrong about them? Because despite her view that he was some sort of fire angel, the elders clearly didn't trust him that much. Still, this was a world away from not trusting him. Suddenly it seemed they had decided to get rid of him.

And it seemed they had been getting rid of problems like him for a long time.

On a hunch Sam bent down to study the crunchy sand under his feet. He scooped up a handful and let it slip through his fingers like rain. Sure enough it glittered as though it was beach sand with tiny pieces of shell mixed through. But this was no beach and mixed in with the sand was no shell. It was bone. Bone that had become almost powdered with age and dryness. This had been a killing ground for a long time. How long did it take for bone to powder? Surely hundreds, maybe thousands of years. And given its size Sam had to wonder just how many men had died here over the years. Thousands? Millions?

Could it be an underworld of some sort? The idea struck him suddenly, and it worried him. Not least because it made sense. It would be a perfect place to send an unruly wizard. And it looked much as one did in his imagination. But where it was didn't matter as much as where he wasn't. For he was no longer with Ry. And since he didn't know how he'd gotten here, or even where here was, he had no way of getting home.

But he had more immediate problems. Because if this was an underworld then that meant that somewhere nearby there were demons.

Sam started drawing all the fire he could find as fast as he knew how. He realised it was only a matter of time until whatever had killed the others came for him. Also, if this place was truly set aside for unruly wizards, fire alone might not be enough to protect him, and so he began trying to attune himself with the land. Normally that was something he never needed to do as he was always part of it. But wherever this was, it wasn't home, and he didn't feel a part of it.

Earth magic wasn't his most powerful weapon by any stretch of the imagination, but sometimes it could be his most useful. Over the years as he'd studied the fire and ice magic for combat, he'd practised the shapes for earth magic as well, finding it an invaluable tool for crossing terrain or entering strange places. With it he could build or level walls, create passages through solid rock, reshape the land itself so that it became liquid and then reform it to trap enemies, or even alter the structure of armour or weapons to make them stronger. While it wasn't strictly a combat magic he could use it to his advantage in a fight. And he suspected he was going to need everything he had to survive whatever was coming.

Reaching out with his thoughts, Sam soon had the feel of the land flowing through his blood. It felt like a slow deep pulse, and he allowed it to fill him. After a while he felt both the slow rhythms of the earth and the furious heat of fire balanced in harmony, like a two piece orchestra. Double base and flute perhaps.

He also had some limited ability with nature magic. He

could use it to call and sometimes command creatures, or to make them feel friendlier towards him. Sometimes it helped him to see into a person's soul or to spot deception and malice. But that was as far as he'd ever got with it. Still, this seemed like the perfect time to find out all it could do. If nothing else, if the enemy came at him on horseback he could make the horses disobey their masters. Horses were quite easy to command. Did demons ride horses?

In time he added the last string to his magical arsenal, as he reached out for the life force of whatever creatures were nearby, though there were precious few. Deep in the soil he could feel the worms and a few insects going about their business. Further up in the sky he could feel small birds soaring, while a few more slept in trees some leagues away. But no larger creatures were nearby. Nevertheless, he let the song of life merge with the rest of the music pouring through him until finally he felt complete. Complete and strong.

That he knew, was as much as he could do. Others could also bend the will of water and air, and they had powerful weapons in them, but he had no affinity for those elements. To him they had no soul. Nor did he have the magic of the mind that illusionists seemed to live with. And though it would have been wondrous in this place, light was not his to command either. Still, what he did have was enough to make him a dangerous enemy to anything that dared approach, and for a while he could almost make himself believe that that would be enough. Enough to get him out of this strange place. That feeling however, didn't last long as the darkness and feeling of isolation of the place began to wear him down.

Knowing he was as ready as he could be, Sam decided it was time for him to leave this place. Though where he would be going to was unclear. He had no idea where he was, no idea of which direction to travel, and he couldn't sense any other place within this dark, threatening land. But neither could he stay in this one spot forever.

He decided to keep travelling in the same direction he had already started in when he had approached the first torch, and mentally he plotted out a course from one torch to the next. It was almost a straight line. Cautiously, he took his first step along the path he had set out for himself, and soon was heading towards the unknown.

The next torch he reached proved to be no different to the first. A single fire brand, it stood as high as his head from the ground, and burned brightly in the gloom. At its base he found more skulls, bleached bones and white powder mixed in with the dirt. Turning around briefly, he could see his footsteps in the dust, a sign of the fifty odd paces he'd walked in this strange place. But other than that there was no sign of anything different in front of him or behind. He had the horrible feeling that no matter how far he walked there might never be.

Carrying on he walked to the next torch and then on to the next one and the next, finding still more bones as he went. He found the sight of so many bones disturbing. It kept making him wonder just how many people had perished in this dark world. More he suspected, than he could count. He also found himself wondering about other things as he walked.

For instance who looked after the torches? It would take an army just to maintain them. There were surely hundreds if not thousands of torches surrounding him on all sides. And where were the stars? If it were truly night then surely he should be able to see the stars? Or was he inside some sort of gigantic cavern as he'd feared? If he was then it was a cavern large enough to contain a desert – and that didn't seem possible. And was this even part of his own world? Or had he somehow been sent directly to the underworld? Even though he had no memory of dying, he still couldn't shake that idea.

A full half hour of wandering went by like that as he kept

trying to answer impossible questions, without any sign of change. He was almost becoming bored by this place. Suddenly a scream pierced the darkness. A woman's scream. It came from somewhere ahead of him, and without thinking he ran towards it, knowing only one thing; that he wasn't alone in this nightmare after all, but that if he didn't hurry he soon might be.

"Hanor!" Having run at least three hundred yards toward where he had heard the scream coming from, Sam still could not see the woman. Nor could he see an enemy. In fact he couldn't really see anything much past each torch, and he began to despair that he had run past the woman, or in the wrong direction.

Another scream though told him he was heading in the right direction after all, and the woman was still alive, whoever she was. Four more torches came and went, until Sam could suddenly hear other noises. Strange noises. He could hear the rustling of wings. They sounded a bit like bat wings, though if they were then they were very large. He could also hear a sound like the squeaks that rats made when they were excited. Again though it sounded very loud. No rat ever born could have the lung power needed to make these squeaks. And then there was the sound of the air parting rapidly as things flew through it, diving and swooping. Very large things.

"Fire bright."

Realising that before he could do anything at all he needed to be able to see what he was facing, Sam uttered the childhood incantation he had been taught so many years before. On cue the entire area around him for hundreds of yards became brightly lit by the torches, their glow no longer yellow and orange, but white as they burnt so much hotter. What it revealed though, almost made him wish he had remained in the dark.

A woman was running towards him. She was a proper woman as his father would have described her. A lady perhaps. Well dressed, attractive, and obviously a lady of means. Just then though she was dishevelled, her dress ripped and torn, and blood leaked from a dozen or more cuts to her arms and face. Razor sharp slashes. That was bad enough, but behind her was what had caused the slashes, and they were far more worrying.

Imps was his first thought, because they looked like some of the artists' paintings of them in Fall Keep. But imps he had always thought of as small and ungainly. Not a true threat. These on the other hand looked deadly. Their leathery wings seemed to have some sort of serrated bones along the front, and their talons were covered with blood as they weaved and dived their way down onto the woman and ripped another piece out of her skin. But even worse than their appearance was their number. There had to be hundreds of the flying devils flitting through the sky.

Almost without thinking Sam launched a fire ball at the ones nearest the strange woman, and then watched as half a dozen of the flying creatures turned into orange explosions as they crashed down on the dirt behind her. It was enough he figured, to get the woman to safety, or to the relative safety of him. But even as he was congratulating himself on having saved the woman, a sudden sound and a tearing made itself known and he felt something sharp slice through his right cheek. He didn't even need to turn around to realise there were more of them behind him. He also discovered that their talons were sharp.

Without thought he flung another fire shape over his head, this time a chained fire lightning spell that cast its fire from one creature to the next, and was immediately rewarded by the sound of imps screaming as their bodies dropped to the ground. That accounted for at least a dozen more of them. But there were still plenty remaining.

By then the woman had reached him, and automatically he erected a fire shield around them both. A dome that sheltered them from attack. He thought it should provide them with some reasonable protection, and if necessary he could hold it all day and all night.

"Are you all right?"

He bent down to the woman who had fallen to her knees, worried about her injuries. That worry grew when she collapsed the rest of the way to the ground in front of him, her strength seemingly gone. In truth it didn't surprise him, as he had already noted the extreme pallor of her face and the terrible amount of blood she had lost. It was only luck and determination that had kept her going this far. He also realised that if he didn't fight well, they might soon both be dead. They might soon become more bones in the sand.

Imps he remembered from his days studying under Master Smythe, had magic of their own. The magic of confounding. They could wear down any spell or enchantment over time, and that most definitely included his fire shield. It was pity really as the fire shield was one of his most useful defences. Now though it seemed that he couldn't afford to keep using it or any other defensive spell, as the effort involved in holding the spell active would sooner or later exhaust him, leaving the imps free to attack. His only option was to attack and destroy the imps before he ran out of strength.

Leaving the fire spell unattended – it would continue to hold for a while longer – he readied his attack, an ice crystal barrage. It was a good attacking spell for this particular enemy. Speaking the incantation to focus his thoughts he froze the water vapour in the air around him into thousands of tiny ice shards, and spun them crazily around his head as though he were the centre of a tornado. As time went by and the fire shield lasted longer than he expected even without his effort, he kept increasing the power of the ice crystal spell, adding ever more ice crystals to the rapidly spinning mix and increasing the speed with which they spun.

It was a heady feeling, shaping and holding the spell in the midst of his fire shield. Ice and fire were two sides of the same magic, but they always had to be kept separate. But it was no more difficult than many other spell combinations he'd tried. His only problem was the surprising amount of time the fire shield was holding. He could feel the imps' power as they eroded away the bonds of the shape and with hundreds of them working together in harmony he'd expected the spell to fail much earlier. Perhaps they weren't as strong as he'd thought, or maybe that was a sign of the advances he'd made in the previous weeks as his shapes had become more solid.

Finally though Sam felt the shield give way. It was the imp's cue to attack as one and they streaked toward him and the unconscious woman at his feet. But it was also his cue to attack. Even as the masses of imps began their charge he released the shape holding the spinning ice shards and watched as they shot out in all directions like arrows.

It worked perfectly. The imps and the ice shards met head on, and in the blink of an eye the imps were reduced to piles of bloodied meat as they fell lifeless to the ground. Not a single one escaped despite their ability to confound magic, because he'd used such a directionless spell. No matter how they tried to alter the trajectory of the ice shards with their magic, there were still too many, and at least one was always going to hit.

"Yes!" Sam pumped his fist in delight, as the light of the illumination spell revealed at least a hundred imp bodies surrounding him and the woman. He could still see bodies lying dead at a distance of seventy or eighty yards, and there were no live imps any further out. Not that he could see that far, but his magical senses told him that. He knew that he and the woman had passed the first barrier between them and freedom from this place, and he was more than happy. Better yet, he wasn't even tired. If need be he could repeat this attack all night long when he hoped the imps would leave as sunlight burned them. Then again, that was assuming this place had a morning, or a sun. Somehow he doubted it.

But perhaps he'd celebrated too soon? He realised that the moment he heard the sound of thunder in the distance and knew it was not the sign of a storm coming. Not when the thunder was in the ground. This was the thunder made by heavy feet. Hundreds of them marching out of step. And they were all marching in his direction. He knew they weren't friends.

Even as he wondered what new monster was coming, Sam saw the first of them coming into view, and tried not to cringe. Stone trolls. Where the hell had stone trolls come from? They lived in mountains not deserts, and they didn't like the dark or fire. But he didn't have time to wonder about the wrongness of it all. He had to prepare to fight, and to fight hard.

Stone trolls were tough opponents. Their rock skin absorbed almost all blows from weapons with ease and most magic attacks, particularly fire. Moreover they were stubborn, and once they attacked they wouldn't stop. Fortunately they were both slow and stupid. It was his only edge. Especially when he couldn't take advantage of their slowness to run away, because even if he didn't have the woman to carry off as well, they – like the imps before them – were coming from all sides. There was no direction to run in.

He quickly decided that the best weapon against them would be their own weight, and without even thinking about it he sent out a ripple of earth magic that liquefied the ground around. It still looked like dirt, but anything that tried to cross it would soon find itself swimming. And stone trolls to the best of his knowledge, couldn't swim.

His plan of course depended on the stone trolls not realising the land ahead of them was fluid. They weren't bright, but seeing the trolls in front of them sinking out of sight might be a give away even for another troll. Fortunately the fire and ice fog shape gave him a way out of that. It was an expensive spell in terms of magic and required intense concentration. It required the spell caster to hold both fire and ice together but separate, while keeping the ground liquid, but it was the only way he could create a truly thick fog.

Focussing first on turning the ground around the perimeter of the liquid earth into a frozen waste, Sam then fired an array of flame shards directly into the ice. The result was everything he'd hoped for as the two magics collided and exploded, creating a blinding fog that quickly enveloped the land all around them.

Maybe thirty heartbeats later he listened to the first of the trolls, already stumbling around in the fog and fighting one another, fall into the liquefied ground with a splash. Due to their weight he hoped they would sink all the way to the bottom. It was about twenty feet or so and without any way out there fate was likely to drown. Not a particularly nice way to die, but then stone trolls weren't particularly nice creatures.

"Hanor!" Sam bellowed out his family war cry. Having waited for far too long and heard only a few dozen splashes, Sam began to wonder how many of the trolls were still outside the liquefied earth. But he figured if there was one thing that would bring a troll running through fog, it was the sound of its prey. And so Sam called out to them, magically enhancing the sound with the feel of prey trying to elude them. He was right and a few heartbeats later he began to hear an increasing number of splashes as more and more of the trolls fell in.

It was just as well, since it was becoming difficult to maintain the earth spell along with the fire and ice fog. But in time, as the sound of splashing became less frequent even when he repeated his cry, and he knew he'd caught most of them and let all the spells go.

It had been hard work holding all those separate magics together and Sam took a few moments to recover. While he did so he watched closely as the fog lifted to reveal a once more mostly empty darkened plain.

Still, more of the imps had appeared in the distance, and even as far away as they were he could feel the illumination spell he'd shaped dissipating, and realised as he stared into the distance that they were slowly undoing its order. Soon he would no longer be able to see them. But he decided however, that there was no point in trying to maintain it against them. The torches afforded enough light that he could see them when they got close, and he couldn't afford to waste his strength trying to maintain it against them.

It was just as well since a little while later he saw the first of the reddish glows that he knew meant trouble. Fire spawn. Imps and spawn both – that was all he needed! Worse yet, he realised they were working together. The imps were degrading his spells, while the spawn attacked. And the imps were far enough off that they didn't need to fear his ice shard attack this time.

For the first time Sam felt despair as he realised a pattern was forming. The attackers were becoming more powerful and smarter with every raid, while he was slowly but surely being drained of strength. While there was no logical reason for it, he knew that when he had defeated these assailants, another even stronger group would come, and then another after them. Sooner or later he would lose. He didn't need the blood trickling down his cheek to tell him what would happen then.

Regardless he had to try. With fire spawn he knew there was only one recognised magical attack that could work; ice shears. The spawn had their own fire magic, and so were resistant to any but the most powerful spells. Worse, their scaly skin was nearly as tough as the stone of the rock trolls – a blast of ice shards would only scratch them. But most troubling of all, once they got close enough they could launch fireballs at him and his charge. And with the imps so near, he couldn't maintain a proper ice shield against them for too long. They would undermine it.

His only hope therefore was to attack the spawn with the shears at a much greater range than he would normally, and hope that the effort didn't wipe him out.

Using every ounce of concentration he could muster Sam began sucking the fire out of the air and freezing the water vapour in it into a pair of circular shears, each about five yards wide. That was the easy part. Next he had to propel the shears at the spawn, still three or four hundred yards away, in a perfectly executed scything motion. Fire of course was the only way to do it, and using the shape of a flaming arrow he set the ice shears in motion, the top one leading the bottom one by a foot.

Twisting where he stood, he began spinning like a top, always facing the shears as if they were on the end of a rope, while trying not to let his natural dizziness interfere with the spells. Then, as if the shears were tied to him, he slowly let them move further and further away from him.

Five perhaps six turns later the shears were at least two hundred yards from him, and though he was now only spinning slowly, at that distance they were moving faster than an arrow. Another four turns and they were three hundred yards away from him. It was at that point that he felt the first impact as they touched the closest spawn. It worked perfectly as the leading shear sliced through the main body of the lizard like creature, while the lower ice shear severed its legs. And then as the shears turned the lower shear became the leading shear, as the top one tracked it like a blood hound.

In the next rotation he felt three more of the spawn meet the icy death he had planned, their fire magic and scaly skin no match for the sharpness of the shears. But at the same time he could feel the effect of the imps on the shears, as it became harder and harder to control them. The shears no longer wanted to fly their spherical dance of death. But Sam held them together – just – and in two more rotations another thirty or so of the spawn met their end. And that, as far as he could tell, was that. He couldn't see any more of the glowing red lights that warned of their presence. But the imps were still out there. Armed with the power of flight, they had never been in danger from the shears.

For a few moments Sam stood there, breathing deeply; trying with his most sensitive nature magic to work out where the imps were. He couldn't see them in the dark now that the illumination spell had largely failed, and he was worried they might take advantage of his tiredness to attack anew. But they weren't that brave he discovered, as he eventually found them roughly four hundred yards away. Nor did they need to be. They could wait.

Having been given a chance to breathe, Sam took advantage of the time to refocus himself. Fear, as the saying went, was a mind killer. It also undermined concentration, and a wizard who couldn't concentrate wasn't a wizard. As he stood there collecting his wits about him, he could feel the sweat slowly dripping off him, running down his armour, and collecting in a puddle by his feet. But he paid it no attention. Losing sweat was normal. It was losing blood that he had to worry about.

Samual

Sadly it wasn't long before he felt the next menace on the horizon. In fact it was far too soon. But this one was different. It wasn't a horde as he'd expected. His heightened nature magic told him that there was only one creature. But it was big. Very big. Something that thought of him as dinner. He couldn't see it yet, but he knew through his magic that it could see him, and even now it was sizing him up as a meal. Make that a snack. He wasn't big enough to make a meal.

It didn't take long for the creature to decide he was as tempting as he looked, and a heartbeat later, Sam felt it coming toward him. Coming fast. And he still couldn't see it. Against an unknown assailant flying at him Sam had to rely on his strongest attacking spell – the fire ball – and hope that the creature wasn't resistant to fire or able to dodge. Sam concentrated on building one as powerful and tight as he could while he waited for it to arrive.

The instant he saw the creature's glowing red eyes flying at him, Sam let it go in a single powerful throw. It was a good, clean shot, and he watched as it flew faster than any arrow directly at the red eyes. He didn't even have time to be nervous. Not then anyway.

The strike was everything he'd wanted, and the explosion when it came lit up the night sky as though it was daylight. But what it revealed was not what he'd expected. He'd thought some sort of demon perhaps. Maybe another fire magic monster. But this was a dozen times worse. As the fire slowly dissipated and the creature once more came into view, he saw its sinuous head and knew he hadn't done enough. He'd knocked it out of the sky, but he hadn't really harmed it at all.

It was a drake. Probably a fire breathing, nightmare drake. Nearly the size of a dragon, but much more savage, he knew no fireball was going to stop it. The creature had its own fire magic. Even as he watched the creature was getting up, barely stunned.

Time! That he suddenly realised was what he needed. He needed time to prepare. No sooner had he realised it then he knew how to get it. Before the drake had a chance to again take to the air, Sam liquefied the ground beneath it, and watched with some pleasure as the creature suddenly sank and screamed in shock. Of course it instantly began to try and reach for the sky. Drakes had fast reactions, but in this instance not fast enough. Even as he saw the drake beginning to rise Sam solidified the ground around it, trapping the drake's legs. It wouldn't hold for long. The creature was tough and strong even without its fire magic, and it would soon escape its stone prison. Already he could see dust rising around its haunches as it fought against the stone's embrace.

He just hoped it was long enough.

But long enough for what? Against a drake, most magic was next to useless. All it did was generally make the creatures angry. He had read that the fabled ice mountain spell could hold it. But with imps around, eroding at the spell even as he shaped it? That did not bode well. They would undo every magical shape he could cast. First he had to get rid of the imps.

With so many of them around and all of them as far away as they were there was only one spell he knew that would work. The fire ring. The one time he had tried it however, the effort had left him exhausted for days. Now he had to form the fire ring once more? In this place? Still, it didn't seem that he had a choice. He would worry about whether he had any strength to form the ice mountain spell after that. And after that he just had to hope that there weren't any more creatures coming.

He began drawing every ounce of fire he could find around him. Drawing it from the torches, the heat in the ground and even the sky. Soon the temperature all around began to plummet. But he didn't care. It only mattered that he had enough. Once he did Sam began shaping the ring into his hands just as he had before, all the time keeping a close eye on the drake as it continued trying to tearing its way loose. Pieces of stone were already flying around. Soon those pieces would be large chunks. And shortly after that he would be lunch. He didn't have much time.

Despite his haste and distraction, the fire ring quickly grew in his hands. In fact it grew even more quickly than it had when he'd first shaped the spell, and in less than a few score heartbeats he could feel the power surging as it tried to pull his hands together, straining to be released.

Enough. Sam knew by then that he had gathered as much fire into his spell as he ever could. He was right on the edge of losing control. And if that happened he would lose his life in the process. It was time for the hard part.

Slowly, or as slowly as he could when the magic pushed so hard, he brought his hands together, feeling the ring shaping around his head with every inch closer they came. Then in a sudden rush they touched, not as smoothly as they had the first time, but then the fire coursing through his hands was far greater than before and he was far more tired.

For a few incredibly long heartbeats it was all he could do just to release the fire as smoothly as he could into the ring circling above his head without releasing his life with it. It was beyond difficult and pushed him to the very edge of his strength as he strained with every fibre of his being to keep it from exploding between his hands. But then in a glorious instant it was done and he released it and he thanked the All Father as he watched it leave him that he had survived. Again.

But even as he fell to his knees in reaction, he couldn't help but admire the magnificence of the ring. This one was even more powerful than before. Instead of a raging fire wall racing away from him faster than an arrow, this was a towering inferno at least fifty yards high, and it raced away from him like a stampeding heard of bison. The imps didn't stand a chance. In fact even the drake was likely to be badly hurt he thought.

As it hit the drake, Sam watched the creature scream with impotent fury, as it struggled to free itself. But it still wasn't enough to kill it. Although the ring caused terrible burns to it, after it had passed an angry charcoal coloured drake remained. It was still alive, but it was in terrible pain. He also suspected that the beast had been blinded. Its red eyes had turned as black as the rest of it. Surely its eyes couldn't be as tough as its scales?

Then it was the imps turn and he watched with joy as just like the steel rats before them, they exploded, unable to flee in time. Many had taken to the air as fast as they could when they saw the ring coming, but such was its speed and their poor flying ability that they couldn't escape its wrath. Even those who had flown upwards of forty or fifty feet exploded in mid-air, and fell to the ground in a fiery rain on their fallen comrades. And they were the ones who were at least half a league away.

But unlike Shavarra, this ring wasn't stopping at such a meagre distance. Instead it carried on, growing ever larger and more deadly and destroying everything in its path. He estimated that it had to have travelled at least a league and a half before it gave out with a fiery wail.

A league and a half of completely safe ground, with only one surviving threat remaining behind, and it was wounded! Sam would have celebrated if he'd had the strength. Instead all he could do was kneel there and survey the destruction around him while trying to catch his breath. The sweat was running off him by the bucket load, he couldn't stop shaking, and no matter what he did he couldn't seem to find enough air to breathe. But he was happy. And he was safe. For the moment.

In time he remembered the threat the drake posed as it continued its insane screaming and to struggle against its rocky prison. Soon it would be free and blind or not, he and his charge would be dinner.

Slowly, as for some reason he couldn't seem to draw the cold any faster, Sam began shaping a prison of ice around the drake. He was finding it hard now, but he kept pushing to build it faster. Every angry roar of the drake encouraged him and the mountain grew surprisingly quickly.

It wasn't until Sam had buried it under a hundred foot tall mountain of ice that the drake finally stopped screaming. The cold coming of the prison walls probably hadn't killed it. He wasn't sure that there was much that could kill it. Instead he suspected it was simply going into its winter sleep as a result of the sudden drop in temperature. For the moment though it posed no threat, and without the imps the ice mountain would endure many weeks before it finally melted. He just hoped that no more drakes were coming.

As he finished off the ice mountain spell Sam felt the pinpricks of blackness creeping into his sight and he knew, he was going to pass out. He had no choice. Sam had used all his magical strength and this time he thought it might be many days or even months before he was once again strong enough to wage a battle on this scale. But he didn't have weeks or months before he guessed the next set of enemies appeared. He might have hours if he was lucky.

The best he could do he realised, was to create a fortress around himself and the woman. Fortunately he still had some earth magic remaining. As long as he could remain awake long enough to create the spell that was.

Digging his nails into the soft skin around the inside of his wrist, Sam managed to pull himself far enough back from the brink of sleep, and the world once more grew a little brighter. Then he began forming the ground around them into a single round stone wall at least six feet thick. A wall which kept growing higher and higher and which curved back in on itself until it formed a dome. A forty foot high dome. Remembering his lessons one last time, he left a very small opening in the very top, just big enough to let some air in, but hopefully no imps.

That he hoped, coupled with the damage from the fire ring, would have removed all traces of the two of them from the land. No footprints, no smell, nothing. When the next set of enemies appeared they would have no clue that this dome was anything other than a giant stone formation. There would be no scent to tell them that a meal was inside, and no surviving enemies who would remember. Best of all, once he had released the magic that shaped it, the stone would have no magic residue for the imps to degrade. It was just solid stone.

By the time he had finished Sam had fallen from his knees to his back, and the world was growing black once more. But even as the darkness took him, he knew he had done everything he could and more to protect the woman and himself. If by some unfortunate chance the enemies did detect them and they were killed, at least he would die well knowing that no more could have been expected of him.

It was a surprisingly comforting thought as the world left him.

Chapter Eleven.

"Good afternoon love."

Sam woke to the sound of a woman's voice he knew well. Ryshal's voice. His heart celebrated even before he opened his eyes. And when he did the reality was even better than he could have hoped for. Ry was there and smiling as always, a cup of some herbal tea in her hand which she handed to him. He could smell the camomile and rose hip in it, and knew it was a restorative. But when he gazed at Ry and realised that he was home he knew it wasn't necessary. She was all the restorative he needed.

Beside that the darkness, the imps and the drake, were as nothing, and he pushed the memories aside.

"How long?" In truth his curiosity was only minor, as his joy at having Ry looking so happy swamped his ability to wonder about anything else. But he knew it had to be a number of days since he had last set eyes on her. There was the beginning of some true health shining through her skin, her cheek bones though still prominent were looking more normal, and her hair was finally starting to look like hair instead of bristles.

"Three days love." Sitting beside him on the bed, she made him sip his tea. "Three long days while the elders have all visited and wondered if they pushed you too far with their test, and the healers told them off."

The healers had told them off? Somehow Sam found that hard to accept. Whether she meant either the elven healers or the human priests who followed Phil the White, somehow he doubted either would have dared tell off the elders. They were as a rule a respectful group.

And then there was the other part. A test? Could that be what it had been? But he didn't ask it out loud. He didn't truly want to know right then. But to think that the waking nightmare he had been through was all some sort of test was just bizarre. It was one of Alder's jests surely. He could have been killed! As could the woman. And that was just a test! But he let it all go, knowing that sooner or later he would learn the full story, and just then he couldn't bring himself to care.

"You did well by the way, as I knew you would. So well in fact that the elders have been visiting daily and lamenting with one another about how best they can complete your tuition. You already have the power of the strongest. It is only the study they say you are lacking, and they worry that you are too proud and too wild to take their direction."

She smiled tenderly to soften the criticism, but he still heard it.

"I'm not too proud and I will happily learn all that they may teach me. I will do whatever I have to do to be here with you and your family. As for my wildness," he reached out, wrapped his arms around her waist and pulled her tight so he could kiss her properly, "that's only for you!"

A long while later he asked her how she was feeling, more curious, than worried as he could see that she was happy. There was a certain playful spark in her eyes. Sam had no doubt that she was recovering.

"I feel good."

She did too. He could hear it in her voice and see it in her eyes. She was starting to sound like the Ry of old and it filled his heart with gladness.

"You do feel good!" He kissed her some more and felt her respond in kind. "And you look very good."

"Every day that passes I feel a little stronger, a little healthier, and a little luckier to have married you. No one else could have got me out of that cell. And no one else could make me feel so happy. So it was nice to be able to look after you for a change instead of the other way around. It made me feel like a wife again instead of an invalid."

"A very wonderful wife." He took one last sip of the tea and then put the cup down on the floor beside him. Then he pulled her down again and kissed her thoroughly, knowing they would be doing far more than that shortly. Already his hands were wandering over her body, finding so much to enjoy. For some reason he felt strong and hungry, and she was so beautiful and so near he couldn't help himself. He wasn't alone in his passion. But he still felt guilty.

"I'm so sorry," he told her once they both came up for air. "If I'd been stronger or smarter you would never have been sent to that dungeon in the first place."

"You cannot blame yourself for the crimes of your brother. You are a good man and he is neither of those things. And you've grown so much. Your strength now is at least that of a master, which is unheard of for someone your age. I remember enough of what I saw at your brother's keep to tell me that. Then there was the battle at Torin Vale which the people keep telling me of, and the way the elders themselves whisper among themselves about you. And you are still only twenty eight! There has never been a master of fire so young. Usually they look like dried up old prunes before they achieve mastery. Seventy is considered quite young for a master. You have achieved a goal that others could only dream of in a mere five years. Be proud of yourself. I am."

"Some days I feel like a dried up old prune! But I'm far

more proud of you Ry. For surviving long enough in such a hell for me to rescue you. I don't know how you did it, but I will be forever grateful that you did."

"How grateful?" She had the cheekiest smile on her face as she asked, and then she wrapped herself around him, leaving him in no doubt as to what she meant. He couldn't help but want it too.

"Come and find out." Several long joyful moments later he released her briefly, but only so that she could remove her dress and crawl under the covers beside him. A heartbeat later they were lying next to each other, skin to skin, and the excitement was making them both shiver.

His hands wandered all over Ry, exploring and loving all that they found. Her hips were still too bony, but now they were starting to find their womanly shape again. Her breasts were once more breasts, not yet full but getting there, while her legs had the beginnings of some shapeliness returning.

She was also stronger, and passionate in her excitement. He found that out when her legs suddenly wrapped around him like an anaconda, and she rolled backwards, pulling him on top of her, demanding to be pleasured by him as they had of old. He willingly gave in to her plea, and soon they were moving together in their usual blissful harmony, oblivious to everything else.

For Sam it was a revelation. The one time they'd made love since leaving Fall Keep, he'd been so careful, terrified of hurting her. This time Ry gave him no such leave. She was stronger and she demanded all that he had to give. With every thrust her hands on his buttocks urged him on, while she cried and moaned as a woman possessed. And with every thrust the excitement grew, while he lost a little more control. Soon his heart was screaming in his ears, while the blood raced in his veins, and the sweat poured off him. The same sweat that was pouring off Ry, even as she licked his off his face, and laughed happily.

Soon, very soon he was at his moment, and he knew he could not hold back for long. But Ry was also there, her needs and desires every bit as great as his own, and he felt her go rigid underneath him, even as her legs locked around his, holding him to her as he gave her his seed in waves of unbearable pleasure.

Afterwards, when their heartbeats had returned to something approaching normal, Ry let him roll her once more so that she was on top. It was not her favourite position, she much preferred being pinned by his weight, but it gave her more freedom to play with his chest hairs as they talked. And for once they could truly talk. Ry showed no sign of the exhaustion that had plagued her for so long, something that pleased him immensely. Not just because it was another indication of how much healthier she was becoming, but also because he had always loved to just hold her and talk afterwards.

They had been wed young. He had been twenty three, Ryshal only nineteen, and their wedded life had been cut brutally short. Barely three months after they had become husband and wife Heri had turned eighteen. He had then assumed the throne and betrayed them. But those precious few months had sustained him for the five long, lonely years while they had been kept apart. There had never been a thought within him of giving up. Of finding another. There could be no other. He suspected that that had been the truth from the day they had first met. Perhaps that was why the priests had been so happy to wed them after such a short courtship? After all a year was not long for nobles to court, and both of them had been very young. Whatever the truth, they had been apart for too long and they had a lot of catching up to do.

For hours it seemed they chattered, as they hadn't since they had first become husband and wife. Perhaps not surprisingly most of their conversation was of that wonderful time. Everything since then had been a nightmare, one that had only become more difficult since he had rescued her. And of course they spoke only of those things that made them smile. They put aside all the hardships and fears for the future. It was not the time for them. It was time to be young and carefree again.

Yet even their happy banter couldn't last forever, and slowly but surely Sam felt his eyelids grow heavy, his breathing slow. But he wasn't alone in that, as even as his eyelids drooped and he succumbed to sleep, he saw that Ry was already ahead of him. Her head was by then into his shoulder, one arm was draped over his waist, and possibly, though she would never admit to it, the faintest of snores was coming from her delicate throat.

Chapter Twelve

"Ah hem!"

The somewhat cranky tones of a man trying to attract his attention were what first woke Sam, and even as he heard them he realised he'd been hearing them for some time. He also realised that he knew the speaker. But he didn't really want to wake up and converse with the Elder just then. He was far too comfortable. Too happy.

Still, the Elder would not be ignored and eventually Sam knew he had no choice. The man was not going to go way. So reluctantly he opened his eyes.

He was still in the covered wagon at least. And he was grateful for that as in the back of his mind there was a dark desert full of monsters somewhere out there where he was sure he should still be. Ry lay sound asleep beside him, unaware of their guest and happy for it he guessed. Or she would be when she awoke. Then again if she had been awake she would probably have been watching and laughing, quietly, as the Elder bothered him. She loved him unconditionally but that didn't mean that she wasn't happy to take a little amusement in his misfortunes from time to time.

"Elder Bela."

Sam greeted the Elder as he was supposed to he thought. But his thoughts were still a little groggy. And he couldn't help but wonder why it always seemed to be Elder Bela who annoyed him. Or for that matter why the Elder was in their wagon. It seemed a little improper.

"Samual Hanor. It's good to see you awake at last, though perhaps dressed would have been better."

Really, Sam thought. He'd come and woken him up and then had the nerve to complain that he wasn't dressed! But he knew it wasn't his place to say anything. Not to an elder.

"Of course Elder." Sam sat up and started hunting around for some clothes. If he had any. He couldn't see his clothes anywhere, and his armour was gone.

"You did well in our test Fire Angel." Typically Master Bela showed no sign of embarrassment as he started talking. Unfortunately he also showed no sign of leaving the covered wagon, not even to let Sam dress in peace. And dressing was going to be an issue.

Sam was still annoyed at having been told that he'd lost his armour, even though it was apparently for only a few days while the smiths reworked it to make it look more elven. He knew it was a necessity if he didn't want to look like a knight of Hanor to the casual human observer. Yet still it hurt. Armour was a personal thing as much as any other set of clothes. More so. He had worn that armour since he had first reached his full growth, more than ten years earlier, and he had worn it every day for the past five years. Which was perhaps a part of the reason the elves of Torin Vale had been wary of him as Ry had pointed out. Armed strangers in town were never welcome. Still, his armour had become a part of him. Almost like a second skin. Without it he felt distinctly naked.

Meanwhile Ry, bless her, was still snoring away gently. She had the most contented look on her face. She was lucky he thought, not to know they had a visitor. But he also suspected that she would not have cared if she had. She was a true elf. While they always worked hard to show a refined and polite appearance, when things went wrong as they occasionally did, it didn't seem to trouble them. Pitiril sela. Accidents happened as they said.

Sam deciding that there was no point and even less dignity in sitting there while the Elder would in all likelihood continue lecturing him once more, crawled over Ry, and then staggered to his feet on the wagon's wooden floor. It wasn't easy since the bed was little more than a straw stuffed mattress on a creaking wooden floor while for some reason he felt kitten weak, but at least he didn't fall on his face in front of the Elder. That would have been humiliating. Not that Master Bela would have said anything. Then he grabbed a towel to cover his private parts and started hunting in earnest for some clothes.

"Master Lavellin was most pleased with your ability to draw and shape fire, and says that in only a very few years your mastery should be assured. You already have the strength, the feel and concentration of a true master, which is highly unusual for someone so young. It's only your lack of experience with some of the other shapes that lets you down now."

Sam listened with half an ear as he concentrated on finding something to wear. Eventually he spied one of the elves' favoured white robes hanging over the side rail and hurriedly started putting it on. But being a robe made for an elf it didn't fit well. Though he might be much the same height as the typical elf at around six foot or so, he was far from the same shape. Thinned down as much as he was from a good diet and regular training, his shoulders, chest and hips were still simply too large for the robe, and he heard what sounded suspiciously like stitches bursting as he struggled into it. Then having finally got it on he thought he looked rather like a sausage bursting out of its skin in the frying pan. Maybe later he hoped, he could persuade Alendro to let some of the material out for him before it ripped completely.

"Fire and ice are more than just weapons," Elder Bela continued, apparently completely oblivious to Sam's wardrobe troubles. "They are powerful tools, and should be looked upon as such. With ice as with earth you can create bridges to carry you across ravines, walls to shelter from winds, and nets to trap fish. Also, you can cool those suffering from fevers with ice water. Fire on the other hand gives you warmth and light as well as weapons, beacons to bring others to you, heat to forge metals and warm water, and spectacular illusions to warm people's hearts."

"Master Lavellin says to tell you that in a couple of days when you're feeling stronger, he looks forward to completing your training."

Sam meanwhile looked forward to being able to breathe fully. The robe really was much too tight. Still, he managed to nod politely as he concentrated on thinking small thoughts.

"Master Riven says your command of the earth magic is still only at the level of an adept, but your perfection of so many shapes speaks of much practice, which is good. If you are willing and have the time, he will be happy to show you those few shapes you have yet to learn, and to help you practice with the rest. Your strength may never be as great as that of a master, though he believes it will grow further as you learn to appreciate its wonder. There is always plenty of work for a well-trained adept in the earth magic. Your skill will be most welcome."

Sam tried to look on attentively to Master Bela as he spoke. It was difficult though. He was already feeling drained and weak just from having stood up, and he wanted desperately to sit down before his legs gave way. He knew though that if he did the robe would surely tear in some embarrassing places. So instead, he leaned against the back wall, which was really just the back of the front seat of the wagon, and tried to look relaxed and attentive.

"Your skills in the natural magics are far less developed

than the others, and yet some of the elders believe you have more promise there than you realise, myself included. Especially when you wield that magic in combination with the others. Humans often fail to see the value in the magic of the natural world, and their knowledge of it is limited, as was your library. In time you may well become an adept, and with many more shapes to learn than you yet realise exist. This too can be a powerful weapon for a soldier as well as a tool. You will be welcome to train with the other novitiates when you have the time."

"Last and by no means least, you are an enchanter, a rare and useful talent, and as with your other gifts, this is one that cannot begin to be fully understood without much training. So far you have used it only for warfare, and as such barely begun to understand its true value. But once you have learned more of the other shapes of fire, earth and nature, you will find its value to be immense. All of us will be most pleased to aid you in discovering all of the gifts you have been given."

For Sam that was all very interesting and welcome. He just wished he could get the Elder to leave the wagon before the robe split.

"Please tell them I would be honoured to accept any and all the training they can give me Elder." Sam was actually grateful for the offer of training, particularly from the elves. They were far more accomplished in the magical arts than most humans, and especially those from Fair Fields. They could teach him a lot, and with the likelihood of more battles ahead if his fears were correct, he needed that learning if he was to become as powerful a soldier as he could.

But it was more than that. He also thought that undertaking their training would help him become more accepted among the elves. That was a necessity given that his wife had now returned to him and he was living among the elves. Ry would expect it of him. For years he had lived beside but not truly among them, as the Elder had rightfully pointed out weeks before. Now, with Ry back in his life and the possibility of a family one day, he had to find a place among them, because he knew he would not be leaving. He would never take Ry away from the comfort and safety of her kith and kin again.

"I will if you insist young Samual, but I think it might be better coming from you. The Masters have after all been quite patiently waiting for you this last half hour or so." Caught by surprise, Sam lowered one of the canvas flaps on the side, and peered out. Sure enough half a dozen elders were sitting just outside the wagon on a fallen tree, quietly chatting among themselves and drinking tea while they waited for him to get up and join them. He groaned quietly.

"Perhaps though it might be best if you wore your own robe instead of your wife's. It looks a little tight." The Elder pointed to another white robe that had been lying on the bed before he turned and stepped off the back of the wagon.

Sam stared in horror at the guilty artefact which had been right in front of his nose all the time. He had the strangest feeling Master Bela was smiling for the first time as he left. All but laughing in fact.

"Another few moments' patience Elder!"

Sam called out after the Elder's rapidly disappearing back, and for a response got merely a wave of the arm. But it was enough, as he hurriedly tried to squirm his way out of one robe and into his own one. He guessed he would have a little time at least. The elders like every other elf in the caravan, had been taking things slowly these past few days.

After the mad rush from Shavarra had ended with the defeat of the second wave of the rats, progress had slowed considerably as the scouts continued to report no new enemies giving chase. And it had slowed ever more as the caravan had grown in size. Then progress had almost stopped once they had reached Fair Fields, as wagon after wagon needed food and provisions. So now they stopped every day for a few hours while traders from all over the realm came visiting. Apparently the word of the elves' plight, and more importantly their coin, had spread fast.

Thus far prices had not reached the level of highway robbery, though from what Ry had told him, they were higher than he was used to. That was only because the goods they were seeking were still in plentiful supply, even for a caravan of such size, and because they were passing through some of the best farming land in any realm. The war masters had already purchased more than fifteen hundred horses, and all the food that the traders could bring, and their provisions were holding up well.

The result was that the caravan had moved into a new mode of travel. They started late each morning to allow for a good breakfast to be cooked, took a two hour lunch break during which the people engaged in trade, and then stopped well before sunset so that they could prepare the evening meal. And of course to conduct yet more trade. They were lucky to cover more than a couple of leagues a day.

As Sam could smell food cooking, he guessed that it must be just on dinner time. That being the case, Sam knew the elders wouldn't be staying long. They would want to get back to their wagons to eat. But he would still have enough time to dress and try to at least appear a little respectable in this elven travesty of a costume.

Why did the elves wear these robes? What was wrong with leggings and a good vest, he asked himself as he dressed. Just as he had asked it a hundred times before. And why always white? Yes it was clean and looked neat. But what was wrong with some colour? Some Hanor blue like his armour?

Of course he had no answer. Save of course the same one he had for why the priests were always around – to annoy him!

A few moments later, after having carefully tucked Ry back into bed, Sam found himself with his next challenge of the day – attempting to get off the back of the wagon. It was a task more difficult than normal as he discovered anew just how high off the ground a wagon was, and how weak he was, and he nearly collapsed in a heap at its rear even before he made it to the wagon's edge. In his current condition he knew he couldn't jump down as he normally would. It would prove a little more exciting than he would want and he'd likely end up falling flat on his face. Instead he levered himself down by hanging on to the wagon's tray and avoided at least that embarrassment. Once down he headed on wobbly legs over to the elders. It was surprising just how weak he was, but he was determined not to show it. Ironically, if he had been wearing his armour as he'd wanted he would have done just that.

Before he'd made it even halfway there however, he felt strong arms grabbing him around the waist as Pietrel helped him the rest of the way. In turn he watched Alendro scurrying for the wagon where Ry was sleeping. Apparently they'd held back while the Elder was there. Sam wondered briefly just how long they'd stayed away before that – not that they would have minded.

Elves had many differences from humans, not least in the way they viewed such things. In Fair Fields had they been caught in such a position, he would have been expected to later regale his friends with tales of his manliness, while Ryshal would have been publicly humiliated for some time to come. But in Shavarra such things were never discussed, neither by those caught nor by those who caught them. Instead they would all go about their business, and would quickly forget that anything had happened. Perhaps they had the right of it. What occurred between a husband and wife should stay between them.

"Thank you."

Pietrel dropped him off on a seat that had obviously been put out just for him, then handed him a small cup of cooling herbal tea before making himself scarce as he headed for the wagon. Like most elves he didn't want to intrude on the elders unless specifically asked for.

It was amazing just how respectful the elves were of their elders. They treated them almost as if they were kings likely to chop their heads off if they said the wrong thing, while often making small amusements about them behind their backs. Yet the elders themselves acted as anything but royalty and would have enjoyed the jests. They didn't rule by fear; in fact they barely ruled at all. And they didn't demand or even seem to want that respect. For them leadership was both a duty and a burden. They accepted it solemnly and with dignity, but never sought it out.

Whether they were wizards, scholars, soldiers, artisans or even members of the Ruling Council itself, they behaved as if they were no different from any others. It was almost a mark of pride with them to be viewed as no different from anyone else, even if the rest of the people couldn't seem to accept it.

For all that the various councils carried out most of the duties that a king or a lord might, and did it well if incredibly slowly. They spent most of their time settling disputes and hearing petitions. Decisions were made by consensus of the appropriate Council, usually after weeks or months of debate. Council hearings were all open to the public and all elves were free to speak.

To make it even more complex the various councils all had complicated titles and even more complicated procedures. So the Ruling Council was actually the Coming Together of the People – or the Indowin nella mi Ellish. The Magic

Council was Galana – or the Awakening. It was very confusing, especially when there were so many different councils.

It was not a fast system of rule, nor always a particularly efficient one – especially when the priests were involved – but it was indisputably fair, and they carried it out with the highest standards of honour and care.

Though he might never fully understand the elves' system of rule, it was something he found wondrous after having seen Heri in action. Heri sat on his throne like some overly pompous toad clad in excessive finery – though he wouldn't be doing that again any time soon Sam thought snidely. He made decisions on the spot and while he sometimes listened to advisers, he often ignored them. He also had a habit of throwing people into the dungeons for the most minor of offences. His brother had always seemed to embody the worst aspects of a ruler. And that had been when he was still only a king in waiting! He was probably worse now. By comparison it was unsurprising that the elves respected and even loved their elders. But a somewhat larger one that the elders didn't take advantage of their respect. It would have been only human. Though there of course was the difference.

Today though it looked like he had half the Magic Council waiting for him. In fact one of them – Elder Bela so Ry kept reminding him – was also a member of the Ruling Council. These people were the key to his future among the elves, and it behoved him to remember that. So Sam sat quietly in the seat provided and nodded respectfully to the elders. It would be best he decided to let them start the conversation.

"So, what did you think of our examination young Samual?"

An elder he didn't know opened the discussion with probably the first thing Sam had wanted to ask about. How could all that he had been through have been some sort of test? Where had it been? How had he gotten there and back? And what had happened to the woman? The questions poured out of him in a tumble of words though he tried to remain respectful.

The answer of course, was as nothing he would have guessed. According to the elves there had been no world, no enemies, no woman and no danger. Instead the examination as the elders called it, had happened entirely in his head.

Actually it had happened in many people's heads. All the elders from all the schools of magic had been there to witness his battle; in fact it was only through them that the test arena had been made real to him. It was they who had decided which opponents he should face and when, and they against whom he'd wielded his magic. It was also they who had judged him.

His strength and control had surprised them. In fact Sam thought it might have even worried some of them, though they would never say it. These weren't people who would admit a lot. Four true masters of fire and twenty adepts had held the arena against him, and still they had worried that he might break through; such was the amount of fire he could draw upon and use. But his knowledge was sadly lacking, and despite his youthful vigour the arena had held firm.

As Elder Bela had said, his knowledge of the earth magics was much more impressive, and much more pleasing. He did not have the power as he did in fire, but he had the control and had learnt many of the forms, probably because he had studied the different types of magic for different reasons. In his thoughts fire was for fighting while earth was useful as a tool, though clearly they didn't agree. But the traps he had launched against the stone trolls were what had really impressed the elders. In using both the earth magic and the fire magic together in a single trap, he had shown a control the equal of any master, and they welcomed that.

His knowledge of the living magic was woeful as he was informed, and had hardly even needed to be assessed. Still, he guessed he had surprised them that he could use it at all.

Most mages would have some ability in at least one other field of magic as well as their main one, but three was unusual. And very few could consciously use those different magics together. He could use two, perhaps even three simultaneously. But then as he already knew, few could enchant either, and weaving different magics together as one was an essential skill for an enchanter.

Overall he suspected that they were pleased with the results, and perhaps a little surprised. For his own part Sam was simply curious. Why had they tested him? There had been no need to as far as he could see. Or was it something to do with this Fire Angel that they kept referring to him as? He was beginning to think that he needed to learn more about that.

Normally as he was told, such testing would only be done once a year for all the novitiates and apprentices as the elders gathered from far and wide in Shavarra to conduct the examination. But occasionally, such as when they had discovered a new talent with the potential for mastery, and when all the elders happened to be together anyway, they could make an exception. When that same candidate had already saved many of them from a painful death at the hands of an army of steel rats, they didn't need much persuading. Though if the truth be told Sam thought, they might have done it out of curiosity even if the rest wasn't true. Staring at the sea of eyes staring back at him, he knew that curiosity was a powerful driver for these master spell casters.

But was there something more than that? Looking around him at the thoughtful and worried faces, he suspected that there just might be. No doubt if there was they'd tell him in time. For the moment he simply had to accept their words and thank them for their time and effort. That provoked a response he hadn't expected.

"Why so respectful Samual?" a woman asked. "You have not been so before. Polite yes, but never willing to actually do as we ask."

Sam didn't know her name, but he did recognise her slightly tongue in cheek accusation even though she didn't seem offended. He also understood that there was another more important question being asked of him. Could he be relied upon? Or was he just going to make trouble?

"My apologies Elders. For the longest time I had troubles that overrode everything else in my life. I was angry and bitter, and a poor excuse for a man, either elf or human. While I listened to all that was said, my wife's imprisonment came first. I could not have stayed away from her once I learned that I had the strength to rescue her. I hid that because I feared that if I told you, you might ask me to stay. I hid my name because of the assassins that plagued me and worried that they would have thickened like flies around a corpse had they suspected my whereabouts. Then when I was told that Ryshal had been murdered I was incapable of restraining my anger. Now I am freed of some of that burden at least."

"I have always tried to obey your people's laws, and I will listen to all you say and shall do my best to follow your instructions. But I am first, last and always, a husband. I cannot be anything else." He said that because it was true and because they had the need to know. It would save on misunderstandings later.

"We would never ask you to be. No more would we go against those same duties ourselves. We are all family minded, and we welcome that in you. But we do worry about the hurt and pain you have endured. There is still much anger in you child."

Her words spoke true. Ry's survival and improving health had released him from the worst of his anger, but he still had five years of loneliness and rage bottled up somewhere inside him together with the terrifying images of her shattered health when he had first rescued her. Those things would be with him for a long time to come.

"I understand that Elder. I am working hard to purge it, and to control what I cannot get rid of, but for what was done to Ryshal I can neither forgive nor forget." Be honest Ry had told him. And watching the reactions of the elders now he knew her advice was good. In any event the elders would have known if he had lied.

"I hope that time, together with my wife's improving health will help to lessen the rage that still burns within me. For now though I live with it, and I would not have you believe otherwise."

"We know of your rage. And of your frustration and fear. Some days it hangs over you like a thundercloud, making all elves avoid you. And we agree that it will pass in time, though it may never leave completely. But the cost to you while it lingers may be higher than you know."

"Anger is a two edged blade for a spell caster Samual, as I'm sure you know by now. In the short while it may make you stronger in magic as well as body. But in the longer while it may weaken you, as well as making it difficult to learn that which we would have you learn."

Sam had already worked much of that out for himself. The anger that had allowed him to advance to such power so quickly had also held him back for years. Because the other side of anger unable to be released was frustration and

220

despair, the very things that had held him back for years. Maybe if he had kept those at bay he would have been able to rescue Ryshal even sooner. And maybe too that was where the impossible increase in his magic had come from – frustration finally released.

"But worse, it hinders your judgement. It can make you squander too much magic where less would achieve better results. These things we all saw in you in the testing realm. In fighting the golems as well as in our test you showed them as you used your full power. Too much power. A true master in full control could have defeated both enemies without resorting to such dramatic spells such as the fire ring. Even with your limited knowledge of the other shapes of fire, you could have too. Arcs and chained fire could both have worked better."

"Instead you destroyed a large area of our forest, and then left yourself drained for the next attack. You had nothing left. Had the enemy behind the steel rats had a second force, you would be dead."

The Elder was right of course. The soldier in Sam knew that even better than the wizard telling him off. It was just that he'd had no other attack available. He hadn't practised those spells as much as the others, choosing instead to concentrate on the most attacking spells and so when the time had come he'd had no choice available. But even if he had had one, he suspected he would still have gone for the most powerful attacking spell he had. It was his nature. He nodded in agreement.

"It was an unwise attack Elder, but it was all I could think of when facing such a large and powerful enemy alone. Also, when I used the fire ring spell against the steel rats it was the first time I had done so. It turned out to be much more powerful than I'd expected. And it proved to be even more powerful in the test. I had never before drawn such power, let alone shaped it. I hadn't even known I could. And when I released it, particularly the first time, it was all I could do not to lose myself in the spell."

"We sensed that. You have quickly gained the strength and control of the strongest fire masters, but the knowledge of only a student. We will help you with that, teaching you new shapes and better control. But you will have to commit yourself to the training."

Sam nodded, knowing that that had always been the case. To learn the intricacies of spell casting was a long and difficult task. Thus far he'd avoided much of the work by concentrating only on those magics useful in combat. But they were only the smallest part of shaping even fire. He predicted years of study ahead if he was truly to become worthy of the title of master. But then he had Ry back with him after so many bitter years. Now he felt as though he could do anything.

"I am more than willing to do so Elder. I must protect my wife, her family and our people, and that is surely the best way I can. On my honour and soul I give my word that I will train as hard as I can."

"And that is all we could ask of you as a spell caster. But as elders we must ask one thing more. We will train you gladly, and our people will welcome you as you have now been told many times. But as elves trying to guide our people in this crisis we also need your support."

"Your pardon?" That caught Sam by surprise. They weren't expecting to go into battle again? So soon?

"In this last month our people have lost not only friends and family, but also their homes. They have witnessed sights that no elf should ever have to see, and they spend their days torn between grief, loss, anger and fear. But worse than that, they have lost many of those they look up to. Those they want guidance from in this terrible time. The elders. Half our Ruling Council is dead, as well as many other elders. Those of us who survived must now try to keep their spirits up. We also need to keep them moving – sometimes we have to stop them from fighting – while at the same time they keep asking us how we could have failed them so badly. It is a question we ask ourselves, and for which we have no answer."

"Against such an enemy –"

Sam was going to say that there was no way they could have triumphed without warning, but the Elder cut him off as she raised her hand. She knew all that he would say. She had probably said it herself, and failed to find comfort in the words. He knew from experience that it simply didn't help. He had not foreseen what his brother would do and he had always known him to be a monster.

"We do not need, want nor ask for any excuses. We only want answers so that we may do better in the future and our people may once more have confidence in us. You however, are not tainted with that failure. Moreover, you are seen by many as a defender. A soldier and wizard of tremendous strength. A guardian."

"There is a legend from our most ancient of tales, a story from our people's childhood which speaks of one similar to you. It resonates with our people and they have cast you in the light of this tale. They believe you to be the Fire Angel."

"Your pardon Elder?" Sam was getting used to the title. Elder Bela had even used it in the wagon and Ry had said the same. However, other than as a mark of respect he'd had no idea that they meant anything more by it.

"According to our most ancient legends, when the elves and even the world were new, our ancestors were raised, taught and protected by four angels. They were the angels of earth, air, fire and water and were sent by the Goddess herself. Others say that they were ancients, the last survivors from the Dragon Wars. These angels kept our people safe from the terrible demons that then ruled the lands."

"Their power was unimaginable and yet even greater than that was their goodness, as they fought day and night to protect every single elf, until no demons remained. They fought so hard that at the end they died of exhaustion, their magic and their very souls consumed in the battle. And yet even at the end, when the lands were finally cleansed and they were breathing their last, they cared only that our people were safe."

"Though the story is surely just that, they still call you Fire Angel. It is a sign of our people's respect, and the hope they place in you. A sign that we must use."

"Ryshal has told me something of this. But I am only a man."

"As are we all. But in the people's hearts and souls you are more than that. Half elven, half human, you are the most powerful and unpredictable of all people. Vero eskaline the most wild and dangerous of storm bloods. A soldier who rides alone into battle covered in fire when all others are fleeing. You are a fire mage of strength as powerful as any master, yet with the years of a novice. And a man who will rescue his wife from any enemy, even an entire kingdom."

"Our people whisper all of these things about you and far more. Indeed the gossip fairly flies around the campfires at night. More than even your power it is your spirit that impresses them most. You show such strength and loyalty as only the best among us do, the bravery that can only come from love and a pure heart. You more than any of us, carry their hopes."

The strange thing was that Sam had the feeling he carried the Elder's hopes as well and that worried him.

"How may I help you?"

"Simply by supporting us. We are charged with bringing our people safely through this nightmare, no matter how unworthy we may be for such a responsibility. All we ask is that you do not oppose us in front of others on any important matters. If you did it would divide our people as sharply as any knife. And this is a time when we must remain as one."

"You know much of the lands through which we must pass, you have the training of a soldier as well as a mage, and we must respect your opinion. All we ask is that if you believe we are making an error, that you raise it with us in private. We will listen."

Looking at the Elder and seeing her staring directly back at him Sam knew that she was serious in her offer and that she spoke for the entire Council. Though it seemed inappropriate for him to lead the elves in any capacity, it seemed that the Council was willing to offer him much of that responsibility. But then he realised, they were desperate.

It was at once frightening and flattering. It was surely unacceptable for a knight, and yet it was also his sworn duty to help. For a brief time Sam struggled to say anything at all as he tried to make sense of the conflict. Finally though, his father's lessons in statecraft came back to him as well as his grandfather's lessons in the knighthood and he knew what he had to say.

"Well over a hundred and fifty years ago, my great, great grandfather Hanor of Melniborn, a battlemaster betrayed by his lord, began the school and the Order of the knights of Hanor. I am proud to be a member of that Order as were my father, grandfather and my great grandfather before me. Our vows were always to the people rather than the King. This is why it was such a surprise when my father was made king by the people."

It was also why he had not wanted the position, but had also been unable to put it aside. The people had needed a king to protect them from their own nobles, and his father had understood that. Even though it had cost him his life when an assassin sent by one of them had felled him with a poisoned dart.

"We are sworn to protect the people, with our lives if need be. To bring them justice tempered always with mercy, and to ease their suffering where we may."

"Though as a knight of Hanor I may not offer you my sword to the Council, any more than I could offer it to a king or an emperor, I freely give my sword to the people. I give it to all of them including yourselves. I take their defence as my sworn duty, as I take yours. And it is clear to me that these elves are a people badly in need of guidance and wise counsel in the months and years to come. Your guidance and your wisdom.

"I Samual Hanor, knight of Hanor, give our people my word that I will support the Council both publicly and privately, in bringing the elves of Shavarra to safety. I will give you whatever knowledge I have of the lands ahead."

And though he didn't speak it, he silently vowed that he would destroy this new Dragon, whoever he was, and bring Ryshal's people home. But that was ambition beyond reason, and he did not speak the words aloud. Only in his heart.

Chapter Thirteen.

Tyne Keep was the first of the Fair Fields fiefdoms to cause trouble for the elves, which came as something of a surprise to Sam.

By then they had already passed the Barony of the Fallbrights and the Principality of Griffin Dale without incident, which was unexpected given their mercenary ways. Then again the black flags prominently displayed throughout their towns told him that the Fallbrights were in mourning. Under those circumstances a bunch of elves crossing their northern lands didn't really concern them. They had revenge to plan. It appeared that Heri had won his duel after all, though Sam didn't ask any of the locals about it. He didn't even show his face anywhere outside of the elven caravan.

The smiths had done a splendid job of removing the last of the crest of Hanor from his armour and reworked it to look like that of the border patrols. Now wearing it he felt reasonably sure he could pass as a somewhat oversized elf, though he felt like a clown in the green and silver. He missed his Hanor blue. The elves had even made some adjustments so it no longer pinched in the places where he'd filled out over the years.

Of course not all the changes to his armour were welcome. In particular, his armour no longer had the full plates along his arms and legs, and it left him feeling distinctly vulnerable. Instead he was wearing the stiffened chain with padded vest and leggings underneath more typical of the elven cavalry. Elves liked to be freer in their movements. But while it was lighter and he definitely had more freedom to move with his weapons, the armour was much hotter than before, and several times a day he had to strip down to his undergarments, just to feel the cool air against his skin.

The smiths had done one thing though that pleased him immensely. They knew he had to be as inconspicuous as possible, and therefore could not wear the markings of Fair Fields openly. But they also knew he was a knight of Hanor and the son of King Hanor, and that he was proud of both. So they had forged him an arm shield for his trailing sword arm, and a cloak, both with the crest prominently displayed and the blue showing proudly. The cloak was for formal occasions and the shield for battle. Of course as neither of them were normally needed, they were stashed away in the wagon.

In fact He needed very little in the way of armour. He hardly ever left Ry's family's wagon. There was little for him to do elsewhere, especially when the elders kept coming to him to give him his lessons and check on his progress. Even the Ruling Council sent riders to him rather than sending for him when they needed advice about matters in Fair Fields.

That suited Sam fine. For the past three full weeks he had been doing little more than caring for Ry and her family, practising with magic and swords, studying the history of the Dragon wars, and above all else celebrating his wife's continuing improvement.

And she was doing well. In fact by the time they had reached the lands of Tyne Keep she was very nearly back to full health. Certainly a month or more of good eating had returned her weight to nearly what it should have been, while her skin was once again the well-tanned golden colour it used to be. Even her hair while short could finally be called hair. She was still weak, her muscles having done far too little for far too long, but she was starting to sing and dance again, regaining more of her natural grace with every day that passed. Soon, she promised, she would return to her duties, teaching the children the dances of the people.

Often, and for long periods of time, Sam found himself

watching her, overwhelmed by the simple joy of being able to see her again. He wasn't alone. Her parents often did much the same, and he couldn't blame them. Their daughter was once more alive and with them and there was little else that mattered.

It bothered him sometimes to be so happy in the midst of such tragedy. It bothered Alendro and Pietrel as well, and they often chose to aid others as best they could; their undeserved guilt getting the better of them. Alendro spent her days knitting and weaving rugs and blankets for others, while Pietrel gathered a handful of tools each evening to help others with the repairs to the wagons. A lifetime spent as traders had made them well used to the life on a wagon, something that few other elves were.

For his part, Sam had started spending his lunch hours assisting the healers as they tended to the sick in the nearby wagons. Heating water for bathing, calming fevers with ice and even cauterising wounds under their careful guidance. It was a welcome break from the continuous study and – as Elder Bela had pointed out – it showed him another side to the magic. A useful and constructive side. It also gave him an opening into elven society that he had previously lacked. A chance to realise that they truly accepted him. He wasn't an outsider any longer.

In fact they were accepting a lot of outsiders. There was now an entire contingent of priests of Phil the White riding with them. But there was still no shortage of people needing the services of the healers so even with them there was plenty of work to be done and so every additional hand was welcome.

Their arrival had surprised him. Not because they were humans from Fair Fields, so much as because they were priests. Normally the elves didn't like the presence of other faiths among them. They followed the Goddess, and to an extent Draco, the Father of Dragons. But those like him who followed The All Father kept their observances discrete and the shrines were few in number.

Still, they had need of the healers and the elves were a practical people.

Unfortunately his work also gave him a chance to truly know the horror of what the people of Shavarra had been through, and it rekindled his anger. Seeing the terrible injuries that many of them bore was bad enough. Hearing the grieving for missing relatives was worse. And listening to the services of the priests as they spoke the rights for those who had died as they travelled was truly awful. And still so many of their number died each day of their wounds.

He was a soldier. He had been trained from birth in the ways of the sword and then raised in the Knighthood. He had been taught the conduct of battle and war until he could recite all its many and terrible rules in his sleep. But what these people had been through was something much worse than war. It wasn't just the enemy's power or numbers that made it different; it was the way this enemy's soldiers had targeted the women and children. They had acted like rabid dogs, killing everything in sight. But no dog even so infected could be organised into an army. Nor could any dog be so deadly.

Time and time again he was told tales of how loved ones, usually the weakest, had been pounced on by the steel vermin and then torn apart in front of their families. Often it seemed the rats had avoided the soldiers, no doubt wanting an easier target, and had hunted the children instead. They had killed those still asleep in their beds, attacked the unarmed and the elderly, leapt upon the sick like wolves, and even murdered the priests and monks as they tended to the sick and dying. But it was the children who had been lost to those steel teeth that caused the greatest suffering.

For the longest time Sam had been unable to accept what he had been told. The absolute wrongness of such deeds made it impossible to believe anyone could do them, even when he read of the same horrors in the accounts of the Dragon Wars themselves. But as the days went by and he kept hearing the same tales from so many different mouths, he'd had no choice but to accept it as the truth. And that just made him angry.

It made the elves angry too. It had taken over a month for them to let their anger loose. They had initially been too busy fleeing in fear while they dealt with their grief and shock. Now though Sam was starting to hear the righteous anger coming through.

He understood it. The fear had subsided, and the grief had been dealt with which left the anger to start bubbling up from the depths. It was now boiling over like a cauldron in a fire. And in exactly the same way, it was creating a hissing, spitting cloud all over the camp, but was unable to be released against those who had committed this terrible evil. So it was striking out at everyone.

The women especially were starting to show it as they coped with their losses, and the men – even those who were used to the ways of the warrior – weren't far behind. Even worse, the children were starting to show its signs. Parents were talking constantly about their children's tantrums, screaming fits and nightmares. Many were even fighting.

As were their parents. They were travelling in overcrowded wagons and under difficult circumstances, heading for an uncertain future. It didn't take much for tempers to fray. A perceived slight, perhaps a small mishap, and the words and sometimes fists would fly. Sam knew it was only natural that the anger that they couldn't focus on the enemy was released somewhere. But that didn't make it right or easy to deal with. Especially when so many of the combatants lost control and physically had to be dragged apart lest there be more injuries or deaths.

The city guards and border patrols spent many long nights doing nothing more than breaking up fights. But often the whole caravan felt like the fire ring he'd twice held between his hands; an explosion simply waiting to happen. All that was needed was a spark.

Tyne Keep could be just such a spark Sam knew. Lord Cameral was a complete bastard, and if the situation was to his advantage he would happily murder the entire party. And right then he thought he had the advantage, and he wanted blood. More accurately he wanted gold, and lots of it, in return for the privilege of the elves wandering across his lands. In short he was charging a toll, and according to the guard who had come to see him, a large one. One gold piece for every ten elves.

Of course it was both an outrageous amount, and something the elves couldn't afford to pay even if they had that sort of wealth with them. Twenty thousand gold pieces would buy a new herd of horses, enough food to last them for many months, repairs to all the wagons, as well as enough weapons to equip an army. In short it would cover all the things that the elves needed. All the things that Cameral was determined to steal from them.

When he heard the news from the messenger, Sam realised the likely danger, and instead of relaying the information through the messenger, leapt on Tyla's back and raced for the front. He paused only long enough to grab the man's helmet which he donned even as they galloped insanely past the other wagons.

A third of a league ahead he found the wagons of the Ruling Council. The elders were sitting around a large fire preparing tea and food for Lord Cameral's party, something that seemed wrong to him. You didn't offer tea to people who had come to steal from you. And then there was the ceremony itself. The tea ceremony was a tradition that Sam had always found frustrating, being an often impatient man as Elder Bela had repeatedly told him. And when it came with blessings from the priests it was a thousand times worse. But right then it was worth all the frustration he had ever suffered, as it meant that nothing of consequence had been spoken thus far. It gave him time.

Leaving Tyla and his sword in the hands of a Council guard stationed behind the wagons, Sam grabbed the man's golden spear and vest with little more than a hurried thank you. The vest would at least cover the green of his repainted armour. He then lowered his visor and walked calmly towards the elders as if he was one of the guards himself. He even remembered to hold the oversized spear diagonally across his chest with both hands. It was a strange weapon to Sam. Guards trained in the use of spears should have shorter stabbing spears and round shields. The eight foot spear was unwieldy and without a shield the guard was vulnerable. But then the Council guards were there more for show than for any actual military reason, but adorned as he was in his newly whitened armour and vest he looked much like all the other guards. Save that was for his breadth of shoulder.

In only a few heartbeats he stood before the elders, who true to form were huddled together in a small circle discussing Lord Cameral's impossible demands. They barely even noticed the new guard come to meet them, and Sam had to quietly clear his throat a few times before they looked up.

"Yes?"

Incredibly, War Master Wyldred – who was acting as the intermediary for the war masters – hadn't realised who he was, despite the fact that he had personally brought his reworked armour to him not long before.

"Elders, it's me, Samual."

As quietly as he spoke, his coarse accent must have gotten through to the elders, and he watched several heads pop up quickly from their huddles like gophers to stare at him. Thankfully none of them were from Lord Cameral's party, who were all clustered around a group of chairs laid out for them by the fire. But then they were as usual more interested in bragging about their wealth and power than worrying about others, and so were speaking loudly, making sure the elves overheard their tales of massive armies already preparing to march. It wasn't a subtle tactic, but then neither were they, and they hoped that by it they would persuade the elves to part with more of their precious gold.

As soon as he had the elders' attention Sam began telling them what he knew. What they needed to know.

"Cameral's a short wind. He talks a good fight, but he doesn't have the numbers to back his words. His keep is run down, with perhaps five hundred men at arms in it, and maybe another two thousand across the entire province he could call on, if he truly needed to. And they would take many days to assemble and then march. He also has a problem with dire wolves which ties up his patrols. That's why he desperately wants your gold, and he believes that you have plenty of gold as well as mithril."

"His real strength is in his markets, which bring in more trade from across all of Fair Fields than any others, and in his spies, of which he is reputed to have legions. He also has some of the strongest mages around, and the reason that he's happy to walk out here and meet with you in the open is that several will be nearby, readying their most powerful magics to protect him."

That raised a few eyebrows. Among the nobles of Fair Fields Cameral was almost a legend for his paranoia, and for his flock of highly expensive wizards he kept at his beck and call. In fact it was reported that they were the reason his keep was so run down. They took all his gold. But among the elves Sam suspected, his spell casters would prove to be less impressive.

"It's to his advantage for his people to trade with you, as much of that money goes into his coffers as taxes. Any commitment you can make to him about purchasing from his markets will be well received."

"Unfortunately he's also a bully and greedy with it. If he finds weakness he will go for the throat, and by every means possible. Magic, armed force, deception, even sabotage; he will use any and all of them just to steal the people's wealth. He also will not care how many innocent people he hurts along the way. He cares nothing for anyone but himself. But if he finds strength he'll back down fast and take whatever you offer."

"The key is to make him feel vulnerable. I advise you to first look for his mages. They won't be far away though they may be hidden with spells of concealment. Then bring them back to the table and accuse them as acting as spies. While you do so point out their weakness against true elven mages, of which you have hundreds if not thousands. At least that's what you must let him believe. Without his protection he'll take anything you offer just to get out of here."

Sam felt absolutely no guilt in betraying Cameral's self-serving nature to the elves. Once, as the son of the king of these very lands he might have, though as a knight of Hanor he probably wouldn't. Knights protected the people, and Cameral was every bit as bad as the rest of the nobles. But he trusted the elves to do the right thing, and he'd never liked this particular lord. He had a barbaric sense of justice that he inflicted upon his subjects, and a crude sense of humour with which he regaled the other nobles, usually while stabbing them in the back through the actions of his agents.

It was a strange thing to have to admit, but while he found the elven system of rule frustrating and confusing, of the two dozen or so fiefdoms, baronies and principalities that comprised Fair Fields, he could think of none that were fairer to their people than them. Nor any that as a commoner he would find easier to live under. But that could be because of the elves themselves rather than their strange and convoluted system of governance. They were an inherently decent people, little concerned with things like wealth or power. Instead, they seemed to have a driving need to help one another. It was almost as though they were a large family rather than an entire people.

His message given, Sam backed up a dozen or so paces and stood guard by one of the wagons, exactly as another eight or so were doing, trying not to look out of place, and awaiting any sign he might be wanted. Despite the fact that the guards seemed to do very little most of the time, it wasn't easy. They had to stand stiffly to attention for many long hours while the elders and the lords spoke, remembering to always keep their spear properly positioned, and hope they didn't cramp up.

Still, it had its rewards. For Sam at least. Because while standing there he was able to listen to the Lord's account of what had gone on in Fall Keep just a few short weeks before. The elders claiming their usual curiosity, asked him about it at length. That didn't surprise Sam as he knew the elders were still a little concerned about the brevity of his report back to them as to what he'd done there. However, Lord Cameral was more than willing to oblige.

His extensive network of spies meant he had a very accurate picture of the night's events. The only thing he had wrong was that he believed that Sam and Harmion Fallbright had acted together, and that once Harmion had fallen, Sam had apparently fled. Though why someone who could ring an entire keep with an eighty foot high wall of fire for over a week would flee, wasn't clear. Presumably whoever his agents had bribed for information had been unwilling to admit that Sam alone had had them all at his mercy. But at least none of the keep's soldiers had died, which was a relief to Sam as he'd never really considered them to be enemies, and surely a relief to the elders. It had taken some three days to chip the last of the soldiers out of the stone floors into which they had sunk and a few were still in care.

Of more interest to Sam, was what else the lord knew or believed. Things like how the fight had gone, and the price of treachery being paid by the rest of the Fallbright House. For a start his brother had cheated, using a poisoned dart someone had apparently managed to smuggle in. Trust Heri to cheat in a matter of honour, was Sam's first thought when he heard of it. It was almost Heri's only talent. Certainly it was his greatest. But surprisingly for once Sam couldn't accuse him of having won unfairly as he hadn't been the only one to cheat. Harmion had coated the tip of his sword with dragon bile, and Heri's armour had begun to rot and fall off him from the very first blow. It had actually been a fair fight in the end. The most cunning rat had won.

After the battle Heri had quickly placed the entire blame on the Fallbright House and had demanded recompense. Thus, as well as burying a son and brother, the family were paying for the repairs to Fall Keep. The bill was so large it was rumoured that the Fallbrights would have to sell large tracts of arable land, and their finest herds to pay it. And that was before they even began to look at the punitive damages which Heri was still adding up. Yet none of that would have hurt a fraction as much as having to publicly declare their dead son a traitor, as Heri had demanded of them. They were not a nice family, but they still cared for their kin.

Sam on the other hand had been publicly declared as a

traitor to Fair Fields by Heri himself, something he would no doubt have enjoyed immensely. A sizeable reward had also been placed on his head. Sam didn't think it was any coincidence that Lord Cameral was asking for twenty thousand gold pieces, a sum that matched exactly the price on his head. No doubt that was the real reason the Lord was so eager to discuss the matter. He knew Sam was half elven, and probably that his mother had come from Shavarra. Putting two and two together, he was trying to work out if Sam might be among them. If so he presumably guessed that that the elves might hand Sam over in lieu of paying the twenty thousand gold pieces, so that Lord Cameral could then claim those reward monies for himself. Of course he didn't stand a chance of being paid the reward, and even he should have understood that.

Heri had put out the reward in all likelihood simply to save face. Branding Sam as a dangerous criminal was simply a cover for his own crimes. To not do so would be a tacit admission of his own guilt, or worse his fear. A king could not show fear. But he had no intention of actually hunting Sam down. He would be terrified by the thought that his people might actually find him. That's why the reward was only offered to Heri's personal guards; he offered it as a way to atone for their failure in Heri's own words. Cameral presumably had a way to hold Sam and then claim the reward for himself, presumably while ingratiating himself to Heri and at the same time finding a soft spot in his back to stick his dagger in.

The one thing Sam was certain of was that none of those guards were ever going to be free to do any bounty hunting. Heri wouldn't allow it. And since all of them had seen him in action, even if they did become free one day, they weren't likely to take up the offer anyway. Nor, if they truly had been imprisoned by his fire wall for more than a week, would any of the soldiers from the keep. And Heri's assassins for much the same reasons, had all been recalled. Heri had at last learned fear.

Cameral though had a different lesson to learn. Disappointment.

The elders, in keeping with their people's great love of honesty and sophistry, told Lord Cameral that there were at least two hundred thousand elves in their caravan, and it was quite possible that Sam could be among them. He was welcome to search, provided he didn't delay their progress or upset any elves. The people were upset and it was unclear how much more strife they could endure before something gave, and then the consequences could be dire.

That set Cameral's teeth grinding away in anger. He'd obviously hoped that they would simply bring Sam out to him to be led away. Clearly they weren't so inclined. That meant if the Lord was to find Sam he had to search through the caravans, and hope that his actions didn't cause a riot. All his soldiers put together couldn't restrain such a large group of angry elves and he knew it. Yet he had to at least appear cordial. His face flushed with anger as he continued his tale but he said nothing untoward.

In the weeks that had followed Harmion's death, Heri had raised the taxes and demanded new measures from his lords to show their loyalty. Primarily they included having one child from each of the noble families to remain in Fall Keep at all times. Heri apparently, had decided to take hostages. Faced with a ruined keep, and one example of brazen treachery, Heri had chosen to reign in his errant lords by any means necessary.

To Cameral it was merely a way of retaining power, even though one of his own kin was also now a hostage. Sam though saw it as a sign of true evil, as Heri was now using the same weapon he had previously levelled against him. If he had said it once he had said it a thousand times; Heri had all the cunning of a rat in a dung heap, and even fewer morals.

Cameral's news made Sam sad as well as angry. Sad not only for the people who would now suffer, but also for his brother who it seemed still had learned nothing of right and wrong. There seemed little hope that he would ever become a man their father might be proud of. And while those he would be holding as hostages might for the most part be no better than him, there would be some who were entirely innocent. Meanwhile the taxes Sam could guess weren't going to be used to repair the throne or the castle. Instead the money would be used to bolster his army.

It was another sure sign of a paranoid king, which was exactly how Cameral saw it as well. What neither he nor Heri could seem to understand was that it would be the people who would suffer for that paranoia, as they would have to work ever longer hours to pay those taxes, and then would no doubt be killed when hostilities broke out. A paranoid king taking hostages? That had to end badly.

Meanwhile the Fallbrights, openly angry at the loss of their youngest son, were actively talking about sedition from Fair Fields. It was just talk though; angry words which would never become actions. They didn't have the resources to back such an act. Their lands were fertile, and they had some very fine herds of both horses and cattle, but they had no metal. Their lands were not blessed with any mines other than a few clay pits. Thus they would have to buy steel, weapons and armour if they wanted to fight, and their few market places weren't popular with outside traders because of the high fees they charged for setting up a stall.

Heri's rule was safe for the moment and their bluster was mainly simple anger – and perhaps a hope of stirring up some of the other lords against him. But while his rule was secure for the moment, Heri's life wasn't so safe.

Though he doubtless had had no choice and everyone knew it, when Heri had killed Harmion he had created an enemy for life out of his family. An enemy that would use whatever means they had at their disposal to kill him. They might not be able to go to war with the entire kingdom, but they could happily weave a trail of chaos and anger through the entire court, and they would. They could spread rumour and gossip, leaving his subjects disenchanted with him, undermine his rule in a thousand ways and even belittle him discretely. Likewise they could hire agents and assassins to destroy Heri's achievements and if possible kill him. Meanwhile a court that was already angry at Heri for holding their kin hostages would be more than a little receptive to their actions.

His brother would not sleep easy for many years to come, and when he tried to enforce his will he might well find it challenged by the various nobles. His only solution would be royal decree, which basically left every lord with the choice of either obedience or outright betrayal and war. But Heri had neither the soldiers nor the wealth to enforce his every command. No more could he use the hostages. The moment he did, war would ensue. They were of value only while they were kept safe. He would have to pick and choose those commands he really wanted followed. He would also have to surround himself with guards and pray that the various families didn't think of a way through them.

The kingdom of course would be the real loser, as Heri's decisions – both the good and the bad – were stymied. Anarchy would ensue as each province went its own way, even if in name they remained loyal. And no doubt the numbers of peasants conscripted for the guards would double or triple as Heri found himself an outsider in his own realm. His use of hostages would prevent the other houses from going to war with him, but it would not guarantee their loyalty. If anything it would do the very opposite as they plotted against him behind closed doors. Yet Heri had bound himself to that course of action. If he released the hostages he would look weak. If he harmed – or worse, killed them – open rebellion would result. If he continued as he was, he would have no willing support in the kingdom, but would remain king until he was finally assassinated.

In such a realm of course, Cameral fancied his prospects. His army might be small, but his spies and wizards gave him a huge advantage. He could manipulate the other houses with ease, sow his own brand of discord, and profit greatly. In time, if he could arrange things just right, Cameral could even challenge for the throne. And unlike Sam's brother, Cameral was not a complete coward. Evil and manipulative certainly, but he would fight when he had to or when the odds were in his favour.

Today however he suddenly found his luck to be in short supply.

The arrival of a group of guards with five human wizards in their midst broke Cameral's tale in mid-stream, and he like the rest turned to see his servants taken as prisoners. It was a bad sight for the lord. His skin turned deathly white and for a while he seemed to stop breathing. Sam wondered briefly if he was going to collapse and drop dead on the spot. But in time he regained his composure, and much of the rest of the meeting went as planned. Just not as the lord had planned.

Cameral quickly explained that they were his servants whom he had left behind as he did not wish to cause a problem for the elves by bringing such powerful wizards with him to a meeting. All of the elders promptly, in what had to be a rehearsed move, laughed politely as they tried to explain that his wizards were surely no more than students. Even Samual who had all but levelled a keep and overcome an entire army alone, was but a student by comparison, though they looked forward to receiving him one day in their halls of magic, and even training him.

If Cameral had gone white already, he lightened a few more shades at their well-chosen words, while it was his wizards' turn to whiten. They did not like being called students, though with arrows at their throats and their magic all but quenched, they could say or do little.

One of them – Master Silden as he called himself – was a master of fire. In fact Sam recognised him as one of his first teachers. Unfortunately the wizard made the mistake of beginning to draw his fire magic. He had always been a proud man, too proud though to be a good teacher. Naturally he had no chance as he fainted dead away a heartbeat later. In the evening Sam knew, he would awaken and no doubt scream down the castle in his anger. But he wouldn't return. He wasn't completely stupid.

Naturally the elders suggested he was surely suffering from an illness. Perhaps some form of food poisoning? Of course everyone knew the truth; that he had tried to draw fire and had been taken out in a heartbeat by another mage. But that didn't need to be said. The look of terror on the lord's face was enough.

It was about then that Cameral generously offered to forgo his tariff as a measure of concern for their plight, if the elves promised to trade at his markets, something they were already set on doing, and the atmosphere lightened considerably.

After that it took an almost indecently short time for the meeting to finish up as the lord was in a hurry to leave. In fact as he and his people mounted up, it was apparent that they would have preferred to have galloped madly away rather than trotted. Only the intense need to show no fear and always seem in control held Cameral back.

His wizards on the other hand were in no hurry to leave with him. They could already feel the days, weeks or even months of abuse which he would no doubt give them as they tried to explain their failure. Though he wouldn't dare fire them – for he couldn't allow them to go to his rivals and share his secrets – their salaries were likely to be cut as he would use the extra monies to try and find even stronger spell casters to defend himself. As if there were such creatures among his people.

One thing was certain though; he would never again think to challenge the magic of the elves with his own spell casters. Nor was he going to cause them any more trouble.

As Cameral rode off hurriedly, Sam let a smile creep over his face. It had been a good day.

Chapter Fourteen.

It was a bad day for Heri. He was sitting in his nearly empty throne room, enjoying the comfort of his newly restored seat for what he feared might be the last time. Outside he could hear the sounds of fighting coming from the rest of the keep as his own soldiers killed one another in their fear.

And of course listening to the endless reports of the first of his enemy's armies approaching as aides kept rushing in and out with news. The prince's army was almost close enough to begin setting a siege. The arrival of his spymaster Tommas, Heri suspected was only going to bring more bad news.

"Highness." The spymaster looked worried as he approached Heri. Professionally concerned would perhaps be a more flattering term, but frightened might be more accurate. "Your enemies are closing in on the keep, and as you know, it's in no state to hold against them. We need to consider our tactics. Strategy. An alliance maybe."

"An alliance?" Heri wasn't fooled by Tommas' silken words. Even as the man walked the last few steps down the centre aisle of his throne room, Heri could tell that the man was here to tell him lies. To deceive him in some way. And maybe to do more than that. Why else would he be flanked by a pair of soldiers as he approached him?

"With Prince Venti. It's his army that leads this first assault, and he is the strongest of the nobles. He is the one most likely to take the throne. But it will not be easy for him to keep. Some words from you, an alliance of strengths and armies, and his ascension would be assured. Without that he would not be strong enough to fight off all the others alone. Not by himself. He could be convinced of your value. He could let you remain as an ally. With your forces and his, the others could not stand against you." Tommas came to a halt with the two guards, ten feet from throne.

Meanwhile Heri noticed that the guards at the door were looking nervous. And not because of any threat from without. They understood that the threat was within. They knew something serious was about to happen.

"My value? And what would that be Tommas?" Heri stared angrily at the man as he wrapped his fingers around the cords attached to the arms of the throne. It was unfair, but it seemed he had just run out of spymasters. The man had turned on him. He just didn't know how exactly. Yet.

"As Regent perhaps. You could inaugurate the new king. Support his rule." Tommas was sweating a little as he said it. His voice not quite as steady as it normally was.

"Regent in name only. A figurehead. Is that what you're suggesting Tommas?"

Heri was angry that the man had even suggested the idea to him. But then he guessed Tommas hadn't come up with the idea. He was just using it as an excuse to approach him. The three of them had something planned, and it wasn't something good for him. The chances were that they planned to use him as a hostage. Something to bargain with when the Prince's army came marching into the keep.

"That seems harsh Highness. And you know you cannot remain here as you are. You will be hung. You need an alliance."

"So you're now my political and strategic adviser?" Heri raised an eyebrow in quiet disbelief. But in truth the man almost was. When Heri's major-domo had fled and his generals couldn't be found, it seemed he had only his spymaster left. Now it seemed he wouldn't have him much longer either.

"I wouldn't presume Highness." The spymaster bowed.

"And so you wouldn't presume to have a different opinion if I said no?"

"Of course not Highness." Tommas managed one of the most insincere smiles Heri had ever seen. The man was no performer. Not even a street performer from the poorer districts.

"Good. Then that is my answer Tommas. You may leave and have this proclaimed from the city streets. There will be no dealing with traitors!"

"Of course Highness." Tommas bowed low. "But there is just one thing. A document. Might I show you it?"

It wasn't a document Heri knew as he watched his spymaster reach into his coat for something. Or if it was it had nothing to do with the deal he claimed he was making. It was something else. Something dangerous. Heri's throat suddenly became dry. This was the moment when his spymaster was about to betray him.

"No!"

"Highness?"

Everything happened in a blur after that. The spymaster managed to sound surprised, but that didn't stop him continuing to pull out whatever it was he had under his jacket. The soldiers with him lowered their weapons as they prepared to attack. And Heri pulled up the two strings in his hands.

A heartbeat later at most there was a massive explosion as

the spymaster and his two soldiers disappeared in a cloud of cannon shot and smoke. The soldiers at the entrance to the throne room were hit by it too, and collapsed to the floor. Whatever plans Tommas had had died with him.

No doubt he had intended to capture Heri and hand him over to whoever first came through the keep's walls. He would do whatever it took to save his skin. Now though Tommas would have to make a deal with the All Father. Heri stared at all that remained of his spymaster and the two soldiers who had stood beside him. A gigantic smear of blood and three indistinguishable lumps of flesh. He had fired from a mere ten feet away, and the cannon apparently didn't leave much behind at that distance.

In the distance Heri could also see the remaining parts of the two soldiers who had guarded the door. Maybe they had been innocent of the crime – Heri didn't know. The cannon however did not take account of guilt or innocence. They destroyed everything alike. He was suddenly glad he'd had a new cannon throne built before everything else. It was literally the seat of his power after all. And he felt vulnerable in court surrounded by his enemies.

Sounds soon intruded on his still ringing ears and he watched as more soldiers dashed into the throne room, took a look at the carnage, and then grabbed the door handles and pulled them shut as they stepped back. Moments later he heard the thunk of a heavy beam as they swung it into place, ostensibly locking him in It was clear his rule had come to an end. His loyal soldiers had just deserted him and intended to leave him locked up in the throne room until the next person came to claim it.

"To the underworld with all of you Alder loving swine!" Heri yelled at his traitorous soldiers, angrily. He then followed it up with a few more obscenities. Whether they even heard him through the heavy wooden doors he didn't know. And it wouldn't have really mattered if they had. Eventually he gave up shouting at them. There was no point.

After that, he sat for a while in silence on his newly rebuilt throne, grinding his teeth in fury. And despite knowing it was pointless, every so often he swore out loud, cursing all of the worthless soldiers in the name of Alder, the god of mischief. Truly he thought, this had to be the work of the divine pest. And not just this final betrayal either. All of it. It had all gone so wrong, and so very quickly. Too wrong and too quickly to be a mere mortals' doing.

Forty one days! That was all it had taken. But it had always been coming he guessed. From the moment Samual had taken his hand and destroyed half the keep he had been doomed. Worse than that he had forced him to kneel before him. He had been shown to be weak. And there was no place for weak kings in Fair Fields.

Now everything he had dreamed of – everything he had grasped and made his own – was about to be taken away from him, and he hated that. Seven years of his life – gone! Two as the King in waiting while his mother acted as regent. Five as King Heri. All gone. He hated that. He hated that there was nothing he could do about it. But most of all he hated his half-brother for causing it. Why couldn't he just bloody die!

All his life Samual had been the favoured son. The apple of their father's eye. And he had lived up to that position by doing everything his father had asked of him. He had become a knight of Hanor. He had inherited his mother's magic and studied diligently. Samual had spent his whole life being the perfect son, and there was no room left over for a second son in their father's life, even if he was legitimate. Heri might as well have never been born.

Of course Heri had tried to do those things too, but he simply wasn't able. He didn't have the same natural skill with the blade and he had no magic as did his older brother. He couldn't seem to make people like him the way Samual did though he had tried by affecting a shortened name and smiling genially. And just to add insult to injury Samual was tall and powerfully built. The ladies had swooned whenever he walked by. Heri had to settle for being quick and clever. By the gods how he hated Samual!

Taking his whore and locking her away had been a huge satisfaction for Heri. Even if she wouldn't lie down with him, just the knowledge that his brother didn't have her had been pure joy. But now Samual had taken her back. He had stolen the whore from him and had humbled him publicly. He had then taken his hand as well, leaving him with a stump where he once had fingers. He had made him a cripple. And now he had robbed him of his throne.

"May the All Father curse your worm infested hide!" Heri cursed Samual angrily. The sounds of battle outside the throne room were getting closer all the time and Heri knew his time was short. But there should always be time to curse his half-brother.

He knew he had to leave and that time was running out. Soon his enemies would be upon him, and then it would be too late to run. And yet he couldn't quite leave yet.

It was all Samual's fault!

That bastard half-brother of his had brought the keep to its knees. He'd terrified the people by building a wall of fire eighty feet tall which had surrounded the keep and the entire city for seven long days. The sight had frightened the great unwashed. In fact there had been rioting in the streets for days. Samual had also embarrassed his army. He'd made them look like children playing with sticks as he had simply rode in, picked up his whore and attacked the king. He'd destroyed the keep and then calmly ridden out, taking sixty thoroughbred horses with him! That last had truly hurt. The slap to his face had been every bit as terrible as if Samual had used his hand.

His hand! Just the thought reminded Heri once more of his injuries, and the pain and suffering Samual had caused him. The missing fingers hurt all the time as if they were actually there. It felt like the torturer was pulling them off with his ice-cold pliers. And it was his leading hand too that Samual had lopped off. He couldn't draw a sword or hold a pen. Worst of all, every time he raised his hand to give a command the ruin of his flesh was made visible for all to see. Everyone knew he had been disciplined by his older brother. Beaten as easily as if he had been a baby. He had been thrashed for disobedience. Samual hadn't even done him the courtesy of killing him. Instead he had left Heri behind like unwanted refuse dumped on the side of the trail. He had been made the laughing stock of his realm.

In that one act Heri had lost all the respect of his subjects. No longer had he been the king. Instead he was just the naughty child thrashed in public by his older brother. His name was a joke on the lying lips of a thousand bards in a thousand inns across the realm. His reputation something the peasants joked about in the streets. King Heri the Bold had become Heri the Weak.

There had of course been only one thing he could do in the face of such gall; impose his authority. And he had done it. Guards in the streets of all the towns had been increased. Crimes had been punished speedily and without mercy. Taxes had been raised and the numbers of collectors doubled. Anyone openly speaking against him – even in jest – had been thrown in the dungeons, which were now full to bursting. The people had to know fear at his hand. They had to know he was their king. Soldiers, all of those who had been there at his defeat, had been flogged in the courtyard in front of the crowds, and then beheaded. Their heads had been stuck on polls along with all the others who in the past had failed him. Heri didn't tolerate failure.

As for the nobles who were all forever scheming, plotting and conspiring against him, he had demanded a price of blood from them all. He had required their nearest and dearest as "guests" in the keep. It was a strategy he'd considered before but had never risked because of the likely outcry. But it was too late to worry about that when he had become a joke.

He had been harsh and brutal. He had demanded fealty and if it wasn't given quickly enough he had harshly punished anyone who hadn't lived up to his standards. And it had seemed to be working.

But then everything had gone wrong again, and all in the space of a single morning. Assassins had struck and all his "guests" had been slaughtered. Who had paid them to act he didn't know though he suspected they were in the pay of the Fallbrights.

That was the end of course. He'd known it the instant his major-domo had brought him the news, and he'd wanted to kill the man on the spot just for speaking the words. What use were dead guests save of course as motivation to kill those who had killed them?

The noble houses had all taken the news badly. Their favoured sons and daughters had all been killed, butchered under the king's nose if not by the king's hand. They were angry. More than that, they were desperate that no other kin should ever be his guests. If their own kin could not be kept safe in the keep even when they were the king's "guests", then how could they ever trust him again? Especially with more of their precious children. And that was assuming they didn't think Heri had killed them himself. They could certainly never again allow their sons and daughters to be held by him. Heri knew that that one act had united all the lords against him. They had decided that he had to go and they weren't considering sending him off to another realm. Unless it was the realm of the dead.

So war had been called and the battle drums had started their relentless beat within days. A dozen armies from a dozen fiefdoms had been hastily assembled, and they now all marched on Fall Keep, proclaiming his coming defeat. A keep that thanks to his poxy, bastard brother, had no walls. Without them his army could not mount a solid defence, least of all against twelve armies, and his soldiers weren't as loyal as they had once been. Apparently seeing their comrades in arms executed had gone down badly. Watching a wizard simply wander through their defences untroubled had also been poorly received. And knowing that a dozen armies were now marching on them while they had no walls to protect them; that had been the final spike in his crypt.

They had deserted. Run away like stinking little cowards, and taken half the people with them. Those who remained in the keep were either too stupid to run, well hidden, or likely to join his enemies even as they proclaimed their loyalty to him. Though they went through the motions of fighting the few renegades and spies who had started the war early, they were in truth paying lip service to him while they planned out what their next move should be in order to survive. Heri had no doubt they would save their skins by handing the enemy his.

Briefly Heri considered the toys in his sanctum. His most powerful weapon, the sun burst, could only be used once, and only on a single target. Activating it would also cause the user's death. Because there was no way that whoever activated it could get away before it exploded. The next weapon – the bronze golems the azure stone conjured – were slow and stupid. They were also few in number and would not be effective against an army. As for the blade of the dark assassin, it too would work only on one enemy at a time and only from a short distance. He would be lucky to kill more than two or three with it. Still, it might be a good toy to take with him.

But in the end it was his canon that had proved the most useful. And there was perhaps a lesson for him in that. The magical would not save him.

It seemed that neither his spymaster nor the soldiers who had locked him in had realised that the base of Heri's throne, a pair of miniature bronze cannon, were kept loaded at all times while he sat and heard his subjects. And even if the new throne hadn't been completely finished, they had been. Clearly Tommas had never been a disciple of the Red God. He did not think like a soldier.

No doubt the spymaster had thought the canon were ornamental. But then he'd also never informed him that the Fallbrights were planning to slaughter his hostages. He hadn't proved to be much of a spymaster in the end.

Augrim would die soon too, though he didn't know it yet. Sand scorpion venom took days to act when ingested. But it would not fail. Not like his pet wizard had. Augrim had spoken all the right words. But he too had lied to Heri's face and then fled with everyone else. No doubt he planned to reveal any and all of Heri's secrets to his enemies if it would work in his favour. He might even tell them about Heri's sanctum and the ancient magical treasures it contained. Augrim could see the writing on the wall. Unfortunately for him, Heri had seen his treachery coming, and made certain the wizard enjoyed a good last meal. And though Augrim had taken the precaution of using a taster as he did for all his meals, that had not been enough. The taster was now slowly dying as well.

So what did he do now?

He could perhaps fight his way out. He could reload the

cannon and blast the doors down. But that would be suicide. He was not about to die no matter how gloriously. That was Samual's noble dream. Heri wanted to live. And then to hurt those who had hurt him. To make them bleed.

Besides, he didn't know who among those fighting outside the throne room he could trust. His thought was that it would be very few of them.

He knew that outside the huge double doors leading to the throne room there would be armed men waging pitched battles. That was already the case throughout the rest of the keep and the citadel beyond. They people were fighting, but more out of confusion as to who was on whose side than to protect him. Some he thought would still try to protect him, though there were precious few left. Some would be waiting outside the doors to either kill him or hand him over to his enemies. Most though were probably just waiting to surrender and save their worthless hides. And he had no idea which of them was which.

What he did know was that when those double doors swung open next, it would not be a good omen for him. And as the guards had heard the cannon roar, they knew he was armed. His enemies would be prepared.

It would be best to leave before then. And he had to leave.

He didn't want to. Heri loved being king. He loved the power, and he loved seeing those others who were also powerful bow before him. He loved making them do his bidding. And he loved watching them suffer under his reign. Especially those who defied him. He loved sitting on his throne and commanding them all. That was why the first thing he'd had rebuilt after Samual's attack had been the cannon throne. But he loved living more than all of those things.

It was time.

Reluctantly Heri got to his feet, said goodbye to his newly rebuilt throne for the last time, and stuffed his crown and new sceptre into a makeshift ermine sack he constructed from the furs draping his throne. Gold was gold after all. Then he walked around to the rear of the dais on which his throne sat. Heri lifted the concealed lever that opened the stone trapdoor leading down to the floor below and hoisted it up with an effort. He'd never been the strongest – strength was for soldiers and soldiers were fools – but even with only one and a half hands he managed it.

After that it was just a short distance down the ladder after letting the trapdoor fall shut behind him, until he was safe in the secret passageway. A passageway that no one knew about since he'd had the artisan who designed it and all his craftsmen killed once the job was complete. There was no point in letting them live when they knew about his escape tunnel. Their work had been done.

It was dark and dirty of course – no one knew of the passageway so no one cleaned it – but he carried a small tinder with him to light the waiting torches that were hanging from the wall on both sides of the ladder, and soon he had enough light to see by. And all he really needed was enough light to be able to walk along the passageway and find the stairs at the far end. They in turn would take him down to an underground tunnel which would take him right out of the keep and to the public stables where he hoped to find a horse.

But before then he decided, he had some scores to settle with his loyal subjects. For his soldiers who had turned their backs on him. For his servants who had run away. And for the noble houses marching on the keep at this moment, planning to steal his throne and kill him. They would get nothing. No throne, no title and no keep. If he couldn't have them then no one could.

When he'd had the underground tunnel carved out, he'd made some alterations to the keep's foundations as well, and now fifty barrels of gunpowder were lashed to the joists and columns, with a long fuse leading from the base of the staircase to them. Just in case something like this happened. He had always intended that no one would take the throne from him. Or that if they did they wouldn't live long enough to enjoy it. And wasn't he just so lucky as to have a flaming torch in his hands!

He hesitated though, just for a moment as he weighed up his alternatives. If he didn't light the fuse his choices became two – running and hiding. He could flee the city – but he would be hunted and might well be caught. Or he could try hiding out in his sanctum with all his treasures. But even assuming he could survive down there, how long would he have to hide in it? Weeks? Months? Years? And of course he would still be hunted. And there would be the added risk that to get to it he'd have to exit this tunnel through the stables, then rush around to the gardeners' hall and down through the secret tunnel to his sanctum. He could be seen.

Of course if he did light the fuse it would mean he couldn't try hiding in his private sanctum. It would probably survive the blast as it was underground and some distance from the castle. But there was no certainty that it would, and Heri didn't want to be buried alive underground. And the gardeners' hall might well be destroyed making it impossible to get in and out. He would have to run. But he would also be dead as far as anyone knew, killed in the same blast that destroyed the keep. No one hunted dead men.

Destroying the keep was his safest option. And in the end that was what mattered.

Decision made Heri pulled loose the stone that hid the end of the fuse, and saw his prize in front of him. It took less than a heartbeat to set the fuse alight, and then he watched the pinpoint of flame and smoke slowly travelling away from him into the darkness beyond the stone wall. It was a good sight to see, knowing that it would destroy his enemy's prize and punish his disloyal soldiers, as well as rob his enemies of their victory. It would also cover his escape. He wished he could have watched it for longer. But to do that would end in his being crushed alive when the keep collapsed. The sight, no matter how cheery, wasn't worth that.

Instead of staying he hurried down the underground passageway until he reached the fake stone wall at the end, which led to the stables. A simple tug on the lever and the trap door opened, and he was in the stables themselves. Looking around he saw that there was only a stable boy there to see him. He looked surprised, the more so when Heri threw a knife at him which even with his modest skill found his middle. He might not be good with a sword, but long ago he'd trained himself in using a knife with either hand. It was a useful weapon and easily concealed.

The boy cried out and fell to the ground clutching at his belly, blood flowing over the straw and dirt. And then he lay there crying some more. Heri ignored his pleas for help. The boy would die now or when the keep exploded. It didn't matter what killed him. What mattered was that Heri lived. Instead he helped himself to a working man's robe that had conveniently been left hanging on one of the stalls, and a horse, a good riding mare. After that it was simply a matter of riding out of the remains of his gate, looking for all the world as if he was simply another peasant leaving the citadel. In the end he need not have even bothered wearing the soiled garment. There was no one patrolling the remains of the gate anyway. But he kept it on just in case.

Heri was at least five hundred yards outside of the citadel walls and heading down the road, when he finally heard the sound he'd been waiting for. It was the sudden roar of thunder in the ground that told him the gunpowder had ignited.

Heri looked back to see a glorious explosion of orange fire bursting loose from the very heart of the keep; a fireball ascending for the heavens themselves, and lighting the entire sky for as far as he could see. Pieces of burning debris sprayed out in all directions, raining a fiery death down on any of his enemies who had survived the initial blast. Heri smiled at the sight, knowing his work was done. Briefly he wondered if he should make an offering at the temple. Though he did not care for the gods or their priests, he had always found it appropriate that he should follow only the All Father. The king of the gods. And now he had proven himself the king of kings. The All Father if he even looked on as the priests claimed he did, should be proud of him.

Meanwhile those cursed nobles riding on Fall Keep would get nothing now. All their planning and scheming had been rendered worthless. All his disloyal guards and servants would meet their end in flames and falling rubble. Better still, everyone would hopefully believe him dead, buried in the remains of the keep with the others. It would be a long time if at all before they thought to send hunters after him. It gave him the time to make his escape.

Of course, he eventually realised, the explosion had probably killed his mother as well. Locked away in her cell in the west tower she had never stood a chance. Not when he could see that the tower was now gone along with most of the rest of the keep. But he felt no loss. She too had betrayed him as she had tried to make his throne hers. It hadn't worked. She had taught him everything she knew of politics and strategy and he had taken those lessons to heart. He had seen through to the truth of her ambition. She wanted to rule through him, and in time through his children. In any case if he had been able to take her with him she would only have slowed him down. A quick death was a good end for her.

In time, once the roar of the explosions had died away and

the smoke had thinned, Heri could see the keep as it had become. A mound of rubble surely fifty feet high peeking over the remains of the wall his brother had destroyed, burning brightly and sending a huge plume of dark smoke rising into the sky. On the ground he could see people running. He thought he could just make out their screams and cries as they carried buckets of water to douse the flames. As busy as they were they would have no time to look around and spot him riding away. It was a good sight.

Unfortunately, judging from the flames leaping not just from the mountain of rubble that had once been the keep, but also from behind it, the city was also burning. That he hadn't wanted. If the city burnt and the people left, who did he have left to rule? But he supposed they would put the fires out in time and he would rule them again one day.

It was just a shame he couldn't go back and empty out his sanctum. Gather together some useful relics for the ride. But for all he knew it was buried. And he didn't want to be seen by anyone trying to enter it. Fleeing had to be his choice for the moment. It would be months before he could return to the city in safety.

Heri turned back, and with a gentle flick of the reigns set his horse to trotting on down the road, away from the dead and dying. Away from Venti's approaching army too. Now he had only one more thing to do before he could begin his new life with the gold in his saddlebags. Before he could put in place his strategy to reclaim the throne.

He had a miserable worm of a bastard half-brother to kill. Before that though he had to make him suffer for what he had done. Samual would suffer as no man had ever suffered before. It would not be easy, but he knew there was a way. There had always been a way. The assassins had failed because they had attacked him directly. They hadn't guessed he was such a powerful wizard. The ease with which Samual had shrugged off those attacks and his subsequent show of strength forty one days ago showed the folly of that approach. But Heri knew exactly what Samual was, and he knew how to defeat magic as well as swordsmanship. He also knew Samual's greatest weakness. After all, he'd kept her locked away in his dungeon for five years. It was time to make use of her again.

Heri chuckled a little as he rode away from the keep, already savouring the feel of the dagger that he would stick in Samual's back, the slipperiness of his warm blood running through his fingers, and the sound of him gasping his last. He kicked the horse's flanks to get her to move a little faster. Samual had already lived for far too long; it was well past time that he put him in the ground. And he had a fair idea where his brother could be found. He even knew where to go to find what he would need to do the job.

His spies had in the end been of some use. Maybe one day, when he got his kingdom back, he would rehire a few of them. Those that still lived. And of course the assassins. There were any number of noble hearts that had to be pierced or poisoned. And he couldn't wait to get started.

Chapter Fifteen.

"Have you heard of the shade faun?"

Sam shook his head carefully as he concentrated on the shape of the ice castle. It was tricky using fire magic to build ice structures, more so than using earth magic to build earth structures. Because instead of adding ice to create a wall or a roof, you had to remove all the fire from an area and then let the water in the air freeze to form the structures. Every fire wizard could do it, but it required immense control to do it well. And he wasn't building a simple structure like a bridge. He was shaping a castle out of ice. Just then he was shaping the inner walls along with outer walls, floors and ceilings. But even that wasn't enough for Master Lavellin. He'd given him more commands. Like the fact that the entire structure had to be taller than he was and yet every wall within it could be no thicker than a sheet of paper Doing it while standing out in the intense heat of the sun didn't make it any easier. But still the castle was coming together and Sam was actually quite proud of the intricate construction.

He was slowly learning the more varied and useful aspects of his talent, while practising his control and visualisation under Master Lavellin's tutelage. And though the Elder's question had surprised him he'd half expected him to make some remark or raise a question just to test his control as he held the complex shapes together. He was good at doing just that. But shade faun? The term was actually vaguely familiar, though Sam couldn't quite place it.

"They're close cousins to us. So close in fact, that some say they are merely a different tribe of our people. But where we have tanned skin and gold or silver hair, they have dark hair and skin that merges well with that of the darkened forest. Neither dark brown nor green, but rather a strange mixture of both, and blotched as though a child had thrown paint on them."

"Shadelings?"

The Elder's description matched that of the fabled deep forest people perfectly, especially his statement about the skin which blended so well into the forest. The names were similar as well.

Shadelings were creatures or people from among the oldest legends Fair Fields. But they had not been seen by any in the realm in living memory. In fact the legends were so old that whether they had ever truly existed had become a cause for debate. What was certain was that if they did exist, the fact that they didn't mix with the other races suggested they weren't friendly, and it was a foolish man who would venture too far into the lands they were said to call home. Whether it was because there were shadelings there or not he didn't know. He only knew that they were dangerous.

"If you like. Others also call them dark elves, tree lords and forest wraiths. But whatever you call them they are hardly ever seen, and when they are, few if any survive to tell of them."

There was no surprise in that for Sam. The few reports they had of them from the occasional surviving rangers and explorers who ventured into their forests long ago, told of arrows coming out of nowhere, blood curdling screams and growls, and then savage people suddenly appearing and then vanishing into thin air. But even those who had given the reports couldn't swear to exactly what they'd seen.

"So why are you asking me about them Elder?" Especially when it was still his magic training time, and the elders were always so particular to make sure he studied and trained hard.

Of course there was one possible explanation, though it didn't make any sense. That the shadelings had something to do with the machina. Except that such magic combined with technology would be an anathema to them. According to the legends they worshipped trees and hated all forms of technology with a passion like that of the dryads. But unlike them, they were violent in their rejection of all things technological, not to mention the people who used such devices. Still, he had to ask that too.

"In a strange way, perhaps they are connected."

"With what? The machina?" That had to stand as one of Master Lavellin's most cryptic remarks to date Sam thought. And there had been a lot of them already.

"Perhaps. But rather we think that they know something about the attack."

"Why? How? And what?"

"The shade faun live in the very deepest reaches of the most impenetrable forests, and can be found in all the lands, including the great forests of Shavarra. They wander freely throughout them, though they make an art out of remaining unseen. If anybody might have seen the evil doers in person yet remained safe from the machina, it is they. And one of our soldiers as we were first fleeing the city, thought he saw one watching the exodus."

"No more than that do we know. However, there are shade faun living in the great wilds of the Borovan Wastes, which we will be passing in a few days."

"Yes." Sam agreed, remembering the tales. "I've heard tales about the shadelings living there for years. But none of them are more than the bard's tales spun for coin. And none ended well."

Actually they were very bad. There had been reports of hunters being hunted. Of foresters being run out of the forests. And travellers being chased. There had also been reports of a lot of other people who had travelled too far into their territory and who had gone missing over the years.

As for the Borovan Wastes, they were a range of small craggy mountains surrounded by some of the thickest, most densely tangled forest known in all of Fair Fields. League after league of forest. It was filled with wolves and other predators, while the land itself was thick with mud, and little of any worth could grow there. Just trees and scrub. No one other than the most dedicated ranger or hunter would ever venture in there. And of those who did too many had not returned.

"The forest itself is considered all but impassable," Sam continued. "Certainly it can't be entered on horseback. The mud, the collapsing rock cliffs and the thickness of the trees make it all but impassable. The terrain is treacherous underfoot, the various denizens inhospitable at best, hostile more often, and it's impossible to see more than a few feet in any direction because of the trees. The bush is so thick a horse could not pass, and even a man on foot would have great difficulty. A party would have more trouble. It's too easy to get separated and lost."

"To add to that it's one of the few parts of Fair Fields where snap wolves may still be found. They were hunted and driven out of the realm everywhere else, but in the Borovan Wastes the forest was simply too thick. Riders couldn't get through."

"There are also some who claim that the Alder Stone lies somewhere within the wastes."

"Alder Stone?"

"A legend. Possibly true. The stone is variously said to be an ancient shrine to the pox ridden God of Mischief, an ancient artefact, or the workings of the unseen wizards. No one knows. All that is known is that if a woman spends the night in sight of the stone she will waken with child. But the child will not be hers. It will not be of her people. But it may be of any other race."

"The true cruelty of the jest is that husbands upon learning what their wives give birth to reject both mother and child. They assume infidelity. And sometimes there is violence." Which would be the perfect jape that Alder would love to play, hence Sam assumed, why people claimed it was his doing.

"In any case the shadelings are said to be hidden. Unable to be seen unless and until they want to be seen. And the shadelings aren't considered friendly. The tales say they have attacked parties without warning, and often without reason."

"It's also at least a hundred leagues back to Shavarra proper, so what could these shadelings know anyway?"

"I did not say it would be easy to meet with them. But neither should it be impossible, or as dangerous as you fear. We elves have a means of meeting safely with the shade faun. And just as the elves have ways of speaking word to word across many leagues, so too we believe can the shade faun."

He was speaking of fire talking Sam knew. An ancient art known only by a few. Usually as he understood it, those who could do it were priests and priestesses of the Goddess. It seemed unlikely to him that the shadelings would have a similar art but he did not want to contradict the Elder.

"We have to try." Master Lavellin added the last with a tone of finality.

Unfortunately Sam agreed with that. Before they could even hope to fight the enemy they had to know who he was, and if the shade faun had knowledge of them then they had to find out. Sam nodded his agreement somewhat reluctantly.

"In two days, Elder Bela and War Master Wyldred are going to make the attempt. They have specifically asked for your company on the journey."

"I would be honoured to accompany them," Sam answered automatically, while trying to suppress an instinctive groan. Those two were not his favourite elves at the best of times, and though they both seemed to have eased off on him over the previous weeks, to spend an extended period of time with them would be a trial. Still, it wasn't a choice.

When an elder asked something of an elf, compliance was expected. Failure to do so while not treason as it would be under Heri's rule, nor even a crime, would be cause for much shame. Both for the individual concerned and for his family. There was no way Sam could allow Ry and her family to be tainted with such a stain, nor in fact himself. Since he was now by and large being accepted as an elf, he had to act as one or risk being ostracised.

Worse, to refuse would be to place the so-called Fire Angel against the will of the Council, and that could lead the elves into discord and even panic, something he had already promised he wouldn't do.

Besides, the idea made sense. If the shadelings could contact their brethren in Shavarra, assuming they survived and assuming they had some knowledge of what was happening there, it could be a valuable tool in the coming war. And while only a few of the elders even now were willing to accept that the golems that had attacked them were true machina, even they knew that what had started in their home was only the beginning. There was a war coming.

If Sam was honest with himself, he was also curious about the shadelings. He had never seen one, had never met anyone else who had, and had never even thought it possible – or wise – to seek them out. But if the elders were right, and they usually seemed to know what they were talking about, he was going to be given that chance. It might not be a pleasurable journey, but it would be interesting.

Then again it might be tricky explaining it to Ry. She had always accepted that he had other duties as a knight which sometimes took him away from her, but she had never been happy about it. To her it was simply wrong that her husband should leave her to go off and play soldier alone. She was an expert with the long bow and a natural woodsman, as were all her people. Her place was at his side.

Now, after a month and a half back with her family and getting better with every day, to learn he was heading into danger without her would not be well received. In fact the shadelings themselves might be easier to deal with.

It was about then that his concentration finally failed – as did his ice castle.

Chapter Sixteen.

"We're being watched." Though Sam couldn't see a single thing out of place in the forests around them, let alone someone spying on them, he was sure. He'd been feeling the presence of others all around them for some time, and right then he could feel them closing in. It didn't make it easy to relax which somewhat defeated the point of their having set up a camp. The tea he was drinking wasn't particularly soothing either.

"I know that!" Far from appreciating his warning Elder Bela almost snapped an irritated reply at him. But then he was a master of nature magic, whereas Sam was scarcely a novice. He'd probably felt the watchers hours before.

War Master Wyldred however, was a different story. Though he said nothing, Sam watched as his hand slowly moved to his sword hilt and stayed there. He, like Sam, was less trusting than Elder Bela of the shade faun and their likely response to having outsiders in their woods.

It was an unusual dynamic between the two elves, and Sam had watched with interest over the previous days as they'd sparred. It had begun from almost the moment they'd left the caravan, but things had really intensified the moment they'd left the horses behind at the clearing before entering the forests of the Borovan Wastes. That was when the tension had truly begun, as they'd left not just the security of the horses, but also the comfort of lands they knew behind.

That had been two long days ago, and the two of them had been bickering ever since. Politely of course, and with a deeply ingrained sense of humour and friendship. There simply wasn't any animosity between the two elves. In fact they quite liked each other as far as Sam could tell. They just had very different views of the world. Elder Bela wanted to enter the forests completely unarmed, determined to show their peaceful intent to the shade faun, whereas the War Master would have preferred to take an entire troop with him. Bela believed in the power of words and the strength of magic; Wyldred valued his steel. Meanwhile Sam, caught between the two of them, and with a foot in each camp by virtue of his own background, was almost forgotten as the two bickered.

For him the journey had been a revelation in many ways, though not perhaps in the way the elders would have wanted. Elder Bela had perhaps hoped to show him the true value of magic and openness and assess his potential as a wizard and one day maybe even a Magic Council wizard. War Master Wyldred meanwhile was busy examining his potential as a soldier in any upcoming battles. But instead Sam was learning a different lesson entirely. He had been learning the true nature of power in the elven community. It wasn't what he'd expected.

The two elders were in fact both of similar standing in Shavarra. Both were at the top of their professions. Elder Bela sat on the Magic Council and War Master Wyldred was a member of the Warriors Guild Conclave. Both were members of the Ruling Council as well. Thus he was travelling with two of the most respected elders in all of Shavarra. Despite that, neither of them had ordered him around even once. Unless it was something essential to their mission or to his training, they asked.

No more did they try to deny each other their opinions. There was no power struggle between the two of them as there would have been between competing nobles in Fair Fields. Rather there was an ongoing debate about how best to achieve their goal, and its outcome as always, was a compromise.

These two, Sam guessed, embodied a tiny model of how the entire elven government worked. Representatives from all the professions and guilds, members of their own councils, elected by their peers to sit on the Ruling Council came together to debate the important issues. Thus at the same table, there would be twenty one elves; three spell casters, three soldiers, three artisans, three priests, three farmers and three married couples, all politely voicing their concerns and debating the motions brought before them. They were seen as representing all parts of elven society. And their purpose was always to try to reach a consensus on everything from tax rates to what crops should be planted next season.

Of course he'd understood in principle how it worked for many years. But he'd never experienced it. And somehow he'd always imagined that it would be a battle of wits and wills. Just as it was in his homeland.

Such a system could never work in Fair Fields, where all such decisions were made by the king. Supposedly he consulted with the nobles. In Heri's case the reality was that whenever he brought them together it was for the specific purpose of glorifying himself and making sure that none of the noble houses were growing too strong. That none could threaten his rule. If that involved stabbing one's fellow nobles in the back in order to advance one's own status in the court, so be it. Of course the nobles also had other agendas, usually related to their family's wealth and holdings, that they liked to advance. But they could only advance them with the consent of the king, and he only gave it if he got something in return; more soldiers, a display of fealty and so forth. Had the nobles been given any true say in matters of the realm, it would have been complete chaos, as they would have quickly traded principles for advancement.

Bela and Wyldred though did no such thing. Instead they debated the issues without a trace of animosity or rivalry. And when they did disagree on something, be it what wood should be used to make a fire from or what to eat, then they generally arrived at a compromise. And if one still felt that they had ceded too much, then all that would occur would be a few barbed comments that were more jest than serious. It could have been just that the two were old friends, something that Sam had quickly become sure of, but he suspected it was more than that. It was part of their very elven nature. They cared nothing for power, and they hated the very concept of deliberately causing harm to another, whether with weapons or words. If only his own people could be so decent.

They were even decent to him. Despite the fact that he was but a commoner in both their society and in the party, they included him in their decision making and general conversation as if he was of no different rank.

Of course that didn't extend to his training when Sam was suddenly reduced to a novice once more and subject to Elder Bela's rather sharp tongue. The fact that they were in the middle of a nearly impenetrable wood didn't seem to dissuade him. Nor the fact that the light above was almost blocked out by the forest canopy. Or even the high probability they were surrounded by possible enemies. Regardless of any of these Sam was expected to train. And so he did each evening while Wyldred stood guard.

A war master standing guard while a soldier sat and played with magic; surely it was unheard of? And yet it kept happening. Moreover Wyldred took the duty very seriously and paid very careful attention to the surroundings, all but ignoring the two of them. Something told Sam that despite his years and rank, he too was not unused to the hardships of a soldier's life. But then he had said as much many times.

If Elder Bela was often sharp of tongue and somewhat private, Wyldred was the opposite. Though he had never shown any sign of weakness with it, he had happily discussed his hopes and fears with Sam. He too was married, and had

had some difficulty explaining to his wife and family why he was leaving them for a short while, perhaps even risking his life. Sam only wondered if his wife too had thrown him against the wagon floor and ravished him, even as she beat him up, and then begged him to be careful. Ry had only let him loose after he had sworn several times to return safely.

The other thing that had surprised him was the fitness of Elder Bela. Some of the country they found themselves wading through was incredibly tough. They had had to scamper over large banks, ford streams, and battle thick bush to make it to the meeting point. Yet the Elder was charging through it like a teenager, often leaving the others struggling in his wake. He had to be a hundred and fifty if he was a day – an age at which even an elf should be starting to take things more slowly – but no one seemed to have told him that. Then again, he was also the only one not wearing armour and carrying heavy weapons as well as a hefty pack.

Regardless, by the time they had stopped and set the evening fire for the second night, Elder Bela had looked remarkably relaxed, while he and Wyldred were exhausted. The Elder even looked clean, as he'd somehow avoided the worst of the mud, while Sam and Wyldred's armour had turned dirt brown. He had to be using his magic Sam had decided, to make the path easier for himself, and perhaps to give himself some extra strength and stamina. And yet Sam had felt no such spell, and despite his lowly ability in nature magic, he would normally sense such magic anywhere nearby.

But he did sense the shadelings. And as they came closer and closer even Elder Bela finally began to look a little concerned. Sam could feel them closing in, like a pack of wolves stalking their prey. They stayed hidden and moved silently. Still, Sam could sense the tell-tale wisps of their emotions as they closed in. They seemed satisfied with their concealment from the enemy. That didn't bode well, and his hand like Wyldred's found his sword hilt and stayed there. He didn't draw it though. Nor his fire. A single stare from Elder Bela made sure of that.

"By the spirit of the mighty oak and ash, we come in peace." The Elder barely raised his voice at all, another indication of just how close the shadelings were. Yet still Sam and Wyldred could see nothing no matter which way they turned.

"By the honour of Shavarra and the Pact of Whisparal we claim safe passage for the night and ask for an exchange of words."

"The pact is agreed, and the honour of Shavarra known to us. Passage is granted and our Wisdom also seeks discourse."

The voice came from barely ten feet in front of Sam, causing him to jump – and still he couldn't see a thing. That troubled him. The shadelings could be an invisible enemy. But at least they had agreed to the Elder's bargain. Then the shadelings showed themselves and he jumped again.

"Alder's balls!" The expletive was drawn from him as he watched the tree in front of him suddenly ripple as though it was a reflection in a pond and then divide to reveal two extremely skinny elves with long bows pointed directly at his head, a mere body length or so away from him. He was supposed to be a trained soldier and as such should always be on guard, and he had known they were near, yet he hadn't seen or heard a thing. It was an impressive display and he suddenly understood what all the legends about shadelings had tried to describe, and failed.

But they weren't as frightening in the flesh as he'd expected. Especially once their bows had lowered and the tension in the strings released. They were elves, exactly as Elder Bela had suggested, though very different from the elves of Shavarra.

For a start they were both thinner and taller than the elves he knew. Taller than him. Their skin was dappled green and dark brown. But they had the pointed ears, raised eyebrows and fine features of elves, and their sense of grace as they moved was akin to a dance. Yet if they were truly elves – and his senses told him they were – then they lived as no other elves he had ever seen.

In place of the long flowing clean white robes he was used to seeing were tight fitting thin leather garments that exposed much of their skin around the middle as well as their arms and legs. Crude, torn leather garments that were also dappled green and brown, and showed off too much of their skin for his liking. No tailor he was certain, had ever been near their clothes. They were simply cut from the animal's hide, dried, tanned and crudely stitched together. No elf he knew would ever wear such rags. But a troll might – if they wore clothes at all, that was.

They wore no shoes upon their feet, nor did they carry any metal. Their weapons and tools were all wood and bone, and were strapped to their arms and thighs with thin leather ties. More ties held their long straight black hair tight against their necks, while what looked like mud had plastered it against the skin of their backs. Their teeth were pointed, but rather by intent than by nature. Sam suspected they sharpened them. And their finger nails and toe nails had also been shaped into claws.

The skin that they did show revealed more scars than healthy flesh. Life could not be easy for them in the depths of the forests, and yet he also realised that as tough as their life was, some of those scars were deliberately inflicted. All of them, men and women both, had diagonal scars running down the outside of their arms; scars that looked as though they had been made with knives, while several also had vertical scars running from their cheeks to their chins. Some sort of ritual perhaps? Or maybe a way of simply showing the world how tough they were? Sam wondered how they could mutilate themselves in such ways and yet still go about their lives and even fight.

They might be elves, but he knew it would be wrong to assume they were anything like any other elves he had met. Once, he had been told, someone had written a treatise claiming that trolls were wild humans who had retreated thousands of years ago to the most inhospitable mountains they could find. Once there they had given up the last of their humanity as they became ever larger and hairier. It didn't explain the grey skin or the huge tusks in their mouths, but many believed it. If that was true, then perhaps these were elven trolls, skinny and wild instead of large and savage, but trolls nonetheless. Or perhaps this was what happened to a people living even in the vicinity of the fabled Alder Stone.

It was a troubling thought. Trolls were savage creatures who preyed upon the weak. They saw no difference between humans and animals. Or even between other trolls and animals. All were meat. And they treated them all as their next meal. Nor were they particularly interested in cooking. Although it was said that some still knew the basics of fire and roasting, they were just as happy eating their prey while it was still alive and struggling. They also ate their own kin when the chance arose. The idea that the shadelings might be similar creatures was far from comforting, especially when they had such strong magic of concealment at their disposal.

"Should we follow you to the meeting place?"

"You are already here."

The leader of the group answered the Elder. He was so thin that he looked almost like a giant stick insect, yet the intensity in his eyes said he was far more dangerous than any insect that had ever lived. As did the way his hand kept fondling the curve of his long bow and the hilts of his bone knives.

"Ohh?" That seemed to have caught Elder Bela off guard.

"With such a mage as this forest murderer here in your party, we could never allow you near our home."

Suddenly all eyes were on Sam and he realised he was in trouble. He had made an enemy of these people long before he'd even arrived. The Elder had told him that these people worshipped trees as did the dryads. Suddenly it seemed that they took the entire worship idea to a new and militant level. His blood turned to ice in his veins. Fortunately Elder Bela seemed to have expected the accusation and had prepared for it.

"Samual Hanor's actions were both foolish and accidental. Raised among the humans, he had little idea of his true strength and he was caught off-guard by the enemy's numbers. They came in their hundreds and he stood alone, surrounded. Still, he saved perhaps many thousands of our people with his act, and the forest will recover in time. If and when we are fortunate enough to return there some day, we will see to its recovery and he will help. That is our honour, and his duty as our charge."

Sam nodded his agreement carefully, still seeing too many hands on bows. He didn't mind helping to replant a forest, not that he would have had any choice in the matter if he had. And he didn't want to have these people angry at him for long. Should they choose to fight, he doubted whether even with both a war master and master wizard beside him he would survive. That invisibility of theirs was a powerful weapon. But he was also left with a question. How did they even know about his fight? Had one of their number been near enough to witness it, and somehow survived? Or was it by some other, yet unknown form of magic?

"It is your honour and you are held to it."

A new voice entered the clearing. An older male, filled with strength and confidence. Sam, like the others turned to see another shadeling appear out of thin air. He was perhaps seventy or eighty – assuming he aged like the elves he knew, but he had not the first trace of grey in his hair, or slowness in his gait. In fact he moved like a young man. Above all else his voice radiated confidence, and Sam knew he had to be the Wisdom that had been mentioned. Unlike an elder among the elves though, none of the others appeared to defer to him. He clearly commanded and they obeyed, but there was no show of respect at all. Just as these people had done away with the refinements of life he guessed, so too had they done away with manners.

On some level these people reminded Sam of wolves in a pack. The strongest acted as the leader and spoke for them, while the rest followed as it suited them. But sooner or later, the leader would fall and a new one would take his place. Normally among wolves there would be a battle and the loser would limp away into exile if he survived the fight. These people he guessed, would follow a similar pattern, respecting strength and cunning rather than wisdom and age.

"Before we can do so however, we have to return to Shavarra, and at present that is beyond our ability. The enemy holds our home in his steel grasp. Unless there is something you can tell us to aid us in our return?" Elder Bela turned the conversation to the reason they had come.

"At least you're direct for your people. The few other elves we have met want to converse at length about the beauty of the world while boiling water for tea."

The Wisdom was right. Caught up in the likelihood of

being skewered by these people for damaging a forest, Sam hadn't even noticed that Elder Bela hadn't gone through the normal rituals. But then the Wisdom didn't seem to appreciate those things anyway and he probably knew that.

"This is what we know of the enemy – and he is our enemy as well as yours. His golems have attacked our villages, and even our spells of concealment do not seem to do much good against them. The steel rats are immune to illusion. We think this is because they have no minds and are therefore unable to see such things."

"Were there many deaths?"

"A few hundred perhaps. Those too slow to seek the safety of the great forests. But once out and away from the villages, our people can climb trees far better than the golems, and drop heavy stones on them from high above. It has proved an effective technique, and shown us the error of our ways. We should never have established villages in the first place. There is no need. The forest provides all that we could ever want."

Except that without a physical village of some sort, the shadelings would lose touch with one another Sam thought. That in turn would mean they would soon lose their sense of community, which was probably all that they had left of civilization. Barbarism would not be far away. But Sam didn't say it. He was already in trouble with these people, and he had no thought that they would ever accept his concerns.

"The battle continues with few of our kin hurt any longer, while many rats die. But many more continue to come, making the battle seem without end. We meet with you only because we hope that you will seek to end it."

"We do so seek. But the enemy is strong. Stronger than any we have ever known."

"True. But sooner or later his strength must fail, especially as he attacks more and more lands. No one can fight everyone, though he is trying. But of more importance to you now is the fact that the enemy has struck once more. Harder than before."

Sam heard that and had to suppress a groan. It was exactly as he'd feared.

"Seventeen days ago his steel rats and also some larger steel spiders, attacked the human port city of Ragnor's Rock in the kingdom of Yed, over a thousand leagues to the south west."

Even though he had never been anywhere near there, Sam knew where Yed was. It was the southern most tip of the continent and home to an army of traders and seafarers, as it was the access route to the twelve major island nations to the south. It was also a natural fortress.

Though he had only ever read about it in history books, Ragnor's Rock was reputed to be a natural bastion, one which no army had ever successfully assaulted. The city itself was perched on the top of a cliff overlooking the port, with a commanding view of all the surrounding lands. They could not be crept up on. To add to their defences, the city walls were lined with canon, able to decimate any attacking army.

"The battle lasted two full nights and a day, and many hundreds if not thousands of the steel things were destroyed. But in the end the humans were defeated, and have fled inland towards their dwarven neighbours. Their own wizards and steel weren't enough when the spiders could spit fire further than an archer's arrow could fly and the rats came in their tens of thousands."

Tens of thousands? Sam couldn't quite bring himself to believe that, and yet if the stories were true, that was what it would take to assault Ragnor's Rock. It was also what the ancient Dragon had assembled to do it. For he too had taken the city once before.

"And of the master behind the rats?"

Trust Wyldred to remember the important questions while he was still reeling in shock, Sam thought. He was not acquitting himself well here.

"We know little, except that he comes by sea, unloading his deadly vermin by night along the shores. He uses a fleet of gigantic sailing ships, fully three sails high each, painted out in black. Even the sails are black. Ship after black ship comes, each carrying hundreds of his steel servants, finding old and disused wharfs to dock at."

"In the black of night they are unloaded, walking off the ship, along the wharf and then along the shore until they find a suitable spot, where they simply collapse down into huddled balls and sleep. Row upon row of them, hundreds wide and dozens deep. Then when there are finally enough of them, the Master gives the order and they awaken and as an army they march towards their target."

"Our people saw it first at Beckenridge to the south east of Shavarra, but they did not know then what these things were. So they watched for a while, and left. It was only days later when the steel army came to life and attacked that any of us understood what was happening. A tragic mistake that harmed us all."

Beckenridge! Or to give it it's proper name in High Elvish, Willen mi Becken or Sea of Becken. Sam knew the town, or rather, its reputation. It was part of the realm of Shavarra, but its people were a strange mix of elves, dwarves, humans and gnomes. Some said there were also sylph and fairy among them. The town was so mixed up in race that for someone to claim they were from the little port town was almost considered a roundabout way of saying that their blood was mixed.

"At Ragnor's Rock he used another abandoned wharf; Little Rock. It had previously only been used by fishing boats in the spring. From there he assembled a force so large it took eight nights for all of the black ships to arrive and unload. At least so our people have heard. And then, once his army was in place, he marched them nearly fifty leagues south, through deep forests and over mountains, to reach the city. As they did in Shavarra the rats attacked by night, scaling the cliffs and fortified walls, and then descended like a plague on the city guard."

"But they did not have the element of surprise on their side for long. The alarm was soon raised, and hundreds and then thousands of soldiers met them on the battlements before they could enter the city proper. Mages among them took a terrible toll on their numbers, but for that they paid an even more terrible price. The steel rats singled them out, and began concentrating their attacks on the mages themselves, heedless of how many of them were destroyed. It was an effective strategy. All the spell casters were killed."

"Once the mages were gone, the rats retreated back down the cliff, and the steel spiders began their assault. Perched on the cliff itself, perhaps twenty feet below its top and beyond the range of archers, they began firing flaming balls of fire high into the air and over the walls, causing many deaths and setting the city alight. What had been a natural fortress became a burning prison and the people were trapped in it. This they did for a day and a night."

"In the end, once enough of the city was destroyed or in flames, the rats once more advanced through the lines of spiders, and entered the city proper. There they caused immeasurable death and chaos, as those who had survived the rain of fire couldn't see them through the fire and smoke. Battles that should have been easily won as the people used their spell casters and heavily armed soldiers to destroy their enemies at a distance, became confused hand to hand fights in the street and the fighting was more even. And the rats kept coming, no matter how many fell."

"In the end it was the numbers of the steel rats that proved decisive, and a retreat was called. The gates and the bridges between the city and the land were opened and the people fled, chased every step of the way by a steel army."

"The city was home to over two hundred thousand humans, but scarcely fifty thousand made it out alive. And not all of them survived. They were pursued relentlessly. For a full three days and three nights the enemy chased them, a swarm of steel teeth and glowing red eyes that didn't need to rest, cutting down any stragglers mercilessly. And then, on the dawn of the fourth day, for no reason at all, they stopped pursuing. The humans do not know why, no more do our kin. It was as if the rats were on a chain, and they had suddenly reached its limit."

It had been the same with the elves, Sam realised. The numbers of both people and rats had been smaller, and after his battle the rats had been slowed. But they had not stopped chasing them. In fact they had continued their hunt for a good three or four days. Until the caravan was well on its way to Fair Fields. And then for no obvious reason they had stopped. So at least the scouts had reported, as had the villagers from the various towns and villages that had been hastily emptied out as the steel vermin advanced on them. But he said nothing. They could wonder about that later.

"The strangest branch of the whole copse is that we have never seen a single man or elf with any of them. No one leads them. The ships seem to sail themselves. Certainly there is no one at the helm, and the steel servants unload themselves.

Their master may not even be on the ships. No more is he in Shavarra, though even now the rats gather there and in the large towns. They are slowly amassing their numbers, presumably readying themselves for the next big battle."

"And are they truly golems? Or do you call them machina?" Everyone turned to stare disapprovingly at Sam as he asked the question he most badly wanted answered. The shadelings obviously wanted nothing more than to forget he even existed, while the elders were upset at having their conversation interrupted. But he still had to ask. Especially when he had no idea just how much these people might know of such things. He suspected it might be more than would seem probable. After all, he didn't know how they knew what they had already revealed.

The shadelings were a contradiction in many ways. Though they professed to follow the ways of the forest and forego the tenants of civilization, they still clearly had both strong magic and considerable learning at their disposal. That surely involved reading and the written word, yet he couldn't imagine any of these people ever having owned a book, let alone read one. He couldn't answer the riddle but regardless he still thought that they might know more than others would expect. If they knew of what was happening hundreds and thousands of leagues away, did they also know of the ancient past? Did they know of the Dragon Wars and the machina?

"You speak of the Dragon, and you may have good reason. Though our legends of the Dragon Wars are little more than rhymes and fire side tales, we know enough to know that these are no mere golems. The magic and alchemy that is behind them is without peer. It has not been seen before in our lifetime. Yes. They are machina as far as we can tell, but we have not tried to divine their nature. Only to escape or destroy them."

"As have we."

"Our most ancient stories tell of the cavern of the Dragon where he created the machina. Andrea, home of the dark death. Perhaps more answers will be found there, though it is a long and difficult journey. But if this is the Dragon returned, you will need more than answers. You will need allies. The ancient tales spoke of the Dragon's army being fought by the dragons themselves. Of their flaming breath scorching the machina on the ground and in the air. Perhaps seeking them out would be a wise strategy, especially when others have already explored the cavern and found little."

Wise perhaps Sam thought, but also a lot more dangerous even than facing the enemy unarmed. Never trust a dragon. And never disturb one. That was something every child knew.

Though the entire continent was named for the dragons – it was the Continent of the Dragon's Spine after all, and the dozen southern island nations were collectively known as the Dragon's Claws – that was purely because of the shapes the lands made on a chart. It had not been named out of respect for the great creatures. They weren't respected. They were feared.

Most dragons were solitary creatures, living out their unending lives sleeping in great mountain caves. They didn't care to be disturbed. Mostly they only ventured out to catch a meal – a troll or an ogre or two – and then returned to sleep for a few more months or years. And that was the way anyone with any sense would like it.

Though dragons were powerful and intelligent creatures who might be willing to fight if their home and kin were threatened, they were far from friendly, and only a fool or someone truly desperate would seek them out. And most of those who did would die. But it was news to him that they had fought the machina before. The books and scrolls had said they had attacked them, but only when the machina had entered their caverns, not as part of any organised campaign. That too was something to ponder later.

"There is one more thing you should know. One more thing we have seen, a thing which we would have you know. Not all that they attack are killed. Some from Shavarra – and we would guess, some from Ragnor's Rock – were taken back in chains to the ships. Perhaps only a few dozen, perhaps more. We do not know how many, nor why. We do not know what the enemy does with them. But we fear it. That even more than the rest."

Sam could understand why. A shiver went down his spine at the thought of hostages being taken by whatever enemy it was that they were facing. Someone so evil would most certainly not treat them well.

"And do –"

"No!"

The Wisdom's tone suddenly became forceful, even though he did not raise his voice in the slightest, and Sam knew the conversation such as it had been, was over. So did the other shadelings as they stood once more to attention, preparing either to attack or leave. Even they, he guessed, weren't quite sure which.

"Now all is said. All know the same as we wanted. But be warned. Though this enemy must be fought by all if any of our people are to survive, this does not make us friends. It only means we share a common enemy. Our truce will continue for now, but we do not seek more of your presence. We will hold to the old ways, and if more is learnt we will send word. But other than that we seek only to be left alone as always. It is time for you to return to your people, as it is time for us to leave as well."

It was some sort of signal. And even as Elder Bela looked to be about to object, the shadelings vanished in front of them. A quick step backwards perhaps, into a tree or a shrub, and they were gone as if they had never been there. It looked for all the world like magic, and yet Sam had the strangest feeling that it was simply practice and the outfits they wore. The forest was their home, and they truly had become a part of it.

In a matter of heartbeats they were alone.

"That was quick." Wyldred spoke for them all as he too looked around, trying desperately to find even a trace of them and failing. "Do we wait, cook some tea and see if they return?"

"No."

Sam, and he guessed the War Master too, was relieved to have Elder Bela dismiss the idea so quickly. Neither of them truly wanted to stay in these dark woods any longer than they had to.

"Everything has been said and we have been dismissed. And though the Pact of Whisparal has been spoken and accepted, I would rather not rely on it for any longer than I have to. We are at best unwelcome guests in their territory, and it might be wisest to leave before our presence becomes an affront to them."

The Elder didn't have to do much persuading. It was late, and though they had set up camp for another night when the shadelings had arrived, suddenly both Sam and Wyldred felt that a few more hours travel might well be in order before they retired. In short order they had all their belongings packed up again, the fire was well and truly out, and they were making their way back through the forest. Back to the clearing where they'd left the horses.

Samual

Back to safety.

Samual

It was a strange thing Sam decided as he walked in silence with the others. Some allies were more worrisome than your enemies.

Chapter Seventeen.

"I think we have company."

Sam looked up from the surrounding mountains to see that Wyldred was right. On the crest of the nearby grassy hill, coming at them fast were three riders. Yet even from the moment he saw them, Sam wasn't worried. He could tell they were elves. They wore the typical white elven armour, and all had long bows slung across their shoulders. He felt nothing threatening about them. That was a pleasant change after the forest they had just left where with every footstep he had imagined one of the shadelings was just behind him, waiting to stick a knife in his back. Or a snap wolf was about to leap on him. They weren't a friendly people and they had ample cause to dislike him. They would make dangerous enemies. Far more dangerous than the armies of assassins he had already faced over the years.

But wasn't that the way of life? There was no safety. There was no one who could not be killed. He had become one of the most powerful spell casters of fire there was. A truly dangerous wizard. He could fight an army if he had to. But now he had become even more vulnerable than before, with a potential enemy he did not even know how to face. Best that he not provoke them.

"Messengers?"

"In a way." It was Elder Bela who answered the question. "Though I think the message they bring might be best stated as 'how dare you just wander off and leave us like that!'"

"Hmm?"

"The lady in the middle. That's my wife Ellise, and I

would assume that I'm in trouble."

Sam stared at the Elder in surprise, for long moments wondering if he had heard him correctly. Somehow he'd simply never thought of Bela as the marrying type. And certainly the Elder had said nothing to him of his family as they'd travelled. Meanwhile on the other side, Wyldred was making strangled noises as he clearly tried to hold back laughter and failed. He at least should have known better.

"I wouldn't laugh so loudly my old friend. The lady on the grey is Amerindel, and you're in the same trouble."

"Oh!"

Sam would have laughed in turn as Wyldred practically chocked on his own laughter, except that he suddenly realised that the third horse was a large black steed, surely one of Tyla's kin. Which meant, he suddenly realised that the rider had to be Ryshal. It would be just like her to do something so foolish as to ride off into unknown territory to meet him when she was still not fully recovered. But he couldn't blame her for it.

Without even thinking about it, he spurred Tyla into a gallop and they all raced directly for the riders, Sam screaming Ryshal's name at the top of his lungs all the way. Beside him, Wyldred and Bela did the same, and the gap between them shrank surprisingly quickly. It had been a long five days apart from their families.

Less than a heartbeat later all three men were holding their wives tight and kissing them soundly as they no doubt deserved. It had to be the best possible reward for a successful mission.

"I love you." They both spoke the words together, knowing they were true, and then kissed some more. It was a long time before either could pay any attention to the others, and then it was only to see that they were doing much the same. Except that for the elders, there was an eye opening difference. Elder Bela was being alternately kissed, hugged and thumped by his wife, and he wasn't lucky enough to be wearing any armour. Meanwhile War Master Wyldred was on the receiving end of a tongue lashing, and losing badly. Sam's eyes nearly popped out of his head as he saw the two elders being publicly abused.

"Don't laugh too loudly my love. You have much apologising to do as well." But Ry kissed him again to make sure he knew she wasn't angry.

"Until the day I die." He meant it too. Leaving Ry had been the hardest thing, and he never wanted to do it again, even though he realised that he would probably have to. They both did. It was a soldier's lot.

"Where did you get the armour?" He was curious. It was the simple, white stuff that a town guard might have, suitable for taking a blow from a drunk, not the heavier, more defensive and coloured armour of the various border patrols, but still he hadn't realised she had any.

"It's my mother's. When we heard you were near, Ellise decided she'd had enough waiting around for you all to return. So Mother gave it to me, unhitched Aegis, and we took off after her. Amerindel joined us before we'd made it half a league, and we've been riding ever since. It's been a good day."

"That it has." Not only because Ry was once again back with him, but because she looked so healthy and happy. It had only been five days, but he could see some real colour in her cheeks, and feel some true strength in her arms as she held him. Ryshal had been making noises for some days about returning to her duties as a teacher, and for the first time he started to think she might almost be strong enough. And by the All Father did he love to see her dance. There was true artistry in her feet.

"The front of the caravan's six or seven leagues back, and the Council wants to see you all the moment you return. We though wanted to see you first. We also wanted to find out what sort of trouble you'd got yourself in."

"No trouble at all love. Except that I have to replant an entire forest in Shavarra if I want to keep on breathing."

"What?"

"I'll tell you about it later beloved." And then he picked her up and kissed her again for good measure. The forest could wait. In fact everything could wait.

It was barely late morning, a long way still to lunch, however the women decided it was time to eat. And as Sam was beginning to realise, what Ryshal wanted she mostly got. In the end he was only the husband in the marriage!

In short order they found themselves sitting around a small camp fire eating the breads and meats the women had thoughtfully brought with them, and telling tall, and plainly ludicrous tales of their adventures with the shadelings. Tales that became ever more fanciful as the telling progressed. In fact they sounded like the tales told by those worshipping Vineus, the Lord of Wine.

The strange thing was that even as they peopled their adventures with giants and ogres – and even some unicorns and flying pixies for good measure, they also managed to leave out all the important bits. Neither Bela, nor Wyldred, nor even himself, even touched on what they had been told of the enemy, or what they had learned of Ragnor's Rock. None of them mentioned the people who had been abducted by this new Dragon. And none spoke of the war to come. Those were things perhaps best left for another time. They were matters both serious and dark. This was not the time for either of those things.

Chapter Eighteen.

"And there it is." Elder Bela could have been talking about the end of the world instead of the entrance to the Dead Creek Pass, from his tone. But then as a nature mage he probably had more reason than most. He could feel the deadness all around.

Even Sam could feel it.

His training as a mage had been advancing well, especially in the nature magics, and his instructors were well pleased with his progress. He had increased not just his repertoire of spells, but also his strength and sensitivity. Now with time and practice, he could call his horse to him from up to half a league away. He could call the birds from the trees to sing for Ry, something she enjoyed a lot. And he too could feel the terrible emptiness of the lands ahead, like a room where the air was starting to run thin and yet heavy. He would never reach the status of a master but in time he might well become an adept after all.

"We'll get through it," Sam replied.

And they would. If nothing else, the elders had prepared their people well for this torturous leg of the journey. They had extra horses, now almost one for every man woman and child. Their artisans had spent their evenings building water wagons, while the people themselves had all been building barrels and oil skins to hold their own supplies. The order had gone out the moment they'd entered Fair Fields; five gallons minimum water carrying capacity for every man woman and child, twenty for each horse. And the people had prepared well. If anything they had exceeded that.

In Sam's own wagon they had four large barrels, each able

to hold forty gallons, all full to the brim and many more skins and jugs. For the four of them and their three horses, it was more than enough to last them through the wastes provided they rationed it carefully. Their load however did mean that they had some trouble finding room to sleep on the deck.

In addition they had built sun shades to allow them and the horses to all to rest comfortably during the hottest part of the day, while they would be travelling through the night. In all, Sam had confidence that they would get through all right.

They were fortunate in that it was fall, which was probably the best possible time to cross the wastes. The days would not be so hot, the nights not so cold. The slow pace they had taken as they crossed Fair Fields had worked to their advantage. Two and a half months to cross one hundred and fifty leagues was almost slothful. But they were better prepared now. And they would not be stopping every day to purchase supplies and trade as they crossed the wastes. It would be a much faster leg of the journey.

"And then what?" For once the Elder was uncharacteristically direct.

Sam understood what he meant. He and the rest of the elders had discussed that even more than the hardships ahead. They could prepare for the hardships. What they couldn't prepare for was a life in another province. No more could their people.

After three long months of travelling, there was only one more month to go. The end was in sight. But the end wasn't really an end. It was just a new beginning. And one no one was sure they wanted to start on. Everyone seemed to now be focused on that. Some of the people were lucky in that they had kin in the Flats, and would be able to stay with them. But most had few if any family there and were effectively refugees in a strange land. They would be cared for, there was no doubt of that, and a place had been set aside for them to set up a township, which in time might become another province. But it wasn't home.

"And then we begin anew. A new city, a new land, but with a strong people. We will survive, mourn our dead and start again."

They were hard words but true. In saying them Sam was actually only saying what had been said a hundred times before in Fair Fields during the land wars before the kingdom had united under its first king. Then too people had said those things after their lives had once more been destroyed. It was simply the price of war. It wasn't just the soldiers who died.

"You forget young Samual. Even if we do find a place and settle down, there is still an enemy out there that we have to fight. He may come for us and our kin again. There is no true end in sight until he is defeated."

"Elder, I have been reading and rereading the accounts of the Dragon Wars day and night, as have the scholars and the war masters. And while much is unclear, some things are obvious, especially when viewed from the information that the shadelings gave us. The enemy comes by boat. His armies can only travel so far from him before they must stop. He will attack up and down the coasts first, driving one and all into the inland provinces. Then presumably, if he makes it that far, he will set up his bases before he strikes further inland. But that will be many years away." Sam left unspoken the fact that the Golden River Flats where they were headed had no coastline. And that the nearest coast to Shavarra – the town of Beckenridge – was thirty leagues from the city. The rats had marched a very long way before attacking the city. He didn't really know just how far the machina would be prepared to march to attack their targets. He just hoped that the Flats would be far enough.

"The original Dragon Wars lasted nearly a decade, and in all that time he attacked and held only twenty seven coastal provinces. Each new territory he gained cost him many more resources, and that meant each following attack was further away in time as he had to build more machina. That's why in his later conquests he hired mercenaries to flesh out his armies. The people will be safe for many years in the Flats even if the worst happens and he takes all the coastal cities. There will be time to prepare."

"Ahh, the naiveté of youth. Wanting to trust in hope where the facts are not certain."

It was unlike the Elder to be so gloomy and Sam guessed the emptiness of the lands must be harder on him than he'd thought.

"No old friend. He gives the analysis of a soldier born. One day we may yet make a war master out of young Samual here. He sees the battle ahead very clearly."

Wyldred had joined them at the entrance to the pass, and he, like Sam, saw the same likely pattern of attacks occurring. Whether it was the Dragon returned or some evil successor, the enemy was so far following the same campaign. He had to. He had the same armies and they assumed the same method of transport. He was probably also sending out his armies from the same place.

The only question for Sam was why the Dragon was attacking the coastal cities if, he was working from Andrea as legends had it? Andrea was nowhere near the sea. And if he was based there surely he should have sent his first armies straight into Fair Fields and Ore Bender's Mountains. They were the closest lands after all. Was he trying to hide his true home? Or had it in fact been that the caverns to which he had finally retreated had not been his origin, only his safe harbour at the end? There was of course no answer but it was a question that desperately needed one.

"What's that?"

Sam was pulled out of his reverie by the guard's abrupt question, and it took him a moment to see where the guard's hand was pointing. Sam let his gaze follow the guard's hand and looked south, across the boundary between Fair Fields and the Dead Belly Wastes. He saw nothing other than sandy hills and more sandy hills for as far as the eye could see.

"Where?" But even as he asked he saw that the guard's hand was pointed not just south, but also slightly upwards, and as he followed his arm, he soon saw the black smudge in the air above the hills that the guard was asking about. Unfortunately, he had no answer. To him it was just a black smudge. It was the same to the others. It was simply too small and too far away. But something about it troubled him. It could have been a bird – a small griffin or even a cloud – but for some reason Sam felt threatened by it. Looking around he saw he wasn't alone.

"Do we have a telescope?" Even as he asked, one of the Council guards pulled out one of the copper tubes from his saddle bags and handed it to him. Another was given to Wyldred and carefully they began studying the skies. The telescopes were amazing instruments, the secret of their construction known only to a few master artisans, all of them dwarves. As always Sam marvelled at the fact that they could bring a man's face into view from more than a league away. It was as though he was just outside the window. But they were difficult to use, and both Sam and Wyldred spent considerable time playing with the small wheels at the instruments' bases before the beast came into view. Then he wished it hadn't.

"Alder's hairy tits! It's a steel drake."

Sam was the first to identify the creature, his nightly

reading of the history of the Dragon Wars telling him exactly what it was. But knowing what it was, and knowing what to do about it were two completely different things. Steel drakes had been the ancient Dragon's terror weapon, and paradoxically his undoing. Nearly unassailable, they attacked from the air, often completely without warning, raining fire down like a dragon upon anyone unfortunate enough to be out in the open. They had struck in the lands that weren't yet under attack, creating chaos and confusion, and preventing them from sending armies to help others under siege.

If the steel drakes hadn't been seen as an affront by the dragons themselves, who had then begun destroying them in their hundreds, they would have ensured the Dragon's victory. The dragons however, would not tolerate another ruler of the skies and when the steel drakes had flown over their lairs they had struck them down.

"Sound the alarms. Get the people down below their wagons. Tether the horses and for the Goddess' sake get the weather mages here as fast as possible."

Fortunately Wyldred was nowhere near as slow as Sam as he started yelling orders, and Sam remembered with relief, that there was an answer. Towards the end of the wars it had been found that weather mages, the most practical and yet least war like of all spell casters, could effectively bring the steel drakes down. The drakes didn't fly well and even a relatively small cross wind could bring them crashing to the ground. If they hit hard enough they would then explode in a fiery heap.

Immediately horses began galloping back toward the rest of the caravan as riders obeyed their instructions. Meanwhile Sam concentrated on building his fire within him. According to all the reading he'd done, it would be of little use to him as the steel drakes like all dragons were immune to fire spells. Still it was his best weapon. In fact against such a nightmare, it was his only one.

Steel drakes chose to attack from the air, staying safely out of range of both archers and fire mages, while it was said their flame could spray for hundreds of yards, incinerating not just a few soldiers, but an entire army. To face them was to die, and to run the only accepted defence, as long as everyone ran in different directions. But if the caravan scattered, Sam knew they would be picked off one by one and not all would return.

Fortunately Sam's lessons suddenly paid off as he realised that while fire magic was not that useful in attacking a steel drake, it could still be a potent defence. Because it could still be used as a way of hiding.

Sending out a spray of ice arrows as far as the eye could see down the caravan, and then hitting them with flame strikes, Sam began creating a fog over the elves. It might not stop the steel drake's flame, but what the machina couldn't see it couldn't spray with fire. And while such creatures might not be affected by illusion, the fog was no illusion.

Slowly he began thickening the fog as he added more and more ice and fire to it. And while the process was painfully slow, thanks to the early warning from the sharp eyed guard he had time. Steel drakes were not fast flyers either, travelling not much quicker than a man on a horse, and this one had been at least a league away when the guard had spotted it. Meanwhile he could hear the sounds of bells clanging furiously all the way down to the caravan's rear, a quarter of a league back. The early warning system had been sounded.

In the middle of the caravan a sudden explosion of fog billowed out. It seemed the other fire mages had seen what he was doing, and had followed suit. With nearly twenty of them – four of them masters – they were doing a much better job than him. Sam felt a wave of relief wash over him as it gave him the chance to concentrate his fog on the parts of the caravan nearer him and thickened it up quickly. It wasn't long before the sky was turning grey all around them.

Soon the fog around them was so thick that they could barely see ten feet in front of them, and Sam could feel it rising hundreds of feet into the air and covering them all in a blanket of cloud. It was just as well, as he could hear the shouts of the sentries hiding just on the edge of the fog, calling that the drake was finally overhead. It had been a nervous wait.

From then on it became a waiting game for Sam. He concentrated only on maintaining and increasing the thick cloud of fog all around them, while the drake flew overhead, looking for anyone to attack. According to the sentries it was circling, like a buzzard over a dying animal, blinded by the fog, but still somehow aware that its prey lay within.

Meanwhile Wyldred had galloped off with a group of soldiers looking for the weather mages, who had somehow disappeared on them. Or at least he'd started off galloping for them. That was the problem with the fog. Even as it protected them it limited their own ability to see one another within it. Nor did the horses run, but trotted slowly, as their riders carried torches and called out to any who might be ahead.

Of course the real danger would come when the weather mages finally acted. If they weren't careful, they could blow their protective fog away as they tried to upset the machina's flight. That could be deadly, but he was certain that Wyldred, would discuss that with the wizards. Once he found them!

The other worry was that the wizards would be successful and the steel drake – easily the size of a six horse wagon – would come crashing down to the ground in the midst of the elves, and promptly explode. If it did so it would kill everyone within a hundred yards as the magic within it was released in a blast of fire. It might even kill Ry. The thought was terrifying but there was little else that could be done. If the creature wasn't destroyed, it could kill all of them.

But at least they had the fog to hide them,

Unfortunately it wasn't enough. The drake apparently decided that it didn't matter what it could or couldn't see. It only mattered that its targets were somewhere in the fog. And so it struck. There was a blast of something, fire and orange light making the clouds glow, and then an explosion as it laid down its fire breath, that was followed by screaming. The drake had attacked!

For a moment Sam was struck almost senseless as he realised what had happened. And then his heart started thumping as he understood they were all in danger. This thing didn't care that it couldn't see them. It was going to strike at them again and again until it had found and killed them all. And there was absolutely nothing he could do.

He couldn't strike at it. Even if his fire would have some effect on the creature, he couldn't see it to hit it. His fog had blinded him too.

He didn't even know if the drake had hit anyone. He couldn't tell where it had struck. If it was anywhere near the people. All he knew was that it had attacked and people had screamed in terror. And that it was going to do it again and again.

Sure enough fifteen or twenty beats of his heart later he saw the sky turn completely orange once more and heard another explosion followed by more screaming, and he knew that if no one had been hurt, sooner or later they would be. And Ry and her family were somewhere out there!

How could he be so helpless? He was one of the most powerful spell casters there was, and yet there was nothing he could do against this enemy. Nothing except create more and more fog and pray to the All Father.

While Sam waited, as helpless as the other elves around him, he concentrated on keeping his calm and maintaining the fog. There was nothing else he could do. He wanted to run to Ry. He wanted to destroy these beasts. But he could do neither. The worst of it all was that he had no idea how long it would be before those who could do something finally acted.

So he kept putting all his magic into creating the fog and praying each and every time the sky lit up and the ground shook that Ry was safe. He couldn't lose her. Not now. Not after everything they had gone through.

The time passed achingly slowly as he worked, with the only knowledge he had of the drake coming from the nearer sentries who reported the drake's position as it flew overhead, hunting them, and the direction of the flashes of light. Nothing however seemed to change. The drake wasn't yet wobbling in its flight or falling out of the sky according to the look outs when they spotted it. Instead it continued to circle above them, searching for targets and raining down fire on them every so often. Sam's nerves began to stretch. Because the longer this went on he knew, the greater the chance it would hit Ry.

Sam could hold the fog shape all day and night if he had to, though it would soon start to get cold and wet inside it. But the interminable waiting for the weather mages to strike back was eating him alive. He had always been a soldier, a man of action. Waiting for a battle was the worst of all possible times, especially when the enemy was already striking at them. And still there was nothing to do.

An age seemed to pass that way, and for the longest time Sam began to worry that the War Master had been unable to find any of the weather mages. Maybe the fog was simply too thick. By then it was hard to see your hand in front of your face. Even the scouts trying to rush to the edge of it to spot the drakes, were useless. The edges of the fog were simply too far away for them to be heard as they shouted back what they saw. Especially when people kept screaming as each new blast shook the ground and lit up the sky. Their screams drowned out whatever the scouts shouted.

Maybe the wizards were right at the rear of the caravan, a full half a league back. If so, Master Wyldred would have a long slow trip as he searched for them.

He wasn't alone. All around him he could hear the Council guards talking to each other, wondering much the same as him, even as they waited for one of the drake's blasts to hit them. Some of them came close. Close enough to deafen them. But none hit.

And then finally, just when Sam was beginning to wonder if it was ever going to end, the mages acted.

The first any of them knew of it was when they heard the sound of the wind whistling. It sounded much as it did when it whipped around the sides of buildings in the larger cities. But there were no buildings nearby, no wind either, or at least none that he could feel, and despite his fear, none of the fog seemed to be blowing away. The breeze was blowing either above or outside of the protective fog.

Rapidly the sound became louder and louder, until even where he was, which was presumably a long way from the weather mages, he could hear nothing other than the wind. He couldn't even hear his own voice when he shouted his questions at the sentries. Doubtless they couldn't hear him either. But though he couldn't hear anything and he couldn't see anything either, the one thing he did know was that the attacks had stopped. The sky was no longer turning orange every so often.

Then, just when he thought things couldn't get any stranger, he heard a new sound entering the mix; thunder. It rolled around them as though it was coming out of the very ground beneath their feet, while above them the fog kept turning white with the flashes of lightning. While he had no idea what was going on outside the fog, one thing at least was certain. Wyldred had found the weather mages.

The storm continued unabated for what seemed like ages while Sam and the others stood there and fretted. It seemed impossible that a storm could rage like that for so long. Surely it had to abate eventually? But finally, as with everything else, it began to ebb. First the thunder and lightning seemed to lessen, and then even the roaring of the wind around them began to fade. The battle he realised, was over. He just hoped they'd won. And that not too many people had been hurt. He began praying some more to the All Father, desperately hoping that Ry and her family were alright.

Unexpectedly a gentle rain began to fall on them, falling out of the greyness above, and despite his sudden alarm as he tried to rebuild the fog, the sky above them started clearing. Even as he threw all his magic into turning the rain itself into more fog, the last of his ability was taken away when a gentle breeze came out of nowhere to blow the clouds away. Against that he had no answer. The fire mage had been bested by the weather mages in a magical battle, something that normally wouldn't be possible. But then weather was their bailiwick, not his.

Knowing his defeat, Sam instead released the last of his fog shape, and started drawing ever more fire into him, just in case he needed to launch a fire ball or two, though he feared it would be a waste of time. Drakes were said to be fireproof. But then he remembered the black drake in the test realm after it had been hit by his fire ring. Real or not, that creature had been hurt by his magic, and surely the steel drake couldn't be

306

as tough despite the legends? It was spelled to be fire proof rather than naturally immune as were its flesh and blood cousins.

Shortly after that the skies above cleared completely, and Sam like everyone around him desperately started hunting for signs of the drake. But they couldn't see it. Wherever it was, it wasn't flying above them.

But the caravan had been hit. He could see smoke rising from half a dozen fires, and he knew that where they blazed the steel drake's fire balls had struck. He also knew that people there would be dead and more would be injured. He could hear the distant cries of men and woman searching for their loved ones; maybe even mourning them. It wasn't total devastation. It was nothing like what had happened in Shavarra. And this time the enemy had been destroyed. But it was bad enough. Unfortunately while his instinct was to go to them, he knew there was nothing he could do for them. He was no healer. He was a soldier. His job had to be to find and kill the enemy – wherever he was.

He couldn't even go to Ry to make sure she was alright. His place was with the soldiers. And if she wasn't, what could he do? He wasn't even sure where their wagon was in the confusion all around. There were people everywhere, running around crazily, shouting and crying. More were rushing around with buckets of water as they put out the fires. Horses were running wild too, panicked by the battle. The entire caravan was a picture of chaos and he had no idea where anyone was within it. Logic told him that she was probably fine. There were only half a dozen fires and it was a huge caravan. The odds were surely in her favour. But logic didn't bring him the comfort he craved. He wanted certainty. He wanted to know she was well. And he simply couldn't know that. Not yet. How could he be so powerful and so helpless at the same time?

"Look!"

The call came from one of the guards, and Sam like the rest turned to see him pointing at the distant sand hills, where a still smouldering blackened husk could be seen half buried in them. With a sense of unbelievable relief he realised that the drake was down. More than down, it was dead.

Then, as he saw more people calling out and more hands pointing, he realised it was also in pieces. The storm had torn the drake into three massive pieces, and they had been scattered everywhere. Whatever the mages had conjured up had been more powerful than anything Sam had ever known they could do. Maybe he should stop thinking of them as simply farming wizards.

But then when he turned around to stare at the pieces of the drake, Sam realised that two of them had heads and the awful truth dawned. It had not been one drake sent to attack them but three. Even as the elves all around him were beginning their celebrations, Sam felt a shiver of cold running up and down his spine. Three steel drakes! It was unheard of in the Dragon Wars. Normally they were sent off on their own to harass villagers and keep the various armies busy trying to hunt them down. No more than one had normally been needed. And even at the end of the wars, when it had been discovered that weather wizards could bring them down, they'd been sent out in pairs to attack columns from opposite directions, their prime target the wizard himself. But three? Never.

Which meant one of three things. This new Dragon was very, very angry with them, very worried, or – and the thought sat like a lump of burning lead in his gut – the Dragon had so many of these things that he didn't need to send them out alone. All of the options were bad. Very bad.

While he sat there on Tyla, brooding and worrying about

his wife, Sam noticed an exodus of soldiers from the caravan wandering over to the giant steel corpses, and almost on instinct he joined them, heading towards the nearest one. It was partly curiosity. After all, it was the chance to see something close up that hadn't been seen in thousands of years. But it was anger too. He needed to satisfy himself that these things were truly dead.

The elves he guessed felt the same, though unlike him they saw this mainly as a victory. Three steel drakes had been slain, few of their people had been hurt, unlike the last time the Dragon had struck, and now they had the chance to gloat over their fallen enemy and study his remains. Some were singing, many were smiling and talking excitedly among themselves. Many were brandishing weapons as if they meant to attack whatever remained of the drakes. None seemed to share Sam's sense of dread, and he hadn't the heart to break their festive mood. This was a victory and they needed it. Now more than ever they needed something to cheer about as they headed into a wasteland, destined for a life unknown while still carrying the memories of too many loved ones who had passed on. Later he would share his thoughts with the elders, assuming they didn't already know them.

It was a lengthy trip as the creature nearest to him had hit the sand nearly half a league south of them but Sam felt no desire to hurry. Unfortunately the slow trip gave him more time to worry about what three steel drakes attacking an elven caravan of refugees could mean for the future. But in time, when the beast was only a few hundred yards away, his thoughts lifted from the danger posed by the enemy to curiosity about the beast itself.

It was massive! That was his first and only thought for quite a while as he stared at it. To have read the tales and to know the descriptions of the creatures off by heart still didn't come anywhere close to explaining the impossibility of the steel drake before him. It was easily as long as a six horse wagon and as high as a man on a horse, even lying on the ground. Its back had been broken by the fall and, yet for all that it was still sinuous and sleek. And somehow this enormous creature of steel had flown! He couldn't imagine that. It would have taken at least a hundred and fifty men just to lift it off the ground. Yet he had seen it soaring, if not gracefully, then still in the air.

It was also deadly. He would have known that the instant he saw the head of the creature, even if he hadn't known that it was a fire breather. Its face was the very soul of ferocity and had a permanent snarl locked in to its five foot long jaw. A snarl that showed off all of its hundreds of needle sharp steel teeth, since the creature had no lips to hide them. Nor did it have skin to cover the gigantic talons on each of its four stubby legs. Six or seven feet long, each talon glinted wickedly in the sun, showing its razor sharpness to anyone too near. Then there were the wicked steel spines that began at the top of its head and ran all the way to the tip of its tail, like some sort of crest.

This was a creature that had been built solely to fight. Its main weapon might be the fire storm it sprayed out, but even on the ground this would be a formidable foe. The head on that massively long neck could whip round to bite a man and a horse in half, while the tail could probably decapitate anyone foolish enough to be within striking distance. To approach it as a warrior would be to face the wrath of its terrible talons, and the soldier would have few tools that could even scratch its surface. Axes might not be enough.

The red eyes that he'd seen on the steel rats were also there, but these were the size of dinner plates. What's more they were still glowing, a sign that the creature still had some life left in it. Which was the reason that he and the others stopped some distance from it. Even the bravest knew enough to know the creature wasn't finished yet. Its back might be broken, two of its legs smashed beyond recognition, but it wasn't dead.

Looking around at the other two drakes further down the way, he could see they were both in worse condition, showing the effects of their fall clearly. They had exploded on impact. This one for some reason, had survived. Perhaps it hadn't had quite so far to fall. Perhaps it was simply tougher.

"Stand clear." Sam called out the command even as he dismounted, knowing that while he intended to get closer, no one else should. If the drake was immune to a fire wizard's magic, so too was a fire wizard immune to the drakes fire, provided he held an ice shield tight around him. Others wouldn't be so lucky. He began drawing the ice as quickly as he could.

It was a strange looking shield. And in fact it wasn't really a shield at all. It was the opposite of one. His fire shield was a wall of fire so hot that it turned anything flammable to ash and melted steel in a heartbeat. And because fire could stream, it could also deflect and repel physical forces. The ice shield was the exact opposite. It was a zone around him where every last scrap of heat and fire had been removed. The water vapour in the air had become tiny little ice crystals that looked like fog. And anything that had even a trace of heat in it would be drawn to it. But if the drake attacked him with fire, the shield would do the one thing that his fire shield couldn't. It would absorb the fire completely. He might look like a man in a personal cloud of ice crystals, but he was completely protected from fire.

Once his shield was in place, he approached the creature slowly on foot. He wasn't going to risk his horse's life in such a contest when he didn't have to. It was enough that he would risk his own. Shivering slightly with the cold and his nerves, he drew his ice shield so tight around him it was almost like a cloak. A frost cloak, that hung in the air before him.

As he walked toward it he watched intently for any sign that the creature was readying its fire. Fortunately there was none. Perhaps it couldn't breathe fire any longer with a broken back? He could but hope.

After what seemed like ages, he came within twenty feet of the creature's head, and stared into its ruby red eyes, knowing with some dread that the creature was staring back at him. It might never have been truly alive but it still wasn't dead, as whatever magic had made it kept it going, and it knew him.

"Do you speak?"

Despite his best intentions his voice came out as surprisingly thin and squeaky, which bothered him. He'd wanted to intimidate the creature. A pointless desire as the creature had no emotions. It didn't know what fear was. He also clearly didn't succeed as the beast failed to respond. But then could it? Could any machina actually speak?

It was a question he couldn't answer, despite the fact that he wanted to. Certainly no golems could speak. They had no intelligence that wasn't that of their master. This thing was probably brighter. But was it bright enough to speak? He doubted it. To speak was to have some ability however limited, to think. And to think was to be able to question, to rebel. The beast's master would never have allowed that. All it could do was obey.

"Can your master speak through you?" It was a better question. Not because the creature understood him, but because it recognised one word; master. That, and the fact that it was now in pieces, would be strange enough for the creature to ask for instructions from him. And that in turn was enough for Sam to feel the magic that was its master responding in surprise and shock. He clearly hadn't been watching his creatures closely. He therefore hadn't realised that the drakes were down, let alone that a mere half elf was approaching one on foot. No doubt he was busy preparing another attack somewhere else.

Naturally his first response, as before, was to attack. It seemed to be the master's only command. But his order was largely disobeyed as the drake found it had no fire in its belly, and couldn't move its head or tail far enough to reach him. Instead it just lay there, moving its head as far as it could on twisted screeching hinges, snapping its remaining teeth at him threateningly, but all in vain. It was helpless, which let Sam breath another huge sigh of relief – quietly. And then to remember that wars were also fought with words.

"Don't think so evil one. Your creature's broken like its comrades and soon you will be too." He even smiled as he said it, not truly as confident as he tried to appear, but determined to upset the creature's master, who somehow he guessed, could hear every word through his creation. He could even feel the Dragon's shock and rage as he listened to himself being threatened, and futilely ordered his drake to attack again and again. This new Dragon was not a very well controlled person.

"Temper, temper foul child. Tantrums aren't going to help. Or didn't your mother ever teach you that?" This time Sam's smile was genuine as he felt the creature's master losing the last of his self-control when he discovered his creature wasn't obeying him. No doubt he would be throwing things around and foaming out of the mouth like any mad man. And while he couldn't speak through his creation, he could still tell Sam a lot about himself without realising it.

"Well then, don't listen to me. Just know that we now know about your ships. We're tracking them even as you soil yourself, and soon you'll be ours." The Dragon's reaction was just what Sam wanted, as his incredible rage suddenly turned to outright fear as he heard Sam's blatant lie and panicked. He obviously hadn't realised that they knew of his ships, and he'd never even thought about the possibility of them being followed home. For a brief while Sam felt the Dragon's attention vanish from him, and knew he was busy ordering his creatures around.

Sam could just imagine him issuing commands to his ships not to return to his base ever again, never realising that that was exactly what Sam wanted. With no returning ships he would have that much more difficulty attacking new targets, though from the fact that he could order them, Sam understood that even his great black ships were machina. He also had no idea that he'd just confirmed to Sam everything the shadelings had said.

Sam waited patiently, his smile growing broader. Finally, there was some hope on the horizon.

"We know about Andrea too!" The moment he felt the Dragon's attention returning he threw the statement at him, and got a response he didn't expect – confusion. This new Dragon, whoever he was, didn't quite know what he was talking about, though after a moment Sam could feel the wheels turning in his mind as he recognised the word. He knew the caverns, knew their history and the Dragon's, he just didn't live there. And a no was as good as a yes to Sam as it also told him more of their enemy.

"We know that you have the knowledge contained within the caverns. Soon it will be ours too, and your machina won't be the only ones waging war."

It was another complete lie and Sam was almost stunned that the Dragon didn't see through it. Clearly he wasn't a very clever man. He was however, a coward and Sam felt a new wave of fear running through him, a sign that he at least knew exactly what knowledge was contained within the caverns. But this time he gave no orders; there were none he could give. Clearly neither he nor his creatures were anywhere near them, though Sam would have bet every last gold piece he had that the enemy's knowledge came from them.

But then came the question Sam most wanted answered, and he thought he had a way to make the new Dragon tell him. It was going to require all his meagre acting ability, however.

"Oh and by the way, even without that knowledge we will win. The original Dragon lost, and lost badly to our ancestors. He wasn't very bright. We're a lot more powerful than them and you're only a pretender. Someone who found his secrets and tried to use them."

This time he felt a whole raft of emotions coming from the machina's master as he spoke. There was more shock and fear at the thought of losing. Somehow this creature had never considered himself vulnerable. Then there was anger at being labelled a pretender, and a strong hint of false denial at being told he'd simply found his secrets. The enemy considered himself as more than that even if he knew the truth. But the important thing was that there was no sense of anger at being told the original Dragon had lost badly because he was an idiot. This one wasn't the original. He didn't like being called a pretender, a copy of the Dragon, but he wasn't the Dragon himself.

That question now answered, it remained only to scare the enemy, and to scare him badly. Sam though had a plan for that. One that he knew would work because this new Dragon was no disciple of the Red God. He knew nothing of tactics or strategy. Nothing of war.

"So you think the magic of your steel drakes makes them immune to fire?" For an illustration he let a small flame appear floating just above his left hand. Immediately he sensed the enemy watching him intently, more than slightly curious as to what he was going to do with the fire. Exactly as he wanted him to, while all the time the fire surging through him was growing and being shaped into a sword in his hands.

"Did it ever occur to you that there's no such thing as true immunity to magic? Just the strength to resist. But strength – all strength – has its limits and enchantments of fire protection are no match for a true fire wizard. Elven mages are a hundred times stronger than any others in the lands. You took Shavarra by evil and skulduggery, while Ragnor's Rock was also unprepared and with only human wizards at their side. Never again will you strike so easily at the elves. And you will pay for your crimes!" As he uttered his curse Sam couldn't help but shake. It wasn't just for effect, or because of the anger that was once more fighting to be released. It was because of the massive bolt of fire that was coursing through his body, almost out of control, desperate to be released. He didn't try to hold it back.

Sam let go a blast of pure fire at the stricken steel drake. Shaped into a fiery sword, it was as strong as anything he'd ever tried, and the heat from the blade almost cooked him where he stood. Which was nothing compared to what it did to its target. But just in case it failed, he reformed the ground under the creature into a swamp of liquid earth. One way or another the creature was about to die, while its master believed it destroyed by fire.

Happily the earth magic wasn't needed. At the first touch of the flame blade the steel creature began screeching, as its twisted remains buckled under the incredible heat which was easily hot enough to melt and forge metal. Its eyes, those massive ruby cut crystal eyes, instantly blackened, and then shattered as if a hammer had been dropped on them. Even its six foot long polished steel talons twisted up into unrecognisable shapes.

Scarcely a heartbeat later the creature exploded – if that

was the right word. In truth what it did was so much more powerful than anything he'd ever seen before, that calling it an explosion was like referring to the sun as a candle in the sky.

The sound was like a cannon blasting barely a foot away from him, while the ground underneath him buckled and shook with its force. The fire and flame that screamed out in all directions was so bright it even lit up the bright daylight sky. The pieces of steel, sand and flame that came at him like a million flaming arrows were thankfully soaked up by the ice shield he'd been growing around him for all that time, but not without almost knocking him to the ground despite his being in the calm centre of the fire.

For a while Sam thought he was going to die, the ferocity of the fire all around him was so great. But it didn't truly matter right then, because more important than that was feeling the creature die. Or rather, he felt its strange link with its evil master shatter. And somehow when he heard the screams of the machina he realised that whatever the strange link was that connected master and machina, it could transfer just a little of the creature's suffering back to him. At least when he was concentrating on them. Using them as his eyes and ears. He wasn't just angry for once, he was hurt. It was a good feeling as far as Sam was concerned, even if it only lasted a heartbeat or two.

Too soon it was all over. The battle was ended and the victory his. One moment the evil one was there, then the next the ground shook with thunder and it was gone. Sam figured the Dragon wouldn't be sending any of his machina back in their direction in a hurry.

A few moments later the smoke had cleared enough that he could see once more the outline of the shattered steel drake. But this time what few parts of it were still recognisable were twisted and blackened. The rest was simply missing; in its place a pile of embers, some puddles of steel, and mounds of blackened earth smouldering away. The sight of it, burnt, broken and above all dead, confirmed to him all he wanted to know. He was truly gone.

It was an enormous relief to have the Dragon gone from his thoughts, and Sam breathed deeply of the fresh air, amazed at how good it tasted in his lungs. But as well as the relief, a feeling of triumph was slowly growing within him. He had defeated the enemy, even if it was only at a great distance and through his servants. Better yet he had destroyed the remains of a steel drake with fire despite the supposed impossibility of doing so.

And the Dragon had been told a pack of lies and had apparently swallowed them completely, showing his true naivety in war. Now Sam felt sure he would be slowed down in his campaign of conquest for fear of his ships being followed back to his base. Nor when he next attacked, would he go for an elven province. He was too scared. He would find smaller, weaker targets, hoping to gradually increase his power on the land.

It was a strange thing to understand, but this new Dragon, powerful as he was, wasn't impossible to defeat after all. He could be fooled, his armies beaten, and eventually, he could even be hunted down and killed. After three long, painful and hard months of misery and despair, for the first time the elves could have some hope.

Hope not just that they would find safety in the Golden River Flats, but also that the enemy could be defeated, and that they might one day return to their beloved Shavarra, though it might be many years away. He couldn't wait to tell the elders, even though he knew it would become an interrogation. They still didn't quite believe that he could feel the machina's master through his creatures. But they would.

Even more he wanted to tell Ry and her parents. The smile

on Ry's face would warm him down to his very toes, while her parents would celebrate as only travelling elves could. There would be feasting, music, singing and dancing. Or at least what they could manage of such things on the trail.

Of course, first he had to find her somewhere in a caravan filled with frightened people, and then pray she hadn't been hurt. Fire Angel or not, it seemed he had his own lesson in humility to learn. No amount of magic could guarantee safety let alone victory.

Chapter Nineteen.

The cavern was dark much as Heri had expected, lit by only a few torches hanging from the walls. And the walls themselves were very cold to touch owing to the fact that the water flowed down them in winter. It was never the sort of place that a man wanted to be, and Heri shuddered a little in the cold, damp air. He worried that some disease might already be attacking his lungs. But he had expected all of that and it wasn't as if he had a lot of other places where he could find what he needed. His spies had told him long ago exactly what he would find in this black market, and how to gain access. Most of them were probably dead by now, some by his own hand. Still, they had been useful.

He pulled his fur a little tighter around him, flicked the reigns lightly and had his horse trot slowly, further into the darkness. She snorted, not liking the dark or the smell, but she obeyed him. If only his subjects had been so obedient! But then she was alive and many of them weren't. They were ashes in the remains of Fall Keep. They had paid for their treachery with their lives, and that was as it should be. The memory still brought him pleasure. It might have been more than a month ago that he had lost his throne, but it was good to know that his enemies had not prospered from it.

In fact the news on the trail had been all bad for his enemies. The keep had been completely destroyed, and the resulting fire had levelled much of the city behind it. What was left of the citadel was now little more than ruins, and no one knew what had happened. More importantly no one knew he was alive.

With no king to usurp the throne and no citadel to capture, the nobles of Fair Fields and their armies had quickly fallen into their old bad habits, and had started fighting. Most of them blamed the others for destroying the keep. Prince Venti was the one most commonly blamed. It had been his army almost on the doorstep of Fall Keep when it had happened after all. And so the strongest of the noble houses had become the first target for the wrath of the others. Several of the towns of Griffin Dale were now under siege and the prince was said to be desperately recruiting soldiers to defend the rest.

But the Principality of Griffin Dale would not be the last to go to war. Because even when there was nothing left to fight for, the noble houses would fight each other purely for spite. Fair Fields was once again in a state of near anarchy. It had always been a realm that had needed a strong king. Without one it was falling into ruin. Maybe that would teach the nobles something about how useful a king he had been, Heri thought. Not that he planned on letting any of them live long enough to truly regret their treason. First he would kill his verminous brother, then it would be their turn as he reclaimed his throne.

Meanwhile refugees from Fall Keep were flooding the roads and the towns in their thousands, looking for somewhere to live and generally causing chaos. But that had worked in his favour from the start. With so many refugees on the roads, what was one more? So after a few days on the road by himself, with his stubble starting to show through and hiding his face, he had simply joined them. No one had recognised him. Now no one would recognise him. Not when the king was dead and he now sported the start of a full beard and was dressed in a peasant's cloak. No one was even looking for him.

Two hundred paces in the cavern narrowed just as he'd been told it would, and at the far end was a huge dark, heavy, oak door with huge iron hinges. It was the sort of door that would be used on a castle to withstand the blows of a battering ram, and it was here for exactly the same reason. The people on the other side of the door lived in constant fear of attack. Why else would anyone live in such a gloomy cavern?

Dismounting, Heri approached the door and thumped it as hard as he could with his good fist. Three good solid thumps, a brief pause, and then three more. It was the first part of the code his spies had told him to use. The information turned out to be good as a few moments later a small, steel barred slot opened in the door and a pair of eyes stared back at him from the other side.

"Yeah?"

It was more a grunt than a word, but Heri understood the guard perfectly.

"Alder Lives." He gave the password and then promptly worried that he'd got it wrong when the eye slot snapped shut. But a heartbeat later he heard the noise of huge bolts being slammed open, and then the door itself swung inwards. Not feeling anywhere near as confident as he appeared, Heri strode through the open doorway and led his mare into the black market.

His spies had told him what to expect, and yet he still wasn't prepared for what he discovered in front of him. For a start the narrow cavern had suddenly opened out into a huge chasm in the middle of the mountain, with a domed ceiling surely as high as the grandest of towers. He thought there was actually enough space to fit his old keep and the parade grounds as well.

There was plenty of light in the great cavern, though no sunlight. Instead it came from glowing crystals embedded in the walls. Great purple crystals that cast a somewhat sinister glow on everyone and everything inside. His spies had never been able to tell him what they were made of or how they worked, but it was enough that they did.

To the side was a small shrine to Alder, the only god most of these people would ever worship. Even most of the mercenaries were his followers rather than those of the Red God. But then they fought for coin, not victory. As long as they got paid they didn't care whether they won or lost.

The sculpture of the God of Mischief was a particularly ugly one. Someone had gone to great lengths to show all of the grotesque lord's deformities in their full glory and had succeeded wonderfully. All those parts of men and woman, people and animals were shown woven together into a whole that was more hideous than any creature that had ever lived. Heri threw a copper piece into the offering bowl as was expected and walked on into the market, trying not to stare at the statue.

The market itself was just like any other. It was comprised of simple stalls and the traders competed with each other to get the peasants to buy their wares. In fact many of the traders that had once visited his kingdom might also have set up here. He might well have bought from some of them. But none of them he was certain would recognise him. Though even if they did, none would do anything about it. Not when they had as much to lose as he did. This was the fabled black market of Fair Fields, a place where the lawless and the black of heart did business, and there was no such thing as a good, honest merchant. Everyone here had a price on their head if they were caught. Though it was probably a mistake, Heri felt almost safe among these brigands and rogues. At least he understood them. Besides, there was no price on his head. Everyone thought he was dead.

"No trouble." An oversized guard, a human with some form of tusked beast blood in his past, grunted the order at him. Heri might have thought he was part troll save that his tusks ran down from his top jaw instead of the other way around.

Heri ignored him as he strode hurriedly towards the waiting stalls, almost dragging the mare with him. They were the reason he had come and their wares, illegal and probably unobtainable anywhere else, were what would allow him to cause the trouble the guard didn't want – for his brother.

The first stall he came to was run by an ageing mercenary of some sort, too old to fight anymore, but still showing all the scars of his past on his bare flesh. He was a grizzled man with hard eyes and plenty of long ropey muscles in his arms. No doubt he had once been a man to fear, and he probably would still pose a risk to the unwary. But Heri had no interest in him. His wares were mainly stolen weapons, many of them poisoned or carrying other curses that would never have been allowed in the more civilised realms. His armour selection was poor. Most of it was old and rusting, but the stuff that was still serviceable included quite a few pieces that a burglar or assassin might wear. Blacked out, light weight for ease of movement, and well-oiled for silence. Heri could have used some of it, but he had to come to his brother openly, and being dressed as an assassin would not help. He moved on.

Further down the row of stalls he found a sylph merchant with a wide assortment of poisons and potions. And the man was pure blooded. The pointed shape of his skull was too marked for him to be anything else. That surprised him. Sylph seldom left their cities and the company of their own people. No doubt he was a dark wizard, cast out from his people for some crime or other and trying to make some easy gold. Heri didn't like either wizards or the sylph. They were an arrogant people. And their magic threatened him. But Heri didn't care about that when he discovered the merchant had a vial of clouded azure, something no other wizard would ever carry. It was the one substance known that would block a wizard's magic. The trick of course was to get it into the wizard. They didn't tend to like being poisoned. Still, Heri bought the vial for what was an outrageous price, and felt better for it. Finally he had something to remove his half-brother's magic. Without it Samual would be far less dangerous.

At the next stall he found a trap-maker, and quickly made a pair of knife throwers his. They were intricate and highly illegal devices in every realm he knew of. After all they were one of the favourite weapons of thieves and cut-throats everywhere. Heri wasn't a swordsman, but he had always been very deft with a knife. Until Samual had destroyed his hand and taken that skill from him. The knife throwers though would make up for his missing fingers as they hurled the knives for him, and they were easily concealed in sleeves.

It seemed that Heri's decision to visit the black market had been a good one, and for the first time in ages he found himself smiling as he stowed away his purchases. But there was still a lot more to buy, if he could find it. And top of the list was something to take out the elves who were sheltering Samual. He was absolutely certain that Samual would be with the Shavarran elves. After all, that was where his whore was from.

The bestiary further down the row looked like it might provide some answers for him, and he quickly scurried over to it and the rows of exotic and deadly creatures locked away behind its bars. His horse though had other ideas as she smelled some of the creatures behind the bars and knew them for the predators they were. He had to spend some time calming her.

Eventually they made it to the pens, and Heri had to admit that he liked what he saw. Giga monsters, wyverns, blood trolls, snap wolves and so many more. The beast-master and his handlers had scoured the world to stock their bestiary, and possessed the most dangerous creatures imaginable. None of them of course would have been seen in a normal market. None of them would have been allowed to live.

Heri though was disappointed. Although all of them were true monsters, none of them could kill his brother. Not when he had such powerful fire magic at his fingertips and could see them coming. And not when he was sheltered by the elves. Two very big problems.

"Like what you see?" The beast-master had apparently decided to join him, hoping to sell some of his creatures. But he didn't sound enthusiastic.

Heri guessed he didn't look like his normal customers, most of whom would have been buying the beasts to stock the arenas that also weren't supposed to exist in a civilised land. Those customers the trader knew had coin. And they probably also bought a lot of creatures. However it was fairly quiet and he was the only customer the man had. So the trader was going to be nice and hope he still might have coin to spend. Others might use his beasts after all. Mostly those who needed a monster or two for some nefarious purpose.

Creatures could be very useful. Often they were used to kill someone and make it look like an accident. Sometimes people just wanted to create a scare, either to drive others away or to create business for themselves as protectors. And occasionally an army would use a few beasts as shock troops. There was always a market for a well-trained monster. And there were monsters and beasts that could deal with elves.

The beast-master was a big man, dressed from head to foot in rough leathers, and carrying a pair of whips large enough to reach from one end of the cavern to the other. He was probably the only man large enough and strong enough to use them. That was probably the way that he controlled the deadly beasts. That, and his smell, which was bad enough to make a strong man faint at twenty feet. Heri held his breath as best he could, knowing that he needed him.

"Not enough. I have an elf problem." And that was his

true problem. Samual could be overcome easily enough once you knew how and what he was capable of. He might have become a powerful fire mage, but a knife in the belly would still kill him. It was getting that knife into his belly when he was surrounded by elves who would all rush to his aid that was the problem.

"Elves?" The beast-master looked puzzled for a heartbeat, then let a slow, calculating grin slide over his face, something that looked more than a little disturbing on his swarthy features. "Tell me about it. How many elves? How badly do you want them dead?"

Heri stared at him, beginning to hope that maybe all of his problems were able to be overcome.

"Very many elves, and it's not them that I want dead. It's the man they shelter. They're just in the way. And they might try to stop me leaving as well." He let a smile grow on his own face. "I can reach my target and kill him. But after that I'll need a way out. Something to keep the elves busy and which they won't see coming."

"Tell me what you can do for me and how much it'll cost."

"I can do a great deal for you. But it'll cost a great deal as well." The man's smile grew unnaturally broad. So broad in fact that he almost looked a little like one of his beasts.

In the end everything came down to gold – it always did – and Heri had plenty. He'd stashed it away over the years – just in case. And it would go further now that he wasn't paying for an army of assassins who had all failed time and again to find and kill Samual. This time he was going to do it the way he always should have. He was going to do it himself.

Chapter Twenty.

"Elder Bela has asked to see you Samual Hanor."

Sam started at the sound of the woman's voice coming from immediately behind him, unsettling his horse. Yet he shouldn't have been surprised. He'd heard the hooves clip clopping their way up from behind him. He just hadn't paid them any attention, lost as he was in surveying the barren wasteland that surrounded him.

Four weeks on the trail through the Dead Creek Pass, and the land hadn't improved since they first entered it. Not even now that they were nearly at the end of it. Some days he thought it was all there was to this place; sand and dirt which ran for league after league in every direction without end. It appeared to be a dead land and staring at it constantly somehow sapped at his strength. Perhaps it was the training in nature magic which was making him more sensitive to such things, but the desolation of the land clutched at him almost like a sword at his throat, and he spent hours just staring at it in horror and wishing he didn't have to see it.

Then again it could have been the sand and dust itself which tormented him most. It seemed to get in every crevice of a man's flesh, left the throat dried out and scratchy, and the eyes red and sore. The heat just made everything worse. After a month of it he dreamed of bathing in cool clear rivers.

And the terrible thing was they weren't actually in the wastes themselves. The trail they were following lay on the border between the wastes and the Fedowir Kingdom. A narrow strip of land perhaps a league and a half wide and bordered by shallow hills. The wastes themselves if they headed south into them, were hotter and drier again. Anyone who entered them soon expired from the harsh heat unless they were prepared. If they went north of course things got better, but only a little. The southern part of the Fedowir kingdom merely exchanged sand for dry packed dirt. People would still die there. The trail through the Dead Creek Pass was just harsh.

For anyone attuned at all to the magic of the natural world, this place was like a wound on the world and to wander through it was to experience pain. It wasn't just the scarcity of living things that caused it. It was that so much of what life there was twisted somehow. The wastes were home to manticores and basilisks. Unnatural and deadly creatures created by magic in the ages before the Dragon Wars. Sand scorpions thrived here. So did giga monsters and shaded cobras. If it was poisonous and deadly, it could be found in them. And even what little decent life there was, was twisted. The plants themselves were harsh and dried out, surviving only by virtue of the fact that they too weren't natural.

According to some of the ancient histories, the wastes had not always existed. Not as wastes anyway. But at some point during the time before the Dragon Wars, some great and terrible spell had been cast that had turned a vibrant and healthy land into this waste. Others claimed that it was the wars themselves that had ruined the land. Sam didn't know if that was true or not. No one did. But it certainly felt like it. The land felt cursed. Even the trail that ran alongside them felt the same.

Sam didn't like this place. In fact the only good thing about the wastes that he could find was that they were nearly out of them.

For the last month he'd spent much of his time trying to think of other things. He concentrated on his duties and practised his magic. He'd even flicked through the texts covering the legend of the Fire Angel – Pietral had obtained a copy of the collected tales from somewhere – and it had made for some interesting reading.

The Fire Angel could apparently not just draw and cast fire, but breathe it like a dragon. He could walk on it too. And in what had to be the most amazing thing he'd ever heard, the Fire Angel could apparently call a phoenix to ride on into battle. Or was that summon one? There were no phoenix after all, so surely you couldn't call one. You had to bring one across from another realm. And didn't the writers know that the phoenix fire would turn even a fire mage to ash as he rode? Even if you could somehow ride a giant bird made of fire, death was assured the instant you got on its back.

He would have thought the writers would have known better since they were elves. The phoenix after all was the favoured companion of the Goddess.

As for the battles the Fire Angel had supposedly engaged in, they were even more fanciful. Apparently he'd defeated armies of giants, ogres and dragons, burning them all to ash. No one seemed to have remembered that the dragons were said to be completely immune to fire. That they even kept their eggs warm with it. But maybe the facts about the children of Draco weren't so important to elves. Draco wasn't their god after all.

The tales were outlandish and obviously written by those who had little understanding of the truth. Still, they were something to read and have a chuckle over. Provided that no one took them seriously. Especially when they took his thoughts off the land all around them. Still, it was probably fortunate that someone had come to give him something to do other than sit there and bemoan his fate now that he'd finished reading them.

He turned to greet the speaker and thank her for her message, but stopped when he realised he had seen her before, and forgot what he was going to say. Though it had been some months since he had seen her, he recognised her. It was the stern faced woman who had first brought him to Ry's parents. Now though, here in this dead wasteland, stern was an understatement. Her face was drawn with tiredness while despair and worry had traced their own lines around her eyes.

"I know you, don't I?" It wasn't what he'd meant to say. He'd meant to give a polite thank you, but it was what he'd been meaning to ask since that very first day he'd met her. He'd never seen her before, and yet there was something very familiar about her.

"We've only met the once Fire Angel." And yet when he looked in her eyes he knew she too knew him. She was simply evading his question with a simple truth, a blatant sophistry and something elves normally didn't engage in if it would lead to deception. But he wasn't about to allow her to get away with it.

"Perhaps, good soldier, and yet I still know you. What is your name?" It was a direct question, perhaps too direct for an elf to ask, but then he was not entirely an elf, and he left her no room to evade his question.

"Mayvelle Ellosian."

"Ellosian? My mother's name?" And yet as he looked at her he suddenly knew why she looked so familiar. She looked like his mother would if his mother had eaten some particularly sour lemons. He might have only been four when she died giving birth to her second child, his brother or sister had the baby survived, but he still remembered her face. And if he'd ever forgotten, her portraits had been hung throughout his father's bedchamber and his own. He'd married his second wife – though in law she was his only true wife – the Lady Dreasda a mere six months later. She had been a woman of high status as he had to give the kingdom a legitimate heir, but it had been a marriage of necessity. He had never loved her. And the fact that he had never taken down the pictures of his true love had likely not made for a happy marriage.

She nodded. "My mother and yours were sisters in law, my father your uncle by blood. We are cousins."

Her words caught him by surprise, and yet looking at her he knew them for the truth. He wasn't sure he liked them though. It should have been a good thing, finally finding kin among the elves, but for some reason it wasn't. Perhaps it was simply the terrible bleakness that surrounded them, but the look in Mayvelle's eyes told of no joy, only regret, and even a coldness that worried him. Still, there were formalities to be considered on meeting kin, especially for the first time. Customs he had practised for five long years as he'd waited for this day even while he'd put it off.

"It is an honour to meet you cousin." He reached out and clasped both her hands in his, bowing his head to her as was proper and tried not to notice the way she flinched and nearly pulled completely away from his clasp, almost as if he was diseased.

"I am Samual Hanor, son of King Eric Hanor the First of Fair Fields, and Alliye Ellosian of Shavarra. Though both are now passed on from this mortal realm, in their names I welcome your company with pleasure."

"And I am Mayvelle Ellosian daughter of Ellree and Mauric'ell Ellosian of Shavarra. In the name of our family I greet you."

If he could be blunt, then apparently so could his new found cousin. Blunt to the point of rudeness. For she had greeted him only. There was clearly no welcome stated or implied. She acted as if he were a new found acquaintance rather than kin or even friend. That was shocking and very unelven. The haste with which she let go his hand clasp was more so. Nor had she even met him with either honour or pleasure, suggesting she wanted nothing to do with him. Their meeting was a matter of duty, no more.

Her greeting cut like a rusty dagger straight into his heart. Just when he was starting to feel accepted by the elves, truly welcome among them, his own family rejected him. The only kin he had except for Ry and her family.

"Have I given you cause for offence cousin?" He couldn't think of any way he might have, but he could think of nothing else that might cause such coldness towards him. "If so I apologise, as a man, as kin and as a knight of Hanor."

"You have given no offence knight of Hanor. This is simply not the time or place for such things. Elder Bela has asked for you to attend to him."

Once more she addressed him by a formal title rather than as kin, something that wasn't lost on him. Nor was the fact that she kneed her horse's flanks and made to leave without giving him even the chance to reply. Her message had been delivered and apparently there was nothing more to be said.

"I understand. Please inform Elder Bela I will be with him as soon as I have spoken with my family, good soldier."

Sam called it after her retreating back, and though she gave no sign, he knew she had heard. Heard and no doubt wondered which family he meant. She didn't slow down though to ask. Clearly she wanted to be as far away from him as soon as possible. It was almost as though he had become a plague carrier once more.

Knowing that he might never truly understand all the subtleties of elven custom, Sam did exactly as he had said. He tapped on Tyla's reins and headed directly for Ryshal and her family. Not only might they at least have some idea of what such a response might mean and what to do about it, they were also naturally inquisitive. And though some less tactful elves might call them nosey, they might well know the reason for his cousin's apparent dislike of him. But even if they didn't, they would quickly find out.

Cantering back to the wagon, he soon found his father in law re-packing a pair of ball bearing wagon wheels, and went to help him. Pietrel might know more about workings and repair of wagons than anyone else alive, certainly more than Sam, but he still could use help. Wheels, especially the metal shod ones, were incredibly heavy, and it was a two man job to take them off and put them back on a wagon, and regrettably there was a lot of work to do. Pietrel could have been kept busy repairing their wagons from morning to night for the next year, as they – never having been intended for such long journeys – constantly needed to be repaired. Most of the repairs of course involved repacking the bearings, as once the dust got into them they started squeaking and made the wagons much harder to pull.

"I met my cousin just now." Not quite knowing what else to say, Sam opened the conversation with his news, even as he reached for the nearest wheel to begin rolling it back to the wagon. Pietral raised his eyebrows in surprise.

"Really. Who?" Pietrel was tired of course – repairing so many wagons he had every reason to be – and that probably explained his parsimony with words. But at least with him Sam knew he meant nothing impolite by them.

"Mayvelle Ellosian, daughter of Ellree and Mauric'ell Ellosian. A woman with a harsh demeanour, and little time for me."

He could have said more, could have mentioned the way she had recoiled from him but he didn't need to. Pietrel understood him, understood that whenever distant family met there should always be time for greetings and conversation at least, even during these trying times. Especially during such times.

Nothing was said for a little while after that as together they lifted the wheel up to the axle, and then started hammering it home with the large wooden mallets Pietrel carried with him. It was hard work on a hot day, and it was a welcome thing when Pietrel could finally knock home the locking pin and then get the horse to pull the wagon off its blocks. But finally it was done and his father in law looked at him with a small nod.

"Your family is ours. Alendro and I will speak with them."

"My thanks." Sam was grateful, that they would, though a little worried about what they might learn. Could it be something to do with the death of his mother as an unmarried woman and the shame that had brought upon the family? There had been little choice in the matter when his father had been king and bearing the weight of an entire realm upon his shoulders. But that did not make it either right or proper. It had been one of the reasons Sam had been so determined to marry Ryshal the moment they had become close. There would be no shame for her because of him. It was also another reason why he had never wanted the throne. He would choose his love over the throne any day.

Still, he had no time to worry about such things. The Elder had summoned him, and Elder Bela was not a man who enjoyed being kept waiting. So with the work done Sam gave his apologies and left for the vanguard at a canter.

His first thought when he approached the elders was that they had visitors, and that had to be a good thing since it had to mean that they were close to the end of the trail. He knew they were guests because of the way the elves wore their hair.

All elves wore it long – he was letting his grow long at Ry's urging – but the elves of Shavarra wore it either free or in long open plats. These newcomers sitting with the elders had their hair tied up in long, thin, tightly wound plats in the way that the elves of Golden River Flats did. They weren't from Shavarra. Their armour indicated the same thing. Rangers had joined them judging by their sigils. And rangers of the order of the blood bear. It was an order he didn't recognise. Blood bears did not dwell in Shavarra, and no one he knew wore their image as a sigil. But the fearsome creatures were found throughout the Golden River Flats.

His next thought was that the group seemed troubled, which was worrying. If they were so close to the end of the trail between the wastes and the Fedowir Kingdom they should be happy. Relieved that the worst of their long journey was over. And the Master of the natural magics should be happiest of all. But Master Bela looked the most troubled of all.

Still, he knew he would find out what was wrong shortly – and then with luck be able to deal with it.

Sam cantered the last of the way to the elders, dismounted and then approached the camp on foot. "Elders." He nodded as was proper, and waited to be welcomed.

"Samual." War Master Wyldred greeted him and even managed a weak smile. But he looked no happier than any of the others. "Come join us."

"This is Elder Frolan from the Golden City."

The Golden City itself? Sam was surprised. There were three cities in the Golden River Flats. Although the "Golden City" wasn't actually a city at all. Most claimed it was merely a large town. But according to legend it had once been the first city in the realm, and that it had shrunk over the millennia as the people had left it to make new homes elsewhere. Homes that in time had become cities while the original city had shrunk.

Despite being only a town it was still well known. It was one of the places that the bard's often sang of in their endless ballads. They called it magical and mystical and above all else, mysterious. It was also well known because it was reputed to be the home of the most powerful and knowledgeable of elven spell casters. It was there that the greatest of elven spell casters trained. As did the archivists, historians, priesthood and lawmakers. It might only be a town but it was the spiritual heart of the Golden River Flats. It was also where people went if they had a magical problem that could not be resolved elsewhere.

"I'm honoured to meet you Elder." Sam greeted the Elder as was expected and wasn't surprised when Elder Bela managed a wry smile in turn. No doubt he found it unusual that Sam should be so respectful to another. Unfortunately there was some truth in that criticism.

"And I you Samual Hanor. You would be the Fire Angel we have heard so much about."

It wasn't a question and he was no Fire Angel but Sam nodded regardless, wondering why this new elf should be so interested in him.

"Good. The Lady Meriana wishes to speak with you when your people have settled in."

All around him Sam could hear the sounds of breaths being drawn in in surprise, and wondered why. He guessed it would have something to do with the mention of the Lady's name, whoever she might be. But if she was as famous as she seemed to be, he still hadn't heard of her. No doubt the others would inform him later.

"I would be pleased to meet with any who might help our people in this time of trouble." As long as it didn't keep him too long away from his family, but he didn't add the last.

"You might not be so happy in time. Especially when she has said that she wishes to test you. But I will pass on your words anyway."

Test? Why did that sound suspiciously like what the elder wizards had done to him when he'd first returned with Ry? Though it had been months ago, he had no wish to go through such an ordeal again. And the elf's words strongly suggested it would be exactly that; an ordeal. Yet was it more than that? Looking at the elders around him, he realised that from the stunned looks on their faces, that the testing was obviously important. He thought he'd better find out.

"Test?"

"Yes Fire Angel, test. The Lady believes you may have some summoning potential, and she wishes to know if it's so."

Suddenly the troubled looks on the elders' faces made perfect sense to Sam, as he surely wore the same expression on his own face. A chill ran down his back.

Summoning! Sam felt ill. Though people often used the word loosely, to summon was vastly different from when a wizard drew magic to him or called a beast. It was a specific magic where creatures and objects from other realms were brought into theirs. Things that were not part of the world and which never should be. And of course some of those creatures were demons.

Summoners were dangerous. Not just because of what they could do, but because of how they thought. Creatures from other worlds thought in other ways. Ways that were foreign. And some of that strangeness became a part of the thoughts of those who made contact with other realms. It was almost like a contamination of the mind and the soul. In the end it was said, summoners who went too far were no longer human. Not inside.

It was as nothing he had suspected, and even less anything that he'd ever wanted. But it made perfect sense in a strange way. He could hear the thoughts of the enemy through his servants, the machina. No one else could, which was why the elder spell casters had had such a hard time believing him. After all, golems didn't have thoughts, and they didn't obey silent commands. They were ordered verbally and they obeyed until either the job was done or something had changed making it impossible to complete. But the machina were nothing like that. They had much greater intelligence, and they could be commanded silently from afar.

So what if the true difference between machina and golems wasn't simply in their construction, but rather their soul, for want of a better word? What if their master wasn't a spell caster as they'd all believed, but rather a creature from one of the other realms? A demon? Or another summoner? What if this wizard was bringing demons into the world and commanding them?

He didn't want to believe it. Summoners were regarded as among the darkest of spell casters, and thankfully the most rare. Against them only the necromancers were considered more evil, and thankfully, equally rare. At the feet of the two dark wizardries lay the blame for much of the death and destruction over the previous thousands of years of recorded history as their practitioners again and again sought power at the expense the people. As such they had started wars, created false religions, summoned monsters, and raised armies of the undead. Creating an army of machina was exactly what they might do, if they could.

It made sense but Sam didn't believe it. He couldn't allow himself to believe that he was such a wizard. And yet on the other hand, he was the only one who could hear the machina's master, something that wasn't lost on him or apparently the others. Already he could feel the divide between them growing as they started regarding him with suspicion. He couldn't face the elders and instead spent his time staring at his feet, wondering what to do. Surely they would never allow a summoner to remain among them? And he couldn't take Ry or her family away from her people. Not again; ever.

"I can't be a summoner! I've never felt a demon in my life, and I'm not evil!"

The words came out almost by themselves, as he felt his whole life slipping away from him. But he was preaching to the deaf, as even he feared he might have some summoning power. Enough to hear the thoughts of demons at least. Perhaps on some level, he truly was evil?

"The Lady knows that. Nor does she think you have any ability of command, only sensing. If you did you would have told the machina to leave. But you seem to have the power to hear them, and because of that it may be that you can know the enemy as few others. She has heard the reports, and she hopes you can tell her a little more of what you know."

His words sadly didn't fill Sam with confidence. A summoner of any stripe was not something he wanted to be.

"Samual. Summoners are not regarded as evil by elves." Elder Bela finally returned to the conversation.

"Rather we regard them as imperilled. Their gift makes them vulnerable to dark thoughts, to temptation. They can hear the thoughts of creatures not of this realm. Creatures with feelings utterly opposed to our own. And those few who can command them must then contend with the temptation of the

340

power of actual life and death over these outsider creatures."

"Because of those risks, we have developed ways of helping those few who are identified as summoners. Meditation techniques. Tests which can reveal to the spell caster the state of his own soul. And the stones of Ivor'll which can show the same to all others."

"With these and other means we can keep summoners on the good side of life. Which is why there has never been an elven summoner so corrupted or tormented as those of human and dwarven history. But then all spell casters are imperilled to some extent by their power, and we use many of those same methods to watch over us all. No one here believes you evil."

Imperilled? Sam wanted to believe him. Desperately. Yet the faces of the others as they stared at him said otherwise. They might not believe him evil, but they were worried. And he was worried too. Maybe they could keep summoners from turning to darkness. But still those with the magic would always be at risk. And everyone would know it. Even if the Elder was right, it was still a mark of shame. A reason to be feared and distrusted.

The one thing he realised he couldn't do however, was wait with this sort of anxiety in his heart. He couldn't leave his wife and family waiting either. He would go to the Lady Meriana immediately and get the test over and done with. And he would pray to the All Father that it would show him free of the taint.

But at least he now knew why his cousin had reacted so badly to seeing him. A summoner in the family? That had to be shameful.

Chapter Twenty One.

Four long days later Sam arrived at the Lady Meriana's tower, and his first thought was surprise that it really was a tower. That he hadn't expected, despite the fact that Aralor – the Lady's representative who had escorted him to see the Elder – had told him as much.

It wasn't an elven construction. Elves built in forests and often in their canopies. They built of wood. And this was an elven land and lady Meriana he was sure was an elf. So why did she have a tower, and a stone one at that? Or for that matter, why did she choose to live in one?

Towers were impractical at best for most purposes. The narrowness of rooms, the excessive number of steps to get from one room to the next. They certainly weren't ideal accommodation. But they did have a couple of advantages for specific groups. They made excellent lookout points, and so soldiers often had one attached to a barracks or a castle. And their elevation could also be used as a means of isolation. For that reason wizards sometimes used them. If they called forth something dangerous they could simply escape, knock down the stairs and leave whatever it was trapped inside – as long as it couldn't fly. Perhaps that was why the Lady Meriana had built it? The All Father only knew what monsters she might summon from the other realms. Though it still didn't explain why she lived in one.

Her tower however, was different from others he had seen. For a start it wasn't attached to another building let alone a fort. Instead it stood alone in a large clearing. It was also broader than many he'd seen, especially around the base, and he quickly guessed she had her living quarters there and her wizard chambers at the top. A sensible arrangement, though he personally would have preferred to have a house

Samual

elsewhere. Preferably a long way away from any wizard tower.

It was also made of white marble instead of the darker stone of which human castles and towers normally seemed to be built, which gave it quite a lovely aspect. Sitting on the brilliant green grass of the meadow that surrounded it and against the back drop of the dark green forests and the perfect blue sky, it almost seemed to shine. It was as though it was alive, and had grown out of the ground like a magnificent tree. Or a gigantic button mushroom.

Yet he did have to wonder. Was it really so odd for an elf to live in a tower? He had only ever once travelled to the Golden River Flats, and then he had only visited a single city – Tori' Less. He had never been to the Golden City or Vern mi Dall as it was properly known – the city of gold. How did he know that the elves in these parts did not build in this manner?

The sight of the tower didn't fill him with happiness though. Instead he felt apprehensive, because it would be here that he would find out the true extent of his magic, and he wasn't entirely sure that that was something he wanted to know. But he had come because he needed to know it, if only to know what to do about it. He dreaded the possibility that he might have some summoning ability, regardless of what Elder Bela had told him. No matter how he looked at it, consorting with demons was darkness.

As they'd ridden there, he on Tyla and Aralor on a unicorn of all creatures, he'd alternated between taking two choices. The first choice was to give up on the mission and go home to his family, without ever finding out if he had any ability. Though he would still be tainted by the rumour, at least it wouldn't be proven. The second was to get to the tower as fast as possible and have it shown that he had no summoning ability. If he did then he would know he could not be evil. The

343

trouble was that he feared that the test would show that he did have that gift. It could damn him as easily as save him.

Elder Bela's words had helped him a little as he journeyed, while his present to him of the stones of Ivor'll had made him more comfortable. Still, the journey hadn't been easy. For though the stones mostly stayed a beautiful blue, they changed colour whenever he was feeling a particularly intense emotion. He didn't want them to do that when the colours showed him and the whole world the truth of his feelings. Feelings of anger and rage he still kept trying to bottle up inside. Fear too.

Every time he thought about Ry and how she had been mistreated over the last five years the stones darkened, something that wasn't lost on either Aralor or himself. He was still angry about what Heri had done, sometimes very angry, and it showed in the stones even when he did his best to hide it. They turned red when he was worried – usually each time he thought about what the test would reveal. Fortunately his moods didn't last and the colours went away quickly. He didn't know what colour the stones would turn if he started summoning demons.

Now however, the journey was suddenly over, and the stones were red once more. No matter how difficult the journey had been, he could still wish himself back on it.

"The Lady is expecting us."

Of course she was. The one thing Sam was certain of was that a summoner would know when visitors were arriving, from whatever realm.

Still, as they rode towards the tower and he spotted a woman in front of it sweeping the stone courtyard, he wondered if they had made a mistake. Because he couldn't imagine the Lady sweeping her own courtyard, even though elves generally didn't have servants. He didn't fully understand how she could have a title – obviously the elves of the Flats were a little different to those of Shavarra – but he understood nobility. And nobles didn't sweep floors. Perhaps summoners were different?

Aralor told him otherwise however, when he asked. The woman sweeping the courtyard wasn't a servant at all but rather the Lady Meriana herself. Regardless she put down the broom to greet them as they approached and even managed a polite smile.

"By the creator you look frightened!"

The woman who greeted him with an easy manner and her hands on her hips was anything but what he had expected. Though what he had expected he didn't quite know. Still, it wasn't a middle aged elven woman with a broom in her hands and wearing an apron and scarf to keep the dust off her as she cleaned. She looked like a typical human housewife. Where, he wondered, were the elegant robes and precious medallions? Where was the menagerie of demons dancing at her beck and call? Where were the horns sticking out of her head? Naturally there was no answer.

One other thing he did notice though, as they led their animals across the last few yards or so to her tower, was that she wasn't fully elven. She had the pointed ears all right, and her accent was perfect, but her form was just a fraction too broad, her hair a trifle too dark and curly. She was clearly also part human. Just like him. But then Elder Bela had told him long ago that the strongest wizards had some human and elven blood both. Apparently that applied to summoners as well. And maybe that explained her title too. Maybe she was from a noble human family.

"Lady Meriana?"

"Of course young Samual Hanor. But you already know that."

There was no doubt in her tone and he guessed she saw him as clearly as a hunter saw her prey. But she was a devastatingly pleasant hunter, and somehow he couldn't imagine her ever doing harm to another. Not to a man and probably not even to an animal. Instead she was the sort of woman who would serve tea to her guests with a smile and make certain they were comfortable. How he wondered, could she possibly be a summoner? It just didn't make sense to him.

"Aralor, would you please help your father in the house. He's trying to prepare a late lunch, and with his penchant for the fire we'll be lucky if he doesn't burn the house down." With a peck on his cheek she sent Aralor – her son it seemed – into the house to help his father, while indicating a small wooden bench to him.

Sam sat down as asked, feeling anything but in control here. A few moments later he was joined by the Lady. At least she'd put down the broom.

"So, the Fire Angel has come to my home. I'm honoured. But shouldn't you have been riding a phoenix here?" She smiled to show she was jesting.

"He was moulting." Despite all his worries her jest actually helped a little.

"Really. Those would be some interesting feathers!" Her smile grew wider. "So tell me of your dreams?"

Her words caught Sam by surprise and it was all he could do not to splutter like a child as he wondered what she meant.

"My dreams?" At least his voice was even, but despite knowing that it was an order, he didn't know what to say.

What dreams did she mean? His idle daydreams and fancies, or those dreams that came by night, and which he forgot each morning once he woke.

"When you were a child. When you first felt the magic flowing through you. When your night time became a whole new world."

Suddenly he understood her. She meant the so called dreams of primacy, the dreams which spoke of the magic being passed into each new child from an unknown father. Every spell caster had them, and most would surely remember them for their intensity if nothing else. But no one ever understood them. Or almost no one. There were a few who said that they did; that the dreams told them about their casting abilities. But most scoffed at such claims. The priests though had different views. Certainly those of the All Father said they were important. That they reflected the will of their Lord as he instilled his magic into the chosen child. He assumed the priests of the Goddess regarded them as significant as well.

Finally knowing what she wanted though not her reasons for wanting to know of them, Sam dutifully told her all he could remember of those days and his dreams of magic. It wasn't easy. He had been only five at the time, young for a wizard's gifts to show up, and as vivid as they had been the dreams had long since been forgotten. And of course they had gone away as he had started learning of his gifts.

For all spell casters the dreams were the first sign of magic. Many believed that through them, a good oracle could tell exactly what gifts a child had been given. But Sam had never been able to see the relationship between the dreams and his gifts. All they had been to him were some exceptionally vivid dreams which had occurred at much the same time as his magic had started to show.

He had never dreamed of fire, or heat or cold. Nor of the earth under his feet, or the natural world. Instead his dreams had mostly left him in a garden. A strange garden full of beautiful creatures and plants, and where glorious fountains sprayed while gentle music played. Sure, some of the fountains had shot fire into the air and were entwined somehow with the water, while others had had creatures playing in them, and he even remembered seeing a small man made of mud serving food. But he had never approached the man or drunk from the fountains, or played with the fire. Instead he remembered playing with the animals all around. Small pets, and larger fiercer creatures like lions and tigers, all of which only wanted to play. Even now he could still feel the softness of their fur under his hands. It was easily the clearest of his memories.

As he told the Lady about his dreams though, a little more of them came back to him. Just talking about it once again he remembered the long soft grass, the puppies playing under the great oak tree, and the feeling of happiness that had overwhelmed him. It had been so intense that he remembered that he awoke each morning filled with energy and joy. They might have made no sense to a five year old child, nor to the man who dimly remembered them, but they had been pleasant enough that he had enjoyed going to bed each night.

Once he had finished he looked up to see the Lady looking at him with a thoughtful expression on her face as she studied him. He wondered what she had learned from his fragments of dreams, since it was clear she had seen something. But she didn't tell him.

"They say you are an enchanter as well as a master of fire. Tell me of that."

It was an order he knew, and dutifully Sam told her of all his abilities and how he could shape more than one magic at a time, and even combine them. All the while he noticed, her stare became ever more intense, and he began to feel more and more like a child being watched.

"And the voices you heard from the machina?" No sooner had he told her of his gifts then she had moved on in her interrogation, and it was time for him to tell her of the battles he'd faced, and most especially of the steel drakes.

It was a long tale, made longer by the fact that she insisted on stopping him repeatedly and making him describe things in even greater detail. Was this the test Sam wondered? It seemed too easy if it was. Or was it just a discussion before the real test began? Though he hadn't really heard voices so much as understood what was being said, something that was difficult to explain.

Eventually though it was done and he knew a sense of relief. He had told her everything he knew. From here on it was up to her.

Lady Meriana took her time, saying nothing. Instead she continued to sit on the seat beside him, staring off into the distance. After the time had stretched for too long he grew impatient and felt the need for some answers.

"Lady Meriana?"

"You're not a summoner. Not at all." She began with the words she surely knew Sam most desperately wanted to hear.

Her words caught him by surprise. With all the questions she'd put to him, and with the lack of any other explanation he had for hearing the enemy's thoughts, he'd thought he had to be that at least. Even if only to the most minor degree. To be told he wasn't while good, didn't fit with what he'd been fearing she would tell him, and for a brief while he wondered if she could be wrong.

But there was nothing in the Lady's face that suggested anything other than certainty. Unless it was disappointment? For whatever reason it seemed she had wanted him to be a summoner just as strongly as he had wanted not to be. But why?

"Then how –?"

"Because you're an enchanter. Moreover, an enchanter in the two schools of magic that the enemy also uses. Nature and Earth. Your inability to summon confirms everything I had feared. The enemy is also an enchanter."

"I thought he was an alchemist."

"He may be that too, as well as an artisan. But above all he is an enchanter in the schools of Earth and Nature. Thus he can imbue a sort of life into an inanimate object, as can you imbue fire into one. The fact that you can hear his commands through his creations proves that beyond doubt. But then he must also be a master artisan to create his monsters in the first place, and a master of spells and potions to give them movement, fire and the power of communication."

"Well, that's good isn't it? I mean at least he's not a demon, or a summoner creating steel demons."

But clearly it wasn't. He could see that in the Lady's eyes. Whatever else it was, the enemy being an enchanter was very, very bad.

"No it's not good. It's not good at all."

Sam let her say what she would without interrupting. If there was one thing he knew, it was that she knew of what she spoke. It shone in the painful certainty in her eyes.

"Demons for all their fierceness and power are not always

350

evil. Nor are they always unstoppable. Most are simply creatures from distant and strange realms, lost and frightened when drawn into our own. Given the choice between killing and going home, most would choose to return home in a heartbeat. Our world is often not just frightening to them but also deadly. Some can't even breathe our air, and need powerful spells just to survive even a short time. And their magic too is often not all that powerful. It is just strange and because we are not familiar with it, it makes it difficult to defend against. At the same time however, that difference leaves them vulnerable to our own."

"But this new enemy is no demon or summoner. He needs no spells to keep him safe in our world. He has no foreign talents or freakish strengths. He is mortal like us. And that is far worse than any demon."

"He has great gifts and great knowledge. And the creatures he has fashioned are machina rather than golems, as much as the elders might want to believe otherwise. They have a form of life, even perhaps a soul if you will, though one that is heavily borrowed from their creator. Thus when they are killed he feels it. When they need directions he can give it to his creations even many leagues away. And he can see through their eyes. The machina and their creator are linked."

That much Sam already knew about the enemy and his servants, but he didn't want to cause offence by mentioning it to Lady Meriana. Instead he let her continue.

"Worst of all though, the Dragon of old was also an enchanter of nature and earth. Five thousand years ago he showed the people of all the lands just what he could do with that power. He wanted – nay he ached – to show those who had spurned him what he could do. For he was rejected from formal training and he sought vengeance for that."

Sam's eyes widened so greatly that they nearly fell out of his head as he realised that the Lady had more knowledge of the Dragon than he'd ever known existed. Certainly much more than he did. But then she lived close to the Golden City and was obviously one of the most respected of mages. She likely had access to much more information than he did. Briefly he wondered just what sort of libraries they might have in the city itself. But Sam didn't ask. It was time to listen carefully instead.

"According to legend, and there is little else left to us, he was a rogue wizard even before he became the Dragon. And like you, one of mixed blood. Part human, part elf. But unlike you he was also part dwarf and part troll."

"It was his troll blood that caused him to be rejected by the schools of magic, even though his talent was strong. They would not train a troll, not even a part troll. They worried what he might do with such training, and whether the other students would be safe from him."

Or whether the other students might be eaten by him, Sam thought, though he kept his thoughts to himself. The Lady probably guessed his views anyway since they were no doubt her own. Trolls were bad news no matter which way you looked at it, and for any to have troll blood in them suggested rape somewhere in their ancestry, and probably more rape and cannibalism in their future. Trolls were savage creatures.

Sam was more interested though in her reference to schools of magic. Immediately he heard that it made him think of classrooms and masters. While it seemed they may have had schools of magic in the past, there were no such schools now. Not in Shavarra or Fair Fields. Nor in any of the other provinces and realms he'd visited. There simply weren't enough wizards and those with the talent for any such schools of magic to exist. Most provinces had an apprentice system. Sometimes governors and governesses were hired by the rich to teach their young spell casters. But before the Dragon Wars there had apparently been schools. At least according to what the Lady was telling him. That meant there had to have been a great many more with the magic in their veins. Again though, he didn't interrupt.

"Being of part troll blood however, gave him another form of magic that no elf, human or dwarf has to this day. He had the magic of permanence. Though we understand it only a very little even now, it is something that is inherent in troll blood. It is part of them, and all trolls have it, whether they have any other magical ability at all or not. Some say it is how they learn, how they are raised, and even what gives them their purpose in life. Over the centuries and millennia the trolls have cast their thoughts, their memories into the rocks and mountains themselves. Thus to each troll, each and every rock or mountain is a book of memories that can be read, a history to be learned."

"It may be even more than that. Rocks and mountains and anything of stone are sacred to trolls, and with good reason. For above all else it is the trolls' belief that when they die, their souls are cast into the rocks themselves, there to be kept safe for all eternity. It is also clear that when the Dragon died he also cast his thoughts, memories and perhaps even his soul into the mountains and caverns of Andrea. Ever since then those lands have become a holy land for the trolls. A shrine to the troll who nearly destroyed the world."

"For the most part they know little and care nothing for the machina, or the Dragon Wars. But they worship the troll who cast his soul into the mountains. They respect his power, his anger and hatred, and above all his savagery, all of which to a troll is the essence of life itself. They worship the memory of his blood letting, and the way he very nearly destroyed an entire world. No other troll before or since has had such strength, nor such single minded devotion to slaughter."

"Now this newcomer has not only some of the Dragon's knowledge and ability, but also his intent and savagery. He has the Dragon's skill and magic, and uses his strategy. He seems to have the same goal. To kill everyone. That speaks strongly of one with some troll blood in him. But this newcomer also has enough blood of the other races that he has far greater intelligence than is usual for a troll as well as the magic of the other races. He has access to both the memories of the original Dragon and the histories of those times. He will know how the original Dragon lost and will plan for it. He will not make the same mistakes."

"There will be no mercenaries this time. No one who is willing to change his allegiance for a few coins. There will be only machina, and they will not be short in number. He will not expose himself to a great battle at the end, allowing himself to be shot with a poisoned spell. Nor will he allow those who have escaped his battles to reform into armies to oppose him. He will strike them hard until all that remain are corpses. And in the end I believe that his purpose is the same as his predecessor's. To destroy all the other races. Not to conquer them, not to take their lands, but to destroy them utterly until no more remain. Enemies must be completely destroyed. That has always been the troll's highest calling."

Conquest by blood. Sam knew that that was what she meant, even if it wasn't quite how he had heard it put before. But trolls had their own god – Crodan the Mountain – and the one command he laid upon them all as his people was that there was no victory save the complete destruction of their enemies. For a troll it was seen as entirely appropriate to eat one's enemies. It was often not so much about food as it was a statement of their triumph. This seemed beyond that but not too far beyond it. After all, the more death the greater the victory for a troll.

"And you are certain this new Dragon is the same as the

Samual

old?" Eventually Sam asked the only question that really mattered.

"I wasn't until I met you. But the fact that you could hear his commands through his machina proves it. You aren't a summoner so his machina cannot be demons. If they were you couldn't hear what they said. And the Dragon's armies are not golems. I wish it were otherwise."

So did Sam after what he'd been told, even though he suspected that the Lady wished him to be a summoner for other reasons. He suspected it was simply because she didn't want to be alone. It had to be a hard life being a summoner, even if what Elder Bela had said was true. Every spell caster, whether mage or wizard liked to know others with the same art. Someone to understand their life. And just as he knew no other enchanters, she was also the only summoner he had heard of. For her to have others to share her gift with would have been a blessing. Still, he was glad she had determined he was not a summoner. But he was confused too. And though she had given him part of an explanation for it, there was one question he badly needed answered.

"I still don't quite understand why I can sense this new Dragon's commands, my Lady."

"Because you too are an enchanter. A spell caster able to cast the magic of one of the magical realms into the manifestations of another. Actually several. But you have not been well trained. That at least is not surprising. Enchanters are very rare, and the secrets of their training even rarer. No living human wizard that I know of could claim to be an enchanter, let alone train one, while the number of elven enchanters in the entire world could be counted upon the fingers of one hand."

"Suffice it to say you are entirely untrained in what may prove to be your most useful talent in the war ahead. You perform your enchantments more on instinct and practice than true understanding. And you are unaware of much of the scope of your gift."

Did she know that for sure Sam wondered? Or was she simply surmising? Because he suspected she was right. He had had a few masters train him as a child. His father had brought many to the land just for that purpose. But none had been able to train him in his enchantments. None had that gift. And so he had had to teach himself. Tentatively he asked.

"Enchanters are not limited to imbuing fire into earth as you do. An enchanter of fire and air could well cast fire magic into a hurricane to create a whirlwind of fire. An enchanter of water and earth can cast water magic into a castle and create liquid walls or even an evaporating castle. He might even cast earth magic into the lakes and create solid walls of water. The limits of enchantment are not known, though some magics do not mix well. I've never heard of an enchanter able to cast fire magic into water for example, since the two realms would tend to work against each other."

What allows you to hear the Dragon is that like the enemy you are an enchanter of nature and earth. As well as imbuing fire into solid objects, you can also imbue that same sort of life magic that he does, into earth. Thus you too could create machina, though you perhaps would need many years of training and then many more of craftsmanship."

The very idea of creating such creatures took Sam's thoughts away, and yet even as he thought of the evil she was suggesting, he had to accept that her words made sense. Strange but fascinating sense.

"But more importantly, you can interact with his creations. If another enchanter gave you a sword imbued with fire magic, you would feel it. You would know it, even be able to use it. This is no different. As an enchanter of nature and earth as well as fire and earth, when one of his machina comes near you, you feel the magic that created it. You hear the creature's thoughts. And through it you hear him, or at least, that part of the enemy's commands that the machina itself hears."

"But I can't use the machina."

Actually he didn't know whether he could or not. He'd never tried to, never even thought about it. But certainly he'd never sensed any sign among the enemy's servants that they would have taken orders from him.

"I would have been surprised if you could. The enemy is probably both much more powerful and more experienced than you in the art, and even if you do one day find the strength to match his, you would still have to overcome the loyalty of his servants. Besides which you would need training – many years of it – and there is no one I know of who could teach you the skills, except perhaps the enemy himself."

Which brought him back to the same old riddle: Who had shown this new Dragon what he could do? Despite her certainty, Sam still couldn't quite believe that this new Dragon could have learned all he had simply from reading the thoughts of the last Dragon in the caves of Andrea. Trolls weren't that bright to start with. But then he had never thought much of trolls. To him they had always been savage subhuman creatures, cannibals, monsters and rapists; things best killed.

"But there are still things you can do and that you need to do. I will write a letter to your elders explaining to them what I can see in you, which I ask you to carry back to them. I'm also going to give you a book from the only other enchanter I've ever heard of who could combine nature magic and earth; Sinselli Longstride. It will sadly tell you only a little of his magic, but much of his journey nearly a thousand years ago."

"He never used his skills to create machina, he considered it a misuse of his gifts to even try, though it was widely believed at the time that he could. But what he did learn to do was to create living structures. Castles, fortresses and manor houses that seemed to live only for their occupants. Thus they would open and close, and even lock doors and windows depending on the needs of their charges. Enemies would be locked out or imprisoned. Guests would find their quarters always comfortable. Walls were said to be impregnable and the gargoyles he shaped into each new building, acted as a defence force of considerable strength. Because of his magic he found most of his work outside of the elven realms, and he was a much travelled elf. He was also a source of much pride to his people."

She was speaking of the Standings Sam realised. Half a dozen of the greatest and oldest castles were imbued with such magic and were called Standings, basically because they were – well – still standing after hundreds of years. There were also a number of smaller Standings scattered throughout the land. Though he'd never spent much time learning about them, Sam knew the basics. That they were living structures, some claimed even breathing. That they could do everything the Lady had claimed and more. Some said they even moved. But most important of all, they were considered miracles of magic and life that cared for and protected their occupants as no other building could. Until just then however, he'd never known who had created them let alone that he was an ancient elf, and that surprised him.

"For you however, the most important thing you need to do is to study your nature magic far more urgently than the other magics. As one raised among humans you have neglected that realm of magic terribly, and it is past time to correct that mistake. Long past time. You need to go beyond the simple magics and shapes you have learned and interact with nature. You must learn how to draw on its raw power and mould its shape.

"I can't even begin to tell you how vital this is. In the first Dragon Wars there were no other enchanters of nature and earth, and there have been very few since. It is auspicious that you should be here now, coming into your mastery early and just in time to face this danger. Though I am no oracle, I would suggest that there is a reason for your being here now; a reason related to this new Dragon. The Goddess surely grants us her grace in this at least."

"In time, it would be my hope, that as a natural enchanter, you will begin to learn how to do at least a fraction of what the enemy does, even without anyone to teach you. And that in turn, may give you some insight into how to fight him."

"I fight with fire," Sam told her simply.

"Yes. I know. But so do many others. Your gift of fire makes you powerful. But it may not be enough. There are others who have the same magic. There are no others who are enchanters of nature and earth. And we do not want another Dragon War. You need to learn to fight as the Dragon himself does. You need to be able to use the same magic. In the end that may be your most powerful weapon."

She sighed heavily and then slumped a little on the bench as if she was tired.

"But enough of this. With a little luck my husband has not burnt the house down and the tea is ready. The sun is shining and the birds are singing. We should speak of happier things. You have a wife I understand. Children perhaps to come? Tell me of them."

With that she stood up and gestured that he should join her as she walked towards the front door. Sam dutifully joined her. He would have preferred to sit and think on what she'd told him. And then to ask more questions of her. But maybe she was right. Maybe this wasn't the time for them.

Besides, he was curious as to what a summoner's tower might look like.

Chapter Twenty Two.

"Mother? Father?"

Ryshal was puzzled as they walked slowly away from the Ellosian's wagon. She was annoyed too. She had felt the Ellosian family's hostility, even as well concealed as it had been underneath their manners. It had been clear enough. The lack of a smile or a greeting. The use of formal names and titles rather than family names as if they were strangers. The unwillingness to discuss anything of even a vaguely personal nature. And the excuses for why they should leave soonest and not return. Ryshal and her parents were clearly unwelcome among the Ellosians. What she didn't understand was why.

The had done nothing more than pay a social call and share a mug of camomile tea around a fire as they introduced themselves to their new family. It had been the perfect time since Samual was away visiting the summoner, and he could be less than tactful. In fact she suspected he had said or done something to offend. He wouldn't have meant to – he had a good heart – but sometimes he simply didn't know what was acceptable and what wasn't. That same directness that made him a good soldier could upset people. So a quiet visit by the Moonmissel family had seemed like the best approach.

Now it seemed she owed her husband an apology. He had already told them of his cousin's hostility to him. Strangely, though she occasionally told her husband that he was making too much of things and that he simply didn't understand the ways of their people, in this case it seemed he had been conservative in his telling. The hostility shown to them was shocking. But as far as she could tell there was no reason for it. Not for the hostility against her parents anyway. Even if the family counted her as much an enemy as her husband, surely that could not extend to them. Could it?

"Do you –?"

"Do we understand why they were so short with us? So dismissive?" Her mother finished her question for her.

"Yes." Ry nodded.

"Because of a little baby girl. And perhaps because of too much fear and secrecy. A life time of it. Pietral?" Her mother unexpectedly gave the duty of explaining it to her father. She did that sometimes, and it was usually because there was something she didn't want to say.

"They were defending their daughter. They consider us a threat to her."

"A threat?" Ryshal didn't understand that at all. They intended no harm to them. No harm to anyone. In any event Mayvelle was the last person anyone would want to threaten. She was a soldier and clearly gifted with weapons.

"Not one of intentional harm to her. But one perhaps of revealing a secret they have been hiding for many years."

"What secret?" Ryshal was confused. Did they know any secrets?

"Tell me what you saw of Mayvelle. What you have heard."

Ryshal sighed a little as she realised her father was going to make a challenge of this. He did that too often in her view, but he liked to teach her things in that way. As a trader and one who drove a wagon through a great many lands, he understood a lot about people. He saw deeply into them. Both her parents did. It was what made them so good at their work.

But more than that, it was part of what they loved about their work. And he wanted her to know the same understanding.

"She is a proud soldier. Tall and straight and true of arm. An adjunct commander with the Griffin Troop that once patrolled the borders of Shavarra."

"True." His father wrapped a comforting arm around her shoulders. "But there is more. She is tall and straight. But is she not just a little too tall and straight? Her hair falls in long blond plats as it should, but is not its colour just a little too dark? Darker than that of other Shavarran elves? And is not the copper of her skin a little lighter? She also shows great strength in her sword arm. But is not the strength contained within it just a little more than you would expect?"

Ryshal nodded, agreeing but not sure what her father was hinting at.

"Next think of her age; twenty three. She is four years younger than Samual."

"I still don't understand." Actually Ryshal had thought her older than that. Older than her certainly. But maybe that was just the years of a hard life etched into her face. And what did her age have to do with Samual? Hesitantly she asked.

"What happened when Samual was four?"

For a moment Ryshal was about to retort that she had no idea. How could she possibly know what had happened to her husband when he was such a young child and she had never even heard of him. And then she realised what her father was referring to. It was one of the things that had most profoundly affected him. Something that still remained with him.

"His mother died."

"In childbirth."

Her mother returned to the explanation suddenly, though for a moment Ryshal didn't understand what was so important about how she'd died. Until she put it together with Mayvelle's age.

"By the Goddess!" It was all suddenly clear. Mayvelle was taller, straighter and stronger than other elves because she wasn't the same as them. For the same reason her skin and hair colour were slightly off. The blood that flowed through her veins was not pure elf. She was half human. Vero eskaline. Storm blood. And she could not have been that if both her parents were pure elves. There could be only one explanation.

"Then she is Samual's sister? Not his cousin?"

"We think so. Even Samual understands something of this. He said that he saw his mother's face in her. That he recognised her before she gave him her name. A brother knows a sister."

"Praise the Goddess! How?"

"At a guess, the brother and his wife attended Samual's mother's second childbirth, knowing that it would be a hard one. But then when she died, they must have spirited the baby away, claiming that she too had died. And ever since they have raised her as their own, praying that she never found out the truth. And the one thing they do not want is for their daughter to have contact with Samual. They fear that he might guess the truth."

It made sense Ry realised. In fact it explained so many things she hadn't even thought of. But it was a large leap to make based on a few observations and a family's rudeness. And yet her parents were extremely capable when it came to seeing into people's souls.

"Do you think Mayvelle knows this? And if she does, why is she so hostile to Samual?" Eventually Ry asked what was probably the most important question.

"It's likely she has been told terrible tales about her mother or aunt and the marriage to his father. Things that would make her not want to have any connection to Samual."

"Praise be to the Goddess!" Ry was appalled, but also worried. Because the one thing she knew they would have to do was to tell Samual about this. But if they did, then the first thing he would want to do was to talk to them. To talk to Mayvelle. It would create trouble but it was still the natural thing to do. And yet what else could they do?

The Fair Fielders had their God of Mischief – Alder – who they were forever using as a curse word. It was always by Alder this or that. Even Samual used his name sometimes. She had been trying to get him to stop the practice since before they had even wed. It was unseemly. But in any case they were elves. He should be worshipping the Goddess. But just then she felt like using the god's name herself. Somehow it even seemed appropriate. If there was anything about this situation that wasn't some sort of divine misadventure she didn't know what it was.

But in the end she was an elf. One of the people of the forests. And there was always and ever only one place they could turn to. "We should speak with the priests before Samual returns."

Chapter Twenty Three

Mayvelle was practising with her weapons when Sam saw her. He had to admit that she impressed him with her skill. Though she was only rehearsing her moves with sword and shield, she was light on her feet, quick and obviously strong. She wore the armour of the border patrols as if it was simply skin. More than that she was obviously skilled, almost seeming to dance as she lunged, spun and kicked back. The Red God obviously favoured her. Though he had trained all his life with his own weapons Sam knew he would have difficulty defeating her with a blade.

Sam was nervous as he approached Mayvelle. More nervous than he had been in many years. But not because he feared a fight. In fact the last time he could remember feeling anything like this was when he'd first approach Ryshal and had worried that she might spurn his advances. This felt similar. Except that he was almost certain she would spurn him. And all he wanted was her friendship.

But Ry's parents were right about her he realised. She was tall and strong and too fast. Too fast to be of simply elven blood at least. And as she practised her lunges and parries with her sword in the clearing, he knew she was good. The sword was heavier than an elf would normally carry. Especially an elven maiden. And yet she swung it as though it was a part of her. The All Father only knew how deadly she would be with her blade in an actual battle.

Vero eskaline. Storm blood. Her gift was with weapons. And as he approached he knew it was a powerful gift. He suspected that she might also have other gifts. The Elder had said that the gifts of those with mixed blood were unpredictable. But did she know? Did she even suspect? And was that why she was so bitter?

Could she really be his sister? He had spent the entire night wondering about that. He respected Pietral and Alendo greatly for their insights into people. They saw further into others than he could understand, and some days he wondered if it was their own very special sort of magic. But this still seemed like such a huge leap to make from so little evidence.

And yet were they wrong? Or could they be right? That was the part that kept hitting him. It could be.

He remembered little of the days when his mother had died. For him it had mostly been a sad time when his mother had gone away and his father had wept. He had only been four at the time and he truly hadn't understood death. He only knew that she had gone away and that he missed her. But he had understood the truth when the new woman – Heri's mother – had come into his life. His mother wasn't coming back. Even as a four year old he had understood that terrible truth.

And what was he supposed to say to her? That was the other question that troubled him. He had to say something. Yet he knew his family were right. He could not simply speak what he feared was the truth. That she was his sister. It would only cause trouble and pain. Especially if it was true. And there had been too much of that already. These people had recently lost their home. Probably friends and maybe family as well. Just like so many others. How could he add to that?

People were still recovering from their losses. And now that they were through the wastes and once more in a fertile land with trees and forests and fields, spirits were lifting. The arguments and the open displays of suffering were fading. But it would be a long time before the people would truly recover. Especially those who had lost loved ones. He knew from personal, painful experience that those losses stayed with a man.

Should he even talk to her? The thought suddenly occurred to him just as she turned around and saw him. It was too late then of course though he suddenly wished it weren't. He could already see the look of disappointment or disdain on her face as he trotted the last few yards towards her.

"Cousin." Sam greeted her as family, even though he was almost certain he should really be calling her sister. But at least he didn't address her by title.

"Samual Hanor." She didn't address him as family – a calculated snub. "Is there ought that you need?"

"Need? No." Sam ignored the snub. He had almost expected it. "I merely came to bring you some news that I hope will be of some relief to you."

"News?" She stopped her practice to listen to him.

"In case you were worried that I had some summoner blood within me." But even as he said it he knew that it hadn't concerned her at all. It had terrified him, but she had no care that he might be one. He could see it in her eyes. He was plague ridden either way as far as she was concerned.

"I was not concerned." And she still wasn't.

"And you have no reason to be. I returned only yesterday from seeing the Lady Meriana, and she pronounced me clear of the magic. There can be no thought that you share blood with one."

"That is good to know."

But it wasn't really. He could see it in her face. Hear it in her voice. She had never cared about it. What she cared about was something far darker. And it was then that he knew what his path had to be. He couldn't tell her what his family suspected. Ever. It was hard to accept, but she was not ready to hear the truth – if truth it was – and she probably never would be.

"Good. Then I would ask a small boon in return if I may."

Mayvelle didn't respond. She simply stood there staring at him, as if worried by what he might ask and fearing it might be something too painful for words. In seeing that he suddenly knew what he had to say.

"You and your family clearly consider me tainted in some way. Bad of blood. Guilty of some crime. Ridden by disease."

"I –." She started to object.

"Enough!" He hushed her with a wave of his hand. "I have no interest in whatever fault it is that you find in me. My only interest is in the well being of my family. They are good people. Loving and kind. And I owe them all that I am. You and your parents were unfailingly rude to them when they visited on my behalf. That was unworthy."

"I will ask them to keep their distance from you and yours. I would ask you to do the same. And if a meeting does occur by chance, it should be polite and respectful. No more is required."

"That's –."

" – All I came to say." Sam cut her off, knowing he had no more he wanted to discuss with her. He could say many things, but none of them would help. None could span the chasm between them. And if by chance that chasm was one day crossed, it would be to her detriment. She was perhaps better off in ignorance.

"Good day soldier." With that he nodded politely and tugged on Tyla's reins to turn her around. And then he left, aware that her hatred of him had likely grown enormously just then. He wasn't worried though. She was angry and her blood might make her very dangerous, but she was still too well trained to do something stupid. Even so, he was glad he was wearing armour.

Had he done the right thing? He wondered about that as he headed back to the wagon and his family. Or had he simply done the only thing he could? He strongly suspected it was the latter. But these days it seemed that was all he ever could do. The Fire Angel was just as powerless in these things as everyone else.

Chapter Twenty Four.

"Concentrate Samual, concentrate."

Sam sighed quietly as he heard Elder Bela ordering him on once more. As if he wasn't already concentrating! As he had been every other time the Elder had given him that same command. It was the Elder's most common instruction – and his usual complaint; the fact that his poor student was failing to try hard enough. Despite that Sam knew, or at least hoped he knew, that he was trying. Moreover he was making good progress in learning nature magic. And exactly as Elder Bela had told him it would, with every day its strength and versatility continued to surprise him.

Now, only two months into rebuilding the city of Shavarra in this new land he was already becoming adept at shaping trees so that they could support the new structures. He had to be because he like all the other Nature mages was in demand, day and night. The elves for the most part were still living in their wagons on the ground far below and were showing signs of frustration. They loved their trees and they would not be content until they once more could live among them. Consequently there wasn't a Nature mage around – from the masters to the lowliest apprentices such as himself – who wasn't being pushed to his limit.

Sam didn't mind however. With the restoration of Ry to him only five or six short months before, something had changed deep within him. He no longer thought only in terms of battle and fighting. He was still angered by those who had done this evil to them, and sometimes the rage ran wild in him, but he no longer lived in fear of an enemy attack. Without that fear and equally the anger that had been there before, he no longer needed to think about his magic solely as a weapon.

Naturally, the process wasn't complete. It would take many more months – perhaps many years – before he was able to lay down his hackles completely, if even then. But in the meantime he was relaxed enough that he was again finding the joy in practising magic as well as the power. It was something he hadn't known in a very long time.

Of course with every ounce of joy had to come an equal measure of sorrow as one of his father's aids had long ago quipped, and with his joy had come the burden of being trained directly by Elder Bela. A most demanding taskmaster.

He still didn't know what exactly the Lady had written in her note to the elders – perhaps it had been somewhat foolish of him not to have read it on the way back – and probably then to have burnt it. Whatever it was though, it had suddenly meant that his training schedule had become much heavier, and he was now being trained nearly every night and day, and only by the most learned of all the nature and earth mages. And so every day that he was asked to help with the rebuilding, he would be accompanied by Elder Bela, Master Riven and Master Lavellin who would instruct him in great detail about every aspect of his work. Often they would make him do and undo things a hundred times until he got them just right. Then they would huddle together like a gaggle of geese and moan about how their student simply wasn't trying hard enough, while he was forced to listen, unable to defend himself.

The only relief he got was at meal times, when he could scurry back to Ryshal and her parents and pretend he had a normal life, and those evenings when the war masters spent some time with him. With them it wasn't so much a master student relationship as it was a sharing of information, as he passed on what he knew of the various matters they were getting in their reports, and they in turn told him of their own understanding. It seemed that they now accepted that he was well versed in the military arts.

Ry for her part thought it was all quite fun. She saw his suffering as a sign of how completely he was being accepted into the community. She viewed the fact that he was being trained by the elders as a mark of great respect, and she felt proud of him. In fact some mornings she was so eager for him to get to his training that she pushed him out of the wagon half-dressed. And as winter was now upon them some of those days were quite cold! But as she was looking so healthy and beautiful lately he would have forgiven her anything.

Her hair had continued to grow and it was now nearly as long as the second knuckle of his smallest finger. But he took the greatest joy in her improved health. She had almost fully recovered. Her shape had returned to the womanly form he had so loved. And he could see muscles in her arms and legs. She was even dancing once more, though not yet as energetically as she had done in his memories, and by the fire light she would weave her dance of love all around him. It might be winter, but to him it was summer every time he saw her.

Ry though and her parents like all the other elves were not always so happy, and Sam knew that the reality of moving to a new and foreign home was finally setting in.

It was a strange thing and yet in hindsight, it should have been perfectly obvious that this was coming. For months the elves' daily lives had been about the journey, coping with the hardships and the fear of another attack and of course grieving for all that they'd lost. That had consumed their thoughts. But when they'd arrived a lot of their problems had gone away, and suddenly they'd had time on their hands. Time to realise that they'd reached the end. And now it was no longer about leaving their old home, but about starting anew. Understanding that this might be their new home for life. Giving up on their dream of going home.

Nightmares were common according to the healers, and many had tears in their eyes as they woke each morning. Tempers had eased which was a blessing, but the sadness had grown so great that at times all the people had to spend time apart, simply to mourn.

Songs of sadness and suffering had been written and were now sung around the fires at night, filling the air with their mournful sounds. The priests were everywhere too, trying to bring hope to the people, and to help them celebrate the lives of those who had been lost and forget the pain of their losses. And while the anger might have lessoned, it was still there. It still came out at unexpected moments.

Yet it wasn't a total disaster. There was joy as well as sorrow. The moment their journey had ended, hope had started to burn in the chests of some.

It was as if the land itself was a healer. A healer of the very soul. It wasn't Shavarra, but it was the next best thing. From its magnificent trees, pristine flowing rivers and lush pastures and fields, it was much that Shavarra had been. So much so that when a name had been called for their new home, the elves had named it Shavarra. If they couldn't go home, then maybe they could rebuild their home here.

The people were caught. Trapped between the acceptance of their terrible losses and the hope for a better future. And maybe Sam thought, that applied to the elders as well. Or maybe Elder Bela was simply a naturally difficult man.

"I am concentrating Elder. It's all under control."

And it was too. As he and the Elder sat there on the end of the outstretched branch while it gradually lowered, inch by inch, he could feel the tree responding to his magic, almost like a man stretching his muscles out under the pressure of a massage. Meanwhile the words from the carpenters hanging off ropes from the branches all around them, seemed to confirm everything he believed. They were measuring the relative heights of all the branches he'd moved into position, and constantly telling him that things were good. In between the calls for him to move the branch to the right or the left or higher or lower, they added phrases like 'just a little bit' and 'gently' as the branch came closer and closer to where they wanted it. And when he was done they told him as much.

In working his magic Sam wasn't actually bending the branches. That would be extremely difficult with a two hundred foot high cedar, if not impossible. In reality he was actually growing the branches in the desired direction. That was one of the differences between nature and fire magic that had had him at his wits end for a long time. With fire and even with earth you could shape it and watch it respond exactly to your will. With nature magic it was more a question of persuasion and encouragement. You couldn't force it to your will. Instead you had to let it think your will was its own, and then let it do what you wanted for itself.

The same was true of all the animals he was learning to call and command. They had their own minds, and while they would come when asked and do as he wanted, it was only as long as they also wanted to. Often the simplest things could interrupt a spell. Especially with the most simple creatures. Mice, small rodents and birds could all be distracted easily by either food or a threat. The instant either was noticed the command would be broken as they scurried off, the caster and spell completely forgotten. Fish were even more stupid and would forget any spell within moments of having been commanded, if they could remember them even that long.

"Yes you're doing well Samual, but you keep forgetting the water."

That was another difference between the magics. With fire

and with earth the magic was always there, ready to be used at a moment's notice, but with nature you had to consider the whole creature. The tree couldn't grow without plenty of water for it to drink, and so a chain gang of workers was hauling buckets and wagon loads of water to the tree's roots, while he concentrated on helping the tree drink it as fast as possible, filling its sap to the limit and letting it grow.

Still, it was a useful skill to know and one day, if and when they were lucky enough to return to Shavarra, he hoped he'd be able to use it to extend his own humble cottage. The mighty oak in which it sat had three or four massive branches which could easily be shaped to form a rather large platform extending out on both sides of it. It could become either a large balcony or a couple of new rooms. Perhaps even a whole new cottage could be built on it. The sad thing was that if he'd known of this ability, he could have done it years ago and his own cottage would have been far grander.

"That's perfect!"

The cry came from several of the carpenters at almost the same time, sparing Sam the duty of telling the Elder he had the positioning under control as well. But with the job done, he looked around him to survey his handiwork, and despite himself was impressed.

Where once the massive cedar's branches had grown at a steep angle to the ground, spreading out wide only at their tips, now the magnificent tree had spread all its branches wide in a radial pattern, like a man with his arms outstretched to the sky. It was the perfect framework for the carpenters to begin building their great platforms on. Once they were built they would begin on the walkways and buildings. The timber for that was already being milled.

Down below on the ground thousands of elves were busy cutting lumber taken from fallen and dead trees into planks and beams. Many more were painting them with the special preparations which would stop them from rotting or wilting. Another army of artisans was involved in the weaving of the thousands of leagues of ropes that would be needed to support walkways and hold the city together. Ropes that varied in thickness from the width of his thumb, to that of his waist. And all the while the designers drew their plans for each additional tree to be added to the city as it grew, and then gave the orders for each new beam, joist and rope to be crafted. The All Father only knew how they managed to plan such a feat of engineering down to such tiny details, and yet still create a beautiful vision of how an entire city should be. Or the Goddess he supposed.

He didn't even know how everyone managed to work in the freezing cold. And some days it was truly bitter. There was ice and snow on the ground in the mornings. Those were the days when he wanted to remain in bed. Of course Ry wouldn't let him. The city had to be built and he had to train. That was her final word on the matter.

Building an elven city was an art as much as a science, but the end result was a pure beauty greater than either could create alone. Sam like most of the other elves had only seen a fraction of the city so far. No more than the few trees he'd been assigned to work on. But even that little was enough to tell him that this was to be no hurried shanty town. Instead the master artisans had planned out a massive city large enough to hold two hundred thousand elves in comfort, all set out in two giant concentric rings of trees forming a circle nearly half a league in diameter.

On the inside of the rings of houses and buildings were the rope walks that would link the different parts of the city to one another, while below them were the clearings provided by nature herself. This was where they would have their bush walks, parks, stables, parade grounds and meeting arenas. The larger clearings were reserved for the farmers, who were already busy planting vast orchards and fields of crops in the fertile soil. Most of the horses and nature mages were busy helping them, and in only another few months the first real bounty from the lands would become available.

No doubt there would be a celebration then. When the priests would be out in force. They were already everywhere anyway. It was another of the differences between the realm of Fair Fields and Shavarra. Everything in Shavarra had to be blessed in the name of the Goddess. The very tree Sam had just finished working on had been blessed before he had begun working on it. It would be blessed again shortly before the artisans began building. And then it would be blessed for the third time when it was finally ready for people.

"Elder! Fire Angel! The Council asks to see you."

The call came from the ground and Sam looked down to see one of the Council guards calling out to him and Master Bela. The two looked at each other wordlessly. They didn't need to ask to know what was so important that his training should be interrupted. They knew. Somewhere, the enemy had struck again. They'd been waiting for the news for so long.

Like a well-trained team they staggered to their feet, not an easy thing for Sam who had been sitting for several hours on the tip of a branch in full armour, and made their way toward the trunk where a set of wide spiral stairs had already been installed, complete with a rope hand rail.

For a man raised among the human cities the trip was a strange one at best, and somewhat frightening. To be walking along a wide flat branch forty or fifty feet in the air with no hand rail was more than a little disturbing. The more so when he watched all the elves literally running and jumping along the other branches, even swinging from ropes like acrobats. But he was slowly adjusting, his elven blood granting him a much better sense of balance than he'd ever realised he had.

He missed the solid stone walls of the keep more than he could say. He missed solid floors and hand rails too. But the elves would soon have this tree converted into a dozen homes, several shops and storehouses and an inn according to the plan, complete with solid wooden platforms and proper timber hand rails. He just had to survive until then. Of course by the time that happened he'd be working on other trees.

The work came with its compensations though, as he daily saw sights he'd never imagined possible. On the last tree he'd finished working on, he could see one of the wind wizards at work, and not for the first time he envied them their magic. To be able to fly, or at least to be able to raise yourself on a spinning column of air – it was surely a miracle. And a very useful one as the wind mages were used to lift the vast piles of lumber and rope into position for the builders to work with. Without them the elves would have had to carry the materials up the stairs by hand, and that would have slowed them down considerably.

Several of the nature mages too were able to fly, but for them it was simply because they could transform themselves into giant birds, eagles and hawks with truly terrifying wingspans and the ability to speak. They were also much in demand, carrying small items such as ropes between trees. Sometimes they also acted as scouts flying out over the land, just in case the enemy did come back.

Already more than thirteen dozen great trees had been finished and at least as many were in their final stages, while four thousand or more elves were settled into their new homes. They were mainly the families with the youngest children, although Sam and the elders had all been offered homes from the first batch. They had all refused saying that the homes should go to the most needy first, and that the children needed to be properly housed and have a school to attend. Though in truth the children didn't mind the hardship. Nor he suspected, the lack of a school.

For them this had all become one great adventure, and this was simply its latest stage. As the healers kept reminding them, children were tougher than they seemed. Moving them into their new homes had been and still was a joyous duty as the children explored their new home as only children could; getting into trouble and causing much mischief and consternation to their parents. But nobody begrudged them their fun. The sound of children's laughter was probably the greatest blessing the elves had known since arriving in this new land. It had been a long time missing, and now they heard it daily.

Reaching the ground they found their horses waiting for them. They too were enjoying their new home, and were putting on weight as they grazed the lush pastures, and enjoyed the freedom of not being ridden night and day. Yet they were loyal – more so than Sam would have ever realised until he'd started practising with his nature magic – and they immediately came to them. In fact they were so loyal that it never occurred to them to disobey. Obedience, work and the simple companionship of people were part of their lives. It was all part of being a member of a herd.

It wasn't far to the Council. Nor were there yet any street corners or obstacles between them as there would be in a city. No walkways to take. Though the builders and artisans were numerous and the work was progressing at an incredible pace, little of the new city had yet been built. So they were at their destination in only a few minutes, ready to hear the news.

As usual the elders were standing around on the grass underneath what they one day hoped would become the Fiore Elle – the Gathering People or the new Council chambers. But that day would be a very long way off. First came the homes and the schools. Then the businesses and common areas. And at some point all the finishing work had to be done. The netting under the walkways. The rope restraints around them and the platforms. The polishing and sanding. Building the Council chambers wouldn't even begin until then. It simply wasn't a priority. Until then the elders had to be happy meeting out in the open.

For the moment what the elders had was grass, a few wagons, some long fallen trees to sit on, and time. Endless time. Time enough to hear petitions, settle disputes, and receive visitors. It was the last that they were doing as the two of them approached.

A party of soldiers in armour had arrived, most of them still mounted on their horses while their leader spoke to the elders. A shorter man who had his back to Sam as he rode up. But strangely he cut a somewhat familiar figure in his ermine court robes. A disturbing one. Even as he rode toward them Sam knew there was something wrong. He felt it like a chill wind across his back. And he didn't like the fact that Ryshal and her parents were standing to one side of the group, presumably having also been summoned by the elders. But what he most disliked was the look on Ry's face. Her face was filled with horror. And the priests who were always in attendance, hid their horror better – but he could see it in their eyes.

Then the man turned as he heard them approach and all of Sam's worst fears were proven correct.

"By the All Father!" Though it was improper here, the words were ripped out of Sam's mouth as he saw who was waiting for them.

"Heri!" Sam was shocked to see his half-brother standing there in what would eventually become the Fiore Elle. More than shocked. It was something that simply shouldn't have happened. Something as nasty as his half-brother should never be allowed in a town full of good people. But more than that he was worried. The calculating smile on his Heri's face was almost an admission of guilt. Except that he knew nothing of such emotions. Where others might know shame or guilt for what they'd done, Heri would know only joy and victory.

He had soldiers with him too. A dozen mounted knights dressed from head to foot in full plate, far too heavy to be useful against elves with longbows and steel headed arrows that could pierce the steel. It would just slow them down. But he supposed they looked quite intimidating in their armour, though it had to be uncomfortably hot with their visors down. Maybe that was what he wanted. Heri was often more concerned with looking the part of the king then actually being him, in his opinion. Like his mother before him.

"Brother."

If anything Heri's cold smile grew broader, and Sam felt more threatened.

"Why are you here? What have you done?"

"Me big brother?" Heri smiled with all the warmth of a venomous serpent about to strike. "What have I done? When it was you who destroyed my keep, and then took my throne and my hand? I think the question should be the other way around." He sounded like a courtier, his words far too smooth and well practised for most.

Sam knew it was a trap of some sort – that evil smirk on his brother's face proudly proclaimed it as such – but he couldn't work out how it would spring shut on him. And until he did show his teeth, Sam knew he couldn't strike him down. The elders would be upset if he did. He had to let Heri speak to find out instead of just striking him down on the spot as he deserved.

"I didn't destroy the keep, only knocked down a few walls." Sam had to defend himself, until the other part of what he'd said suddenly hit him. "Did you say you've lost your throne?"

If he had why was he dressed as a king? Why was he attended to by these knights in full armour? Why did he have advisers in their formal court robes with him? Why was he meeting with the elders at all? And why was he even alive? In Fair Fields the loss of a throne was normally associated with death. The king either died, leaving the throne available to his successor, or someone took it and killed the king. It was a simple, somewhat bloody and barbaric system. But what else could you expect in a land where the noble houses were constantly at war with one another?

"As you well know. Tell me brother, do these good elves know of your crimes?"

"What crimes?"

Even as he said it Sam knew he was falling straight into Heri's trap. He had expected his response. And all the time he was wondering how Heri had lost his throne, and why he thought it was his fault.

"Murder, of my soldiers and subjects. The destruction of Fall Keep, levelled by your fire magic, killing who knows how many. Insurrection and treason, as you overthrew your rightful king. The list of your crimes is endless."

"I have done none of those things." He had to deny it, and of course Heri knew that. He'd planned on it.

"The guilty always deny their deeds." Heri abruptly looked up and started speaking to all those around him. "But the truth always finds a way to be heard."

"Behold, my witnesses." With a flourish he waved at his soldiers, and they bowed to him, rather too easily for Sam's liking. There was something wrong with them, something in the way they moved he thought. But they were still just soldiers, and Heri was the one on the ground closest to him. He had a dagger in his belt and in all likelihood murder in his heart.

"I'm sure they will say whatever lies you have told them to say, and no elven court will count their words any more truthful than those from your lying tongue. So why have you come for me little brother? Did you doubt my word when I said what I would do to you if you ever bothered me again?" And the one thing Sam was certain of was that he'd heard him.

Heri should be frightened. But he wasn't. In fact if anything he looked like a man who thought he was winning. And while Sam couldn't see how he could possibly think to defeat him, that troubled him. Fortunately more and more soldiers were taking up positions around the clearing, just in case. No doubt they too understood there was some sort of threat.

"I did not come for you brother."

That caught Sam completely by surprise and for a moment he didn't quite know what to say.

"Is that what you really think? That I would hate you so greatly that I would risk my own life to have you condemned for the traitorous piece of spit that you are." Heri continued, his face a mask of sorrow that everyone could see was false.

"No. You are a criminal, but all the heavens know you are beyond the reach of my law to judge. Here in this elven land, my word as a mere king carries no weight. But the word of the faithful still does, and as evil as you are, there is one more who must be judged first. She who made you do these terrible things. Ryshal Hanor."

There was a gasp, and it took Sam a moment to realise it was his. And then his anger cut loose.

"How dare you –."

"– How dare I? How dare I brother?" Heri pretended outrage as he spoke over the top of him. But there was a smirk in his eyes and Sam knew that he was closing his trap.

"I suppose that you do not know that she has consorted with demons! I suppose you do not know that she is a summoner! I suppose you do not know that she was kept under lock and key because of her evil! Kept alive only because of my concern for your heart should she die!"

It was insane, vile and utterly mad, and yet as a story it made sense, in a most twisted fashion. His brother knew how to weave the facts into a convincing lie. He always had.

"Liar!"

"She is demon tainted."

"Filthy liar! Alder take you!" Sam hated himself for losing control, but Heri's accusations were intolerable, and he would not stand for them.

"Mind yourself big brother. You are held to your honour and I came in peace." Heri pointed to the flag carried by the knights. "And I came for justice. Not a battle."

"This one –." Heri raised a hand and pointed it straight at Ry, "– is a wanted criminal. She is to be brought back to Fair Fields where she can be properly tried by the Court and then hung."

"Never!" Sam gave up on any pretence of calm as he yelled it at his brother. "You will never lay your filthy hands on her again!"

And it wouldn't just be him who stopped Heri this time. There were soldiers all around guarding the elders, making sure nothing untoward happened. In fact they were gathering quickly. Every soldier who had been in ear shot was hurrying for them. Heri, whatever lies he spoke, would not steal Ryshal away again.

"Do you deny me my right?" Heri smiled cruelly as he played to the audience.

"What right?! You said you've lost your throne!" And if Heri was no longer king what right did he have to demand anything? Sam wasn't always the quickest when it came to matters of state, but he remembered that much at least.

"But I still speak for the Court. And I will be king again in the fullness of time."

"How can you speak for the Court when you've lost your throne?" Sam didn't understand that. And even with all the rage and fear rushing through him, that question hit him. This all had to be some sort of elaborate scheme. He didn't understand it. But nothing else made sense.

"Ahh, you've got me there, big brother. But too late as always." Heri's secret smile suddenly became a grimace of mocking triumph.

"Now that everyone's here!" Heri waved his arms above his head in some sort of prearranged gesture, and the trap was sprung as his knights reached for their weapons. And after that everything seemed to happen in a heartbeat.

The soldiers weren't soldiers at all. Sam realised that immediately he saw them move. Their subtle changes in body position as they reached for their swords far too quickly told him their bones were not as solid as they should be. They moved far too fluidly in their armour to be human or elf. But none of that mattered when there was apparently about to be a battle.

It was a trap.

Sam called out the warning even as he drew his own blade, and jumped lightly to the ground. No matter how fast they thought they were, he was faster. So many years of training, so much anger and hatred coursed through his veins. He was always going to be faster. And there might be a dozen of them, but that would not be enough.

The elders scattered like the wind as they should – none of them were warriors – but the guards took their place, longbows drawn in the blink of an eye. A dozen soldiers against surely a hundred elves, Heri's guards had never stood a chance. But Sam had not properly considered Heri's evil and cunning.

Instead of actually drawing their swords, the soldiers hissed, a sound akin to that of a snake about to strike, and between one blink of an eye and the next, he knew a feeling of torture. It was the sound of a termite mound screaming in each ear, loud and discordant, and somehow crippling. Almost as if the termites were eating out the very centre of his head.

Arrows were loosed and flew in all directions. But none of them hit their targets as those who had loosed them collapsed.

Sam cried out in shock and torment. He wanted to drop his sword and cover his ears, but somehow he didn't. He was alone though. As bad as the noise was for him it was worse for everyone else. The elves screamed. Weapons were dropped and hands covered ears as the elves cried out in pain and fell to the ground in agony all around him. It wasn't just the guards either, it was all of them. The elders, the onlookers, and his beloved Ryshal and her family. None of them could stand the noise. And it was then that Sam finally understood why Heri had been grandstanding. He'd been bringing all the elven soldiers to within range of the soldiers' hissing.

But none of that mattered when Ryshal was down.

Panicking Sam ran to her, all his years of training and discipline forgotten in a heartbeat as he saw Ry writhing in agony on the ground with the others. It was only when he felt the pain of a knife biting into his back that he realised his terrible mistake. He'd turned his back on Heri.

Instantly he spun. The wound was bad but not bad enough to stop him slaughtering his half-brother there and then. The noise wasn't going to stop him either. Sam simply reached for his fire and prepared a blast. But it didn't come.

That shocked him. The fire always came, and he could feel it roaring furiously away in his core. But still it wouldn't come. The shock must have shown on his face, as he looked up to see Heri approaching him, knife in hand, laughing like a madman.

"What, no magic brother?" He mocked him, enjoying his apparent powerlessness, savouring his coming victory, and Sam knew he was in desperate trouble. A knife in his back, his magic somehow gone, and that terrible noise attacking his head; Heri had sprung his trap and it was devastating.

"Naturally I coated the blade with a tincture of clouded azure. Even now the poison is flowing through your blood, blocking your magic. It'll return of course, in a day or two. But you'll be long dead by then." Heri laughed some more, his face twisted up in triumph until it resembled something inhuman.

"And the noise. The hiss of the shadow vipers. The

weakness of all the elves, and through your harlot mother, you with them. Imagine that big brother; the same blood that gives you your devastating magic, leaves you powerless against a bunch of armoured snakes."

"Stupid of you really not to have prepared. But then you always did underestimate me. You always did think that with your muscles and your magic you were better than me. Father did too. But I'm smarter."

And just to prove it he raised his arm, and Sam had just enough time to see another knife strapped to the inside of his forearm before it shot at him like an arrow. But that was all the warning he needed, and somehow he managed to twist around a little, just enough that the knife didn't hit his breastplate cleanly and instead bounced off to go flying into the trees. At least some of his training was still with him. Enough to dodge a knife thrower.

That didn't please Heri at all, and he snarled at him like a rabid dog, words apparently failing him. But he still had a knife in his hand, its blade dripping with some sort of black liquid that ate the light around it, and Sam knew he was in trouble. Sam gripped the hilt of his sword tightly, assuming a defensive stance. At least he was armed, even if he could barely see for the pain in his head.

"There is no fear. There is no doubt. There is no pain. There is only the battle." It had been a long time since Sam had spoken the creed of the warrior out loud. He'd seldom had the need. But it was good to hear the words again, and better to feel their strength flowing through him. A warrior was always ready. There were no excuses. There could be no failure. Years and years on the parade grounds being drilled in his weapons every day and being pushed to breaking point had taught him that.

As Heri advanced on him he pushed aside the noise trying

to tear his head apart, pushed aside the pain and weakness in his back too and even forgot that he had no magic. None of that mattered. Instead he focussed only on the battle and the sword in his hands.

Heri must have seen that in his eyes, and he started goading him, determined to break his concentration.

"You know your own mother and your nearly born sister died at my mother's hands. She poisoned her just as she was about to give birth. There could be no more half elf bastards running around the kingdom."

Heri lunged at him, hoping his words would distract him, but he was out of luck. There was only the battle and only the blade in his hand, and Sam simply deflected his attack with a simple flick of his sword. He left the words for later.

"You know I'm going to kill Ryshal." Heri tried another lunge with the poisoned blade, and Sam deflected it again, spinning him around.

He might be weaker than normal, but his technique was still working perfectly.

"After I have her." This time Heri used a surprising twisting spin blow, hoping to come under his guard, but it was easily enough blocked.

"Again."

There it was, that last nasty accusation designed to throw Sam off just as he took aim with his blade and hurled it at him with all his strength. But Sam had expected it, and he would never allow Heri to distract him. A simple twist and the blade shot straight past him to land somewhere among the trees. Suddenly Heri was unarmed.

His half-brother looked up at him, suddenly frightened as he realised he was helpless and about to die. Sam could see the fear in his eyes, and though it was wrong he knew a moment of intense pleasure at the sight. But of course it wasn't over. He still had to take Heri's head.

Heri though had other ideas and he spun on his heels like a dancer and dashed frantically for the horses, thinking either to flee or to grab another weapon. Whichever it was he was out of luck. Seeing him break and run Sam simply raised his greatsword over his head, and with a two handed cast, hurled it straight at his retreating back with all the strength he had.

It was a good throw. The blade cut through the air, spinning like a top, before burying itself hilt deep in the small of his back with a thump. Heri went down with a gasp, collapsing on the ground in a bloody tangle of limbs and leather, and Sam knew the blow had been a serious one. He might not be dead yet, but he soon would be. Surely by the All Father he would soon be gone from this world!

Before Sam could celebrate though, he had some snakes to kill.

Calmly, still somehow putting the pain in his head out of his thoughts, he walked over to his horse and drew his crossbow from her pack, Shadow vipers were nasty creatures, and as Heri had said, especially dangerous to those with sharp ears such as the elves and the sylph. But they were also incredibly rare and very hard to control. Just squeezing them into the armour would have been a struggle, and then getting them on top of the horses another. The horses wouldn't have liked it either. Somewhere in amongst them he knew, would be their handler. A wizard gifted with some sort of control over them. It had to be one of the advisers, both of whom were staring at him with a look of fear and horror on their faces. Things weren't working out as they had expected. Everyone was supposed to have been overcome by their creatures. Suddenly they were facing a warrior and their creatures had no real power other than their hiss.

The advisers clearly thought they were about to die. They assumed that Sam was going to put a bolt through their hearts and were panicking. It was ironic really. They'd brought what they had thought was an army that was all but unassailable by the elves, and they were right. But against a single half elf with a crossbow and a sword they were helpless. To add to the irony Heri had brought them for his defence, but when he'd fallen they'd discovered that they needed him as much as he needed them.

"Get down." He gave the order and the two advisers obeyed without so much as a word of protest. No doubt they thought he was going to kill them on the spot but they were still too frightened to disobey him. In truth he wanted to kill them. The pain was terrible.

But he couldn't kill them yet. To kill the handler would be to release the vipers from their control, and then they would run wild, killing any elves they found still lying helpless on the ground.

So instead he put his first bolt straight through the centre of the nearest creature's breastplate, fairly much where a man's heart would be. He wasn't completely sure that these foul things had hearts, but it must have been enough as the viper suddenly screeched madly and fell off the horse, before writhing away on the ground in its death throes.

Bits of its armour fell off as it writhed, revealing the true horror of the creature. With the gauntlets gone, he could see the snake like tentacles it had for arms bursting free, and once the helm rolled away, its viper like head popped out. In fact it even had a forked tongue like a snake sticking out between its fangs.

Though he'd never seen one before, he knew from the tales that the creatures were built like starfish, with four snake like tentacles where a man would have arms and legs, and a viper's head on what was another tentacle. They were truly frightening creatures, especially in the distant swamps of Arusid where they lived. Their bodies didn't allow them to walk, but they didn't need to. They used their tentacles to pull themselves quickly along the soft ground, and the poison from their fangs to kill their prey before they wrapped it up and crushed it into a pulp to drink.

The vipers had weaknesses though, and the greatest of them was that they weren't strong fighters. They would never attack a creature that hadn't fallen victim to their hiss. They couldn't use weapons, and wrapped up head to foot in armour as they were, they were almost helpless. Save for their hiss. Their hiss was a weapon they used to great effect against creatures with sharp hearing, which was why the elves with their acute hearing were so vulnerable. As a half elf Sam was apparently far less vulnerable.

The response to the first viper guard's death was immediate as the advisers and the remaining vipers all spun around on their heels and tried to mount up and gallop for safety, hissing all the way. Their handler was hoping to use their hissing as a shield as he fled the town. But there could be no escape for them.

"Stop!" Sam bellowed it at the advisers at the top of his lungs. By then he already had the next bolt loaded. "Let go of the reins or I put the next bolt in your back."

Of course he could only kill one of them, and if they'd been thinking clearly they would have realised that. But they weren't soldiers and they didn't think like them. They didn't even realise that they might have had time to flee between each bolt as it took him a few moments to reload each one. One of them might get away. So instead they just turned back to him and stood there staring at him, paralysed with fear.

"Now lie face down on the ground."

They did it, their terror preventing them from understanding that the only reason he was doing it was to slow them down. To make it harder for them to run away. It worked.

But what worked even better was when an arrow suddenly found its way deep into the chest of another viper. It wasn't his. He had a crossbow firing heavy bolts. This was a full three foot length of wood with a metal tip loosed from a long bow.

Sam turned to see Mayvelle standing there, longbow in hand, a pained look on her face, but determination in her eyes. She too could resist the hiss. And she was already reaching for another arrow.

That was Sam's cue to release a second bolt into a second viper chest.

After that it was straight forward. One by one they put the vipers down in front of them. And fortunately they died easily enough while their masters lay there in terror, knowing that when the vipers were gone they'd be completely defenceless.

Both of them he realised were minor wizards. Untrained and with only a few spells to their name. But those spells they'd learned thoroughly. Neither of them though could use a weapon. Neither of them had so much as a fireball to their name. And neither of them could plan their way out of a tent. If they'd been thinking they would have sent half the vipers his way for him to deal with, and used the other half to make their escape while he was busy. But they weren't soldiers. Just black hearted rogues. And they were too frightened to think.

So they lay there, their faces in the dirt, while he and Mayvelle destroyed their army soldier by soldier.

Each viper that fell to the ground lessened the noise in his head, and all around he could see the anguish on the faces of the others lessening as well. In time as they kept killing the creatures, some of the elves even managed to get to their feet and draw their weapons. And so by the end the creatures were falling thanks to his bolts and a number of other elven arrows.

After that the battle was over. Heri was still lying on the ground and dying slowly. The vipers were all dead and only the two advisers remained to be dealt with. One was the wizard who had controlled the vipers, and the other at a guess was a wizard who had managed to hide their nature from the elves and had presumably kept the horses under control. Had the elves realised what they were they would have been dead long before they reached the town.

Neither of the men stood a chance against the elves. They were swiftly gathered up and dragged away from their mounts, bound hand and foot and brought before the elders for judgement. Judging from the elders' faces, it would not be a pleasant fate that awaited them. The pain from the creatures' hissing was still with them. But Sam didn't care about any of that. Nor that Mayvelle had fairly much proven that she had human blood in her veins. He didn't even care about Heri slowly dying on the ground in front of him. He went to Ryshal instead, and helped her and her parents up.

They were pale and shaking, much as he had expected. Much as he probably was himself. That hiss was a dreadful thing. But they were unharmed.

"Aylin mi elle, are you all right?" It was the only thing that mattered as he held his wife tight, and finally let some of the emotion that he'd been holding back, run free.

"Praise the Goddess I'm well husband. But you need the healers immediately!"

She was right as he suddenly realised that he'd somehow forgotten about the knife in his back in the heat of battle. Or maybe it was simply that with that terrible hiss gone, the relief had robbed him of any ability to feel pain. Ry though was staring at it as though it was a demon. Though to be fair it wasn't hurting as much as it had at the start. That of course might not be a good thing. But as the tears of relief trickled out of the corners of his eyes and ran down his cheeks, he didn't really care.

After that things became a little confused. Healers turned up out of nowhere, and started tending to those who still weren't able to get up. One of them pulled him away from Ry and swiftly had him lying on the ground as they pulled the knife free. It hurt, but only for a few heartbeats as they pushed their healing magic into his flesh.

They told him that the wound was nasty but that he would make a full recovery, so he didn't really care that much. He was more curious that a thrown knife – even one thrown by a mechanical device had managed to pierce his back plate. In time he'd have to look at that device, just to see how powerful it actually was.

At some point someone returned his greatsword to him, and he gathered that they were now healing Heri. If he had still been alive at the time that they pulled it out of his back. Of course he was sure he was. Demons didn't die easily. Sam vehemently hoped that the removal of his greatsword from Heri's back had at least caused him sheer agony.

Then someone dragged out a stretcher from nowhere, and they tried to make him lie down on it. Sam tried to refuse, telling them he could walk, and that it was undignified to be carried away like that. But Ry would have none of it. She pushed him down onto it and after that he was swiftly carried away, though four elves were needed to lift his bulk off the ground. In all his armour it wasn't surprising. But at least Ry was with him, holding his hand and telling him everything was going to be all right. With her beside him he was sure it would be.

The only sour note in fact was that as he was led away he could hear his brother's voice somewhere in the distance, and knew that somehow he still lived. Weak and thin, he was begging for mercy and promising to tell anyone who would listen all sorts of secrets. And though it would be a mistake, Sam knew enough of his wife's people to know that they would consider it even after all he'd done. Sometimes he thought the elves might be a people too decent for their own good.

Certainly they were too decent for his.

Chapter Twenty Five.

"Samual."

Sam looked up as he heard Elder Bela calling his name to see the Elder standing there on the grass by their wagon with War Master Wyldred beside him. They were his two most regular and most annoying visitors. He sighed, wondering why they were bothering him again. He was supposed to be resting while he recovered from his injury, and was not to be disturbed. Or so the healers had instructed. But really he felt fine. His magic had returned as he had known it would. And mostly he was simply enjoying being fussed over a little. Ry was very good at fussing. And it was cold outside.

Unfortunately it seemed that that time had passed. It had been six days. He felt fully fit save for a few minor twinges. And there was undoubtedly work to do. But from the looks on his visitor's faces, not pleasant work.

Naturally there was only one matter of late that could make them look so unhappy.

"The toad's made a full recovery hasn't he?" Sam could tell that from the somewhat sour expression on the Elder's face. It was a disgrace to let Heri live, and probably a mistake, and they all knew it. Heri would be back to cause more trouble sooner or later. But the elves weren't cold blooded enough to kill a wounded man in cold blood. They'd tended to his wounds instead.

"No. Not full. But enough to be on his way. And we have agreed to let him go." Elder Bela shook his head. "But he will never be able to harm you or your family again. I promise you that."

Promises were being given too freely these days in Sam's opinion, and too often they couldn't be kept. But instead of railing against them for making them he held his temper. After all, he had promised never to cross the elders. But still a little of his bitterness escaped.

"You should have let him die. Why didn't you Elder? It would have been for the best. It would have been justice."

"Because he had information. Knowledge of crimes against our people. Brigands who have crossed us. Even some knowledge of the rats and their master."

"He always has information," Sam told him bitterly. Information was always one of his little brother's most valuable weapons. But at some point he thought, you had to stop trading for it.

Yet his true bitterness wasn't for them or their deal. He understood them. It was for himself. For once again underestimating his brother. And for letting himself belief the tall tales about the Fire Angel that everyone kept spouting. He might be a powerful mage. He might have fire magic as powerful as any other. But he still had huge weaknesses. And he kept forgetting that. Heri had exposed one of them, he could be tricked as easily as any other. He should never have allowed himself to fall prey to Heri's trap. He should have killed him the instant he saw him.

"Nonetheless, it is time for him to be released according to our deal and we thought you should be there for that if you're strong enough."

"I'm strong enough." Physically that was the truth. In his heart though he didn't know if he could stand to see Heri go free. Still, it had been agreed, and he mounted up and followed the elders back to the Council clearing.

Nothing was said as they rode. Sam was in no mood to speak and he didn't completely trust himself to say the right thing anyway. The others seemed no more talkative than he was.

At least Heri looked less like a king than he had Sam decided when he finally set eyes on his half-brother. The knife he had put in Sam's back had hurt. But the greatsword Sam had put in Heri's had done far more serious damage and Heri was still largely bedridden. In fact he was lying in the middle of the clearing, surrounded by elders, on a light weight cot. It seemed that they had simply carried him here from the healers' tent.

Gone too were his robes. The expensive ermine had been removed, his armour as well, and he had been clothed in typical day wear for an elf. If there was one thing he didn't look like just then, it was a king. But then he wasn't a king. Not anymore. According to what they had learned from him, Heri had destroyed his castle and his city, pretended to be dead, and had run away. If he'd had any sense Sam thought, he should have simply kept running. But he didn't. He had too much hatred to listen to common sense. Hatred that showed itself even as Sam and the others dismounted.

"You plague ridden wart!" Heri started abusing Sam the instant he laid eyes on him and didn't stop until he ran out of breath.

What came out of his mouth though was more of a screech. The healers had done their best work to keep him alive, but even they had their limits. Heri would never walk straight again. Too many of his back and stomach muscles had been severed for that. And for some reason his voice no longer worked as it once had either. Added to that he had only half of his good hand remaining. He was a rather pathetic figure lying there on his cot. But again Sam had to remind himself, he could never underestimate Heri again. He could never again let himself believe the stories of the Fire Angel again either. He wasn't invulnerable.

Sam ignored him. He had expected his little brother's tirade. There was in fact only one thing the two of them agreed on. Their hatred of one another.

"Elder, might I be permitted to burn out his tongue at least?" Really he wanted to burn off his entire head, but he could restrain himself. And just keeping his brother completely silent would be a blessing. Especially when Heri heard him and started screeching about the deal he had made. He was panicking.

"Regretfully not." Elder Bela shook his head. "We did unfortunately make a deal with him that included healing his injuries and not harming him. But still, with a viper's tongue like his I do wonder if we were too generous."

Too generous or not, his words shut Heri's mouth very quickly as he was reminded once again that he was not among friends.

"Letting him breathe was too generous."

Sam couldn't help but let his bitterness show. Ever since the confessions Heri had made had been brought to him, he had discovered a whole new level of hatred for his little brother. For his entire lineage.

Heri had claimed during the battle that his mother had poisoned his own mother. That she had died in childbirth but not of childbirth as he had always believed. Apparently Lady Dreasda had had designs on the throne from the start and his mother had simply been in her way. Heri had also claimed that she had later poisoned his father as well. There had been no assassin with a poisoned dart who had somehow escaped the guards. Heri had maintained that story during his questioning. Even when the elders had had soothsayers there to hear every word. It seemed that the Lady Dreasda had ruined his life and murdered his entire family. And she had raised her son from the start to be the same as her. No doubt she had fed Heri her poison in her very milk. Which made it somewhat ironic that Heri had killed her. There was no love lost among vipers.

"Perhaps, but there is at least no reason to fear his return. He will not be coming back. And he will never be able to cause harm to you or your family again. We had a very powerful geas placed upon him. One that will endure for a lifetime. To even raise a hand against you or ask another to do so will cause him terrible pain. To attempt to do more than that will be far worse for him."

"Thank you Elders." Sam bowed respectfully to them though there was no joy in his heart at the news. Whether it would be enough to stop Heri forever he didn't know. But at least it was something.

"Young Samual." Elder Bela was smiling as he gently mocked him. "Do you truly imagine that we could ever allow Heri to harm you again? That would be shameful. And we worked hard to find a suitable sentence."

"Sentence?" Heri looked up at the Elder from his cot, suddenly worried. His face was completely white. "There was to be no sentence. I am to go free. That was the deal."

"Of course young Heri." Master Bela smiled at him in what had to be the least genuine smile his face had ever worn. "Perhaps I misspoke. I did not mean to suggest that we would be punishing you for your crimes. We did give you our word after all. But there will be retribution and restitution made for your crimes regardless. Justice will be done. Of that you can be certain."

Heri looked confused and frightened. Sam on the other hand was just confused. He didn't truly fear his brother's return anymore. Not when he had had such a powerful geas placed on him. Heri might hate him, he might have wealth and power, but against an elven geas he was powerless. Besides, he still looked completely helpless. His body was broken, and the healers said he would not walk easily again.

A broken body. A powerful geas placed upon him. His throne gone. Sam did not fear his brother's vengeance. Mostly.

Any questions Sam might have had though were taken from him by the unexpected thunder of horses hooves in the distance, and he turned to see a patrol galloping furiously towards them.

"Ah, right on time." Elder Bela smiled some more and even Heri probably realised that he was planning something. He would have been more worried if he'd seen the smiles on the faces of the other elders.

"What have you done?" he screeched at the Elder in panic.

"Why exactly what we agreed upon of course." Elder Bela managed a suitably surprised expression. "We are setting you free. And these men are here to witness the fact that you have been freed. In fact they have expressed some interest in escorting you safely all the way back to Fair Fields."

Free to die was Sam's thought. And die badly. He could suddenly make out the pennant of the Fallbrights flying proudly over the heads of the riders, and it was all he could do to keep from laughing. The elves had delivered him straight into the arms of his enemies. Sam might have held back his laughter but he couldn't stop a smile from finding his face. He had always found the elves passion for word games strange and somewhat unexpected in a people with a love for the truth, but sometimes sophistry was its own blessing. This it seemed was one of those times. His brother didn't find it so amusing however, and instantly started shrieking in terror. He had a fair idea of what was going to happen to him when the riders had him.

"No! I gave you everything you asked for!" Heri was almost out of his mind with terror, and though it was probably something he should not do, Sam found pleasure in that. A lot of pleasure. But after all the terrible things Heri had done he figured it was at least something.

"Yes you did Heri. And we are giving you your freedom in return."

Sam could feel the quiet anger in the Elder, burning slowly but steadily. And he had every right to be angry. If what Heri had said was correct, the Elder had every right to want to kill his verminous little half-brother on the spot. Heri it seemed had been secretly capturing, imprisoning and torturing the elves of Shavarra for useful information for years. And he had sent in assassins after Sam who had killed many more in their quest. Any elf would be outraged. So would be the dwarves of Ore Bender's Mountains, who had been similarly targeted. And the gnomes of the Fedowir Kingdom. In fact any people from any land where Heri thought there was something to be gained. Sam was outraged. He had had no thought that Heri would go so far. But as did any true elf, Elder Bela held it back and maintained his calm. And he kept his word. He would have made a fine knight.

Sam was saved from having to think any further on his brother's villainy as the riders pulled up in front of them, and he was grateful for that. Even when he saw the leader pull off his helmet and recognised his face. More importantly the man recognised him.

"Samual Hanor?" He seemed surprised, and behind that,

suspicious. But then he was Galan Fallbright, the elder brother of Harmion, and if he knew nothing else he knew Sam had cut half his brother's hand off. They were not friends. But on the other hand Galan was a soldier. He respected the laws of the land.

"Galan." Sam nodded politely. There was no reason not to. But he was surprised to see him. After all, it had only been a week since Heri's attack on him and the elves. There was no way that anyone, even if they'd known of it immediately it had happened, could have made it all the way from Fair Fields. He must have already been in Golden River Flats for some reason. Perhaps he had been visiting the Fallbright family's trading outposts. They had a number of them.

"Are you here to argue for your brother?"

Of course he would think that. Galan had actually liked his brother. Even if the whole family were a pack of greedy robber barons extorting traders and robbing the people blind, they still had a bond of family. Sam envied them that.

"No. Not by Alder's balls or his tits!" It was crude and out of the corner of his eye Sam saw some of the elders' faces fall as the words slipped out. But it was the truth.

"No?"

"No. Heri should face justice for his crimes. A proper trial where he can be judged fairly and then given a swift execution."

Galan's eyes widened a little in surprise when he said that and Sam wondered why. Did he truly not know of all the terrible things Heri had done to him and his family? But it didn't matter. Neither did his brother's screeching as he lay on the cot. In the end he just wanted to be rid of him. One way or another.

"You will not …?" Galan's words trailed off as he stared at him, maybe a little nervously.

"What, rescue him? Defend him?" Sam was surprised that he could imagine such a thing. But then he guessed that Heri had hidden a lot of what he'd done from the rest of Fair Fields. "By all the gods no. Heri is a monster. He has done terrible harm to me and my family, and disgraced us all. He imprisoned my wife in his dungeons for five years, until I rescued her. He exiled me and sent numerous assassins after me for all that time. A week ago he made another attempt on my life, bringing assassins with shadow vipers to this land, harming many, He again threatened my family and stabbed me with a poisoned blade. He is Alder's very right hand!"

"No I will not protect him in any way."

"You can't do this!" Heri abruptly started screeching again. "I'm your brother!"

Sam almost fell over in shock when he heard Heri say that. And all around him he could see the other elves staring at one another in disbelief. The sheer effrontery of it was beyond belief. And yet he had said similar things before. Did Heri not understand what he'd done Sam wondered? It was almost as though he had no concept of right and wrong. He recalled having wondered that very thing before. Was he truly so blind? Or was he simply desperate? Either way no one answered him.

"Now Heri," Elder Bela turned to the fallen king, "Our deal is complete and you are free to leave as agreed. We will even provide you with some crutches to help you on your way." The instant he said it a healer rushed over with the promised crutches and started to help Heri to his feet.

"And you can go with these men, or alternatively if you

choose, run away. We don't care. We just want you gone."

"But they're going to kill me!"

"That is between you and them. Our deal is done and you are free to go. But perhaps you should start running then."

Heri gaped at the Elder. At all of them. And then, suddenly realising that he had no hope that anyone would rush to his aid, he started running exactly as he needed to. But his running was a short lived event as Galan simply nodded to his men and a moment later Heri was caught, knocked to the ground, bound, thrown over a horse and quickly lashed to it. Heri never stopped screeching as they did so.

"Elders." Galan nodded respectfully to them as Heri screeched in terror. And they in turn nodded back.

"Samual." Galan nodded to Sam.

"Galan." Sam returned the farewell. But then thought he should say something more.

"I'm sorry for your loss. Harmion was not a good man, and he like Heri harmed my wife terribly in his ambition. But at least he was a brother and I sorrow that mine took that from you."

Galan didn't answer him. Sam wasn't sure he had expected him to. But it had had to be said. And he was glad he had as he watched the young Fallbright lord mount up and then ride away with his troop and his prisoner.

Was it over? Sam wondered about that as he watched them ride off into the distance. The Fallbrights would not be counted among his friends he knew. But they had Heri and he doubted that they cared half so much about him. And as for Heri, though the odds were against him he doubted that he could ever say he was safe from him. Not until he was finally dead.

But at least it was over for now.

Chapter Twenty Six

Ryshal sat on a flat rock on the side of the river that flowed through their new home, her feet in the water as she worked patiently on the laundry.

Laundering clothes wasn't a particularly difficult job. It was just a matter of soaping the clothes, squeezing them against the rocks to get the foam to wash through them, and then rinsing them in the flowing water before pounding them on the rocks to get the water out. Routine, boring and repetitive drudgery, but still good exercise for muscles that had done too little for far too long. And it was good to grow a little strength Ryshal thought. To breathe a little heavily from time to time and feel the blood flowing. And it could be quite pleasant when the sun was shining as it was. Then again the water was icy cold on her hands and feet.

Some days it was also quite a social event as the river was filled with women doing the same as her while the river flowed white with little soap bubbles. It would be good though when eventually they had houses and tubs. Especially once they had warm water. But those days she suspected were a long way off. For the moment they had to do things as simply as possible. You couldn't get much simpler than a bar of soap, some flat rocks and a river.

Today though the river was nearly empty. But from the sound of footsteps behind her she was about to have company. Ryshal looked around to see Mayvelle walking towards her and immediately had to suppress a surprised sigh. If there was one person she had never expected to see again it was her. In fact after the way she and her family had been treated by Mayvelle and her parents, she would have been grateful for that. Even though she guessed the reason for their rudeness, she didn't want to see the Ellosian family again. She had been grateful that she had not seen them since that day. Save for Mayvelle who had been there when Heri had attacked. But she had noticed little of her or anyone else then.

Yet it seemed she was about to see Mayvelle again regardless of what she wanted. But at least it was Mayvelle alone. She wasn't certain she could endure the parents' barely concealed hostility as well. On the other hand she did wonder about the timing. Samual had just returned to his proper duties and studies with the elders that morning, leaving her to do the laundry alone. Was that a coincidence? Somehow she thought not. The two of them had a fractious relationship at best.

Ryshal concentrated on washing the clothes as the woman approached, deciding not to change her routine just because she had a visitor. And besides, laundry wasn't a task she particularly enjoyed. It was best to get it over with as quickly as possible.

"Ryshal?" Mayvelle greeted her.

"Mayvelle." She could have been rude and ignored her she supposed, but Ryshal saw no point in that. Besides, her parents would have been unhappy with her if she had done that. "I didn't expect to see you here."

"And did not wish to either, at a guess."

Ryshal didn't answer her. There was no answer she could give that was both polite and true. Instead she concentrated on her work, pressing the clothes against a flat rock to squeeze the soapy water out of them, then dunking them again in the river before repeating. Eventually Mayvelle seemed to understand that she wasn't going to get an answer and carried on.

"I came first to apologise."

"There is no need for apologies among family," Ry answered her automatically.

"Yes, but sometimes there is a desire. And my family and I were unfailingly rude to you and yours. I desire to repair that failing."

"It is repaired and forgotten." Ry finally looked up to see her standing there looking awkward. No doubt Mayvelle didn't do a lot of apologising in her life. But she also looked nervous. Annoying and direct as she was, Mayvelle was never a nervous woman. This was not about a mere apology. Something else was weighing on her mind.

"Thank you. Your husband was most … certain in his words to me." Mayvelle said it awkwardly.

"My husband is like you, a soldier. He can be very direct. Especially when he believes his family has been wronged in some way." Ry managed a small smile. If Mayvelle was apologising than she had to be gracious. "But I will speak to him, and I apologise on his behalf if he was too direct."

"He was not. Sometimes it is good to hear the truth plainly spoken."

"Then I will tell him that, and thank you for your understanding." Ry returned to her work, knowing that there was more that Mayvelle wanted to say but also that it wasn't her place to ask.

"You are well after the attack? Your parents too?"

"Yes. It was painful, like someone shredding the bones of our skulls from the inside, but thanks to yourself and Samual it ended quickly enough and no harm was done." It would have been if the vipers had not been stopped, and probably many would have died as the vipers bit them while they lay there, helpless. But that had not happened, praise the Goddess.

"Samual was able to fight because he is vero eskaline?"

"Yes." Ry heard the alarm in Mayvelle's voice as she asked the question and abruptly understood why the soldier had come to her. This was about blood. She had doubts about her heritage. "As one of part human and part elf blood his hearing is not so sharp as some. He heard the hiss and it hurt, but not so greatly that it could prevent him from doing what he had to."

"Nor I." Mayvelle lowered her head. "And I wonder why."

But she didn't wonder. Not really Ry knew as she stopped working once more and looked up at her. Mayvelle had guessed the truth and the pain was written all over her long face. She just wanted it confirmed. But that could not be done by her, Ryshal knew.

"Among our people there are some with sharper eyes and some with poorer. The same is true of hearing. Perhaps your hearing is simply not as sharp."

"And perhaps there is a reason for it. As there is for my speed and strength. My stature."

Ry sighed quietly, knowing that she could not give the soldier the answers she wanted because, firstly it was not her place, and secondly all she had herself was supposition. Mayvelle didn't know that of course. She suspected Samual had more knowledge. And that because of that Ry would. That was why the soldier had come to her. But she didn't and yet she had to say something. Eventually some words came to her.

"I'm sorry but I cannot answer your questions. I simply

don't have the answers. The only ones who do are your parents." She guessed though that they would not want to provide Mayvelle with those answers if they were what she suspected.

"But you can guess." Mayvelle suddenly looked up from the ground to stare straight at Ryshal, her eyes at once both pleading and accusing.

"What you are speaking of is a matter too important for guesses. You need the truth."

There was silence after that as neither of them knew what to say. How to broach the difficulty that lay between them. But eventually Ry saw Mayvelle's shoulders begin to relax as she realised that she had told her all she could.

"You are right and I thank you for your wisdom." Mayvelle nodded politely to her. "But I need to return to my duties. I just wanted to see that you were well and to apologise for my rudeness of the other day."

With that the soldier abruptly turned and left her, leaving Ry with a view of her departing form and endless questions. She didn't know what Mayvelle would do. Whether she would broach the matter with her parents. It was not an easy thing for a daughter to do. Not even for an adult daughter. Nor did she know what Mayvelle's parents would say. Most of all she didn't know what the outcome would be if her parents did tell Mayvelle what Ry was sure was the truth. But she feared that things would not be easy in the Ellosian wagon for a while. It would be best that none of that was laid at their feet.

Still, she knew as she returned to her work that it was something she could do nothing about. She had said what she could and had been very careful in it. All she could do for the moment was wash the clothes. And speak to her parents and her husband in time so that they knew what had happened.

Maybe too she would say a prayer to the Goddess for the soldier. In the end it was the Goddess who had allowed her to survive for so long in that prison cell. Had she not held to her faith she would have died early on. And she was certain that the Goddess was behind Samual's incredible growth as a mage. That the Fire Angel was her servant even if he did not know it.

Surely she could do something for the Fire Angel's sister as well.

Chapter Twenty Seven

Heri smiled grimly as he plunged the dagger into the last soldier's throat and then watched his lifeless corpse collapse back. He was pleased that the battle such as it was, was over. But he was annoyed that it wasn't Galan's gurgling he was listening to.

The man was an annoyance. His entire family was a plague. They had opposed him from the start. They had threatened his rule, and ultimately they had taken it away from him. Heri was certain that it was their assassin who had killed the hostages. No one else would be so ruthless. No one else hated him so greatly.

The Fallbrights had to die. All of them.

But his vengeance would have to wait for a while. He was back in Fair Fields, not too many leagues from their own barony. Soon he knew Galan Fallbright would be back with his entire verminous family, no doubt in a hurry to throw a rope over a suitable tree branch and hang him from it. They were going to be very unhappy he suspected when they returned to find their entire patrol dead. Especially Galan when he'd raced hard through the wastes to get him here as quickly as possible.

Really though, it was their own fault. They had restrained him and searched him thoroughly for weapons before taking him away. And they thought they had done their job well. But they had been stupid. The Fallbrights had always been an unimaginative family. Slow witted and quick to anger. It had never occurred to them to check for poisons.

It had never occurred to them either, to guess that as they had brought him back through the wastes to face judgement in

Fair Fields that he had let them. His beard was growing nicely into a bush. His hair was longer now and unkempt. His wounds were healing. And they were actually escorting him through a dangerous land and away from his enemies. Enemies who had proven surprisingly dangerous. Now as King Heri was dead, no one would be looking for him and he would be safe enough in Fair Fields. As long as word didn't get out that he was alive. Which was another reason he was angry that Galan wasn't there to die with his men.

Still, it was only one man. One noble anyway. The soldiers, those who had ridden with Galan, didn't count. And Galan was a Fallbright. A family that were already in deep trouble with the other noble houses. The word had spread that it was they who had sent the assassins into the keep and arranged the killing of their loved ones. After that the stories of his survival would look like the desperate attempts of a noble house to deflect blame.

So really, while Galan had imagined he was bringing a condemned man back for execution, in truth he and his soldiers had been escorting the former king home. Back to where he had his gold.

A man with gold could do a lot. His mother had taught him that.

She had taught him a lot. The ways of power. The art of deception. And of course the science of poisons. In fact it was a pity she was dead. Still, she would have died quickly. If he had been overthrown and tried then she would have been tried too and her execution would have been by stoning. That would have been a far crueller fate. This had been better for her.

And in the end she had betrayed him. She had in fact planned his poisoning with bale root. He had found the plants in her private garden and understood her plan immediately.

And removing the plants had not been enough. She would have done so again. It was simply the woman she was. She wanted the throne. She would have done anything she could to get it. And if she couldn't be queen because the laws of Fair Fields did not allow for a woman to sit on the throne, she would have settled for regent for a son laid low by long term sickness. In time she could have ruled through her grandchildren after he'd finally died of whatever unfortunate malady she'd intended for him to contract. In time no doubt, they would have died too. She could have been regent for life.

Another soldier suddenly gurgled one final time before collapsing at Heri's feet, catching him by surprise. He'd thought they were all dead already. Hearing him he checked the rest of the corpses just to make sure. When he found that one solider still had a pulse he slit the man's throat again just to make sure. After that he was done.

Soldiers! They had to be the most stupid men alive! Who but a fool would take coin to fight for someone else when they should be fighting for themselves? And now look at them. All dead. And for nothing.

Heri wiped his hands on the coat of the nearest dead soldier before going to sit by the fire and plan his next move. Naturally he didn't touch the stew. Not after he'd dropped a bulb of scorpion venom in it while the others weren't looking. That was the other failing of soldiers. They looked for threats with weapons. They never thought to think of things like poisons. And they had paid for that mistake with their lives.

But what next? That was the question. He couldn't go after Samual. Not again. Not yet. The elves would never let him go near them again. Once more his brother had proven himself too strong for him. Even without magic. And the elves would not be lied to either. Not twice. They were an irritating people, but not completely stupid. So for the moment his brother would live. It was time instead to start thinking about the rest of his enemies. And about his throne.

He had gold, and gold was power. It wasn't the throne and he couldn't buy it back with it. But it could be used as part of his plan to get it back. He'd always been careful to stash some away in little repositories throughout the kingdom, just in case. There might be some digging involved since many of those repositories were graves. But that just meant it would take time.

What he didn't have and what he needed most were allies. The gold could buy him property and servants and guards. But not allies. And thanks to the Fallbright's one clever idea, he never would. Not among the nobles of the Court. They too like the soldiers were stupid, though their foolishness related to family rather than force of arms. They would never ally themselves with someone who had killed their loved ones. And though they were now warring with one another as they fought for the throne, if they knew he lived they would all come together to destroy him. It was foolish and short sighted. But it was who they were.

His mother had taught him better than that of course. Caring for others was weakness. Love was a mistake. His mother had proven it repeatedly as she had arranged time and again for her husband to die. Finding ever more difficult and dangerous battles for him to fight and enemies to face. And why? Because his father had never loved her. His heart had always belonged to that elven whore. And so true hatred had been born in her heart. While love for a dead whore had killed his father.

It had been tricky of course. She could never have let him guess it was her behind all the attempts on his life. Or that she had killed his first love. And she had had to make sure that the kingdom would hold together after he was gone with her as regent. But she had been determined. It was simply that he had been even more determined to live. Something that had infuriated her as nothing else could, though she'd always had to hide it behind a forced smile and fake tears of relief. His mother had really hated his father.

But really as he recalled, the hardest thing she had had to face was her joy when she had finally succeeded. When his body was being lowered into the ground. She had finally realised that her subtle machinations were never going to work, and resorted to acting directly, poisoning his food and then pretending that he had been struck by an assassin's poisoned dart. And when she had finally succeeded the smile had scarcely left her face for weeks.

He had been dead. She had been regent – queen in all but name. And life had seemed wondrous. At the time the only dark spot on her horizon was him. That had been a trans-formative moment in his life. When he had seen her smile and realised her plans. He had been sixteen. In two short years he would have been old enough to claim the throne for himself. And her short reign as regent would be ended before it even began. He knew then that she was never going to let that happen. Seeing his father lowered into the ground and his mother's grin hidden behind the black veil, he had known his life was in mortal danger. It was then that he'd known that he would have to act against her.

False charges, accusations of infidelity, rumours of further tax reductions – all had played into his hands as he'd undermined her rule. And of course he'd had her watched. Made sure he knew every plant and poison she had. Destroyed most of them. She had never known it was him. Not until after it was done. She had taught him well.

But those strategies would not serve here. The noble houses were already at war with one another. It was not about reputations anymore. It was about blood and strength of arms. And the throne along with the city and its keep were gone. Now he would have to create a new throne. His own throne.

And he would have to do it with allies who didn't want to kill him on sight. Allies he hadn't harmed.

There were only two.

The first were the thieves, outlaws and miscellaneous brigands and black market merchants he had dealt with over the years. But they were all by their very nature, untrustworthy. They would betray him the instant it served their purposes.

Which left him only with the second. This new Dragon.

He had bargained away some of his knowledge to the pestilent elves to save his life. He had had to after his plan had fallen apart so badly. And he had taken a secret joy in telling them of what he had done to some of their people. But he had kept a lot hidden. And then the elves had surprised him with their betrayal in turn. It had been surprisingly unelven of them. They were such an honest people. So straight forward. Now it seemed they were also capable of deception. He hated them for that. And yet it was also the only time he had ever respected them for a single decision they had made. But his deception was still greater. He had not told them all. And the most important thing he had not told them was that he knew where the Dragon could be found. And how to contact him.

His former spymaster might have betrayed him at the end. But his army of spies had been extremely effective. When the Dragon had struck they had been able to learn a lot about him. And Augrim had divined a fair amount as well. All of which meant that Heri was now the only man on the entire continent of the Dragon's Spine that knew who the new Dragon was.

Not his name of course. Heri wasn't even sure that troll bloods had names. But he knew where he could be found and how to contact him. And that was far more than anyone else knew.

He had not told the elves that of course. He had scarcely told them even a fraction of all that he knew about the Dragon. He had really just given them information about the Dragon's attacks across the entire continent. The strategies he had employed against different cities. The different creatures he had used. And what had happened to those realms he had conquered. They had been particularly concerned about Shavarra and he could tell them what the rats had done to it – nothing. Once the people were gone, dead or fled, the Dragon hadn't cared about it. His goal was murder, not conquest. In the end he was a troll blood.

Heri had not tried to make contact with the Dragon thus far, because there had seemed no point. And dealing with troll bloods was always bad for your health. But looking at the dead soldiers and knowing the pain of his ruined back muscles and missing half a hand, he knew the time had come. It was time to use the Dragon.

It was dangerous but necessary. The alternative was to run away and give up his dream of taking the throne once more. He could not do that. So he had to take a chance. His mother had in the end realised that she had to take a chance and risked revealing herself as she had set about poisoning his father herself. That had worked out well for her. He would have to do the same and hope for the same outcome. He needed an army now that some of the people knew he was alive, and the Dragon's army would do. After all, even if most didn't believe Galan's story, they would still investigate. They would start hunting for him, just in case. And he couldn't expect to poison them all, pleasing as that would have been. So he had to destroy his enemies before they succeeded in killing him, and that would require an army. Or some steel drakes.

The thought made him laugh a little. His enemies would not know what had struck them until it was too late. And when they did, those few survivors would never be able to link the attacks to him. It was the Dragon after all. And that was what he did.

Then, after his enemies were dead he would unite the survivors under his banner. The Dragon would conveniently go away once the noble houses had been left in disarray. The troll blood would be easy enough to control. Heri would make up some story about having beaten back the Dragon. And maybe a story about why the Dragon might return if he wasn't made king again. The people would not be able to argue against him. And by the time he was finished with them what remained of the noble houses wouldn't even think of trying.

"You should have bowed to me soldiers!" Heri shouted at the dead men, a feeling of triumph overcoming him. "This is what happens when you fail to acknowledge your king!"

Heri would gather his strength. Rebuild his armies. Take back his throne. And once he had rebuilt his castle and his kingdom he would find a wizard and have this hideous compulsion removed from him. Then he would arrange to have Samual slaughtered. And all the rest of the accursed elves with him.

Samual

He might even mount Samual's damned head on a wall!

Chapter Twenty Eight

Sam walked the last few dozen paces to the Council meeting, choosing to leave Tyla behind to graze. The horses tended to wander a little when the elders were meeting, sometimes intruding on what was being discussed as they hunted out the best grass.

He had hurried here. Today he had the feeling that there was something important to be discussed. Mostly because of the way in which the messenger had spoken to him as he'd brought him word that his presence was required. The man had seemed somewhat anxious and been insistent that he hurry.

Sam was happy enough to comply. After another long morning of doing nothing more than reshaping the great trees so that the artisans could start working with them, he was bored. It was work that he could almost do in his sleep. And he still had no great love of heights.

But as he approached the meeting he understood some of the messenger's insistence. This was no normal meeting of the Council. The Fiore Elle was full, and not just with elves.

The Shavarran Ruling Council was there as he'd expected, along with an assortment of other elders, wizards, warriors and sages. But they were far from alone. Mixed in among them were dwarves. By the looks of things a scout party had arrived, and were decked out in their solid steel plate and sporting battle axes as large as any he'd ever seen.

Standing proud among the elves, none of them over five feet in height but all well over two hundred pounds in pure muscle and bone, they looked distinctly out of place. But for all that Sam knew that they were supremely confident in their physical prowess, to the point where every one of them would have believed himself the equal of at least a dozen elves in a fight. And they did love to fight. They would never have considered themselves as being out of place even in an elven land. Rather, for them it was the elves who were far from home.

The dwarves weren't alone. Also among them were a group of humans, all dressed in rough sewn outfits of leather and fur with riding boots and leather gloves. Judging by their outfits he thought they had to be hillmen, and if the dwarves were many leagues from their home the hillmen had come from even further afield. Hillmen were often called rangers or mountain men, and their truest home was always on horseback, riding the alpine lands furthest from civilization. It was a very long way from this new Shavarra.

For them to be here, in the lowlands as they called them – and moreover in the midst of a forest instead of wide open mountain steeps – meant that something had to be wrong. Very wrong. They weren't traders, and they weren't great explorers of other lands. Moreover, they had hurried here. He could see that when he saw they hadn't packed for the trip. Instead of dressing for warmer climes, they still wore their shaggy pelts proudly, despite the fact that they had to be melting in the warm sun. The worst of winter was passed, and though it wasn't yet spring, it was still far warmer than the alpine lands. Their horses also looked to be carrying few provisions in their empty saddle bags, and the animals themselves had obviously been run hard for many days. Despite their natural fitness, they were tired.

All of that together could only mean one thing: The enemy had struck again. That understanding came with a whole new set of questions, since the hillmen didn't live anywhere close to the sea. Their lands, wherever they were, were always a long way inland. So if he had struck them, he had changed his pattern. But how? Where could he have landed his ships? Or had he marched his army over league after league of inhospitable terrain just to reach them? And why?

Walking quietly Sam joined the group, wondering if his presence was required simply for protocol or if something more was required of him. Naturally no one was going to tell him if it was, and by the look on his face Elder Bela standing to one side didn't look like he knew what was going on either.

"Good. All are here now for the telling." War Master Indolan acknowledged Sam's arrival.

Sam gained the distinct impression from the War Master's tone that not only had he and the rest of the elders waited for him, but that he was late, though how he could have come any quicker was beyond him. He nodded politely but said nothing, knowing there was nothing he could say that wouldn't sound like some sort of excuse.

"This is Lochar Stonewright of the Bronze Mountain Clan to the south east of us, and Halibur Swift of the Straight Arrow Pride, their neighbours these past many years. They have a tale to tell."

Lochar launched into his tale a moment later, automatically assuming the position of the leader as was his people's nature. For their part the hillmen stood around, watching, listening and waiting patiently, apparently completely unconcerned by having a dwarf speak for them. But then they were nomads by nature, all their worldly possessions and their homes carried on horseback, and fixed to no particular place or allegiance. As such they were always remarkably calm about all things that couldn't be changed according to the tales, choosing to leave rather than argue when things became difficult. There was always another mountain range to settle. But apparently they couldn't do that any longer. In fact if Lochar was correct, the hillmen were just as trapped as those who had built great cities or fortresses, bound not by their own walls, but by the enemy's armies.

It seemed the enemy had changed his approach with the hillmen, very likely after having had his conversation with Sam. Gone were the sailing ships. Instead he had found great ships of the air to carry his armies. Balloons. Great black bags of gas that held aloft baskets in which the rats could be carried. And instead of worrying about the vagaries of the wind, he had the balloons tethered to one another and towed a dozen at a time by a steel drake. It was a frightening development. And it was new. He hadn't read that in the histories of the Dragon Wars.

This new Dragon was learning. And he would be even more dangerous because of it. If each drake could tow a dozen balloons and each balloon could hold four or five rats, then each landing left fifty or more of the steel vermin on the ground ready to attack, with a drake in the air to rain down fire from above. In that way his armies grew fast.

No more were the steel rats his only soldiers either. At least as far as the open ranges went. Instead, he now had an army of spiders that spat balls of fire the size of a man's head further than an archer's arrow could fly. Worse than that, when the fire balls landed they exploded, spreading fire and fragments of steel everywhere, and taking out as many as a dozen people at once. In short he now had mobile artillery. The same mobile artillery he understood had been used to such devastating effect against Ragnor's Rock.

Infantry supported by air power and artillery. The Dragon had obviously started to improve his tactics.

Against them the hillmen had had their traditional advantage of speed as they stayed in the saddle. They had always thought themselves safe thanks to that. But for once it hadn't been enough. The enemy's drakes were even faster, and could strike silently from above without warning. They would cast great swaths of fire down upon the hillmen's unsuspecting heads, leaving more than a few charred corpses still in their saddles. It was a vicious tactic, but an effective one. The drakes kept the various clans bottled up tight in the forests where their horses' speed was limited, while the rats, the enemy's foot soldiers, made the forests their own, turning them into a series of traps rather than a refuge.

Attacked from the air mercilessly and finding no safety in the forests, the hillmen had been forced to retreat, and for the first time ever, to find shelter from the open skies. It was something they had never done before. Something they had never even considered. Consequently they hadn't been entirely sure what they should do. They had no skills to build great castles, and there were no such structures among their lands. Nor could they flee great distances to those lands where such structures existed. The drakes would have caught them the moment they left the shelter of the forests. So they had found themselves a place among the dwarves of the Bronze Mountain Clan.

And then the enemy had found them there too.

In the tunnels and corridors of their great underground city the enemy's rats had made a reappearance. There they had truly found themselves at home. They loved the dark, and they could squeeze themselves down into the tightest of places, cunningly letting the dwarves pass them by only to attack from the rear. And as before they had numbers on their side. It seemed that however many of them the dwarves killed, they were replaced by dozens more.

But in turn the dwarves had their battle hardened steel weapons and armour, and the archery of the hillmen to call upon. The fight had soon become a pitched battle for the city which nobody could win. Yet. Instead both sides had formed siege lines and established fortifications, and currently they were waging a battle of attrition.

The real danger for them however, wasn't the rats that were already there. The dwarves might even win against them. It was that they were trapped within their underground city. The steel drakes and fire spiders were unable to break through into the city itself, but they stopped the dwarves leaving as they set up a perimeter around it. A barrier that prevented the dwarves both being resupplied and escaping to safety, while the enemy kept growing in strength up top.

As a soldier Sam could see the strategy of the enemy, and even be impressed as he turned his opponent's strengths into weaknesses. It was a well thought out campaign he'd launched and it appeared he'd started studying tactics. But as a man, he found it disgusting. What had happened at Shavarra was terrible, but this was worse. Far worse. It showed the enemy's purpose. It was clear that he wanted no survivors. Then again perhaps he hadn't wanted any at Shavarra either, they'd just fought back a little better than he'd expected. He had trapped the dwarves in their own cities, knowing that they couldn't escape since his drakes would have torn them apart in the open, and then settled back to win a battle of attrition. In short the battle had become a siege, and a siege that the enemy would win.

In time the dwarves and the hillmen would be forced out, slowly but surely as hunger and desperation forced them either to assault the rats, or flee. In both instances the dwarves would come off second best. They weren't suited for a fight out in the open, and the rats had turned their own defences against them.

It was only the construction of hidden entrances to the city that had allowed these dwarves to escape and the speed of the hillmen that had got them through the wilds to the new elven homeland. And all the while as they had desperately made their way to the new home of a people they'd heard had fought a battle against the enemy and perhaps even drawn it, the battle behind them continued towards its inexorable end. Food and supplies were running lower by the day, while ever more rats arrived to replace the fallen.

But the question was what to do about it. Or more accurately what did they want Sam to do about it?

Clearly his fame, or at least the legend of his battle with the rats had made it as far as the dwarves, and they hoped that once more he and the elves could turn the tide. But at the same time, how much could they actually know about the battle he'd fought? Did they understand that it was magic that he'd used? Something the dwarven people weren't especially fond of, except for their own enchantments of course. Did they understand that his most powerful weapon, the fire ring, couldn't be used in an underground city – it would kill everyone out in the open, the dwarves and rats alike. It would also likely smother the dwarves and any buildings that fell as a result, would make barricades for both sides. A siege would become trench warfare. And that was the best result assuming he got into position in time. Long before they got there Sam and any others he travelled with would have to contend with an army of spiders and drakes.

Despite all the problems though, Sam wanted to help. How could he not? He was a man as well as a knight, and he could not sit back and let others die, especially women and children, while he stood back and did nothing. He suspected he wasn't alone either. All around him he could see the soldiers and guards bristling with anger, while the war masters were obviously well into planning their own campaign.

But could they dream one up sufficient to wipe out such a scourge? And was it even a choice?

Chapter Twenty Nine

Riding through the forests in the rain and fog was far from a pleasant experience, though Tyla didn't seem to mind. Sam though was tired of the wet and the cold, even though he knew the weather protected him. But he would truly have welcomed some sunshine. The last of winter was still with them and the cold and wet was the last thing he wanted as he rode into battle. In fact after a week of this, he would have given away everything he owned just to enjoy a couple of hours of blue skies and sunshine.

But it wasn't to be and he knew that it was for the best. They were riding into battle, and he knew they had to be close to their destination. They had ridden hard to get here and in a week and a half of riding an army could travel a lot of leagues.

The Bronze Mountains he thought couldn't be many more leagues ahead. Of course when they got there the battle would begin. Maybe a little rain and fog wasn't such a terrible thing after all.

"Spider." The soft call came from just in front of Sam, startling him, and it was a few heartbeats before he realised the intent. It was a warning and he cursed the elves for their soft voices. Often their warnings were no more than murmurs in the background, and if he wasn't paying attention he could miss them altogether over the noise of the rain and hoof beats.

Still he did his part, pulling on the reins to stop Tyla in her tracks, while Forellin, the youngest master of earth magic, drew alongside him with his great bow in hand. And what a bow it was – nearly as tall as a man standing and bursting with magic. It took all of the forty something year old elf's strength to pull back the cord and release the arrow, and yet despite that and the fog, he was deadly accurate. More importantly, he was a powerful mage and the arrow that he fired would completely destroy a spider, or even a drake should it happen to be on the ground.

Its stone tip was magically hardened until it was stronger than the best steel – far stronger. It would pierce even the steel sides of the massive spiders. But the real genius lay in the metal shaft just behind the head, which would explode on impact, tearing the steel beast apart. Before they'd left, Sam had enchanted over two hundred of the arrows under Master Forellin's watchful eye, each at least four feet long, and Aegis who proudly carried the master and the arrows looked as though a giant porcupine had attacked her. Still, she could bear the weight of the elf and his oversized quivers with ease where other horses would have struggled.

It was an odd thing he thought, but the strength of the force they'd brought to the rescue to the hillmen and the dwarves was far stronger for being diverse than he would have expected. Forellin and the arrows were merely the beginning of that strength.

Further back in the party, nearly a third of a league behind them, the weather mages were creating the constant mist and fog that hid the party's approach from the steel vermin, and coincidentally grounded the drakes. That was an unexpected blessing. Until now, no one had realised the beasts couldn't fly in the rain, and Forellin's arrows had already turned nearly two dozen of them into piles of smouldering steel rubbish along with at least fifty of the spiders as they sat there like wounded rabbits.

There was no doubt the enemy had noticed their approach, but given that all his machina they had encountered had been destroyed, he could have no real idea who they were or exactly where they were coming from. His rats which he'd sent out in droves to search and destroy, were also disappearing by the hundreds as the elves' long bows were taking a deadly toll on them. On the rats they were using slightly different arrows. These ones just had hardened heads. But that was enough. They might not destroy a spider or a drake, but the smaller rats were no match for them.

Meanwhile the hillmen, armed with their own short bows, were riding horses which had all been gifted with extra stamina and speed by the nature mages. They too were cutting a mean swathe through the outer patrols of the machina as they attacked and ran, pulling the enemy forces in every direction as they tried to give chase and failed. The rats and spiders were too slow to catch them, the drakes and balloons were grounded, and the hillmen's arrows destroyed them as they too were hardened. The end result was that the enemy forces were in chaos, as their master gave into his every vicious impulse and chased every attacking party without realising it was a fool's move. One thing was certain; he was no military man. He was like an angry giant swatting at flies, never realising he was just wasting his own strength.

Their real weapon though was being readied by the dwarves even now as they approached to within range of the army. During the week and a half that they had ridden here, the dwarves had been building, their own war machines. Giant trebuchets which were mounted on some of the spare wagons the elves had had left over, and which were being pulled by the incredibly strong war horses of Fair Fields. Each night when they stopped the dwarves went to work, and each morning the giant war machines were taller and heavier.

Sam would have preferred it if they could have brought cannon with them, but the dwarves had none with them and the elves would never have tolerated such weapons at all. They didn't have a foundry either. The only cannon there were, were all in the city itself. So they were having to fall back on weapons they could make without a foundry. Still, the war machines were powerful weapons and the dwarves were impossibly quick builders. It helped that their numbers were being boosted as they took a path through some of the dwarven outposts, but even so the progress was amazing.

And the war masters had come up with a plan of attack that was inspired. One that used all their different strengths. The plan was that while the hillmen used their speed to keep the steel army busy and the elves wiped out their scouts and hunting parties, the dwarves would be setting up the score of war machines on the ridges surrounding the enemy encampment. With an expected range of six to eight hundred yards thanks to yet more magic and the surprisingly small size of the stones they would fire, they would rain down death upon the steel army, while Sam and the other elves would become the final assault force, should they be needed.

Somehow, he didn't think they would. The steel army encampment when the dwarves and hillmen had escaped had been around ten thousand strong, all of them simply sitting there, waiting their turn to enter the tunnels and attack the underground city. Hopefully that wouldn't have changed. And they had five thousand elves armed with longbows if it did. Before that happened though the enchanted stones the dwarves would fire into their massed troops would take a devastating toll on the machina. They were some of his best work, and he had spent each evening simply imbuing the stones with the chained fire spells the elders had encouraged him to study. It was simply incredible how much fire he'd been able to enchant into each rock. The earth mages had found and quarried only the best rocks for ammunition, and each of the fifty pound rocks held at least ten times as much magic as each sword or axe he carried. Sam was looking forward to seeing them on the battlefield.

Of course, the real battle would come later. Because there would be two battles, not one. Once they had destroyed the machina on the surface, they would have to go below and attack the rats underground, something that Sam was less confident of. On the surface, the enemy was a sitting duck, even if the Dragon didn't realise it. Underground, the steel rats would have an advantage. Several advantages. Darkness to hide in. Narrow twisting passageways which would limit the effectiveness of long bows. And perhaps numbers too.

A bird whistle stopped his thoughts in their tracks, as he realised it was time to put another steel monster into the ground. For a moment he stopped even breathing as he waited. Then he realised the sound was an owl's hoot. That meant it was time to put two of the beasts away.

It was hard for him to just sit there and let another take the battle to the enemy when every stretched nerve in his body was telling him to rush forward and attack, though as a soldier he knew it was the right thing to do. It was made that much harder because he could see nothing ahead. The forest was heavy and the fog thick. In fact in places it was so thick that he wondered how Forellin could even see his target fifty paces ahead. Especially in the fog. And yet he did. Perfectly.

As had happened dozens of times already, he heard the sudden twanging of a bow, followed a heartbeat later by a gigantic explosion which shook the trees all around them and sent a wave of glorious yellow and orange fire soaring high into the grey skies above them, almost like a sunset. Two more heartbeats passed and then a second explosion rocked the forest around them, and the already golden skies brightened once more. Two more spiders or drakes down.

After that it was simply a matter of waiting, and Sam like the rest of the elves sat there, nervously twiddling his thumbs and listening for the all clear. It would be a while he knew. Two large steel beasts had been destroyed, but that didn't mean that there might not be more around. Also, it was possible that others might be drawn closer by the noise of the explosions. And then of course there were the rats. They were sneaky little things and loved to pounce on the unwary. But the elves were wary. More importantly, they were prepared.

The rats would quickly hone in on the noise of their larger brethren being destroyed, but they would be met with hardened arrows as well. Probably another two or three dozen rats would end up as lumps of scrap metal in the next half hour or so, and then the party would move on while the rats' master hopefully had another fit of uncontrolled rage.

Best of all though, the Dragon would never realise that as he hunted them, the dwarves were moving their war machines into range, preparing for a massive counter attack. And when they struck Sam hoped the new Dragon would learn a lesson in humility. Thus far he'd won through thanks to his numbers and attacking those not ready for him. This would be the campaign where his forces were finally crushed. Where he learned that he wasn't as powerful as he thought.

With a little luck maybe he would die of a heart attack as he understood how badly he'd been outplayed. Maybe he'd even choke to death on his own bile.

Now that was a thought to enjoy Sam thought as he waited for the all clear to sound.

Chapter Thirty

Dawn was approaching when everyone was finally in position and ready for the attack. The black sky was just beginning to turn blue. Soon Sam knew it would be glowing orange with fire as the machina burnt.

And there were a lot of machina to burn. That was the thing that Sam couldn't quite believe. But in front of him, or in the valley just below, there were so many rats and spiders and other steel machina that they filled the valley floor. Sam couldn't understand it. The ships had stopped sailing. And the balloons as large as they were, could only carry a few machina at a time. But as he had been told, there were at least ten thousand machina sitting on the grass. Possibly a great many more than that now. They were all just sitting there, calmly waiting to enter the caverns of the Bronze Mountain Clan as soon as their steel comrades were destroyed and needed to be replaced.

The dwarves and hillmen had told them of the numbers to expect, and the soldier part of him had heard the words and planned for them. But he'd still never seen an army of that size before. Battles in Fair Fields were mostly skirmishes. Small forces attacking one another, maybe raiding a village of a neighbouring lord. This was different.

It was a sea of steel and glowing red eyes. With this many above ground Sam wondered how many they would find below.

How were there so many? And why? It was the second question even more than the first that troubled him. Because it suggested to the soldier in him that this wasn't just a simple attack. An extermination. Instead it could become a base. Once he had claimed it, the Dragon could use it as a place where he could build up his forces in safety, and then periodically send them out army by army to conquer the surrounding lands. He no longer had ships and ports, but he might perhaps have a beach head regardless.

Sam had to keep reminding himself that this was a new Dragon and not the old one. He would not use the same tactics and strategy as those in their history books. And though he had a temper problem, he was still learning how to wage a war with the forces he had. Sam had to stop underestimating him.

Whatever the Dragon's plans for the Bronze Mountains were one thing seemed clear: He truly wanted the dwarven home. Because it looked like he was committing everything he had to the battle. Which perversely meant that if he lost here, his plans would be hurt. That was something Sam could hope for. And despite the enemy's numbers Sam thought they still had the advantage.

Still, he was nervous. He was always nervous before riding into a battle. But this was a battle far larger than any he'd ever been a part of before and a lot of lives were at risk. Normally as a knight he'd faced just a few enemies at a time, maybe a party of brigands. And then he'd have his brothers with him. Men who he'd stood beside and fought with a hundred times before. Losses and injuries had been few. Victories had been normal as they were better armed, trained and prepared than their foes. As an exile he'd faced one or two would be assassins on his own. But even then he'd been stronger and it had only been his own life at risk.

He kept thinking that this would be the perfect chance to use his fire ring. Simply draw his fire, everything he could, ride out alone into the heart of the enemy, and unleash it. But he couldn't. Even if the shadelings would have forgiven him and the rest could have got far enough away, there was an obvious problem. He would be seen. The machina were unaffected by spells of invisibility and illusion. Once again the magic of the Fire Angel was being shown to be useless. He was beginning to wonder what the point of having such power even was.

So here they had to use strategy and tactics. They had to fight according to a plan. And they had to hope it was enough. But this was different to anything any of them had ever been involved in. No war master in a thousand years had fought a battle like this. Not one of this scale. This was a major campaign. There were many thousands of rats and other machina pitted against thousands of soldiers. It could all go horribly wrong and in a hundred different ways. And if it did there was little he could do about it. He only hoped that they were prepared for whatever happened.

Just then a horn sounded in the still air and it was too late to worry. A heartbeat later a score of war machines sprang into life and he watched as the first group of the enchanted missiles sailed up high into the air before beginning their glorious descent into the army of machina.

He watched them hit and then heard the explosions as his enchantments of chained fire ripped out through the machina. It was glorious. The entire valley seemed to come alive with fire. Orange flames leapt like birds given flight into the air, and a whole valley of steel and red eyes rippled like waves in an ocean squall.

It was a devastating strike, and the machina would have felt it – if they felt anything – and Sam started screaming with triumph just like everyone else did. He was almost willing to imagine that the battle was over. But of course it wasn't. Their score of war machines had destroyed maybe two or three hundred of the steel beasts. But there were thousands of them. And worst of all the trebuchet took time to reload.

He could see the dwarves working furiously as they

wound the levers and wheels back, pulling the giant swinging arms back down. And as the flames cleared below he could see the machina still sitting there in their somewhat disorganised rows, waiting for instructions. Sam knew that this was the moment they had worried about. The moment when the machina struck back. Because by now the Dragon knew his army had been attacked. He would be looking for the attackers.

Before that could happen though a squall hit as the wind and mist arrived from out of nowhere to cover the entire battlefield. The weather mages were making sure the machina were blind. They'd needed to be able to see to find the range and position of the machina for their war machines, but from here on out, everyone had to be blind. That way as their master stared through the eyes of his creations he would see nothing but fog, and he wouldn't know what was happening as his army was destroyed. He would know it was an attack, but he wouldn't know from which direction it was coming. He wouldn't know which way to send his army.

Of course they were blind too.

It seemed to work. And as time passed painfully slowly, Sam saw no sign of any of the machina emerging from the fog as they charged towards them. Finally though, he heard the twangs as more of the rocks took to the sky and flew down into their enemy's midst in the valley below. He heard the explosions as they hit. And he saw the flashes of orange fire below as the entire valley seemed to glow with fire. It would have actually been quite beautiful if he hadn't have known the danger.

It was then that he finally heard the machina, or more accurately their master, yelling in fury. The sound that wasn't a sound, just an understanding inside his head, spoke of his rage and confusion. It was clear that he didn't know what was happening. Still, he was demanding that the steel beasts go out and destroy their enemies. He just had no idea where to send them and the machina had to have a target or a direction. They couldn't charge their enemies if they didn't know which direction to charge. Which left them still sitting there with nowhere to go while their master screamed and yelled at them like a petulant child.

For what seemed like ages, things continued like that. The war machines continued to send their deadly missiles down into the valley below, and the machina exploded in great balls of orange fire that lit up the mist. Until finally the Dragon thought about the problem and gave the only order he could. He told them to charge – in all directions.

That was Sam's cue – he was the only one who could hear the Dragon speaking with his steel beasts and so the only one who would know what he was planning. Sam stood up tall, reached for his horn and blew three quick blasts on it to tell everyone that the enemy was coming.

Immediately thousands of soldiers – elves one and all – took up positions between the war machines and the enemy, and stood ready with longbows in hand. When the machina broke through the fog, they would not last long. Not against the arrows with their especially hardened heads. Sam joined them, crossbow in hand. One day he'd master the longbow, but not this day.

Then the first of the machina emerged from the fog fifty or a hundred paces in front of him, and instantly exploded as an arrow caught it.

After that the battle was joined. The machina emerged in numbers from the fog, and the archers took them down almost as quickly as they showed themselves. Meanwhile the war machines continued their assault, though Sam had no idea what if anything they hit. The spiders started spitting their own fire back at them. It wasn't aimed – they were firing from inside the fog at enemies they couldn't see – but it was still too accurate.

Men screamed in fear and pain. He saw some in the distance fall and burn and he even saw one of the war machines catch fire. A towering pyre that seemed to set the fog ablaze. But he had no way of knowing how many of their own were dying that day, nor how many machina were being destroyed. These were his brothers in arms, living, fighting and dying, and he could do nothing to help them save what he already was. He felt so helpless. But the soldiers nearer to him kept firing and the machina kept exploding, none of them reaching their lines, and he did the same. That had to be enough for him.

For what felt like an age that continued to be the shape of the battle, and Sam almost dared to believe that they were winning. Surely thousands of the steel beasts had been destroyed. How many more could there be? But then the Dragon struck back with a new tactic and Sam knew things had just taken a turn for the worse.

The first he knew of it was when he saw the silver and black silk of a balloon rising above the endless mist, a ball of glowing light lit by the fire that heated the air in it, and for a moment it meant nothing to him. Until he realised that the Dragon was trying to see where they were. The moment he did that he could send all his machina straight at them as one organised army.

Sam hurled a fire ball at it, the only magic he had that could span the distance between them, and it hit turning the glowing orb into a fireball. But even as the silver balloon started falling in flames, he didn't know if he'd been quick enough. And he knew that even if he had been, the Dragon would try again. He had to stand ready for when that happened.

The battle intensified after that, with more and more of the machina emerging from the fog to charge their lines, and more balls of fire blasting at them from out of the fog as well. But though more men fell, the elves were up to the task, and they kept the machina back from their lines.

In time the machina became a line of burning steel bodies, as high as a wall and as deep as a house, and Sam began to worry that the flames would spread through the trees and drive them back even when the machina couldn't. But there was nothing to be done about it. They would just have to face that problem if and when it happened. Until then it would hamper the rest of the machina from reaching them just as it stopped them from destroying them as they once had. The destroyed machina had become a barricade for both sides.

Then the first of the steel drakes appeared in the sky and Sam knew they had more problems. Fortunately the weather mages spotted them quickly and started hitting them with unstable air, causing them to fly erratically. Unfortunately that meant they were no longer controlling the fog and it quickly began dissipating. Soon it was thin enough that he could see through it and past the piles of flaming steel beasts to the rest of the army of machina, and he knew things weren't good.

There had to be at least a few thousand steel beasts remaining. Worse still, the beasts could see them. They were coming from all directions. Running for them.

Sam started launching fireballs at them, destroying as many as he could, but they were so spread out that he couldn't get as many as he wanted. Someone else laid down a storm of lightning with similar results. And the archers continued to take a heavy toll on any of them that came within range. But the spiders were more dangerous once they knew where to aim, and Sam heard many more of his brothers in arms crying out as they were hit. To add to their woes more war machines were being taken out. Whatever remained of the enemy in the valley below – and it was hard to be certain across the distance and through the remaining mist and black smoke – would soon be safe from their attack.

Then as he'd known it always did, the battle started to close in. Sam was less able to pay any attention to the wider battle as he had to focus on the rats charging towards him and those nearer to him. They were getting closer, bursting through the barricade of their burning steel comrades, and charging their lines, while the spiders' fireballs kept hitting the ground all around them.

He struck back of course, sending out blast after blast of chained fire at them, and destroying hundreds. But his magic was hampered by the way the rats were spread out. If they'd been coming at them in organised lines his magic would have been so much more effective. But this was never that sort of battle. It had become a close quarters ranged battle, and soon he feared, it would become hand to steel claw.

Still, they had numbers. They had archers with proper weapons. And as the front lines of the rats came closer and closer, he thought they had to have a good chance.

Then a fire ball landed somewhere in front of him and Sam was sent flying backwards, and he had to wonder about their chances even as he hit the ground. But as he got up, mostly just scratched and bruised, his armour having saved him from the worst of it, he knew he didn't have time to worry. He just had to fight.

So that was what he did, sending blast after blast of chained fire into the enemy, while the others took a devastating toll on them with their longbows, and all of them waited for the moment when they'd have to draw their swords.

That moment seemed to be coming closer and closer, as ever more glowing red eyes appeared in front of them. And it seemed very close when more fireballs started crashing down around them. Sam was knocked over a second time. Others were too.

But he got up again and returned to the fight, and most of the others did too. And little by little, the tide started to turn. The numbers of machina charging their lines started to thin, and those who got close didn't get as close as before. The fireballs grew fewer. And in time what had been an army became a collection of individual steel soldiers. The steel drakes – those that were still flying – buffeted by ever stronger winds fell out of the sky and exploded when they crashed into the ground. And a storm of falling rocks from one of the war machines took the last of the steel spiders out. The rest of the steel beasts, mostly rats, were taken out by the archers as they came within range. Many simply blew up as they tried to clamber over the wall of burning steel beasts, unable to deal with the fire.

At some point what remained were so few in number that everyone began to realise it was over. And that was when the cheering started. It started slowly at first, hesitantly, but it was a sound that slowly grew until finally it began to echo across the entire valley.

Sam cheered too. Even as he went to the others to start helping with the wounded – and there were many who were down near him – he cheered. He didn't mean to. He didn't think about it. The sound almost seemed to come out of his mouth by itself. And he didn't regret it.

Many were dead. Many more were injured. And there was another perhaps even tougher battle yet to come as they had to make their way into the city itself. But still, it was a victory and they had survived. An entire army of steel beasts had been destroyed. And it was simply human nature to want to celebrate that. Especially after so many of them had already suffered terrible losses in Shavarra.

But finally it seemed the elves' Goddess and the All Father seemed to be blessing them. Maybe even Alder had favoured them. What greater mischief could there be than war after all?

So they cheered and they screamed and they yelled their victory to the blue sky high above. And for a while they managed to put the pain of what they'd lost behind them. The fear of what lay ahead was briefly put aside. For a while.

Chapter Thirty One

The mood in the camp was buoyant after the battle. Even Sam was letting a little of that cheer flow through him. Drinking a little cider. Singing songs he didn't know the words to along with the others – though only quietly and while always trying to maintain a little dignity. He was a knight of Hanor after all.

After the battle had been won, they'd claimed the field of battle and set up camp in the valley that the machina had once held. Riding on to that valley floor among the mounds of steel wreckage that had once been their enemies, had been a moving event for all of them. It brought home the realisation that despite their losses they had won through.

When the field had been claimed, they'd started tending to the hundreds of wounded, and burying the dead. Readying themselves for the following day. Eating, resting, and preparing the weapons and tactics they would need for the next phase of the battle. Fighting underground in tunnels was going to be very different to fighting above. They couldn't use the war machines for a start. And the weather mages would be useless. But they also wouldn't be facing steel drakes, and even the steel spiders would be limited in what they could do thanks to the low ceiling heights. To launch their fire any distance they had to fire it up at an angle.

Luckily the caverns were well ventilated and there wasn't much underground which could burn. Otherwise his magic would have been completely useless and the enemy would have had an entirely new weapon to use. He could have suffocated them simply by setting fire to everything in sight. The dwarves though had long ago realised the dangers of fire underground and designed accordingly.

The plan was to use shields. Massive wheeled ones that the dwarves were assembling while the rest of them relaxed. These would allow them to enter the tunnels safely while the archers could shelter behind them and rain down death on the enemy.

Mages would be vital, and they would also stand behind the shields where they would send their magic into the enemy, destroying them before they could reach their lines. The rest of the army would be pushing the massive steel shields yard by yard further into the tunnels, ploughing their way through the bodies of their fallen foes as they advanced. It was a simple plan, but Sam had faith in it. After all, that was how the dwarves fought in their own cities and they should know what worked.

Mostly though, they hadn't been thinking about the battle ahead. They'd been celebrating. Eating, drinking and singing. There had been a lot of singing. There had been a lot of ale and cider drunk too.

As the day had progressed they'd all discovered a sense of triumph, Sam included. Never had an army so large and so powerful been destroyed so easily and quickly. Not in living history, not in the books, not even during the fabled Dragon Wars. And this was the same enemy that had destroyed their home and driven them from Shavarra. Victory over them had been so very sweet. But it was more than that that drove them to celebrate. It was the thought of the coming battle. Elves had no love of enclosed spaces and darkness underground. They liked wide open spaces and sky. So when faced with the prospect of an underground battle ahead of them, they chose instead to celebrate. It was better than fearing the day to come.

Still, Sam kept telling himself the odds had to be in their favour. The enemy had to be hurting badly, and his last few thousand or so rats wouldn't last long against the magically enhanced bows of the elves and the hillmen, while their lines would break on the shields. They had the numbers and the plan.

Sam should have remembered however, that pride was ever a mistake. He rediscovered that that afternoon. The first he knew though was when men started shouting in alarm. Sam looked to the men and then to where they were pointing and his blood ran cold as he saw the enemy.

Huge steel beasts were unearthing themselves from the ground in the distance all around them and he understood then that they were in the teeth of a trap. They'd claimed the field of battle, never realising that in doing so they'd wandered right over the enemy' defensive lines. Suddenly they were surrounded. Surrounded and in trouble.

Horns blew frantically as men began reaching for their weapons. Arrows started to fly at the nearest of the machina. But these creatures were big. Very big. Even the arrows with their hardened heads bounced off their thick steel hides.

It seemed that the enemy had discovered a whole new form of shock troop. It was some sort of burrowing termite the size of a mammoth, and they were rapidly rising out of the valley floor all around them, pushing aside mountains of dirt and the remains of their steel comrades as they formed a new, more powerful army. Worse still, these termites could spit fire like the spiders, and Sam watched them fly high into the air before beginning their deadly descent. More than a few men fall to them. Fortunately, high above them the dwarves were still with their war machines. And they had seen the same. Quickly they began arming the remaining trebuchets and the sounds of them firing were soon heard once more.

The second army quickly began dying as Sam and the rest began a panicked retreat for the mouth of the city, picking their way carefully over the destroyed machina in their way. It was the safest place even though they had their backs to the enemy inside the underground city. They needed as much distance between them and the enemy as possible for the dwarves above to be sure of hitting the enemy and not them. And they also needed to come together as an army once more. To form lines and start acting in concert – as an army instead of a rabble.

But even as he ran, as vulnerable to the fire falling on their heads as everyone else, Sam kept thinking that they'd underestimated their enemy – again!

Despite the shock of the ambush, only a few hundred of their troops were killed by the termites in the initial volley, mainly because they were quick on their feet. But that was still hundreds more than should have been killed, and as he listened to the sound of more men screaming and dying he knew it could quickly become so much worse. The enemy had foolishly struck too soon, not waiting for them to move fully into his trap. But that was his only mistake. If he'd been smarter he would have waited until nightfall when they would have been sleeping. And luckily the range the termites could spit fire was limited. By retreating to the centre of the battle field they were increasing the distance the termites had to fire. Those mistakes Sam promised himself when he finally reached what he hoped was safety and began launching fireballs at the steel termites, would be his downfall.

The main problem the dwarves faced was that they'd squandered most of their ammunition already. Each catapult had had only forty or fifty rocks to fire, and most of those were already gone. Also, they had only a dozen of the war machines left and none had full crews as many of the dwarves were down in the valley with everyone else. The trebuchets were slow to fire. Worse still, these new creatures were as tough as the spiders and drakes themselves, and the explosions of fire that streaked out from each impact weren't as deadly. To destroy a termite each one had to take a direct hit, and war machines weren't known for their accuracy. Even Sam's fire balls weren't completely effective. These things had massive steel hides, and often he had to hit each one two or three times to cause it to explode. If he'd had more time to draw his fire – but that was the point of an ambush. But what protected the enemy most of all was that they were spaced widely apart. When one of the massive steel termites detonated, it died alone. Where the rats had exploded in their hundreds each time, these died only in their ones and twos. That left many hundreds still to destroy when the catapults began to fall silent.

The Dragon was also much more wary with the termites than he had been with their rat cousins. Once it had become clear to their master that they were being attacked once more from the air, while still having no clue where the enemy was, he had them start burrowing once more, seeking the safety of the protective earth above. The catapults were soon falling silent not only because of reduced ammunition, but also because as their prey disappeared from sight.

But that was a tactic that also worked in the elves' favour. The enemy had no idea they were low on stones, and so while the termites kept burrowing after each new assault, their master presumably thinking he was protecting his army, he was really failing them as it actually gave them time to start preparing a new attack. He should have pressed his attack. He would pay for that mistake Sam promised himself as he drew more fire and prepared for the next round.

Sam's worry though was that while the termites didn't move above the ground – obviously they were too large for that – he did wonder if they could burrow under it and sooner or later appear beneath their feet.

The silence after the termites had reburied themselves stretched and stretched, and so did the tension as they all waited for the next attack. But it gave Sam the chance he needed to finally start drawing some fire.

Finally, after what seemed like hours, the first of the termites began emerging once more from the earth. This time though they didn't emerge fully but stopped half way. That wasn't like before.

For a long time Sam didn't understand quite what was happening, as he watched the termites rise halfway out of the ground, and then stop. Was it some new and even stranger enemy ploy? Had the creatures simply broken down? But then he saw the earth wizards with their arms extended as they shaped their powerful magics and he felt the magic flowing from them and understood. The mages had trapped the creatures in the ground, turning the soft earth into solid rock around them, preventing them moving and leaving them as perfect sitting targets. But for what? He had the feeling as he launched fireball after fireball at them, that it wasn't for him. Nor for the war machines.

Someone had a plan.

Even as he and the others stood there wondering, Sam felt the first delicate touch of a breeze and was surprised. Until then it had been a perfectly still day, which was strange considering that the sky above was filled with thunder clouds and rain. But then that was magic. The remnants of the squall they'd created earlier on to blind the enemy. Then again he slowly realised as he saw the first dust motes rising out of the ground in front of them, so was this. Weather magic. True to their nature the weather mages were whipping up a storm. In this case though, it was several storms and they were like nothing he had seen before.

Four miniature hurricanes, each only a hundred feet high or so, could be seen coalescing in the distance, their nature revealed by the dust and dirt they were rapidly funnelling upwards. Each of them was darkening as it strengthened and more and more dirt was added to the funnel. Still, the hurricanes didn't seem to grow as they should. Instead of becoming funnels reaching high into the clouds, they remained tiny twisters, mere shadows of what they should be, but for all that terribly powerful. In fact they just seemed to become more solid and angry as they spun faster and faster.

In a surprisingly short time, the sound of the whistling of the winds could be heard across the entire valley. The sound of the wind funnels wasn't the deep continuous thunder he would have expected from a full sized hurricane or typhoon, but then these weren't normal. Instead, being so much more compact and spinning so much faster than a normal hurricane, they sounded like the shrieking of angry hawks; lots of them. And the sound only kept growing until it hurt their ears, as far away as they were. Yet still there was nothing more than a gentle breeze playing across his skin.

Some sort of signal must have been given soon after, just as everyone was holding their hands firmly over their ears because of the noise, and all four hurricanes abruptly took off as though they were wild animals suddenly released. But if they were, then at the same time they were also perfectly controlled. This was no panicked stampede. He knew that because he watched the four tiny twisters suddenly form a giant circle and then start spinning around one another like children dancing around a maypole. But these were no children and this was no dance he'd ever seen before.

The circling twisters headed directly for the trapped steel termites, bearing down on them like hunters. And when they hit he knew, there would be war. The only question on Sam's mind though was whether they would be capable of destroying the beasts. It was the question on everyone's mind. Wind against steel. It didn't seem like a fair match, though the shear ferocity of the wind suggested otherwise.

Sam and the others though needn't have worried. The first

hurricane only had to touch the first termite and instantly it was destroyed in a glorious explosion of fire that itself was blown away by the furious wind. For a moment though the twister itself was a column of fire. Sam's spirits lifted at the glorious sight. They lifted some more when the twister moved on to the next termite, leaving only bare earth in its wake. No doubt the steel termite's metal innards had joined the whirling mass of air and soil above it, the better to batter its brethren to death, because that was the secret of the twisters' devastating power. The mass of spinning air was bad, but the rocks and dirt held aloft in those spinning columns were what was really tearing the metal beasts apart.

Like a quartet of drunken dancers the twisters began a dance of death as they started circling the valley, sweeping from one termite to the next. They quickly turned the steel termites and anything else that happened to get in their way into a collection of airborne flotsam, while their very bases became a continuing explosion of orange fire that covered the valley floor, scouring it clean. Meanwhile the music to their deadly dance was provided by the Dragon himself who Sam could hear in his head, screaming in rage.

It didn't take very long for the termites to be destroyed. The dancing hurricanes simply scoured the valley from one end to the other, destroying everything in their path, until very soon, the valley was completely devoid of them. In fact it was devoid of most things. Such was the savagery of the dancing twisters. All that remained was bare dirt, and the occasional broken tree stump or patch of battered grass.

That was the last time Sam quickly decided, that he would ever dare doubt the effectiveness of weather mages in combat. Those twisters had destroyed an army far more effectively than even his own fire ring could, though in fairness he told himself, like his own fire shape they too would have also destroyed a forest had there been one around. Besides, there were four weather mages and only one of him.

Still, he knew as he finally started breathing again, they had been lucky. The Dragon had out thought and out planned them. And they had been over-confident. They should have checked the battlefield before advancing on to it. And they should never have started celebrating before the final battle was one. In the end the thing that had saved them was the Dragon's impatience as he struck too early, and his poor tactics as he tried to protect his soldiers instead of pressing his advantage.

And even so they had paid a bitter price. More were dead and injured. Many more. He watched as the bodies were picked up from where they lay and carried to the priests. As the injured were helped to the healers' tents. So many more of them. And every soldier who fell here would be unable to fight in the morning.

Over the hours that followed, Sam and the rest of the soldiers moved out over the valley floor, looking for survivors of the attack and quickly destroying them. There weren't that many. What few of the termites that had survived the war machines and fire balls mostly hadn't survived the twisters, and the only ones that had were a few termites that had had the sense to remain buried. The earth protected them even against the hurricanes. But not against the slow and methodical destruction he and the other mages brought against them. A master of earth would find them and uncover enough of them to expose a steel nose, and then Sam would drop a white hot fireball right on it. The resultant explosion was like an earthquake as it was contained almost completely by the ground, though black smoke would rise from the grave.

As the others enjoyed themselves, destroying the last of the enemy's army, Sam's thoughts kept returning to one single question: What else was coming?

Already the enemy had surprised them, making up for his

pitiful command of his armies with sheer numbers and a cleverly concealed second army. Only good luck, speed and training, plus the unexpected and clever use of magic had saved them this time. Next time they might not be so lucky. Could he possibly have yet a third army in reserve, or an even tougher type of foot soldier?

Already he'd used a steel beast never mentioned in any of the histories. What else was in his machina army? And how much study had he now done on the tactics and strategy of war? Because it was clear that he was learning. And if he became a master? Then this new Dragon might not only be a terrifying monster; he could actually become more deadly than the first.

The other question that troubled him during those long hours, was the fate of the dwarves and hillmen below. Did they still survive? The sheer size of that first army of steel rats had shocked him when he'd first laid eyes on it. Never before had he seen such a massive force, and despite the reports they'd received of the battle for Ragnor's Rock, he'd somehow not truly imagined the sheer scale of the enemy until just then. He wasn't even sure it had been ten thousand. He suspected it had been far more. And if this was what waited for them above the ground, what would it be like below?

He hoped that the dwarves and hillmen still lived. The enemy must have known of the elves' coming for some days now from the loss of his soldiers, and he had probably kept the bulk of his forces back to destroy them. Especially if he suspected Sam was among those coming. The enemy hated him with a passion born of fear. In any case the last thing he could have afforded was to be attacked from the rear as he assaulted the dwarven caverns. Even a complete idiot would know that much. Therefore he would have left his army underground in defensive positions, holding the dwarves back but no more, while he prepared for another attack above ground. Then once he had won through above ground he would have continued his war below. It was the smart thing to do.

But Sam had to reconcile that hope with the realization that the enemy was no war master. He might not have thought to have to strengthen his above ground forces. He might well have chosen to keep battling the dwarves below ground as hard as he could while thinking his forces above ground would be enough on their own. In which case what lay beneath their feet?

It was a long few hours as they walked the perimeter of the valley, destroying all the termites they could find. A time made longer by his worries. And by the looks on the faces of the others as they continued killing the termites Sam suspected he wasn't alone in his worries.

By late-afternoon the last of the termites had been destroyed as far as anybody could tell. Certainly Sam could feel no trace of them anywhere nearby, and no more could the other mages. Surely the best part of five hundred of the great steel beasts had been destroyed and he couldn't imagine that the Dragon had any more. Of course the entire region was thick with the tang of strong magic and there could be no guarantee of what there could truly be.

Nevertheless, the war masters were confident enough of their safety by then that he and the other mages and commanders were gathered together to plan out the next battle, while the men returned to their camp on the valley floor. Celebrations were put on hold. Ale and cider bottles were capped. And the singing died away as the soldiers took up defensive positions. There would be a large number of sentries kept on watch that evening, and sleep might well be in short supply, but it was a start.

The real question to be answered as far as they were concerned, was what waited for them below? They had planned for the surface forces in the valley, and had been caught off guard by the enemy's cunning and the sheer scale of his forces. They couldn't afford to make the same mistake twice. But how could they know the size of the force that truly awaited them below? Or what other traps he might have left for them? And now they knew he had soldiers that could burrow. They hadn't planned for that.

The original plan had been a simple one. They would simply wander down into the tunnels and destroy the enemy from behind the safety of their shields. Now they had to revise it. They couldn't risk the original established tunnels because there could be steel termites in the walls, just waiting for their forces to go past them and then launch an attack from behind.

The new plan was to use the masters of earth magic to open up new tunnels to the underground city, and then use those tunnels either to allow the people trapped below to escape, or to open up a new front to attack the steel rats. It would be slower and a battle that had been expected to last a day or two might take a week or more. Each new tunnel would be only just wide enough to allow one of the huge wheeled shields passage and perhaps a few of the people trapped below might be able to slip around the side and escape the city. But there would be no mass exodus. The city's original tunnels which were much wider would be blocked. In that way they hoped they could not just control the battle but shape the battlefield to their advantage.

Unfortunately the plan came with its own risks, as each time the mages created a new tunnel down into the city, they would have had no idea as to whether they were reaching the dwarven occupied sector of the city or the parts the steel rats held. They would have no idea either as to whether they should send down a rescue party or an assault force until the tunnel was ready. And by then battle might well be joined.

And now there was a new problem. After the day's battles

they realised that they didn't even know what they would be facing or how large their assault force would have to be, or even if there was anyone left to rescue at all.

It should work. At least, that was what Sam kept telling himself. Against what they had thought was down there it should have been completely effective. But that was before the termites had shown their faces. Now they had to face the very real possibility that all their forces might not be enough. After all, nobody had any real idea of the termites' true capabilities or how many there were. All they knew about the steel termites was that they could tunnel in soft earth, but not solid rock when it encased them. Everything in between was unknown. Worse still, they could already be there, waiting for them in overwhelming numbers.

The most terrible possibility – the one that everyone was thinking about but no one mentioned – was that they could be too late. The dwarves and the hillmen could already be dead. This could all be for nothing.

When the party had escaped the Bronze Mountains, four long weeks before, no sign of the termites had been seen, and only the rats and spiders had gone below ground. The dwarves had been holding them off. The termites had clearly been brought to this land sometime between then and now, specifically to dig down into the city and add their own brand of horror to that of the steel vermin. How long had they had to kill the trapped dwarves, and how much death had they dealt? It wasn't a pleasant thought, and it also meant they might well be risking their lives for nothing, though no one dared speak the words aloud.

The debate on tactics raged among the war masters for hours, as everyone had their own ideas as to how to fight the enemy underground. Slowly the afternoon became the evening and then the evening gave way to night. Time though wasn't a problem. They'd always planned on having the second phase of their assault start the following morning, giving the mages enough time to recharge their magic, and the soldier's time to dress their wounds and recover their strength.

But it also gave the enemy a chance to recover.

As night fell and the smell of tea began wafting over the valley, the meeting broke up with little resolved. They had prepared for what they could and the rest was in the hands of the gods – something that only the priests seemed comfortable with.

Sam, along with most of the others, made his way over to one of the nearer camp sites to groom and feed Tyla before the battle the next morning, and then to get some hot food inside him. He had eaten nothing since breakfast – many hours and two large battles before – and the grumbling of his stomach and the saliva growing in his mouth told him dinner would be very welcome. After that he thought, he would go and spend some time with the healers, heating water and doing what he could to help the wounded. The All Father only knew they had enough of them.

It was then that the enemy struck for the third time, and the only warning he or anyone else had was the lone cry of a sentry, standing guard by the main entrance to the city.

But that scream was enough. Even as he heard the scream, Sam understood it and had to curse himself for his stupidity. Of course the enemy would strike at them instead of waiting for them to take the battle to him! It was his standard gambit. He attacked, and then he attacked some more. And all the while that they had spent foolishly debating the relative approaches to combat underground, he had been quietly moving his third army into position. Waiting for the time that would favour his own soldiers: Night.

The enemy had possibly been slightly too eager, and had

attacked while there was still enough light to see by, but that was his only mistake. And it wasn't enough to save them. Unfortunately the elves had been caught completely flat footed by his attack.

Many were scattered across the entire valley, still looking for termite heads to pop up out of the ground, so that they could kill them as quickly as possible. Everyone else was camped, eating their dinners and maybe even daring to imagine they could get a good night's sleep. Few were anywhere near the entrance to the city, as the battles thus far had not been fought there. And they weren't dressed or armed for battle. Sam like the rest of the wizards had only a little of his magic on hand. The rest he had let slip after the worst of the battles had seemed won, hoping to rest up for the morning. But what he did have he remembered with some thanks, even as he started drawing heat from the surrounds, was a battle axe and a greatsword, both fully powered.

Sam vaulted onto Tyla's back and with a kick to her side, galloped madly toward the cavern entrance where he could see a dozen or more soldiers already being overrun by the steel vermin, which were coming out of the entrance like a river. A silvery steel river of death and glowing red eyes. As quick as he was – and it was only luck that he'd been anywhere close to the entrance himself – Sam was too slow as he saw the elves ahead of him start running for their lives.

They weren't nearly fast enough, and the rats were on them in moments, tearing into their flesh, even while he was still the best part of a hundred yards away. But the battle wasn't one sided, entirely. Two dozen or more rats had been taken out by the elven arrows even as they attacked, and at close range they were effective too. The elven swords had been swapped for heavier blades, and he could see more explosions as they took a heavy toll on the steel vermin.

An instant later Sam was upon the rats, riding straight into their midst no matter the recklessness of the attack, and, raising his battle axe high above his head, he released the magic held within it in a blinding ball of fire and lightning. He hoped and prayed that the elves that still lived were far enough back that the spell wouldn't hit them, but he knew he had no choice. Just as he knew if he didn't use the enchantment they would be dead soon enough anyway as the rats overran them.

The result was everything he'd hoped for as fifty or a hundred of the rats simply exploded even as they charged down the sentries, giving them enough time and room to make a better stand. A score or more of them were down, probably dead, but perhaps another dozen were on their feet and running for safety. Meanwhile others were forming a line as they raised their long bows. And with the closest rats destroyed Sam knew that that was his chance to retreat with the others. To fall back behind the line. He took advantage of it. What he had done had simply been too reckless, and Tyla could have been killed.

With the first wave down, the soldiers were able to switch once more to long bows; always an elf's truest weapon. Another two dozen fell to their arrows even as Sam joined them on the line and switched from battle axe to greatsword. Then he unleashed his favourite fire scythe spell.

The rats had no chance. Attacking them in a column formation, the shape dictated by the fact that they had just emerged from a long narrow tunnel, Sam was for a while, able to destroy them all. The narrow beam of fire that shone from his sword cut directly into them, and destroyed them all the way back to the tunnel entrance, and even inside it. But soon he knew, the sword's magic would be used up, and he didn't have another shape ready. With only a hundred yards between the tunnel entrance and their position there wasn't a lot of time to prepare one. It might however, be enough time to hold off the attack while his brothers in arms formed into a proper line and more soldiers arrived.

"Fall back and line up! Defensive lines!" He bellowed the command even as he used the sword and simply hoped the men obeyed him.

For what was surely the longest few dozen heartbeats of his life, Sam sat there astride Tyla, and kept playing his sword's scythe spell back down the column of rats that were still trying to emerge from the tunnel entrance, and held the rats on his own. And all the time he was waiting for one of the rats to leap on him and tear him to pieces. But though he didn't dare turn his head to look, he heard the sound of feet disappearing behind him, hopefully to do as he wanted, and that was everything. He doubted though that they'd have time to fall back as far as they should. Two hundred paces would have been best considering the range of the long bows, but there was no chance of that. For the moment the continuing explosion that was the tunnel mouth told him the rats were dying by the score had to be enough. For a while. Still, every pace they made was a victory as far as he was concerned.

Finally the sword ran out of magic as he'd known it had to, and he had barely enough of his own drawn by then to manage a good chained fire shape or two. There just hadn't been enough time to prepare. Again!

Sheathing the greatsword, Sam watched the rats start emerging once more from the tunnel mouth, and he knew that while perhaps hundreds had already died, it was nothing compared to the thousands behind them. Numbers were always the enemy's greatest strength.

Knowing he had to be as effective as possible with his magic, he let the head of the rats approach to within fifty yards of him and Tyla. In fact they felt so close that even the horse had the good sense to be nervous as she saw the column of silver and steel running straight for them. Then he released

463

his first shape of chained fire, and watched with infinite relief as all the rats coming toward him died as a unit. A column perhaps fifty yards long and over five rats wide suddenly turned into a glorious river of exploding fire in front of him, and he thanked the elders for having made him study that particular shape day in and day out. Not only did it not require the same amount of effort to hold and shape it, but it was far quicker to use than the fire ring, and time was critical. Even as he watched the first river of fire dying down, and saw the sea of glowing red eyes behind it trying to run over their fallen comrades, he could feel enough magic roaring within him for a second blast. It was a good feeling.

He felt even better a dozen heartbeats later when he heard the sounds of hoof beats somewhere behind him, and knew the battle was being joined.

"Archers, take positions!"

Sam didn't know whose voice it was that shouted out – he was too busy releasing his second chained fire shape – but when he heard the call he knew that it was his turn to retreat. A heartbeat later he had wheeled Tyla around and was galloping madly back for the lines, where at least a hundred elves were already in position.

The first volley of arrows flew past his head just as he reached them. Fifty or a hundred arrows flew and he guessed as many rats had just burst into flames. The elves didn't miss.

By the time he'd once more reined in Tyla and returned to the line, all he could see of the rats was a burning column of steel, a hundred yards long. He had no idea how many of them had been destroyed, but he knew it was a lot. But still more were coming. He didn't know how many, but as he watched ever more rats pour out of the cavern mouth, he feared it would be far more than they'd expected.

Still, it was not a soldier's place to surrender to fear. And as he took his place on the line with the others and drew his magic to him, he promised them all silently that he would not. No matter what happened, no matter the odds, he would fight.

For a little while he didn't have to. Though the rats kept coming, a river of steel and glowing red eyes, the soldiers were up to the challenge. And so the numbers of dead rats kept growing while the column of rats bursting from the cavern scarcely grew any larger. And all the while he was drawing his fire to him.

The air was chilling all around, the fires from the torches were dimming, and the sky above and the ground below were growing cold. He tried to draw more from above and below, shielding the elves from his magic, but still he knew they must be cold. Yet it was the only way he could fight – and sooner or later he knew they would run out of arrows.

Then he heard the sounds of hoof beats assembling all around him, and watched out of the corner of his eyes as more elves took up their positions. They were being joined by more and more elves as they came from across the valley floor to join the fight and he praised the All Father for that mercy.

Soon they were hundreds strong. Surely two hundred stood on either side of him and another hundred were astride their horses. And as the commanders started shouting instructions they formed up into formation, ready to take on the rats. A giant semicircle with himself in its middle, and the tunnel mouth at the centre.

It was just as well. The rats were coming faster by then. Instead of a column five or six wide they were a dozen at least running at them side by side, and they were moving even faster. The river was fast becoming a torrent.

Still they came and still they died. And though every so

often as the column of rats emerging from the cavern mouth grew longer, he loosed a good hot fire ball at them. One that would not just destroy them but send the pieces of their steel corpses flying high into the night sky. And each time they did he heard cheering from all around.

In time they found a rhythm. The archers on his right would loose a volley. Then when more rats emerged he would send a spell of chained fire screaming down their middle. Next the archers on his left would take their turn. And all the while more soldiers and more supplies, mainly quivers of arrows, would be brought to them.

It was a good system. It gave them all a chance to rest between attacks and conserved arrows. But as the rats kept coming and coming Sam kept wondering when they would run out. By then he was sure that several thousand had to have been destroyed. The land all around for hundreds of yards was littered with burning steel corpses. In places they were starting to form piles. And yet they kept coming.

Still, as long as they kept being destroyed.

And so the battle went on for what seemed like ages. The sun, long since set, finally let the last of its light leave the land and the sky grew completely dark around them. But another mage had an answer for that – a vast orb of shimmering silver appearing in the sky above, giving the archers all the light they needed to keep sending the rats to a fiery death. Meanwhile step by step the elves fell back as a unit, making the semicircle ever larger and allowing more archers to stand with them. Soon they were thousands strong, and for maybe the first time ever, the machina were outnumbered as they burst from the tunnel mouth. It gave the men more time to pick their targets and loose their arrows. And it turned what had been a panicked retreat into an attacking formation.

Not to be outdone, the masters of earth magic soon arrived

to stand beside Sam and the archers with a plan of their own. One as deadly as any he could ever have asked for. As the soldiers fell back, they turned the good earth where they'd just been into liquid, in effect creating a giant, unseen trench fifty yards deep, which, if and when they decided to let the rats advance fully out of the tunnel, they would fall into, never to be seen again. All that was needed was the command. It was the same shape he'd used when the elders had tested him, and that others had used before him. And he guessed that it was a shape that would become more common as the war against the machina progressed. Who said that earth magic couldn't make a useful weapon!

Meanwhile above his head Sam could feel the gentle wind that marked the very edge of a gigantic tornado hovering high above them, as the weather mages made ready. No doubt they would hold off for a while, since their magic was likely to be as dangerous to anyone caught in it as to the enemy, but if and when the time came Sam knew they too would be used.

Over the next half hour or so, though it seemed longer to Sam, what had been a desperate defence and holding of the line against the enemy, became an organised campaign. The war masters somewhere behind them began sending their messengers along the lines, coordinating the attack so that the most damage was dealt to the steel rats for the least effort. At the same time the rats began to pay a heavy price for their attack. Where initially they had been destroyed in their scores, in time that became in their hundreds and even thousands. In fact so many were being destroyed that their still burning steel remnants were forming a gigantic hill over which their fellow rats had to climb to get to the elves.

But at the same time, while Sam was feeling good about their success, he was also starting to worry about the sheer numbers of rats that kept emerging from the underground entrance. They didn't seem to be slowing down. They had thought that there would only be a few thousand underground.

But he was starting to think that that was yet another miscalculation. Just how many were there?

"Fog in five! Fall back twenty paces on the horn when it arrives."

A messenger screamed it at them even as he galloped by on his horse. His words could barely be heard over the constant thunder that was the death of so many rats, but for everyone who heard him it was a major morale boost as they knew what was coming. It was time to see just how effective the earth mage's trench could be.

Exactly as promised, a little while later a fog began to descend on the rats, and Sam like every other soldier there began to feel a trace of excitement as they waited for the horn. This could be the decisive moment in the battle! The killer blow that would decimate the enemy and give them a chance to rest. Or, though he didn't want to imagine it, the rats could finally come in such numbers that they would completely fill the trench and the rest would then come running over the bodies of the fallen.

Just as they'd hoped for the fog began thickening, starting at the cavern mouth and then spreading out back towards the elves, covering the liquid trench the mages had built so that it was completely hidden. And when the fog finally reached them Sam knew that everything was in play. So did the war masters, and as promised the horn sounded.

With a final blast of fire and a volley of arrows aimed in the general direction of the cavern mouth and the rats, the elves fell back the required twenty paces like a well drilled unit. And waited.

It wasn't easy waiting. Staying calm and not attacking the enemy, even though they couldn't see him anyway, but it was necessary. The rats' master had to believe they'd retreated under the cover of fog, fled against his insurmountable numbers. They hoped it would be the bait he needed to make a mistake. To order his soldiers to charge ahead blindly, heedless of the risk. And that he was just stupid enough to take it. To send his army running heedlessly and blindly into a trap. The real question was how long would he keep doing it once his rats began sinking? How many would he have left after he'd realised his rats were all being destroyed?

Naturally there was no answer, and Sam like everyone else there simply had to wait it out. But at least while he waited he had the chance to once more draw the fire he so desperately needed. It had been tight for a while as the age spent battling the rats had used up so much of his fire, leaving him without enough magic burning within him, and using nearly everything he had with each blast. Now that he had the chance to draw more fire he used it for all he was worth, fanning the barely glowing embers into a raging bonfire.

By the time the first of the plopping sounds could be heard, exactly as though the rats were diving into a river, the bonfire was singing sweetly in his flesh. Meanwhile thunder in the skies was beginning to grow and Sam guessed the weather mages were also preparing themselves for something spectacular.

Suddenly the plopping sounds became a symphony of falling water. It was almost as though the skies had opened up and unleashed a deluge on to a pond. But it wasn't rain drops that were making the noise. The rats, finding the ground ahead of them free of elves and arrows, were charging toward where they thought the elves were, and sinking in their hundreds. The noise brought a smile and a small cheer to Sam's lips and he wasn't alone. All around he could hear the sudden, quickly suppressed roar that were the thousands of elves standing with him cheering. He could see their white teeth and the whites of their eyes glowing orange in the fire lit sky.

In time the noise of the rats ceased, as they'd always known it had to once their master finally realised his foolishness. But by that time having listened to the rats hitting the water almost continuously, surely thousands if not tens of thousands had to have been destroyed. Meanwhile Sam and the other mages had rediscovered their magic, the archers had rested and reloaded their quivers, and tired arms had been stretched. No matter how many rats remained, this had been a victory for them.

"Count off a hundred then cheer!"

The rider thundered by, giving the next command, and Sam could see the logic. In theory the rats had stopped running blindly into a trap in pursuit of an enemy they couldn't find. It was time to give them a target to chase, though of course they would remain blinded by the fog. Meanwhile they could rest for a little while longer and recover their strength. Immediately the count began.

Soon – though whether the full hundred had been counted Sam wasn't sure – a cheer rang out from dozens and then hundreds and thousands of throats. A cheer which quickly became a roar of triumph that filled the entire valley itself. A roar that the Dragon surely heard even in his homeland, wherever that was. And sure enough, in time more plopping sounds could soon be heard through it, as more rats ran for their prey and sank into the earth. This time those plopping sounds didn't became a deluge, but that was expected. Even the most stupid commander would have realised his mistake eventually.

But as time passed and the silence continued, Sam like all the rest, finally began to hope. Could it be that the enemy was finally out of soldiers? Or was he simply becoming smarter? Sam had no answer, and neither, he suspected did anyone else. They simply kept cheering and hoping.

A sudden touch of earth magic raised the hairs on the back of Sam's neck, and he realised that the earth mages had sealed their trap, entombing the rats in their rocky grave. A few moments later a gust of wind blew away the fog as if it had never been and the light from the fire mages suddenly revealed a rocky landscape, bereft of steel vermin. In truth it was bereft of anything as even the grass that had once covered it had sunk into its strange liquid embrace, never to grow again. A ring of bare dirt surrounding the cavern entrance and the arena surrounding it filled with piles of burning steel bodies. But more important than the death of the land was the complete lack of steel vermin even behind the trap. No new ones were emerging from the cavern. None were running for them, trying desperately to cross the ring of bare dirt in which their brothers were entombed.

Where the cavern entrance popped up out of the ground no more glowing red eyes could be seen. No more steel glowed in the silvery light – it was all blackened. No more fires burnt either. No more threat remained above ground as far as they could see.

But what remained under ground? That was the question. How many more of the rats remained? How many more would they have to fight their way through in the morning? And in the longer term, how many more armies could this new Dragon raise?

It was a sobering thought, as Sam tried to estimate the numbers of his steel vermin they'd already destroyed that day, and failed to even find an estimate. Certainly it was something in the many tens of thousands, but no closer than that could he begin to guess. And if the Dragon could raise armies like that, even afford to lose them and then raise more, what hope was there in truth? What hope at all?

But even as he was thinking such morbid thoughts a new

cheer erupted from all around him, and he wondered why. But he understood when he caught sight of arms pointing and followed to what they were pointing at. To the new figures that had emerged on top of the mountain of destroyed steel vermin surrounding the cavern entrance. Short stocky dwarven figures.

There could only be one explanation. The rats were gone. They had used all their numbers up in this final attack and the dwarves had destroyed whatever remained below before chasing them all the way back up the tunnels.

The battle was over and they had finally won. A province had been cleared of the enemy. The Dragon had been defeated if only on a single battlefield.

But it was a start.

There were simply no words to express how powerful the emotion was that overcome him. But the tears of joy that began streaming down his cheeks were a start.

Chapter Thirty Two

Riding home after a war was an unusual experience for Sam. He guessed it was the same for everyone. It was actually more difficult than he would have expected. On the one hand he still felt like celebrating over a week later. He felt like throwing his head back and shouting the joyful news to the skies. They had won a major victory and it was time that the entire world knew it. It was time that the people knew that the Dragon could be beaten. And though the celebrations and drinking had largely ended he kept thinking that they should still be doing that.

On the other hand it was also a time when the price they had paid for that victory sat heavy in his heart. More than eight hundred men and women had perished. Nearly a thousand more had been badly injured, and would only return home once the healers had finished tending to them. If they survived. Another thousand carried the scars and minor injuries of battle.

A tenth of their army was dead. Another quarter would not soon return to the fight if at all. And at that he knew, they had been lucky. They had been stupid too, and in battle making stupid mistakes got you killed.

So what were they to do? Celebrate or mourn? And what would they say to the families whose loved ones had perished? How did one tell a wife or husband that their partner had died? How did you tell the children that their father or mother was now with the Goddess? And most terrible of all, how did you tell parents that their most beloved children were gone? Especially when so many had already lost loved ones already?

And yet if the price the elves had paid for their victory

was too high, it was so much worse for the dwarves of the Bronze Mountains. Their losses were in fact so great that they could never place a true figure on them. All they could truly guess was that nearly a quarter of their clan or around thirty to fifty thousand – had died. There would be no family he guessed that had not suffered some losses. Some families might have been wiped out completely.

And all because of one man. One part troll. A man who wasn't yet finished either. He might have had his nose bloodied, but he was far from down. Even now Sam knew, he would be building his armies once again. Preparing for the next attack. And no doubt next time he would be stronger.

The people had a song they sang constantly as they marched – Rowell ni mar – the gold is going, and while on the face of it it was simply a ballad about the end of fall, it was about much more than that. It was about the falling of the golden leaves and the coming of winter to the land. Only in this case the falling golden leaves were the people and they were falling in numbers, covering the forest floor.

"So, tell me about my parents, brother."

Sam started as he heard Mayvelle's voice come from just beside him. He hadn't heard her approach. But then he hadn't been paying attention to much as he'd been riding. Mostly he'd just been wallowing in his own dark thoughts. In fact he hadn't even known she or her troop were with the army. It took a few moments to redirect his thoughts to the question asked. And then to realise he had no idea what she was talking about.

"I don't know anything about your parents."

Why he wondered would she even think he did? And then the last word hit him and sent his thoughts spinning in a whole new direction.

"Brother?" Ry and her family had said she might be his sister, and maybe they were right. He didn't know. But he hadn't broached the subject with Mayvelle back in their new home. Not even after Ry had told him about her visit. He'd barely even seen her around the new Shavarra. And when he had the topic hadn't come up, for which he had been grateful. Because it wouldn't have been good for anyone. So why was she?

"I discussed the matter with my parents before we left. They told me the truth." Her face though said it had been a bitter truth.

"What exactly did they tell you?" Sam stalled, trying to work out what she thought she knew and more importantly what she felt about it.

"That they took me from my mother's dying arms. That she'd been poisoned. That your father and his mistress killed her."

"What?!" Sam was instantly outraged. The very idea was appalling. In fact it was worse than that. So much worse that he didn't know what it was. But he knew he couldn't allow his father's name to be so badly tainted by lies. "My father would never do any such thing! He was a good man. An honourable man. And he loved my mother with all his heart."

Clearly Mayvelle didn't believe him. Her face said it all. Maybe she thought that he was lying to her for some reason? Still, he continued. He could not allow such a falsehood to go unchallenged.

"When she died it broke my father. He hadn't expected it. He never wanted it. And he wept at her funeral. He was a strong man, a brave knight and a king. But he wept for her."

It was one of the few memories Sam had of those days. He'd only been small at the time, confused at why his mother hadn't come home. But he remembered that. He remembered his father standing there at the graveside while the priests intoned their prayers, and the tears running down his face. He'd been too young to truly understand what was happening. He only knew that his mother had gone away. But that image still stayed with him. Sometimes it even haunted him in the quiet times.

"He wed the poisoner not six months later." Mayvelle said it without emotion, but it was an accusation as deadly as any he'd ever heard.

"He had no choice. He was the king and a king in Fair Fields can only rule with the support of the Court. He had no wife and no heir. The nobles were unhappy about that. And they were already unhappy with his rule. He had brought about sweeping changes to the kingdom. Ones that would leave the nobles without much of their power and would cut their income. They were very unhappy. There was talk of a coup. If he wanted to keep his throne, not to mention his head and mine, he had to have at least something he could show them. An acceptable wife from a good family. There were few choices that would not leave the kingdom in disarray."

Of course Lady Dreasda had been a poor choice of Queen. She had been a lying bitch, and if what Heri had claimed was true, the murderer of both his parents. It was less than noble, but Sam was glad she was dead. And he found it ironic that it had been by her own son's hand, but also fitting. Heri after all had been her route to the throne – or so she had thought. It was just a pity for her that Heri had not wanted to be someone else's route to power. Not even his own mother's. And especially not the route to what he considered his own power. He did not share.

"So you say." Mayvelle clearly didn't believe a word of it.

476

Sam's face whitened with anger and he had to suppress the urge to draw his sword. He couldn't though stop his fists from clenching tight. Now his father was a monster and he was a liar? How in all the hells could she suggest such a thing?!

"Well believe this. In my father's private bedchamber there were half a dozen portraits of my mother hanging in pride of place on the walls. He visited her grave regularly to speak with her and placed flowers on it on each anniversary of her birth and her death. And when he died, his only request was that he be buried beside her. My step mother despite years of trying, never managed to change a single one of those things. Theirs was not a happy marriage." Of course it had been even more unhappy than he had known until recently, and it had ended in disaster. The price of love had been high. The price of wedding the wrong woman, death.

Mayvelle's response was a distinctly unelven grunt, something that surprised Sam. And the expression on her face was one of true disbelief, bitterness and barely suppressed anger. She might have learned the truth, but she wasn't happy about it. And Sam realised there was nothing he could do about any of that. But his anger in turn also did not help. Sam took a few deep breathes to still his anger before speaking again.

"Mayvelle, you may be my sister or not. I don't know. And you may share my parents. I don't know that either. The one thing I do know however is my parents. And you can choose to believe me or not when I tell you what I know of them. And I have nothing but love for them and sorrow that they are gone. I would thank you not to cast falsehoods on their graves."

"Have a care before you ever dare speak to me again!"

"How dare –!" It was Mayvelle's turn to grow angry and to

raise her voice.

"– You should return to your patrol now soldier." Sam didn't care if she was angry. He didn't care about much at all just then. He wanted her gone. Out of his sight. And damned be whatever the priests might say about such a thing. No doubt they would say something. They always did.

"As you wish Fire Angel." It was some time before Mayvelle managed to squeeze the words out. And when she did her face was filled with thunderclouds as she realised she'd been dismissed. But she said nothing as she flicked the reins of her horse, wheeled around and rode off.

Sam's face he expected, was not much different to hers. To have such baseless and horrid aspersions cast on his family! It was unacceptable. So what had she expected to get back from him? Agreement? Love and respect? She was lucky he hadn't thrashed her for such rudeness as she deserved! And it wasn't as if he didn't already have enough troubles on his mind.

Still, now he knew that when he returned to Ry he would have to tell her how badly he'd failed with Mayvelle. And she'd be unhappy with him. Then she'd tell him all the ways he should have handled it. The polite ways. The elven ways. After that she would no doubt ask him to speak with the priests.

Damn! He cursed the gods. He cursed Alder above all. Because this was surely his doing. It was beginning to look as though he was going to have to endure a bad peace following a bad war.

Chapter Thirty Three

Fall Keep was gone. Not just the keep which had become a mountain of rubble. But the city behind it, which was little better. Fire had raged through the entire city, and after it was finished, little had been left. Certainly nothing was intact.

But while the keep had been destroyed by the explosion, Heri was pleased to find that his private sanctum had survived very much intact. He was relieved too. He had always intended that it should survive even such a catastrophe as the destruction of the keep. So he had built his sanctum to the rear of the keep and had buried it underground. In fact it was accessible only through a secret passageway beneath the gardeners' hall. But he had still not known for certain that it would survive. Not until just then. And it had survived even better than he had expected.

The gardeners' hall itself had been burnt out and suffered a partial collapse. That was no great loss considering that there were no gardens and no gardeners left anymore. And he'd had to push aside some rubble inside the hall to reach the secret passage. But once he'd reached the passageway everything else had been in perfect condition. There wasn't even any dust.

The sanctum was intact. That was the first thing Heri had noticed as he entered it from the long dark steeply sloping hallway. It was also the only thing that mattered. That and the treasures contained within. There was no rubble on the floor. No holes in the ceiling. Even the paintings were still hanging on the walls. It had survived the destruction of Fall Keep completely and he was grateful for that. He needed this place. Because without the sanctum he would have had no hope of regaining his throne.

But it was intact, and he let that wonder fill him with hope as he went around the huge circular chamber with his torch, lighting the candles on the wall shelves so that the light could once more shine in it. And the light showed that not only was the sanctum intact, but so too were his treasures. Hanging on the walls, sitting on shelves, or even on the floor. But all of them were intact, and presumably all of them still had their magic. All of them could still be used.

It seemed something of a minor miracle after the explosion he had caused. Perhaps it was a blessing from the All Father? Maybe that worthless god had finally done something for him. He had spent enough time in the temples to the god after all. It wasn't that he wanted to or that he even really believed in the All Father or any of the gods. As far as he was concerned the gods were for the simple minded peasants. Something to keep their minds off their troubles as they worked. And hopefully something that stopped them rebelling. But as king he had had to be seen to pay his respects to the god of the kingdom. The last thing he had needed was upset priests and temples as well as everything else. So he had prayed and paid his tributes. Perhaps it had been worth it?

Of course the real reason the sanctum had survived was probably because it was underground. Buried deep beneath the solid earth and protected by it. Heri felt fairly good about his foresight in building it there just then as he collapsed into the welcoming arms of the huge leather armchair. It was intact and he was safe here. No one knew about this place.

If they had, treasure hunters would have long since descended on this place in packs. Wizards too. Because the ancient treasures he had obtained over the years were worth a fortune in gold. They were probably worth even more to the wizards. The ancients – before they had been torn apart by the Dragon Wars – had been a powerfully magical people. And they had not been peaceful. So what he was surrounded by included an arsenal of some of the most deadly weapons ever created. But it also held some of the most useful tools and a large number of amazing curios that might or might not be of some use. And all of them still worked despite the thousands of years that had passed since they had been created. All of the artefacts were priceless too. He could sell some of them if he had need of gold.

Despite his need for weapons and tools to help him maintain his rule, Heri had collected a lot of other ancient treasures. Things which were precious in their own right. So he had an ancient golden hoe that would return life to barren soil. He couldn't even begin to imagine what the gnomes of the Fedowir Kingdom would pay for that if they knew he had it. And the horn of Aural which would call unicorns to him. Augrim had been particularly keen that he get that one as he recalled. Hanging on the wall to one side was the Drum of Hester. If he was to beat it during a riot it would immediately turn into a festival as people started losing themselves in the dance. He had a horse's head that would transform a man into a horse. That one could be useful for getting rid of your enemies without leaving a blood trail.

Of course there were other ancient curios in his collection that were of even less worth as far as he could see, but which Augrim had collected for him anyway. There was a painting on the wall which regularly and randomly decided what pictures to display. Beside it was a candle with no name that when lit would transform the sky into a sea of rainbows. He could think of no use for it but had no doubt it would sell for plenty of gold if and when the time came. And it was pretty. There was also a knife that for no reason he could determine turned your hand scaly while you held it.

These things were not of any use to him. But they were valuable and if ever his rule was threatened and he needed gold, they would bring a lot of it when he sold them.

Having surveyed his treasures and found them all intact Heri collapsed into the huge leather arm chair in the centre of the chamber and let a feeling of euphoria wash over him. Here at least he could sit surrounded by his treasures and know that everything was in order in at least one little part of his kingdom. Everything else was gone. But not this place. And after the last few months it was important that he had something left to him. Some little piece of his kingdom remaining.

He had lost so much, and the pain of his miserable brother's sword in his back was with him as a constant reminder of that. But it was also instructive. Because it told him that now was the time when he had to start reclaiming all that was his. To do what he couldn't do when he'd first fled the keep. Then he had had to hide. To make sure that no one saw him. And he had let his hatred for his brother take hold. Now there was no one to see him. No one who knew he was alive. And he could no longer go after his brother no matter how much he hated him. It was time.

It was strange being back in the keep. Or at least underneath what remained of it. But Heri could be there because there wasn't much of a keep left and because the city itself was largely deserted. There was no doubt that when he'd blown up Fall Keep he'd destroyed most of the city as well. He hadn't intended that. But it seemed that the explosion had set the city ablaze as well. Now all that was left behind the damaged city walls was blackened stone and ashes. There was actually little left to fight over and few to do the fighting.

He was saddened by that. Destroying the city had never been his intention. He wanted to be king once more and a king had to have a realm and people to rule over. Now the largest city in the realm was gone and the people with it. His kingdom was less than it had been, and he would be less of a king because of it. Still, the destruction had made it safer for him to return to Fall Keep.

Of course the other reason he could be there in complete safety was that he looked nothing like the Heri of old. Nothing like the king. If someone did see him they would simply assume he was someone else. Maybe a noble. Maybe a merchant or even a scavenger. But the king was dead so he absolutely couldn't be him. In fact for the whole month that he'd spent on the trail riding here, no one had stopped him or asked him any questions. The land was just coming through the end of winter, and people were shaking out the cold and preparing for a busy spring. The noble houses were threatening one another with war. One more stranger on the road simply didn't matter.

He'd even revisited the black market to purchase some more knife throwers – the elves still had his old ones – and no one had said a word to him. They hadn't even recognised him from the previous time he'd visited.

Heri hadn't had to return to Fall Keep and his sanctum. After realising that he was completely unrecognisable, he knew that he could have chosen instead to ride off somewhere else. Made himself a new home somewhere and a new name and lived on his gold. He had thought about it. After all, he had lost so much. And it would have been an easier life. Especially now that he was carrying so many injuries. He could have bought himself a mansion somewhere. Had healers attend to him. Lived comfortably. But in the end he had to rule. He had to be king. And he had to have his vengeance. And his sanctum was the only place where he could begin that journey again. Because it was here that he had kept his most prized possessions. Not gold, though there was plenty of that here as well. Not wealth of any sort. But those things that would protect his rule. Or in this case, restore it.

Augrim, bless his worm infested corpse, had been more than just his magical advisor. He had been his purveyor of the most powerful and dangerous, and highly illegal items. He had found for him magical treasures from ancient times. And he had been extremely good at his work.

Despite what people thought, Heri wasn't averse to magic. He just didn't like wizards. He hated that they had power which he didn't. He was especially averse to his brother having magic. But there were many magical items that a man without magic could use, and he had purchased a lot of them over the years. You never knew when a good magical weapon might come in handy.

Sadly, though as he sat in his grand leather armchair surrounded by them, he realised that even the most powerful weapon couldn't keep you warm and fed. He had only trail food to eat and watered down wine to drink. The keep was gone and so were his servants. Most he suspected were buried somewhere in the keep's remains. Just then he would have loved to have been able to call out to one of them and have him come rushing to do his bidding. Perhaps serve him a hot meal. He would have loved the comfort of a soft bed too and a few wenches. But none of that was possible anymore. And it would be a long time before it was again.

Rebuilding the keep would take years. Rebuilding the city behind it probably a decade or more. And absolutely none of that could even begin before the noble houses were destroyed.

So it was best he decided that he begin that task quickly.

That began with the Window of Parsus – his most precious tool. It wasn't actually a window despite its name. It was a mirror. But it hung on the wall looking much as a window would and with a command it showed the outside. Anywhere the viewer wanted to see. The window had cost him a fortune in gold and precious stones, but it was invaluable as it allowed him to see right into the hearts of his enemy's homes. They had often wondered how he could possibly always be prepared for their plans, and had assumed that it was his spies. And his spies were good. But this was his best spy.

The window had allowed him to find the Dragon. It and his spies that was. And Augrim too if he was honest. The spies had told him of the machina and Augrim had connected them to the ancient Dragon, of which he had happened to know a lot. The Window and chance had done the rest.

He'd often used it to spy on neighbouring realms as well, mostly out of curiosity. And one of those realms he had always been fascinated by was Ragnor's Rock. It had been by good fortune that he had been watching when the city had been besieged. That had been nearly a week before he had lost his throne, and then, while he had still had living hostages, he had had only one thing on his mind. Spying on the nobles and trying to work out their plans. But somewhere during that time he had grown tired of staring at them and wanted to see something other than their ugly faces. Something like the greatest city on the Continent of the Dragon's Spine. A city that he had dreamed Fall Keep would one day resemble. But then he'd seen the rats and spiders attacking it.

After that it had simply been a matter of using the window to back track the machina's path back as they marched towards the impregnable city, all the way to the dock where they'd landed, and then to follow the black ships as they came and went. That had shown him the island and in time, the Dragon himself.

He was a disgusting little troll blood buried in a cavern under an island where he created his armies of steel vermin. The miserable little creature was a horror to him, mostly because he was both wizard and troll. It simply seemed wrong that any miserable troll should have magic when he didn't. An insult from the gods themselves, and another reason not to worship any of them. Still, as horrible as the creature was, he might now prove useful.

Briefly though, he did wonder about the wisdom of contacting the troll blood. The foul creature was dangerous. And he was a wizard. He might have a way of finding him. Meanwhile Heri had no actual way of controlling him. Just some threats. But in the end it was the only chance he had of regaining his throne. And without that he was nothing. He could not be nothing.

Before making contact with him though, Heri took some basic precautions. Mostly that consisted of blowing out all the candles that stood between him and the window so that no light fell on his face. He didn't look like the former king and the chances were that the troll blood wouldn't have known what the king of Fair Fields had looked like anyway. But there was no point in taking chances. Then he sat back down and prepared himself mentally for what he had to do.

Quickly Heri used the window to return to the island and the cavern in its heart. And what a cavern! The entire inside of a volcano had been hollowed out somehow. Lava literally pooled in small lakes everywhere filling the cavern with an orange glow. And someone had somehow carved huge stone platforms over each of those pools from which a man might stand and gaze down in wonder. Or in this case a worthless troll blood.

Strangest of all, the machina themselves simply walked out of the lava lakes one by one. Glowing lava creations that slowly cooled and turned to steel. Somehow they were created from the very fire of the molten rocks. He didn't understand that. Mostly he suspected it was something of the ancients left over from before the first Dragon Wars. But he understood that this was how the troll blood could create his armies. The entire cavern was some sort of ancient workshop that could produce machina. He also knew that the Dragon hadn't created this wonder of the world. He had just somehow found it and then made use of it. There was no way a troll blood could have built this.

It wasn't long before he found the troll blood casting his magic into a batch of steel spiders. He only wished it had been so good at finding Sam. He could have killed the Alder worshipping bastard years ago and been done with him before he had grown so powerful. But finding a man who could be anywhere was a much harder thing than finding a town or an island. He had tried. He had searched the streets of every city he could think of that his brother might go to. But he had not found him. The troll blood had been much easier to find.

Heri didn't want to use the troll blood. Trolls were dangerous enemies and this one would always be his enemy. But he was out of choices. It was this or nothing. And it couldn't be nothing. He had to get his throne back, and he needed an army to do that. The Dragon's army was the only one he had available.

Once he'd found the troll blood, Heri spoke the words that opened the window. That allowed him not just to see the new Dragon, but to speak with him. And unfortunately to be seen and heard by him. That was why he hadn't risked making contact with him before. It was bad enough that he was troll blood. But when he could send armies to crush a realm it made speaking with him that much more dangerous. The time for caution though was over. He wanted his throne back and there was no other way to get it. Besides, he was sitting in a darkened chamber with all the light from the lamps and candles coming from behind him. The troll blood would be able to see very little. And trolls were stupid.

"Troll blood! Attend to me at once!"

Heri snapped his command at the troll. Partly it was because he didn't like the foul creatures. But partly it was because he knew that you had to always be in control with any troll blood. If they sensed submission they would kill you.

Samual

They only respected strength. As a strategy it seemed to work.

The new Dragon and would be master of the world leapt into the air in shock. He also managed to look suitably worried when he landed. It wasn't an expression that came naturally to his features. Troll mouths didn't work the same way as others owing to the upturned tusks that protruded from their lower jaws. It meant that they couldn't show a lot of normal emotions. They couldn't smile or show sorrow for example, and when they laughed the sound was more animal than human. Still, he thought he saw fear in his eyes. That pleased him.

"Who are you?" The troll blood yelled the question out angrily, his words slurring together as he forced them out too quickly.

"Your new master of course." Heri smiled and watched as the troll blood grimaced in fury. That was one expression a creature such as him could always manage.

"Never! I serve no one! Especially not a filthy human!"

"Oh well then, I guess I'll just have to destroy you and most of your miserable race."

Heri managed a smile even as he reached for the blood red orb on the table beside him. The moment his hand touched it the orb began glowing gently, casting a blood red hue right around the chamber. Naturally the troll blood recognised it. He was magical after all, and there was no wizard who wouldn't know what it was.

"Where'd you get that?" Despite everything, the troll blood was impressed. What Heri was holding in his hands was power. Ultimate magical power. An ancient weapon that had been built to destroy cities. Or in this case mountains.

Samual

"This? You mean them don't you?" Heri smiled some more, lying through his teeth and pretending a confidence he didn't have as he patted the orb. Pretending he had more of them. But he needed this troll blood frightened. "And why should it matter where I got them from? What should matter to you is what I'm going to do with them."

That got through to the creature. Its defiance died away a little and it started thinking. Slowly of course. It was troll blood after all. Tusks, greying wrinkled viciousness, and apparently magic. But not intelligence. Eventually it came up with some more obvious questions.

"You can't kill me with that. You can't get it on the island. My machina would destroy you before you got here."

"Kill you?" Heri managed a confident laugh. "Why would I kill you? That seems entirely too much work for something as worthless as you. Especially when it's so much easier to destroy you."

"Destroy?" The Dragon suddenly looked anxious, an almost comical expression on its wrinkled face.

"Of course. You see I know your secret. The secret of all trolls." And he did. Bless Augrim's rotting corpse! The man might have been expensive and ultimately disloyal, but he had had his uses.

"What secret?" The troll blood tried for defiance once more. But it sounded false on his lips.

"About your precious mountains of course. You know, that little thing you've never spoken about in all the centuries that your kind has been a plague on the world? That the mountains aren't just a home and a place where you store memories. That they're the place where your souls reside."

It was a guess. He didn't know that. No one did – not for sure. Even Augrim hadn't been certain, despite studying the issue extensively. But the trolls believed it. It was the heart of their religion. It was the truth that they shook their ancient bones at. And once he'd known he was dealing with a troll blood Heri had known what levers he would have to use to make him do what he wanted.

"That's just the shaman talking."

But he didn't believe that. Heri could see the uncertainty in the troll blood's eyes. Hear it in his voice.

"Really? Well I guess we'll know soon. Because I've already had the first of these placed in one of your ancestral mountains. The caves of Andrea. And with just a word from me, the mountain will be no more. It should be interesting to see what happens to you. The soul of your ancient Dragon – you know the real one that you're copying. The souls of all those others. A thousand years of your people's memories and lives, all gone in the blink of an eye. I wonder what'll be left of you? And of all the knowledge you've gained from it?"

"Will you lose your magic? It is the Dragon's magic after all. Your knowledge? That too was his first. Your intelligence. And that would be bad because you're only troll blood. Small and weak. The others, the true trolls would eat you. And after all, Andrea is your spiritual home isn't it?" Heri managed another amused laugh, but really he was no more certain of what he was saying than the troll blood was. This was all a bluff.

"I'm not from Andrea."

In the instant he said that Heri knew he had the new Dragon. Because he knew that the troll blood was lying. He didn't have the wit to lie ably.

"Well I guess we'll see in a few hours, won't we?" He smiled confidently. "I'll check back in a few hours to see what's happened to you after I've sent a message to my people shall I?"

"No!"

"No? Why ever not? I mean you've already said you won't do as I command. So what use are you to me? To anyone? Best I think to wipe your ugly race out. Don't you?"

"What do you want?" The new Dragon with his massive armies of machina gave in abruptly, and no doubt hated himself as he did so. He probably hated every word that came out of his mouth. But he'd realised he had no choice.

And he didn't as long as he didn't know that Heri was lying through his teeth. Because if he ever guessed the truth he would come after Heri with everything he had. And he had armies of machina. Heri would not survive against them. The troll blood would destroy the entire kingdom to get to him.

"Oh well then, isn't that better?" Heri mocked him. It was vital that he retained the upper hand. That the troll blood believed he had all the power. There could be no lapses. And the troll blood could never guess who he was either. He could never be given a target to strike at.

"All I want is such a small thing. A few little deaths when you already have so many. A couple or three of your steel drakes."

"Who do you want killed?"

"Well, let's start with the nobility of Fair Fields. They all need to die. There's a family called the Fallbrights. Do you know they once tried to hang me as a thief?! They said I shouldn't be stealing the magic of their ancestors. As if necromancy is so terrible!"

Heri continued with his lies, pretending to be the one thing he wasn't – an unseen wizard. But it was an easy enough deception when he was speaking to the troll blood through a magic mirror and holding a sun burst. And when trolls were stupid.

Even as he was giving the troll blood the first of his list of enemies to be destroyed however, Heri was thinking that maybe he should actually have the sun burst brought to the caves of Andrea. After all, if the troll blood truly believed that destroying them would harm him in some way, maybe there was an element of truth in the shaman's stories. And at some point he had to kill this foul creature anyway. Before he reclaimed his throne. Because the moment he did the troll blood would know who he was and would have a target to send his armies after.

That was the problem with trolls and their thirst for blood. They always wanted to kill you. Friend or foe. Human or even another troll. They always wanted you dead. They wanted everyone dead. They were nothing but savages. And now he had one with magic who would want to do nothing more than hunt him down and kill him if he could. But there had always been a price to be paid for taking this path.

Which was why he had a second plan to save himself. Reveal the Dragon's location to those who could do something about the troll blood.

Heri laughed quietly after he'd finished with the troll blood and shut the window, pleased with how things were going. He was back and he was safe. He had the beginnings of power once more. And he could put his plan into effect. It was a simple four part plan. Destroy his enemies. Reclaim the throne. Kill the Dragon. And then kill his pestilent big brother.

Each step of course had its difficulties. Destroying his enemies always had to involve not getting killed in the act. But at least it was started. Reclaiming the throne would require finding allies. Killing the Dragon came with the basic problem that he had no idea how to do it. And he had no idea if others could either. He just had to hope that they could. And killing his brother was a bigger problem than ever now that the damned elves had laid a geas on him preventing him from doing it. He could want to. He desperately wanted to. He could curse Samual until the end of time and threaten him too. But when it came to the moment to stick the knife in, he would be unable to do so. He was also unable to give the command to others to do so.

But that, he decided as he felt the ache of the torn muscles in his back, would not stop him from trying. Samual had to die.

Chapter Thirty Four

The great house of Bainbury was quiet. Nestled in the heart of the town, it was at peace along with everyone else. It was past the middle of the night and everyone was asleep. But even during the days lately the house had been calm. A few soldiers would patrol the walls and the roof of the great house. Perhaps walk the courtyard. Maybe some of the Fallbrights would take a ride or wander into the town surrounding their home. But that was it. There were no noble visitors coming and going. No balls being held. And even their court was held only once a week.

The entire barony was quiet. Save for the soldiers of course, who were guarding every town. It had been quiet for a long time. Ever since the former king had escaped the clutches of their son, Galan. It had to be quiet because once word of the escape had reached the other noble houses, the Fallbrights had found themselves pariahs.

First their son Harmion had tried to usurp the throne – not that anyone objected to that. But the other nobles objected to the way it had worked out with Fall Keep being badly damaged. The other families didn't care that Harmion had died. They cared only that the failure had resulted in a damaged prize and that their own family members being taken hostage. They cared about that very much.

Then their kin had been slaughtered, and though there was no proof that the assassins had been in the pay of the Fallbrights, many suspected their hand. That was not something that would be quickly or easily forgotten.

After that Fall Keep had been destroyed, and though no one knew who had done it or why, again suspicion had fallen on the Fallbrights. Of that at least they were innocent, but it wasn't about innocence or guilt. It was about what people believed.

When the throne had been destroyed and the noble houses had fallen to feuding and occasionally open warfare as they battled for power, anything that reminded the other houses of the Fallbrights and their possible role in what had gone wrong, was unwanted. This was a time when the house wanted to go unnoticed. When they wanted to be forgotten. Let the other houses destroy one another. The Fallbrights needed to stay out of that until they were stronger.

But then things had become worse. For a while the family had reason to hope that all the damage that had been done to their name could be repaired. They had had the former king in their clutches. They had had proof that it was he who had destroyed Fall Keep. How else could he be alive? And they had had the chance to bring him to justice in front of all the other noble houses, proving their innocence. They had sent word to their son in the Golden River Flats trading outpost to bring Heri back, alive. They had sent word to all the other noble houses of his capture and upcoming trial. For a while it had seemed that the sun was once more shining on them.

But then Heri had escaped and they had been left with nothing. Less than nothing. No one believed their claim that the king was still alive. They assumed it was all some deception that had gone wrong. A way of diverting suspicion from them. Now the other houses were preparing to attack. The barony of the Fallbrights had become as hated as the king himself had once been.

Because of that soldiers now patrolled the lands and the towns. Armies were standing ready to defend the city. Defences were being shored up. And they were waiting for the first enemy to come marching on to their land. They were ready for them. At least for the first army to attack.

But they weren't ready for an enemy that came from the sky.

It was in the dark of night when the steel drakes came, striking fast and silently from above. No one saw them. No one raised the alarm. Not the guards on the outer walls surrounding the great house. Nor those on its roof patrolling the battlements. Of course it couldn't have helped much if they had. Three steel drakes diving down out of the darkness and then spewing all the fires of the hells upon the house were too many to fight.

The cannon couldn't protect them. Even if they could have been angled upwards to fire into the sky, the drakes were flying far too fast to hit. Archers were useless. And the wizards who came rushing out in their night clothes to help were little better.

So the drakes struck and there was nothing that could be done to stop them. Instead they had to endure the attack. But even that was more difficult than any would have believed. The steel drakes' fiery blast wasn't just fire. It was heavy falling down like rain and it came with terrible force. It burst through windows, smashing them apart and broke down the walls surrounding them. And then the fire poured into the rooms, destroying everything in its path and setting it ablaze. It knocked the crenelations off the battlements on the roof and incinerated the soldiers standing guard. It knocked the watch towers over sending burning sentries flying.

Far too quickly the entire great house was on fire. Four stories of stone mansion was alight, with flames shooting out of a hundred different windows. Those who hadn't been killed in the initial attack had fled for their lives, some of them on fire as they ran. But they had no hope of escaping. The drakes when they saw them running struck at the fleeing people, and caught them inside the courtyard as they ran for the gate. Scores fell to each blast of fire. Those as yet unburnt were left in a desperate situation as they could either take shelter in a burning building or run. Both options were deadly.

And then things actually got worse as the drakes set fire to the long grass of the courtyard, creating an inferno that completely surrounded the great house. They could either stay where they were and burn, or run directly into the flames.

But just to make sure that no one could escape the inferno the drakes began knocking down the walls surrounding the estate. Blasting them with fire before smashing into them with their steel bodies, and bringing the walls crashing to the ground as piles of rubble. Rubble that they set on fire, making sure that no one could clamber over them to safety.

Soon there was no great house left. No courtyard. No walls. There was only fire. A huge inferno of it in the heart of the town of Bainbury. There were also no survivors, or very few anyway. Some had made it to the basement of the great house and were sheltering down there as the world above them burnt. But even though they were safe from the flames they knew they were in danger as the air burnt. They could well suffocate.

And as they sheltered there, shaking with shock, fear and confusion, wondering what had happened and where the great steel beasts had come from, not a one of them suspected that they had been sent by the king. Not a one of them would have imagined that the former king was even now sitting in his private sanctum, watching the entire battle on his magical window, and celebrating even as he planned the next house's demise.

Mostly they just prayed that they would somehow survive the night.

Chapter Thirty Five

The Fallbrights were gone! Dead! Heri crowed to himself about that. In fact it brought a huge smile to his face as he sat in his sanctum and chewed on his trail bread. He had been celebrating all night long. In addition to destroying his enemies' home and killing all who resided within the drakes had taken out half of Bainbury as well. He hadn't asked or wanted that, but the steel drakes had been thorough and the town had burned. Still, though he hadn't asked for it, it could prove useful. If any Fallbrights survived their people would be angry with them. Raising an army would be that much harder for them because of it. They wouldn't be a threat for a long time to come.

It had been a good night.

Still, he guessed there were at least a dozen more noble houses that had to be destroyed, and next on his list was Griffin Dale. The self-styled principality was home to the Venti House, and while the Fallbrights might have been his most annoying rivals for the throne, the Ventis were the most powerful. In fact they'd held the throne until his father had assumed it from them after the attack that had nearly levelled the kingdom and killed the old king. The stupid old fool had actually led his soldiers onto the field of battle. He wouldn't do that twice! And while the Ventis had tolerated Eric Hanor – they'd had to when the people so openly supported him – Heri's rule had been far less tolerable to them. He wasn't quite sure why. He had reversed many of his father's decisions, allowing the noble houses to prosper once more. They should have been grateful. But instead they kept objecting to his rulings in Court, all but openly defying him. And with six large towns – three of them cities in all but name – they could raise a massive army. The Ventis house was the largest of any of the houses. And really, just the fact that they addressed their lord as "Prince" was an offence. Prince Venti had to die.

"Troll blood!"

Heri activated the window into the Dragon's cavern and the moment he spotted the Dragon at work, yelled at him. Once again he made him jump. It was good to see the troll blood jump. But he wasn't surprised by it. The Dragon wasn't physically the largest and most powerful of trolls. And trolls often ate one another when they weren't beating each other to death. He would not survive long among his own kind, and very likely the only way he had even made it to adulthood was by being quick on his feet.

"Again?" The troll blood turned to him, his wrinkled face even more hideous than Heri remembered. "I did what you wanted."

"You did and it was a good start. But there are a lot of nobles in Fair Fields to be killed and your drakes are nearby." He assumed they still were. It had taken them nearly a week to arrive in the kingdom. They weren't fast flyers. Certainly not as fast as pigeons.

"And when they're gone you can take the throne?"

"There is no throne left. No king, no throne, no city." Heri responded instantly with the answer he had always known he needed. Because he could never afford for the Dragon to know who he was. But even as he said it he was thinking that the troll blood was quicker mentally than others. He was not just a troll. But then he wouldn't be. He was a wizard. And he was already trying to work out who his new master was.

"Let's just say that I have reasons for wanting the entire Court dead. You destroy the houses and I'll take care of the rest."

"And is that it?" The Dragon looked upset as well as angry. He sounded it too. But he knew he didn't have a choice – for the moment.

"For Fair Fields yes. But there are some elves that need killing too."

"I'm not going to war with the elves!" The Dragon responded instantly.

But was he a little too quick? Heri thought he might be. There might even have been a touch of alarm in the troll blood's voice. Even his wrinkles betrayed a trace of panic.

"Is there a problem with the elves?" Heri asked casually. But inside he wasn't casual at all. He was thinking that if there was a weakness there he needed to know about it. Because at some stage he was going to have to kill the troll blood. Or get someone else to do it. Maybe the elves could handle that for him.

"They are not my enemy."

That was a lie Heri knew. The Dragon was no master of the deceptive arts. That required intelligence. "You destroyed Shavarra."

"We have reached an understanding."

Another lie! Heri knew he was on to something. The Dragon was frightened of the elves. And that could surely only mean that he had reason. That he'd had his nose somehow bloodied by them. It was time he decided to start spying a little more on the elves. But for the moment he didn't need to push it.

"Alright then. You destroy the nobles of Fair Fields and I'll destroy the elves."

The Dragon didn't answer him, but Heri saw his eyes widen as he heard him say he'd destroy the elves. Partly in surprise, but partly he suspected in hope. The troll blood wanted them dead. But it was beyond him. And there Heri had his weapon. He would use the elves to kill the Dragon. The Dragon to kill the nobles. And in the ruin of both lands he would retake the throne. And maybe he would even take Shavarra too. There was little of it left and no one guarding it after all.

"Who next?"

"The Venti Family of Griffin Dale. They once threw me in a dungeon when I was very young. They claimed I was an enemy wizard. I think it's time they burnt for that crime, don't you?" He lied to the Dragon about his motives, wanting him to have no clue who he was. He doubted the troll blood had any idea at all he was being lied to. He really was a simple creature.

"Where?"

"Griffin Dale. The town of Griffin Hold. And you should know they have cannon. Your beasts should attack at night, unseen."

Heri gave him the rest of his instructions – they weren't really that complex – and then cut the connection. After that he collapsed back into the heavy leather embrace of the chair and celebrated with a little more watered down wine. He had a point of attack to use with the Dragon. And he had the Dragon's services until then. It was now only a matter of working out how best to use them.

Destroy the noble houses. Kill the Dragon. Take the throne. Get this accursed geas lifted from him. And finally kill his brother. At last things were starting to come together.

Chapter Thirty Six

Winter had loosened its grip on the land and the difficult weather of spring was taking hold. And while spring wasn't always the easiest of seasons Ry for her part was glad of its arrival. The storms, wind and rain weren't always the most pleasant but the cold of winter spent in a wagon was worse. She didn't want to spend a second one in it – though the chances were that she would. But at least they would be better prepared for it. More rugs, warmer clothes. More food and more firewood. Their new Shavarra was coming along well and with it the gardens and farms. Of course there was always a chance she would be with child by then, and she didn't want to give birth in a wagon if she could avoid it. But that might not be a choice either. Building a city for nearly three hundred thousand people took time.

At present they had homes for maybe twenty thousand, and they were the families with the most and/or the youngest children. The ones in most need of shelter. They hadn't even started building the shrine to the Goddess. The people cried out for it. They needed a place to go to worship. She did too. But even that had to wait. The priests and priestesses had to work from a small grove they were busy planting in their free time, as they wandered among the people bestowing the favours of the Goddess. It wasn't a choice for them either.

As for the elders, it would be years before there was a Fiore Elle. And until then they would have to meet in the little clearing where they had decided it would one day be built as they decided the matters of the day. They had no choice in that.

And it seemed that keeping the elders away was not to be a choice for her and her family in turn. Not when her husband was the Fire Angel. They simply had to live with them. Not that she minded Elder Bela. He was actually a warm and friendly man once you got past his gruff exterior, and his wife was fun to talk to. In fact she rather liked Ellise. But there was so much formality in dealing with the elders. And though they didn't want it and refused most of the trappings of hospitality, they were respected elders and it had to be done. Ry would not shame her family by being less than respectful to any elder.

So the table was always set out for Elder Bela when he came and he was given blankets and cushions. The tea was the best they had as was the food they served him. And they always addressed him respectfully. It didn't matter what he wanted. He was an elder.

It would have helped if Samual was with her when he visited. Most of the Elder's words were for him anyway and she and the rest of her family could make themselves scarce while they spoke. But Samual had been called away by War Master Wyldred only a few moments before, leaving Elder Bela sitting there all alone and needing to be attended to.

Her father was speaking with the Elder about the state of the wagons in their new home as they prepared for the coming summer, something Elder Bela probably didn't know a lot about or want to. But he listened politely, regardless. Meanwhile her mother was preparing some food for the Elder and she was serving him tea. But really, they were all just waiting for Samual to return.

"Elder Bela."

A man's voice came from behind her, causing Ry to jump a little. She hadn't known anyone was there. And it was somewhat rude to creep up on people. But when she turned to see who it was, it was to discover that things weren't as she'd expected. There was no man standing there behind her. Instead there was a window. Or rather, it was the only thing she could describe it as. A window hanging in the middle of the air with no wooden frame and no wall to support it. And through that window she could see a man sitting in a darkened room, his face concealed in shadow.

But she thought she knew him regardless. There was something about the voice that she recognised. And that something she didn't like. He was human too. He was speaking trade, not Elvish as everyone here did.

"I am. And you would be?" Elder Bela responded easily, as if this was something that happened every day.

Maybe it did. He was a wizard after all. But it was shocking to Ryshal and her parents who had never seen anything like it before.

"Someone who has a little information you might want to hear."

And someone who had the tone of a meddler Ryshal thought. He sounded arrogant and somewhat amused. As if this whole thing was some sort of game. A jest he was playing. And she was becoming ever more certain she knew the jester.

"Which would be?"

"The location of the Dragon of course." The man in the shadows laughed as if he had said something amusing. Or maybe he thought it amusing that he knew something that the Elder didn't.

"You know where he can be found?" The Elder sounded interested but still calm, despite learning that this stranger could tell them what was surely the most important piece of information there could be.

"Of course," the man in shadows responded smugly.

"Where?"

"There is an island roughly a hundred and fifty leagues south east of Ragnar's Rock. It is a giant volcano in truth, with two smaller mountains on either side. They rise up out of the ocean and are known by sailors as the Three Sisters. The sailors avoid them because of the rocks and the frequent storms that assail the coast. There are also stories of terrible monsters that lurk on the island."

"However, if you arrive from the east and sail close to the coast, you will see that there is a hidden cove where scores of black sailed ships are moored. If you dock there, there is a path leading up into the volcano itself, and a great series of caverns inside it. That is where the Dragon creates his armies of machina."

"The Dragon himself is a troll blood, forced apart from the rest of his kind because of his small size. He would have been eaten early in life were it not for his magic. For decades he has been alone, building his armies in secret. Dreaming of the day when he can destroy the entire world."

"He believes that day is at hand. Or he did until your people handed him a stinging defeat at the Bronze Mountains. He still has plans on his tables of the attack and no thought as to how he could have lost the battle. Now he is busy rebuilding his armies, determined to become even stronger. Determined to crush you."

Determined to crush them? That filled Ryshal with fear. But it also sounded disturbingly accurate. The Dragon had come for them twice. Once at Shavarra where he'd destroyed their home. And once at the beginning of the Dead Creek Pass, where his steel drakes had been destroyed. She had no doubt he would want to try again. Especially after their victory at the Bronze Mountains.

"And how would you know this? Unless perhaps you know the Dragon?" The Elder seemed unmoved by the thought of the Dragon coming for them again. In fact he calmly took a sip of his tea as if it was simply a normal meeting.

"Is it not obvious?" The man in the shadows gestured in front of him, presumably at the magical window. "I am one of the unseen."

"No. I don't think so. There is no magic in you. Mischief, but no magic." The Elder denied his claim almost casually despite the fact that he was speaking to them from a window hanging in the middle of the air. "So who are you? And how do you know what you claim?"

"King Heri Hanor," the man in the shadows began. Then he started. "Alder's hairy tits! Why did I say that?" He sounded frightened.

"Because it is the truth and you want to tell the truth," Elder Bela told him simply. "And that unless I am mistaken is a Window of Parsus. It requires no magic to operate. Just a few words. Please continue."

Heri! It was him Ryshal knew. She knew that superior tone only too well. And she knew a moment of pure hatred for him. For the dungeon he had thrown her in. For the way he had torn her from her husband's side. But for him she should already have children and a happy, growing family. Why wasn't he dead?! Yet she had to hold back her anger. Not only would it go against the Goddess' teachings, but it would also have served no purpose when he had information they needed. So Ry swallowed her fury while Heri's confession continued.

"I tracked the Dragon down by following his ships with

this window after the attack on Ragnor's Rock."

"And you have done more than just find him, haven't you?" The Elder accused him of more crimes. "What exactly have you done?"

"Yes," Heri grudgingly admitted the truth, and then started telling the Elder all that he had done. And every so often when he paused to take a breath he kept asking how it was that he could be telling Elder Bela everything. But the Elder started him speaking again with just a few words.

That made Ryshal smile. The fool had contacted an elder with the magic of nature and thought to use him as a tool. But he had forgotten something so simple. If he could speak and be heard, the Elder could do the same. And a lot of his magic was in his words.

It was a terrible tale that Heri told. Half a dozen noble houses in Fair Fields had been destroyed by Heri through his deal with the Dragon. And the towns around them had been burnt. They were monstrous acts in a time when the entire kingdom was already at war. And yet she had already known that he had destroyed his own keep. He had admitted the destruction of Fall Keep when they had first captured him.

Was there no goodness in him at all she wondered? And was this all because he hated Samual? It seemed too much. Or were his actions the result of his nurturing? Samual had been raised by his father to be good and noble in his heart. Heri had been raised by his mother to crave power above all else. Could it be that simple? No doubt she would have to discuss that with the priests.

Naturally the tale grew worse as he started telling the Elder everything else he had done. Where he was and what other ancient treasures he had in his underground chamber. How he had obtained them. And all the other crimes he had committed.

She knew some of them of course. Samual knew some of them and had told her. But there were so many more. And even though the elders had interrogated him after the attack on them, even Elder Bela seemed taken aback by them. It seemed that each crime had led to another. Each atrocity had made the next one easier for him. So easy in fact that it meant nothing to him that he had killed his own mother. He had let her be killed in the destruction of Fall Keep. That she hadn't known. Neither had Elder Bela she guessed from the way his calm visage slipped a little when he heard the words trip off Heri's tongue.

Still, the Elder carried on, quickly controlling his shock as he listened. Until finally Heri was done.

"And now Heri, you will start atoning for your crimes. And it will begin with never speaking to the Dragon again. You will not converse with him, nor will you ever try to use his creatures again. Is that understood?"

"Yes."

It was understood. But it wasn't liked. Ryshal could hear that in Heri's tone. He didn't want to do as the Elder demanded, just as he hadn't wanted to say what he had said. And if his face hadn't been concealed in shadow she would have guessed it would have been wrapped up in fury. But really it was his own foolishness that was at fault. He had opened a window to an Elder, not realising that the wizard's ability to command the beasts of the world with a few simple words could cross through the window and command him in the same way.

"Next, all of the magical treasures you have collected will be delivered to us. We do not want the gold. That you will give to the people you have hurt. All of the gold. But every one of those ancient artefacts you will wrap carefully. You will place them on the back of a wagon and transport them to the Fair Fields side of the Dead Creek Pass as quickly as you can. A patrol of elves will meet you there to carry them on. Is that understood?"

"Yes." Heri agreed instantly. But he really didn't want to do that. Every tortured syllable out of his mouth screamed that he hated the very idea. But he seemed to have no choice.

"Good. Then you may begin." Elder Bela dismissed him and a few heartbeats later Heri shouted something and the image of him and the window vanished. But it left the Elder sitting there looking as sour as anyone had ever been.

"Elder?" Ryshal interrupted him cautiously when he didn't move for a bit.

"That young man is beyond understanding." The Elder shook his head sadly. "He lacks any sense of right and wrong. Any compassion. And I cannot help but believe that we acted hastily when we made our deal with him. We have let loose a monster upon the world. That cannot happen again."

"Yes Elder." Ryshal bowed her head. She agreed with him completely. It was a shameful thing to even think of killing a man, but in this case it seemed the only thing to do. If he was free he would only cause more suffering. That was his nature.

"This poison was fed to him by his mother in his very milk." Ryshal's father abruptly spoke up startling everyone. He had been completely silent until then. "He is undoubtedly guilty of a great many crimes. But a crime was done to him before he was even old enough to understand."

"True." The Elder nodded sadly. "But it does not change things."

"It does perhaps suggest that he should make restitution to his victims. And that his fate should lie with them. And there is one here with us who has suffered a life time because of the crimes of his mother. One who his words could perhaps heal."

"It would not be right to send Samual to meet him. To have brother killing brother. And he has many duties here."

"I was not thinking of Samual, Elder," Pietral answered him. "I was thinking of Samual's sister."

"Sister?" The Elder sounded surprised.

"Mayvelle Ellosian. A woman of great anger since she found out that her mother was poisoned by Heri's mother. And who believes falsely that her father was responsible. There is a rift in the family because of it. If it is at all possible I would like to see that rift healed."

Her father was right Ryshal realised. And it was a clever idea. To at least heal one small hurt would be a good thing. And she would be grateful if it could in turn heal her husband. He still felt anger for what Mayvelle had said. The charges she had laid at his dead father's feet. He controlled it, tried to hide it from her, but it was there. But Mayvelle might not be so amenable to having her hurt fixed. She was comfortable with her pain. It had become a part of her. And so the chances were that she would simply kill Heri on the spot rather than ask him the questions she needed to.

In a strange way the two of them were alike. Both proud and both stubborn. Both prone to anger. And both soldiers. So she had to believe that if they were the same in those things then they were also the same in having good hearts. And a good heart could make up for a lot of faults.

Still, Ryshal thought there was hope. She would go to the temple such as it was and offer a prayer to the Goddess that

Mayvelle would ask of Heri the questions in her heart – before she killed him! After all the Goddess had kept her alive for all those years in her cell, and shaped her husband into the Fire Angel. She could do something for his sister, surely.

And maybe she suddenly thought, that was why Heri was so different from his brother. Samual believed. He followed the All Father instead of the Goddess, but at least he chose to follow a god. Heri believed in no one but himself. He was godless. Godless and a slave to his own depravity.

Maybe she should say a prayer for him as well. A prayer that he would finally find the Goddess. Even if it was in death.

Chapter Thirty Seven

It had been a hard ride through the desert. Dry and dusty and the heat had been no friend of hers. But despite the hardships they had made good time, managing to reach and then cross the Dead Creek Pass in under a month. She knew she should be pleased with that. But really Mayvelle was quietly groaning at the thought that the journey was only half over. They had to return yet. Almost as soon as they met up with Heri. But they had packed for it. They had good food, lots of water and good steeds. Mayvelle expected that they would complete their mission in the minimum time.

And when she spotted the wagon in the distance as they exited the pass, she guessed that they would be starting their return journey within a matter of hours. There wouldn't even be time to rest.

Mayvelle was surprised that Heri was there already. She had expected to have to wait here at this last watering hole for some time, perhaps even weeks, waiting for Heri to show up. He was in a wagon after all. But somehow he had matched them for speed. Partly she guessed that that was because his wagon was a coach drawn by four horses. But mostly she suspected it was because he was under a compulsion. He had had to get here as quickly as possible.

He did not look well. As they approached the former king she became convinced of that. Sickness showed in his eyes and exhaustion was etched into the lines of his face. It was as if he had driven the horses day and night to get here. That he hadn't rested in all that time. Maybe he hadn't? Elder Bela was a master of the natural magics and she imagined that if he put a compulsion on someone it would force them to do whatever he required, regardless of their physical failings.

She didn't care about that though. She cared only that he was a monster. And that Elder Bela not only knew that she was Samual's sister, but that he had insisted she speak with Heri about her parent's deaths. She didn't want to do that. But she also didn't want to disobey an elder. Or upset her own parents either.

Things had been uneasy in the family home ever since they had told her the truth. For that reason she had been grateful to be able to spend as much time as she could with her patrol. Still, she had had to go home every so often and face the truth that not only were her parents not her parents but rather her aunt and uncle, but that they had lied to her for her entire life. It had not been an easy thing to accept. And if what her brother had told her was correct, they had possibly lied to her about more than just her parentage. She didn't know if she could face the thought that they might have simply abducted her from her dead mother's arms without truly believing that her father was responsible for Alliye's death.

That was why she'd perhaps responded so aggressively to Samual's denials of his father's nature. More harshly than she should have. Because it seemed that either her brother was lying about their father, and she was the daughter of a murdered woman and her murderer. Or her parents were lying and she had been abducted and stolen from a loving father. Neither option was good. And now she was due to find out the truth.

The patrol covered the last little distance to where Heri was sitting on his coach waiting for them. Before going forward she and her patrol checked that there was no ambush waiting for them. It was something they did almost by reflex whenever they arrived somewhere. And if there was anyone who would set one up, it would be Heri. He was nothing short of evil. And he was her half-brother as she had to keep reminding herself.

By the Goddess – how could she be related to this piece of vermin?! It was just plain wrong. She could live with the thought of Samual Hanor as her brother. He was arrogant and short tempered, and clearly he had no understanding of elven sensibilities. But at least he was honourable. But Heri?! That was simply too terrible for words.

There was no trap of course. Though really, she would have thought anyone willing to take on a patrol of sixty elven soldiers would want an army with him. She had no doubt that Heri would have had one with him if he could have. But equally she knew that he couldn't set a trap for them. Apart from the compulsion which she knew would keep him under control Heri was fairly obviously at his end. This was not the arrogant, devious and monstrous creature who had attacked them before. This was a wretch.

"Heri Hanor?" Captain Yossil greeted him. Heri just nodded in reply.

"Is all as it should be?"

"Yes." Heri bowed his head, clearly exhausted. He might even have been expecting to be killed.

And really Mayvelle thought, if there was any justice in their path they would kill him. An arrow through the heart would be quick and clean and it would stop him from harming others. But the Elder had told them not to. Heri had committed many crimes since being released from their care, but none against their people. He was a human and should be tried by his own people.

"Then you may get down from the wagon and depart, after you have answered some questions."

"Questions?" But even as he asked Heri was already

getting down from the coach.

"Ellosian!" The Captain called to her and immediately Mayvelle dismounted and walked towards her half-brother. Meanwhile the others were dismounting and leading their horses to the creek. It was time to drink their fill.

"Captain." She nodded respectfully to her commanding officer.

"You have only a short while. I want to be gone from here as soon as possible."

"Thank you Captain." She nodded again and turned to Heri.

"You know of the deaths of Alliye Ellosian and Eric Hanor. Tell me of them." She put it simply, and didn't care if he recognised that her name too was Ellosian. She didn't even care if he refused to answer. Mostly she just wanted him gone.

"My mother killed them both. Hemlock and blood bane as I understand it. She fed the elven bitch the mixture over several long months, trying to kill her before she gave birth to another bastard child, but she was strong and lived as long as she could. My father she poisoned directly at his breakfast table, and then stabbed him with a dart to make it look as though an assassin had killed him. It was a desperate act, but she truly hated him."

For the longest time Mayvelle stood there staring at him, wondering how he could speak so casually about something so terrible. He was talking about the murder of his own father! It was beyond her ken. And yet the death of his father clearly meant nothing to Heri. What sort of coldness was that? Eventually though an obvious question did cross her mind.

"Why?"

"To rule of course. The elven whore was in her way. She was not and could not be queen but while she lived she prevented my mother from taking that place. She had to go. And then she did not want to have to live in the shadow of the king. So she spent years trying to kill my father. From soon after I was born in fact. She did it so she could be regent – queen in all but name."

"She would have killed me too in time. As soon as she had another heir to secure her position. But I was too quick for her." Heri smiled unexpectedly, the first sign of emotion he had shown.

"It doesn't upset you that she murdered your father?" Mayvelle wasn't sure she wanted to ask the question as she feared the answer. But the words slipped out before she could stop them.

"Upset me?" Heri looked surprised. "Why? My father had no time for me. He was always with his precious first born. The son of his only love. Prattling on about things like honour and nobility. And I had no time for him either. He was stupid and slow. I would have killed him myself when I came of age to claim the throne." He stared straight at Mayvelle as he said it, his gaze unflinching.

It was the truth, Mayvelle knew. Cold, bare and uncompromising. That was who and what Heri was. It was also presumably who and what his mother had been in order to raise him to be that. Samual had been right. His father – their father – had not been the killer her parents had told her he was. They might have been wrong rather than lying. But they had still stolen her from a father who would have loved her. That was a bitter potion to swallow.

"Thank you. Captain." Mayvelle turned and nodded to her commanding officer. Then she walked back to her horse who had by then had its fill of the water and was chewing contentedly on the grass. Her questions had been answered. It was just a pity that she didn't like the answers.

And then she mounted up and waited while others tended to the important things. Checking on the new horses, making sure they had enough water to drink and had not been run too hard for too long. Checking on the contents of the coach to make sure that what had been promised was there and intact. Filling water bags from the nearby creek. Preparing for the journey back. It took a while but soon everything was done and in order.

But there was still one more thing to do before they could set off.

"Heri Hanor." The Captain addressed the wretch standing to one side. "The elders have said that you may go free – but only after you have drunk this." He pulled a small stoppered bottle from his saddle bags.

"Poison?" Heri didn't even sound upset. He sounded broken. He looked it too, and he was scarcely able to meet the Captain's eyes.

"No. Just something to ensure that you commit no more crimes. A blessed vial from the priests of the Goddess."

A potion of adherence was what the priest who had brought it to the Captain had called it. A potion blessed by the temple so that those whoever drank it could never go against the will of the Goddess. And the Goddess did not tolerate murder. Mayvelle had been curious when she had watched the priest bring the potion to them. More though by the priest than the potion. He had been a human. That was unusual though the temple did not discriminate. But what had most marked him out as unusual for her was the man's beard. It had been a curious mass of curls and ringlets that she was sure had to be cultivated somehow. Hair simply did not grow like that. But if the potion worked as promised and Heri was prevented from committing any more crimes, then that was all that mattered. Not the strange grooming of a strange priest.

"I do not believe in the gods. What have they ever done for me?" Heri looked as though he wanted to refuse.

"Well then my orders are clear." The Captain waved and instantly sixty longbows were raised and the arrows pointed at Heri's chest. "You will either drink this or you will die here where you stand."

Heri stared at the longbows and the arrows pointed at him, and seemed to think things over. But it wasn't courage that made him stand there defiantly Mayvelle thought. It was tiredness. He was at his end and he saw little hope ahead of him. Eventually though some remaining thought of self-preservation took hold.

"Fine." He walked awkwardly toward the Captain and took the bottle from his hands. Then he unstoppered and upended it, swallowing the contents in front of them.

Nothing happened after that and Mayvelle was disappointed. It would have been nice to have seen him start clutching at his throat and fall to the ground, breathing his last. Or better yet if he had burst into flames. But the elders would not do that she knew. Nor would the priests.

"And so you are now bound to the Goddess' law," the Captain told Heri, as if he had passed sentence upon him. And maybe he had. "You may go."

"Be quick soldiers! I want to be gone from this place before I grow old." The Captain turned to the rest of them and gave the order and most of the rest of the patrol mounted up. The rest hurried whatever they were doing.

Mayvelle was happy to go. More than happy. She didn't want to be here any longer. Not even when she saw the small, broken figure of her half-brother trudging dispiritedly away with only the clothes on his back.

This had not been a good day. And there were worse ones ahead. The day when she would have to approach her parents with this truth. And the day when she would have to apologise to her brother.

Chapter Thirty Eight

Heri was bone tired. He'd never walked so far or for so long in his life. The accursed elves had stolen his horses along with his wagon and left him on foot. He hated them for that. As he did for making him drink whatever foul concoction they'd prepared. It had tasted like water but he knew better. The damned thing was a brew of magic. He didn't yet know what sort of magic, but he was sure it would be bad.

And it had all happened because of that miserable Elder! Elder Bela. Heri would have cursed his name to all the heavens but every time he tried the words just wouldn't come out of his mouth. That was more accursed elven magic he guessed. The Elder had decided he didn't want to be cursed and had made sure he wouldn't be.

Now he had nothing. All his treasures had been taken. Stolen! The things that he'd hoped could have brought him back his throne. But that hope was gone now. All he had left was gold, and that wasn't enough. Assuming he was even able to keep it. And he had a horrible feeling that the compulsion placed on him would have something to say about that. The Elder had told him as much.

He could do nothing now except live a normal life. A miserable peasant life with maybe enough gold to make it bearable. But he would never rule again. He would never have the nobles of the land bow before him. He would never have balls held in his honour. Not that he liked the balls – he hated them – but still they were held for him and he valued that. People would no longer tremble before him when they saw him on his throne. Nor would they come before him begging.

Everything was gone. Taken from him by the elves and that miserable half-brother of his! They had left him with nothing. In fact now he *was* nothing. That was one lesson his mother had taught him very clearly. Power was everything. To be without it was to be nothing. A nobody. And that was now who he was. Another miserable nobody trudging his way across the endless fields and rolling hills back to Fall Keep. The only difference between him and so many others was the direction he was travelling in and the fact that he knew there was a crypt there stashed with gold.

Things couldn't get any worse.

But typically just as he was thinking that they did. A party of riders crested the hill in front of him and came charging in his direction. Heri knew a moment of fear when he saw them. And that fear only grew when he saw that they were flying the flag of the House of Cameral, one of his most annoying rivals and one of the few houses still standing. Because they were so weak he hadn't gotten around to sending the drakes after Tyne Keep before everything had gone wrong. Now the house looked like becoming one of the new powers in the realm. Maybe Lord Cameral himself would even become king in time. After everyone else had been killed off. His riders were out. Even now they were scouring the lands looking for survivors of the other noble houses and killing them. There was no room in Fair Fields for rivals who couldn't defend themselves. They were probably killing off any peasants who got in the way as well.

Meanwhile all he had on him was a knife against a score of heavily armed riders. And a ruined hand. He wasn't going to fight his way out of this Heri knew. And even if he'd had some poison, that wouldn't have been a possibility either. All he could do was bow and grovel and hope they ignored him as worthless.

As the party rode towards him though, he feared that they might not. They looked like they were riding to war. They were certainly dressed for it, with all of them decked out in their best armour and carrying their finest blades. Had war been declared somewhere?

"You! Who are you and where are you going?" The leader of the band called out to Heri even before they'd pulled up.

"Just a homeless wanderer heading for Stonebridge."

He shouldn't have said it. Heri knew that even before he felt the touch of a boot on his face. He shouldn't have dared to look directly at the leader. Nor should he have forgotten to address him as "Sir". The touch of his heavy boot sent Heri flying to the ground while all around the soldiers laughed. He needed to remember to be more respectful. And as he sat up holding his face and wondering how many teeth he was going to lose, he knew it was probably a valuable lesson for his new life.

"That's Sir to you! Or didn't your mother teach you any manners?!" The leader told him off while his troops kept laughing.

"Sorry Sir." Heri didn't try to get up. He knew that that would be a mistake. And he kept his gaze averted. Staring at the man would be a mistake. He was no longer King. He was a nobody. He kept forgetting that.

But why had he said he was going to Stonebridge? That wasn't where he was going. Why would anyone go there? It was just a bunch of ruins. Not even a village any longer. But the name had simply slipped out when he had meant to say Fall Keep.

"Better." The leader managed a cruel smile. "Seen any riders?"

"Just elves Sir. Heading into Dead Creek Pass. This morning." Heri wanted to rip out his tongue when the words came out of his mouth. Why had he said it? He should have said no. That he'd seen no one. It was the quickest and easiest path to safety. But again his mouth seemed to be betraying him. What was happening?

"Elves?"

"Fifty or sixty of them Sir. Riding west. And with a wagon." The words just kept coming out of his mouth! Someone else had control of his tongue! It was the only thing he could think of. It had to be more accursed elven magic!

"How long ago?"

"Five or six hours Sir." Heri wasn't even surprised when the words came out of his mouth by then. He couldn't seem to stop them.

"More damned elves!" The leader spat on the ground and for once Heri could only agree with him. They were a plague race. But he lay on the ground in silence and waited to be spoken to. He was smart enough to realise that that was the only way he was going to avoid a beating.

"Captain?" One of the other soldiers spoke up.

"The elves are no concern of ours. Lord Cameral made that clear. We head south." With that the Captain waved his hand and the party wheeled around. He had given his decision and that was it. Heri of course was completely forgotten as they thundered off south leaving him sitting there nursing his jaw.

He hated them. He hated the Captain most of all for kicking him in the face. One day when he had some sort of power back, he would hunt down and kill that man. But he also understood them. They had power. They could do what they wanted. He had none and he could do nothing. He simply had to do as he was told. It was humiliating and humbling. But it was how the world worked and he had to remember it if he didn't want to get beaten again.

There was a bigger problem though he realised as he got to his feet. His feet. They weren't taking him due east to Fall Keep he suddenly realised. They were taking him very slightly north east. In the direction of Stonebridge. He had not only lost control of his tongue but also his feet!

"Al –!" He tried to curse the elves in the name of the god of mischief, but the name died on his lips before he could even get it out. Apparently even speaking the name of a rival god was unacceptable to whoever controlled his tongue. Which left him having to curse silently as his feet started carrying him in the wrong direction.

What in all the hells had the poxy elves done to him?!

By the All Father, why had he ever got involved with the damned elves?! The whole miserable race was more trouble than they were worth. And now he would never be able to kill them.

Why did the gods hate him so?

Chapter Thirty Nine

It was late and everyone who had any sense had retired for the night. The only ones left awake were those who had to be. Mostly they were guards. Allivre had the honour of being one of those guards. And the honour of being awake at such an unwelcome hour. A plague on all the damned honours he thought! It was too damned cold!

Still, someone had to watch over these ancient treasures. According to the elders they included some of the most powerful weapons ever created. One in particular which could destroy entire cities. They could not be allowed to fall into the wrong hands. Though there were no hands here save for those of his people, and they were never the sort to do stupid things.

Meanwhile a young sage was sitting in front of the Window of Parsus, watching the Dragon as he created his armies. Of course it was late where the Dragon was too, and he wasn't doing anything at that particular time either. The troll blood had collapsed into a chair and fallen asleep. There was nothing for the sage to report on save that he snored like a wild animal.

The Dragon didn't look like much of a threat to Allivre. Certainly he didn't look like a creature who could destroy the world. He was troll blood not pure troll. Though that might be what gave him his magic, it also stole from him the size of his trollish ancestors. His tusks were smaller than those of true trolls, though they looked just as sharp. And he did not have the breadth of shoulder or length of arm that his cousins did. Even the axes he carried strapped to his belt were under sized. Allivre fancied that he could stand against him with spear and shield if he had to. Of course it was the armies of machina that made him dangerous.

And yet this was the miserable creature that had attacked Shavarra and driven them from their home. Who had murdered so many of his friends. He might look somewhat unimpressive, but he had to die!

"Ginseng and wild herb tea?" A voice came from out of the darkness startling Allivre, and he looked around hastily, worried that an enemy had crept up on him unawares. But it was only a young priest carrying a pot of hot tea.

"Thank you priest. And praise to the Goddess." Allivre accept the cup with good grace. He was actually grateful for it. It had been a long night already. And even though he knew it was a minor breach of the rules for the priest to be there, he decided not to say anything. The priest might not return another night.

He was a strange one for a priest Allivre thought. Mainly it was the beard that seemed odd. Most elves didn't grow beards. They didn't have the full facial hair that the humans did and so what grew was often wispy and patchy. But the priest had a full beard of tightly curled ringlets. In all likelihood he wasn't a full elf. He might even be human though it was hard to be certain when he had his hood up.

That was not an issue though. The temple had no rules about who could serve and who couldn't. The belief in the Goddess and the desire to serve was their only concern. And if the priest was bringing tea to the weary on watch in the middle of the night, that was surely a sign that he served.

"It is a cool night," the priest commented. "Surely you should have more braziers than that."

"It would be nice," Allivre agreed. But really he knew they had two braziers, one each for the two of them. They were actually doing well. And they weren't getting any more so there was no point in complaining about it. Still, he decided as he looked at the little copper basket full of burning coals beside him and pulled his cloak a little tighter around him, a man could dream.

"A little chill is good." The sage spoke up. "It keeps us alert when we have important work to do."

"Always true, praise the Goddess. Especially when you keep watch on her enemies."

The priest gestured toward the window floating in the air just in front of them. "You know he is such a small creature for one who has caused such terrible pain. So much pain. He looks so weak."

"Be glad he can't hear you Priest. His armies seem to grow and grow without end." Allivre was glad the Dragon couldn't hear them. That he didn't know they were watching him. Because his greatest fear was that the Dragon would send another army for them. He was not alone in that.

"Have faith child. The Goddess has provided her most powerful warrior to us and he has defeated the Dragon's armies three times. Destroyed them completely. In Shavarra he beat them back. The steel drakes at the edge of the wastes were destroyed. And in the Bronze Mountains he devastated an entire army. He grows ever stronger. The Dragon ever more doomed. It is only a matter of time until the Fire Angel completes his work and the world is returned to its rightful order."

That was the day they all prayed for. Allivre as much as anyone. So he wasn't disturbed by the way the priest subtly chided him for his fear. Fear was doubt, and those who followed the Goddess should never doubt. He nodded his thanks for the reminder.

"I pray that that day comes soon."

"It cannot be far away child. After all, we now know where the Dragon may be found. It is only the distance to his island that holds us back. And the Fire Angel grows in strength all the time as he prepares. Soon he will ride for him and the Dragon will be no more. When he is done I doubt that any of that island will remain above the southern ocean."

"He, his twisted machina and the island all will be a spectacle for the fish to enjoy." The priest managed a reassuring smile. "But in any case I have tarried too long. There are others I must attend to on this cold night."

With that the priest nodded politely to them both and then continued on his way with his kettle of tea. As he disappeared into the darkness Allivre could only hope he returned again. Not only was the tea welcome, but so was having someone to speak to during the long night hours. The sages weren't as a rule so cheery. And the one who was keeping watch over the window was even less so.

A few hours later as dawn finally found the sky once more and their replacements arrived to take over their places, he discovered something else about the sages. They weren't that capable at their work. Somehow the sage had managed to activate the window so that it worked both ways. The Dragon could see and hear them as they could see and hear him.

The sage swore to the elders that he had done nothing. That he hadn't activated the window. But he was young and uncertain.

Whether the Dragon knew they were watching him no one could say. After all the Dragon had been asleep in his chair the whole time. Allivre could attest to that. But still, it had been dark. He could not see if the Dragon's eyes had been open or closed. And Allivre worried that he might have been awake. That he might have been feigning sleep. And that could be bad.

What would the Dragon do if he realised he was being watched?

It didn't occur to him to wonder what he would do if he had heard what the priest had said about the Fire Angel coming to destroy his island and kill him. Not until much later that was. And then when it did, the questions were finished and the elders had left them.

But what could it matter? It was only the comforting words of a priest after all.

Chapter Forty

"A copper for your dreams my love."

Sam looked up to see Ry's smiling face and he gave thanks once more for her survival. Without her life had almost not been worth living. With her little else mattered. Especially when she sang as she had been doing for most of the day.

"They're not worth that much beloved."

And in truth they weren't, and hadn't been for far too long. Though it wasn't fair to her or anyone else, ever since he had heard that Heri had survived he had been walking along a precipice on the edge of despair that threatened to swallow him whole. How did Heri keep surviving? Why did the gods allow it? And now he had learned his brother had even been consorting with the Dragon! It was like some sort of celestial joke that mortals couldn't understand. Only the gods could. Maybe only Alder himself. It was some sort of mischief after all.

As if that wasn't enough his sister had gone to meet with Heri. And though the party had returned weeks before with all the magical sundries Heri had gathered over the years, he had not seen her since. So he didn't know what Heri had told her. He didn't know what she believed. And he wasn't sure he wanted to find out. His last few meetings with her – in fact all his meetings with Mayvelle – had gone badly. Each one worse than the last. The next one could be disastrous.

To be honest though ever since returning from that great and terrible battle of the Bronze Mountains, even though they had been victorious Sam's thoughts had been sour. That was three long months ago. He wasn't alone in that either, and many of the elders had hidden themselves away simply to stop themselves upsetting their families as they ruminated upon the future.

For most it was a victory and little more than that. Officially over twenty thousand of the enemy had been destroyed, though no one had actually counted, and he put it at more like thirty. Some put it higher still. Nothing of the machina's master had been heard of since. Save of course for what his half-brother had been doing with his steel drakes and what the elders saw of him through the Window of Parsus. Sam did not get to hear much of that.

Many dared to hope it was over. But for those who studied tactics and war, as great as what they'd achieved was, it was only a holding action in a war, and no more. In fact the war was only going to get worse. Even now Sam knew the Dragon would be readying his forces for a new target. Amassing his armies and planning his tactics. He would be stronger next time, and though the likelihood was that he would strike far away from the elves of Shavarra hoping to find easier prey, Sam knew that sooner or later he would return.

Against that day, Sam and the elders had been preparing their defences. Now not a day went by when Sam didn't enchant at least a few hundred to a thousand or more arrows and weapons in addition to his other duties. He wasn't alone. The elves had called in every known enchanter in all their lands, and they were all spending day and night enchanting weapons both in their own lands, and those of their nearer neighbours.

But the question remained. If the Dragon could send an army of twenty or thirty thousand machina so far inland to strike at a relatively unimportant target, how many more did he have available? And where would he send them next? When?

"So be it sour puss! Come and say hello to your wife."

Before he could even respond Ry grabbed his hand and started pulling him to his feet. And one thing about Ry; she was strong now. Even without his willing assistance she would very nearly have pulled him up all by herself. Her hair thus far was only a few inches long, but it was golden and thick, and it complemented the growing vitality of her skin. These days she shone with health, vitality and happiness, and he couldn't refuse her anything, least of all that. He guessed her students couldn't refuse her either, and she spent most of her afternoons now instructing the children in the dances of their people.

Ry took him in her arms and kissed him passionately, setting his heart beating a little faster. Maybe later he thought they could do something more than just kiss. They probably would. Now that she was so much recovered, she liked spending as much time in his arms as possible. And he liked it too. In fact it was some considerable time before they let each other go. And then it was only so they could breathe. And maybe laugh a little.

"Now that was worth a copper my husband!" She laughed happily, enjoying both the passion and the power she had over him. And Sam laughed with her. It was most definitely worth a copper.

"It was. But I think I should be the one paying you!" He pulled her tight and kissed her some more. By the All Father she felt good in his arms! Warm and soft and with all the right curves where she needed them. And she smelled even better. "In fact, I think I should be paying you more."

"How much more?"

"Everything I have of course.

"Then you should have everything you want."

Sam was left in no doubt as to what she meant when her hands started exploring him. But then there had never really been much doubt to begin with. It was lunch time. They were alone. The wagon was parked behind some trees where others couldn't see them. And they enjoyed themselves most lunch times when they were able to be together.

Now that Ry was so fully recovered from her ordeal, it seemed she was making up for everything she'd missed out on for all those years, and that most definitely included the pleasures that a husband and wife should share. There was not an evening that went past of late that they did not make love, and many lunch times too that they had spent in one another's arms. Some nights, while her parents were asleep in the wagon, they took some furs out by the fire and spent the entire night doing nothing more than being husband and wife under the stars.

Though he hadn't asked, ever since the healers had pronounced her fully recovered he suspected she had been trying to become pregnant, a goal which he shared. Their family was too small, and death of late had been too close a companion. A baby would be a most welcome blessing in such a terrible time, as well as a testament to the importance of the struggle for life itself. He hoped it would also be a way of keeping Ry safe at home and happy when he was away. Unfortunately he feared there would be more trips for him ahead.

Maybe it was time to ask.

"So beloved," he slid his hands around her waist until he had her belly in them, "how long do you think it will be before we can have this filled with an ellwyn mi fore?" He used the elvish phrase for baby which translated roughly as "promise of spring." He much preferred the term. And since it was actually spring it seemed somehow appropriate.

Ry laughed and coloured a little. But she didn't pull away.

"And how do you know it isn't already full?" She managed a cheeky grin.

"Is it?" He asked, more than a little curious.

"I don't know, but I don't think the day can be too far off. If that's what you want." She suddenly dropped her gaze, as if afraid to meet his eyes.

"That's very much what I want." He gently lifted her head up and kissed her as she wanted to be kissed. "And I notice that your parents are away for a while. The wagon is empty. We could get started now. If you approve."

Judging by her cheeky grin Sam gathered she very much approved. Quickly she grabbed his hands and started to lead him back to the wagon – not that she ever had to do much leading.

"Samual Hanor." The messenger's voice came from out of nowhere, and stopped Sam in his tracks. "The elders have asked for your presence."

Sam groaned quietly. The wagon was only a dozen paces away. And Ry was looking so eager. But he also knew it wasn't a choice. He had given his word.

"Please inform them that I'll be there shortly." He didn't want to say it. Not just then. But he had to. And it seemed to be enough for the messenger as he turned and headed back.

"I'm sorry beloved." He turned back to Ry.

"Don't be." Her cheeky grin broadened unexpectedly. "You've still got to change and that'll take at least a little while!" She started tugging at his hands again, pulling him the rest of the way to the wagon and then all but ordering him in to it.

It was more than a little while before Sam finally made it to the elders, and poor Tyla was breathing hard when they made it. She had had to gallop hard to get there.

No one said anything about his tardiness though. Nor did they comment on his somewhat dishevelled appearance either. They were too busy staring at the Window of Parsus. Ever since the Griffin border patrol had returned with it, the ancient artefact had become a favourite toy of the elders as they used it to spy on their enemy.

Heri had given them the location and description of the island as well as the window, and with that and a little time they had found the Dragon.

They'd found his secret too. The way he could build his massive armies. But the secret wasn't what they'd expected. It seemed that he didn't have to build each one himself. Instead, he built one of each type of machina, and then through some form of magic they didn't understand, the volcano copied it. Endlessly. There was a pit of lava in the heart of the lair that seemed to be as much molten metal as rock. And all the Dragon had to do was march one of his machina to a stone plinth above it and in short order an identical steel beast would march out of the lake of orange fire. When it cooled of course, another machina would be ready for his commands.

It wasn't the Dragon's magic at all. Because though he built the original and controlled the copies, the actually engine that built his armies was something from the ancient world. Probably something that had been around before even the first Dragon had appeared. In fact Sam was sure the first Dragon had simply found this place and used it as well. The only thing he didn't know was who had built it. Because the ancients had been incredibly powerful. Their knowledge and their magic had been beyond anything that existed any longer. It had to be for so much of it to survive five thousand or more years. But this seemed more like something of the gods themselves.

In the end though, who had built this ancient engine of production didn't matter. Though he might not have built the armies himself, the Dragon still had control of them and the magical engine that he could use to build ever more of them. And he would.

He was also a troll blood as they'd thought. That was the other thing they'd learned through the window. Though some had argued that anyone with troll blood couldn't possibly have the intelligence to do what he was doing, the Dragon clearly did. And he had the intelligence to learn. As they watched him they saw his designs for new machina. They saw his workshops where he built them one by one to assess them, then tore them down and rebuilt them until they were perfect.

They also saw his study and his books. His tables overflowing with maps and plans. They realised that he was learning the art of the war master. Studying campaign strategy and tactics. He might not be the most stable of souls – he was a troll blood after all – but he was determined to become an ever more dangerous enemy. More dangerous even than the first Dragon.

But there were other things they saw that chilled the soul. And perhaps the worst of them was the fate of those the Dragon abducted. It wasn't good. The Dragon considered himself a warrior. The troll equivalent at least. And as such he wanted to test himself. So the men were being given weapons and forced to defend themselves in a makeshift arena while the Dragon slaughtered them with a pair of hand axes he carried everywhere. Then he would offer prayers to Crodan, cut out their hearts and eat them. The women he accepted as his prize for his victories.

Of course it was never a fair fight. The Dragon was small being only troll blood, but still he was part troll. He had the strength and speed of his blood and the natural savagery. And those he fought generally weren't fighters. Some were little more than boys. Most looked to have never held a sword in their lives. They didn't last long. But then the Dragon had never intended that they should.

Since discovering the Dragon's island someone had always been stationed at the window to watch him. Sam didn't envy them that duty. But it had to be done. They had to check what he was doing, what creatures he was making, and most important of all try to work out where he was sending his next army.

The last they still didn't know. But they did know that his next army was big. Every bit as large as the one he had sent against the dwarves and the hillmen in the Bronze Mountains. And he had a new beast as well; wolves. They were slightly bigger than the rats and had longer legs and snouts filled with sharp steel teeth and razor sharp claws. Sam guessed that they would become the foot soldiers in his next army. They would also be much faster runners than the rats and would be able to chase down their victims. Sam had no doubt that few would escape once a wolf set its sights on its prey. And that was always the Dragon's goal; to kill everyone.

"Elders." Sam bowed respectfully to the elders as he approached.

"Samual." Elder Bela greeted him on behalf of the Council as he usually did. But for once there was a different expression on his face. Sadness perhaps. "We know the Dragon's next target."

If they did then that should have been a good thing Sam

thought. If you knew where he was going to strike you could prepare for him. But it didn't seem to be in this case. Elder Bela's face was longer than ever, and the rest couldn't even seem to look at him. That worried Sam.

"Where Elders?"

"Fair Fields. He's coming for Fair Fields."

The moment he said it Sam's legs went weak as he realised what he was saying. His family home was about to be destroyed. And there was nothing anyone could do about it. Thanks to Heri the entire kingdom was in chaos. The noble families had withdrawn to their various little corners of the land. And many of them were licking their wounds after Heri's attacks. None of them would come together to stand as one against an army of machina. And none of them were strong enough to stand alone.

He understood why the troll was constructing the wolves too. Fair Fields was a realm of flat lands and shallow hills, farms and open spaces. The forests were few and far between. The mountains uncommon. And the towns were largely undefended. In short, it was a land set up for wolves to roam. The wolves would run in packs and overrun the towns one after another. They would murder any travellers on the roads as well as those with homes in the farmlands. Refugees fleeing the towns would be hunted down and killed. There would be nothing left. No survivors.

"Show me." It was presumptuous of him to just order an elder about, but Sam had to see for himself. And when Elder Bela nodded to the young sage operating the Window for them, he did see.

The sage brought the image of the Dragon's chamber flying back from the massive army he was creating to a smaller chamber inside the mountain where he was sitting at a table. But the Dragon wasn't the sage's target. Instead he turned the view around until they were staring from above straight down at another table. One on which the map of Fair Fields was laid out. Several maps actually since it seemed he had plans of all the major towns. There was no doubt that the Dragon was studying Fair Fields extensively. And with the massive army he was building, little doubt why.

There was also no doubt that the Dragon knew he was being watched. The fear that they had been discovered had been confirmed. When every single map had all the names scrawled over and scratched out so that they couldn't be read, it was obvious that he didn't want anyone guessing where they were. But Sam knew the realm. He knew the contours of the land and the positions of the towns. He would not be so easily fooled. Nor apparently would the others.

Sam resisted the urge to bury his head in his hands. But it wasn't easy. Especially when he already understood why the Dragon was focussing his armies on Fair Fields. Heri!

Obviously since Heri had not been heard from for some time by the Dragon, he had decided his threats no longer held any weight. And he wanted Heri dead at all costs. Presumably he had decided that if he destroyed all of Fair Fields, murdered every man, woman and child he would have a good chance of doing just that. It was a simple plan. But it would work.

Why did it always have to be his little brother? Sam asked himself the question silently as he had so many times before. Whenever things went wrong of late, it always seemed to him that it was Heri's fault. Once it had just been him and Ry who had suffered. With Ryshal locked away and a continual string of assassins arriving in the middle of the night his anger and outrage had been purely personal. But lately it had grown worse. Heri was ruining everyone's lives. He had completely destroyed Fall Keep killing probably thousands. He had then gone on to destroy a number of the noble houses, probably killing thousands more in the process. The kingdom was engaged in civil war thanks to Heri, and the death toll from that would be beyond counting. And now there was an army of machina bent on wiping out every Fair Fielder. All of it was Heri's doing, and there could be no thought at all that he had not intended for it to happen.

Sam should have killed him long ago. It might have been murder. It might have been shameful as well. It might even have gone against his father's wishes – he had always hoped and prayed that Heri would have one day grown into a better man. But it would have saved so many lives.

Now though, they had to save as many more lives as they could.

Sam didn't even need to see the plans on the Dragon's table to know how he would mount the attack. There was only one way. Fair Fields was land locked. The nearest ports were the ones in Ore Bender's Mountains south east of Fair Fields. But there were only three of them and all were beside massive dwarven cities. All of them had heard about the attack in the Bronze Mountains, and had prepared defences in case the machina came for them. Plans that would no doubt begin with sinking the ships that carried them. No ships meant no enemy armies. It was that simple. Which was why their docks were now lined with cannon.

So the Dragon would not do that. Instead he would send his armies by air. He would land them somewhere where there would be little opposition. If Sam was to guess it would be at the ruined city of Fall Keep where few people remained. There he would build his forces up, behind the remains of the city walls. And finally once he thought he had enough he would send them out to destroy the realm town by town.

There would be no one to stop them. No thought of a

common defence. Not when thanks to Heri the kingdom was at war. The noble houses were all fighting one another. Many had been badly weakened. So even though Fair Fields was not a particularly useful strategic target such as the Bronze Mountains had been, it would be an easy victory for him.

Or could there be a strategy he wasn't seeing? In the Bronze Mountains the Dragon had sought a base from which he could grow his armies of machina. A realm surrounded by other realms which his armies could strike at. There were few realms that the Dragon's armies could strike at from Fair Fields. Just the dwarves in Ore Bender's Mountains and the gnomish of the Fedowir Kingdom – and that was a long trek. Neither was there a protected mountain home where his armies would be safe while he grew them. The only fortified city in the kingdom had been destroyed by Heri. Its walls had holes. Would this Dragon really launch such an invasion just to kill one man for no strategic advantage? Sam didn't know. But it did occur to him as he stood there worrying, that he might be missing something.

"How long do we have?" Sam asked what was in the end the only question that mattered, and got no answer. He wasn't surprised. They didn't know. They couldn't hear the Dragon without opening the window and revealing themselves. And they weren't going to do that. But even if they could have heard the Dragon it wouldn't have helped. The troll blood had no one to talk to. He didn't speak with those people his armies abducted. He fought and killed the men and raped and killed the women. That Sam thought, did not bode well for them. And of course the Dragon was not writing his plans and dates down for them to read. It was just lucky that he had some maps on his table for them to see.

But one thing Sam did know was that the attack would be soon. The chamber of the volcano was packed full of wolves, and he knew that they had to number in the many thousands. Thousands more were outside on the grass, lined up and waiting to be picked up by the balloons. Thousands of balloons!

"Elder we must stop him!" Sam spoke from the heart, frightened and desperate. "We cannot let the slaughter happen."

"How?"

"Can you not use your magic on the Dragon? Compel him to stop?"

"He is a mage of nature as am I. He may not have the command of others as I do, but his gift grants him protection against such magic just as yours does against fire."

Of course it did. Sam knew that. He had known it before. Others had asked the same question and the same answer had been given.

"Then amongst Heri's stolen ancient treasures? Surely there must be something?"

"No." Elder Bela shook his head sadly. "There are a great many weapons, but none that can destroy from such a distance. All we can do is warn the people. The window will allow us to do that at least. And we will continue to try to forge alliances where we can. But it will be with limited success. The realms are so divided. By distance. By people. By rulers. And by trust."

"The sylph of Racavor are the most powerful of the magical. The ones who could perhaps stop the Dragon. But they will not get involved. In fact they refuse to speak with us. They have even found a way to prevent the Window of Parsus from seeing into their Kingdom. The city of Istantia is dark to us."

"The dwarves of Ore Bender's Mountains are the strongest fighting force remaining, but they will not leave their cities. They fear the Dragon will return while their forces are divided. The gnomes of the Fedowir Kingdom have neither the fighting strength nor the magic to wage a war against the Dragon. The elves of Golden River Flats cannot reach Fair Fields in time. And both Shavarra and the Dead Belly Wastes are empty of people."

"It is sad but Fair Fields it seems must stand alone."

Elder Bela was right Sam knew. But the tragedy was that if Heri had not destroyed Fair Fields it would at least have made a credible stand. They had walled cities and towns and cannon. Even an army of steel wolves could not have broken the walls of Fall Keep. And now that they knew the steel drakes' weaknesses they could have hired weather mages. The termites could have been stopped by earth mages. Enough at least for the larger towns. But the city had been destroyed, the lords of the realm had gone to war with one another and there was no thought of mounting a common defence.

"Then I must go to the island and destroy him myself."

"It's more than five hundred leagues to the nearest coast and then there is a sea journey as well. You could not make it in time," the Elder told him sadly, his long face hanging even lower than normal.

He was right Sam knew. The distance was far too great. Even using his magic it would take over a month of hard riding just to reach the south east tip of the continent. And the sea journey after that posed even more problems. Possibly he could hire a ship, but a hundred and fifty plus leagues over open ocean was a big journey. Few would risk it. And he had no idea as to how long it would take. It depended on the winds he supposed. But that still wasn't good enough.

They needed to fly. But there were few who could, and none of them could fly such a distance. The weather mages who could lift themselves on a curtain of wind, could only manage that for short periods of time. Those who could shift shape into the form of a bird were equally limited. And of course, he could do neither.

"We must do something Elder!" But even as he said it he knew that they were just as helpless in this as he was. He could see it in the elders' faces as he looked around. They had brought him here to tell him the news because he had a right to know. But not because there was anything they thought he or they could do.

"And we will. As I have said, we will send warnings. And with luck those who heed our warnings will escape to other, nearby realms in time."

But how many would that be? That was the question. Sam could not see the noble houses fleeing. They would not abandon their homes. Their seats of power. It was who they were. And many of them would not allow their people to flee either. What was a fiefdom without people after all? They would stand and they would fight – and they would fall and they would die.

As he stood there, trying to think of something, anything to do, Sam slowly realised the awful truth.

Fair Fields was doomed.

Chapter Forty One

Stonebridge. What a miserable ruin it was, Heri thought as he wandered in to the ancient village. And what a waste of a journey. He'd spent a month at least crossing Fair Fields on foot to get here, and every one of those days had been a torment.

His feet ached as they never had before, and his soft boots had been reduced to shreds. His back hurt too; the injury of his brother's blade was always with him. He was twisted as he walked, and bent a little to one side. And though he could use a staff to help him walk in a more upright position, it just wasn't as it had been. He was crippled.

Yet worse than that, his mind had gone as well. He didn't know exactly how, though he did know it was the elves' doing. Them and he assumed the cursed potion they had made him drink. Thanks to it he could no longer speak the name of another god. Nor could he lie. In fact too often the truth would just come pouring out of him when he was asked a question. He also had no control over the path his feet chose to travel – which was why he was here. He could not even draw his knife. Not in anger anyway.

But by far the biggest curse he had had to deal with was his complete lack of ability to hold on to his coin. If he saw someone in need he would be compelled to give his coin to them, regardless of the fact that it was his! He needed his gold! And yet he kept giving it away. Even worse than that he'd seen a healer tending to the injured in a small village a while back and had suddenly found himself walking to him. Once he reached him the first thing he had told him was the location of one of the crypts where he had stashed some of his gold. Similarly he had seen a priest of the All Father tending to his flock and had immediately told him the location of another stash. There had been others.

Soon he would have no gold left. And it was his gold! By right!

Before he had drunk the potion he had at least had some hope of ending his days with enough gold to see out his days in comfort. Now even that hope was gone. He was a complete peasant with not a coin to his name. If he wanted a hot meal he had to scrounge it for himself. Occasionally he had no choice but to eat the things that others had left behind or thrown away. Sometimes he even had to beg. It was humiliating! He had never begged in his life. But if he was to eat he had to.

And now here he was. In an ancient ruined village surrounded by no one. There was no one around to beg from. No one who could even put him up for the night. He could see no orchards from which he might steal some fruit. He couldn't even see a place where he could find a roof to shelter him from the rain. The only thing he could see in the village were stones. Piles and piles of stones.

To the right an ancient stone bridge spanned a narrow river chasm. It was all that was left of the ancient village and the structure for which it had been named. All around him he could see hundreds of piles of collapsed rubble that had once been peoples' homes, however many thousands of years ago. There were also acres upon acres of scrub and tough looking grass surrounding them. That was all there was, save for the wind that never seemed to stop blowing.

The place was dead. It had been dead for a thousand years. Maybe even two thousand. Some even claimed it was older than that. That it had been destroyed during the Dragon Wars. Heri didn't know. He didn't even care. All he knew was that it had been dead for so long that even the ghosts had left.

Samual

"All right I'm here! Now what?!"

Heri yelled it at no one. Because there was no one around to hear him. Then again maybe there was – whoever or whatever was controlling him had brought him here for a reason. But either way he wanted to be gone from this place. Whatever reason he had come here for, he at least wanted it to be over and done with. After that maybe whoever or whatever controlled him would be done with him. It was a faint hope but it was all he had. And he was hungry. That was something he had never known before. People had always brought him food when he wanted it. He needed to leave this place and find some food.

Unfortunately no one answered him and his feet refused to let him leave. Every time he tried they just marched him in a circle back to the bridge. Which in the end left him with nothing to do but sit down and wait – and hope he wasn't going to be here long.

It was a long wait. The sun reached the zenith of its arc and then started heading down the other side while he sat on the grass leaning against the crumbling stone blocks of the bridge. And while he sat there all he could do was stare at the ruins that had once been buildings and wonder what they had looked like before they'd crumbled away. It wasn't much of a mystery to set his mind to. The sages had spent decades arguing about how the ancient world had worked and what sort of people they had been before the Dragon Wars. Not that this was necessarily built by them. And they had never found an answer they could agree on. But it was all he had to do. And by the time the sun was settling into the distant hills he couldn't even be bothered thinking about it anymore. Who cared? He certainly didn't.

What he did care about was that just as the sun touched the hills he suddenly felt the need to get up. And then once he was up to wander through the piles of rubble that had once been a village to the far end. He walked toward a small copse of trees that had grown up in what he suspected had once been the entrance to it.

Why he was there he didn't know. It looked like any other small copse of trees he had ever seen. Maybe a sage or a forester would have seen something special in it. But he didn't. All he saw was a small stand of tall trees. Fir trees that looked like any others.

But obviously there was something about them. He didn't know what. But why else would his feet suddenly start carrying him into the copse? Why would they force him to work his way around and through scrub and weeds as high as his chest? That wasn't something any normal man of normal wit would do. Especially when the scrub was so thick that it tore at his already ragged clothes and scratched any skin it could reach. When there were thistles as well. And it wasn't as if he could weave his way around any of them. His feet wouldn't let him.

Heri pressed on, doing his best to push away the branches of the offending foliage, but still taking a lot of cuts and scratches as he forced his way through the scrub. The only blessing he was given was that the copse was small. Because by the time he reached the middle of it, he was bleeding from a hundred different scratches.

In the middle of the copse he found nothing other than a rotten tree stump and he realised with surprise that it seemed to be his destination. His feet were heading straight for it after all. And the rays of the setting sun, were playing directly on it – something that he was sure was no accident. But why? There was nothing there. No altar or shrine. No one waiting to speak to him. No structure of any kind. Just a rotten tree stump sitting out in the middle of a scrub filled copse by itself. Why would anyone want to visit a tree stump?

He was still wondering that when he reached it and saw fairly much what he'd expected to see – nothing. It was old and rotten. Hollowed out to an extent by time, but with nothing inside it. It might have been a good place to hide a treasure, but there was no treasure to be seen.

He was disappointed by that, though really he knew he would never have been allowed to keep it anyway. Still, to have walked all this way for nothing seemed hard.

A growl suddenly pierced the air and sent his heart racing. He looked up to see a huge pair of eyes staring at him. Eyes attached to a head full of fur and teeth. A head as high off the ground as he was. He saw fangs and razor sharp teeth as the mouth opened and then snapped shut with a bony crack. And his blood chilled as he knew he was staring at a snap wolf. Cousin to a dire wolf but bigger. Much bigger. Big enough that the beast could bite him in half with just one snap of those jaws. This then must be the reason he had been called here. To die. The snap of those jaws was death. It was generally the last thing anyone ever heard before they died. But why bring him all this way to die?

Heri was terrified. He'd never seen one of the beasts before. They weren't even supposed to be in his lands. Not in Fair Fields. He'd had them all hunted down. But suddenly he was staring at one, and it was close enough to just reach over and bite him in half. Close enough that he could smell its foul breath so very clearly. The odour of rotten meat and filth was nearly overpowering.

But then instead of running as he should he reached across the stump to the far side where a small, spiral shoot was growing up out of it and he knew he hadn't come for nothing. He knew it even more clearly when the instant his fingers wrapped themselves around it he felt some force flowing through them. Mostly though he knew it when the shoot came instantly free in his hand.

And though the snap wolf was still standing there watching, and it had been close enough to bite his hand off as he'd reached for the shoot, it did nothing. Maybe it wasn't going to? Maybe it was also controlled in some way? He had come here to retrieve this shoot. The wolf had been left here as its guardian. And for some reason he was allowed to take it.

That helped Heri. It let his heart stop racing a little. Because in the end despite everything that had happened to him, he didn't want to die. And the snap wolf was death on four legs. But he still didn't trust the beast. It was a predator. A savage creature. Even if it wasn't meant to kill him, it could still do so in a heartbeat should it change its mind.

The sooner he was away from it he thought, the better. But unfortunately his body didn't seem to think the same thing. Because all it wanted to do was stand there and stare at the shoot.

What was it? He stood there staring at the shoot, wondering. He even managed to put the wolf out of his mind as he did so. Because it didn't look like anything much to him. If it had been a stick with a sharp point on the end it could perhaps have worked as a dagger. But really he thought, the wood of the shoot was too soft and springy. It would bend before it pierced someone's body. And though it was likely some sort of magical sundry, it was nothing like any of the treasures he had once owned. Those had all been crafted and spelled. They showed the work of the artisan. This was just a shoot.

Still, it was clearly important to whoever was controlling him. He knew that when instead of simply tossing it aside he carefully tucked it inside his vest. It also seemed that it was what he had come for. That too was obvious when he turned around and started forcing his way back through the scrub and brambles to where he had come from. Now he had somewhere else to go it seemed.

It also seemed he had a companion. Heri discovered that when he finally escaped the copse to discover with some shock that the snap wolf was right beside him. He hadn't heard it forcing its way through the undergrowth. And it wasn't covered in rips and scratches as he was. Clearly despite its size it was far more agile and able to walk though scrub than he was. But as he headed back to the bridge it walked beside him. It stuck to him like a shadow.

Heri groaned quietly. At least he still had the freedom to groan. Why did he have to have a companion? And why this one of all creatures? He would never be safe with it around. Especially when he realised why the snap wolf was accompanying him. It wasn't. It was the guardian of the shoot. He was just a pair of hands to hold it and feet to transport it. Everything was about the shoot!

And yet he knew as he walked back to the bridge, he didn't have a choice. He was a king! And yet somehow he had become a peon. A slave. Even less than a slave. No one could have truly understood the anger he felt at that. Or the helplessness.

Chapter Forty Two

Sam stood in the clearing patiently waiting as he searched the sky. He knew his creature was coming – he could feel it – but he couldn't see it. And considering the creature's size that seemed wrong. He was impatient for its arrival.

Of course others were going to say that what he was doing was wrong. Ry was absolutely going to be one of them – which was why he was grateful that he hadn't told her. But she would have tried to stop him. Tried to tell him he was one man alone. That he couldn't fight the Dragon on his own. But it was Fair Fields! It was his home even if he never lived there again. He had to protect it. And he had a plan. Sort of. But everything hinged on his arriving before the Dragon. And of course arriving there in one piece – preferably not inside his mount.

"Samual."

Elder Bela's voice came from behind him, catching Sam by surprise. He should have expected that the Elder would realise he was doing something. He would have felt the magic when he'd cast the shape and come running. It was significant nature magic after all. And a spell that Sam shouldn't be able to cast.

"Would you like to tell me what you're doing?" It wasn't a question.

"What I have to do. I have to stop the Dragon. Permanently."

"You can't do that! Not on your own. And you can't get there in time." The Elder repeated what they both knew to be true. Or what they had believed was true until Sam had woken up this morning. From the moment he had opened his eyes he had understood the truth.

"Elder, I won't be alone. And I can get there in time. Because I know where the Dragon is going."

It had come as a surprise to all of them a week before when they had seen the Dragon unexpectedly get into a giant balloon. Or rather, a gondola as large as four baskets, held aloft by six balloons and towed by a pair of steel drakes. They had expected him to send his army for him while he stayed behind on his island cavern where it was safe. It was what after all he had always previously done. But this time it was different. Sam didn't know why. None of them did. But he had awoken this morning knowing exactly where he was headed.

"Fair Fields."

"Yes but I know exactly where in Fair Fields he's going. Mount Andrea."

"Mount Andrea?" The Elder sounded surprised. But then he started considering Sam's idea, staring off into the distance as he thought.

"Why?"

"I don't know exactly. I woke up this morning knowing where but not why. But I think it's because Mount Andrea and especially the caverns underneath it and the surrounding peaks, are similar to the cavern beneath his island. That there is some form of ancient magic there. And that from them he can continue his campaign."

"I think that's why the original Dragon fled there at the end. He too was using the island originally. But at some point he knew it wasn't enough. He needed a base on the Continent of the Dragon's Spine. And so that was where he ran to."

"He didn't run fast enough and so the spell took him down. But he still made it there, and was there long enough to prophesise his coming victory. To scribe it into the cavern walls. But he died before he could complete it. This new Dragon is following the same path. But he's not injured or dying."

"And your plan is?"

"To destroy the caverns before the Dragon gets there. If I destroy them then Dragon is left helpless, or at least no more powerful than before. Then it's just a matter of killing him."

"Destroy –?" The Elder stopped in mid question when he spotted the bundle by Sam's feet. "Is that …?"

"Yes." Sam nodded. "I took it from the wagon this morning. How else can I destroy a mountain?"

"By the Goddess!" The Elder paled. "You know that's a one way trip?"

"Maybe. But I have a plan for that too." And even as he said it he could see his plan arriving. Finally. It was just a smudge in the sky. But it was a big smudge.

The Elder turned as he saw where Sam's eyes were looking, and then stopped for a bit and stared. Not many people had ever seen a Roc before. Not many would see one again.

"You called a roc?" He said it as if it was a surprise. But really he should have felt the power of the spell and guessed. Actually he had felt the power. That was why he'd come. He just didn't know what the power was being used for and hadn't expected that this was what he would find.

"Again, I woke up this morning knowing the shape of the spell I needed."

Sam didn't understand how he could have woken up with such knowledge, though he suspected it had something to do with the various deities who it appeared were getting involved. Perhaps the Goddess. Maybe the All Father. He hoped it wasn't Alder. Or the Red God. But whoever it was he was almost sure that they were acting in some way. And if they were choosing to act through him to stop the Dragon, then that was fine as far as he was concerned. The Dragon had to be stopped. He had given his word to Ry that he would protect her people. He had more or less said the same to the elders. He was a knight of Hanor. Sam would never go back on what he had sworn.

Still, it worried him. He had never been used by the deities before. Very few had. And there were always stories about it happening and most of them claimed that it had ended badly for the one used.

Just then though as he watched the roc grew larger in the sky, he realised he had a more immediate problem. The giant bird – an eagle grown to enormous size – was no domesticated steed. He needed the bird's power of flight to get him where he needed to go in time, but he didn't want to be bitten in two by its massive beak before he even took off. And it had only come because he had called it; not because it liked him or felt any desire to obey. Rocs were wild. As wild and free as the dragons themselves. And nearly as dangerous.

"Are you sure about this Samual?" Elder Bela was surprisingly restrained as he asked the question.

"Only that it has to be Elder. I was given this spell for a reason. I have to have faith in that." But his throat was dry and his hands were threatening to tremble as they held on to the rope. It only got harder to control his fear as the bird grew ever larger.

The roc was enormous. Easily as large as a steel drake. And far faster. The steel drakes were slow and awkward flyers. The roc was fast, agile and powerful. More than a match for them in the air. Its enormous talons would shear through steel plate with ease and it could easily dodge their fire. Then Sam looked at the roc's wings as it spread them out wide as it prepared to land and gulped. The wingspan was enormous and the blast of air that blew off it as it banked buffeted them all.

Despite that, when it alighted in front of him, there was barely a sound. The giant bird was truly graceful.

Sam gathered up his pack, swung it over his shoulder, and wrapped the rope around his arms before walking toward the great bird. He realised that if he was going to do this he had to do it quickly – before his nerve gave out. He was not actually a fearless warrior after all. Not when he was facing a bird that could kill him in a heartbeat. Not when he was powerless before it.

With every step he took toward the roc he kept his eyes firmly fixed on its nearest eye. While he could see the fierceness and savagery in it, he was mainly looking for any sign that it was about to attack. He also noticed with every step he took closer to the bird how much higher off the ground that eye seemed to get. The bird had to be standing at least twelve feet tall, even when it wasn't completely upright.

Luckily the roc didn't attack him. Instead it stood there calmly while he approached. Soon he was directly under its neck, standing in the shade.

The next part was a little tricky as he had to use his Earth magic to raise the ground underneath him a little so that he could reach what he needed to. And he worried that it might startle the creature. But it didn't. The roc seemed remarkably accepting of the ground rising beside it, if not completely calm.

Soon he was standing at neck height, and unwound the rope as he prepared himself for the next step. This was the part that he thought would upset the roc most. It was a wild animal. It did not want to be tethered. If it had been a horse he would have expected it to start bucking and kicking. But it had to be done. He could not ride on the back of the bird without something to hold on to. And so, carefully, with his heart thumping furiously in his chest, he tossed the rope around its great neck, and prepared to be bitten in half.

But he wasn't. The rope twirled around the roc's neck and the end almost ended up in his own hand by itself. It didn't quite, slipping out of his grasp as it swung away. But then it swung back and he caught it. After that it was simply a matter of tying it so that it became a collar.

Sweat was trickling down his forehead by the time he had finished. But despite his fear the roc did not attack him. Maybe that had something to do with the gods as well. He didn't know.

Then came the tricky bit. Clambering on to its back. He had prepared for this as best he could. And so he was wearing soft leather forester's boots instead of a proper soldier's heavy boots so he didn't upset the creature. His armour consisted of only his breast plate and back plate to save weight. The rest was his normal wear, though the clothes were heavy and warm to allow for the cold wind he guessed he would feel high up. He also carried no shield and no battle axe; only his favourite greatsword strapped to his back so it didn't get in the way.

Gingerly he climbed onto the bird's back and despite his fear the roc allowed him to. It seemed accepting of him, despite his fears.

After that he found himself lying there on the bird's back, hanging on to the rope as the angle threatened to send him sliding off, relieved that it seemed the bird wasn't going to kill him. It took a little while to come to terms with that. And then a little longer to look across to where the Elder was still standing, and realise how small he looked.

"Elder," he called down to him. "Can you please tell my wife where I am and that I will do everything I can to return to her as quickly as I can. Also, please give her my apologies for this."

And he knew he had to apologise. Ryshal had been gone by the time he had awoken with the understanding of what he had to do. She was teaching some of the children the art and meaning of dance, and he had woken knowing he had no time to find her. But maybe he also hadn't tried because he hadn't wanted to face her? To tell her he was once more running off into danger. And to have to see the fear in her eyes and hear the pain in her voice. In some things he was just a frightened man like any other.

"I shall." Elder Bela nodded to him, never taking his eyes off the roc as he did so.

"Thank you."

With that done Sam gave the command and instantly felt the muscles of the bird tense beneath him as it spread its wings wide. Then he was all but squashed into the roc's back as it leapt into the air, something that caught him completely by surprise.

But then he hadn't known what to expect. Sam had had no thought at all of what flying would be like. And his first thought was that it was surprisingly uncomfortable as the wings beat the air and the bird's mighty back muscles danced and flowed underneath him. But at least in flight he was lying flat, the bird's tail no lower than its head. He wasn't going to slide off.

The next thought he had after he came to terms with being so high above the ground, was how small everything below looked. It had only been a matter of a few moments surely and already all of the new city of Shavarra was laid out beneath him. If he fell he thought, he would be falling for a very long time before he hit the ground. He did not like that idea at all. In fact it made him feel ill, and his hands tightened on the rope until his fingers were white.

Still, he had to endure. And as the roc rose ever higher into the air he tried to concentrate on its feathers just in front of his face. And on how long the journey would be. His best guess was two days. The Dragon had left his island nearly a week before. His drakes were much slower than the roc and the distance they had to travel to reach their destination was much greater. Added to that they had to tow the great balloons. If he was lucky Sam hoped, he would have time. Time to do what he had to do.

But it would be close.

And to think; the Fire Angel of old had apparently flown around on the back of a phoenix! Sam couldn't even begin to imagine what that would be like. Warmer he suspected. Though the rope collar would probably have burnt through in a hurry – along with his bones!

This was safer. And though he hated the sight of the ground far below, his only chance. He just had to hang on.

Chapter Forty Three

Mount Andrea. Heri wasn't sure he wanted to see it. Not this close. Not ever. The Caverns of Andrea were a cursed land according to the stories. The mountains were filled with trolls and other deadly creatures; the caverns beneath them a honeycomb filled with ghosts and spirits. As for the mountain itself in the middle of the series of peaks, it was the original Dragon's ancient home. And while everything he knew could be attributed to the tales of the bards who spun them for coppers, there were enough stories of the place that Heri knew there had to be some truth in them.

Still, here he was. He was also exhausted. His shoes had long since worn out and now he was barefoot as well as dressed in worn out rags. He was sure he'd lost a lot of weight as he'd walked across the realm to get here. He didn't even know how many days he'd spent walking here. One day tended to drift into another after a while when all you did was walk from dawn to dusk.

Now though he was here and the next stage in his torture began. After all he had stopped walking. It had to be time for something new. Something probably even worse than the endless walking on his badly blistered feet.

That something began with his pulling the twisted shoot he had gained in Stonebridge out of his jacket pocket and holding it up in front of him. He wondered why. And despite his exhaustion he started paying attention. This could be the thing that finally got him killed after all.

The snap wolf hadn't. That had surprised him at first as the monstrous beast followed him around. He'd expected it to kill him at any moment. And going to sleep that first night after Stonebridge had been terrifying. He'd wondered if he'd wake up. But he had, and in time realised the simple truth. It was guarding the shoot. So it would make sure that no one tried to harm him as long as he was carrying it. But it would also stop him from trying to run off with it. And the gods only knew what it would do when it was time for him to put the shoot down somewhere. Would he then finally become its dinner? And had that time finally arrived?

"It is time." The words came out of Heri's mouth but they weren't his words. He wasn't at all sure whose words they were. Only that it was obviously those of the one who controlled him.

The words were also powerful in some way. He didn't understand how exactly. Maybe it was magic? But he felt the power in them, almost like the roar of thunder echoing in the distance.

Another thing occurred to him. The words weren't spoken in common. He didn't know what language they were spoken in – the tongue was one he had never heard before – but still he somehow understood them. That had to be magic of some sort. More foul magic ruining his life!

No one answered Heri at first, and that seemed to annoy the one controlling him. Enough that a couple of moments later he or she raised Heri's voice a little more and repeated the statement after prefacing it with a very distinct 'I said'. Whoever the 'I' was Heri didn't know. But he gathered from the way he emphasised the words, that the speaker thought it should mean something to whoever he was speaking to.

"I heard you."

Another voice answered him or her, and this time at least it wasn't someone using Heri's mouth. He was grateful for that. But not so grateful that the voice was coming from somewhere just in front of him and all he could see was empty air. More accursed magic!

"Then why didn't you answer?" Heri's master seemed unhappy.

"I was enjoying a pleasant little nap. And anyway it can't be time. It's too soon." The other voice sounded tired, as if he wanted to return to his nap.

"It's been five thousand years!" Heri's master snapped at the other voice.

"As I said, too soon." The voice let out a disinterested yawn. "Wake me in another ten."

"There will be no world in another ten thousand years!" Heri's master sounded annoyed. "Or had you missed that. And show yourself!"

Ten thousand years? Heri wasn't sure he wanted to believe that. Or anything else that was coming out of his mouth. But he had no place to object in this conversation. And in any case he forgot the matter completely when the other speaker finally appeared in front of him. Or rather a part of him did.

An eye unexpectedly appeared, hanging in mid-air maybe fifty paces from him. But how did an eye do that? Unless it was attached to an invisible body! A body that had to be absolutely enormous. The eye was huge and golden and had a slitted black pupil. And it was definitely a creature not a man. Not anything even remotely human. Even ignoring its size, that eye was not of any man or race he had ever seen before. In fact if he'd had to guess he would have said the owner of the eye was a giant lizard.

"Fine!" The eye sounded somewhat irked, as if it was being forced to do something it didn't want to do. "I'll wake my children. But really, it seems unnecessary. And why are you wearing that form? It seems so … tiny."

Heri knew the golden eye was speaking about him – as if he was merely a set of clothes. But he chose not to feel offended when he was staring at an eye the size of a blood bear hanging in mid-air by itself.

"Because it was available. And he offended me. Besides which, many prayed for his punishment. I was thinking about turning him into a flea. He was already something of a blood sucker. But then I thought that would be too quick. And he could serve me. For a while."

"You don't have to answer them you know."

"No – *you* don't have to answer them." Heri's master emphasised the 'you' somewhat forcefully. "But have you forgotten what happened the last time you stopped paying attention? Your workshops were seized by the grey vermin. The world was almost overrun by the steel armies they built in them. And now they stand poised to try again. Just as I told you they would."

Grey vermin? Did he or she mean the trolls Heri wondered? They were grey skinned after all. And he couldn't think of a race more deserving of the title of vermin. But overrunning the world? Then again, it had been five thousand years since the Dragon Wars had raged. And the current Dragon was a troll blood.

"They are a nuisance. Always trying to eat my children's eggs." Golden eye agreed with Heri's master. But he didn't sound particularly concerned.

"As is the fact that you didn't close down your ancient workshops."

"I was busy!" Golden Eye defended himself. "And he

swore he wouldn't have his creatures do it again."

"And now you're going to be busy again." Heri's master ignored Golden Eye's protests.

"It's almost the same as last time. Another champion has been called and he's coming here with a sun burst. He will place it in the caves and that will hopefully stop any more of these grey vermin from arising and making a nuisance of themselves."

"If things go as I hope, he may also return one of the lost to the world. My servants tell me that the knowledge surges within him. Our sister's doing no doubt. But it will be nice to see them return to the world. He must be protected."

"And of course at the same time the grey vermin comes with a steel army. They must be destroyed. The champion must be protected."

So the vermin were the trolls! And the particular vermin his master was speaking about was the Dragon. Heri was glad of that. Glad that the horrible little creature was going to be destroyed. At least one enemy of his would be gone. Heri would have cheered, save that he had no control over his mouth just then.

"My children will be there."

With that the golden eye vanished and Heri was left standing there, wondering what happened next. Mostly he wondered about what would happen to him. Was his work done? Had he finished his duty? Was it time for the snap wolf to enjoy a meal? And if there was to be a battle here, could he run away?

Apparently not was his answer as he unexpectedly found himself walking toward the mountains. It seemed his suffering

Samual

was to continue.

He hated the gods!

Chapter Forty Four

Sam was overjoyed when he saw Mount Andrea in front of him. Partly because he could see no army of steel in front of him. But in truth mostly because he had had enough of flying. More than enough.

It was hard and uncomfortable. The ground was a horribly long way down and he had tried to ignore it by keeping his face buried in the roc's feathers. And the roc didn't care for him. It didn't dislike him. But it was no friend of his either, and it had no concern that he might fall off every time it banked and turned. And so after two days of lying flat on its back his hands were white from having gripped on to the rope so tightly for so long. He was exhausted from not having slept at all. And he was frozen through. The air up high was colder than he would have believed and unlike his steed, he didn't have a thick coat of feathers to keep him warm. He had dressed warmly but apparently not warmly enough.

Still, he had crossed a hundred and fifty or more leagues in two days. That was beyond what he would have ever believed possible before the knowledge had come to him. And much of that had been spent crossing the Dead Belly wastes.

Now the central mountain surrounded by its smaller sisters was lying in front of him, the peaks lost in the grey clouds that forever shrouded them while the caverns of the ancient Dragon lay somewhere beneath it. Somewhere in the endless honeycomb of warrens, tunnels and chambers that criss-crossed the entire region. Finding the cavern was of course his next challenge, but he figured that it would be nowhere near as difficult as it should be. Sir Haggard had spent a lifetime exploring those tunnels. He would not need to do the same. Not when it was clear that he was being guided.

Sam guided the roc towards the nearest plateau in the mountain with a tap on its neck, knowing somehow that it was where he needed to begin work. He was also aware that just as he was guiding the roc, he in turn was being guided. He didn't know by whom. He just hoped it was by someone who wanted the same things he did. And thus far that had proven true.

The plateau was a striking part of the mountain. It was actually a rocky terrace in the mountain's side. An enormous terrace. But what was truly amazing was the sheerness of the terrace and the cliffs both above and below it. The straightness of the cuts and the sharpness of the angles. It looked for all the world as if some giant had simply grabbed an enormous shovel and cut a huge wedge out of the side of the mountain. But what sort of giant could tower so high that it could simply cut a wedge out of a mountain that's top half was lost in the clouds?

As they flew closer its size became ever more apparent. The plateau stood atop a massive cliff that he would have guessed towered a thousand or more paces above the more gently sloping foothills that were the base of the mountain. And it was at least five hundred paces deep and a thousand wide. Where the inner part of the terrace reached the side of the mountain there was another vertical cliff towering up above it which he would have guessed was much the same height as the one it sat on. It was almost as though the plateau was a flat floor in a home, and the cliff a vertical wall. It was that straight.

There were other such terraces in the mountain and in its smaller sister peaks. Sam took note of them as they flew. And though none of them were as large as their destination, he could not imagine that any of them had occurred naturally. Not when the sides of the cliffs were so straight and the terraces so flat. But short of his theory about giants and shovels he couldn't begin to guess how they had been built.

As they flew closer Sam realised that some of his thoughts had been a little off. The terrace was flat and the cliff faces above and below it sheer, but they weren't as smooth as he'd thought. Closer up he could see that there were huge cracks criss-crossing the terrace, while the cliffs had pieces missing from them. Time had weathered the dark stone and he guessed large parts of the cliffs had crumbled away and were now part of the foothills. Still, he thought they were too straight to be natural.

Landing on the terrace proved to be trickier than he'd expected. The roc simply alighted gently as it should, but then when it straightened up he found himself once more hanging on to the rope collar he'd tied around it, not wanting to slide off. Eventually though he realised that that was exactly what he needed to do. He could have tried raising a column of stone in the same way that he had done when he had mounted the bird, but it was dense rock. It would take time. So in the end he chose to slide, and eventually ended up sitting on the cold stone and nursing a sore ankle after he hit the ground awkwardly.

Still, he was down and that, he decided as he sent the roc away, was what mattered. He was here. The Dragon hadn't arrived. All he had to do now was find the cavern. That part however, wasn't up to him.

When he'd awoken two days before with the shape of the call for the roc and the beginnings of a plan in his head, he'd also known that he would be shown the cavern as he wouldn't be able to find it by himself. So, nursing his ankle, he clambered awkwardly to his feet and waited for the information to come to him. It had to because he could spend weeks just looking for the entrance to the underground caverns, and then months or years searching them for the one he needed. And presumably the Dragon already knew the location.

There were other things he could be doing. Eating, drinking, shaking the stiffness out of his body, even undertaking the normal ablutions of life – something that he'd had to use his nature magic to help him put off for all that time. After all, he'd done nothing for two days except hang on to the back of a giant bird and he was mere flesh and blood. But time was critical. He could do everything he needed to do later.

"I'm here." Sam announced his arrival to the mountain, as if it was the mountain that had brought him here. Naturally it didn't answer him. But as he put down his pack and started gingerly putting some weight on his injured ankle, he did get an answer.

It wasn't in words. It wasn't writing or anything so civilised. It was only a thought. A suggestion. A direction. But as he stood there he suddenly knew where the cavern was. He could feel it. He suddenly knew the angle he would have to cut through to reach it. He even knew the depth. And that was the plan. It wasn't a complex one. In fact it was so simple a child could have come up with it. He would drill down to the cavern and then blow it up.

In theory it was no different to digging a well for water. Except that it was a lot deeper, through solid rock and it couldn't be hit and miss. He had to actually aim at what he was drilling for. But thanks to whoever was guiding him he had a target and he also had magic.

Sam was tired. He was cold and hungry. He was sore too. But he didn't have time for any of those things. So he used his nature magic to provide him with a little more strength and vitality, then put everything else out of his mind as he began sending his magic streaming into the rock beneath his feet. And thanks to all the hard work he'd been doing with Master Forellin the stone gave way to his will much more easily than it once would have. It was almost like digging through loose soil.

Still he couldn't help but think that this wasn't right. Master Forellin or any of the other masters of earth magic could have done this far more quickly than him. He was a fire mage. Why bring him all this way if not to use his fire? Naturally that knowledge wasn't given to him. And he realised, as weak as he might be compared to a true master of earth magic, he was still the only wizard with that magic here. So it had to be him.

As he worked the roc kept watch over him, taking up a post not far away, occasionally taking a flight around him as it spotted enemies from the air. He wasn't quite sure why – it was no doing of his – but it was good to know that it was there looking out for him. Unless of course it was simply there waiting for the right time to eat him. But he had to assume that whatever it was doing was the will of whoever was guiding him – and he didn't want him dead.

Soon he had a channel half a pace across and a good three or four paces deep, aimed straight at the heart of the cavern. But he knew that there was a long way to go and that it was not soft earth. It had been easier at the start. But as he dug deeper, the rock became tougher. The stuff on the top had been weathered by millennia of wind and rain. What lay ahead of him was going to be tougher still. The cavern was deep in the bedrock underneath the mountain and he would have to push all the way down to it. He had probably days of concentration ahead of him.

Still, he would do it. He had to. And then he would activate the sun burst and drop it down the well he'd dug, and jump on the roc's back and fly as if all the demons of the underworld were chasing him.

Hours later, he wasn't quite sure how many as he'd lost

track of time, he was interrupted by Ryshal. By her calling to
him.

At the sound of her voice he lost concentration, as for a
moment he thought she was somehow there with him. But of
course she wasn't. Instead he could see her face and those of
some of the elders hanging in a window in the air to his side,
and he realised she was still in the city. The elders had known
where he was going and once he had stopped and started
digging it had simply been a matter of them searching for him
with the window.

"Beloved." He greeted her with a smile in his heart as he
always did, happy to see her, but equally aware that he had to
continue with his work. He didn't know how long he had
before the Dragon and his army showed up. He had to be done
before they arrived.

"Don't you dare "beloved" me! You ran off! You oaf!"

Ryshal was upset. She was also worried. Sam could see
that in her face. She'd probably been living in terror ever since
she'd been told he'd gone flying off on the back of a giant
bird, heading into battle. He knew a lot of shame for that.

"I know, and I'm sorry. But I woke up with this plan in my
thoughts, and I knew there was no time. I did not have time to
find you."

"Or you knew I'd stop you. This is madness! You can't
fight an army on your own. Fire Angel or not, it's just too
much!" Her fear showed in the tremor in her voice and the
way she had paled. She wasn't that far from tears.

"And I don't intend to. Believe me Ry, I have every
intention of returning to you. I just need to destroy the ancient
Dragon's cavern below, and then run. And if it does come to a
fight, I won't be alone."

"You are alone!"

This time she finally let her fear loose and Sam could see tears starting to run down her cheeks. But he actually had an answer for her. One that he hoped might bring her some comfort.

"No. I'm not. I don't know who's with me, but I'm not alone. This is not my plan. It was given to me in my sleep. And the magic to call the roc was given to me as well. The location of the cavern below was given to me when I arrived here. And in the same way that I have so far known all of these details, I also know that I will have allies if and when I need them."

"I have no idea who's guiding me. The All Father I hope. But I have faith. And you've got to have faith too. There is a plan here. A purpose greater than you and me." He wished he could tell her more. He wished he could promise her that he would come home. And most of all he wished he didn't have to see the fear in her eyes. But he could only tell her what he knew.

Fortunately he was saved from having to plead with her by one of the elders who gathered Ry up in her arms and escorted her away from the window. They understood that he had to concentrate on his work. And they didn't want to see her burst into tears either.

Unfortunately that just gave others the chance to speak.

"Guided?" Elder Bela was the first to ask the question. But others in the window looked like they were about to ask the same one.

"I don't know. But I have this certainty that this is what has to be done. That it's not just about Fair Fields. I also know that this is my task and that it has been since the moment I was born. Even the damned bird knows it. It's keeping watch over me – and I didn't command it to do that."

The Elder pursed his lips in concentration as he considered Sam's claim, but said nothing for a while, allowing Sam to return to his work. But eventually he could no longer endure the silence.

"What can we do to help?"

"I have to concentrate on this. I can't keep watch. But if you can use the Window of Parsus to check the surrounding lands and tell me when the Dragon arrives, that would help."

With that Sam returned fully to his work, knowing that time was precious. Knowing also that more was at stake than he was aware of. And that his wife was hurting and it was his fault. That more than anything else, wounded him.

But he had to dig.

Chapter Forty Five

Ryshal sat on the ground in the Fiore Elle, staring at the window hanging in the air and her husband in it, worrying. But also wondering. It was late, night had fallen and she was exhausted just from watching and worrying. But her husband still stood where he had been. He was a silent figure. In fact he looked almost a living statue with his head bowed, but Ryshal knew he was working furiously. He was sending his magic streaming into the rock beneath him. He had been doing it for hour after hour and in all that time he had never moved. He never said anything. He never did anything but concentrate. And she was sure that wasn't possible. No one could maintain that sort of concentration and stillness for so long? At the very least he should be cramping up. Shifting his weight about on his feet to relieve some of the strain. And yet he just wasn't.

The elders were no help. In fact she guessed that as they maintained their own vigil around the window with her that they were just as confused as she was. And not just by Samual's unending concentration.

Even though they were huddled about in their own small groups, she had heard Elder Bela tell the others several times that Sam could not possibly have called the roc. That it was a calling far beyond his ability. It was beyond that of most masters. And yet he was only an apprentice.

She had heard several others say that what he was doing was of the Goddess. The priests had even been called to consider the matter. She hadn't unfortunately heard what they'd decided. But she had heard one of the elders say in passing that this was the calling of the Fire Angel. That he was finally doing what he had been called for. That scared her perhaps more than anything else. After all, the last Fire Angel had died according to the legends. He had given his everything to the battle and it had destroyed him. This seemed very much the same to her.

"You should eat something."

Ry looked up to see Mayvelle standing there with a cup of something hot in her hands for her. The warrior woman had turned up several hours before – why Ry didn't know – and had stayed ever since.

"I can't eat." Still, she accepted the cup. Tea helped she had discovered. Maybe it was simply the act of holding something in her hands and having something to do. Maybe it was the smell.

"I understand." Mayvelle unexpectedly sat down on the grass beside her. "It is always this way before a battle."

"You think there will be a battle?"

"I know there will be a battle. I am vero eskaline. Storm blood like my brother. And my gift is in war. There will be a huge battle. But I doubt your husband will be fighting it."

"What?" That had caught Ryshal's attention where nothing else had.

"It's one of the things that I saw when I first saw your husband. My brother. Before I knew him as either of those things. And before he knew me. It was the night after the battle for Shavarra. We had lost and were retreating, and we passed by Samual's home. And when we did I felt it. Not him. The war."

"It was chilling. We had already lost a terrible battle. A great many of our loved ones were dead. Many more were injured. Our home was gone. And we were running. I thought then that there could be no worse day. But when I saw your husband standing on the balcony of his home with a torch, calling out to us as we passed, I knew it was only the beginning of something worse."

"I went to him then, telling him what he needed to hear. That there was an enemy chasing us, and that he needed to flee. But even as I did so I knew that I had to. Not because it was my duty, though it was, but because it was part of a greater plan that he be told. That it would be the calling of him. And I did not even know who he was then."

"I have felt this same thing every time I have been near him since then. I can feel the forces swirling and aligning themselves around him. And when I saw Heri I felt the same thing. He is a vile creature, but he too is caught up in this somehow. He has a part to play and he cannot and will not be allowed to pass from this world until he has played it."

"Heri?" If there was one person that Ryshal would have thought not involved in this war it would have been Heri. He would not risk his life in any battle. In fact he despised those who were willing to do so. Fighting to him was a foolish endeavour. He only cared about winning.

"You thought it was by chance that he happened to have the ancient devices that will be needed to destroy this cavern? That he found the Dragon before we did?" Mayvelle's eyebrows rose in question.

"That was not chance. That was part of a greater plan that we do not know. And maybe we will never know it. This is a war between sides we do not see. Fought by players we do not know. Gods, ancients, maybe others. And it is fought to ends we can only guess at. The priests might one day claim it is a war between the Goddess and Crodan the Mountain. I don't know if that's true."

"But what I do know is that both sides have called on their champions. Those who will do what needs to be done when it needs to be done. And so the Fire Angel is called to one side, the Dragon to the other. But these champions are not the warriors who will fight the battle. Nor are they the commanders of the armies. We do not see the commanders. The champions are in large part figureheads. The foci of the sides. And they will both be stoutly protected. It is a bit like when the humans go to war. When the king falls the battle is lost."

"They cannot be allowed to fall."

"You are speaking of what you hope, not what you know." Ryshal didn't want to say it, especially to the warrior woman, but it was the truth.

"Perhaps, but I have faith. You should too." Mayvelle managed a smile, and for the first time her face became something other than hard. In fact she could almost have been described as beautiful – in a stern way.

"I did not think you were the type?" And truthfully she hadn't thought that Mayvelle was a woman of faith. Rather she was a woman of steel. She believed not in the Goddess, but in what she could do herself with sword in hand. A lot of soldiers were that way.

"I wasn't. But then I met a man." Mayvelle managed another smile.

"I'm happy to hear –." Ry had been about to give her her congratulations, but before she could, Mayvelle cut her off.

"Not that sort of a man. They run from me. A trader, human with a strange beard and a good ear for listening. A good mind for asking questions too. And as I told him my tale, he asked the questions I should have thought of."

"Questions?" Ry didn't understand.

"For you. Because it isn't only the champions who have been called. It is all the pieces on the board. And you are one of those pieces."

"Me?" That Ryshal couldn't quite believe she'd heard. Because she was no soldier and no king. No lord and no elder. She was just a frightened wife.

"You." Mayvelle nodded to emphasise her words. "Because as the trader said, you have done two things that do not make sense. The first is that you did not see Heri for the threat he was to you and your husband. Yet you are an elf. The daughter of traders. You see people as they are. You see to the heart of them. So how did you not see his dark designs?"

"I did, but …" Her voice trailed off as she thought about it. And as she realised the woman was right. She had seen. But she had not spoken out as she should have. And she didn't know why. She should have gone to Samual. She should have begged him to leave early. She should have told him all that was in her heart. He would have listened. He would have done as she asked. But she hadn't.

Eventually she thought of something to say. "And the second?"

"You survived. And as my friend pointed out, that was a hard thing to do. Human dungeons are terrible places. Especially for an elf. But you survived. How?"

"I had faith. In the Goddess. She brought me comfort. And she told me that Samual would come." And that was the truth. Was it proof of anything more though? She didn't think so.

"Exactly!" Mayvelle almost seemed to pounce on her words. "You had faith. But did it ever occur to you that you had a reason for that faith? Certain knowledge?"

"Pardon?" That Ry truly didn't understand.

"Think of this as a war. An ancient war with players preparing their forces. And think of Samual as one of those pieces. You were the impetus that drove him to become the Fire Angel. First you were captured and imprisoned. And from that moment on he could do nothing more than grow in strength as he prepared himself for the battle to rescue you."

"And then you survived. Because had you died he would have been broken. He could not have become the Fire Angel."

Could she be right? Ryshal didn't know. It didn't seem right. And yet she couldn't put her finger on where it might be wrong. Because it made sense in a way. But it would mean that she had been used. Maybe by the Goddess herself. And she didn't like that.

For ages she simply stood there, thinking about it. Trying to work out what she should even think about it. And she would have kept doing that save that Mayvelle finally interrupted her.

"Now you should drink your soup and then you can tell me about your husband. And about how best I can apologise to him."

"Apologise?" Ryshal was caught by surprise. Somehow she hadn't thought Mayvelle the type to apologise for much. She was a proud woman.

"I spoke to Heri and I saw the truth in his eyes. I heard it in his words. He is a heartless creature raised by a heartless mother. A child spoiled by his very birth. He knows only the lure of power. And if a mother can do that to her only child, then what must she be able to do to a woman who stands in her way?"

"My parents were true in their belief that the king had some hand in his wife's death. But it seems they were wrong. And now I am left wanting to know something of my first parents. Things that only my brother can tell me. A man I have given grave offence to."

"He will forgive you. Have no fear." Ryshal put down her tea and reached for the warrior woman's hands. "For all that he may be a soldier with a soldier's manner, he has a heart as good and pure as any I know. It is why I love him."

"And this –" she indicated the Window and Samual in it "– is done for love. He does not fight out of anger or fear. There is no thought of gain or glory in his heart. No righteous crusade even. He fights only to protect those he loves. So simply speak from your heart and he will forgive you. He will tell you whatever you wish to know."

It felt good to be able to tell Mayvelle that. To give her perhaps a little comfort. But even as Ryshal spoke she felt a touch of fear. Her husband fought for love. He fought for those he loved. And if he died he would die for them too.

He would die for her. And even if Mayvelle was right, that didn't guarantee he would live. If there were gods on both sides there were no guarantees. And in any case, even those on his side only needed him to live long enough to do whatever they needed done. After that he was on his own.

Chapter Forty Six

"Samual!"

Sam started as he heard his name called. But even as he did he realised the Elder had been calling him for some time. He just hadn't been listening. He had been lost in concentration as he focused on his work. Forcing his Earth magic ever deeper into the stone, and using it to push it apart and create a round shaft. He had to concentrate. Partly because he was so tired after having stood there working at it for so long – two nights had passed while he did nothing but concentrate on the task. And partly because as the shaft went down ever deeper into the mountain and further away from him, it became harder. If he'd had the strength of a master it would have surely been quicker. But even a master he thought would have had difficulty exerting his will on stone more than a league beneath him.

"Elder Bela?" Sam didn't take his thoughts off his work.

"You're out of time. The steel drakes are on their way."

Those words robbed Sam of his concentration. It was too soon! But as he turned around to face the southern skies where he knew they would be coming from, he knew the Elder's words were true. He could see them in the distance. At the moment they were little more than a collection of sparkling wisps in the distance. But he could see an entire cloud of them.

"Alder's balls!" He cursed.

Obviously the Dragon had landed his army somewhere to the south of here, unhitched the drakes from the balloons they were towing, and sent them to the mountains. They would be faster if they weren't towing the rest of the army. Did that mean the Dragon knew what he was doing and had sent them to kill him soonest? Or was he just in a hurry to secure his new base?

Either way it didn't matter. The drakes would arrive long before he was ready. They would spot him and battle would ensue.

It was simply too damned soon! Sam almost screamed with frustration and panic when he saw how close the steel drakes were. He needed more time. At least another half an hour. Probably two hours. But he had at most a fraction of that time. The drakes were slow flyers, but not that slow, and he was out in the open. Exposed.

What should he do? Should he simply activate the sun burst, drop it down the not quite complete shaft and hope it did what it needed to? He wanted to. Because then he could simply climb back on the roc and fly away to safety. But he couldn't do that. There was only one sun burst and he had no idea how powerful it was. If it failed because it wasn't close enough to its target that would be a disaster. There would be no second chance.

To add to his problems if he stopped digging and put all his strength into fighting the drakes, he couldn't win. There was no chance he could hold off so many steel drakes. Not on his own. And the roc couldn't either. It looked ready to try. It sounded ready as it screamed its battle cry. The sound was piercing and damn near boiled his blood. But the roc was still only flesh and blood against steel. It would destroy some of them. Maybe many of them. But in the end it would fall. And if he instead kept digging he still wouldn't reach his target and the sun burst might still fail while he would die waiting to use it.

His magic simply wasn't enough. Fog wouldn't work,

because even if he could generate enough the drakes would simply blast the entire region with fire. The Dragon would command them to do so. He had learned that lesson once already. And sooner or later they would hit him. A simply breeze could have taken them all down, but he had no trace of weather magic. And as capable as he was with his Earth magic he couldn't create a dome large enough and strong enough to defend himself against them in the time he had available. And an ice shield would not hold against concentrated drake fire. It was force as well as fire. Their fire ultimately overwhelm it.

If he fell the cavern would survive. The Dragon would claim it. And in time his armies would spread out across the entire world. He would not be stopped. And eventually everyone Sam knew or loved would be killed. Ryshal would be killed. He could not let that happen.

The whole thing was a riddle with no right answer. Every choice was wrong. Every choice led to failure. And now everything was falling apart. If only the drakes hadn't arrived so soon!

Sam was desperate. Frantic with worry. Barely able to think. But it didn't matter that it was too soon. It only mattered that he had to do something. But what?

And then it came to him. A whisper. An idea. The answer to a prayer he'd been too desperate to even make. A shape that he hadn't ever seen before. A magic that wasn't even possible. No wizard could do what he was considering doing. It was a desperate gamble. But he was desperate and it was the only chance any of them had.

Sam called the already raging roc to him, and despite the fact that his nature magic was waning it came. It even lowered its great head into his arms when he ordered it to. Maybe it knew his plan. And then he gave it fire.

It was a shocking enchantment. Sam had no idea whether it would work. Whether it even could. But all he did know was that he had to try. So he drew all the fire he had and pushed it into every muscle and fibre of the great bird. And it took so much. His sword when he enchanted it, could hold a powerful spell. His axe an even more powerful one. But against the roc they were nothing. This was taking every ounce of fire magic he had. As much as the fire rings had.

Still he continued to draw on the magic and force it into the roc no matter the pain, and somehow he filled it. There was no room left. No part of the roc that was not filled with fire. And finally when the entire plateau was a flat lake of ice and every trace of fire in him was gone, he knew it was time.

He spoke the word. A word he didn't even know. It was simply there in his head. Mostly it seemed like just a sound; a collection of syllables that might not even have been meant to be uttered by a human throat, and the fire was released. All of it. And it was glorious.

There was light and power, flames and fury, and the roc caught fire in front of him. It exploded as it burnt from the inside out, and yet even as he was hurled back from the beast by the blast to come crashing down on the ice, Sam saw that it wasn't consumed by those flames.

But then it couldn't be. The phoenix had been reborn.

As he lay there on the stone terrace, staring up at the flaming beast, Sam found himself all but overwhelmed by the sight. Staggered by the understanding that he had done this. Created this. Because this was magic that surely no wizard could ever have. It was simply too much.

But he also understood that it didn't matter. The phoenix was reborn and it had been reborn for a reason.

"The drakes. Destroy them." He gave the command and on some level understood that he was giving the beast its final command. The calling of the roc was ended. The phoenix was free. Free from him. Free from everyone. It would never be commanded again. Because that was its nature – freedom.

Sam didn't see the phoenix leave – it was too fast for that. Instead he saw a trail of fire in the air from where it had been, much like the trail that came from a cannon when it spoke. And when he turned his head in the direction in which it had travelled he saw where it had arrived. Or rather, he saw the after effects.

There was a glorious orange explosion in the air about half a league away. He could just make out what he thought were huge hunks of burning steel beginning their long, painfully slow, descent to the ground, trailing fire and black smoke. And even as he watched there were more explosions and more falling steel corpses.

It was so fast. Far too fast for the eye to keep up with. All he could see were the explosions, one after another, and the streaks of fire between them that he knew were the phoenix flying from one to the next.

"Samual?"

The elders were calling him, but for the longest time Sam couldn't pay them any attention. He couldn't do much at all except lie there and stare in wonder at the impossible creature he'd somehow wrought. At the complete destruction of the steel drakes. But finally he managed to tear his eyes away from the sight and give his attention to the elders in the window.

"I don't know elders. It just came to me, but it's not my doing." He didn't know what else he could tell them. And soon his eyes returned to the battle in the distance.

Sam lay there watching the battle for a good little while, wondering how he could possibly have brought this magnificent beast into existence. How in any way he could have shaped the phoenix. But mostly he was just amazed at how dangerous the beast was. Stunned as the distant sky turned orange with the bodies of the steel drakes tumbling out of the sky.

He was relieved too because he knew none of them were going to make it to the terrace. None of them were going to come anywhere close before their remains rained down on the land.

But it wasn't all good news. Staring out to the horizon, he could just make out a distant wave of steel flowing towards him that he knew were the wolves. The wolves were fast, and though they couldn't climb – he hoped – the distance meant that he had only a couple of hours before they arrived. And when they did the mountain would be completely surrounded. He had also lost his ride home. When the wolves arrived, he would be surrounded. Trapped.

To add to his problems he was exhausted. Calling the roc and commanding it had been exhausting. His fire magic was all but spent. Nearly everything he had, had gone into the phoenix. His nature magic was running low too. He scarcely had enough magic left to keep himself going. All he had left was his Earth magic and that was waning as he dug ever deeper.

But still he had to continue. The phoenix had bought him the time he needed. Now he had to make that time count.

Somehow he staggered to his feet, and then walked like an old man back to the shaft he was digging. He was drained, but as he focussed on the task at hand, he determined that whatever he had left he would make certain was enough. The Dragon would not claim this cavern. Fair Fields would not fall. His loved ones would not surrender their lives to the steel vermin.

Once again he sent his magic streaming into the well. Pushing the stone aside as it dug ever deeper, always aiming straight for the cavern. And though the magic did not come as easily as it had, it still came. He just had to focus. To ignore the pain and tiredness, put aside his fears, and let it flow through him into the distant rock.

In time he could feel the shaft biting ever deeper into the stone, and he knew the end was in sight. It gave him hope.

Hours later he could feel it almost within his grasp. It was a matter of only a few paces, and the nearness of his goal almost undid him. The excitement was nearly too much. But he held on, pushing the stone aside as he forced his magic down the shaft, until finally in a moment of absolute wonder he felt it push through.

It was done! He would have screamed his triumph to the heavens above if he could have. But he couldn't. He had no strength left. None in his flesh. None of his magic either. And yet that didn't matter. The last part of his mission did not require either of those things. It only required a word.

He limped slowly across to his pack, feeling as though he'd aged a century in only a few days. But he felt stronger when he pulled the sun burst out of it and held it in his hands.

It was an impossible device. An orb of orange and yellow fire that he didn't really understand. But he understood power. He could feel it, just as he could the warmth of the sun. There was so much magic flowing through it. Far more than any mere wizard could ever possess. How had the ancients ever managed to contain that power within an orb? It didn't seem possible.

Not for the first time he wondered how his brother could ever have laid his hands on this ancient weapon. He hadn't even known they existed save in the ancient tales. And the tales were wild. They called them city wreckers and mountain destroyers. Things that couldn't really be true. The devices couldn't be that powerful. Nothing could be. Which was suddenly important to him since he was standing on a mountain with one of the impossible devices in his hands. Could it destroy a mountain? He had to hope not.

But in the end he knew that only one thing mattered. That the device was powerful enough to destroy a subterranean cavern. He just had to hope that its power wasn't such that it would reach him. And surely it couldn't. Not through the best part of a league and a half of stone above it? Praise the All Father he would be safe up here.

Because he wouldn't be safe on the ground. That much became obvious when he finally looked around to see a sea of steel flowing towards him. The wolves were now half way between the horizon and the mountain, and getting closer all the time. And somewhere behind them he knew was the Dragon himself. The general was coming to claim his base on the continent and from there to build his armies. That could not happen. If he achieved nothing else Sam knew, he had to stop him here. No matter what.

Sam walked back to the shaft, the sun burst cradled safely in his arms, uttered a quick prayer to the All Father and then spoke the word as he stared into the red orb.

Did it work? For the longest time Sam didn't know. He studied the device with all his senses, trying to detect a change. And then after heartbeats that had seemed to drag like years he felt it. The magic contained within the ancient weapon was starting to build. He saw it too. The gold and red of the orb was starting to brighten. It was working.

Sam dropped the orb into the shaft and watched it vanish into the depths with a feeling of relief as he knew his job was done. The device would work or not. That was now out of his hands. He just had to pray that it worked as the ones in the ancient tales claimed it did – save for the mountain destroying part. But the one thing he did notice as the time crawled by, was that the inky blackness of the shaft was no longer inky black. Though the orb fell further and further with every beat of his heart and was soon completely out of sight, the orange and gold fire still streamed up out of the shaft, becoming ever brighter.

Soon the light became blinding and he had to step back and look away from the shaft. But even that wasn't enough and as the light kept growing brighter he had to move further and further away. And in time even that wasn't enough. The ray of light bursting from the shaft and streaking for the heaven was starting to cook him.

"Alders whoring tits!" Sam turned and began running, suddenly realising that he was in trouble. Clearly all his doubts about the power of the ancient weapon had been unworthy. It had all the power the ancient legends said it did and more. Meanwhile even while fear was starting to lend his legs a little strength, he knew he was in danger. A lot of danger. This thing might actually level a mountain.

And when he felt the heat on his back as he ran he began to realise it was worse than he had imagined.

Sam was soon sprinting like a frightened deer with a lion on its tail, using all the strength he had, and all the magic he had as well to lend his legs more strength, but he knew it wasn't enough. He could feel his back starting to burn. He could feel the mountain underneath him beginning to tremble. And worst of all he could see the edge of the terrace in front of him getting ever closer. And suddenly he was faced with a shocking decision. What should he do? Jump and fall to his death? Or stay and burn?

When he risked looking behind him though, he realised it wasn't a decision at all. Not when he could see the entire terrace behind him starting to melt. It was turning into a lake of molten rock. And he knew then that he couldn't stay. The pain as his armour started burning into his back was simply too great.

So when he reached the edge of the terrace he leapt, screaming as he did so. And he prayed as he had never prayed before. It was all he had left. Prayer. He had no magic left to him. No Roc to save him. No real hope at all. Just the promise of death rising up to meet him.

So he prayed and he fell. The wind whipped him around and blasted into his face. And every time he spun around it was to see the entire cliff face behind him beginning to melt like butter left out in the sun.

This wasn't supposed to be happening he told himself as he tumbled out of control. He was supposed to be able to escape the doom he had unleashed upon the mountain. But he couldn't escape anything. He was falling to his death. And the best he could hope for as he spun around wildly, was that it would be quick. And that Ry would forgive him and move on with her life.

He wanted her to be happy. He desperately wanted that. He also wanted her to be safe. But he didn't know if what he had done would be a critical hit for the Dragon. Now it seemed he wasn't going to find out. So he offered a prayer to the Goddess for her. Ryshal was always a follower of the Goddess so it seemed only right.

Then he surrendered himself to death on the rocky ground

far below him. Ground that was coming ever closer.

But death didn't come. Teeth did.

Between one heartbeat and the next Sam found himself trapped within a cage of giant teeth. Completely surrounded by them. Worse, it seemed that he was lying on a tongue. It took time to understand that – he'd already had too many shocks that day – but he finally realised he was inside the mouth of a giant beast. He was being eaten!

How could that happen? How could a man both burning and falling to his doom suddenly be eaten in mid-air? And by what? Sam had no idea. He couldn't even make sense of it. But as he was suddenly squashed brutally into the embrace of the scaly tongue he realised it didn't matter. He was about to be swallowed.

Again he was wrong. Instead of heading down the creature's throat he unexpectedly found himself being launched towards the cage of teeth in front of him which magically seemed to open just in time, and he realised he was being spat out. Just before he saw a tree in front of him and crashed into it.

Branches snapped, his clothes ripped, his skin was torn and lashed, but at least he survived. He hurt all over, but the very fact that he was hurting meant that he was alive.

And the fact that he could see the ground just ten paces below him meant he was hanging in a tree branch.

Sam hung there for the longest time, simply trying to make sense of what had happened. But there was no sense to be had. There was only pain, saliva that seemed to be covering him from head to foot, and the smell of carrion that he assumed was the creature's breath lingering. There was also hysteria which kept threatening to bubble up from the depths of his thoughts and claim him. But somehow he held it back – just.

There was one other thing too – roaring. It sounded almost like the roar of a lion, but so much louder. In fact it was everywhere, and it was coming closer.

It was then that he realised he had to get down. He had to find the ground and somewhere away from the tree where he could see what was happening. Because all he could see from where he was, was the ground and endless pine needles.

Climbing down wasn't easy. When he'd been a child he remembered climbing up and down trees all day. He remembered loving it. But sometime during his life that had changed. His feet were nowhere near as confident in finding branches to support his weight. His hands had nothing like the strength he remembered them having. Several times he came close to falling.

But somehow in a series of awkward gyrations and lunges, he made it to the lower branches of the tree and then to the ground. It was fortunate he thought. Because it would have been embarrassing to have killed himself falling out of a tree after having survived a mountain exploding underneath him and then being eaten by some great beast.

Once on the ground it didn't take long to make his way through the copse of trees in which he'd been deposited, to see the land unfolding in front of him. And when he was finally able to take it all in, he wondered if he'd hit his head too many times.

There were dragons in the sky! Dozens of dragons. Flying through the air in an intricate aerial dance, laying down huge columns of fire on the steel wolves beneath them. He could see iridescent scales sparkling in the sunshine. Huge wings beating surprisingly gently in the air. Long sinuous necks and tails weaving through the skies. And cascades of fire streaming down.

The wolves for their part were running around in all directions. They no longer had a destination and their master had doubtless only instructed them just to run away from the dragons. It was all they could do. There was fire everywhere. Leagues of fire that seemingly went all the way back to the horizon. Thousands of steel corpses were burning and had set the fields on fire as they burnt.

Meanwhile when he finally managed to tear his eyes away from the spectacle unfolding in front of him it was to discover that half a league behind him Mount Andrea had gone. It had vanished from the middle of the other mountains, almost as though it had sunk into the ground. And the mountains that had surrounded it looked to have been melted a little as well. Like candles with wax running down their sides. Where Mount Andrea had once been there was now a sea of flames. As for the cavern beneath them he could only imagine that it had been destroyed. The sun burst had done everything the ancient tales had said it would and had actually melted the entire mountain. Now it was a bubbling lake of molten rock nestled between its sisters.

No one would ever again visit the ancient caverns underneath it. Not even if they still survived. But the chances were that they were now simply flooded with molten rock.

But the caverns didn't matter anymore. Spectacular as a molten lake was, it wasn't going to kill him. A wolf might. Sam returned his attention to the spectacle unfolding in front of him. Dragons fighting steel wolves. No one was ever going to believe that. He wasn't sure he believed it himself. He wasn't sure he believed any of it.

A phoenix reborn to fire. A mountain that had actually melted. And now the dragons destroying an army of machina.

This could only be the work of the gods he decided. Draco, Lord of the Skies, was sending his children into battle. The Goddess having her precious symbol – or was that pet – restored to her. And wherever the phoenix was now, he was sure it would be being seen. A glorious flaming bird wasn't the sort of thing that was easily missed. And gods liked their works to be seen.

Perhaps the sun burst wasn't of the ancients either? Perhaps it too had been built by the gods? That at least made some sense. Though not a lot. The gods seldom acted. They had priests for exerting their will on the world if they needed to.

In time another thought crossed his mind. The shadelings had better never see this! As he watched the dragons continue their work and the land turn to fire for as far as he could see, Sam knew they would be distinctly unhappy. Or if they did see it they had better never imagine that this was his doing. Because he couldn't even begin to imagine how upset they would be. This might not be a forest, but it was still widespread devastation that put his fire ring to shame and they would never accept such a thing. And who would imagine that this was the work of dragons?

Where had the dragons come from? He could see at least a score of the beasts dancing and weaving through the air as they set the world ablaze. And dragons tended to be solitary creatures. Very few ever saw a dragon. But if you did, you only ever saw one.

Could this really be the work of Draco? Lord of the Skies and Father of the Dragons? Could a god truly be getting involved in the affairs of mortals? Sam kept returning to that question as he watched. It was the only answer he had though it seemed fanciful. But was it any more fanciful than a score of dragons incinerating an army of machina? And as he eventually recalled from his reading, the dragons had become involved in the first Dragon Wars.

Was it over? Sam wondered about that in time as he stood there staring at the distant battle. He wondered about it some more as he eventually gave up on standing and collapsed to the ground to lean back against a tree. He'd run out of strength as well as magic. In fact he doubted that he would even be able to draw his greatsword should one of the wolves make it close enough to be able attack him. Fortunately they were some distance from him and he figured there were very few left by then.

It seemed that the battle was over – for him at least. The dragons were ridding the world of the wolves. The phoenix had rid the sky of the drakes. And he had destroyed the ancient Dragon's cavern. There was only one enemy remaining – the Dragon himself – and Sam had no thought at all where he might be. The only thing he knew for sure was that he would not be with his armies. He did not fight his own wars. He did not stand with his soldiers. That was not his way.

No doubt in time he would start making his way back to his island to start again. But the chances were that he would be on foot with the steel drakes gone, and they could begin a hunt for him. And with the Window of Parsus they could pass the word to others about the Dragon. That would make the hunt far easier. It also wasn't as if they didn't know where he was going. After all there were only a few places where a man could hire a ship to take him to the southern islands. And a part troll blood would stand out. He would likely be caught.

As for himself it seemed he was safe for the moment. No one was coming for him. The wolves weren't heading his way since their master had no idea where he was or even who he was. And while he was weak, he would recover. In time, after he'd rested, he could begin his long journey home. Back to Ryshal. And then maybe they could begin working on the things that really mattered – like starting a family.

That was a pleasant thought to sleep on. And it became obvious to him as he sat there that that was all he could do. So as his eyes began to close he clung to the dream. After everything that had happened he needed to cling to something good.

Chapter Forty Seven

"Aylin mi elle." A woman's voice came out of the darkness. One filled with love and promise.

Even in his sleep Sam smiled when he heard it. Because he knew the speaker. He knew her whether asleep or awake. He would always know her.

"Samual, it's time to awaken." She raised her voice a little, becoming a tiny bit more insistent.

But Sam was simply too happy in his dreams to open his eyes. He let the soft, wonderful words flow over him like a soothing blanket.

"Get up Samual!" This time it was a man who spoke and he sounded annoyed. It was that that finally managed to persuade Sam to open his eyes.

When he did it was to discover that he was still where he had fallen asleep. Still propped up against the side of a tree. Somehow even in his sleep he hadn't managed to collapse completely. Time had passed. Clearly quite a lot of it. Night had fallen and if he was any judge of the moon's position on the horizon, dawn could not be far away. But while the sleep had helped him, he was still nowhere near his normal strength. His magic was subdued. His flesh felt bruised if not completely broken. Worse still he could still smell carrion. That accursed smell would just not go away. He needed to find a river.

"Elder?" He was actually almost glad to hear the Elder's voice, crotchety as he was. And he was very glad to hear Ryshal's. Glad to see both of them staring back at him from the window in the sky which was hanging just in front of him.

"Samual Hanor, do you have any thought of how much trouble you have put us to?"

"I'm sorry Elder." It was an instinctive response that came out of his mouth. He actually had no thought what the Elder was talking about. "I will try to do better."

"See that you do," the Elder humphed. "And see that you apologise to your poor wife as well. After all the pain you have put her through this night. I will give you two a little while to speak." With that the Elder walked away leaving Sam sitting there staring at only his wife.

"Elder Bela is right beloved. I owe you a great many apologies."

"And we will speak at length of how you may give them aylin mi elle. And how often." But she smiled to show that she wasn't angry. She was relieved.

She had been upset. Even in the darkness he could see the traces of tears on her face. But the tears had dried. The upset had gone away. In fact, though Sam thought he could see worry in her eyes, she looked happy. That was a good thing. Wasn't it?

"For the moment though we must speak of your journey home."

"I will begin the moment the sun rises," he promised her. She was right. It was time to come home. "I will not let myself be kept from you a day longer than I must. I promise."

"And I will wait impatiently for your return. But the elders say you will have to make a stop along the way at Fall Keep."

"Fall Keep?" Sam hadn't expected that. Fall Keep wasn't

on the direct path back to Ryshal. And there was nothing left there anyway. The keep was gone, the town burnt to the ground. There were no people left there. Why would he go there? He asked.

"Because the elders have asked and I believe they are right to do so. The Dragon is heading there and he still must be stopped."

Sam didn't respond to that. Instead he simply sat there wondering. He couldn't imagine why the Dragon was heading there. If there was nothing there for Sam there was nothing there for the Dragon either. It was a ruin. But she was right. If they knew where the Dragon was it was his duty to hunt him down if he could. Before he returned to his island.

But on the other hand it was a fifty league journey and he was on foot. He was also nowhere near his full strength. Stranger still, why would Ry want him to go into danger? She hated it when he left her and risked his life. Carefully he asked his wife that.

"Yes, but you are stronger now and you will continue to recover. By the time you reach the city you should be as strong as ever. You should be the Fire Angel again. And no mere Dragon will stop you. Especially now when he's weak."

"I am no god that victory should always be mine."

"You are the Fire Angel. I did not truly believe that until yesterday. And for that I am truly sorry. But now I understand. Even the Dragon understands as he flees in terror from you. He knows he cannot face you. That no one can."

"Ry I ..."

Sam wanted to tell her that she was giving him too much praise. That he was not the unstoppable warrior she believed.

That he could be killed far too easily. Just like any man. But the words stuck in his throat when he saw the faith in her eyes. She had been very frightened. And that was his fault. He had scared her. Now she had found something to believe in. He could not take that from her just now. Later when they were once more together he would tell her the truth. Instead he turned his words to practical matters.

"The Dragon is weak?"

"He only has a small army. Smaller than the one you destroyed in Shavarra. But in two weeks he will be stronger. All the rats from Shavarra are marching to Fair Fields. The war masters say he will go to Fall Keep. That he will repair the walls and wait until they arrive. Then he will march south with a much larger army as he heads for his island. Samual he cannot be allowed to return to his island. In time he would only send more armies to destroy us all and we can't have that. Especially not now."

"Not now?" Sam didn't understand.

"Not now." Ryshal turned side on so he could see her belly and then patted it and smiled. "Not when we have so much to protect."

"Are you saying …?" Sam's question trailed off as he knew exactly what she was saying. There was no sign of a bump, but she surely knew if she was with child. And suddenly he was gloriously happy.

"You are the most perfect wife a man could ever hope for!"

"And you are the champion a wife dreams of." She smiled broadly, tears in her eyes. "But now you will have to be once more the champion our child needs to protect him or her."

In that moment Sam understood why she was asking him to go into battle, when always before she wanted to keep him from it. She was going to be a mother and she had a duty to protect their child. The Dragon threatened their baby just as he threatened everyone else. He had to be stopped. And she believed he could do it. That in fact he was the only one who could.

"I will not fail you," Sam vowed.

"I know that." Ry smiled happily. "You have rebirthed the phoenix. Called the dragons to war. And levelled a mountain. The entire world surely trembles at your feet. The feet of the Fire Angel."

"Ry, I didn't really do any of those things. The phoenix was reborn through me, but not by me. I cast the magic but I don't know where the shape came from. And Mount Andrea was levelled by a sun burst. I do not have that sort of power. As for the dragons I have no thought at all where they came from." He felt terrible telling her that. Letting her know that he wasn't as powerful as she believed. But it was the truth and she had to hear it. From him before others made it clear.

"Then you also did not leap off a thousand pace high cliff and fly to the ground?" She shone like the sun with happiness as she said it.

"Alder's hairy tits!" Sam let swore as the memories came flooding back. He couldn't help himself. And then he stuttered like a village idiot as he tried to think of something intelligent to say. But there was nothing he could say, and eventually he ended up sitting in silence.

"If you didn't fly there then how did you not fall to your death?" Ryshal seemed somewhat curious. Maybe even a little worried. "That was when we lost you. You ran too fast and we couldn't keep up. I spent half the night looking for you at the bottom of the cliff. It was only that there was no body lying there and that the priests swore you still lived that kept me from weeping in terror."

"Praise the All Father, Ryshal I'm so sorry for that. There was no time and I did not think. And then when it was over I was too exhausted to do anything but sleep. I should have told you I lived. I should have found a way."

"But you do live and that is what matters. The Fire Angel lives. The father of my baby lives. He has learnt to fly."

"I cannot fly." Sam understood why she believed it. It was actually easier to believe than the truth. But it wasn't the truth.

"Then how did you reach the ground from such a height?" She looked puzzled, and maybe even just a little bit worried.

"Ry my glorious wife, could we choose not to speak of that – ever?" The last thing Sam wanted to do was tell anyone of that journey. He didn't want to even remember it. But when he saw the determination in Ry's face he knew she would not be kept from finding out.

"Then at least can you promise me that no one will ever hear of this please?" He pleaded with her a little and finally got at least a nod from her.

"I was falling when a dragon caught me."

"That doesn't sound so bad." But clearly she realised it wasn't the full story.

"In its mouth," Sam added to complete the picture. "And it spat me out in this copse of trees."

"A dragon ate you and spat you out?" Her eyebrows rose in disbelief.

Immediately she said it Sam could hear laughter coming from somewhere out of sight and he guessed his secret was out. It was quite a lot of laughter actually.

"It was unpleasant. And I was covered in saliva. Even now I still stink of carrion. The whole world stinks of it. I need a bath."

He shouldn't have added the last. Immediately the words left his mouth he could hear people around her exploding with laughter. Some obviously tried to hide it behind coughing fits. But others didn't even bother. Soon the only thing he could hear was laughter. Even Ry gave in and started giggling – though she tried to hide her amusement behind her hands.

Meanwhile Sam had to sit there and wait for them to stop. It was a long wait. But at least Ry was happy. In fact whatever trace of fear she had been holding seemed to have vanished as she gave in to her merriment. He supposed that was for the best.

"Oh my beautiful husband, you bring light to the world in dark times." She eventually managed to speak through her laughter, though she nearly choked doing it. "You truly do."

"I live to please you," he told her a little sarcastically. Because just then as he sat there red faced, he would have preferred not to have brought so much pleasure to so many.

"Samual, you should be happy."

"About being eaten by a dragon? Less than you'd think!"

"About being saved by a dragon!" She told him a little sternly. But she was still laughing quietly. "No man has ever been saved by a dragon. And it means you will defeat our enemy. You can't fail."

"Huh?" Sam didn't see the logic.

"Beloved, if a dragon saved you it can only mean that it was commanded to, and only Draco could do that. Husband, the Father of Dragons saved your life."

No wonder she was happy Sam realised! She thought he had the gods on his side. Even if she was still laughing.

"Or I just didn't taste very good!" He shouldn't have said it. Sam knew that the instant the words left his mouth. But it didn't stop him saying them. And nothing at all he guessed was going to stop the laughter that followed.

Maybe it would have been better if the dragon had swallowed him!

Chapter Forty Eight

It was daylight when Sam finally reached Fall Keep. And he was glad to see at least some of it still standing in the sunshine even if night would have been a better time to attack. Mostly that was because he was aching from having ridden for so long. Moose were not good riding animals even when you had magic. And though he could keep the animal calm, he could do nothing about the hardness or shape of its back or its natural gait. He couldn't simply create a saddle for it either. Three days on the back of a moose was hard on a man. But unfortunately there were no horses around. No doubt they had all been taken as people fled the realm.

Still, the beast was actually quite quick when it wanted to be, and they had made good time. Thus far there was no sign of the rats.

The Dragon had beaten him here – but then he was in a light wagon being pulled by a pack of steel wolves that could run night and day without pause. He had always been going to beat him here. Luckily he had not got far with his repairs to the walls. They had begun; the Dragon had started using his magic to shape the stone and lift the walls up. But he had not yet had time to complete the job.

As for the wolves, they were patrolling the walls. Sam could see them through the massive hole where the gate had been. A hole he had created. A small wall of steel teeth and claws replacing the missing stone. But they would not last long. The elders had said the Dragon had come with an army of only a hundred and fifty to two hundred wolves. It had been what he had presumably thought would be his personal protective squad as he rode to claim his prize after his army had captured it. Now it was his entire army. It was also about to get smaller. Much smaller.

Sam was still nowhere near his full strength. In fact he had the strange feeling that his fire would not return as powerfully as it had before, but he still had enough magic to launch a fire ball at the wolves standing in the remains of the gate. A moment later at least a score of the steel beasts were gone. His fire ball was nowhere near as hot as it should be and it would certainly never knock over a city wall as his best ones once had. But the wolves weren't the most powerful of the machina and it was more than a match for them. The Fire Angel had announced his arrival. Even if he was no longer the master of fire he had been.

"War Masters," he spoke to the window in the air beside him, "can you give me some targets to aim at please."

The Window of Parsus was an incredibly useful tool he thought. Especially when your enemy was hiding behind huge walls that he couldn't see through and didn't have the strength to knock down. And so as he watched the window abruptly streak away from him at great speed heading for the keep, he felt a small thrill of victory. The Dragon had never prepared for this.

Soon the window was back and the war masters had a list of targets for him to hit. Naturally he sent fireballs at all of them, surprised at how easy it was. And a few moments later when they returned from checking out the damage he'd done he was given the welcome news that at least two score of wolves were gone.

A third of the Dragon's army – gone before he'd even approached the keep! Sam suspected the troll blood had to be hiding somewhere inside the city, trembling with fear. Soon though Sam silently promised him, he would no longer be afraid.

Over confidence though was always a mistake. A lesson

Sam learned anew when he heard a sound he had not expected to hear. Cannon fire. Obviously the Dragon had been busier than he'd realised.

Sam raced for cover behind a farm house, annoyed at his oversight. But thankfully the cannon shot came nowhere near him. It wasn't surprising in hindsight he supposed. The Dragon might have raised the cannon into position and loaded them, but he had no one to aim and fire them. An army of steel wolves could not operate war machines. He was just firing them wherever they sat.

How was he lighting them though? The Dragon had no fire magic as far as he knew. Only nature and earth magic. Had he set up some elaborate fuse system? Or was he running along the walls himself with a torch in his hands?

Either way it didn't matter. The front walls had once had thirty or forty cannon on the ramparts. And Sam had heard thirty or forty blasts. Now that the cannon had been fired they had to be reloaded. Who did the Dragon have to do that? Only himself. That meant that for the moment they were useless.

Once again the Dragon had struck too early. If he'd had any military training he would have waited until Sam was in his sights before firing. But he hadn't and so he'd weakened himself.

But he still had more soldiers that Sam hadn't prepared for. And they began with the three steel drakes that he had used to decimate Fair Fields with. Sam had forgotten about them. Everyone had. But as he watched them climb into the sky from somewhere within the keep, he remembered them anew.

Luckily Sam had a weapon too that the Dragon didn't know about. And when he pulled his sword and aimed it at the nearest of the three drakes, he knew the Dragon was going to be upset. Some time ago he'd found out that the steel drakes weren't nearly as fire proof as they were supposed to be. That was a weakness. And by focusing the fire scythe spell, he planned on exploiting that weakness.

When the closest drake was within two hundred paces he released the spell and played the thin ray of fire over its wing. The wing was the drake's most vulnerable point since the metal there was thinnest and without a wing the drake couldn't fly.

It took a few moments for the spell to cut into the wing as he wanted, but then he was heartened by the sight of a small explosion in it, followed by the sight of the drake tumbling out of the air and then hitting the ground where it exploded properly.

The second drake proved just as easy to destroy. But the third was too close. It laid down a blast of heavy fire at the building he was hiding behind, knocking over its front walls and setting it ablaze. But then it made the mistake of continuing to fly over the burning building. Right over Sam's head. In a heartbeat he had a perfect target as the drake flew away from him, and Sam took advantage of it.

Heartbeats later the third drake came tumbling down out of the sky, only to explode when it hit the ground, sending shards of burning metal flying in all directions. They were actually more of a risk to him than the flames the drakes had launched.

Three drakes down, sixty wolves destroyed. The Dragon had to know he was in trouble. It was time Sam thought to make him understand that. Because the more frightened he was the more mistakes he would make. It was time to let him taste fear.

Sam sent the window flying back in to the city, but this time with only one target for the war masters to find. The

Dragon himself. He was in there somewhere, hiding; hoping he would not be found. It was time to take that hope from him.

While the war masters searched the city, Sam set about restoring the magic to the fire scythe spell. It was a very effective spell and he wanted to have it ready when he needed it. He was nowhere near his full strength, so he needed to be prepared for whatever awaited him.

The war masters returned with a target for Sam just as he had finished restoring the spell to its full power. Apparently the Dragon was hiding in the wine store abutting the west wall. It seemed like an odd place to hide Sam thought. The wine store had only half height walls with poles supporting the clay tile roof above them, and there was nothing in them. No furniture, no food, no drinking water or places to bathe. It really was just a place where barrels of wine were stored. But if the war masters said that that was where the Dragon was, Sam was happy enough to take them at their word. Immediately Sam sent a stream of fireballs aimed at the inside of that wall. And then waited to hear back from the war masters.

When they reported back though it was to tell him that the Dragon was out in the open in the front courtyard and running around in a blind panic as he looked for new places to hide. There were also a number of wolves racing for the gate and presumably toward him. Sam saw it for the diversion it was. The Dragon needed to stop the fireballs landing on his head. But still, as another score of wolves rushed through the front gate, Sam was more than happy to destroy them. The more he got rid of the less the Dragon had left to call on. It was a simple equation.

The Dragon quickly settled on a new direction to run – away from Sam – and when the war masters told him that, Sam smiled. In that moment he knew that he had the Dragon.

If he had run behind the pile of rubble that had once been the keep and into the city itself, then it meant he was no longer watching the front wall. It gave Sam the chance to approach the keep.

Sam began his approach, walking slowly up the road toward the gap where the front gate had been. And despite his certainty that he was safe he was relieved when no cannon fired at him and no wolves attacked him, even though he took his time covering the half league or so.

Just inside the remains of the gate he stopped, spotting a few wolves in the courtyard. They quickly fell to his spells, long before they had a chance to reach him. It was scary seeing the huge steel monsters almost the size of snap wolves running at him, but he was a soldier. He had been trained to deal with fear.

So another half dozen more wolves perished while he crossed to the side of the keep and the crudely repaired staircase leading up to the ramparts behind the walls. Going up the ramparts was his plan for dealing with the wolves. Because unlike the rats the wolves couldn't climb. They could ascend stairs which was why he was so keen to destroy the stairs after he'd reached the ramparts, but they couldn't reach him. Meanwhile he had complete access to the outside of the city. He even crossed the gap in the wall he'd created along the side of the courtyard, simply by using his magic to create a stone bridge.

After that the battle was his. He walked the ramparts which completely surrounded the city, destroying wolves wherever they appeared, while the war masters used the window to keep finding targets for him. It was slow – Fall Keep was a good sized city and the Dragon had plenty of burnt out buildings to hide in – but in only a few hours he was sure another sixty or so wolves had perished.

What did that leave the Dragon with he wondered? A pack of fifty or so wolves at most, he figured, and because his fireballs were levelling buildings one by one, they had fewer and fewer places to hide. It was only a matter of time.

Of course over confidence was always a weakness, and once again Sam had to remember that when he saw a shambling figure in rags – a beggar – suddenly walk around a corner. Why was the man here? The city was deserted. Or so he had thought. The walls were gone, the buildings burnt out. There was no food left. No resources. No riches of any kind. Multiple armies had threatened to invade it. And currently there were still steel wolves loose in it. Wolves that would surely kill anyone they saw. So why was there a beggar wandering the streets? Who was he going to beg from? How was he even still alive?

And were there others? He hadn't seen any, and the war masters looking on through the window hadn't reported any either, but that didn't mean there weren't any. They could be hiding in the ruins of their homes. In fact with the wolves running around the city, that was probably where they would be. While he was bringing the houses down on their heads one by one.

Sam didn't like that last thought very much. How could he level the city building by building and conduct a battle if there were innocent people in it? He could kill them. And what did he do about the one he had spotted? He had to get him out of the city obviously. But he also had to find any others. And both were impossible to do when he was standing on the battlements on the walls high above the houses, raining down destruction on them.

Sam sighed heavily, knowing his duty. And then he used a little Earth magic to extend a stone walkway from the rampart he was on to the roof of the nearest house. From there it was only a short jump through the already broken roof and then down through the house's internal staircase to the ground and the street outside. From here on he would have to face the wolves on the ground, one by one. He would have to search the houses before he destroyed them. And he would have to hunt the Dragon on foot.

But first he'd have to find that beggar he'd seen and get him out of the city.

That proved harder than he'd expected. By the time he'd made it to the street the beggar was gone. He'd either turned a corner or ducked into one of the houses, and since Sam hadn't seen which, he was going to have to check both.

Sam continued walking down the street, checking the buildings as quickly as he could and calling out to anyone who might be in them. As he'd expected his actions drew the wolves to him. Those that were left had taken up positions hiding in the burnt out ruins. A man alone on the ground would have looked like an easy target. So they charged him and he destroyed them one by one, though it was harder than it should have been. They were much faster on the ground than the rats and more cunning as they waited until he got close before rushing at him.

Sam however, held his fire shield tight as he walked down the streets and it seemed to work. The wolves exploded when they touched it and most of the debris went flying away from him. He took a few scratches and his armour – as minimal as it was – a few more, but after an hour he guessed a dozen wolves had fallen to it and he was still standing.

But he hadn't found the beggar. Nor any other civilians. No more had the war masters as they scoured the streets through the mirror. And all the time the Dragon remained hidden. Sam had however, levelled two more streets and scores of burnt out buildings that had once been homes and small businesses. It was slow, but this way he knew that sooner or later the Dragon would be forced out into the open. There would be nowhere left for him to hide.

"Two streets up, to your left." War Master Wyldred's voice suddenly interrupted him in his work, and immediately he heard it Sam started running in the indicated direction.

"The beggar or the Dragon?" It didn't matter which, he had to find them both.

"The beggar."

Two streets up Sam turned the around the corner and got a glimpse of the beggar in the distance. He saw a dark, shambling figure ducking into a building. Sam started running harder. His blood and his training made him quick on his feet. But still he wasn't fast enough and to add to his worries a wolf came from out of nowhere to attack him. Happily it exploded on his fire shield, but still, it had caught him by surprise and he didn't like that.

When he reached the building, breathing a little more heavily than he would have liked, there was no sign of the beggar. But Sam was sure he was inside.

The building was a warehouse. Actually it was the burnt out remains of one. It stood three stories high, though he doubted it had any internal floors left as they would have been wood. All that was left was the building's skeleton which had been built from stone. Most importantly though it was dark inside. Pitch black. The roof was slate and still intact. The windows, those that hadn't melted, were covered with char. And the walls were fire blackened. There was no light inside and he didn't like the thought of entering the darkened space. Even with his fire shield he would have felt vulnerable.

Getting rid of the slate roof though proved easy as Sam fused the slates together, and then snapped all the nails holding them to what remained of the beams and purlins. He then let them slide off and fall to the ground where they shattered with a pleasing sound. With the roof gone there was plenty of light inside. Even on the ground floor. As he'd suspected, the internal floors had burnt out.

The light revealed about a dozen wolves as he walked in, something that sent his heart racing a little. They were perched in the corners of the building or lodged on the remains of the joists that had once supported the floors, gleaming in the newly arrived sunlight, and all ready to attack. But once the light had been shone inside the building and their element of surprise had been lost, they gave up on any plans of an ambush. Instead they rushed to attack him as he stood in the double width doorway staring at them.

Sam tightened his fire shield as he saw them charge. In short order the wolves threw themselves at it and exploded barely ten feet in front of him.

A matter of heartbeats later it was over and all the wolves were gone. All that was left was a large open expanse of dirt floor littered with burning pieces of twisted steel on the other side of a ruined door frame. And as he stood there staring at them Sam realised he'd found the Dragon. This surely had to be the last of his army, kept close to protect him. Which meant he had to be close.

"War Masters." Sam indicated the warehouse. "The Dragon has to be inside."

He let them do the search since they were safe behind their Window of Parsus, while he stood there and let the hope wash over him. It was nearly ended. And while it seemed odd to him that he should have chased the beggar in here only to find the Dragon, in the end that didn't matter.

What did matter was when a moment later a steel clad

form abruptly swung down from above, burst through his fire shield and tried to put an axe through his head.

Sam dodged the attack – barely – and then pulled his own greatsword from his back as the Dragon came at him again. Instinctively he countered another vicious attack designed to cut his legs out from under him. And again he barely succeeded. The Dragon was fast, his fury powering him as nothing else could. More than that, he was trained. And Sam had been caught by surprise. He didn't like that.

Sam hadn't expected the Dragon to be so capable. He'd seen the Dragon in the Window of Parsus and known he was troll blood. He'd seen him murder those unfortunate men his machina had abducted. But still he'd thought of him mostly as an enchanter. That was what made him dangerous after all. So to have the Dragon in front of him, dressed in some sort of steel armour that obviously protected him from fire and swinging a pair of heavy hand axes was distinctly scary.

But in a strange way it seemed right that at the end he would have to face him sword against axe and tusk. And it wasn't a choice. After all, the Dragon's armour protected him somewhat against fire and Sam's magic was at a low ebb to begin with. He had more strength with his Earth magic, but the Dragon had the same magic. And nature magic wouldn't help either of them. In the end it had to be steel on steel.

Fortunately, though the Dragon had the speed and strength the blood of his trollish ancestors gave him, Sam had years of training in combat. And once he'd dodged the second attack he calmed his nerves and remembered the basics of combat. The third time the Dragon came for him he dodged again but this time swivelled as the troll over extended and planted a boot in his back.

The Dragon went flying, sprawling back into the warehouse only to land on his face. Sam strode after him thinking to end this quickly.

His enemy had other ideas though and he rolled to his side surprisingly quickly before finding his feet once more. Once again the two of them stood facing one another. Knight against troll. Enchanter against enchanter. Fire Angel against Dragon. Standing in what to all intents and purposes was an arena. Sam heard a gasp that he knew was his wife's, but he could not take a single heartbeat to comfort her. Not when he had an enemy to face.

Maybe this was supposed to be how it ended Sam thought. It seemed right somehow. Though he'd never seen a troll in armour before. Nor one that knew how to fight with weapons and armour. Normally they were savage creatures and that was how they fought. Though he might not be a military strategist, he was a clever fighter.

The Dragon demonstrated that a moment later as he bent, half rolled, stuck one axe in the other hand, grabbed up a handful of dirt from the ground and flung it at him. Sam spun, barely managing to keep the dirt from finding his eyes, and knowing this was going to be no easy battle. Fortunately he knew enough to complete his spin, greatsword held out before him, and then catch the Dragon who was already rushing him on the shoulder. The heavy plate took most of the blow, but it still buckled and tore. Sam could see a trace of blood on his blade as the Dragon was knocked aside.

"First blood to me then!" Sam laughed at the Dragon, hoping to goad him into making a mistake. But other than letting out a savage growl, the Dragon didn't seem to fall for the trick. His tusks might look as brutish and animalistic as those of any other troll, but there was a mind behind them. A mind that knew Sam was dangerous with a blade in his hand.

The Dragon tried the move a second time, but this time instead of scooping up dirt he tossed a belt knife at him, hoping to catch him by surprise. It bounced off Sam's armour, but even so the sound told him he had to be wary.

"If you'd had any sense you would have gone for the legs." He taunted the Dragon.

"If you had any sense you'd run!" The Dragon wasn't so good at the game, but he still knew how to threaten.

Unfortunately for him Sam suddenly remembered that he still had some useful magic at his command, and he sent a spray of ice at the Dragon. He figured that the armour might be proof against fire, but that ice was a different matter.

"Foetid whore!" The Dragon swore and shook off the ice, mostly unharmed, but he had bruising to his cheek. "You're nothing without your magic!"

Sam knew then that the Dragon had weak points he could exploit, and not having worn a full helm was one of them. Of course Sam also had weak points as he'd come wearing only his chest and back plates.

"And you're nothing without your armies. But I don't see them around."

"They'll be back. As soon as I've killed you." The Dragon edged to his left, sheathed his axe and drew a long steel knife for his off hand. It seemed he had no end of weapons strapped to his armour.

"Trying to gain position?" Sam laughed as he responded to the move. "Thinking to feint and dive through the door to safety? No such luck. I'll always know which way you'll jump. You're just not very bright."

"Really? You didn't catch me before. I escaped the island before you reached me. And if you hadn't had help you wouldn't have stopped me at Andrea." The Dragon edged another step to his left.

"Escaped the island?" Sam didn't understand. Nor did he really care. But he was curious. And he wanted his enemy distracted.

"I heard the fool priest when he said that the Fire Angel was coming for me. So I made sure I wasn't there."

Sam shrugged having no idea what the Dragon was talking about. Yet it did explain why he'd run to Fair Fields. Still, this was all about distracting him, not having a conversation. And he knew one way to do that. "So I destroyed Andrea instead. It wasn't hard."

That got the response he'd wanted from the Dragon, as the troll blood snarled like an animal at him. "The fire is weaker without Andrea but there are other workshops and you don't have enough sun bursts to destroy them all."

"I don't have to destroy them. I just have to kill you now." Why was the troll blood still edging to his side? Still going for an exit? Or was he turning him? Getting him out of position? Sam didn't know. But he was suspicious.

The Dragon took two more quick steps to his left and then suddenly lunged at him and Sam discovered his plan even as he found his blade hemmed in against the wall. He couldn't swing it as he needed to, to parry the Dragon's knife. Fortunately he could dance back a step and let the Dragon's attack fall short. Then he took half a step away from the wall and countered, striking for his eyes.

It was the Dragon's turn to dance back in fear, dropping the knife and reaching once more for his axe. As he did so Sam sent another blast of ice shards at him. This time when the Dragon had finished twisting and turning there was blood running down his cheek. A lot of it.

There was also fury in his eyes, and it made him dangerous. Even as he was twisting to avoid the ice blast, the Dragon managed a side step and lunged at him, and Sam had to dodge quickly in turn. One thing was certain. The Dragon wasn't letting his injuries slow him down. If anything he was getting faster.

Which was when Sam released the scything spell on the sword, full in the middle of the Dragon's chest. It was spectacular, and for a moment both of them were blinded by the fire. But the Dragon's armour proved tougher than the wings of his drakes, and when he was done his enemy was unharmed. So Sam hit him with yet another ice blast sending him flying backwards and making him snarl once more.

"Whore!" The Dragon quickly returned to the fight. But he looked rattled.

"Ready to pay for your crimes?" Sam goaded him some more, then had to doge and twist again as the Dragon leapt for him, swinging both axes wildly. By the gods he was fast! But it was desperation and fear powering him. And again he overreached and Sam delivered another kick to his back that sent the Dragon sprawling.

"My crimes?!" The Dragon got to his feet and spat in fury on the ground. "I have committed no crimes. I obey my Lord."

This time the Dragon didn't make the same mistake. He spun his axes in a furious set of arcs but never over extended as he advanced on Sam. Unfortunately for him Sam's greatsword had a greater reach and a step before the Dragon reached him he raised it and stepped into the attack, thrusting it straight into his gut.

Three feet of the best tempered steel with a diamond sharpened point would not be stopped by any armour no matter how pretty, and the sword punched through it to skewer the Dragon nicely. When Sam withdrew it there was a good six inches of blood on the end of it. It wasn't a deadly strike – the Dragon had twisted as the blade had ripped into him causing it to miss his target – but Sam knew as he watched the Dragon leap back and scream in pain, that it would cripple him. Certainly it would slow him down.

Others knew it too. Sam could hear the elves cheering through the Window as they looked on. No doubt they thought it was a greater blow than it was.

"Bastard!" The Dragon cursed him. "May Crodan take your soul!"

"You follow the Mountain God?" Sam was happy to talk. Especially now. Partly because he was curious. But also because he knew the longer he kept his enemy talking the more blood he would be losing and the slower he would get.

"I am first shaman!" The Dragon spat on the ground once more. Then he tried a half lunge, dodging towards him but staying just out of reach of Sam's blade, hoping to get him to swing at him and lose position. Sam wasn't that ill-trained though and he guessed the tactic. He held his position, the sword between them and watched as a trickle of red emerged from underneath the Dragon's breast plate and ran down his leg. And if he was leaking that much blood outside his armour it had to be much worse inside.

"Not very priestly are you?" Sam goaded him a little.

"Spoken by a wizard!" The Dragon let his temper loose and tried a feint, dancing to one side and seeming to strike with the axe in his left hand before swapping sides. He wanted to get Sam's sword following him the wrong way so he could slip past it. But Sam was too well trained for that. He'd seen the Dragon's feet move and expected the attack. And that gave him just enough time to punch the tip of his sword through the Dragon's shoulder.

"And a knight." Sam smiled happily as the Dragon leapt back, startled and bleeding from another wound. He smiled some more at the Dragon's look of pain.

Unfortunately it was his off hand that he'd hit and the Dragon responded by hurling his other axe with his good hand at Sam. This time Sam couldn't quite avoid the blow. And though it bounced off his breast plate, it had been thrown with all the speed and strength a desperate and frightened troll blood could muster. It was enough to buckle the plate and knock him back a couple of steps. Enough to make Ryshal scream in terror.

"And a witless servant of the elves' puny Goddess."

"I follow the All Father." Sam felt the need to correct him even though he had no issue with the Goddess. "And now you only have one axe!"

"Really? You returned the phoenix to the world – the Goddess' blessed symbol and pet. And you were protected by dragons, the children of Draco, Lord of the Skies, and the Goddess' companion. At what point did you think that the All Father stood by you?"

"At this point."

Sam flinched a little as a new voice came from the side, as did the Dragon. And then he shifted his gaze just enough to see the beggar standing there. And the shocking thing was that he knew the voice. He even knew the face.

"Heri?" It was him he slowly realised. But he didn't look

very much like himself. He had a full beard that by the looks of it hadn't been attended to with a comb or brush in months. His hair was long and unkempt. The skin of his face had been burnt by the sun. And he was painfully gaunt, his arms showing skin stretched over bone. Sam almost couldn't believe it was his brother.

Unfortunately he'd taken his eyes off the Dragon, and by the time he returned them to his enemy, an axe was already flying at his head. Sam knew then that he was dead even as he belatedly tried to dodge. But he didn't die. Instead the axe stopped in mid-air for no reason before falling to the ground between them, while back in new Shavarra Ryshal's terrified scream slowly died away.

"That is the name of this vessel."

Heri lowered his hand, a small shoot in it, and Sam guessed that he was the reason the axe had been stopped. But he couldn't understand how or why it had happened. Heri had no magic and he wanted him dead. Didn't he?

"But you servant of Crodan, have annoyed me for the last time." Heri turned to the Dragon who was finally looking frightened. But he wasn't moving.

"Five thousand years ago your predecessor tried to destroy the world as your Lord tried to usurp his brothers and sisters. He was stopped by them. And he swore to do better in future. He swore to me! Now despite his word given to me, he has tried again through you, and again he has been stopped. I will not allow this to happen a third time."

Whoever "I" was, clearly wasn't Heri, Sam realised. If nothing else Heri wasn't five thousand years old or claiming to be a vessel. And what was a vessel?

"Tell your deceitful Lord this as he runs away and hides

from me while he licks his wounds. No more! Draco's workshops are now sealed forever from his servants. And his ugly little offspring race may no longer retain his grace. That gift is taken from them, and the ability to bestow it is taken from Crodan. They will return to the beasts they wcre. He will have no more followers."

"But –."

The Dragon's words were cut off with a scream as in the space of a heartbeat he was transformed into burning white light. A column of it that reached for the skies. It was so bright that it forced Sam to close his eyes, cover them with an arm and then turn away. Even then it was painful. He could actually see the bones of his arm in front of him.

Mercifully it ended quickly, though even afterwards he couldn't see anything but brilliant reds and greens for ages. But though he was blinded, Sam knew he was safe. The Dragon was gone. Presumably dead. Which meant that the First Shaman was supposed to give the message to his master in the afterlife. Was that possible?

And Heri was obviously no longer Heri.

But was he the All Father? That Sam couldn't quite believe. After all it was Heri. He had never believed in the gods and he would never willingly serve one. And the king of gods? Here, with him? That couldn't possibly be true. Sam thought about asking, but stopped. Somehow it didn't seem right to ask – and he wasn't sure he wanted the answers. So he stood there in silence and waited – wondering what happened next.

"You did well little one. Though I did have to step in a couple of times. I will see that my servants tell your story with pride."

Samual

With that he was gone in another flash of light, and whether he was the All Father or Heri, Sam didn't know. In any case he still couldn't see anything except impossibly vibrant colours everywhere. But he heard a popping sound and somehow knew he had left.

In time he heard cheering. Laughter and applause. It was loud and uncontrolled and growing all the time in volume as more and more joined in. And despite everything Sam wanted to join with them. Because he knew it could only mean that the war was over. But he could barely see anything at all and the soldier in him knew he could never give in to emotion when there might be an enemy about. So he contained his emotions and did his best to search the warehouse for any trace of the Dragon or his steel wolves.

It felt like years passed before his vision returned to normal and the cheering and applause died away so that he could hear again. And when it was finally as it should be Sam knew enough to finally believe it was over. Enough to sheath his sword. There was no sign of the Dragon. No sign of his half-brother either. The roof was missing too when he looked up. Completely gone. What little of it had been left had vanished along with most of the top story of the building. Now there weren't even half burnt beams connecting the walls together. The Dragon's funeral pyre had apparently turned them to ash.

It was over! The duel, the battle and even the war. The Dragon had been defeated. A god had been defeated!

It took Sam some time to let that understanding wash over him. To let it sink in. And all the time he stood there, staring, hunting for any sign of either Heri or the Dragon. Because it just didn't seem right that they could be gone. They never left. They were always somewhere, making trouble and spreading misery. That was the curse they were. And yet in time he knew that simple fact for the truth. They were gone.

Which left him standing there, wondering what to do.

He wasn't alone in that of course. As the noise from the window slowly died away he could hear the elders starting to discuss things among themselves. Asking questions. Though not the questions he cared about. They wanted to know how the All Father had somehow ended up being involved in this mess. They were elves after all. It should have been the Goddess who had saved them as far as they were concerned. And the dragons were the children of Draco, Lord of the Skies and companion to the Goddess. The All Father was a human god.

Sam though didn't care. Really he was just thankful that there was nothing left to do. It was over. He could go home. To his wife. And to their child yet to be born.

And he realised, he could do one thing more. He could stop being the Fire Angel. But then he suddenly understood, he never had been. That had been something of the gods. They had granted him the extra magic. Made him into a wizard far more powerful than he was. And he didn't know why. Especially when at the end he had defeated the Dragon with an artefact he suspected they had provided, his less powerful earth magic, and his trusty sword. But perhaps it had been necessary to have the Fire Angel walk the land to bring the people hope? To frighten their enemies. And ultimately to rebirth the phoenix. Now those things were done. And it being over, the gods had taken the magic back. He was no longer the Fire Angel. He might not even be a master of fire magic.

But that was a good thing. Partly because he had never wanted to be the Fire Angel, and now that the Dragon was defeated, he had no need to be him either. But mostly because what he wanted to be was a simple husband and father. And if losing a little magic was the price for that, he would have paid it gladly a thousand times over.

Heri would never have understood such a thing. For whatever reason he craved power. And now Sam understood, he was somewhere paying the price for giving in to that craving. Meanwhile Sam intended to be rewarded. And there was only one thing he wanted.

"Ryshal, aylin mi elle." He called to Ryshal and after several attempts finally managed to attract her attention. Things were still somewhat loud on the other side of the window as the elders lost themselves in their conversations. It took her some time to squeeze her way through the elders as they discussed the events of the day at somewhat loud volumes and with arms waving. In fact he thought, they looked distinctly unelven.

"My beloved?" She couldn't stop smiling as she stared at him, and though there were tears running down her cheeks they were only of joy. And though it was unmanly, Sam had tears in his eyes too.

There were so many things he wanted to say to her. Things of his heart and soul. And he almost did. But in the end he was a king's son, and there were people listening to everything he said. He had to always control his tongue. So he limited himself to the only thing that mattered. To what he had promised his wife. And a promise he was going to keep.

"Boil some water for the tea please. I'm coming home. I just have to go and find my riding moose!"

Chapter Forty Nine

Heri was annoyed when he unexpectedly found himself standing on the edge of a lake. Partly because he had no idea where was. But mostly because of what had happened before he had been brought here.

He had had his brother there in front of him. He had had a knife in his hands. And it would have been so easy while Samual was distracted by the Dragon to simply step up behind him and plunge a knife in his back. But he hadn't. He'd wanted to. He'd begged for the chance. But no matter what he hadn't been able to. He had been impotent.

And then as if that wasn't bad enough he'd saved his miserable half-brother's life! That axe would have cleaved Samual's skull in two. All he had had to do was let it. But he couldn't. Instead he had raised the shoot and stopped it. How could he have done that?! Samual had to die!

But when he heard the bone crunching snap of jaws behind him, he knew that he had bigger problems. That damned snap wolf was still with him. Still guarding him. And when he turned to look at it, he knew he was still on the menu. The beast might be controlled in some way, but it still thought of him as a meal.

How could any god be so cruel to him? And the All Father of all gods! He had paid for the upkeep of his temple in Fall Keep. He'd accepted the holidays the temple demanded on behalf of his people. He had even banned some of those temples that the All Father's priests found objectionable. And this was how he rewarded him? Saving Samual and bringing him here to some worthless lake in the wilds? The miserable worm ridden piece of dung!

"Wild root tea?"

Heri spun as the man's voice came from behind him, startling him. And then when he saw him he stopped dead, forgetting his anger at the All Father in his disbelief. He'd recognised the voice. But he hadn't considered who the voice belonged to until he saw the face. And that accursed beard! When he did though Heri didn't know what to think.

"You're dead!" Eventually the words slipped out of him. He couldn't stop them. But he knew they were true. He'd poisoned the wizard himself.

"What, a little sand scorpion poison?" Augrim chuckled quietly as he sat beside a fire checking on the progress of a kettle as it boiled. "You really thought that would harm me?"

Heri's anger flowed at the wizard's mockery. How dare he speak to him like that! And before he even thought about it a curse found his tongue. But he couldn't speak it. The words just wouldn't make it out of his mouth.

"No bad language now!" Augrim's annoying smile grew broader. "That's not allowed."

Unexpectedly the wizard reached out an arm in welcome, but not to Heri. Instead he welcomed the wolf to him, and when it came he started running his fingers through the fur on the top of its head. The wolf actually seemed to like that. So much so that it collapsed down on to the ground to let him continue.

"Now come, sit." Augrim indicated a flat rock beside him. "From what I understand you've had a difficult day and a little tea will help."

Despite not really wanting to Heri did as the wizard said, taking the proffered seat and accepting the mug of tea. He had to remember that Augrim was a wizard. He had power. Power over a snap wolf for a start. And Augrim was right, the tea did help a little. It was strong but still palatable, and the heady aroma returned a little life to his tired brain. It let him start thinking about things again. To start asking questions.

"Where are we?"

"Where we need to be of course," Augrim answered him cryptically.

Heri resisted yelling at him. The man was annoying. But he had always been that. And he suspected that the words wouldn't make it out of his mouth. Besides it probably didn't matter. The only thing that mattered was his freedom. He had been cursed by a damned elf wizard. And Augrim was a wizard. What one could do surely another could undo?

"You know I have been cursed?"

"Cursed?" Augrim raised an eyebrow. "I had not heard. But I would think it very unlikely. You are usually the one doing the cursing."

It was hard not to leap at the wizard for his gall. To reach out, put his hands around the wizard's throat and strangle him. How dare he speak to him like that! As though he was some common beggar! But somehow Heri restrained himself even though he could feel the anger boiling in his blood. But here he was in the company of his former, not so dead wizard. He had to seize the opportunity. He had a chance to free himself. Finally something was going his way!

"A geas was placed on me. I need it removed."

"Remove a geas?" Augrim looked surprised. "What geas?"

"One that compels me to do things I do not want to do. One that the poxy Alder loving elves had placed on me. I want it gone."

"Oh that!" Augrim chuckled some more. "That is no geas. A geas is what wizards do. And that is not of any wizard. It is of the All Father's servants. A blessing and a prayer for obedience. It may not be undone by any save the All Father himself. And he would not do that. Not after you betrayed him."

"Betrayed him? What betrayal?" That at least Heri was sure he hadn't done. It was the All Father who had betrayed him.

"Have you forgotten already?" Augrim stared curiously at him as he absent-mindedly stroked his beard. "When you destroyed the city you destroyed his temple and killed some of his followers. He did not take kindly to that."

"That was an accident!" Heri defended himself instinctively.

"But then you went further," Augrim continued. "You made a compact with the Dragon. The All Father is the king of gods. And the God of Kings. As such he rules over both kings and gods. When you sided with the high priest of Crodan the Mountain against your own people, he found that offensive. That it should be done by one who claimed to have faith in his teachings was more so. A king slaughtering his own people while claiming to serve the All Father! He could not let those crimes pass."

"So he had his servants prepared a potion of divine will and you were given it."

"It was a potion from the Goddess' accursed elven priests," Heri corrected him, not even sure why he bothered.

The wizard didn't seem at all concerned by his plight. Was he no longer interested in gold? Because though Heri had nothing he would pretend to offer him a fortune. Then kill him – properly this time.

"Her priests did prepare a potion for you to stop you murdering people, but that was not sufficient for the All Father. Not when you had betrayed him and murdered his servants. When you had betrayed your duties as king – and done it in his name. Not when you looked to be intent on continuing to do so. And not when you interfered in his plans by trying to kill his servant – the Fire Angel. And so you were given a different potion instead. One that will ensure that you spend the rest of your life atoning for your crimes, not merely incapable of committing more."

The rest of his life? That did not sound good. But could it be true? Heri didn't know. It could be he supposed. Elves were a tricky people as he was beginning to realise. But regardless it didn't matter. He just wanted it gone. He certainly didn't want this to endure for the rest of his life.

"So what? They're only priests! You're a wizard. You have some knowledge of these things. I have gold and I want to be rid of this curse." Heri put it plainly.

"But even if I could remove the All Father's blessing, why would I?" Augrim looked up at him from the fire and smiled easily. "After all I was the one who swapped the potions and made sure you got the right one."

Heri sat there for a heartbeat, stunned beyond measure, unable to believe he had just heard what he had. Then he screamed with fury, threw the cup aside and leapt on the smiling wizard with arms outstretched.

Or he tried to. But he couldn't. No muscle so much as twitched as he willed them to act. Nor did a scream make it out of his mouth. Not even a small one. Though he was tried to do all those things he could do nothing. He just ended up sitting there quietly. The cup of tea didn't so much as shake in his hands. And Augrim ignored him completely, choosing instead to concentrate on scratching the back of the snap wolf's head.

It was a long time before Heri found some calm again. A long time spent just sitting there with the tea in his hands, filled with hate. But eventually he had to accept that he could do neither of those things. That he had to obey if he wanted to have any free will. Even ask a question.

"Why? Why would you do that? Didn't I reward you well for your services?"

"Because my Lord commanded it of course." Augrim shrugged as if it was obvious. And maybe it was to him.

"And perhaps I too owe you a small apology. For deceiving you when I came into your employ. You see I am not a wizard. I have no magic at all. I am the High Priest for the All Father. He grants me whatever magic and knowledge he deems I need."

"But then you did try to murder me, so I think that evens things out!"

The All Father had had his High Priest working for him as a magical advisor? Heri tried to find a reason for that and failed. Though really he didn't want a reason. He wanted blood! But he couldn't have blood and the only way he could even get answers was by being calm. And he needed answers. He needed to know what sort of trouble he was in. So eventually he managed to restrain his temper enough that he was able to ask why.

"Someone had to bring you all those ancient treasures.

They had to be ready, waiting for when the time was right for them to be used." Augrim smiled some more. "After all did you really imagine that any simple wizard could just find them? Or if he did that he would ever give them to you?"

"The gold was welcome though. My Lord's servants made good use of it."

The rage flared once more in Heri's heart and he would have leapt on him and strangled him with his bare hands all over again if he could have. But he couldn't. He couldn't even scream. And no more could he pray for the gods to strike the vile wretch down. Not when he would be praying to the All Father to strike down his own servant. Which left him sitting there, helpless and filled with rage and trying to keep a measure of calm. He was beginning to understand that it was the only way he was going to be able to do anything. Even ask a question.

"The All Father wanted me to have all those artefacts? Why?"

"No. He wanted them all kept together in a safe place for when they were needed. They were never to be yours. You were just their keeper."

"I see." Actually he did see. He had been used as a storekeeper. But it made him angry to realise he had been used. He was a king not a peon!

"Maybe some, but not all."

Augrim offered Heri another cup of the tea and Heri let him refill it. The tea was good and it was calming. He needed to be calm. He needed to listen. And he needed the damned snap wolf to remain calm. Somehow he suspected that it would take it amiss if he started yelling at Augrim.

"The All Father has now restored a little more of the world to rights. Crodan the Mountain has been punished once again for trying to usurp the other gods. Now he has no people, no followers, no High Priest and little power. It will be a hundred thousand years at least before he can even think to challenge the others. And a million before he forgets how easily he was tricked."

"He thought the All Father's servant was coming to destroy his servant. That it would be yet another five thousand years before another Dragon was born to serve him – if even then. He thought that if his servant took the largest of Draco's workshops, he would be able to build a bigger army, faster. So fast that the Fire Angel could not win. Instead he had his servant walk into a trap."

"The Goddess was most grievously hurt the last time Crodan tried to take the throne of the gods, and so she has had a fraction more of her power restored to her. And her symbol the phoenix now flies among the mountains. She will grow in strength once more and in time the scars of the last war such as the Dead Belly Wastes will be healed."

"Draco's ancient workshops have been returned to him, forever beyond the ability of Crodan's followers to seize – now that he has no followers."

"The Fire Angel has been seen once more and the legends of his mighty battles will soon become the songs of the bards and the tales of history. They will bring hope to future generations – and a little faith."

"And in the world of men the ancient treasures have been given to those who will make good use of them. They will help to restore much of what was lost five thousand years ago. Those who have been driven from their homes will in time return to them. Once more a lesson of unity has been taught, as the greatest victories were won by those who stand as one.

The greatest defeats suffered by those who remain divided."

"And lest I forget one corrupt king has been removed from his throne. That will stand as a warning to others. A reminder that even the most powerful must submit to the All Father. Gods and kings both."

Heri gathered he was the corrupt king Augrim was referring to. But for once he held his temper. He was beginning to realise he was in trouble. Especially when he saw the snap wolf yawn as Augrim petted it, and saw the shocking array of weaponry in its mouth.

"But you'll have plenty of time to learn the rest of it."

"How much time?" Heri heard the part about him having time and immediately started to panic. It was starting to sound as though he'd been sentenced and he hadn't even had a trial. But trials were mortal things. The gods didn't generally get involved in such matters as he understood it. They just decided what punishments people would receive.

"Why, the rest of your life of course." Augrim laughed merrily as if it was some sort of joke.

"But that's –."

" – Your fate." Augrim finished Heri's sentence for him. "And it is of your own choosing."

"My –?!"

"You were given the choice. I told you when your brother attacked the keep that he was too strong for you. That he was working with others more powerful still. You could have walked away. You should have. But you chose to let your hatred dictate your actions. And everything has followed from that. Now here you are."

"Be grateful. The All Father could be much harsher. But he still intends to make an example of you."

"Now drink up. You have a lot of work to do and it begins today. There are temples to rebuild, people to bring to them, offerings to be collected, prayers to be intoned and temple floors to clean."

"But I'm not a priest!" Heri objected.

"No, of course not." Augrim pretended to look concerned for a moment. Then his expression hardened. "You're a serf."

"I am not –!" Heri lost his temper and again tried to yell, only to have his voice dry up. But this time he didn't care that he couldn't scream at the wizard and he couldn't move. He was simply too angry to care.

"Yes you are." Augrim started preening his beard some more. "Some serve from love as do the priests. Some serve by their nature as does your brother. And some serve as slaves, as now do you. This is the All Father's judgement."

"For the rest of your life you will be Heri the serf. The people will see you scrubbing the floors of the temples, cleaning out the waste ponds and mucking out the pigs. And they will know that you were once a king who betrayed his family, his people and his god. They will laugh and pelt you with rotten fruit. The bards will sing of your fall for a thousand years and across a thousand realms. Artists will travel the world to paint your image. And perhaps a few of the high and mighty will learn a lesson from your example."

"No!" Heri gave up and yelled at the former wizard, and this time he actually managed to get that one word out before he locked up. But he was a king. He could not become the village idiot. A figure of ridicule. Someone to laugh at. It was just too much.

"Yes." Augrim let that smile of his spread over his entire face. "You should be pleased. You will finally be the king whose name the world will remember!" Augrim finally gave up on restraining himself and burst into great peals of laughter and the snap wolf started growling in agreement.

Heri meanwhile just had to sit there, completely frozen, unable to even object, and listen to his former magic adviser laughing at him. He thought in that moment that his hatred for him almost eclipsed his hatred for his half-brother. But no amount of hatred was going to help him. Because while the anger and the hatred flowed through him like water, he still knew that there was nothing he could do. He was completely helpless. And that he slowly realised, was his destiny.

It just wasn't fair!

Chapter Fifty

Home! After so long spent on the back of a horse Sam was infinitely glad to see the last length of the journey in front of him. A long straight stretch of track with only small trees lining either side. The new city of Shavarra was only a league or so in front of him. He was glad too to no longer be riding a moose. It had taken him a week to find a wild horse to ride, and a week on the back of a moose had felt like an eternity of suffering. It had been a loyal animal and it had served him well, but it simply wasn't meant to be ridden. Now hopefully it was back with its herd, no doubt telling them equally unpleasant things about the human who had chosen to jump on his back and ride him.

Sam was confused as he set eyes on the distant city. Why was the sky filled with rainbows? That didn't look right. One rainbow he could understand. But scores of them? They had transformed the entire sky into something he didn't recognise, though it was beautiful. And where was the rain that went with them?

And where were the people? Normally the stretch of track he was on would have others on it. Foresters hunting logs for the city as it was built. Hunters out looking for food. Traders who regularly plied the routes between the cities of the Golden River Flats. But looking ahead all he could see was an empty track.

Perhaps he had been expecting that someone would be waiting to greet him? The Fire Angel returning from his mighty victory? Then again perhaps that was just arrogance and false pride. Besides, how would they know he was here? The Window of Parsus was an incredible ancient treasure, but it had its limits. It was easy enough to use it to show far away cities. But they were always in the same place. Trying to find a man on horseback who could be anywhere was much harder.

Still, the empty track seemed strange. Then again, they were living in strange times. He didn't understand why or how exactly. But the world was changing. The elders had managed to contact him once as he'd travelled to the Dead Creek Pass and told him a little of what was happening in the world.

The phoenix was now flying the skies. The glorious symbol of the Goddess was now seen over the entire continent and perhaps beyond. And they were no longer certain that it was just one. Dragons were being seen more often now too. They were flying the skies above their mountain lairs. As for the trolls they had reverted all the way back to savagery. They no longer wore clothes – not even the rags they once had. They no longer spoke. And they no longer carried weapons. They didn't even stand up straight. Whatever it was that had once made them like men had vanished. Sam wasn't completely certain whether that made them less dangerous or more. But what he did understand was that it made them no longer Crodan's followers. Crodan no longer had any. And that weakened him.

All of that was in part his doing and yet he wasn't certain he had actually caused any of it. He was certain though that any of it that was his doing he hadn't intended. It hadn't been an accident either. Others had been guiding things. Actually they had been directing them. He'd just been used. And he knew he wasn't alone.

Heri had certainly been used, though no one could explain how it was that he had become a vessel for the All Father. Or when it had happened. Nor could they explain how or why he had had so many ancient treasures – including of all things, the ones they would need to defeat the Dragon.

And Sam suspected that the Dragon had been manipulated

as well. He had left his island because he had thought an attack was imminent. So he had looked for another base. Sam still didn't know why he'd believed that an attack was coming. But he was sure it was the reason he'd moved. It was the only thing that made sense.

It went beyond just pushing and prodding though. The gods had done more than that. He suspected that they had actually empowered him. He didn't know how exactly. Or when or even why. But he had had time to recover his magic on the month and a half long trip back here, and he knew he no longer had the strength he had once had. It was as though they had granted him a little extra magic just so he could do what he needed to, and now that he didn't need it they had taken it back. In the same way he had been granted knowledge. The shape to call a roc and to transform it into a phoenix. That knowledge was gone now. He had done it. But he could no longer remember how he had done it.

All three of them; him, Heri and the Dragon had all just been pieces in some giant game, and had been moved around by players they couldn't see. But what else could you expect when the gods were getting involved? The only real question was who were the gods? Crodan? The Goddess? Draco? The All Father? Or all of them?

And of course there was another, perhaps even more important question. Were the gods finished with them?

Sam didn't know and he guessed he never would. That was the sort of thing the priests would argue over for years. A wise man, he decided, wouldn't concern himself with such matters. Whether the gods were involving themselves in the affairs of the world or not, a man still had to live his life as if it was his own.

And that began with his wife who abruptly appeared from out of nowhere to drag him off his horse, push him down in the long grass and start covering him with kisses. She was happy to see him he gathered. Impatient too since he hadn't even reached the city. The horse seemed a little confused though. Probably because she kept calling him her beautiful man. That was one thing he had never thought of himself as being.

"Ryshal." He murmured her name a few times until she finally gave him a chance to speak. But not a chance to get up. She wasn't having that.

"Yes husband?" She smiled happily and returned to her kissing.

"Isn't this a bit open? I mean someone could see." Not that he really cared. Normally he would. He hated to do anything that could cause embarrassment – especially to Ry. But she felt so good in his arms. Warm and soft and filled with life. And all he wanted to do was make love to her.

"No one will see and no one will care." And then she proved how little she cared by starting work on the straps to his armour.

That was as much as Sam needed to hear and he grabbed her up, carried her to a quiet spot between a few trees a little distance from the track, and laid her down in the long grass as they both wanted. Soon after that they were eagerly renewing their wedding vows, while the light of the sun and the rainbows played over their naked bodies.

Afterwards both of them lay there for a time, enjoying the peace and each other, but saying little. For his part Sam was most curious about his wife's belly, and kept rubbing his hands over it, feeling the very slight bulge that he knew was the promise of their child to come, and wondering how it could finally be. It seemed so incredible after everything else.

But he also found himself wondering why it had taken so long. They had lost five years and those years should never have been lost. Yet this last year for all that it had been so hard on them all, had been wondrous. Maybe it all balanced out somehow. He didn't know.

Ry didn't think as he did though. She had forgotten the pain and hardship quickly and knew only the joy and the hope for the future. It was something he had always admired in her. And something he thought their child would find a blessing in his or her mother. She wasn't thinking of anything but their marriage and their child to come. Or probably he guessed, their children to come. She liked to think ahead.

"I suppose I should visit with the elders," Sam said finally, remembering his duty. Still, he was loathe to leave.

"They don't really have time to see you beloved." She laughed merrily. "They don't really have time for much lately."

"Mmm?" He twirled a little of her hair in his hands, so very glad that he could. It was once more her rowell aylin. Her golden crown.

"It's been six weeks since you killed the Dragon."

"I didn't kill him." He corrected her without thinking even though he hated doing it. "Heri did?" And he still didn't understand that.

"You did defeat him though. And Heri's not going to be taking any praise for the act. Or any praise at all. In fact he's very unhappy at the moment."

"He's – ?! … You've seen Heri?" Sam was surprised.

"Through the Window of Parsus. He's in the great temple

of the All Father in the Fedowir Kingdom. He has been relegated to menial chores and is being regularly pelted with rotten fruit by those of Fair Fields who fled there. And a giant snap wolf watches over him, preventing him from running away. Your brother is a very unhappy man."

"Good!" It might by churlish and less than noble but Sam was pleased by that. Besides, Heri should really have been put to death. Ryshal tittered happily into his chest which he assumed meant she agreed.

"The elders though are far more concerned with the rest. With the sylph who arrived here a couple of weeks ago. They are apparently upset because they have a phoenix problem."

"A phoenix problem?" Sam raised an eyebrow in question.

"The phoenix has nested in the mountain above their city of Istantia in Racavor. They believe it's laid a clutch of eggs and soon they'll be overrun. Their flocks of sheep will be at risk. And they say it's our fault. They want compensation."

"These would be the same sylph who refused to raise a finger to help when Fair Fields was threatened?" Sam wasn't particularly upset by the idea that they would lose a few sheep. Perhaps that showed.

"The elders have made that point themselves. Several times!" She laughed softly. "But the sylph still want access to the treasures from Heri's sanctum as payment for the trouble we have caused them. They are a difficult people."

"That they are." Sam agreed with her, though he would really have described them as arrogant.

"The priests have been difficult too."

"Priests?" He wouldn't have thought of priests as difficult.

Annoying sometimes and occasionally in the way. Actually they were mostly annoying and in the way. But by and large they didn't cause trouble.

"Both the priests of the All Father and Draco are requesting that they be permitted to build large temples within Shavarra. The priests of the Goddess say no. They can have shrines only. They say that this is the Goddess' land and we are her people. They say that the priests of the All Father and Draco have no place here. They are however considering allowing the priests of Phil the White to build a healing chapel. The elders have been hearing submissions on the matter every day."

"I'm sure the matter will die down in time." He wasn't actually though. It was just something reassuring to say when he didn't know what the future held. And really, Sam's thoughts were once more with Heri. His brother had saved his life and destroyed the Dragon! That still seemed impossible. But mostly he thought about what Heri had said afterwards. That he would make sure Sam's story was told. The last thing Sam wanted to be was a symbol or a witness for several faiths to fight over. Was he the witness to the All Father's victory over Crodan, the caller of Draco's Dragons or the Goddess' servant? Suddenly he wasn't so sure he wanted to visit with the elders. Not when three faiths might each want to claim him as theirs. Somehow he suspected he was going to be approached by all of them in time.

"And the rainbows?" Sam changed the subject, not wanting to dwell on matters he could do nothing about.

"Didn't I tell you? It's been six weeks since the Dragon was defeated. And for six long weeks we've been celebrating. The rainbows are created by one of the treasures from Heri's sanctum. And you're just lucky that you aren't close enough to hear the drum."

"The drum?"

"Another ancient treasure. Whenever anyone beats it, everyone within hearing starts dancing for joy. You can't help yourself. It's like some madness that sweeps everyone up. And when it ends everyone's left exhausted. After six weeks of it people are beyond simply exhausted. In fact I think that may be one of the treasures the elders would be happy to give to the sylph!"

"It's good that the war has ended." Sam tried to turn things back to the positive.

"Ended? It's more than that. The Dragon's dead. The war's over. The machina sit rusting in the streets and fields, never to move again. The trolls are mindless. Far less of a threat than they once were. And all of it is your doing. The bards spend endless hours in every inn and alehouse in every land, making up songs of the Fire Angel's heroic deeds and mighty victory."

Sam groaned quietly. But he had always known that that was going to happen and there was nothing he could do about it.

"Best of all the people are starting to reclaim their homes. Returning to their abandoned cities, and starting to rebuild what they can. In fact for the last month we've been debating the same. Do we return to the original Shavarra or remain here in this new Shavarra in Golden River Flats?"

"Only yesterday the elders made the decision that we should go home. That the original city of Shavarra is our home and we will return to it. It will however be up to each person individually to decide whether to stay or go. But the elders will organise a caravan for those who want to return and the rest can continue to build this new city here. Most people I think want to go home though.

Samual

"Ever since the defeat of the Dragon the rainbows have been in the sky and that accursed drum has been playing. The city is filled with unconscious people and many more simply too exhausted to move. As I said no one will see us."

"The whole city?" Somehow Sam couldn't quite believe that.

"That infernal drum is powerful beyond understanding. Most people have collapsed. Thousands are lying on the ground like drunks who've passed out across the entire city. The rest are probably doing the same in their homes. Or if they had any sense, they've run." She laughed. "That damned drum comes from one of the underworlds! It belongs with the sylph!"

Sam laughed with her. He didn't really know anything about the drum or its power. And truthfully he didn't really care, save that he thought it might be fun to see some of the elders cavorting around under its influence. But one thing he did care about.

"And you and your family – our family – will we be returning to Shavarra?"

"We hope to. I hope to. It is our home, and I have not seen it in many years. I ache to return to it. If you're willing?" She asked the last carefully, as if fearing his answer.

"I will go anywhere with you. You know that. And I have – we have – a home near Torin Vale which I want you to see." He took her hand and kissed it. "Besides, I have to return and replant a forest else the shadelings will come after my head."

"As long as I don't have to ride a moose there! Or a roc! Or –," he shuddered as the memory returned, "– in the mouth of a dragon!"

"Beloved, you know none of those things ever happened! When the tales are told you will have ridden on the back of a great dragon with a flaming sword in your hand. Or on the back of a phoenix as you raced into battle. The Fire Angel does not ride on a moose!" She laughed happily.

She was probably right Sam realised. He had read the tales of the previous Fire Angel – the real one – and he had guessed that they had been written by wine soaked bards more interested in a fine story than the truth. But it didn't matter anymore. The war was over and he was no longer the Fire Angel – if he ever had been. He was just a husband and in time a father. And that was a far greater thing to be.

It was a strange thing to realise, but everything he had been through was someone else's intent. He had started out on his journey as an angry man. And that anger had made him powerful. But that power had been a lie in a strange way. It had never been his, just something he had been loaned. And not so he could defeat the Dragon. Just so he could be the Fire Angel. And perhaps also so that the Goddess could have her creature returned to her. Now that the anger was gone and the power had been returned he had become just a normal man again. A man in love, and that was a far greater thing. It was a lesson neither his brother nor the Dragon had ever learned. And he guessed that no matter how many times he tried to tell that tale, it would never be heard. Instead the Fire Angel would have come and defeated the Dragon in glorious combat. Because that was the way that those who had arranged all this, wanted it told.

And he didn't care.

"Aylin mi elle we should go and start packing. I want you to be in our home well before our child is to be born."

"It can wait a few hours husband." She smiled cheekily up at him from the long grass. "You still have a little more riding to do!"

Sam smiled back at her as he reached for his wife. And he suddenly realised that he didn't care about anything else she had said. He only cared that he was with his wife and their family to come. He had finally returned home.

Made in the USA
San Bernardino, CA
06 July 2016